SMEDDUM
A LEWIS GRASSIC GIBBON ANTHOLOGY

James Leslie Mitchell, 'Lewis Grassic Gibbon', (1901–35), was born and brought up in the rich farming land of Scotland's North East coast. After a brief and unsuccessful journalistic career, he joined the Royal Army Service Corps in 1919 serving in Persia, India and Egypt. Thereafter he spent a further six years as a clerk in the RAF. He married Rebecca Middleton in 1925, and became a full time writer in 1929. The young couple settled in Welwyn Garden City where they lived until the writer's death in 1935.

Mitchell published a number of short stories and articles and his first book, *Hanno, or the Future of Exploration* appeared in 1928. Seven novels followed under his own name, *Stained Radiance* (1930); *The Thirteenth Disciple* (1931); *Three Go Back* (1932); *Image and Superscription* (1933); *The Lost Trumpet* (1932); *Spartacus* (1933); and *Gay Hunter* (1934). In the same year Mitchell collaborated with Hugh MacDiarmid to make *Scottish Scene*, which contained three of Mitchell's best short stories, later collected in *A Scots Hairst* (1969).

He adopted his mother's name for his finest work the trilogy, *A Scots Quair*, which comprised *Sunset Song, Cloud Howe* and *Grey Granite* written between 1932 and 1934. Dogged by ill health at the end, Mitchell died of a perforated ulcer at the age of only thirty-four. An unfinished novel, *The Speak of the Mearns*, was first published in 1982.

Valentina Bold is Lecturer in Scottish Studies at the University of Glasgow Crichton Campus, Dumfries. Her publications include a CD-Rom: *Northern Folk: Living Traditions of North East Scotland*, co-edited with Tom McKean. She is currently writing a book based on her doctoral thesis: *Nature's Making: James Hogg and the Autodidactic Tradition in Scottish Poetry*, and editing James Hogg's *The Brownie of Bodsbeck* for the Stirling/South Carolina edition.

Smeddum

A Lewis Grassic Gibbon Anthology

★

Edited and Introduced by
Valentina Bold

★

CANONGATE

CLASSICS

97

First published as a Canongate Classic in 2001
by Canongate Books, 14 High Street, Edinburgh EHI ITE. Copyright © the estate of
Lewis Grassic Gibbon. Introduction and notes
copyright © Valentina Bold, 2001.

The publishers gratefully acknowledge general
subsidy from the Scottish Arts Council towards
the Canongate Classics series.

Set in 10pt Plantin by Hewer Text Composition Services, Edinburgh. Printed and bound
in Finland by WS Bookwell.

2 4 6 8 9 7 5 3 1

CANONGATE CLASSICS
Series Editor: Roderick Watson
Editorial Board: J.B. Pick, Cairns Craig,
Dorothy McMillan

British Library Cataloguing in Publication Data
A catalogue record for this book is available on
request from the British Library.

ISBN 0 86241 965 4

www.canongate.net

Contents

Introduction

Let us go forth and venture beyond the utmost plain!
Beyond the utmost beetling crag where wilting
    sunsets wane!
Beyond the dark, dour valleys where Silence keeps
    her reign:
                    Let us go forth!
                        'Song of a Going Forth'
                        by James Leslie Mitchell

JAMES LESLIE MITCHELL was a literary explorer. Along with his alter ego, Lewis Grassic Gibbon, he made imaginative journeys through time, space, and the human psyche. His work is at once distinctively Scottish and universalist in its concerns; he explores traditional means of expression and is, equally, experimental. Because of this, his writing is equally resonant, and significant, for Gibbon's native North East, for Scotland, and for international audiences.[1]

This anthology allows the reader to make a new assessment of Gibbon's work. It is the most comprehensive collection to date of Mitchell's prolific output of short stories, essays, poems and synopses. This brings together the full range of his work for the first time since the 1930s.[2] Some pieces will be very familiar. Others are reprinted for the first time since their original publication, or from typescript and manuscript sources.

Seen as a set, the shorter work shows Gibbon's willingness to take creative risks. Hard-edged polemic is balanced by fantasy and revealing poetry; caustic criticism is set against sympathetic, but truthful, voyages at home and abroad.

Explorations of local, national and international identities range through the past, present and future. Boundaries between fact and fiction are blurred. The confidence and range of Gibbon's creativity reveals him in his true colours, as a distinctively Scottish writer of international importance.

The present collection is a companion to the longer fiction and prose in print, as part of Gibbon's current, well-deserved revival.[3] Gibbon constantly refined his ideas. He was a meticulous planner, as the synopses show, and redrafted his poetry at least once (usually with minor, but always significant, changes). The uncompleted histories, as much as the short stories, reveal a constant reworking of themes, and a quest for new ideas. This anthology also shows Gibbon's growth and development, during the Scottish literary renaissance. 'The Speak of the Mearns', for instance, goes beyond *Sunset Song* in considering rural identities in the area where Gibbon was raised. 'The Woman of Leadenhall Street' is a more mature response to the theme of cultures in conflict explored in *Three Go Back* (1932). Recurrent themes and motifs are apparent: the way communities change over time, for instance; the foolishness, and also the vulnerability of folk.

Politically, and culturally, Gibbon is extremely astute. His work reflects a range of (very broadly) Communist beliefs, as discussed in detail by William Malcolm in *A Blasphemer and Reformer* (1984). Gibbon exemplifies the forward-thinking Scot of the early twentieth century. He identifies Scotland's role in the modern world, and its possibilities for the future, and Scottish perspectives pervade Gibbon's work. His childhood experiences in Kincardineshire, and his time as a reporter in Aberdeen and Glasgow, irrevocably shaped Gibbon's consciousness. This is particularly apparent in *Scottish Scene; or, the intelligent man's guide to Albyn* (1934), a creative and acerbic tour de force, co-edited with Hugh MacDiarmid, which set out to define and challenge the nation.

Gibbon was one of the last of the Scottish autodidacts. Despite an adequate education at Arbuthnott School and Mackie Academy, Stonehaven, he shows a range of self-acquired knowledge, and an ambition of vision which resembles James Hogg's. Just as Hogg deals with topics as diverse as Borders shepherding and polar exploration, so Gibbon knows no limits in his subject matter, writing with ease about modern and future cultures, archaeology and anthropology, contemporary and historical politics, gender and sexual relationships, religious and class structures. He is as happy (if not always as convincing) in historical treatments of the Maya, as he is in the Mearns.

The first section of the present collection includes all of Gibbon's contributions to *Scottish Scene*. They are amongst his finest stories and essays. MacDiarmid's 'Postlude' is also included, as it identifies the book's aim to find new Scottish prophets (perhaps the co-authors). MacDiarmid and Gibbon, as the 'Curtain Raiser' explains, engage in a form of counterpoint. Their contributions alternate, as the book shifts, elegantly, between past to present; description and analysis; fiction and documentary. The two writers, at times, contradict each other, viewing a 'composite' Scotland, from two different 'angles' (Gibbon's 'village near London'; MacDiarmid's home in the Shetlands). Equally, although this is not stated, the two writers' unique Scottish personae, grounded in culturally distinct areas – the North East and the Borders – foster differing perspectives.

Due to the episodic structure of the book, though – similar to a traditional tale-telling session, held over several nights – Gibbon's essays and stories work well on their own. These 'scenes' (in both the dramatic and argumentative sense), define Scotland and Scottish identity in all its dimensions: urban and rural; political, cultural and literary. Local affiliations are proclaimed without too much sentiment. Literal observations, anecdotes and stories intermingle, sometimes within the same piece. In the original

volume the essays by the two authors offer implicit comments on the stories, just as the stories illustrate the essays.
In this collection, however, it's useful to look at Gibbon's
pieces in thematic groups.

'The Antique Scene' is reviewed idiosyncratically, but
with as much confidence as 'The Unfurrowed Field' in
Sunset Song. As a diffusionist, Gibbon's history is a series
of lows, highs and turning points, governed by the over-
arching principle that: 'barbarism is no half-way house of a
progressive people towards full and complete civilization: on
the contrary, it marks a degeneration from an older civilization'.[4] An eclectic group of heroes and villains is identified,
unified by an 'awareness of blood-brotherhood and freedom-right', and characteristic of Gibbon's work. The Picts
represent Scotland's Golden Age whereas the Celts are
gangsters. Wallace, Cromwell, Lincoln and Lenin are
grouped together for their republican sympathies and Knox,
too, is presented as a revolutionary, who wandered Europe
in exile, like Lenin. The Covenanters are 'the People's
Church'. Gibbon was raised close to Dunottar Castle with
its Covenanters' prison, the Whigs' Vault. Perhaps, like
Hogg in *The Brownie of Bodsbeck* (1818), he draws on oral
tradition in his depiction of the 'criminal degenerate' behaviour of those who opposed the Covenanters. Gibbon calls
for a rewriting of Scottish history, to celebrate: 'the lives of
millions of the lowly who wiped the sweats of toil from
browned faces and smelt the pour of waters by the Mull
of Kintyre and the winds of autumn in the Grampian
haughs'. This is a powerful statement, setting the scene
for the stories which follow and highlighting Gibbon's agen-
da. The stories – 'Greenden', 'Smeddum', 'Sim' and 'Clay' –
celebrate, and analyse, the life of ordinary folk in North East
Scotland. This is the fermtoun culture of Flora Garry's
'Bennygoak'.[5] They are located in a circle centred around
Bloomfield farm, where Gibbon was raised. He presents a
turn-of-the century Scotland in agricultural transition.

While it is possible to walk out these locations today, compared to Gibbon's time, it is an empty landscape; the bothy billies are gone. Only the stark beauty of the land remains as, strangely, Gibbon predicts in 'Clay'.

In writing about the Mearns and its environs, Gibbon is at his most cartographic. He maps out the world of his childhood with confidence, offering a precise picture of its history, landscape, customs, people and social (or antisocial) interactions. This is the land of the bothy ballad, where people are summarised roughly and accurately; where the mean-spirited are swiftly dismissed, and people are exhausted and exploited by service to the land. However, Gibbon goes far beyond mere ethnographic details, compelling the reader to adopt the role, almost, of participant observer, experiencing North East life from multiple perspectives. In Gibbon's North East, the land always wins and the people, usually, are broken. As in the bothy ballads, it is rare to find a good tenant farmer.

'Greenden' decries the smallness of country life among 'the dour red clay of the den'. Greenden is isolated, 'fair smothered away from the world', surrounded by a closed community characterised by vituperative gossip or – depending on perspective – telling a 'story in a neighbour-like way'. It is all highly allegorical, and wonderfully detailed. Ellen Simpson, the 'town-bred' heroine has moved to the country with her husband – who has 'clerking lungs' – because of the hymn, 'There is a green hill far away . . ./ Where the dear Lord was crucified'. To the country hantle, this is ridiculous: 'hymns were just things that you sang'. Paradoxically, the hymn is almost a prediction of Ellen's fate among the larch woods of Greenden. The tragedy here (and the ending is close to a religious passion) is that those who are spiritually closest to the land (perhaps Chris Guthrie was in this category) come dangerously close to madness. (There are links with the Christ of 'Forsaken', too, discussed below.)

'Smeddum', on the other hand, explores the qualities that allow people to survive, whilst retaining their individuality, in the hostile environment of the Mearns. Meg's smeddum is hard to define, but easily understood, combining thrawness and endurance; she resembles Nan Shepherd's heroines, at their best. A hard worker, Meg is likened to 'a big roan mare' constantly busy on Tocherty toun. Her daughter, Kath, who also has smeddum, is equally described through images of nature: she is compared to a 'swallow' as she leaves home. She creates a natural longing in John Robb, too, as he cycles out on a summer's day, 'the Grampians rising far and behind, Kinraddie spread like a map for show'. The powerful punchline to this story, however, is Gibbon's best definition of smeddum.

'Sim' explores another Scots characteristic: the tendency to be 'sweir'. Sim Wilson has the ability to become school dux for a pound's prize, but later rejects lessons, as *'they're not worth the sweat'*. His 'sweirty went like a mist in June' to win the Manse maid, Kate Duthie. He turns the clay soil of Haughgreen farm into productive land, first for his wife, and later for his children, 'chaving like daft'. The story goes further, though. The feel of 'Sim', like 'Greenden', is of Biblical parable. It is headed by Ecclesiastes i, 4: 'What profit hath a man of all his labour which he taketh under the sun?' Sim is cruelly disappointed by life. His wife turns out to be far from the 'angel' he thought her; and his beloved daughters disappoint his expectations. As predicted (almost foretold), 'he had better look out, 'twas fell unchance to show over-plain that you thought over-much of any bit bairn'.

The most despairing story in this set is 'Clay' which, like 'Greenden', is based in a Biblical image: flesh is the clay which surrounds the spirit. Rob Galt is 'a fine, frank childe that was kindness itself' until he is possessed by the 'chave, chave, chave' of the toun of Pittaulds, by Segget. Galt talks about his farm like a woman – *'Man, she's fairly a bitch, is*

that park . . . But I'll kittle her up with some phosphate.' His
wife and daughter Rachel (a quintessentially North East
woman, like Chris Guthrie, 'over thin to be bonny') are
sacrificed to his ambitions. Poignantly, Galt's wife (victim
to the same disease as the neglected wife of *The House with
the Green Shutters*) understands, '*He just doesn't think, it's not
that he's cruel, he's just mad on Pittaulds.*' Rachel too realises,
'there was something in him that tugged at herself, daft-
like, a feeling with him that the fields mattered and mattered, nothing else at all.' Poignantly, this story is a lament
for the land as farming life changed, even in Gibbon's
lifetime: 'All life – just clay that awoke and strove to return
again to its mother's breast . . . no other would come to
tend the ill rigs in the north wind's blow.'

Clay is followed, self-consciously, by a lyrical essay on
'The Land' (balanced by MacDiarmid on 'The Sea'). Like
Henryson's *The Testament of Cresseid*, this opens in Winter.
Gibbon identifies his Land as distinctively Scottish. While
his 'task of voyaging with a pen' in Scotland is pleasing, 'I
balk at reaching beyond the Border, into that chill land of
alien geology and deplorable methods of ploughing . . . I
shrink from geographical impropriety.' The beauty, and
brutality, of the Land is explored through the Seasons.
Autumn, in particular, makes Gibbon realise, 'how very
Scotch I am . . . how much a stranger I am, south, in those
seasons of mists and mellow fruitfulness as alien to my
Howe as the olive groves of Persia.' Bervie Braes are
present for Gibbon, even when he is not there. As in
'The Woman of Leadenhall Street', time is a spiral of
present and past: 'the hunters are *now* lying down their
first night in Scotland, with their tall, deep-bosomed sinewy mates and their children, tired from trek.' For Gibbon,
revelations are found in natural places; here he comes into
contact with the numinous.

It is within this context that the writer's views on Christianity should be placed. His short story 'Forsaken'

considers the confusion of Christ as he comes unrecognised into the present. He is like King Arthur awoken, with his knights long-changed. The story is set, perhaps, in Aberdeen; Market Square and the Gallowgate are mentioned; *Grey Granite* (1934) is recalled with the stallholder Ma Cleghorn, whose goods are knocked down by 'wee Johnny Tamson'. Equally it could be Glasgow or Dundee. Incidentally, MacDiarmid wishes that Dante should be brought back in Dundee,: 'he would add a sensational new circle to his Inferno.' Christ, too, had already visited Dundee in James Young Geddes' 'The Second Advent' from *The New Jerusalem* (1879) and it is possible that Gibbon knew this poem. In a form of eternal recurrence, Christ's old companions, and his beliefs, have latter day counterparts. There is a sense of mutual recognition, too, sometimes expressed with humour. As Christ eats smokies and oatcakes, rather than fishes and loaves, even the child Pete recognises the former 'joiner' who should be able to plane a bookcase. The ultimate tragedy of the tale though is that, despite these continuities, all has changed. Pa may be Christ's old 'Comrade'; Communism and Christianity are seen as alike: '*All things in common for the glory of God*'. Hard-working Ma is Martha and Jess, the daughter of the house, is a latter day Magdalene. However, since the crucifixion, people have undergone an irrevocable 'change of heart', losing their 'faith and trust, hope even'.

The paradigm is pursued by Gibbon, (as it was by MacDiarmid in *A Drunk Man Looks at the Thistle*) in his essay on 'Religion' which defines the state of Christianity in Scotland from the starting point that, 'Man is naturally irreligious.' Basically, 'Religion is no more fundamental to the human character than cancer is fundamental to the human brain.' All denominations are dismissed. The established Kirk is 'the greatest example of an armchair scientific Religion known to the world since the decay of the great State cults of Egypt and Mexico. In the case of all three countries the Gods were both unlovely and largely unloved.' Gibbon acknowledges the appeal of Christianity for 'the bitterly oppressed' but argues that the Kirk made Scots 'the conscienceless anarchist in politics, in commerce, in private affairs', and led to an unhealthy attitude to sex. Catholicism and Episcopalianism are dispensed with swiftly, but most bile is reserved for the Free Church (strong then, as now, in the North East). It is asserted that 'great economic and historical movements' will dispose of religion – initially a 'cortical abortion, a misapprehension of the functions and activities of nature' – although 'there may be long delays'. Chillingly, Gibbon predicts that Fascism, as in Italy and Germany, may prevail in Scotland: 'If the Fascists achive power, the country may see crowded kirks, persecutions and little parish tyrannies, a Free Kirk minister's millenial dream.' Ultimately, 'Nothing' should replace religion: 'one does not seek to replace a fever by an attack of jaundice.'

Gibbon relishes polemic. 'Literary Lights' considers most contemporary writers with Scottish associations, in assertive ways. With some exceptions, 'there is not the remotest reason why the majority of modern Scots writers should be considered Scots.' A. J. Cronin's work is 'terrifying and fascinating' although Norman Douglas and Compton Mackenzie, writing in English, 'have nevertheless an essential Scottishness'; Cunninghame Graham 'is certainly not of the English Orthodox'. Despite agreeing with the Anglo-Gael James Barke that, 'In Scotland today there exists no body of Gaelic culture,' Gibbon admires the work of Donald Sinclair, Duncan Johnston of Islay and John MacFadyen. Astutely, he adds, with respect to Fionn MacColla: 'his English is the finest Gaelic we have.'

The difficulties facing Scottish writers are described through characteristic aphorisms. Writing in English is akin to translation: 'the truly Scots writer . . . has to *learn* to write in English: he is like a Chinese scholar spending the

best years of his life in the mystic mazes of the pictographs.'
Most of the 'best' Scottish writers, as a consequence, are
merely products of 'the interesting English county of Scotshire'. In this group, Gibbon includes John Buchan, James
Bridie, Edwin Muir, Roy Campbell and Neil Gunn. Praise
is given to Willa Muir, Catherine Carswell, Muriel Stuart
and Naomi Mitchison. Self-referentially, he adds that
Mitchison 'wrote that had she had the command of Scots
speech possessed by Lewis Grassic Gibbon she would have
written her Spartan books . . . in Scots'. Gibbon continues,
'they would undoubtedly have been worse novels – but they
would have been Scots books by a Scots writer.' The writer
defines his own technique as being: 'to mould the English
language into the rhythms and cadences of Scots spoken
speech, and to inject into the English vocabulary such
minimum number of words from Braid Scots as that
remodelling requires'. In conclusion, the 'two solitary
lights in modern Scots Literature' are Hugh MacDiarmid
and Lewis Spence and Gibbon is particularly heartfelt in
praise of his co-editor and those who follow him, like
William Soutar. Quoting 'The Watergaw' in full, he praises
MacDiarmid's achievement in showing Scots was not only
for 'the more flat-footed sentiments of the bothy', sparking
off hopes of a real Scots renaissance.

Gibbon is as vitriolic to those he despises, as he is
generous towards those he admires. James Ramsay Mac-
Donald, 'The Wrecker', is rudely dismissed as all form and
no substance. His greatest sin – summarised in a series of
memorable images – is betraying his party, preferring 'the
seemly shape his calves occupied inside the silk stockings of
Court dress' to Socialism.

Moray-shire born MacDonald, however, was 'characteristically Scottish' with a 'hazy inability to grasp at the flinty
actualities of existence'. Moreover, 'he has never learned to
think like an Englishman . . . He has foisted antique
Scotticisms upon quite alien essentials.' Ultimately, 'There

is hardly a Scotsman alive who does not feel a shudder of amused shame . . . We have, we Scots, (all of us) too much of his quality in our hearts and souls.'

As well as analyses of Scottish history and modern politics, there are descriptive topographies of Scotland's cities. Gibbon's Glasgow is a Victorian hell, in the tradition of James Thomson's *City of Dreadful Night* (1874). He comments, with a characteristic self-referential flourish: 'My distant cousin, Mr Leslie Mitchell, once described Glasgow in one of his novels as "the vomit of a cataleptic commercialism". But is is more than that. It may be a corpse, but the maggot-swarm upon it is very fiercely alive.' He is horrified by life in the slums and, to end it, 'I would welcome the English in suzerainty over Scotland till the end of time . . . the end of Braid Scots and Gaelic, our culture, our history, our nationhood.'

Gibbon is uncomfortable with intellectual chit chat. He dismisses the rhetoric of nationalism, MacDiarmid's favoured Douglasism, as well as Fascism, Anarchocommunism with its 'Gospels according to St Bakunin' and Socialism, 'ruddy and plump, with the spoils from the latest Glasgow Corporation swindle'. His own political daydreams are hilariously satirical: from 'a Scots Catholic kingdom with Mr Compton Mackenzie Prime Minister to some disinterred Jacobite royalty, and all the Scots intellectuals settled out on the land on thirty-acre crofts' to 'a Scottish Socialist Republic under Mr Maxton . . . summoning the Russian Red Army to his aid (the Red Army digging a secret tunnel from Archangel to Aberdeen)'. For Gibbon, though, all such 'parlour chatter' is forgotten in the face of Glasgow's slum-dwellers.

Beyond expressing the belief that Glasgow has potential for change, Gibbon advocates 'cosmopolitanism', rather than nationalism or internationalism, giving credence, for instance to the English ideals of 'decency, freedom, justice, ideals innate in the minds of man'. He declares himself a nationalist only 'temporarily, opportunistically', seeing the potential in Braid Scots of giving 'lovely lights and shadows not only to English but to the perfected speech of Cosmopolitan Man'. Even so, 'I'd rather, any day, be an expatriate writing novels in Persian about the Cape of Good Hope than a member of a homogeneous literary cultus . . . prosing eternally on one plane.'

The city Gibbon knows most intimately, Aberdeen, is described in detail, and subjected to historical and political cartography. As throughout the degenerate Scotland profiled here, 'Agitationally, in spite of its unemployed, Aberdeen sleeps these days.' The writer recalls the Aberdeen Soviet being founded, on the news of the Bolshevik Revolution: 'I and a cub reporter from another paper . . . were elected to the Soviet Council, forgetting we were pressmen; and spent perspiring minutes with our chief reporters afterwards, explaining that we could not report the meeting being ourselves good sovietists.' Such personal reminiscence enlivens the travelogue immensely, typifying Gibbon's vigorous style. Most memorably, he calls Aberdeen: a 'materialisation of an Eskimo's vision of hell', treating it with some rude affection. This city of 'Lauder-imitators' is a joke place, exemplified by a grimly humorous, post-cremation story: ' "What's this?" she enquired. "Your husband, Mem," said the boy, "– his ashes, you know." Slowly, the widow took the package in her hand. "His ashes? Oh ay. *But where's the dripping*?" ' As a man from the country, he ridicules the language of the town: 'the thin Aberdeen patois – full of long *ee's*, and conversions of *wh's* into *f's*'. This is spoken by everyone, except 'the bourgeois speaks English, and, strangely, speaks it.' However, he is not wholly condemnatory: 'the understanding is no easy thing. One detests Aberdeen with the detestation of a thwarted lover. It is the one haunting and exasperatingly lovable city in Scotland.'

This enduring connexion to home is particularly evident

in Gibbon's poetry. The section here is a complete transcription of Gibbon's typescript poems in the National Library, MS 26058, along with one item held by Aberdeen University's Department of Special Collections. Once again, the sequence of the originals is preserved. Most of the poems appear in the typescript as draft and fair copies and, as the typescript listing suggests, Gibbon probably intended an anthology to be made from the second group.

Some of Gibbon's poems are more admirable than others (it should be remembered that he did not have the chance to edit all of these for publication). However, they work well as set, showing Gibbon's wide range of literary, political and personal concerns, and paralleling his ideas in prose. Most of these poems have never been published before and they offer new insights into Gibbon's concerns (political, poetic, religious and personal). 'Songs of Limbo' reveal a deeply ambivalent relationship between Gibbon and the land of his self-imposed time 'In Exile'. The writer lived in Welwyn Garden City for the last part of his short life, settling there after leaving the RAF in 1929. Little of his published work reflects this experience directly. In the poetry, he reflects on the lands left behind: physical landscapes and communities, as well as the personal landscapes of his own past and present. Adopting the perspective of the traveller in exile, Gibbon exemplifies the disquieting experiences of those writing after *The Waste Land*. He was deeply uncomfortable with some aspects of Englishness, despite his appreciation of the best English values, especially the colonial mentality. 'Nostalgia: A Parody' presents an unpleasant picture of an Englishman in Cairo, fondly remembering 'ginger-pop upon the lawn' and 'glistening sandwiches of brawn'. The phrasing, and semi-ironic tone, too, parodies the worst proponents of pre-War English poetry.

There is evidence of a complex belief system here, showing Gibbon's disenchantment with religious faith, or at least people's treatment of God. 'When God Died' and 'Lost' bely the harsh observations of the essay on 'Religion'. 'Dust' takes the reader on a grand tour from Crete (with its Scottish-focussed 'Cretan kine') to the 'terraces of Toltec Yucatan' to see Christ, outcast. 'Michael' portrays the 'Child of Desire, his name a battle-cry', with a great deal of sympathy for the angel who 'cleansed our hearts for Love's own Lovely birth'. Like the story 'Forsaken' ('Lost' treats exactly the same theme in verse) the poems suggest that Gibbon struggled to reconcile a highly spiritual nature with his political and historical beliefs. Losses and sacrifices are evoked too. 'Vimy Ridge' explores the horror of the unsung sacrifice in wartime, a theme pursued in *The Thirteenth Disciple* (1931). MacDiarmid's 'innumerable Christs' are revisited, as 'Crossless, unkissed, unknown'; seven years after the event, the 'poor fools' wait for resurrection. The untitled French poem, immediately translated (I have given the first line as the title) is particularly moving in the light of the writer's own fate: 'La vie est breve'. Images of sunsets and settings 'At Dusk' are as prevalent here as in the prose. Gibbon's visionary tendencies can be seen here in his constant use of the motifs of dream, and dream-self. The most immediate aspect of this poetry is how closely (with the exception of the items of love for his wife) it mirrors the concerns of the prose.

Heroes at home and abroad are celebrated, with poetic tributes to 'Spartacus' (celebrated, of course, in Gibbon's inspirational novel of the same title), Christ, Lenin, Karl Liebknecht, Rosa Luxembourg and 'The Communards of Paris'. Intellectual icons are celebrated, from 'Rupert Brooke' to Ruskin's memory in 'Nostalgia' (incidentally, the section about a walk by Drumtochy Burn in 'The Land' recalls Ruskin on Scottish burns). In these celebrations, too, there are precise parallels to the fiction, with 'Lost' (God lost in London) and 'Christ' (a tourist attraction in

Jerusalem) anticipating 'Forsaken'. There is a nineteenth-
century flavour to much of this, with traces of Robert Louis
Stevenson in items like 'The Rainbow Road': 'Oh, happy
are we who find not what we seek.' Gibbon experiments in
traditional poetic forms, too – in the 'Sonnets' sequence,
for instance – and enjoys playing with the shape of poetry
on the page in 'A Last Nightfall'. He has a gift for the
memorable line; 'The Photograph' recalls, 'The wash and
glide of old tides in your eyes' and, in the draft version of
'Tearless': 'Was it darkness drowned you or light.'

Suprisingly, there is only one poem in Scots; 'Morven' is
a gently nostalgic lyric, in the style of Soutar's 'Bairn
Rhymes', and with echoes of the Ossianic cycle's placing
of Morven as Scotland's lost homeland. Unlike the North
East idioms, mixed with English, of the fiction, this is a
more national form of Scots; again, there is a hint of
Stevenson's poetry in Scots; 'A Mile an' a Bittock' comes
to mind, with its foray 'Abüne the burn, ayont the law' by
moonlight, comparable to Gibbon's 'Ayont the brig and up
the brae' (albeit in the company of 'lads', rather than
Gibbon's 'lassie').

Gibbon is at his most personal in his poetry, and it is
tempting to engage in psychoanalytical speculations. There
is a strong melancholic tendency in poems like 'A Song of
Limbo', where the poet regrets the lost 'days that are dead'
and cries out, in a different way from De La Mare, '*Come
hither*!' 'In Memoriam, Ray Mitchell' is a heartbreaking
tribute to a lost baby, who died within six days of birth. As
so often, Gibbon seeks comfort in nature, 'in the call of
sheep/On windy moors', as well as through communion
with humanity, in 'the benediction of another's tears'.

'Dead Love' is amongst the most disturbing poems here,
chilling because of its directness: 'We part not, my dear and
I/With bitter word'; 'For when I looked within your eyes/
(Once stranger than the strangest skies)/Far down through
all the rayless ways/I came where your soul lies.' However,

at the end it becomes closer to catharsis, as the narrator offers comfort to the lost lover in the dawn, as 'wild purple hills ablaze/Fire the dark valleys'.

There is great joy in Gibbon's work, though, and the lugubrious pieces should be set against the poetry dedicated to his wife. The sonnet sequence, for example, is presented as a gift of love, with his innermost thoughts. The most endearing items include the exuberantly familiar 'Rhea, Remembered Suddenly', and the more contemplative 'To My Lady Rhea'. The nature of love is considered in items like 'The Lovers' where the realisation of love affirms a lasting faith in humanity. There are even lighthearted pieces (and Gibbon was a hilarious correspondent) like 'To Billie on her Birthday'. In short, like the prose, the poetry ranges through a vast array of subjects; the weighting towards the persona, however, is heavier in verse.

Yet another area of activity is Gibbon's exotic writing, fictional and documentary. There are many interconnexions and overlaps between the next three sections, which include Gibbon's factual and fictional discussions. He is subtle in his approach to ideas, as well as to language; eclectic in treating different times and places.

The 'Polychromata' series, from *The Cornhill Magazine* (1929–30), consists of tales of adventure and mystery, based around Cairo and the Nile. These racy, and sometimes mystical, pieces draw detail from Gibbon's formative experiences in the Royal Army Service Corps, between 1919 and 1923, in locations throughout the Middle East. Uneven in quality, they nevertheless illustrate Gibbon's continuing quest for new subjects, and new insights.

'Polychromata' has stylistic parallels with the Scottish fiction. The stream-of-consciousness style Gibbon favours in Scots is in the English pieces here. 'The Road', for instance, opens in frenetic fashion: 'Some procession religious, I think. Ah no, the Warren strikers . . . And look – God mine, here in Cairo! – *a women's contingent!*' There is, perhaps, a sense of the 'translation' Gibbon identified as the fate of the truly Scots writer working in English. The exercise certainly allows him to explore the colonial mentality in detail. However, the breathless, intimate style, at its best – the evocative treatment of 'The Life and Death of Elias Constantinidos'; the 'half-twilight' of London life imagined in 'Daybreak' – makes them compelling reading.

The section 'One Man with a Dream', is near-metaphysical, exploring connexions between the past and present, and alternative states of mind. Edinburgh bodysnatchers are relocated to Egypt in 'For Ten's Sake'. 'A Stele from Atlantis', on some levels, pays tribute to Rider Haggard; in Gibbon's hands, though, the faintly ridiculous plot has a wryly acerbic twist. Gibbon explored the lost world of Atlantis in more detail in *Three Go Back* (1932). The past becomes a terrifying setting for the horrifically lonely tale of 'The Woman of Leadenhall Street'; it coincides with the present, with grim humour, in 'First and Last Woman'. These are nightmare visions of the future, in the vein of *Gay Hunter* (1934). At times they are even bleaker than Huxley's *Brave New World* (1932). There are, equally, uplifting tales: in the gentler 'Roads to Freedom', for instance, a fallen man is rehabilitated through his kinship with nature.

'The Glamour of Gold' shows Gibbon's delight in exploration, as he discusses adventurers of the past, and their modern anthropological interpreters. 'The Glamour of Gold and the Givers of Life' is a capsule foreword for Gibbon's theme here of 'Man the Explorer'; on geographical and anthropological levels. As a diffusionist, Gibbon was fascinated by colonising impulses. 'Religions of Ancient Mexico' shows Gibbon's thirst for collecting data about subjects close to his heart; 'The Buddha of America' adopts an idiosyncratic position on religious history.

Gibbon's Scottish identity is apparent, though, even in the treatments of international figures and issues. 'Mungo Park Attains the Niger and Passes Timbuctoo' portrays a legendary, national figure in his international context, in a documentary style. Gibbon, perhaps, sensed a kindred spirit in Park: 'Cool, impassioned, cowardly, courageous, imperturbable', constantly questing for 'the mystery river to the mystery city'. 'Don Christóbal Colon and the Earthly Paradise' explores the discovery of America and 'The End of the Maya Old Empire' turns to one of Gibbon's pet topics.

The unfinished work promised to be every bit as varied and controversial. The penultimate section here brings together Gibbon's synopses for works he never had the chance to complete. Some are fictional – the notes for a sequel to *Stained Radiance* are of particular interest to those who have read the novel; Garland's fate is surprising. There are histories of the self and of other cultures. 'Memoirs of a Materialist', sketched out like a film, promises to be as wide-ranging as *Scottish Scene*. 'Men of the Mearns' was to have been Gibbon's definitive novel about the Covenanters.

There are also two short articles by Gibbon, showing him to be every bit as opinionated in his journalism as in fiction and poetry. 'A Novelist Looks at the Cinema' has the alternative title 'A Philistine looks at the Films' (elsewhere Gibbon expresses his admiration for the Philistines who, at least, knew how to appreciate a good sunset). Gibbon asserts: 'Like most intelligent people I prefer the cinema to the theatre'. 'Controversy: Writers' International (British Section)' stands in defence of revolutionary writers, and Gibbon proclaims 'I am a revolutionary writer,' advocating the formation of 'a union of revolutionary writers' with the exception of 'paragraphists, minor reviewers, ghastly poetasters and all the like amateurs'.

The final section, 'The Speak of the Mearns', brings this collection full circle, with Gibbon back in the world of 'Smeddum'. Much of this is reminiscent of what MacDiarmid calls, in his essay on the 'Modern Scene' in *Scottish Scene* the thesis-novel, 'markedly propagandist of 'the new Scotland' (he draws attention to Gibbon, the Muirs, Eric Linklater and Nancy Brysson Morrison as among the finest proponents in this style). This is the story of quintessentially North East folk, told in the various voices of the community, but the proposed ending shows that Gibbon envisaged a bleaker fate for these folk than in his previous work. Gibbon's genius lies in his ability to make imaginative journeys both at home and outwith his Scottish experiences, but his work was always rooted in North East Scotland. Whether writing about the *Scottish Scene*, national and local, or voyaging through the realms of personal experiences (particularly in his verse) he speaks with a distinctively Scottish voice. There is a constant willingness to explore, and map out, familiar and exotic landscapes. His work is assertive, encompasses a huge range of subject matter, and is always individualistic. To use one of his story titles, he is 'He Who Seeks' and the journey is as important as the destination.

The work is permeated with 'smeddum'; that story, more than any, epitomises Gibbon's own approach to literature: he is self-sufficient, strong-willed, and his vision is rooted, like Meg Menzies, in life based on the land. Gibbon should be admired, above all, for his experimental approach to ideas, themes and topics, and for his strength in expressing these ideas. It is hoped that this anthology will help readers reach a deeper understanding of the well-loved writer of the *Scots Quair*, and an appreciation of his value as a great Scottish writer of international significance.

Valentina Bold

Notes

1. For more information about Mitchell, visit the Grassic Gibbon Centre at Arbuthnott, website at http://www.stonehaven. org.uk/grassic.htm. See too Ian S. Munro, *Leslie Mitchell: Lewis Grassic Gibbon* (1966), Ian Campbell, *Lewis Grassic Gibbon* (1985) and Douglas Gifford, *Neil M. Gunn and Lewis Grassic Gibbon* (1983). Clarke Geddes, *Nemesis in the Mearns* (1996) is a novel about Mitchell's life between 1911 and 1935.

2. Previous collections have been neither comprehensive nor definitive. Ian S. Munro's out of print *A Scots Hairst: essays and short stories* (1967) does not fully reflect the range of Gibbon's work, printing essays out of sequence, and without links. It does, however, include essays from Gibbon's 'Arbuthnott School Essay Book' and several poems. *Smeddum: stories and essays* (1980), edited by D.M. Budge, is a small volume, with commentaries, and William K. Malcolm includes a few poems in an appendix to *A Blasphemer & Reformer. A Study of James Leslie Mitchell/Lewis Grassic Gibbon* (1984). Ian Campbell has long been Gibbon's champion, editing *Spartacus* (1990), *Three Go Back* (1995), *Persian Dawns, Egyptian Nights* (1997) and *The Speak of the Mearns* (1994), the last mentioned reprinting the complete draft of the book, in its near-complete form.

3. There are several modern editions of *A Scots Quair*, including the Canongate Classics version, edited by Tom Crawford, and J.B. Pick's edition of *Sunset Song*. A variety of Gibbon's novels have recently been reprinted, including his first, social realist novel *Stained Radiance* (1930), the reimagined history of *Spartacus* (1933) and the science fantasies *Three Go Back* (1932), *Gay Hunter* (1934) and *The Lost Trumpet* (1932).

4. As Douglas F. Young shows, in *Beyond the Sunset* (1973), diffusionism is a key element in Gibbon's work.

5. The four short stories, *Smeddum, Clay, Greenden* and *Sim* are available as an audiocassette (1995). *Clay, Smeddum* and *Greenden* were also made into a Play for Today by BBC Scotland

(1976), dir. Moira Armstrong, with notable performances from Fulton Mackay as Webster the grocer, Eileen MacCallum as Meg Menzies and Claire Neilson as Ellen Simpson. Flora Garry, 'Bennygoak, The Hill of the Cuckoo', *Bennygoak and other poems*, 3rd edn (1975), pp. 13–14. On North East traditions, see the CD-Rom *Northern Folk: Living Traditions of North East Scotland*, (eds.) Valentina Bold and Tom McKean (1999) and David Buchan, *The Ballad and the Folk* (1997). For further information on the distinctive bothy songs of North East Scotland see *Scottish Tradition 1: Bothy Ballads, Music from the North-East* (1993), CDTRAX 9001 and *The Greig-Duncan Folk Song Collection*, (eds.) Patrick Shuldham-Shaw and Emily B. Lyle, 8 vols (1995–present).

Acknowledgements

I would like to thank Rhea Martin for her kind permission to include all of the items in this volume. Thanks are also due to the National Library of Scotland for material in the section 'Songs of Limbo', which is all taken from NLS MS 26058 with the exception of the final item, which appears courtesy of Aberdeen University Library, and is from AUL 2377/1/31. I am also grateful to Ian Campbell for his pioneering work in reprinting Mitchell's work, particularly 'The Speak of the Mearns'.

Valentina Bold

I

Scottish Scene

or

The Intelligent Man's Guide to Albyn

Curtain Raiser

MR LEWIS GRASSIC GIBBON proposed the scheme of this book to Mr Hugh MacDiarmid. Then they drew up a synopsis and went their separate ways, each to write his separate sections – one wrote the most of his in a pleasant village near London, the other in the sound of the running seas by the Shetlands. They believed that distance from the Scottish Scene would lend them some clarity in viewing it.

But – though they agree in many matters – their views of that scene are conditioned by many other factors than those of separate geographical focus. The standpoint of the one in controversial matters – and what matters in modern Scotland are not controversial?—is not necessarily that of the other. The one (as these pages will make plain) is seldom a convert to the other's entire beliefs. Yet perhaps this is rather advantage than disadvantage. Viewing the Scottish Scene from such different angles, cultural and geographical, may give the better composite picture.

L.G.G.
H. MACD.
1934

The Antique Scene

THE HISTORY OF Scotland may be divided into the three phases of Colonisation, Civilisation, and Barbarisation.

That the last word is a synonym for Anglicisation is no adverse reflection upon the quality of the great English culture. Again and again, in the play of the historic forces, a great civilisation on an alien and lesser has compassed that alien's downfall.

Few things cry so urgently for rewriting as does Scots history, in few aspects of her bastardised culture has Scotland been so ill-served as by her historians. The chatter and gossip of half the salons and drawing-rooms of European intellectualism hang over the antique Scottish scene like a malarial fog through which peer the fictitious faces of heroic Highlanders, hardy Norsemen, lovely Stewart queens, and dashing Jacobite rebels. Those stage-ghosts shamble amid the dimness, and mope and mow in their ancient parts with an idiotic vacuity but a maddening persistence. Modern research along orthodox lines balks from the players, or renames them shyly and retires into footnotes on Kaltwasser.

Yet behind those grimaces of the romanticised or alien imagination a real people once lived and had its being, and hoped and feared and hated, and was greatly uplifted, and loved its children, and knew agony of the patriotic spirit, and was mean and bestial, and generous, and sardonically merciful. Behind the posturings of those poltergeists are the lives of millions of the lowly who wiped the sweats of toil from browned faces and smelt the pour of waters by the Mull of Kintyre and the winds of autumn in the Grampian haughs and the sour, sweet odours of the upland tarns; who tramped in their varying costumes and speeches to the colour and play of the old guild-towns; who made great poetry and sang it; who begat their kind in shame or delight in the begetting; who were much as you or I, human animals bedevilled or uplifted by the play of the forces of civilisation in that remote corner of the Western world which we call Scotland.

All human civilisations originated in Ancient Egypt. Through the accident of time and chance and the cultivation of wild barley in the Valley of the Nile, there arose in a single spot on the earth's surface the urge in men to upbuild for their economic salvation the great fabric of civilisation. Before the planning of that architecture enslaved the minds of men, man was a free and happy and undiseased animal wandering the world in the Golden Age of the poets (and reality) from the Shetlands to Tierra del Fuego. And from that central focal point in Ancient Egypt the first civilisers spread abroad the globe the beliefs and practices, the diggings and plantings and indignations and shadowy revilements of the Archaic Civilisation.

They reached Scotland in some age that we do not know, coming to the Islands of Mist in search of copper and gold and pearls, Givers of Life in the fantastic theology that followed the practice of agriculture. They found the Scots lowlands and highlands waving green into morning and night tremendous forests where the red deer belled, where the great bear, perhaps, had still his tracks and his caverns, where wolves howled the hills in great scattering packs, where, in that forested land, a danker climate than today prevailed. And amid those forests and mountain slopes lived the Golden Age hunters – men perhaps mainly of Maglemosian stock, dark and sinewy and agile, intermixed long ages before with other racial stocks, the stock of Cro-Magnard and Magdalenian who had followed the ice-caps north when the reindeer vanished from the French valleys. They were men naked, cultureless, without religion or social organisation, shy hunters, courageous, happy, kindly, who stared at the advent of the first great boats that brought the miners and explorers of the Archaic Civilisation from Crete or Southern Spain. They flocked down to stare at the new-comers, to offer tentative gifts of food and the like; and to set on their necks the yoke under which all mankind has since passed.

For the Archaic Civilisation rooted in Scotland. Agriculture was learned from the Ancient Mariners and with it the host of rites deemed necessary to propitiate the gods of the earth and sky. Village communities came into being, the first peasants with the first overlords, those priestly overlords who built the rings of the Devil Stones on the high places from Lewis to Aberdeenshire. And the ages came and passed and the agricultural belts grew and spread, and the smoke of sacrifice rose from a thousand altars through the length and breadth of the land at the times of seedtime and harvest, feast and supplication. They buried their dead in modifications of the Egyptian fashion, in Egyptian graves. There came to them, in the slow ebb of the centuries, a driftage of other cultural elements from that ferment of civilisation in the basin of the Mediterranean. They learned their own skill with stick and stone, presently with copper, and at last with bronze. But, until the coming of the makers of bronze that Archaic civilisation in Scotland, as elsewhere, was one singularly peaceful and undisturbed. Organised warfare had yet to dawn on the Western World.

How it dawned is too lengthy a tale to tell here in any detail: how bands of forest-dwellers in the Central European areas, uncivilised, living on the verge of the great settlements of the Archaic communities and absorbing little but the worst of their practices, fell on those communities and murdered them was the first great tragedy of pre-Christian Europe. The ancient matriarchies of the Seine were wiped from existence and in their place (and presently across the Channel) came swarming the dagger-armed hosts of a primitive who, never civilised, had become a savage. This was the Kelt.

We see his advent in the fragments of sword and buckler that lie ticketed in our museums; but all the tale of that rape of a civilisation by the savage, far greater and infinitely more tragic than the rape of the Roman Empire by the Goth, is little more than a faint moan and murmur in the immense cañons of near-history. In Scotland, no doubt, he played his characteristic part, the Kelt, coming armed on a peaceful population, slaying and robbing and finally enslaving, establishing himself as king and overlord, routing the ancient sunpriests from the holy places and establishing his own devil-haunted, uneasy myths and gods through the efforts of the younger sons. From Berwick to Cape Wrath the scene for two hundred years must have been a weary repetition, year upon year, of invasion and murder, inversion and triumph. When Pytheas sailed the Scottish coasts it is likely that the Kelt had triumphed almost everywhere. By the time the Romans came raiding across the English Neck Scotland was a land of great barbaric Kelt tribes, armed and armoured, with a degenerate, bastardised culture and some skill in war and weapon-making. It was as capable of producing a ferocious soldiery and a great military leader like Calgacus as it was incapable of a single motif in art or song to influence the New Civilisation of the European World.

Yet of that culture of those Picts or Painted Men, those Caledonians whom the Romans encountered and fought and marvelled upon, it is doubtful if a single element of any value had been contributed by the Kelt. It is doubtful if the Kelts ever contributed a single item to the national cultures of the countries miscalled Keltic. It is doubtful for the best of reasons: There is no proof that the Kelts, invading Britain, came in any great numbers. They were a conquering military caste, not a people in migration: they imposed their language and their social organisation upon the basic Maglemosian-Mediterranean stock; they survived into remoter times, the times of Calgacus, the times of Kenneth MacAlpin, as nobles, an aristocracy on horseback. They survive to the present day as a thin strand in the Scottish population: half Scotland's landed gentry is by descent Normanised Kelt. But the Kelts are a strain quite alien to the indubitable and original Scot. They were, and remain, one of the greatest curses of the Scottish scene, quick, avaricious, unintelligent, quarrelsome, cultureless,

and uncivilisable. It is one of the strangest jests of history
that they should have given their name to so much that is
fine and noble, the singing of poets and the fighting of great
fights, in which their own actual part has been that of
gaping, unintelligent audition or mere carrion-bird raiding.

The first serious modification of the basic Pictish stock
did not occur until towards the end of the sixth Christian
century, when the Northumbrian Angles flowed upwards,
kingdom-building, as far as the shores of the Firth of Forth.
They were a people and nation in transit; they exterminated
or reduced to villeinage the Kelt-led Picts of those lands:
they succeeded in doing those things not because they were
braver or more generous or God-inspired than the Pictish
tribes, but because of the fact that they were backed by the
Saxon military organisation, their weapons were better, and
apparently they fronted a congeries of warring tribes in-
anely led in the usual Keltic fashion – tribes which had
interwarred and raided and murdered and grown their
crops and drunk their ale unstirred by alien adventures
since the passing of the Romans. The Angle pressed north,
something new to the scene, bringing his own distinctive
culture and language, his own gods and heroes and hero-
myths. About the same time a tribe of Kelt-led Irish
Mediterraneans crossed in some numbers into Argyllshire
and allied themselves with, or subdued the ancient inhabitants. From that alliance or conquest arose the kingdom
of Dalriada – the Kingdom of the Scots. Yet this Irish
invasion had no such profound effect on the national
culture as the coming of the Angles in the South: the Irish
Scots were of much the same speech and origin as the
Argyllshire natives among whom they settled.

With the coming of the Angles, indeed, the period of
Colonisation comes to a close. It is amusing to note how
modern research disposes of the ancient fallacies which saw
Scotland overrun by wave after wave of conquering, colonising peoples. Scotland was colonised only twice – once

fairly completely, once partially, the first time when the Maglemosian hunters drifted north, in hunting, happy-go-lucky migration; the second time, when the Angles lumbered up into Lothian. The Kelt, the Scot, the Norseman, the Norman were no more than small bands of raiders and robbers. The peasant at his immemorial toil would lift his eyes to see a new master installed at the broch, at the keep, at, later, the castle: and would shrug the matter aside as one of indifference, turning, with the rain in his face, to the essentials of existence, his fields, his cattle, his woman in the dark little eirde, earth-house.

The three hundred years after that almost simultaneous descent of Scot and Angle on different sectors of the Scottish scene is a tangle of clumsy names and loutish wars. Kings bickered and bred and murdered and intrigued, armies marched and counter-marched and perpetrated heroisms now dust and nonsense, atrocities the dried blood of which are now not even dust. Christianity came in a number of guises, the Irish heresy a chill blink of light in its coming. It did little or nothing to alter the temper of the times, it was largely a matter of politics and place-seeking, Columba and John Knox apart there is no ecclesiastic in Scots history who does not but show up in the light of impartial research as either a posturing ape, rump-scratching in search of soft living, or as a moronic dullard, hagridden by the grisly transplanted fears of the Levant. The peasant merely exchanged the bass chanting of the Druid in the pre-Druid circles for the whining hymnings of priests in wood-built churches; and turned to his land again.

But presently, coastwise, north, west, and east, a new danger was dragging him in reluctant levies from his ancient pursuits. This was the coming of the Norsemen.

If the Kelts were the first great curse of Scotland, the Norse were assuredly the second. Both have gathered to themselves in the eyes of later times qualities and achievements to which the originals possessed no fragment of a

claim. The dreamy, poetic, God-moved Kelt we have seen
as a mere Chicagoan gangster, murderous, avaricious,
culturally sterile, a typical aristocrat, typically base. The
hardy, heroic Norseman uncovers into even sorrier reality.
He was a farmer or fisherman, raiding in order to supplement the mean livelihood he could draw from more praiseworthy pursuits in the Norwegian fjords. The accident of
his country lying at the trans-Baltic end of the great trans-
Continental trade-route had provided him with the knowledge of making steel weapons in great number and abundance. Raiding Scotland, he was in no sense a superior or
heroic type subduing a lowly or inferior; he was merely a
pirate with a good cutlass, a thug with a sudden and
efficient strangling-rope. Yet those dull, dyspeptic whey-
faced clowns have figured in all orthodox histories as the
bringers of something new and vital to Scottish culture, as
an invigorating strain, a hard and splendid ingredient. It is
farcical that it should be necessary to affirm at this late day
that the Norseman brought nothing of any permanence to
Scotland other than his characteristic gastritis.

Yet that cutlass carved great sections from the Scottish
coasts: presently all the Western Isles had suffered a profound infiltration of the thin, mean blood of the northern
sea-raiders. In the east, the attacks were almost purely
burglarious. The hardy Norseman, with his long grey face
so unfortunately reminiscent of a horse's, would descend
on that and this village or township, steal and rape and fire,
and then race for his ships to escape encounter with the
local levies. On such occasions as he landed in any force,
and met the Picts (even the idiotically badly-led, Kelt-led
Picts) in any force, he would, as at the Battle of Aberlemno,
be routed with decision and vigour. Yet those constant
raidings weakened the Eastern kingdom of the Picts: in AD
844 the Scot king, Kenneth MacAlpin, succeeded to the
Pictish throne – it was evidently regarded as the succession
of a superior to the estates of an inferior. Thereafter the

name Pict disappears from Scottish history, though, paradoxically immortal, the Pict remained.

From 1034, when Duncan ascended the Scottish throne,
until 1603, when James VI ascended the English throne,
Scotland occupied herself, willy-nilly, in upbuilding her
second (and last) characteristic civilisation. Her first, as we
have seen, was that modification of the Archaic Civilisation
which the Kelts overthrew; this second which slowly
struggled into being under the arrow-hails, the ridings
and rapings and throat-cuttings of official policy, the jealous restraints of clerical officialdom, was compounded of
many cultural strands. It was in essentials a Pictish civilisation, as the vast majority of the inhabitants remained Picts.
But, in the Lowlands, it had changed once again its speech,
relinquishing the alien Keltic in favour of the equally alien
Anglo-Saxon. The exchange was a matter of domestic
policy, a febrific historical accident hinged on the bed-
favours wrung from his consort by the henpecked Malcolm
Canmore.

The third of the name of Malcolm to rule in Scotland, his
speech, his court, and his official pronunciamentos were all
Keltic until he wedded the Princess Margaret, who had fled
from the Norman invasion of England. A great-niece of
Edward the Confessor, Margaret was a pious daughter of
the Church and greatly shocked at the Keltic deviations
from Roman dates and ceremonial incantations. She devoted her life to bringing the usages of the Scottish Church
into harmony with orthodox Catholicism. She bred assiduously: she bred six sons and two daughters, and in return
for the delights of the shameful intimacies which begat this
offspring, the abashed Malcolm refrained from any hand in
their christening. They were all christened with good
English names, they were taught English as their native
speech, they lived to grow up and Anglicise court and
church and town. Of the two great women in Scots history
it is doubtful if the most calamitously pathological influ-

ence should be ascribed to Margaret the Good or to Mary the Unchaste.

Yet this Anglicisation was a surface Anglicisation. English speech and English culture alike were as yet fluid things: it meant no cultural subjection to the southern half of the island. It begat a tradition, a speech, an art and a literature in the southern half of Scotland which were set in an Anglo-Saxon, not an English, mould, but filled with the deep spiritual awarenesses of the great basic race which wielded this new cultural weapon as once it had wielded the Keltic. It was a thing national and with a homely and accustomed feel, this language in which Wyntoun and Barbour and Blind Harry were presently telling the epic stories of the great War of Independence.

The effect of that war, the unceasing war of several centuries, was calamitous to the Scots civilisation in the sense that it permanently impoverished it, leaving Scotland, but for a brief blink, always a poor country economically, and a blessing in that it set firmly in the Scots mind the knowledge of national homogeneity: Scotland was the home of true political nationalism (once a liberating influence, not as now an inhibiting one) – not the nationalism forced upon an unwilling or indifferent people by the intrigues of kings and courtesans, but the spontaneous uprising of an awareness of blood-brotherhood and freedom-right. In the midst of the many dreary and shameful pages of the book of Scottish history the story of the rising of the Scots under the leadership of William Wallace still rings splendid and amazing. Wallace was one of the few authentic national heroes: authentic in the sense that he apprehended and moulded the historic forces of his time in a fashion denied to all but a few of the world's great political leaders – Cromwell, Lincoln, Lenin.

It was 1296. Scotland, after a dynastic squabble on the rights of this and that boorish noble to ascend the Scottish throne and there cheat and fornicate after the divine rights of kings, had been conquered, dismembered and ground in the mud by Edward the First of England. He did it with a cold and bored efficiency, as a man chastising and chaining a slobbering, yelping cur. Then he returned to England; and the chained cur suddenly awoke in the likeness of a lion.

'The instinct of the Scottish people,' wrote John Richard Green, 'has guided it right in choosing Wallace for its national hero. He was the first to assert freedom as a national birth-right.' His assertion roused Scotland. The peasants flocked to his standard – suddenly, and for perhaps the first time in Scots history, stirred beyond their customary indifference over the quarrels of their rulers. Here was something new, a leader who promised something new. Nor did he only promise: presently he was accomplishing. At the head of a force that bore the significant title of the 'Army of the Commons of Scotland' Wallace met and routed the English in pitched battle at Cambuskenneth Bridge in 1297, was offered the crown of Scotland, refused it, and instead was nominated Guardian of Scotland, a great republican with the first of the great republican titles, albeit he called himself a royalist.

For a year it seemed his cause would sweep everything before it. The laggard nobles came to join him. Presently the Army of the Commons of Scotland was being poisoned by the usual aristocratic intrigues, though still the troubled peasants and townsmen clung to their faith in the Guardian. The news came that Edward in person was on the march against Scotland. Wallace assembled all his forces and met the invader at Falkirk. The Scots cavalry, noble-recruited, nobleled, strategically placed to fall on the ranks of the English archers and rout them at the crucial moment, fled without striking a blow. Wallace's great schiltrouns of heroic peasant spearmen were broken and dispersed.

Wallace himself sailed for France, seeking aid there for his distracted country. In 1304 he returned, was captured

by the English, tried and condemned as a traitor, and
hanged, castrated, and disembowelled on Tower Hill. This
judicial murder is one of the first and most dreadful
examples of that characteristic English frightfulness
wielded throughout history against the defenders of alien
and weaker peoples. More serious than Wallace's personal
fate, it murdered that fine hope and enthusiasm that had
stirred the Army of the Scots Commons on the morning of
Falkirk. In a kind of despairing hatred, not hope, the Scots
people turned to support the rebellions of the various
shoddy noble adventurers who now raised the standard
against the English. By intrigue, assassination, and some
strategical skill one of those nobles, Robert the Brus, had
presently disposed of all his rivals, had himself crowned
king, and, after various reverses and flights and hidings and
romantic escapades in company with spiders and Lorne
loons, succeeded in routing the English at the Battle of
Bannockburn. With that victory the Scots royalties came to
their own again, however little the Scots commons.

Yet, in the succeeding centuries of wars and raids,
dynastic begettings and dynastic blood-lettings, the commons of Scotland showed a vigour both un-English and un-
French in defence of the rights of the individual. Villeinage
died early in Scotland: the independent tenant-retainer
came early on the scene in the Lowlands. In the Highlands
the clan system, ostensibly aristocratic, was never so in
actuality. It was a communistic patriarchy, the relation of
the chief to his meanest clansman the relation of an elder
blood brother, seldom of a noble to a serf. The guildsmen
of the towns modelled their policies on those of the Hansa
cities and Augsburg, rather than on the slavish subservience
of their contemporaries in England. Presently the French
alliance, disastrous from a military point of view, was
profoundly leavening the character of Scots culture, leavening, not obliterating it. Scots built and carved and sang
and wrote with new tools of technique and vocabulary to

hand. The Scots civilisation of the fifteenth and sixteenth centuries absorbed its great cultural impulses from the Continent; as a sequence, Scots literature in the fifteenth century is already a great literature while in contemporary England there is little more than the maundering of a poetasting host of semi-illiterates. Despite the feuds and squabbles of noble and king, there came into being a rude plenty in Scotland of the fifteenth and sixteenth centuries. The reign of James the Fourth was, economically and culturally, the Golden Age of the great Scots civilisation. Its duration was brief and its fate soon that which had overtaken the Golden Age of the happy Pict hunters three thousand years before.

The end of James the Fourth at Flodden in 1513, the dark end to the greatest raid of the Scots into England, plunged the country into fifteen years of mis-government, when this and that clownish noble attempted to seize the power through this and that intrigue of palace and bed-chamber. The Golden Age faded rapidly as marauding bands of horse clattered up the cobbled streets of the towns and across the fertile Lowland crop-lands. By the time the Fifth James assumed the power Scotland was a distracted country, the commons bitterly taxed and raided and oppressed, the ruler in castle and keep a gorged and stinking carrion-crow. James, the Commons' King, the one heroic royalty in Scots history, faced a hopeless task with the broken and impoverished Commons but half aware of his championship. He put down the nobles with a ruthless hand, defied the monk-murdering Henry VIII of England, established the Court of Session and the Supreme Court of Justice; he might well have re-established the economic prosperity of his father's reign but for the English invasion of the country in 1542. The nobles refused to join the army he raised – the pitiful Church army routed at Solway Moss. Dying at Falkland Palace a few days later James, God's Scotsman as he has been well called, heard of the birth of a daughter. 'It cam wi' a lass and 'twill gang wi' a lass,' he said, speaking perhaps of his own dynasty; unforeseeing the fact that it was the Scots civilisation itself that that daughter was to see in early eclipse.

That eclipse was inaugurated by the coming of the tumultuous change in Christian ritualism and superstitious practice dignified by the name of Reformation. Into its many causes in Western Europe there is no need to enter here. Nobles hungered to devour Church lands; churchmen were often then, as later, cowardly and avaricious souls; the Church, then as often, seemed intellectually moribund, a dead weight lying athwart the minds of men. So, in apparent dispute as to the correct method of devouring the symbolic body of the dead god, symbolically slain, hell was let loose on the European scene for a long two hundred years. Men fought and died with enthusiasm in the cause of ceremonial cannibalism. In Scotland the Reforming party had been growing to power even in the age of the Fifth James. During the long minority of his daughter, Mary Queen of Scots, it was frequently in possession of the reins of power: in 1557 it gathered together its forces and signed a National Convention for the establishment of the Reformed Faith.

Two years afterwards the ecclesiastic, John Knox, returned from a long exile in England and on the Continent. Knox had served as a slave on the French galleys for eighteen months after the assassination of Cardinal Beaton in 1546, he had definite and clear beliefs on the part the Reformation must play in Scotland, and in the years of his exile he had wandered from haunt to haunt of the European revolutionaries (much as Lenin did in the first decade of the twentieth century) testing out his own creed in converse and debate with Calvin and the like innovators. Once again a Scotsman had arisen capable of apprehending the direction of the historic forces, and determined to enchannel those for the benefit of a Commons' Scotland. The nauseous character of his political allies in Scotland did not deter him from the conflict. In the triumphant Parliament summoned in 1560 the Protestants under his direction established the Reformed Church, forbade the mass, and practically legalised the wholesale seizure of Church property. Knox's intentions with regard to the disposal of that property were definite and unshakable: it would be used for the relief of the poor, for the establishment of free schools, for the sustentation of a free people's priesthood. But, though he had foreseen the direction of the historic forces thus far, history proved on the side of his robbing allies, not on his. The Covenant left the Commons poorer than ever and Knox an embittered and sterile leader, turning from his battle in the cause of the people to sardonic denunciations of the minor moral lapses of the young Queen.

He was a leader defeated: and history was to ascribe to him and his immediate followers, and with justice, blame for some of the most terrible aberrations of the Scots spirit in succeeding centuries. Yet Knox himself was of truly heroic mould; had his followers, far less his allies, been of like mettle, the history of Scotland might have been strangely and splendidly different. To pose him against the screen of antique time as an inhibition-ridden neurotic (as is the modern fashion) who murdered the spirit and hope of an heroic young queen, is malicious distortion of the true picture. The 'heroic young queen' in question had the face, mind, manners and morals of a well-intentioned but hysterical poodle.

Her succession by the calamitous Sixth James, who was summoned to the English throne in 1603, was the beginning of the end of the Scots civilisation. That end came quickly. Not only had temporal power moved from Edinburgh to London (for at least a while) but the cultural focus had shifted as well. There began that long process of barbarisation of the Scots mind and culture which is still in progress. Presently it was understood to be rather a

shameful thing to be a Scotsman, to make Scots poetry, to
be subject to Scots law, to be an inhabitant of the northern
half of the island. The Diffusionist school of historians
holds that the state of Barbarism is no half-way house of a
progressive people towards full and complete civilisation:
on the contrary, it marks a degeneration from an older
civilisation, as Savagery is the state of a people absorbing
only the poorer elements of an alien culture. The state of
Scotland since the Union of the Crowns gives remarkable
support to this view, though the savagery of large portions
of the modern urbanised population had a fresh calamity –
the Industrial Revolution – to father it.

Yet, though all art is no more than the fine savour and
essence of the free life, its decay and death in Scotland was
no real mark of the subjection and decay of the free Scottish
spirit: it was merely a mark of that spirit in an anguished
travail that has not yet ceased. Presently, gathering that
unquenchable force into new focus, came the Covenanting
Times, the call of the Church of Knox to be defended as the
Church of the Commons, of the People, bitterly assailed by
noble and King. That the call was justified we may doubt,
that the higher councils of the Church government themselves were other than sedulously manipulated tyrannies in
the hands of the old landed Keltic gentry may also be
doubted. But to large sections of the Lowland Scots the
Covenant was not so much a sworn bond between themselves and God as between their own souls and freedom.
They flocked to its standards in the second Bishops' War,
they invaded England. For a time the Covenanting Scots
Army at Newcastle dictated English policy, ruled England,
and almost imposed on it the Presbytery. Thereafter, in the
sway and clash of the Parliamentarian wars, it suffered
collapse under the weight of its own prosperity and rotten-
ness. Cromwell forcibly dissolved the General Assembly of
the Scots Church in 1653, incorporated Scotland in the
Commonwealth, and marched home leaving a country

under English military governance – a country chastised and corrected, but strangely unbroken in spirit. Scotland and the Scots, after a gasp of surprise, accepted Cromwell with a wary trust. Here, and again, as once in those brief days when the standards of the Guardian of Scotland unfurled by Stirling Brig, was something new on the Scottish scene – English-inspired, but new and promising. If they laboured under dictatorship, so did the English. If their nobles were proscribed and persecuted, so were the English. If their frontier was down, trade with England and the English colonies was free. . . . It was a glimpse of the Greater Republicanism; and it faded almost before Scotland could look on it. The Second Charles returned and enforced the Episcopacy on the Scots, and from 1660 until 1690 Scotland travailed in such political Terror as has few parallels in history.

The People's Church gathered around it the peasants – especially the western peasants – in its defence. At Rullion Green the Covenanting Army was defeated, and an orgy of suppression followed. Covenanters were tortured with rigour and a sadistic ingenuity before being executed in front of their own houses, in sight of their own women-folk. In the forefront of this business of oppression were the Scots nobles, led by Graham of Claverhouse, 'Bonny Dundee'. This remarkable individual, so much biographied and romanticised by later generations, was both a sadist and a criminal degenerate. He was one in a long train of the Scots nobility. He had few qualities to recommend him, his generalship was poor and his strategy worse. Torturing unarmed peasants was the utmost reach of statesmanship ever achieved by this hero of the romantics. Where he met an army – even a badly organised army as at Drumclog – he was ignominiously defeated and fled with the speed and panic of the thin-blooded pervert that he was. His last battle, that of Killiecrankie, he won by enlisting the aid of the Highlanders against those whom they imagined to be their enemies. His portrayed face has a rat-like look in the mean, cold eyes; his name has a sour stench still in the pages of Scottish history.

That last battle of his marked almost the end of the Church persecutions: the Kirk of Scotland emerged with the Revolution from its long night into a day of power and pomp. So doing, following an infallible law of history, it shed the enthusiasm and high loyalty of all generous souls. From 1690 onwards the history of the churches in Scotland is a history of minor and unimportant brawling on questions of state support and state denunciation, it is an oddly political history, reflecting the dreary play of politics up to and after the Union of the Parliaments, the Union which destroyed the last outward symbols of the national civilisation.

Whatever the growing modern support for repudiation of that Union, it is well to realise that the first tentative moves towards it came from the side of the Scots Parliament, if not of the Scots people. As early as 1689 the Scots Parliament appointed commissioners to treat for an 'incorporating union', though nothing came of it. Scottish trade and Scottish industry was very desperately hampered by the English Navigation Act, in which Scots were treated as aliens; and also by the fact that the Scots lacked any overseas dominion on which to dump their surpluses of wealth and population – though indeed, except in the farcical economics of that time (ours are no less farcical) they had surpluses of neither. The first attempts at Union came to nothing: the Scots turned their energies to founding a colony in Darien.

The attempt was disastrous: the Spaniards, already in possession, and aided and abetted by powerful English influences, beat off the settlers. News of the disaster killed among the Scots people any desire for union with the auld enemy; nor indeed did they ever again support it. The Union was brought about by as strange a series of intrigues as history is aware of: England ingeniously bribed her way to power. There was little real resistance in the Scots Parliament except by such lonely figures as Fletcher of Saltoun. On May 1st, 1707, Scotland officially ceased to be a country and became 'that part of the United Kingdom, North Britain'. Scotsmen officially ceased to be Scots, and became Britons – presumably North Britons. England similarly lost identity – impatiently, on a scrap of paper. But everyone knew, both at home and abroad, that what really had happened was the final subjugation of the Scots by the English, and the absorption of the Northern people into the polity and name of the southern.

There was a smouldering fire of resistance: it sprang to flame twice in the course of the first half-century. In 1715 the Earl of Mar raised the standard for the exiled Jacobite King. He received a support entirely unwarranted by either his own person or that of the puppet monarch whose cause he championed. At the strange, drawn battle of Sheriffmuir the Jacobite rebellion was not so much suppressed as suddenly bored. It was as though its supporters were overtaken by a desire to yawn at the whole affair. They melted from the field, not to assemble, they or their sons, for another thirty years.

This was with the landing of Prince Charles Edward in the Highlands in 1745. Scotland – Scotland of the Highlands, great sections of Scotland of the Lowlands – took him to the heart. The clans rose in his support, not unwillingly following the call of their chiefs. Here was relief from that crushing sense of inferiority that had pressed on the nation since the first day of the Union: here was one who promised to restore the Ancient Times – the time of meal and milk and plenty of the Fifth James; here was one who promised Scotland her nationhood again. In after years it became the fashion to pretend that the vast mass of the Scots people were indifferent to, or hostile to, this last adventure of the Stewarts. But there was no Scotsman worthy of the name who was not, at least at first, an enthusiast and a partisan.

Charles marched from victory to victory: presently he was marching across the Borders with an ill-equipped army of Highlanders and Lowland levies, seeking the support promised him by the English Jacobites. He sought it in vain. To the English Jacobite, to all the English, it was plain that here was no exiled English king come to reclaim his throne: here was something long familiar in wars with the northern enemy – a Scots army on a raid. Charles turned back at Derby, and, turning, lost the campaign, lost the last chance to restore the ancient nationhood of Scotland, lost (which was of no importance) himself.

His final defeat at Culloden inaugurated the ruthless extirpation of the clan system in the Highlands, the extirpation of almost a whole people. Sheep-farming came to the Highlands, depopulating its glens, just as the Industrial Revolution was coming to the Lowlands, enriching the new plutocracy and brutalising the ancient plebs. Glasgow and Greenock were coming into being as the last embers of the old Scots culture flickered and fuffed and went out.

There followed that century and a half which leads us to the present day, a century through which we hear the wail of children in unending factories and in night-time slums, the rantings of place-seeking politicians, the odd chirping and cackling of the bastardised Scots romantic schools in music and literature. It is a hundred and fifty years of unloveliness and pridelessness, of growing wealth and growing impoverishment, of Scotland sharing in the rise and final torturing maladjustments of that economic system which holds all the modern world in thrall. It was a hundred and fifty years in which the ancient Pictish spirit remembered only at dim intervals, as in a nightmare, the cry of the wind in the hair of freemen in that ancient life of the Golden Age, the play of the same wind in the banners of Wallace when he marshalled his schiltrouns at Falkirk.

Greenden

FOLK LAUGHED WHEN they heard of the creatures coming to sit them down in the farm of Greenden that lay west of the Tulloch by Bervie Water. It was a forty-fifty acre place, the Den, wet in the bottom as well it might be so low it lay there in its woods. In the midst stood the biggings; they were old and right dark: from the kitchen door you looked round and up at a jungle, near, lost from the world, so close around and between the trees the broom plants grew, and the whins. But when night came sometimes over the trees and the rank, wild waste of the moor you'd see through a narrow pass in the woods the last of the sun as it kindled a light on the Grampian Hills and went off to its bed. And that light in the mirk was near as much as a man would see of the world outby from the kitchen door of Greenden.

Well, old Grant had farmed there till he died, a steady old stock – fair strong in the hands if weak in the head, was the speak of Murdoch of Mains. For a body hardly ever made out what he said; he would whisper and whisper, whispering even as he girned at his horse in the lithe of the woods that watched Greenden. Soon's he'd been ta'en, the old mistress moved her into Drumlithie and took a bit cottage, and lived on his silver; and sometimes she'd say to a crony at night *It's fine to be here and with sonsy folk*. They thought at first she would miss her man; the minister came, the Free Kirk loon, he snuffled right godly and said through his nose *You'll meet him Above, Mistress Grant*. But at that she gave a kind of a start, near dropped the teapot, she did, when he spoke. *Will I, then? Ay, fegs, I'll confess I hadn't reckoned that.*

Well, that was the Grants gone out of Greenden, there the ill place lay as the winter wore on, not an offer the factor had for it either; a man could sweat out his guts on a better ploy than manuring the dour red clay of the Den. Syne the news went round it was let at last: the factor had let it to no farming body, but a creature from a town, from Glasgow it was; he'd never handled a plough or a graip and Murdoch at the Mains had a story about him. For he'd driven the creature and his wife round the district, and as they went by the parks at Pittendreich they'd seen a roller of old Pittendreich's there, out in the ley the thing was lying. And the body of a woman had gleyed at the thing: *What a shame to let it get rusty, isn't it?* and looked at Murdoch like a fool of a bairn.

Folk took that through hand with a laugh here and there; some said it was surely a lie, though gey witty, for everybody knew that the Murdoch brute could lie like a tink when the mood was on him. True or not, you began to think of the creatures – Simpson the name was – that had taken Greenden and were moving in there at the February end. Ay, they'd find it a change from their Glasgow streets; they didn't know what it was to work, the dirt that came from the towns.

Well, come at last the Simpsons did to Greenden; their gear and furniture came by Bervie, and the Simpson man went there to hire two carts for the carting down of the stuff. Webster the grocer had no rounds that day and he hired out his carts and drove one himself, George Simpson the other, it was late at night when they came to the Den, down through the thick woods, larch it was there, so close the trunks that the night was dark though the light shone still out on the high road that walked by the sea. But they saw in the Den as they wound down there a lantern kindled at last in the mirk, kindled and shining from the kitchen door. And when the carts came rumbling into the close there the wife of Simpson was standing and waiting, the lantern held in her hand.

And Webster took a bit keek at the creature and half thought she must be but Simpson's daughter, no wife she looked, she was thin and slim, bonny in a way, and her eyes were kind. She laughed up at Simpson coming behind, syne smiled at the grocer, and cried up in an English-like voice: *You've been long. I thought I'd have to spend the night down here – all alone by myself in Greenden.*

Alec Webster said *Well, mistress, you'd have ta'en no ill,* And she nodded to that *I know that fine . . . And, of course, the country's lovely to live in.* And she smiled at him like a daft-like quean. He glowered back at her, canny, slow and quiet Alec, he couldn't make head nor tail of her yet, her laugh and that quiver she hid in her laugh.

Syne he loosed and helped them in with their gear, a great clutter of stuff they'd brought up from Glasgow, George Simpson he puffed and paiched right sore, big though he was, with a sappy big face, and a look on that face as though some childe had ta'en him a right hard kick in the dowp. But his lungs were gey bad, he told to the grocer; he'd come out to the country for his lungs, he said. And when Murdoch at Mains heard of that he said: *Faith, the creature's more like to mislay his anatomy than pick up a bit on the rigs of the Den.*

So there were the two of them settled in there, Simpson and the little bit snippet of a wife: she looked light enough for a puff of wind to blow her from the kitchen door at night when she opened that door to come out to the grocer as he drove his van down for her orders on Friday. Alec Webster was a kindly stock, and he cried *Losh, Mistress, you're not in your Glasgow now, you'll fair need to keep yourself wrapped up.* But she only laughed *I'm fine – oh listen to the trees!* And the grocer listened, and heard them sough, and turned him his head and glowered at the woods: they were just as aye they had been, he thought, why should a man stand still and listen? He asked her,

Ellen Simpson, that, and keeked at her white, still stare. And she started again and smiled at him queer. *Oh, nothing. Sorry. But I can't but listen.*

Well, maybe she knew what she meant, he didn't. He sold her her orders – she fair had a lot – and drove away up the February dark; and as he was driving he heard in the dark a hoasting and hacking out there by the barn, and he thought of the Simpson childe and his lungs. Faith, he'd come to the wrong place here for his lungs; it wasn't long likely he would store the kiln.

Mistress Murdoch went down to tea at Greenden. But she couldn't abide George Simpson's mistress, the creature fair got on to her nerves with her flitting here and her tripping there, and her laugh, and the meikle eyes of her in the small doll face that she had. She said it was Simpson she pitied, poor man, with lungs like his and a wife like that, little comfort by day and less in his bed; she herself would rather sleep with a fluff of a feather than depend on *that* on a coldrife night.

And then, as daft-like a blether as ever you heard, the story got about how it was they'd come to move up from Glasgow to Greenden toun. George Simpson himself it was that told it one night he dropped in at the Murdoch house – he would go a bit walk there now and again and gley at the daughter, Jeannie. And the way of their moving from Glasgow had been when his lungs took bad it was plain that he wouldn't last out a long while at his clerking; he was fair for the knackers' yard, you would say. The doctors said he should leave the town, but he'd little fancy for that himself, and his wife had less: she was town-bred, and feared at the country, Ellen: or so he'd aye thought. For next Sunday he'd gone with her to their kirk, and then it was that a hymn was sung, and it fair seemed to change Ellen Simpson's mind. And the hymn was the one that begins with the words:

> There is a green hill far away,
>> Beyond a city wall,
> Where the dear Lord was crucified,
>> Who died to save us all.

So when the Simpsons got back to their house, Ellen Simpson had kept whispering and remembering that tune, and sudden-like she said they must leave the town; they must find a farm where George could work out in the open and mend his ill lungs.

Well, he'd hardly hear of the thing at first, as he told to the Murdochs that night at their house, he thought that work on a farm would kill him. But Ellen had set her mind on the plan, so he set about looking for a place to please her. He'd but little silver to stock up a steading, and land in the south was far overdear, but up in the Mearns he came on Greenden, its rent inside the reach of his pouch. So he'd ta'en his wife up to see it; she'd stared, down in the hollow, and seemed half ta'en back. And then she'd said they must take it, and take it they did, and here now they were; and *she* liked it fine.

And fine well she might, the coarse creature, folk said. It wasn't her had to face up the rains of that year or the coarse ploughing of the ill red clay of Greenden. Ay, Simpson was a fine bit childe, a bit dour, but faith! he was surely a fool as well to let himself be ta'en from a fine town job out to the pleiter and soss of a farm to pleasure that creature his wife and the fancies she'd gotten from hearing a hymn in a kirk. Folk with sense knew that hymns were just things that you sang, douce, and then you forgot the damn things.

Wet it was that spring: March came flooding in rains down the length and breadth of the guttering Howe; every night you'd hear the swash of the water if your place in the bed was next to the wall; the gulls were up from the Bervie beaches and cawing at all hours over the parks. Down in Greenden it was worse than most, and Simpson with his

hoast, poor childe might well have kept in his bed and
blankets, but his creature of a wife wouldn't hear of that,
laughing at him, affronting him into a rage. *Come on, now,
George, the day's half dead! And it's fine, a good day for the
plough.*

So out he'd to get, and out with his pair, and go slow
step-stepping up and down the ley haughs that lined the
deep Den. His ploughing was fair a sight for sore eyes; of a
Sunday the bothy billies would come over, they'd take a bit
dander down to the Den and stand and laugh as they
looked at the drills, they went this way and that: *Damn't
man, they've but little sense in towns!* Syne they'd hear
Mistress Simpson crying to her hens, and see her, small,
like a snippet of a doll, flit over the close on some errand or
another, the poor Simpson childe kept to his bed on the
Sundays.

Well, the spring wore on, fine planting weather came, by
May the sun was blaze of heat, up and down the long Howe
folk shook their heads. With a spring like this you might
well depend that you'd have a summer with sleet, most-
like. But it was well enough while it went, and Murdoch of
Mains took a dander down to the Den now and then to see
how the Simpson man fared. And faith! he'd been kept with
his nose at the grind; he'd his parks as well forward as any
other place. Murdoch hadn't set eyes on him near for a
month, and fair got a shock as he stopped his roller and
stood by to speak. He'd grown thicker and bigger, his face
filled out, you could hardly see the town in him at all.
Murdoch said *Ay man, you're fair a bit farmer.*

And Simpson smiled wan, right patient-like though, with
his sappy red face like an ill-used nout's, and said *Maybe*,
and paiched to listen at his lungs. And then he told that
each night he went to his bed with a back like to break, but
Ellen just laughed, she didn't know what an illness was, he
wasn't the man to fear her and tell her. So Murdoch saw
fine how the thing was going, the Simpson childe working

himself to his grave, with his coarse lungs, too, to please his
coarse wife. There was nothing he could do in the matter,
he thought, but he said they'd aye be pleased to see
Simpson at Mains. He said nothing of Ellen, the bit wife,
in that; there was damn the pleasure to be had in the
creature: with her laugh and her listening and the flutter
of her eyes she fairly got on a body's nerves.

What with rain and with heat the Den was green-lush
right early that year – the grocer thought it came thicker
than ever he minded – the broom stopped up the aisles of
the larch that stretched up the braes from the old brown
biggings of the Den. Ellen Simpson would come running
out to the door as she heard the sound of his wheels on the
close, and cry him good-day, and bring him the eggs, and
stand still while he counted, a slow, canny childe; but once
he raised his head and said: *Losh, but it's still!*

And the two of them stood there and listened in that
quiet, not a sound to be heard or a thing to be seen beyond
the green cup that stood listening around. And Ellen
Simpson smiled white and said *Yes, it is still – and I'll take
two loaves and some tea now, please.*

And Webster took a look at her: thinner she'd grown,
more a wisp than ever, but still with her smile, and he liked
her fine, near the only soul in the district that did. Most said
she'd grown thinner with temper, faith! girning at her man
to get out and start work, and him no more than an invalid,
like.

Just luck she hadn't his death on her hands, and you
couldn't blame him that he fell in the way, nearly every bit
evening he would do it now, of taiking away over the brae
from the Den to the Mains and his Murdoch friends.
Jeannie Murdoch and he would flirt and would fleer –
no harm in their fun, folk 'greed about that: the poor stock
was no doubt in need of a laugh, him and that wife with her
flutterings that fair set your hackles on edge. He was better
than he'd been, he'd confess, would Simpson; all the more

reason why he wanted some cheer when he came in about
to his own fire at night, not aye to be listening to somebody
cry: *Oh, George, do you think your lungs are near better?*

And Jeannie Murdoch would say *No, I'm sure. Sit you
down. I'll make you a fine cup of tea.* And George Simpson
would laugh out his big, sappy laugh *Faith! you're fine as
you're bonny, Jean, lass.*

And Murdoch and his mistress would hear them and
gley, Mistress Murdoch pull down her meikle bit face;
maybe she thought Jeannie went over far with a man that
was married – no more than fun though their speak might
be. If it wasn't for that snippet of a creature, Ellen, you'd
think Simpson as fine a goodson as you'd meet, a bit slow at
the uptake, maybe a bit dour, but a pretty, upstanding
childe he was now.

Folk wondered a bit what she thought of those jaunts,
Ellen Simpson down by her lone in Greenden. But she
never said a word to a soul about them, not that she saw a
many to speak to; she'd just smile, and go running and
bring you some tea, kind enough you supposed that the
creature was, but you'd never get yourself to like her,
somehow; she'd set you at unease till you'd sit and wonder
what ailed yourself – till going up home through the dark
you'd be filled with fancies daft as a carrying woman, as
though the trees moved and the broom was whispering, and
some beast with quiet breath came padding in your tracks;
and you'd look, and 'twas only a whin that you'd passed.
And you'd heave a great breath, outside of the Den, up in
the light of the evening sun, though the Den below was
already in shadow.

But of nights as that summer wore on to its close she took
to standing at her kitchen door while the light drew in and
the dark came close: now and then some soul would come
on her there, near startle her out of her skin as he cried *Ay,
mistress, it's a fine bit night.* And she'd laugh, with her hand
at her breast, daft-like, and then turn her head as though

half she'd forgotten you, and look up and away out over the trees, and you'd look the same way and see feint the thing. And then maybe you'd look harder and see what it was; it was from the kitchen door alone of Greenden that the swathe of the trees and the broom was broken and through the hollow that was left in the gloaming the sun struck light on the Grampian slopes, long miles away and across the Mearns, shining immediate, yet distant and blue, their green earth-hazed in the heatherbells. And that was the thing that she stood and watched as a daftie would, and you'd scrape your feet, and you'd give a bit hoast, and she'd start and switch round, her face gone white, and say *Oh, I'm sorry, I'd forgotten you were here. Was it George that you wanted to see?*

Well, that was in June, and the June-end came, as bonny as ever it came in the Howe; folk meeting the Simpson man on the road would cry to him for a joke *Ay, man, you're fair smothered away from the world in Greenden*. And, faith! they spoke but the truth, so high was the broom with a mantling of bloom, and the trees a wall green-blinding the place. George Simpson made out of it every bit night over to the Mains' new barn they were building; he'd pretend it was the barn he went over to see, but he'd edge away from it as soon as he might, taik round to the kitchen, and Jeannie would blush: *Step away in, Mr Simpson. How are you? I'm sure you are tired.*

Well, that barn it was, Webster was to swear, brought to an end that steer at Greenden. He never told the story in a neighbour-like way, he never did that, and he wasn't much liked, for he'd never much news to give a body when you spoke to him at the tail of his van and would drop a bit hint that you'd like to know why the Gordon quean was getting gey stout, and if Wallace was as coarse as they said to his wife, and such newsy-like bits of an interest to folk. He'd just grunt when you spoke and start counting the eggs, and say he was damned if he knew or he cared. So he told the

Greenden tale to none but his wife; he thought her the same as himself, did Alec. But faith! she could claik a tink from a door, and soon it was known up and down the Howe, every bit of the happening that night at Greenden.

For he'd driven down late, as aye he had done, the grocer, and was coming in by the yard when he met Ellen Simpson come running up the road; her face was white in the fading light, and twice as she ran he saw her fall; and she picked herself up with blood on her face where a stone had cut as she fell. And Webster stopped his horse and jumped off the van and went running to meet her; and he cried *God, mistress, what's ta'en you – what's wrong?*

And she gabbled as he held her, he saw her eyes wild, syne she quieted a minute and covered her eyes and shivered, hot though the June night was. Then she whispered sudden, he shivered himself, *They've done something to my hill, they have taken it away! Oh, I can't stand it now, I can't, I can't!*

And Webster said *What?* He was clean dumb-foundered; and he thought in a flash of old Grant of Greenden – he also had whispered and whispered like that. But she pointed up across the larch-hill and the broom, and he gowked, did the grocer, and saw nothing for a while. Syne he saw that there rose through that howe in the woods, through which you'd once see the light gleam on the hills, the roof and the girders of Murdoch's new barn. He stared at the thing, and then stared at the woman, and at that she broke down and cried like a bairn; she'd no shame before him, she was surely daft.

Oh, I can't stand it longer in this hateful place! It's smothering and killing me, down and lost here, I've been frightened, so frightened since the first hour here. I've tried not to show it, and I know that it's nothing, but the trees – they hate me, the fields, and at night . . . Oh, I can't stand it longer, not even for George, now they've blocked up that sight of the hill that was mine!

And she cried out more of that stite, and the grocer – he'd aye liked her – was fair in a way: *Whisht, mistress, go in and lie down,* he said, but she whispered: *Don't leave me, don't leave me, I'm frightened!* And the dark came then down over the broom, and the horse stood champing and scraping its hooves, and a howlet began to hoot in the larch while Webster sat by her in the kitchen to quiet her. And she whispered once: *George – he's safe now, he's safe, God died, but I needn't, He saved him, not I.* And syne she was whispering again in her terror: *The trees and the broom, keep off the trees; it's growing so dark I can't see it, the hill . . .*

But at last she grew quiet; he told her to lie down. She went ben from the kitchen and he stood and thought. And he minded her man might be at the Mains; he went out and drew round his grocer's van, and got into it and drove up out of the Den, and whipped his bit beast to a trot for the Mains.

And folk told when he got there he went stamping in the kitchen: George Simpson was sitting with Jeannie and her father; the mistress was off to the pictures at Bervie. And Alec Webster cried *Leave your courting until you're a widower; have you no shame at all to abandon your wife night after night in that hell of a Den?* And George Simpson stood up and blustered *You Bulgar—,* and the grocer said *Away, raise your hand up to me, you big, well-fed bullock, and I'll crack your jaw where you stand.* Old Murdoch came in between them then, and he cried *What is't? What's wrong?*

So Webster told Simpson his wife was gey queer; was he or was he not going home? And Simpson scowled and said *Yes,* and went out with the grocer, and that childe swung round his weary bit horse and lashed it to a trot, and out into the road, and so, in their time, by the track to the Den. And there it was dark as a fireless lum, but far off as they neared to the biggings they heard a voice singing – singing so strange that it raised their hair:

> There is a green hill far away,
>   Beyond a city wall,
> Where the dear Lord was crucified,
>   Who died to save us all.

And it suddenly ceased, and Webster swore, and he lashed the horse, and they came to the close, and Webster jumped down and ran into the house. Behind him went Simpson, more slow – he was feared. In the kitchen it was dark and still as they came. Then the grocer slipped, there was something slippery and wet on the floor. So he kindled a match, and they both looked up, and they saw what it was, and it turned them sick. And a waft of wind came in from the door and the Shape from the beam swung to and fro.

And Webster turned round and went blundering out, as though he couldn't see, and he called to Simpson: *Take her down and I'll go for the doctor, man.*

But he knew right well that that would help nothing, and the thought went with him as he drove through the woods, up out of the Den, to the road that walked by the sea and the green hills that stood to peer with quiet faces in the blow of the wind from the sunset's place.

Smeddum

SHE'D HAD NINE of a family in her time, Mistress Menzies, and brought the nine of them up, forbye – some near by the scruff of the neck, you would say. They were sniftering and weakly, two-three of the bairns, sniftering in their cradles to get into their coffins; but she'd shake them to life, and dose them with salts and feed them up till they couldn't but live. And she'd plonk one down –

finishing the wiping of the creature's neb or the unco dosing of an ill bit stomach or the binding of a broken head – with a look on her face as much as to say *Die on me now and see what you'll get!*

Big-boned she was by her fortieth year, like a big roan mare, and *If ever she was bonny 'twas in Noah's time*, Jock Menzies, her eldest son would say. She'd reddish hair and a high, skeugh nose, and a hand that skelped her way through life; and if ever a soul had seen her at rest when the dark was done and the day was come he'd died of the shock and never let on.

For from morn till night she was at it, work, work, on that ill bit croft that sloped to the sea. When there wasn't a mist on the cold, stone parks there was more than likely the wheep of the rain, wheeling and dripping in from the sea that soughed and plashed by the land's stiff edge. Kinneff lay north, and at night in the south, if the sky was clear on the gloaming's edge, you'd see in that sky the Bervie lights come suddenly lit, far and away, with the quiet about you as you stood and looked, nothing to hear but a sea-bird's cry.

But feint the much time to look or to listen had Margaret Menzies of Tocherty toun. Day blinked and Meg did the same, and was out, up out of her bed, and about the house, making the porridge and rousting the bairns, and out to the byre to milk the three kye, the morning growing out in the east and a wind like a hail of knives from the hills. Syne back to the kitchen again she would be, and catch Jock, her eldest, a clour in the lug that he hadn't roused up his sisters and brothers; and rouse them herself, and feed them and scold, pull up their breeks and straighten their frocks, and polish their shoes and set their caps straight. *Off you get and see you're not late*, she would cry, *and see you behave your-selves at the school. And tell the Dominie I'll be down the night to ask him what the mischief he meant by leathering Jeannie and her not well.*

They'd cry *Ay, Mother*, and go trotting away, a fair flock

of the creatures, their faces red-scoured. Her own as red, like a meikle roan mare's, Meg'd turn at the door and go prancing in; and then at last, by the closet-bed, lean over and shake her man half-awake. *Come on, then, Willie, it's time you were up.*

And he'd groan and say *Is't?* and crawl out at last, a little bit thing like a weasel, Will Menzies, though some said that weasels were decent beside him. He was drinking himself into the grave, folk said, as coarse a little brute as you'd meet, bone-lazy forbye, and as sly as sin. Rampageous and ill with her tongue though she was, you couldn't but pity a woman like Meg tied up for life to a thing like *that*. But she'd more than a soft side still to the creature, she'd half-skelp the backside from any of the bairns she found in the telling of a small bit lie; but when Menzies would come paiching in of a noon and groan that he fair was tashed with his work, he'd mended all the ley fence that day and he doubted he'd need to be off to his bed – when he'd told her that and had ta'en to the blankets, and maybe in less than the space of an hour she'd hold out for the kye and see that he'd lied, the fence neither mended nor letten a-be, she'd just purse up her meikle wide mouth and say nothing, her eyes with a glint as though she half-laughed. And when he came drunken home from a mart she'd shoo the children out of the room, and take off his clothes and put him to bed, with an extra nip to keep off a chill.

She did half his work in the Tocherty parks, she'd yoke up the horse and the sholtie together, and kilt up her skirts till you'd see her great legs, and cry *Wissh!* like a man and turn a fair drill, the sea-gulls cawing in a cloud behind, the wind in her hair and the sea beyond. And Menzies with his sly-like eyes would be off on some drunken ploy to Kineff or Stone-hive. Man, you couldn't but think as you saw that steer it was well that there was a thing like marriage, folk held together and couldn't get apart; else a black look-out it well would be for the fusionless creature of Tocherty toun.

Well, he drank himself to his grave at last, less smell on the earth if maybe more in it. But she broke down and wept, it was awful to see, Meg Menzies weeping like a stricken horse, her eyes on the dead, quiet face of her man. And she ran from the house, she was gone all that night, though the bairns cried and cried her name up and down the parks in the sound of the sea. But next morning they found her back in their midst, brisk as ever, like a great-boned mare, ordering here and directing there, and a fine feed set the next day for the folk that came to the funeral of her orra man.

She'd four of the bairns at home when he died, the rest were in kitchen-service or fee'd, she'd seen to the settling of the queans herself; and twice when two of them had come home, complaining-like of their mistresses' ways, she'd thrashen the queans and taken them back – near scared the life from the doctor's wife, her that was mistress to young Jean Menzies. *I've skelped the lassie and brought you her back. But don't you ill-use her, or I'll skelp you as well.*

There was a fair speak about that at the time, Meg Menzies and the vulgar words she had used, folk told that she'd even said what was the place where she'd skelp the bit doctor's wife. And faith! that fair must have been a sore shock to the doctor's wife that was that genteel she'd never believed she'd a place like that.

Be that as it might, her man new dead, Meg wouldn't hear of leaving the toun. It was harvest then and she drove the reaper up and down the long, clanging clay rigs by the sea, she'd jump down smart at the head of a bout and go gathering and binding swift as the wind, syne wheel in the horse to the cutting again. She led the stooks with her bairns to help, you'd see them at night a drowsing cluster under the moon on the harvesting cart.

And through that year and into the next and so till the speak died down in the Howe Meg Menzies worked the Tocherty toun; and faith, her crops came none so ill. She rode to the mart at Stonehive when she must, on the old box-cart, the old horse in the shafts, the cart behind with a sheep for sale or a birn of old hens that had finished with laying. And a butcher once tried to make a bit joke. *That's a sheep like yourself, fell long in the tooth.* And Meg answered up, neighing like a horse, and all heard: *Faith, then, if you've got a spite against teeth I've a clucking hen in the cart outbye. It's as toothless and senseless as you are, near.*

Then word got about of her eldest son, Jock Menzies that was fee'd up Allardyce way. The creature of a loon had had fair a conceit since he'd won a prize at a ploughing match – not for his ploughing, but for good looks; and the queans about were as daft as himself, he'd only to nod and they came to his heel; and the stories told they came further than that. Well, Meg'd heard the stories and paid no heed, till the last one came, she was fell quick then.

Soon's she heard it she hove out the old bit bike that her daughter Kathie had bought for herself, and got on the thing and went cycling away down through the Bervie braes in that Spring, the sun was out and the land lay green with a blink of mist that was blue on the hills, as she came to the toun where Jock was fee'd she saw him out in a park by the road, ploughing, the black loam smooth like a ribbon turning and wheeling at the tail of the plough. Another billy came ploughing behind, Meg Menzies watched till they reached the rig-end, her great chest heaving like a meikle roan's, her eyes on the shape of the furrows they made. And they drew to the end and drew the horse out, and Jock cried *Ay*, and she answered back *Ay*, and looked at the drill, and gave a bit snort, *If your looks win prizes, your ploughing never will.*

Jock laughed, *Fegs, then, I'll not greet for that*, and chirked to his horses and turned them about. But she cried him. *Just bide a minute, my lad. What's this I hear about you and Ag Grant?*

He drew up short then, and turned right red, the other

childe as well, and they both gave a laugh, as plough-childes do when you mention a quean they've known overwell in more ways than one. And Meg snapped *It's an answer I want, not a cockerel's cackle: I can hear that at home on my own dunghill. What are you to do about Ag and her pleiter?*

And Jock said *Nothing,* impudent as you like, and next minute Meg was in over the dyke and had hold of his lug and shook him and it till the other childe ran and caught at her nieve. *Faith, mistress, you'll have his lug off!* he cried. But Meg Menzies turned like a mare on new grass, *Keep off or I'll have yours off as well!*

So he kept off and watched, fair a story he'd to tell when he rode out that night to go courting his quean. For Meg held to the lug till it near came off and Jock swore that he'd put things right with Ag Grant. She let go the lug then and looked at him grim: *See that you do and get married right quick, you're the like that needs loaded with a birn of bairns – to keep you out of the jail, I jaloose. It needs smeddum to be either right coarse or right kind.*

They were wed before the month was well out, Meg found them a cottar house to settle and gave them a bed and a press she had, and two-three more sticks from Tocherty toun. And she herself led the wedding dance, the minister in her arms, a small bit childe; and 'twas then as she whirled him about the room, he looked like a rat in the teeth of a tyke, that he thanked her for seeing Ag out of her soss, *There's nothing like a marriage for redding things up.* And Meg Menzies said *EH?* and then she said *Ay,* but queer-like, he supposed she'd no thought of the thing. Syne she slipped off to sprinkle thorns in the bed and to hang below it the great hand-bell that the bothy-billies took them to every bit marriage.

Well, that was Jock married and at last off her hands. But she'd plenty left still, Dod, Kathleen and Jim that were still at school, Kathie a limner that alone tongued her mother, Jeannie that next led trouble to her door. She'd been found at her place, the doctor's it was, stealing some money and they sent her home. Syne news of the thing got into Stonehive, the police came out and tormented her sore, she swore she never had stolen a meck, and Meg swore with her, she was black with rage. And folk laughed right hearty, fegs! that was a clour for meikle Meg Menzies, her daughter a thief!

But it didn't last long, it was only three days when folk saw the doctor drive up in his car. And out he jumped and went striding through the close and met face to face with Meg at the door. And he cried *Well, mistress, I've come over for Jeannie*. And she glared at him over her high, skeugh nose, *Ay, have you so then? And why, may I speir?*

So he told her why, the money they'd missed had been found at last in a press by the door; somebody or other had left it there, when paying a grocer or such at the door. And Jeannie – he'd come over to take Jean back.

But Meg glared *Ay, well, you've made another mistake. Out of this, you and your thieving suspicions together!* The doctor turned red, *You're making a miserable error* – and Meg said *I'll make you mince-meat in a minute.*

So he didn't wait that, she didn't watch him go, but went ben to the kitchen where Jeannie was sitting, her face chalk-white as she'd heard them speak. And what happened then a story went round, Jim carried it to school, and it soon spread out, Meg sank in a chair, they thought she was greeting; syne she raised up her head and they saw she was laughing, near as fearsome the one as the other, they thought. *Have you any cigarettes?* she snapped sudden at Jean, and Jean quavered *No*, and Meg glowered at her cold. *Don't sit there and lie. Gang bring them to me.* And Jean brought them, her mother took the pack in her hand. *Give's hold of a match till I light up the thing. Maybe smoke'll do good for the crow that I got in the throat last night by the doctor's house.*

Well, in less than a month she'd got rid of Jean – packed

off to Brechin the quean was, and soon got married to a creature there – some clerk that would have left her sore in the lurch but that Meg went down to the place on her bike, and there, so the story went, kicked the childe so that he couldn't sit down for a fortnight, near. No doubt that was just a bit lie that they told, but faith! Meg Menzies had herself to blame, the reputation she'd gotten in the Howe, folk said, *She'll meet with a sore heart yet.* But devil a sore was there to be seen, Jeannie was married and was fair genteel.

Kathleen was next to leave home at the term. She was tall, like Meg, and with red hair as well, but a thin fine face, long eyes blue-grey like the hills on a hot day, and a mouth with lips you thought over thick. And she cried *Ah well, I'm off then, mother.* And Meg cried *See you behave yourself.* And Kathleen cried *Maybe; I'm not at school now.*

Meg stood and stared after the slip of a quean, you'd have thought her half-angry, half near to laughing, as she watched that figure, so slender and trig, with its shoulders square-set, slide down the hill on the wheeling bike, swallows were dipping and flying by Kinneff, she looked light and free as a swallow herself, the quean, as she biked away from her home, she turned at the bend and waved and whistled, she whistled like a loon and as loud, did Kath.

Jim was the next to leave from the school, he bided at home and he took no fee, a quiet-like loon, and he worked the toun, and, wonder of wonders, Meg took a rest. Folk said that age was telling a bit on even Meg Menzies at last. The grocer made hints at that one night, and Meg answered up smart as ever of old: *Damn the age! But I've finished the trauchle of the bairns at last, the most of them married or still over young. I'm as swack as ever I was, my lad. But I've just got the notion to be a bit sweir.*

Well, she'd hardly begun on that notion when faith! ill the news that came up to the place from Segget. Kathleen her quean that was fee'd down there, she'd ta'en up with some coarse old childe in a bank, he'd left his wife, they were off together, and she but a bare sixteen years old.

And that proved the truth of what folk were saying, Meg Menzies she hardly paid heed to the news, just gave a bit laugh like a neighing horse and went on with the work of park and byre, cool as you please – ay, getting fell old.

No more was heard of the quean or the man till a two years or more had passed and then word came up to the Tocherty someone had seen her – and where do you think? Out on a boat that was coming from Australia. She was working as stewardess on that bit boat, and the childe that saw her was young John Robb, an emigrant back from his uncle's farm, near starved to death he had been down there. She hadn't met in with him near till the end, the boat close to Southampton the evening they met. And she'd known him at once, though he not her, she'd cried *John Robb?* and he'd answered back *Ay?* and looked at her canny in case it might be the creature was looking for a tip from him. Syne she'd laughed *Don't you know me, then, you gowk? I'm Kathie Menzies you knew long syne – it was me ran off with the banker from Segget!*

He was clean dumbfounded, young Robb, and he gaped, and then they shook hands and she spoke some more, though she hadn't much time, they were serving up dinner for the first-class folk, aye dirt that are ready to eat and to drink. *If ever you get near to Tocherty toun tell Meg I'll get home and see her sometime. Ta-ta!* And then she was off with a smile, young Robb he stood and he stared where she'd been, he thought her the bonniest thing that he'd seen all the weary weeks that he'd been from home.

And this was the tale that he brought to Tocherty, Meg sat and listened and smoked like a tink, forbye herself there was young Jim there, and Jock and his wife and their three bit bairns, he'd fair changed with marriage, had young Jock Menzies. For no sooner had he taken Ag Grant to his bed than he'd started to save, grown mean as dirt, in a three-four years he'd finished with feeing, now he rented a fell big farm himself, well stocked it was, and he fee'd two men. Jock himself had grown thin in a way, like his father but worse his bothy childes said, old Menzies at least could take a bit dram and get lost to the world but the son was that mean he might drink rat-poison and take no harm, 'twould feel at home in a stomach like his.

Well, that was Jock, and he sat and heard the story of Kath and her stay on the boat. *Ay, still a coarse bitch, I have not a doubt. Well if she never comes back to the Mearns, in Segget you cannot but redden with shame when a body will ask 'Was Kath Menzies your sister?'*

And Ag, she'd grown a great sumph of a woman, she nodded to that, it was only too true, a sore thing it was on decent bit folks that they should have any relations like Kath.

But Meg just sat there and smoked and said never a word, as though she thought nothing worth a yea or a nay. Young Robb had fair ta'en a fancy to Kath and he near boiled up when he heard Jock speak, him and the wife that he'd married from her shame. So he left them short and went raging home, and wished for one that Kath would come back, a Summer noon as he cycled home, snipe were calling in the Auchindreich moor where the cattle stood with their tails a-switch, the Grampians rising far and behind, Kinraddie spread like a map for show, its ledges veiled in a mist from the sun. You felt on that day a wild, daft unease, man, beast and bird: as though something were missing and lost from the world, and Kath was the thing that John Robb missed, she'd something in her that minded a man of a house that was builded upon a hill.

Folk thought that maybe the last they would hear of young Kath Menzies and her ill-gettèd ways. So fair stammy-gastered they were with the news she'd come back to the Mearns, she was down in Stonehive, in a grocer's shop, as calm as could be, selling out tea and cheese and such-like with no blush of shame on her face at all, to decent women that were properly wed and had never looked on men but their own, and only on them with their braces buttoned.

It just showed you the way that the world was going to allow an ill quean like that in a shop, some folk protested to the creature that owned it, but he just shook his head, *Ah well, she works fine; and what else she does is no business of mine.* So you well might guess there was more than business between the man and Kath Menzies, like.

And Meg heard the news and went into Stonehive, driving her sholtie, and stopped at the shop. And some in the shop knew who she was and minded the things she had done long syne to other bit bairns of hers that went wrong; and they waited with their breaths held up with delight. But all that Meg did was to nod to Kath, *Ay, well, then, it's you – Ay, mother, just that – Two pounds of syrup and see that it's good.*

And not another word passed between them, Meg Menzies that once would have ta'en such a quean and skelped her to rights before you could wink. Going home from Stonehive she stopped by the farm where young Robb was fee'd, he was out in the hayfield coling the hay, and she nodded to him grim, with her high horse face. *What's this that I hear about you and Kath Menzies?*

He turned right red, but he wasn't ashamed. *I've no idea – though I hope it's the worse—. It fell near is—. Then I wish it was true, she might marry me, then, as I've prigged her to do.*

Oh, have you so, then? said Meg, and drove home, as though the whole matter was a nothing to her.

But next Tuesday the postman brought a bit note, from Kathie it was to her mother at Tocherty. *Dear mother, John Robb's going out to Canada and wants me to marry him and go with him. I've told him instead I'll go with him and see what he's like as a man – and then marry him at leisure, if I feel in the mood. But he's hardly any money, and we want to borrow some, so he and I are coming over on Sunday. I hope that you'll have dumpling for tea. Your own daughter, Kath.*

Well, Meg passed that letter over to Jim, he glowered at it
dour, *I know – near all the Howe's heard. What are you going
to do, now, mother?*

But Meg just lighted a cigarette and said nothing, she'd
smoked like a tink since that steer with Jean. There was
promise of strange on-goings at Tocherty by the time that
the Sabbath day was come. For Jock came there on a visit as
well, him and his wife, and besides him was Jeannie, her
that had married the clerk down in Brechin, and she
brought the bit creature, he fair was a toff; and he stepped
like a cat through the sharn in the close; and when he had
heard the story of Kath, her and her plan and John Robb
and all, he was shocked near to death, and so was his wife.
And Jock Menzies gaped and gave a mean laugh. *Ay, coarse
to the bone, ill-gettèd I'd say if it wasn't that we came of the same
bit stock. Ah well, she'll fair have to tramp to Canada, eh
mother? – if she's looking for money from you.*

And Meg answered quiet *No, I wouldn't say that. I've the
money all ready for them when they come.*

You could hear the sea plashing down soft on the rocks,
there was such a dead silence in Tocherty house. And then
Jock habbered like a cock with fits *What, give silver to one
who does as she likes, and won't marry as you made the rest of us
marry? Give silver to one who's no more than a—.*

And he called his sister an ill name enough, and Meg sat
and smoked looking over the parks. *Ay, just that. You see,
she takes after myself.*

And Jeannie squeaked *How?* and Meg answered her
quiet: *She's fit to be free and to make her own choice the same
as myself and the same kind of choice. There was none of the rest
of you fit to do that, you'd to marry or burn, so I married you
quick. But Kath and me could afford to find out. It all depends if
you've smeddum or not.*

She stood up then and put her cigarette out, and looked
at the gaping gowks she had mothered. *I never married your
father, you see. I could never make up my mind about Will. But*

*maybe our Kath will find something surer . . . Here's her and
her man coming up the road.*

Forsaken

Eloi! Eloi! lama sabachthani?

FOR A WHILE you could not think at all what strange toun
this was you had come intil, the blash of the lights dazzled
your eyes so long they'd been used to the dark, in your ears
were the shammle and grind and drummle of dream-
minded slopes of earth or of years, your hands moved with
a weight as of lead, draggingly, anciently, so that you
glowered down at them in a kind of grey startlement.
And then as you saw the holes where the nails had been,
the dried blood thick on the long brown palms, and minded
back in a flash to that hour, keen and awful, and the
slavering grins on the faces of the Roman soldiers as they
drove the nails into the stinking Yid. That you minded –
but now – now where had you come from that lang hame?

Right above your head some thing towered up with
branching arms in the flow of the lights; and you saw that
it was a cross of stone, overlaid with curlecues, strange,
dreich signs, like the banners of the Roman robbers of men
whom you'd preached against in Zion last night. Some
Gentile city they had carried you to, you supposed, and
your lips relaxed to that, thinking of the Samaritans, of the
woman by the well that day whom you'd blessed – as often
you'd blessed, pitifully and angrily, seeing the filth and the
foolishness in folk, but the kindly glimmer of the spirit as
well. Here even in the stour and stench and glare there
would surely be such folk—

It was wee Johnny Tamson saw the Yid first – feuch! there the nasty creature stood, shoggling backward and forward alow Mercat Cross, Johnny kenned at once the coarse brute was drunk same as father was Friday nights when he got his money from the Broo. So he handed a hack on the shins to Pete Gordon that was keeking in at a stall near by to see if he could nick a bit orange. *There's a fortune-teller, let's gang and make faces at him!*

You were standing under the shadow of the Cross and the Friday market was gurling below, but only the two loons had seen you as yet. You saw them come scrambling up the laired steps, one cried *Well, Yid!* and the other had a pluffer in his hand, and he winked and let up with the thing, and ping! on your cheek. But it didn't hurt, though you put up your hand to give it a dight, your hand you hardly felt on your cheek so strange it had grown, your eyen on the loon. Queer that lads had aye been like that, so in Bethlehem long syne you could mind they had been, though you yourself never been so, staring at books, at the sky, at the wan long trail of some northing star that led the tired herdsmen home . . .

Johnny Tamson was shoggling backward and forward two steps below where the sheeny stood, he'd fallen to a coarse-like singing now, trying to vex the foreign fortune-teller:

> *Yiddy-piddy,*
> *He canna keep steady,*
> *He stan's in an auld nichtgoon!*

But Pete hadn't used his pluffer again, he felt all watery inside him, like. He cried up *Don't vex the man!* for something hurt when he looked in those eyen, terrible queer eyen, like mother's sometimes, like father's once . . . *Stop it!* he cried to young Johnny Tamson.

Johnny Tamson pranced down the steps at that and

circled round Pete like a fell raised cat. *Who're you telling to stop?* he asked, and Pete felt feared to his shackle-bone, Johnny Tamson was a bigger chap than him. So, because he was awful feared he said *You!* and bashed Johnny Tamson one in the neb, it burst into blood like a cracked ink-bottle and Johnny went stitering back and couped, backerty-gets into the stall they'd been sneaking about five minutes before, waiting a chance to nick an orange. Old Ma Cleghorn turned round at that minute, just as Johnny hit the leg of the stall and down it went with a showd and a bang.

You saw the thing that happened and heard the quarrel of the loons, understood in a flash, had moved down from the steps of the Mercat Cross, but had not moved quick enough, crash went the stall, and there was the boy Pete staring appalled. As you put your hand on his shoulder he gasped, and looked round: *Oh, it's you!* and was suddenly urgent – *Come on!*

The Yid man wouldn't or he couldn't run, but came loping down the Gallowgate fine, Pete breathing and snorting through his nose and looking back at the stouring market din. Syne he looked at the mannie, and stopt, the street dark: *You'll be all right here*, he said to the mannie, *but they'd have blamed you – they aye blame Yids. Well, so long, I'm away home!*

You looked after the loon and stared round you again at the clorted house-walls of the antrin toun. And then because you went all light-headed you leaned up against the wall of the street, your hand at your eyen as the very street skellacht; till someone plucked at your sleeve . . .

God damn and blast it, just like young Pete, coming belting against you out in the streets as you were tearing home for your tea: *Father, there's a Yid chap up in the close – with a nightgown on, he looks awful queer. – Well, I'm queer myself, I'm away for my tea. – Father, I want you to take him home with us – you're aye taking queer folk home . . .* So here was Pa, hauled up to speak to the Yid – and a damned

queer-looking felly at that, fair starving the creature was by
his look.

Ay, then, Comrade!

You saw something in his face you seemed to know from
far-off times, in a lowe of sea-water caught by the sun, in a
garden at night when the whit owl grew quiet, that awful
night in Gethsemane when you couldn't see the way clear
at all, when you were only blank, dead afeared. Comrade!
You knew him at once, with your hand to your head, to
your heart, in greeting.

PETER!

*Ay, that's my name. This young nickum here thinks you're no
very well. Will you come in by for a dish of tea?*

So next you were walking atween the loon and Peter
down one dark street and along another and up dark
twisting stairs. And at one of those twists the light from
the street shone on the staircase and through on you, and
Peter gave a kind of a gasp.

God, man, where was't I kenned you afore?

II

Sick of father and the tosh he piled in the room, books and
papers, an undighted hand-press, wasn't room for a quean
to do a hand's-turn to get into her outgoing clothes. Mr
Redding had called that evening to Jess: *Miss Gordon, come
into the office,* in she'd gone, he was fat, the creash oozed
over his collar, and she'd kenned at once when he closed
the door the thing he was going to do. And he'd done it,
she'd laughed, it hurt, the bloody beast. But she didn't say
so, he sweated and loosed her, paiching: *We'll make a night
o' it, eh, my Pootsy? I'll pick you up in the car at Mercat Cross.*

Oh, damn! She found herself greeting a bit, not loud,
Mother would hear her greeting like a bairn as she minded
that. But what else was there for a lassie to do, if she liked
bonny things and fine things to eat, and – oh, to be hapt in a

fine rug in a car and get a good bed to lie on – even if it was beside that oozing creash in the dark, as it had been afore now. Mind the last time? . . . But she couldn't do anything else, she'd her job to hold on to, a lot of use to find herself sacked, on the Broo, and father with work only now and then and the rest of his time ta'en up with Bolsheviks – he'd be in the jail with it ere all was done, and where would his family be then?

She found the dress and scraped her way intilt, angrily, and heard the whisp-whisp of folk coming in at the kitchen door, wiping their feet on the bass and Mother speaking to them low. She tore the comb through her hair and opened the door and went into the parlour, not heeding them a damn. *Ma*—

You knew that face at once, the long golden throat and the wide, strange eyen and the looping up of the brightsome hair, your heart was twisted with a sudden memory, re-membering her sorrow, her repentance, once, that night when she laved your feet with tears, how she followed through the stour of the suns and days of those moons when you trekked your men to El Kuds, Magdalene, the Magdalene.

She thought, Oh gosh, isn't father just awful? another tink brought into the house, a fright of a fool in an old nightgown. If Mr Redding saw him I'd never hear the end . . . And she looked at the Yid with a flyting eye, but feared a bit, something queer about him, as though she'd once seen him, once long back – that was daft, where could she have seen him? *Mother, where's my crocodile shoon?*

Ma was seating the Yid by the fire, poor creature, he'd been out in ill weather enough in that silly sark-like thing that he wore. He looked sore troubled in his mind about something, the Lord kenned what, men were like that, Ma never bothered about their daft minds, and their ploys and palavers and blether of right, wrong and hate and all the rest of the dirt, they were only loons that never grew up and came back still wanting their bruises bandaged. But she thought the Yid was a fine-like stock, for all that, not like some of the creatures – feuch, how they smelt! that Peter would bring from his Bolshevist meetings.

Fegs, lassie, can you no see to the crocodiles yourself – or the alligators either, if it comes to that? Peter was in fair a good humour the night, warming his nieves, steeking and unsteeking them in front of the fire. *Your Ma's to see to the tea for me and this comrade here that young Pete met up by Mercat Cross.*

Jess banged over under the big box bed and found the crocodiles there, oh, no, not cleaned, young Pete was a lazy Bulgar, Ma spoiled him, he never did a thing for his meat, there he sat glowering at that Yid, like a gowk, as though the queer creature were some kind of sweetie . . . Oh Christ, and they've tint the blasted brushes.

She got down on her knees and raxed out the polish, and started to clean, no body speaking, Ma seeing to the smokies above the fire, Pa warming his hands and Pete just staring, the Yid – Jess looked up then and saw him look at her, she stopped and looked back with a glower of her brows and next minute felt suddenly sick and faint . . . Oh Gosh, that couldn't have happened to her, not *that*, after that night with Redding? She'd go daft, she'd go out and drown herself if there were a kid—.

You could see in this room with the wide, strange lum and those folk who only half-minded you suddenly a flash in the Magdalene's eyes. She was minding – minding you and the days when she joined the band, the New Men you led, while you preached again chastity, patience and love. The Magdalene minding, her eyes all alowe, in a minute she'd speak as Peter had spoken—

Peter said *Those smokies have fairly a right fine guff. Up with them, Ma, I've the meeting to gang to. Sit in about, Comrade, and help yourself. Queer I thought I'd once met you afore – Dottlet, folk sometimes get, eh, ay? Do you like two lumps or three in your tea?*

You heard yourself say *None, if you please,* though this was a queer and antrin stuff put into a queer and antrin drink. Yet it warmed you up as you drank it then and ate the smoked fish the woman Martha served, with a still, grave face (you minded her face in other time, before that birling of dust went past).

Pete thought as he ate up his bit of a smoky, *My Yid chap was famisht as Pa would say. Look how he's tearing into the fish. Maybe he'll help me to plane my bookcase after he's finisht.* And he called out loud, they all gave a loup, *Will you help me to plane my bookcase, chap? You were once a joiner and should do it just fine.*

The loon, you saw, knew you – or kenned only that? *How did you ken that I carpentered?*

—*Och, I just kent. Will you help me? Ma, there's Will coming up the stair.*

Jess got to her feet and slipped into the room, and banged the door and stood biting her lips, feared, but not now so feared as she'd been. If that was the thing that had happened to her she kenned a place where they'd see to it. Ugh, it made her shiver, that couldn't be helped, she'd see to the thing in spite of the Yid . . . Och, she was going clean daft, she supposed, what had the Yid to do with it all? Something queer as he stared at her? If she vexed over every gowk that stared she'd be in a damn fine soss ere long. In a damn fine soss already, oh Gosh! . . .

Will thought as he stepped in and snibbed the door, Hello, another recruit for the Cause. A perfect devil for recruits, old Pa – wish to God he'd get some with some sense and go. And he sighed, fell tired, and nodded to the man that sat in the queer get-up by the table. Looked clean done in, poor devil in that fancy gown of his, some unemployed Lascar up from the Docks trying on the old fortune-telling stunt . . .

Of him you were hardly sure at all – the thin, cool face and the burning eyes and the body that had a faint twist as it moved. And then you minded – a breathing space, an hour at night on the twilight's edge when the trees stood thin as pencil smoke, wan, against the saffron sky, in a village you rested in as a train went through, gurling camels with loping tails, and a childe bent down from a camel back, in the light, and stared at you with hard, fierce, cool eyes. And they'd told you he was a Sanhedrin man, Saul of Tarsus, a hater and contemner of the New Men you led.

Will, this is a comrade that young Pete found. My son's the secretary of the Communist cell. Would you be one of the Party yourself?

Will thought, Just like Pa, simple as ever. Poor devil of a Yid, of course he'll say *Ay* . . . But instead the man looked up and stared, and seemed to think, and syne nodded, half doubtful. *All things in common for the glory of God.*

Pa said *Ay, just, that's what I tell Will. But he will not have it you can be religious at all if you're communist, I think that's daft, the two are the same. But he kens his job well enough, I'll say that. Eat up, Comrade, you're taking nothing.*

You thought back on that wild march up on El Kuds and the ancient phrases came soft on your lips as you looked at the bitter, cool face of Saul, and you heard yourself say them, aloud in the room. *All things in common in the Kingdom of God, when the hearts of men are changed by light, when sin has ceased to be.*

Will thought, Queer how that delusion still lasts, queer enough in this poor, ragged devil from the Docks. Funny, too, how he said the old, empty words as though they were new and bit and pringled, not the grim, toothless tykes they are. Looked in a funny-like way when he said them, one half-believed one had seen him before. Oh, well, oh hell, couldn't let that pass. Agitprop, even while eating a smoky!

That's been tried and found useless over long, Comrade. Waiting the change of heart, I mean. It's not the heart we want to change, but the system. Skunks with quite normal hearts can work miraculous change for the good of men. People who

have themselves changed hearts are generally crucified – like
Christ.

—*Christ? Who is Christ?*

They all glowered at him, Pete fair ashamed, it wasn't fair
the poor Yid should be shown up like that. Ma turned to
the fire again, Eh me, the Jew felly was unco unlearned,
poor brute, with they staring eyen – and whatever had he
been doing to those hands of his? Pa reddened and pushed
the oat cakes over.

Help yourself, Comrade, you're eating nothing. Never mind
about Jesus, he's long been dead.

Jesus? What Jesus was this of theirs, who brought that
look of shame to them? Some prophet of antique time, no
doubt, this man named as someone you knew had been
named . . . Saul's eyen staring with that question in them –
neither the eyen of an enemy nor yet of a frere.

Who was Jesus?

Ma thought, Well, well, and now they'll be at it. Will'll
never get his smoky down at all with all this blether he's
having on hand telling the poor Jew man about Jesus – Eh
me, and the way he speaks, too, right bonny, though no
very decent my mother'd have thought. But that was long
syne, afore you met in with Peter Gordon and his queer-like
notions – scandalized mother off the earth, near, they
had!. . . *Will, would you have another smoky?*

—*No, Ma, thank you kindly . . . So that was the way of it,*
you see, this Prophet childe started with the notion that men's
hearts would first need changing, to make them love one another,
care for the State – he called it the Kingdom of God in his lingo.
And what happened was that he himself was crucified after
leading an army against Jerusalem; syne, hardly was he dead
than his followers started making a god of him, quite the old kind
of God, started toning down all he'd taught to make it fit in with
the structure of the Roman state. They became priests and princes
in the service of the temples dedicated to the dead Jesus, whom
they'd made a God . . . And, mind you, that change of heart

*must have happened often enough to folk when they heard of the
sayings of this Jesus. Thousands and thousands changed – but
there was no cohesion – no holding together, they put off the
Kingdom of God till Eternity: and were tortured and murdered
in Jesus' name.*

You stared in the bright sharp eyes of Saul and saw now
that he had no knowledge of you. Jesus? – many years ago,
he had said . . . And after that last black night, that hour
when you cried to God forsaking you, mad darkness had
descended again on the earth, on the faces and souls of
Magdalene and Martha, Peter and Saul – Peter there with
the old, kind smile on his face, his mind far lost in dreams.
And those banners you had led up the passes against El
Kuds were put away for the flaunting flag of a God – a God
worshipped afar in the strange touns.

Ma cried, *Eh, mighty, the poor childe's no well. Lean back a
minute; Pete, open that window; Fegs you fair gave me a turn,
man!*

III

Jess Gordon came out from the room all dressed, with her
crocodiles on, as they tended the Yid. He opened his eyen
as she stepped in the room, Gosh, what need had he to look
at her like that, as though he both *kenned* and nearly grat?
Well, she didn't care, not a damn, she was going out with
Redding, she would tell them all that, that greasy Lascar
into the bargain. *What's wrong with him, Ma?*

And now you saw she was not the Magdalene – or the
Magdalene after two thousand years with the steel of a
Roman sword in her heart, sharper, clearer, colder than of
yore, not to be moved by glance or touch or the aura of God
that you carried from those Bethlehem days as a loon. This
was Magdalene from the thousands of years that drummlet
and rumblet into the night since the pain tore deep in your
wounded feet . . .

Ma said, *The childe was feeling the heat, just don't vex him and don't stare at him like that, as though he had done you some ill or other. And where are you off to with your crocodiles on?*

—*To meet a chap if you want to know.* Jess dragged her eyen from those staring eyen. (Damn him, he could stare.) *Ta-ta, folk.*

Ta, ta, they called. She turned at the door. *And ta-ta, YOU.* Her look was a knife.

Pa louped up as she banged the door. *What's ta'en the ill-gettèd bitch the night? Glowering that way at the Comrade here? . . . Eh, what did you say?*

You had said only *Peter!* and at that he had turned, for a moment you saw loup into his eyen that love and amazement that had once been his, love and amazement for the leader, not the creed, it died away as he sat down again. And even he you saw now was not the Peter of that other time, weak and leal and kind he had been, but more of the kindness now, little of the love, forsaken of the trust and uttermost belief. No thing in him now you could ever touch except with a cry of despair.

Ma said, *There was nothing to fuss about. Finish your tea, you've your meeting, Pa. Pete, it's time you were off to your bed. Say ta-ta now to the gentlemen.*

—*Och, isn't there no time for my bookcase, Ma? All right, all right, ta-ta, chap.*

The mannie looked and said *Ta-ta.* And again something came twisting in young Pete's wame. He looked back, white-faced, from the bedroom door. *Ta-ta. I – liked you awful, you ken.*

—*Hear that?* said Pa. *He's fair ta'en to you, Comrade. Well, I'll need t'away to the meeting, I doubt. You'll be down there, Will?*

—*Ay will I, worse luck. Is the comrade coming?*

You looked from the face of one to the other, the faces of Martha and Saul and Peter, and you saw, no mist now happing your eyen (that mist from past times), they'd no kinship with you. Saul with the bitter face and creed, a leader once for that army you led up the heights to El Kuds, never for that love you had led it with. Looking into his heart with that ancient power you saw the white, stainless soul that was there, but love had gone from it, faith and trust, hope even, only resolve remained. Nothing there but resolve, nothing else that survived the awful torment your name had become . . . And you saw in the face of Martha even something that was newer or older than you – a cold and a strange and a terrible thing, a mother of men with the eyen of men, facing fear and pain without hope as did Saul, wary and cool, unbannered, unafraid . . . You shook your head:

No. I maun gang to my hame.

They could never make up their minds what he said next that minute when he covered his face with his hands, afore he went out of the house and their lives. Pa said it was something about some Eliot, Will said the poor Lascar devil had mumbled something or other about the Sabbath.

Sim

> What profit hath a man of all his labour which he
> taketh under the sun?   Ecclesiastes i, 4

SIM WILSON CAME of a fell queer stock, his mother a spinner at the Segget Mills, his father a soldier killed by the Boers. When news of that killing came up to Segget the wife just laughed – *Worse folk than the Boers!* – and went on with the tink-like life that she led. In time that fair grew a scandal in Segget, a body wasn't safe to let her man out of her sight for a minute in case he met in with that Wilson creature and was led all agley with her coarse green glower.

Sim was no more than five years old when at last things came to a head in Segget, his mother went off on a moonlight flit with the widow Grant's son and half of her silver, folk wondered which of the two would last longest. Young Sim was left in an emptied house till his auntie that bade in a house by Drumlithie took pity on the loon and had him down there. She came all a-fuss and a-pant with pity, the aunty, a meikle big creash of a woman, and she said to Sim *You're my dawtie now*. And Sim said *Maybe – if you'll leave me a-be*.

Faith, that was his only care from the first, as sweir a nickum as you'd meet, folk said, sweir at the school as he was at his home, it was fair a disease with the ill-gettèd loon. And an impudent creature he was, forbye, with his glinting black hair and his glinting green eyes, he'd truant from school more often than not and be off in the summer to sleep in the sun under the lithe of a whin or a stook. And once, he was then about ten years old, his auntie came on him high on the brae, in the heat, his chin in his hands as he keeked down through the veils of broom at the teams steaming at work in the parks below. She cried, *You coarse brute, why aren't you at school? Aren't you fair black affronted to lie there and stink?*

Well, Sim just sneered, not feared a wee bit. *No, I'm not. I was watching those fools in that park. You won't find me sossing and chaving like that when I'm a man with a fee of my own. The dafties – not to take a bit rest! . . . Lessons? Away, do you think I am soft?*

And he stuck out his tongue and slipped under her arm, his auntie near greeting with rage as he ran. But she couldn't catch up, loaded down with her creash. Sim was soon out of sight on his way up the hill. He spent the whole day lying flat on his back, the only sweir soul in the hash of the Howe.

Folk said that he'd come to an ill-like end, his sweirty would eat to his bones and they'd rot. But then, near the middle of his thirteenth year, he heard the news in his class at the school that the prize for dux that year was a pound; and all of a jiffy he started to work, like mad, near blinded himself of a night with reading and writing and learning his lessons, the hills hardly saw him except back of a book. And he'd cleverness in him, sweir though he'd been, he was dux for that year, and the dominie delighted.

He said to the loon *You'll do even better*, but Sim just sneered in his impudent way. *I'm finished with chaving at lessons and dirt. I've tried, and I know that they're not worth the sweat.* The dominie was fair took aback to hear that, *You'll gang a hard gait through the world, I fear.* And Sim said *Maybe; but I'll gang it myself. And I'll know what I'm getting ere I gang it at all.*

He fee'd his first fee at Upperhill in Kinraddie. Big-boned he had grown and supple and swack, but as sweir as ever and an ill-liked brute. He'd sneer at his elders and betters in the bothy. *What, work my guts out for that red-headed rat? Whatever for, can you tell me that? Show me a thing that is worth my trauchle, and I'll work you all off the face of the earth!*

The foreman there was a canny-like childe, and the only one that could bear with Sim. They both stayed on for a four-five years, Sim sweir as ever, with his glinting, green eyes, he'd a bigger power for lazing around than a pig in a ree was the speak of the bothy. And young and buirdly, well-happed like a hog, he'd doze through the work of the Upperhill parks, good-natured enough were he letten alone. But sometimes he'd stop from making his brose, of a night, when the bothy was lit by the fire. *And to think that the morn we'll be doing the same!* The billies in the bothy would maybe say *What?* and he'd say *Why, making more brose to eat! And the night after that and the night after that. And we'll get up the morn and slave and chave for that red-headed rat – and go to our beds and get up again. Whatever for, can you tell me that?*

And the brute in one of those unco-like moods would go off on a jaunting down to Segget; and take a dram or so in the Arms; and look round about for a spinner to spite. And if there were such Sim would swagger up to him *Ay, man, you've a look on your face I don't like. And I don't much like your face the look's on.* The spinner would maybe look Sim up and down, with a sneer, and call him a clod-hopping clown, and Sim would take him a bash in the face, and next minute the spinners would pile in on Sim; and when he got back to Upper-hill bothy he'd look as though he'd been fed through the teeth of a mill. But he'd say he got in his bed *That was fine. Man, I fairly stirred up that dirt down in Segget!* And next day he'd be sleepy and sweir as before.

Syne he met with Kate Duthie at a dance down in Segget, she was narrow and red-haired, with a pointed chin and hard grey eyes you could strike a spunk on, a quean that worked as maid at the Manse. Well, Sim took a look at her, she one at him; and he fair went daft that minute about her. He waited till that dance was over and said *Can I have the next?* and Kate Duthie said, *Maybe. Who might you be?* And Sim Wilson told her, and Kate gave a laugh, *Oh, only a ploughman.*

As the Upperhill lads walked back that night in a bunch from the dance they had been to in Segget Sim told them the speak of the grey-eyed quean. The foreman said, *And who might she think that she is? A joskin's as good as any damned maid.* Sim shook his head, *Most maybe; not her. Faith, man, but she's bonny, and I wish that I had her.*

Well, that was only the beginning of the stir, his sweirty went like a mist in June, he was out nearly every bit night after that, down at the Manse or hanging round Segget. Kate sometimes saw him and sometimes she didn't, she kept as cool as a clayed-up coulter. At last it came to a night Sim said *I'm thinking of marrying*; Kate Duthie said, *Oh; well I, wish you joy.* And Sim said *Ay, I'll get that fine – if you'll come and provide it.*

Kate laughed in his face and told him plain she wasn't cut out for a ploughman's wife to drag through her days in a cottar house. Sim said there would maybe be no need to cottar, though he'd never thought of the thing before, he spent every meck he ever had made on drink and coarse queens, any coarseness at all that didn't trouble his sweirty too much. But now with the grey-eyed quean in his arms he felt as he'd done that time when a loon and he made up his mind he would win the school prize. *I'll get a bit place of my own. You'll wait?*

Kate shrugged and said *Maybe, you'll have to risk that.* Sim held her and looked at her, suddenly cuddled her, daft and tight till she nearly screamed, just for a minute, and syne finished with that. *You needn't be feared, I'll wait for my turn. That's just a taste of what I'll yet take. What about a kiss?* And she gave him one, cold, like a peck, but he thought it fine, and lapped it in and put her away and went swinging away home the Kinraddie road; you could hear him nearly a mile from the bothy singing as he climbed up the road in the dark.

Well, God! there fair was a change in him then. It was brose and then brose and syne brose to his meat. The other billies in the bothy would laugh and mock at Sim and cry *What's it all for?* But Sim didn't heed, he saved every penny, he worked extra work, and afore two years, what with saving and scraping, he'd enough silver saved for the rent of Haughgreen.

It lies low down by the Segget burn. The clay of the Mearns has thickened down there till in a dry season a man might well think he stood in the yard of a milk-jar potter, the drills just hillocks and slivers of clay. Its rent was low in spite of its size, the most of the biggings just held together, disheartened-like, as though waiting the time to fall in a rickle on somebody's head. But Sim gave a swagger *I'll manage them fine*, the daft-like gaze on his queer green eyes; and was off every night from the Upperhill bothy, not down as afore to Kate Duthie in Segget, but down to Haughgreen with a saw and an axe, pliers and planes, and the Lord knows what. In the last week afore he was due to move in the Upperhill foreman went down for a look, and he found Haughgreen all shored-up and trig, the house all new papered, with furniture in it, the stable fit to take horses again, the stalls in the byre set well for nout – he'd worked like a nigger had that sweir brute, Sim.

The foreman said 'twas a miracle, just; he was glad that Sim had wakened at last. Sim gave him a clap that near couped him at that *Ay, man, and for why? Because I'll soon have the best quean in the Howe. What think you of that? In my house and my bed!*

That night he tramped to his quean down in Segget, and knocked at the kitchen door of the Manse, and Kate came to it and said *Oh, it's you?* And Sim said *Ay*, with his eyes fit to eat her, *You mind what I asked you near two years back?*

Kate said *What was that?* She thought little of him and knew nothing of his slaving to save for Haughgreen. But he started to tell her, as he stood in the door, that he was a farmer, with a farm of his own, and ready to take her there when she liked.

She gaped and said *Sim, it's not true, is it now?* And he said *Ay, it is*. And she fair seemed to thaw, and speired him up hill and down dale all about it, Sim standing and staring at the white of her neck, white, like cream, and he felt like a cat and licked his lips with a hungry tongue.

Well, she soon said *Ay*, she needed no prigging, fore-seeing herself a braw farmer's wife. At the end of the term the two of them married, Sim looked that day as though wedding an angel, not just a quean with a warm, white skin and close grey eyes and a mouth like a mule. Not but that the creature had smiles for the hour, and was awful kind to the ploughmen that came. She danced with the foreman and said *You're a joskin? Maybe my husband will give you a fee?* And the foreman spat, *Well, would he now, then? But you see I'm particular-like about the mistress.*

She would try to put Sim against him for that, the foreman knew, and keeked over at Sim; and he saw his eyes as they fixed on Kate, hungry and daft, more a glare than a glower. And he suddenly minded Sim back in the bothy in the days before he had met with this quean, and that speak of his, *Trauchle the day just to trauchle the morn! But show me a thing that is worth my chave and I'll work you all off the face of the earth*!

Well, he'd gotten the thing, good luck go with him, the foreman thought as he tramped away home up through the grey of the morning mists with the bothy lightless and grey in the dawn, leaving Sim with his hard-eyed quean; you hoped he'd not eat her, that's what he'd looked like.

But faith! she survived, fair the kind to do that. Folk gave a bit laugh at the news from Haughgreen, and shook their heads when they heard that Sim no sooner married was as sweir as before, taking life cool as ever he had done in spite of the nagging and prigging of Kate. The ploughing was on; but Sim Wilson's was not, the parks were lucky did they see him by nine, instead of six, when other childes yoked. Even then he'd do little but stand up and gant or wheeber out loud as he sat on a gate.

Now and then a body would cry to him *Ay, you're ploughing's far back for the season, is't not?* and he'd say, *Damn the doubt. What o't though it is?* And he'd whistle and stare at the clouds in the Howe, his cat-like eyes a-blink in the sun.

The foreman at last took a taik in about and Sim was as pleased to see him as though he wasn't new-married, new-buried instead. Kate snapped from the room like an ill-ta'en rat; she didn't like the foreman, he didn't like her. And he thought as he sat and waited his dram it was more than likely that she wore the breeks.

But right soon he was changing his mind about that. As

they sat at their dram, him and Sim, she came back: *It's dark, and it's time you went for the kye – Gang for them yourself*, Sim said, and never turned. *You enjoy trauchle; well, enjoy some more.*

Kate's face blazed up like a fire with rage, she choked and went out and banged the door. The foreman felt a bit shamed for the quean; Damn't, you could see it wasn't so easy to be married to a sweir, queer brute like Sim; it wouldn't be long that these two together would store the kiln in Haughgreen, you knew.

There were more stammy-gastered than him at the change. For all of a sudden as the May came in Sim seemed to wake up and his sweirty went, he was out at all hours at the work of the parks, chaving like daft at his weed-choked drills. The land had lain fallow, he wasn't too late, and afore folk had well gotten over their gape they saw Sim Wilson was having fine crops manured with the sweat of his own meikle hams. He snored no more in the lithe of a whin and he stopped from ganting by every bit gate.

The reason for that was soon plain to be seen, Kate with a bairn and the creature soon due. The Upperhill foreman met in with Sim one night as he drove from the mart at Stonehive, and the foreman cried up *Ay, man, and how are you?* Sim stopped and cried back *Oh, it's you is it, then? Fine, man, I'm aye fine; I get what I want. Have you heard of the news of what's coming to Haughgreen?*

And he told the foreman of the bairn that was coming, as if half the Howe didn't know about that, his green glazed eyes all glinting and shining. You'd have thought by the way that Sim Wilson spoke 'twas the first bit bairn that had waited for birth in all the windy Howe of the Mearns. He was daft on it, as daft as he had been a wee while afore to marry its mother. And the foreman thought as he wished him luck there were some that had aye to be looking ahead, and others looked back, and it made little odds, looked you east, looked you west, you'd to work or to die.

Kate had a sore time and let every soul know, but the mid-wife said that the queer-like thing was the way that that meikle Sim Wilson behaved, not like most of the fathers she ever had known, and she'd known a fell few; they went into three classes – fools, poor fools, and just plain damn fools. Well, the last were mostly the fathers of first-born, they'd wabble at the knees and whiten at the gills and pay no need to aught but the wife. Sim Wilson was different, with his unco green eyes, 'twas the bairn that took him his first minute in the room. He had it in his arms as ready as you please, and cuddled it, chuckled to it – the great silly sumph – till Kate whined out from the bed where she lay *And have you got nothing to say to me now?* And Sim Wilson said *Eh? Damn't, Kate, I'd forgotten you!*

An ill-like thing, that, to say to a wife, but that was the way the brute now behaved; there was nothing he thought on earth worth the price of daddling his bairn up and down in his arms, and swearing she'd winked, and wasn't she a topper? The Upperhill foreman came down for a look, and keeked at the creature, an ordinary bairn, like an ill-boiled swede; but Sim sat and glowered at her, the look in his eyes he'd once turned on Kate ere she lay in his bed – *Man, but I'll make a braw life for this lass – I'll give her education and make her a lady.*

The foreman said he thought education was dirt; if ever he had bairns he'd set them to work. Sim laughed in a way that he didn't much like. *You? Maybe. I was kittled on a different day.*

So the foreman left him, fair angered at that. 'Twas nearly five years ere he saw Sim again, for he moved down the Howe and took a fresh fee and got married himself and had bairns of his own. And sometimes he'd mind of that sweir brute Sim and the speaks of his in the bothy long syne: *Well, what's it all for, all your chaving and care?* And when he'd mind that the foreman would laugh and know that most likely his stomach was wrong.

Though he didn't see Sim he heard now and then of him and his capers down at Haughgreen. Folk told that he'd turned to a slaver, just, he'd fee'd two men and near worked them to death, and himself as well, and long Kate forbye – faith, if she'd thought she did herself well marrying a farmer and setting up braw she'd got many a sore heart since her marriage-morn. Sim gave her no help, he wouldn't fee a maid, he was up and out at the blink of dawn crying his men from their beds to work. He spared neither man nor beast, did Sim; in his four-five years he'd made a fair pile. But he was as ready as ever he had been to blab what he thought, a sneer or a boast. And he'd tell any soul that would care to listen the why and the wherefore he moiled like a mole. *It's that lass of mine, Jean – faith, man, she's a topper! I'm to send her to college, away from this soss, and she'll lack for nothing that money can bring.*

And neither she did. It fair was a scandal, folk said, that plain though they ate at Haughgreen the bairn was fed on this dainty and that. Sim had bought the wee wretch the finest of beds and he'd have her aye dressed like the bairns of gentry. You'd heard afore this of folk daft on a bairn but he was surely the worst in the Howe. Folk shook their heads, he had better look out, 'twas fell unchancy to show over-plain that you thought over-much of any bit bairn.

And faith! folk weren't far wrong in their speak – the bairn didn't die, she was healthy enough, but just when it came for the time of her schooling they seemed to wake up to the fact at Haughgreen. She was unco backward and couldn't speak well, and had funny-like ways; she would croon a bit song all the hours of the day, staring up at the hills of the Howe, not caring a fig what she ate or what wore, only caring to lie in the sun and to sleep.

Sim sent for a specialist out from Dundon and had the bit bairn taken away south and treated and tested and God knows what. That went on a six months and the cost was a ruin, a time of sore hearts and black looks at Haughgreen.

And he well might have spared his time and his silver, she came back just the same – the bairn was a daftie, and the doctors said that so she'd remain a bairn of three all the years of her life.

Folk thought it awful, but they gave a bit snicker: *Ay, what will that fool at the Haugh say now?* Well, he went in a kind of daze for weeks, but his work didn't slacken as the foreman had thought – when he heard of the thing he had minded long back how Sim had behaved when he married his Kate and found that angel of common enough clay. But slaving was deep in his bones by now and he couldn't well stop though he wished, you supposed. The foreman met him one day at a roup, sneering and boasting as loudly as ever. But there was a look in the queer green eyes as though he were watching for something he'd tint.

He made no mention of the daftie, Jean, that had answered his question *What's it all for?* Sun, wind, and the batter of rain in his face – well, he'd settle now as others had done, and take it all for the riddle it was, not a race to be run with a prize at the end.

Then the news got about and you knew in a blink why he'd acted so calm with his firstborn, Jean. His wife had brought another bit bairn in the world, a lassie as well, and fine and strong. And soon's it was born Sim Wilson was crying *Is it right in the head, is it right in the head?* The doctor knew neither one way nor the other, but he said *Ay, it's fine*, to quieten the fool.

Sim doted on Jess from the day of her birth, promising her all as he'd done with Jean – Jean that now he could hardly thole to look on, any more than on Kate, his wife, thin and old. She'd fair withered up had the thin-flanked Kate, except her bit tongue, it could scoriate your skin. But it didn't vex Sim with his daughter Jess, he would stride in the kitchen when he loosened at night: *Where's ma wee quean?* and Jess would cry *Here!* Bonny and trig, like a princess dressed, nothing soft about her like that thing in the corner, hunched up and crooning, aye half-way in sleep. She was clever and bright and a favourite at college, Jess, and Sim swore she should have what she liked, she never need soss with the land and its pleiter, she would marry no joskin, a lady she'd be.

He bled the red clay of Haughgreen near to white to wring silver from it for Jess and her life, to send her to college and give her brave clothes. Fegs, he was fair a long gait from the days when he'd mock at the land – *Ay, come and get ME – get me if you can – I'm not such a fool*!

The foreman had clean forgot him for years, Sim Wilson the sweir and the fairlies he chased; and when next he did hear he could hardly believe one thing in the tale that came swift up the Howe. That thing was the age of the daughter, Jess. *Why, the lassie is only a bairn* he said. But the childe that stopped to pass him the tale said *Faith, no, man, eighteen if a day. Ay, a real coarse quean, and you cannot but laugh at the nasty whack it is in the mouth for that meikle fool that farms Haughgreen*!

There was nothing unco in the tale when told, the kind of thing had been known to the world since the coming of men – and afore that, no doubt, else all the ill pleiter would have never begun. But for that to happen to the dawtie of Sim! – Jess, the student, so haughty and neat, the maid that had led his question so on, up out of the years: *What's it all for?*

It seems that she carried her shame a long time, and the creature that found her out was the daftie. One night when old Sim came home from the fields the daftie pointed at her sister, Jess, and giggled, and mouthed and made slabbering sounds. Sim had paid her no heed a good twenty years, but something in the wrigglings of the creature took him. He cried *What's that?* and glowered at his wife, old Kate, with her thinning face and greyed hair.

But Kate knew nothing, like himself she stared at Jess that sat red-faced by the fire. And then while they stared

Jess jumped to her feet, weeping, and ran from the room, and they saw – plain enough the way she was in, they'd been blind.

Old Sim gave a groan as an old horse groans when you drive him his last bit bout up a hill, and stood and stared at the daftie, Jean, that was giggling and fleering there like a bairn, like something tint his life long syne, in the kitchen quiet as the daylight waned.

Clay

THE GALTS WERE so thick on the land around Segget folk said if you went for a walk at night and you trod on some thing and it gave a squiggle, it was ten to one you would find it a Galt. And if you were a newcomer up in the Howe and you stopped a man and asked him the way the chances were he'd be one of the brood. Like as not, before he had finished with you, he'd have sold you a horse or else stolen your watch, found out everything that you ever had done, recognised your mother and had doubts of your father. Syne off home he'd go and spread the news round from Galt of Catcraig that lay high in the hills to Galt of Drumbogs that lay low by Mondynes, all your doings were known and what you had said, what you wore next your skin, what you had to your breakfast, what you whispered to your wife in the dead of night. And the Galts would snigger *Ay, gentry, no doubt*, and spit in the vulgar way that they had: the average Galt knew less of politeness than a broody hen knows of Bible exegesis.

They farmed here and they farmed there, brothers and cousins and half-brothers and uncles, your head would reel as you tried to make out if Sarah were daughter to Ake of

Catcraig or only a relation through marrying a nephew of
Sim of High Rigs that was cousin to Will. But the Galts
knew all their relationships fine, more especially if anything
had gone a bit wrong, they'd tell you how twenty-five years
or so back when the daughter of Redleaf had married her
cousin, old Alec that now was the farmer of Kirn, the first
bit bairn that came of that marriage – ay, faith, that bairn
had come unco soon! And they'd lick at their chops as they
minded of that and sneer at each other and fair have a time.
But if you were strange and would chance to agree, they'd
close up quick, with a look on their faces as much as to say
And who are you would say ill of the Galts?

They made silver like dirt wherever they sat, there was
hardly a toun that they sat in for long. So soon's they moved
in to some fresh bit farm they'd rive up the earth, manure it
with fish, work the land to death in the space of their lease,
syne flit to the other side of the Howe with the land left dry
as a rat-sucked swede. And often enough as he neared his
lease-end a Galt would break and be rouped from his place,
he'd say that farming was just infernal and his wife would
weep as she watched her bit things sold here and there to
cover their debts. And if you didn't know much of the Galts
you would be right sorry and would bid fell high. Syne
you'd hear in less than a six months' time that the childe
that went broke had bought a new farm and had stocked it
up to the hilt with the silver he'd laid cannily by before he
went broke.

Well, the best of the bunch was Rob Galt of Drumbogs, lightsome and hearty, not mean like the rest, he'd
worked for nearly a twenty-five years as his father's
foreman up at Drumbogs. Old Galt, the father, seemed
nearly immortal, the older he grew the coarser he was,
Rob stuck the brute as a good son should though aye he
had wanted land of his own. When they fell out at last
Rob Galt gave a laugh *You can keep Drumbogs and all
things that are on it, I'll soon get a place of my own, old man.*

His father sneered *You?* and Rob Galt said *Ay, a place of my own and parks that are MINE.*

He was lanky and long like all of the Galts, his mouser twisted up at the ends, with a chinny Galt face and a long, thin nose, and eyes pale-blue in a red-weathered face, a fine, frank childe that was kindness itself, though his notion of taking a rest from the plough was to loosen his horses and start in to harrow. He didn't look long for a toun of his own, Pittaulds by Segget he leased in a wink, it stood high up on the edge of the Mounth, you could see the clutter of Segget below, wet, with the glint of its roofs at dawn. The rent was low, for the land was coarse, red clay that sucked with a hungry mouth at your feet as you passed through the evening fields.

Well, he moved to Pittaulds in the autumn term, folk watched his flitting come down by Mondynes and turn at the corner and trudge up the brae to the big house poised on the edge of the hill. He brought his wife, she was long as himself, with a dark-like face, quiet, as though gentry – faith, that was funny, a Galt wedded decent! But he fair was fond of the creature, folk said, queer in a man with a wife that had managed to bring but one bairn into the world. That bairn was now near a twelve years old, dark, like her mother, solemn and slim, Rob spoiled them both, the wife and the quean, you'd have thought them sugar he was feared would melt.

But they'd hardly sat down a week in Pittaulds when Rachel that would trot at the rear of Rob, like a collie dog, saw a queer-like change. Now and then her father would give her a pat and she'd think that he was to play as of old. But instead he would cry *Losh, run to the house, and see if your mother will let you come out, we've two loads of turnips to pull afore dinner.* Rachel, the quean, would chirp *Ay, father,* and go blithe to the shed for her tailer and his, and out they would wade through the cling of the clay and pull side by side down the long, swede rows, the rain in a drifting seep from the hills, below them the Howe in its garment of mist. And the little, dark quean would work by his side, say never a word though she fair was soaked; and at last go home; and her mother would stare, whatever in the world had happened to Rob? She would ask him that as he came into dinner – *the quean'll fair have her death of cold*. He would blink with his pale-blue eyes, impatient, *Hoots, lassie, she'll take no harm from the rain. And we fair must clear the swedes from the land, I'm a good three weeks behind with the work*.

The best of the Galts? Then God keep off the rest! For, as that year wore on to its winter, while he'd rise at five, as most other folk did, he wouldn't be into his bed till near morning, it was chave, chave, chave till at last you would think he'd turn himself into an earthworm, near. In the blink of the light from the lanterns of dawn he would snap short-tempered at his dark-faced wife, she would stare and wonder and give a bit laugh, and eat up his porridge as though he was feared he would lose his appetite halfway through, and muck out the byre and the stable as fast as though he were paid for the job by the hour, with a scowl of ill-nature behind his long nose. And then, while the dark still lay on the land, and through the low mist that slept on the fields not a bird was cheeping and not a thing showing but the waving lanterns in the Segget wynds, he'd harness his horses and lead out the first, its hooves striking fire from the stones of the close, and cry to the second, and it would come after, and the two of them drink at the trough while Rob would button up his collar against the sharp drive of the frozen dew as the north wind woke. Then he'd jump on the back of the meikle roan, Jim, and go swaying and jangling down by the hedge, in the dark, the world on the morning's edge, wet, the smell of the parks in his face, the squelch of the horses soft in the clay.

Syne, as the light came grey in a tide, wan and slow from the Bervie Braes, and a hare would scuttle away through the grass and the peesies waken and cry and wheep, Rob Galt would jump from the back of Jim and back the pair up against the plough and unloose the chains from the horses' britchens and hook them up to the swivel-trees. Then he'd spit on his hands and cry *Wissh, Jim!* no longer ill-natured, but high-out and pleased, and swink the plough into the red, soaked land; and the horses would strain and snort and move canny and the clay wheel back in the coulter's trace, Rob swaying slow in the rear of the plough, one foot in the drill and one on the rig. The bothy billies on Arbuthnott's bents riding their pairs to start on some park would cry one to the other *Ay, Rob's on the go*, seeing him then as the light grew strong, wheeling, him and the horses and plough, a ranging of dots on the park that sloped its long clay rigs to the edge of the moor.

By eight, as Rachel set out for school, a slim dark thing with her well-tackèd boots, she would hear the whistle of her father, Rob, deep, a wheeber, upon the hill; and she'd see him come swinging to the end of a rig and mind how he once would stop and would joke and tease her for lads that she had at the school. And she'd cry *Hello father!* but Rob would say nothing till he'd drawn his horse out and looked back at the rig and given his mouser a twist and a wipe. Syne he'd peek at his daughter as though he'd new woke *Ay, then, so you're off*, and cry *Wissh!* to his horses and turn them about and set to again, while Rachel went on, quiet, with the wonder clouding her face that had altered so since she came to Pittaulds.

He'd the place all ploughed ere December was out, folk said that he'd follow the usual Galt course, he'd showed up mean as the rest of them did, he'd be off to the marts and a dealing in horses, or a buying of this or a stealing of that, if there were silver in the selling of frogs the Galts would puddock-hunt in their parks. But instead he began on the daftest-like ploy, between the hill of Pittaulds and the house a stretch of the moor thrust in a thin tongue, three or four acre, deep-pitted with holes and as rank with whins as a

haddock with scales, not a tenant yet who had farmed
Pittaulds but had had the sense to leave it a-be. But Rob
Galt set in to break up the land, he said it fair cried to have a
man at it, he carted great stones to fill up the holes and
would lever out the roots when he could with a pick, when
he couldn't he'd bring out his horses and yoke them and
tear them out from the ground that way. Working that
Spring to break in the moor by April's end he was all
behind, folk took a laugh, it served the fool fine.

Once in a blue moon or so he'd come round, he fair was a
deave as he sat by your fire, he and your man would start in
on the crops and the lie of the land and how you should
drain it, the best kind of turnips to plant in the clay, the
manure that would bring the best yield a dry year. Your
man would be keen enough on all that, but not like Rob
Galt, he would kittle up daft and start in to tell you tales of
the land that were just plain stite, of this park and that as
though they were women you'd to prig and to pat afore
they'd come on. And your man would go ganting wide as a
gate and the clock would be hirpling the hours on to morn
and still Rob Galt would sit there and habber. *Man, she's
fairly a bitch, is that park, sly and sleeked, you can feel it as soon
as you start in on her, she'll take corn with the meikle husk, not
with the little. But I'll kittle her up with some phosphate, I think.*
Your man would say *Ay, well, well, is that so? What do you
think of this business of Tariffs?* and Rob would say *Well, man,
I just couldn't say. What worries me's that park where I've put
in the tares. It's fair on the sulk about something or other.*

And what could you think of a fool like that? Though
he'd fallen behind with his chave on the moor he soon
made it up with his working at night, he fair had a fine bit
crop the next year, the wife and the quean both out at the
cutting, binding and stooking as he reapered the fields.
Rachel had shot up all of a sudden, you looked at her in a
kind of surprise as you saw the creature go by to the school.
It was said that she fair was a scholar, the quean – no better

than your own bit Johnnie, you knew, the teachers were
coarse to your Johnnie, the tinks. Well, Rachel brought
home to Pittaulds some news the night that Rob came back
from the mart, he'd sold his corn at a fair bit price. For once
he had finished pleitering outside, he sat in the kitchen, his
feet to the fire, puffing at his pipe, his eye on the window
watching the ley rise up outside and peer in the house as
though looking for him. It was Rachel thought that as she
sat at her supper, dark, quiet, a bit queer, over thin to be
bonny, you like a lass with a good bit of beef. Well, she
finished her meat and syne started to tell the message the
Dominie had sent her home with; and maybe if she was sent
to the college she'd win a bursary or something to help.

Her mother said *Well, Rob, what say you to that?* and Rob
asked *What?* and they told him again and Rob skeughed his
face round *What, money for school? And where do you think
that I'll manage to get that?*

Mrs Galt said *Out of the corn you've just sold,* and Rob gave
a laugh as though speaking to a daftie – *I've my seed to get
and my drains to dig and what about the ley for the next year's
corn? Damn't, it's just crying aloud for manure, it'll hardly
leave me a penny-piece over.*

Rachel sat still and looked out at the ley, sitting so still,
with her face in the dark. Then they heard her sniff and Rob
swung round fair astonished at the sound she made. *What
ails you?* he asked, and her mother said *Ails her? You would
greet yourself if you saw your life ruined.* Rob got to his feet and
gave Rachel a pat. *Well, well, I'm right sorry that you're
taking't like that. But losh, it's a small bit thing to greet over.
Come out and we'll go for a walk round the parks.*

So Rachel went with him half-hoping he thought to
change his mind on this business of college. But all that
he did on the walk was to stand now and then and stare at
the flow of the stubble or laugh queer-like as they came to a
patch where the grass was bare and the crop had failed. *Ay,
see that, Rachel, the wretch wouldn't take. She'll want a deep*

drill, this park, the next season. And he bent down and picked up a handful of earth and trickled the stuff through his fingers, slow, then dusted it back on the park, not the path, careful, as though it were gold-dust not dirt. So they came at last to the moor he had broken, he smoked his pipe and he stood and looked at it *Ay, quean, I've got you in fettle at last.* He was speaking to the park not his daughter but Rachel hated Pittaulds from that moment, she thought, quiet, watching her father and thinking how much he'd changed since he first set foot on its clay.

He worked from dawn until dark, and still later, he hove great harvests out of the land, he was mean as dirt with the silver he made; but in five years' time of his farming there he'd but hardly a penny he could call his own. Every meck that he got from the crops of one year seemed to cry to go back to the crops of the next. The coarse bit moor that lay north of the biggings he coddled as though 'twas his own blood and bone, he fed it manure and cross-ploughed it twice-thrice, and would harrow it, tend it, and roll the damn thing till the Segget joke seemed more than a joke, that he'd take it to bed with him if he could. For all that his wife saw of him in hers he might well have done that, Mrs Galt that was tall and dark and so quiet came to look at him queer as he came in by, you could hardly believe it still was the Rob that once wouldn't blush to call you his jewel, that had many a time said all he wanted on earth was a wife like he had and land of his own. But that was afore he had gotten the land.

One night she said as they sat at their meat *Rob, I've still that queer pain in my breast. I've had it for long and I doubt that it's worse. We'll need to send for the doctor, I think.* Rob said *Eh?* and gleyed at her dull *Well, well, that's fine. I'll need to be stepping, I must put in a two-three hours the night on the weeds that are coming so thick in the swedes, it's fair pestered with the dirt, that poor bit of park.* Mrs Galt said *Rob, will you leave your parks, just for a minute, and consider me? I'm ill and I want a doctor at last.*

Late the next afternoon he set off for Stonehive and the light came low and the hours went by, Mrs Galt saw nothing of her man or the doctor and near went daft with the worry and pain. But at last as it grew fell black on the fields she heard the step of Rob on the close and she ran out and cried *What's kept you so long?* and he said *What's that? Why, what but my work?* He'd come back and he'd seen his swedes waiting the hoe, so he'd got off his bike and held into the hoeing, what sense would there have been in wasting his time going up to the house to tell the news that the doctor wouldn't be till the morn?

Well, the doctor came in his long brown car, he cried to Rob as he hoed the swedes *I'll need you up at the house with me.* And Rob cried *Why? I've no time to waste.* But he got at last into the doctor's car and drove to the house and waited impatient; and the doctor came ben, and was stroking his lips; and he said *Well, Galt, I'm feared I've bad news. Your wife has a cancer in the breast, I think.*

She'd to take to her bed and was there a good month while Rob Galt worked the Pittaulds on his own. Syne she wrote a letter to her daughter Rachel that was fee'd in Segget, and Rachel came home. And she said, quiet, *Mother, has he never looked near you? I'll get the police on the beast for this,* she meant her father that was out with the hay, through the windows she could see him scything a bout, hear the skirl of the stone as he'd whet the wet blade, the sun a still lowe on the drowsing Howe, the dying woman in the littered bed. But Mrs Galt whispered *He just doesn't think, it's not that he's cruel, he's just mad on Pittaulds.*

But Rachel was nearly a woman by then, dark, with a temper that all the lads knew, and she hardly waited for her father to come home to tell him how much he might well be ashamed, he had nearly killed her mother with neglect, was he just a beast with no heart at all? But Rob hardly looked at the quean in his hurry *Hoots, lassie, your stomach's gone sour*

with the heat. Could I leave my parks to get covered with weeds?
And he gave her a pat, as to quieten a bairn, and ate up his
dinner, all in a fash to be coling the hay. Rachel cried *Aren't
you going to look in on mother?* and he said *Oh, ay,* and went
ben in a hurry. *Well, lass, you'll be pleased that the hay's done
fine—. Damn't, there's a cloud coming up from the sea!* And the
next that they saw he was out of the house staring at the
cloud as at Judgment Day.

Mrs Galt was dead ere September's end, on the day of
the funeral as folk came up they met Rob Galt in his old
cord breeks, with a hoe in his hand, and he said he'd been
out loosening up the potato drills a wee bit. He changed to
his black and he helped with his brothers to carry the coffin
out to the hearse. There were three bit carriages, he got in
the first, and the horses went jangling slow to the road. The
folk in the carriage kept solemn and long-faced, they
thought Rob the same because of his wife. But he suddenly
woke *Damn't, man, but I've got it! It's LIME that I should
have given the yavil. It's been greeting for the stuff, that park on
the brae!*

Rachel took on the housekeeping at Pittaulds, sombre
and slim, aye reading in books, she would stand of a winter
night and listen to the suck and slob of the rain on the clay
and hate the sound as she tried to hate Rob. And sometimes he'd say as they sat at their meat *What's wrong with
you, lass, that you're glowering like that?* and the quean would
look down, and remember her mother, while Rob rose
cheery and went to his work.

And yet, as she told to one of the lads that came cycling
up from Segget to see her, she just couldn't hate him, hard
though she tried. There was something in him that tugged
at herself, daft-like, a feeling with him that the fields
mattered and mattered, nothing else at all. And the lad
said *What, not even me, Rachel?* and she laughed and gave
him that which he sought, but half-absent like, she thought
little of lads.

Well, that winter Rob Galt made up his mind that he'd break in another bit stretch of the moor beyond the bit he already had broke, there the land rose steep in a birn of wee braes, folk told him he fair would be daft to break that, it was land had lain wild and unfed since the Flood. Rob Galt said *Maybe, but they're queer-like, those braes, as though some childe had once shored them tight up.* And he set to the trauchle as he'd done before, he'd come sweating in like a bull at night and Rachel would ask him *Why don't you rest?* and he'd stare at her dumb-founded a moment: *What, rest, and me with my new bit park? What would I do but get on with my work?*

And then, as the next day wore to its close, she heard him crying her name outbye, and went through the close, and he waved from the moor. So she closed the door and went up by the track through the schlorich of the wet November moor, a windy day in the winter's nieve, the hills a-cower from the bite of the wind, the whins in that wind had a moan as they moved, not a day for a dog to be out you would say. But she found her father near tirred to the skin, he'd been heaving a great root up from its hold, *Come in by and look on this fairely, lass, I knew that some childe had once farmed up here.*

And Rachel looked at the hole in the clay and the chamber behind it, dim in the light, where there gleamed a rickle of stone-grey sticks, the bones of a man of antique time. Amid the bones was a litter of flints and a crumbling stick in the shape of a heuch.

She knew it as an eirde of olden time, an earth-house built by the early folk, Rob nodded, *Ay, he was more than that. Look at that heuch, it once scythed Pittaulds. Losh, lass, I'd have liked to have kenned that childe, what a crack together we'd have had on the crops!*

Well, that night Rob started to splutter and hoast, next morning was over stiff to move, fair clean amazed at his own condition. Rachel got a neighbour to go for the doctor,

Rob had taken a cold while he stood and looked at the hole and the bones in the old-time grave. There was nothing in that and it fair was a shock when folk heard the news in a two-three days Rob Galt was dead of the cold he had ta'en. He'd worked all his go in the ground nought left to fight the black hoast that took hold of his lungs.

He'd said hardly a word, once whispered *The Ley*! the last hour as he lay and looked out at that park, red-white, with a tremor of its earthen face as the evening glow came over the Howe. Then he said to Rachel *You'll take on the land, you and some childe, I've a notion for that?* But she couldn't lie even to please him just then, she'd no fancy for either the land or a lad, she shook her head and Rob's gley grew dim.

When the doctor came in he found Rob dead, with his face to the wall and the blinds down-drawn. He asked the quean if she'd stay there alone, all the night with her father's corpse? She nodded *Oh, yes*, and watched him go, standing at the door as he drove off to Segget. Then she turned her about and went up through the parks, quiet, in the wet, quiet gloaming's coming, up through the hill to the old earth-house.

There the wind came sudden in a gust in her hair as she looked at the place and the way she had come and thought of the things the minister would say when she told him she planned her father be buried up here by the bones of the man of old time. And she shivered sudden as she looked round about at the bare clay slopes that slept in the dusk, the whistle of the whins seemed to rise in a voice, the parks below to whisper and listen as the wind came up them out of the east.

All life – just clay that awoke and strove to return again to its mother's breast. And she thought of the men who had made these rigs and the windy days of their toil and years, the daftness of toil that had been Rob Galt's, that had been that of many men long on the land, though seldom seen now, was it good, was it bad? What power had that been that woke once on this brae and was gone at last from the parks of Pittaulds?

For she knew in that moment that no other would come to tend the ill rigs in the north wind's blow. This was finished and ended, a thing put by, and the whins and the broom creep down once again, and only the peesies wheep and be still when she'd gone to the life that was hers, that was different, and the earth turn sleeping, unquieted no longer, her hungry bairns in her hungry breast where sleep and death and the earth were one.

The Land

I WINTER

I LIKE THE STORY of the helpful Englishman who, when shown a modern Scots Nationalist map with 'Scotland Proper' stretching from John o' Groats to the Tweed, and 'Scotia Irredenta' stretching from the Tweed to the Mersey, suggested 'Scotland Improper' in place of the latter term. The propriety of Northern England to rank as a section of Scotland may have political justice; it certainly has no aesthetic claim. If I look out on the land of Scotland and see it fouled by the smoking slag-heaps of industrialism rightwards and leftwards, a long trailing rift down the eastern coast and a vomiting geyser in Lanarkshire, I feel no stirrings of passion at all to add those tortured wastes of countryside, Northumbria and Lancashire, to the Scottish land. I like the grey glister of sleet in the dark this night, seen through the unblinded window; and I like this idle task of voyaging with a pen through the storm-happed wastes of Scotland in winter; but I balk at reaching beyond the Border, into that chill land of alien geology and deplorable methods of ploughing. This paraffin lamp set beside me on the table was lit for the benefit of myself and Scotland Proper: I shrink from geographical impropriety tonight as my Kailyard literary forerunners shrank from description of the bridal bed.

And now that I bend to the task and the logs are crackling so cheerfully and the wind has veered a point, and there's a fine whoom in the lum, it comes on me with a qualm that perhaps I have no qualifications for the task at all. For if the land is the enumeration of figures and statistics of the yield of wheat in the Merse or the Carse of Gowrie, fruit-harvesting in Coupar-Angus, or how they couple and breed their cattle in Ayrshire, I am quite lost. And if the land is the lilting of tourist names, Strathmore, Ben Lomond, Ben Macdhui, Rannoch, Loch Tay and the Sidlaw Hills, I confess to bored glimpses of this and that stretch of unique countryside, I confess that once (just such a night as this) I journeyed up to Oban; and the train was bogged in a snowstorm; and I spent shivering hours in view of Ben Cruachan; and once an Anglo-Gaelic novelist took me round Loch Lomond in his car and we drank good whisky and talked about Lenin; and an uncle once dragged me, protesting, up Lochnagar, in search of a sunrise that failed to appear – the sun hid that morning in a diffusion of peasoup fog; and I've viewed the Caledonian Canal with suitable commercial enthusiasm and recited (as a small boy at concerts) verse about the Dee and Don, they still run on (a phenomenon which elicited complacent clappings of commendation from my audiences); and I've eaten trout by Loch Levenside. But I refuse the beetling crags and the spume of Spey; still I think they are not The Land.

That is The Land out there, under the sleet, churned and pelted there in the dark, the long rigs upturning their clayey faces to the spear-onset of the sleet. That is The Land, a dim vision this night of laggard fences and long stretching

rigs. And the voice of it – the true and unforgettable voice –
you can hear even such a night as this as the dark comes
down, the immemorial plaint of the peewit, flying lost. *That*
is The Land – though not quite all. Those folk in the byre
whose lantern light is a glimmer through the sleet as they
muck and bed and tend the kye, and milk the milk into tin
pails, in curling froth – they are The Land in as great a
measure. Those two, a dual power, are the protagonists in
this little sketch. They are the essentials for the title. And
besides, quite unfairly, they are all so intimately mine that I
would give them that position though they had not a
shadow of a claim to it.

I like to remember I am of peasant rearing and peasant
stock. Good manners prevail on me not to insist on the fact
over-much, not to boast in the company of those who come
from manses and slums and castles and villas, the folk of
the proletariat, the bigger and lesser bourgeoisies. But I am
again and again, as I hear them talk of their origins and
beginnings and begetters, conscious of an over-weening
pride that mine was thus and so, that the land was so closely
and intimately mine (my mother used to hap me in a plaid
in harvest-time and leave me in the lee of a stook while she
harvested) that I feel of a strange and antique age in the
company and converse of my adult peers – like an adult
himself listening to the bright sayings and laughters of
callow boys, parvenus on the human scene, while I, a good
Venriconian Pict, harken from the shade of my sun circle
and look away, bored, in pride of possession at my terraced
crops, at the on-ding of rain and snow across my leavened
fields . . .

How much this is merely reaction from the hatreds of my
youth I do not know. For once I had a very bitter detestation for all this life of the land and the folk upon it. My view
was that of my distant cousin, Mr Leslie Mitchell, writing
in his novel *The Thirteenth Disciple:*

A grey, grey life. Dull and grey in its routine, Spring, Summer, Autumn, Winter, that life the Neolithic men brought from the south, supplanting Azilian hunger and hunting and light-hearted shiftlessness with servitude to seasons and soil and the tending of cattle. A beastly life. With memory of it and reading those Catholic writers, who, for some obscure reason, champion the peasant and his state as the ideal state, I am moved to unkindly mirth . . . unprintably sceptical as to Mr Chesterton or his chelas ever having grubbed a livelihood from hungry acres of red clay, or regarding the land and its inhabitants with other vision than an obese Victorian astigmatism.

Not, I think, that I have gone the full circle and have returned among the romantics. As I listen to that sleet-drive I can see the wilting hay-ricks under the fall of the sleet and think of the wind ablow on ungarmented floors, ploughmen in sodden bothies on the farms outbye, old, bent and wrinkled people who have mislaid so much of fun and hope and high endeavour in grey servitude to those rigs curling away, only half-inanimate, into the night. I can still think and see these things with great clarity though I sit in this warm room and write this pleasant essay and find pleasure in the manipulation of words on a blank page. But when I read or hear our new leaders and their plans for making of Scotland a great peasant nation, a land of little farms and little farming communities, I am moved to a bored disgust with those pseudo-literary romantics playing with politics, those refugees from the warm parlours and lights and policemen and theatre-stalls of the Scots cities. They are promising the New Scotland a purgatory that would decimate it. They are promising it narrowness and bitterness and heart-breaking toil in one of the most unkindly agricultural lands in the world. They are promising to make of a young, ricketic man, with the phthisis of

Glasgow in his throat, a bewildered labourer in pelting rains and the flares of head-aching suns, they are promising him years of a murderous monotony, poverty and struggle and loss of happy human relationships. They promise that of which they know nothing, except through sipping of the scum of Kailyard romance.

For this life is for no modern man or woman – even the finest of these. It belongs to a different, an alien generation. That winter that is sweeping up the Howe, bending the whins on Auchindreich hill, seeping with pelting blasts through the old walls of Edzell Castle, malagarousing the ploughed lands and swashing about and above the heavy cattle-courts where in darkness the great herds lie cud-chewing and breath-blowing in frosty steam, is a thing for most to be stared at, tourist-wise, endured for a day or a week. This night, the winter on the countryside, the crofter may doze contentedly in the arm-chair in the ingleneuk and the mistress yawn with an equal content at the clock. For you or I or young Simon who is taking his girl to the pictures it is as alien and unendurable in permanence as the life of the Kamtchatkan.

II SPRING

Going down the rigs this morning, my head full of that unaccustomed smell of the earth, fresh and salty and anciently mouldy, I remembered the psalmist's voice of the turtle and instinctively listened for its Scots equivalent – that far cooing of pigeons that used to greet the coming of Spring mornings when I was a boy. But the woods have gone, their green encirclement replaced by swathes of bog and muck and rank-growing heath, all the land about here is left bare in the North wind's blow. The pigeons have gone and the rabbits and like vermin multiplied – unhappily and to no profit, for the farmers tell me the rabbits are tuberculous, dangerous meat. Unshielded by the woods, the farm-lands are assailed by enemies my youth never knew.

But they are fewer and fewer, the cultivated lands. Half of them are in grass – permanently in grass – and browsed upon by great flocks of sheep, leaving that spider-trail of grey that sheep bring to pastures. We are repeating here what the Border men did in Badenoch and the Highlands – eating away the land and the crofter, killing off the peasant as surely as in Russia – and with no Russian compensation. If the little dykes and the sodden ditches that rivuleted in the Springs of bygone times with the waters hastening to the Forthie – the ditches that separated this little farm from that – were filled and obliterated by a sovkholz with tractors and high enthusiasm and a great and tremendous agricultural hope, I at least could turn to the hills and the heath – that other and older Land – with no more regret than the sensitive felt in the passing of the windjammers and the coming of the steamboats. But instead there has come here only a brainless greed, a grabbing stupidity, the mean avariciousness and planlessness of our community in epitome. I do not wonder that the rabbits are tuberculous: the wonder is that they are not jaundiced as well.

It was then that I thought what a fine and heartsome smell has rank cow-dung as the childe with the graip hurls it steady heap on heap from the rear of his gurling cart. They sell stuff in Paris in little bottles with just that smell, and charge for it handsomely, as they may well do, for it is the smell that backgrounds existence. And then (having come to the end of the rig and looked at the rabbit-snare and found it empty and found also a stone whereon to sit) I fell into another meditation: this dung that backgrounded existence, this Autumn's crops, meal for the folk of the cities, good heartsome barley alcohol – would never be spread, never be seeded, never ground to bree, but for the aristocracy of the earth, the ploughmen and the peasants.

These are the real rulers of Scotland: they are the rulers of the earth!

And how patient and genial and ingenuously foul-mouthed and dourly wary and kindly they are, those self-less aristos of Scotland. They endure a life of mean and bitter poverty, an order sneered upon by the little folk of the towns, their gait is a mockery in city streets, you see little waitresses stare haughtily at their great red, sun-creased hands, plump professors in spectacles and pimples enunciate theses on their mortality and morality, their habits of breeding and their shiftlessness – and they endure it all! They endure the chatter of the city salons, the plannings of this and that war and blockade, they endure the pretensions of every social class but their own to be the mainspring and base of human society – they, the masters, who feed the world! . . . And it came on me that all over Great Britain, all over Europe this morning, the mean fields of France and fat pastures of Saxony and the rolling lands of Roumania those rulers of the earth were out and about, bent-backed at plodding toil, the world's great Green International awaiting the coming of its Spartacus.

There are gulls in from the sea this morning, wheeling in comet tails at the heels of this and that ploughman, a dotting of signatures against the dark green of the Bervie braes. Here the land is red clay, sour and dour, but south, by Brechin, you come to that rich loam land that patterns Scotland like a ragged veil, the lovely land that even here erupts in sudden patches and brings tall corn while the surrounding fields wilt in the baking clay. The clay is good for potatoes in the dry years, however – those dry years that come every decade or so for no reason that we know of here in the Howe, for we are beyond the 'mountain-shadow' that makes of Donside and Braemar the tourist's camping-ground . . .

In the sunlight, down by Kinneff, the fog-horn has begun its wail, the sun has drawn great banks of mist out of the

North Sea and now they are billowing over Auchendreich
like the soft, coloured spume from a washing-tub. But leftwards the sun is a bright, steely glare on the ridged humps
of the Grampians, hastening south into the coming of
Summer, crowned with snow in their upper haughs – much
the same mountains, I suppose, as the Maglemosians
looked on that Spring day in the youth of the world and
the youth of Scotland when they crossed the low lands of
the Dogger Bank and clambered up the rocks of Kinneff
into a still and untenanted Scotland. The great bear
watched them come, and the eagle from his Grampian
eyrie and scattering packs of wolves on the forest fringes
saw that migration of the hunters seven thousand years ago.
They came over Auchendreich there, through the whins
and heath, and halted and stared at the billowing Howe,
and laughed and muttered and squatted and stared – dark
men, and tall, without gods or kings, classes or culture,
writers or artists, free and happy, and all the world theirs.
Scotland woke and looked at them from a hundred peaks
and stared a shy virgin's amaze.

All winter the cattle were kept to the byres. This morning
saw their first deliverance – cows and stirks and stots and
calves they grumphed and galumphed from the byre to the
park and squattered an astounded delight in the mud, and
boxed at each other, and stared a bovine surprise at the
world, and went mad with delight and raced round the
park, and stood still and mooed: they mooed on a long,
devilish note, the whole lot of them, for nearly two minutes
on end and for no reason at all but delight in hearing their
own moo. They are all of mixed breed, except one, a small
Jersey cow of a southron coldness, who drops her aitches,
haughtily, and also her calves. The strains are mostly
shorthorn, with a dash of Highland, I suspect: a hundred
years of mixed pasturing and crop-rotation weeded out the
experimental breeds and left these satisfying mongrels.
Presently (after racing a grocer' grocer's cart for the length

of the field and all but hamstringing themselves on the boundary fence) they abandoned playfulness and took to grazing, remembering their mission was to provide fat carcases for the slaughtershed—.

We balk from such notions, in Spring especially, in especial as the evening comes with that fresh smell all about it, impregnating it, the kind of evening that has growth and youngness and kindliness in its essence – balk from the thought of our strange, unthinking cruelties, the underpit of blood and suffering and intolerable horror on which the most innocent of us build our lives. I feel this evening that never again will I eat a dead animal (or, I find myself guarding the resolve with the inevitable flippancy, a live one). But that resolve will be gone tomorrow: the Horror is beyond personalism, very old and strange and terrible. Even those hunters all those millennia ago were eaters of flesh.

It is strange to think that, if events never die (as some of the wise have supposed), but live existence all time in Eternity, back through the time-spirals, still alive and aware in that world seven thousand years ago, the hunters are *now* lying down their first night in Scotland, with their tall, deep-bosomed sinewy mates and their children, tired from trek . . . Over in the west a long line of lights twinkles against the dark. Whin-burning – or the camps of Maglemose?

III SUMMER

I cycled up the Glen of Drumtochty today. It was very hot, the heat was caught in the cup of the Howe and spun and stirred there, milkily, by little currents of wind that had come filtering down through the Grampian passes. In the long, dusty stretches of roadway my shadow winked and fluttered perspiringly while I followed in a sympathetic sweat. This till we pass down into the Glen itself, when the over-shadowing hills flung us a cool shade. There the water sparkled and spun coolly, so coldly, a little burn with deep brown detritus winding amidst the broom and the whins. To the left the reafforested Drumtochty Hill towered up dazzlingly impossible in purple. This Tyrian splendour on Drumtochty Hill is probably unmatched in all Scotland, very breath-taking and strange, alien to Scotland: it is a wonder, a flamboyant flaunting of nature that comes for a month on our dour hill-lands and we stare at it, sober, Presbyterian, from our blacks and browns – much as Mac-Diarmid visioned the Scots on Judgement Day staring at

> God and a' his gang
> O' angels in the lift,
> Thae trashy, bleezin' French-like folk
> Wha garred them shift . . .

Beyond the contours of Drumtochty, through the piping of that stillness, snipe were sounding. I got off my bicycle to listen to that and look round. So doing I was aware of a sober fact: that indeed all this was a little disappointing. I would never apprehend its full darkly colourful beauty until I had gone back to England, far from it, down in the smooth pastures of Hertfordshire some night I would remember it and itch to write of it, I would see it without the unessentials – sweat and flies and that hideous gimcrack castle, nestling – (Good God, it even *nestled!*) among the trees. I would see it in simplicity then, even as I would see the people of the land.

This perhaps is the real land; not those furrows that haunt me as animate. This is the land, unstirred and greatly untouched by men, unknowing ploughing or crops or the coming of the scythe. Yet even those hills were not always thus. The Archaic Civilisation came here and terraced great sections of those hills and reared Devil Stones, Sun Circles, to the great agricultural gods of ancient times

– long ago, before Pytheas sailed these coasts, while Alexander rode his horse across the Jaxartes there were peasants on those hills, on such a day as this, who paused to wipe the sweat from their faces and look with shrewd eyes at the green upspringing of the barley crops . . . By night they slept in houses dug in the earth, roofed with thatch, and looked out on a wilder and wetter Howe, but still with that passion of purple mantling it in this month. They are so tenuous and yet so real, those folk – and how they haunted me years ago! I had no great interest in the things around me, I remember, the summer dawns that came flecked with saffron over the ricks of my father's farm, the whisper and pelt of the corn-heads, green turning to yellow in the long fields that lay down in front of our front-door, the rattle and creak of the shelvins of a passing box-cart, the chirp and sardonic *Ay!* of the farming childe who squatted unshaven, with twinkling eyes, on the forefront of the shelvin . . . but the ancient men haunted those woods and hills for me, and do so still.

I climbed up the top of Cairn o' Mount with my bicycle and sat and lunched and looked about me: and found it very still, the land of Scotland taking a brief siesta in that midday hour. Down in the north the green parks, miles away, were like plaques of malachite set on the table of some craftsman of ancient Chichen-Itza or Mexico, translucent and gleaming and polished. One understood then, if never before, how that colour – green – obsessed the ancient civilisation with its magic virtues. It was one of the colours that marked a Giver of Life – reasonably, for those crops are surely such Givers? It is better land here than in my homeland – darker, streaked with clay, but with a richer sub-soil. Between the green of the corn and barley shone the darker stretches of the tattie-shaws, the turnip tops, and the honey brown of the clover. Bees were humming about me: one came and ate jam from my sandwiches, some discontented apian soul unfulfilled with the natural honey of the heather-bells and longing for the tart, sharp tastes of the artificial.

He is not alone in that. In the days of my youth (I have that odd pleasure that men in the early thirties derive from thinking of themselves as beyond youth: this pleasure fades in the forties) men and women still lived largely on the food-stuffs grown in the districts – kale and cabbage and good oatmeal, they made brose and porridge and crisp oatcakes, and jams from the blackberry bushes in the dour little, sour little gardens. But that is mostly a matter of the past. There are few who bake oatcakes nowadays, fewer still who ever taste kale. Stuff from the grocer's, stuff in bottles and tins, the canned nutriments of Chicago and the ubiquitous Fray Bentos, have supplanted the old-time diets. This dull, feculent stuff is more easy to deal with, not enslaving your whole life as once the cooking and serving did in the little farms and cottars' houses – cooking in the heat of such a day as this on great open fireplaces, without even a range. And though I sit here on this hill and deplore the fusionless foods of the canneries, I have no sympathy at all with those odd souls of the cities who would see the return of that 'rich agricultural life' as the return of something praiseworthy, blessed and rich and generous. Better Fray Bentos and a seat in the pictures with your man of a Saturday night than a grilling baking of piled oatcakes and a headache withal.

They change reluctantly, the men and women of the little crofts and cottar houses; but slowly a quite new orientation of outlook is taking place. There are fewer children now plodding through the black glaur of the wet summer storms to school, fewer in both farm and cottar house. The ancient, strange whirlimagig of the generations that enslaved the Scots peasantry for centuries is broken. In times gone by a ploughman might save and scrape and live meanly and hardly and marry a quean of like mettle. And in time they would have gathered enough to rent a croft, then a little farm; and all the while they saved, and lived austere, sardonic lives; and their savings took them at last to the wide cattle-courts and the great stone-floored kitchen of a large farm. And all the while the woman bred, very efficiently and plentifully and with out fuss – twelve or thirteen were the common numberings of a farmer's progeny. And those children grew up, and their father died. And in the division of property at his death each son or daughter gathered as inheritance only a few poor pounds. And perforce they started as ploughmen in the bothies, maids in the kitchens, and set about climbing the rungs again – that their children might do the same.

It kept a kind of democracy on the land that is gone or is going; your halflin or your maid was the son or the daughter of your old friends of High Rigs: your own sons and daugthers were in bothies or little crofts: it was a perfect Spenglerian cycle. Yet it was waste effort, it was as foolish as the plod of an ass in a treadmill, innumerable generations of asses. If the clumsy fumblements of contraception have done no more than break the wheel and play of that ancient cycle they have done much. Under these hills – so summer-hazed, so immobile and essentially unchanging – of a hundred years hence I do not know what strange master of the cultivated lands will pass in what strange mechanical contrivance: but he will be outwith that ancient yoke, and I send him my love and the hope that he'll sometime climb up Cairn o' Mount and sit where I'm sitting now, and stray in summery thought – into the sun-hazed mists of the future, into the lives and wistful desirings of forgotten men who begat him.

IV AUTUMN

I have a daughter four years old who was born in England and goes to school there, and already has notions on ethnology. Occasionally she and I debate and fall out, and her final triumphant thrust is 'You're only Scotch!'

Autumn of all seasons is when I realise how very Scotch I am, how interwoven with the fibre of my body and personality is this land and its queer, scarce harvests, its hours of reeking sunshine and stifling rain, how much a stranger I am, south, in those seasons of mist and mellow fruitfulness as alien to my Howe as the olive groves of Persia. It is a harder and slower harvest, and lovelier in its austerity, that is gathered here, in September's early coming, in doubtful glances on the sky at dawn, in listening to the sigh of the sea down there by Bervie. Mellow it certainly is not: but it has the most unique of tangs, this season haunted by the laplaplap of the peesie's wings, by great moons that come nowhere as in Scotland, unending moons when the harvesting carts plod through great thickets of fir-shadow to the cornyards deep in glaur.

These are the most magical nights of the land: they endure but a little while, but their smells – sharp and clear, commingled of fresh horse-dung and dusty cornheads – pervade the winter months. The champ and showd of a horse in that moonsprayed dark and the guttural 'Tchkh, min!' of the forker, the great shapes of cattle in the parks as you ride by, the glimmer far away of the lights of some couthy toun on the verge of sleep, the queer shapes of post and gate and stook – Nature unfolds the puppets and theatre pieces year after year, unvaryingly, and they lose their dust, each year uniquely fresh. You can stand and listen as though for the lost trumpet of God in that autumn night silence: but indeed all that you are listening for is a passing peewit.

It is strange how Scotland has no Gilbert White or HJ Massingham to sing its fields, its birds, such night as this, to chronicle the comings and goings of the swallows in simple, careful prose, ecstasy controlled. But perhaps not so strange. We Scots have little interest in the wild and its world; I realise how compassed and controlled is my own interest, I am vague about sparrows and tits, martins and swallows, I know little of their seasons, and my ignorance lies heavily upon me not at all. I am concerned so much more deeply with men and women, with their nights and days, the things they believe, the things that move them to pain and anger and the callous, idle cruelties that are yet undead. When I hear or read of a dog tortured to death, very vilely and foully, of some old horse driven to a broken back down a hill with an over-loaded cart of corn, of rats captured and tormented with red-hot pokers in bothies, I have a shudder of disgust. But these things do not move me too deeply, not as the fate of the old-time Cameronian prisoners over there, three miles away in Dunnottar; not as the face of that ragged tramp who went by this afternoon; not as the crucifixion of the Spartacist slaves along the Appian Way. To me it is inconceivable that sincere and honest men should go outside the range of their own species with gifts of pity and angry compassion and rage when there is horror and dread among humankind. I am unreasonably and mulishly prejudiced in favour of my own biological species. I am a jingo patriot of planet earth: 'Humanity right or wrong!'

Particularly in Autumn. At noon I crossed a field off which the last of the stooks had been lifted and led captive away, the gaping stubble heads pushed through the cricks of clay, the long bouts of the binder wound and wheeled around the park, where the foreman had driven his team three weeks before. And each of those minute stubble stalks grew from seed that men had handled and winnowed and selected and ploughed and harrowed the earth to receive, and sown and tended and watched come up in the rains of Springs and the hot Summer suns – each and all of these – and out and beyond their kindred trillions in the other parks, up to the biggings of Upperhill there, and sough through all the chave of the Howe to the black lands that start by Brechin and roll down the coast till they come to the richness of Lothian and the orchards of Blairgowrie . . . This is our power, this the wonder of humankind, our one great victory over nature and time. Three million years hence our descendants out on some tremendous furrowing of the Galaxy, with the Great Bear yoked to The Plough and the wastes of space their fields, will remember this little planet, if at all, for the men who conquered the land and wrung sustenance from it by stealth and shrewdness and a savage and surly endurance. Nothing else at all may endure in those overhuman memories: I do not think there is anything else I want to endure.

The ricks loom tall and white in the moonlight about their yellow bosses: folk are loosening the heavy horses from the carts and leading them tramp, tramp across the cobbles of the close: with a scrape and clatter by the water-trough and a silence and then the sound of a slavering long, enjoyable long suction: I feel thirsty in sympathy with that equine delight of cool, good water in a parched mouth and throat. Then a light blinks through the cobwebs of the stable, an impatient voice says *Wissh!* and harvest is over.

Quiet enough here, because the very young and irre-sponsible are not here. But elsewhere, nights like this, up and down the great agricultural belts of Scotland, in and about the yards and the ricks, there is still some relic of the ancient fun at the last ingathering of the sheaves – still a genial clowning and drinking and a staring at the moon, and slow, steady childes swinging away to the bothies, their hands deep down in their pouches, their boots striking fire from the cobbles; still maids to wait their lads in the lee of the new-built stacks, and be cuddled and warm and happy against brown, dank chests, and be kissed into wonder on the world, and taste the goodness of the night and the Autumn's end . . . Before the Winter comes.

Tomorrow the potato harvests, of course. But somehow they are not real harvests, they are not truly of Autumn as is the taking in of the corn. It is still an alien plant, the potato, an intruder from that world of wild belief and wilder practice that we call the New, a plant that hides and lairs deep down in the midst of back-breaking drills. The corn is so ancient that its fresh harvesting is no more than the killing of an ancient enemy-friend, ritualistic, that you may eat of the flesh of the God, drink of his blood, and be given salvation and life.

Glasgow

GLASGOW IS ONE of the few places in Scotland which defy personification. To image Edinburgh as a disappointed spinster, with a hare-lip and inhibitions, is at least to approximate as closely to the truth as to image the Prime Mover as a Levantine Semite. So with Dundee, a frowsy fisher-wife addicted to gin and infanticide, Aberdeen a thin-lipped peasant-woman who has borne eleven and buried nine. But no Scottish image of personification may display, even distortedly, the essential Glasgow. One might go further afield, to the tortured imaginings of the Asiatic mind, to find her likeness – many-armed Siva with the waistlet of skulls, or Xipe of Ancient America, whose priest skinned the victim alive, and then clad himself in the victim's skin. . . . But one doubts anthropomorphic representation at all. The monster of Loch Ness is probably the lost soul of Glasgow, in scales and horns, disporting itself in the Highlands after evacuating finally and completely its mother-corpse.

One cannot blame it. My distant cousin, Mr Leslie Mitchell, once described Glasgow in one of his novels as 'the vomit of a cataleptic commercialism'. But it is more

than that. It may be a corpse, but the maggot-swarm upon
it is very fiercely alive. One cannot watch and hear the long
beat of traffic down Sauchiehall, or see its eddy and spume
where St Vincent Street and Renfield Street cross, without
realising what excellent grounds the old-fashioned anthropologist appeared to have for believing that man was by
nature a brutish savage, a herd-beast delighting in vocal
discordance and orgiastic aural abandon.

Loch Lomond lies quite near to Glasgow. Nice Glaswe-
gians motor out there and admire the scenery and calculate
its horse-power and drink whisky and chaff one another in
genteelly Anglicised Glaswegianisms. After a hasty look at
Glasgow the investigator would do well to disguise himself
as one of like kind, drive down to Loch Lomondside and
stare across its waters at the sailing clouds that crown the
Ben, at the flooding of colours changing and darkling and
miraculously lighting up and down those misty slopes,
where night comes over long mountain leagues that know
only the paddings of the shy, stray hare, the whirr and cry of
the startled pheasant, silences so deep you can hear the
moon come up, mornings so greyly coloured they seem
stolen from Norse myth. This is the proper land and stance
from which to look at Glasgow, to divest oneself of horror
or shame or admiration or – very real – fear, and ask: Why?
Why did men ever allow themselves to become enslaved to
a thing so obscene and so foul when there was *this* awaiting
them here – hills and the splendours of freedom and
silence, the clean splendours of hunger and woe and dread
in the winds and rains and famine-times of the earth,
hunting and love and the call of the moon? Nothing
endured by the primitives who once roamed those hills –
nothing of woe or terror – approximated in degree or kind
to that life that festers in the courts and wynds and alleys of
Camlachie, Govan, the Gorbals.

In Glasgow there are over a hundred and fifty thousand
human beings living in such conditions as the most bitterly

pressed primitive in Tierra del Fuego never visioned. They
live five or six to the single room . . . And at this point,
sitting and staring at Ben Lomond, it requires a vivid
mental jerk to realise the quality of that room. It is not a
room in a large and airy building, it is not a single-roomed
hut on the verge of a hill; it is not a cave driven into free
rock, in the sound of the sea-birds as that old Azilian cave in
Argyll: it is a room that is part of some great sloven of
tenement – the tenement itself in a line or a grouping with
hundreds of its fellows, its windows grimed with the unceasing wash and drift of coal-dust, its stairs narrow and
befouled and steep, its evening breath like that which might
issue from the mouth of a lung-diseased beast. The hundred and fifty thousand eat and sleep and copulate and
conceive and crawl into childhood in those waste jungles of
stench and disease and hopelessness, sub-humans as definitely as the Morlocks of Wells – and without even the
consolation of feeding on their oppressors' flesh.

A hundred and fifty thousand . . . and all very like you or
me or my investigator sitting appalled on the banks of Loch
Lomond (where he and his true love will never meet again).
And they live on food of the quality of offal, ill-cooked, ill-
eaten with speedily-diseased teeth for the tending of which
they can afford no fees; they work – if they have work – in
factories or foundries or the roaring reek of the Docks toilsome and dreary and unimaginative hours – hour on hour,
day on day, frittering away the tissues of their bodies and
the spirit-stuff of their souls; they are workless – great
numbers of them – doomed to long days of staring vacuity,
of shoelessness, of shivering hidings in this and that mean
runway when the landlords' agents come, of mean and
desperate beggings at Labour Exchanges and Public Assistance Committees; their voices are the voices of men and
women robbed of manhood and womanhood . . .

The investigator on Loch Lomondside shudders and
turns to culture for comfort. He is, of course, a subscriber

to *The Modern Scot*, where culture at three removes – castrated, disembowelled, and genteelly vulgarised – is served afresh each season; and has brought his copy with him. Mr Adam Kennedy is serialising a novel, *The Mourners*, his technique a genteel objectivity. And one of his characters has stopped in Glasgow's Kelvingrove, and is savouring its essence:

'John's eyes savoured the spaciousness of the crescent, the formal curve of the unbroken line of house façades, the regimentation of the rows of chimney-pots, the full-length windows, the unnecessarily broad front steps, the feudal basements – savoured all these in the shimmering heat of the day just as his nose had savoured the morning freshness. It was as good for him to walk round these old terraces as to visit a cathedral. He could imagine now and then that he had evoked for himself something of the atmosphere of the grand days of these streets. The world was surer of itself then, sure of the ultimate perfectability of man, sure of the ultimate mastery over the forces that surrounded him. And if Atlas then no longer had the world firm on his shoulder, the world for all that rested on the same basis of the thus-and-thusness of things. With such a basis you could have that sureness of yourself to do things largely as had been done before. But the modern mind was no longer sure of itself even in a four-roomed bungalow. Its pride was the splitting of its personality into broods of impish devils that spent their time spying one on the other. It could never get properly outside itself, could never achieve the objectivity that was capable of such grandly deliberate planning as in these streets.'

Glasgow speaks. The hundred and fifty thousand are answered. Glasgow has spoken.

This, indeed, is its attitude, not merely the pale whey of intellectualism peculiar to *The Modern Scot*. The bourgeois Glaswegian cultivates aesthetic objectivity as happier men cultivate beards or gardens. Pleasant folk of Kelvingrove point out that those hundred and fifty thousand – how well off they are! Free education, low rents, no rates, State relief – half of them, in fact, State pensioners. Besides, they enjoy life as they are – damn them, or they ought to. Always raising riots about their conditions. Not that they raise the riots themselves – it's the work of the communists – paid agitators from Moscow. But they've long since lost all hold. Or they ought to have—.

In those days of Nationalism, of Douglasism, (that ingenious scheme for childbirth without pain and – even more intriguing – without a child), of Socialism, of Fascism, Glasgow, as no other place, moves me to a statement of faith. I have amused myself with many political creeds – the more egregrious the creed the better. I like the thought of a Scots Republic with Scots Border Guards in saffron kilts – the thought of those kilts can awake me to joy in the middle of the night. I like the thought of Miss Wendy Wood leading a Scots Expeditionary Force down to Westminster to reclaim the Scone Stone: I would certainly march with that expedition myself in spite of the risk of dying of laughter by the way. I like the thought of a Scots Catholic kingdom with Mr Compton Mackenzie Prime Minister to some disinterred Jacobite royalty, and all the Scots intellectuals settled out on the land on thirty-acre crofts, or sent to recolonise St Kilda for the good of their souls and the nation (except the hundreds streaming over the Border in panic flight at sight of this Scotland of their dreams). I like the thought of the ancient Scots aristocracy revived and set in order by Mr George Blake, that ephor of the people: Mr Blake vetoing the Duke of Montrose is one of my dearest visions. I like the thought of the Scottish Fascists evicting all those of Irish blood from Scotland, and so leaving Albyn entirely deserted but for some half-dozen pro-Irish Picts like myself. I like the thought of a Scottish Socialist Republic under Mr Maxton – preferably at war with royalist England, and Mr Maxton summoning the

Russian Red Army to his aid (the Red Army digging a secret tunnel from Archangel to Aberdeen). And I like the thought of Mr RM Black and his mysterious Free Scots, that modern Mafia, assassinating the Bankers (which is what bankers are for) . . .

But I cannot play with those fantasies when I think of the hundred and fifty thousand in Glasgow. They are a something that stills the parlour chatter. I find I am by way of being an intellectual myself. I meet and talk with many people whose interests are art and letters and music, enthusiasm for this and that aspect of craft and architecture, men and women who have very warm and sincere beliefs indeed regarding the ancient culture of Scotland, people to whom Glasgow is the Hunterian Museum with its fine array of Roman coins, or the Galleries with their equally fine array of pictures. 'Culture' is the motif-word of the conversation: ancient Scots culture, future Scots culture, culture ad lib. and ad nauseam . . . The patter is as intimate on my tongue as on theirs. And relevant to the fate and being of those hundred and fifty thousand it is no more than the chatter and scratch of a band of apes, seated in a pit on a midden of corpses.

There is nothing in culture or art that is worth the life and elementary happiness of one of those thousands who rot in the Glasgow slums. There is nothing in science or religion. If it came (as it may come) to some fantastic choice between a free and independent Scotland, a centre of culture, a bright flame of artistic and scientific achievement, and providing elementary decencies of food and shelter to the submerged proletariat of Glasgow and Scotland, I at least would have no doubt as to which side of the battle I would range myself. For the cleansing of that horror, if cleanse it they could, I would welcome the English in suzerainty over Scotland till the end of time. I would welcome the end of Braid Scots and Gaelic, our culture, our history, our nationhood under the heels of a

Chinese army of occupation if it could cleanse the Glasgow slums, give a surety of food and play – the elementary right of every human being – to those people of the abyss . . .

I realise (seated on the plump modernity of *The Modern Scot* by the side of my investigator out on Loch Lomond-bank) how completely I am the complete Philistine. I have always liked the Philistines, a commendable and gracious and cleanly race. They built clean cities with wide, airy streets, they delighted in the singing of good, simple songs and hunting and lovemaking and the worshipping of relevant and comprehensible Gods. They were a light in the Ancient East and led simple and happy and carefree lives, with a splendour of trumpets now and again to stir them to amusing orgy . . . And above, in the hills, in Jerusalem, dwelt the Israelites, unwashed and unashamed, horrified at the clean anarchy which is the essence of life, oppressed by grisly fears of life and death and time, suborning simple human pleasures in living into an insane debating on justice and right, the Good Life, the Soul of Man, artistic canon, the First Cause, National Ethos, the mainsprings of conduct, aesthetic approach – and all the rest of the dirty little toys with which dirty little men in dirty little caves love to play, turning with a haughty shudder of repulsion from the cry of the wind and the beat of the sun on the hills outside . . . One of the greatest tragedies of the ancient world was the killing of Goliath by David – a ghoul-haunted little village squirt who sneaked up and murdered the Philistine while the latter (with a good breakfast below his belt) was admiring the sunrise.

The non-Philistines never admire sunrises. They never admire good breakfasts. Their ideal is the half-starved at sunset, whose actions and appearances they can record with a proper aesthetic detachment. One of the best-loved pictures of an earlier generation of Glasgow intellectuals was Josef Israel's *Frugal Meal* in the Glasgow Galleries. Even yet the modern will halt you to admire the chiaroscuro, the fine shades and attitudes. But you realise he is a liar. He is merely an inhibited little sadist, and his concentrated essence of enjoyment is the hunger and dirt and hopleessness of the two figures in question. He calls this a 'robust acceptance of life.'

Sometime, it is true, the non-Philistine of past days had a qualm of regret, a notion, a thin pale abortion of an idea that life in simplicity was life in essence. So he painted a man or a woman, nude only in the less shameful portions of his or her anatomy (egregious bushes were called in to hide the genital shames) and called it not *Walking* or *Running* or *Staring* or *Sleeping* or *Lusting* (as it generally was) but *Light* or *Realization* or *The Choir* or what not. A Millais in the Glasgow Galleries is an excellent example, which neither you nor my investigator may miss. It is the non-Philistine's wistful idea of (in capitals) Life in Simplicity – a decent young childe in a breech-clout about to play hoop-la with a forked stick. But instead of labelling this truthfully and obviously *Portrait of Shy-Making Intellectual Playing at Boy Scouts* it is called (of course) *The Forerunner*.

The bourgeois returns at evening these days to Kelvingrove, to Woodsidehill, to Hillhead and Dowanhill with heavy and doubting steps. The shipyards are still, with rusting cranes and unbefouled waters nearby, in Springburn the empty factories increase and multiply, there are dead windows and barred factory-gates in Bridgeton and Mile End. Commercialism has returned to its own vomit too often and too long still to find sustenance therein. Determinedly in Glasgow (as elsewhere) they call this condition 'The Crisis', and, in the fashion of a Christian Scientist whose actual need is cascara, invoke Optimism for its cure. But here as nowhere else in the modern world of capitalism does the impartial investigator realise that the remedy lies neither in medicine nor massage, but in surgery . . . The doctors (he hears) are gathered for the Saturday-Sunday diagnoses on Glasgow Green; and betakes himself there accordingly.

But there (as elsewhere) the physicians disagree – multitudes of physicians, surrounded by anxious groups of the ailing patient's dependents. A brief round of the various physicians convinces the investigator of one thing: the unpopularity of surgery. The single surgeon orating is, of course, the Communist. His gathering is small. A larger following attends Mr Guy Aldred, Non-Parliamentary Anarcho-communist, pledged to use neither knives nor pills, but invocation of the Gospels according to St Bakunin. Orthodox Socialism, ruddy and plump, with the spoils from the latest Glasgow Corporation swindle in its pocket, the fee'd physician, popular and pawky, is fervent and optimistic. Pills? – Nonsense! Surgery? – Muscovite savagery! What is needed to remove the sprouting pustules from the fair face of commercialism is merely a light, nongreasy ointment (which will not stain the sheets). Near at hand stands the Fascist: the investigator, with a training which has hitherto led him to debar the Neanderthaler from the direct ancestral line of *Homo Sapiens*, stares at this ethnological note of interrogation. The Fascist diagnosis: Lack of blood. Remedy: Bleeding. A Nationalist holds forth near by. What the patient needs is not more food, fresh air, a decent room of his own and a decent soul of his own – No! What he needs is the air he ceased to breathe two hundred and fifty years ago – specially reclaimed and canned by the National Party of Scotland (and forwarded in plain vans) . . . A Separatist casts scorn on the Nationalist's case. What the patient requires is: Separation. Separation from England, from English speech, English manners, English food, English clothes, English culinary and English common sense. Then he will recover.

It is coming on dark, as they say in the Scotland that is not Glasgow. And out of the Gorbals arises again that foul breath as of a dying beast.

You turn from Glasgow Green with a determination to inspect this Gorbals on your own. It is incredibly un-

Scottish. It is lovably and abominably and delightfully and hideously un-Scottish. It is not even a Scottish slum. Stout men in beards and ringlets and unseemly attire lounge and strut with pointed shoes: Ruth and Naomi go by with down-cast Eastern faces, the Lascar rubs shoulder with the Syrian, Harry Lauder is a Baal unkeened to the midnight stars. In the air the stench is of a different quality to Govan's or Camlachie's – a better quality. It is not filth and futility and boredom unrelieved. It is haunted by an ancient ghost of goodness and grossness, sun-warmed and ripened under alien suns. It is the most saving slum in Glasgow, and the most abandoned. Emerging from it, the investigator suddenly realises why he sought it in such haste from Glasgow Green: it was in order that he might assure himself there were really and actually other races on the earth apart from the Scots!

So long I have wanted to write what I am about to write – but hitherto I have lacked the excuse. Glasgow provides it . . . About Nationalism. About Small Nations. What a curse to the earth are small nations! Latvia, Lithuania, Poland, Finland, San Salvador, Luxembourg, Manchukuo, the Irish Free State. There are many more: there is an appalling number of disgusting little stretches of the globe claimed, occupied and infected by groupings of babbling little morons – babbling militant on the subjects (unendingly) of their *exclusive* cultures, their *exclusive* languages, their *national* souls, their *national* genius, their unique achievements in throat-cutting in this and that abominable little squabble in the past. Mangy little curs a-yap above their minute hoardings of shrivelled bones, they cease from their yelpings at the passers-by only in such intervals as they devote to civil-war flea-hunts. Of all the accursed progeny of World War, surely the worst was this dwarf mongrel-litter. The South Irish of the middle class were never pleasant persons: since they obtained their Free State the belch of their pride in the accents of their unhygienic patois has given the unfortunate Irish Channel the seeming of a cess-pool. Having blamed their misfortunes on England for centuries, they achieved independence and promptly found themselves incapable of securing that independence by the obvious and necessary operation – social revolution. Instead: revival of Gaelic, bewildering an unhappy world with uncouth spellings and titles and postage-stamps: revival of the blood feud; revival of the decayed literary cultus which (like most products of the Kelt) was an abomination even while actually alive and but poor manure when it died . . . Or Finland – Communist-murdering Finland – ruled by German Generals and the Central European foundries, boasting to its ragged population the return of its ancient literary culture like a senile octogenarian boasting the coming of second childhood . . .

And we are bidden go and do likewise:

'For we are not opposed to English influence only at those points where it expresses itself in political domination and financial and economic over-control, but we are (or ought to be) opposed to English influence at all points. Not only must English governmental control be overthrown, but the English language must go, and English methods of education, English fashions in dress, English models in the arts, English ideals, everything English. Everything English must go.'

This is a Mr Ludovic Grant, writing in *The Free Man*. Note what the Scot is bidden to give up: the English language, that lovely and flexible instrument, so akin to the darker Braid Scots which has been the Scotsman's tool of thought for a thousand years. English methods of education: which are derived from Germano-French-Italian models. English fashions in dress: invented in Paris – London – Edinburgh – Timbuktu – Calcutta – Chichen-Itza – New York. English models in the arts: nude models as well, no doubt – Scots models in future must sprout three pair of arms and a navel in the likeness of a lion rampant. English ideals: decency, freedom, justice, ideals innate in the mind of man, as common to the Bantu as to the Kentishman – those also he must relinquish . . . It will profit Glasgow's hundred and fifty thousand slum-dwellers so much to know that they are being starved and brutalised by Labour Exchanges and Public Assistance Committees staffed exclusively by Gaelic-speaking, haggis-eating Scots in saffron kilts and tongued brogues, full of such typical Scottish ideals as those which kept men chained as slaves in the Fifeshire mines a century or so ago . . .

Glasgow's salvation, Scotland's salvation, the world's salvation lies in neither nationalism nor internationalism, those twin halves of an idiot whole. It lies in ultimate cosmopolitanism, the earth the City of God, the Brahma-putra and Easter Island as free and familiar to the man from Govan as the Molendinar and Bute. A time will come when the self-wrought, prideful differentiations of Scotsman, Englishman, Frenchman, Spaniard will seem as ludicrous as the infantile squabblings of the Heptarchians. A time will come when nationalism, with other cultural aberrations, will have passed from the human spirit, when Man, again free and unchained, has all the earth for his footstool, sings his epics in a language moulded from the best on earth, draws his heroes, his sunrises, his valleys and his mountains from all the crinkles of our lovely planet . . . And we are bidden to abandon this vision for the delights of an archaic ape-spite, a brosy barbarisation!

I am a nationalist only in the sense that the sane Heptar-chian was a Wessexman or a Mercian or what not: tem-porarily, opportunistically. I think the Braid Scots may yet give lovely lights and shadows not only to English but to the perfected speech of Cosmopolitan Man: so I cultivate it, for lack of that perfect speech that is yet to be. I think there's the chance that Scotland, especially in its Glasgow, in its bitter straitening of the economic struggle, may win to a freedom preparatory to, and in alignment with, that cos-

mopolitan freedom, long before England: so, a cosmopolitan opportunist, I am some kind of Nationalist. But I'd
rather, any day, be an expatriate writing novels in Persian
about the Cape of Good Hope than a member of a homogeneous literary cultus (to quote again the cant phrase of
the day) prosing eternally on one plane – the insanitary
reactions to death of a Kelvingrove bourgeois, or the
owlish gawk (it would speedily have that seeming) of
Ben Lomond through its clouds, like a walrus through a
fuff of whiskers.

For this Scottish Siva herself, brandishing her many arms
of smoke against the coming of the darkness, it is pleasant
to remember at least one incident. On a raining night six
hundred and fifty years ago a small band of men, selfless
and desperate and coolly-led, tramped through the wynds
to the assault of the English-garrisoned Bell o' the Brae
(which is now the steep upper part of High Street). It was a
venture unsupported by priest or patrician, the intellectual
or bourgeois of those days. It succeeded: and it lighted a
flame of liberty throughout Scotland.

Some day the surgeon-leaders of the hundred and fifty
thousand may take that tale of Bell o' the Brae for their text.

Aberdeen

NO FOREIGNER CAN think of that vulgarisation of Scots
humour and the Scots lyric which Sir Harry Lauder has
brought to such pitch of perfection without a bye-thought
on a Scots city which would seem to breed, principally, if
not entirely, Lauder-imitators. For the benefit of the Eng-
lish-reading public Aberdeen is the home of the typical
'Scotch' joke. In this the Scot is shown as ludicrously mean,

he is the victim and perpetrator of a farcical and brainless greed. And most of the material for those tales and fantasies of so-called humour are exported from Aberdeen itself, as the editor of any light-hearted English periodical will confirm.

Now, a tale may be read, quite consciously and knowingly, as humour-fantasy, and yet have curious repercussions on the mind of the reader. So with Aberdeen: it is impossible that its streets can be thronged with reproductions of this odd caricature of humanity who parades in the jokes. Still – and the good Englishman and the good American display a kind of humorous contemptuous care in their dealings with an authentic Aberdonian, set foot in Aberdeen itself with wary grins on their faces. Recently I received a reply-paid envelope from an American publisher. In the course of the accompanying letter the publisher referred to the envelope (in a business-like fashion, without inverted commas, because the joke in this minor aspect has grown stale and passed into the ordinary vocabulary of American business) as an 'Aberdeen envelope'. Once, in Jerusalem, I struck up acquaintance with an intelligent and interesting Syrian. We talked ethnology; and in the course of the conversation I told him that I was born in Aberdeenshire in Scotland. He was amused and pitiful, though a little hazy. 'Aberdeen – it is the pariah place, is it not?'

These phenomena – Aberdeen's comic reputation and Aberdonian humour itself – are worthy of some investigation, just as the man who laughs too loudly and too long stirs curiosities in the mind of the sceptical bystander. Why so much laughter – and why that steely ring in the last guffaw? Here is an Aberdonian 'funny story':

An Aberdonian died and gave instructions in his will that his body be cremated. This was done. The day after the cremation the widow heard a knock at the door. She opened it and saw a small message-boy standing on the doorstep holding out a package towards her. 'What's this?' she enquired. 'Your husband, Mem,' said the boy, '– his ashes, you know.' Slowly the widow took the package in her hand. 'His ashes? Oh, ay. *But where's the dripping?*'

I choose this example deliberately as that of an Aberdonian story insufficiently padded. You laugh, but (if you have any imagination at all) you have a slight qualm. The grisliness below the humour is insufficiently concealed. You can smell the stench of that burning body, you can see the running human fats – with a dish in appropriate position to collect them . . . You see too closely in this instance the grinning skull behind the large, jolly countenance of the laughing man; you may suspect him, outside the flare of lights in the bar and the help of alcohol, as one solemn and serious enough, uneasy, haunted by an unending apprehension of life as a bleak enough parade.

Bleakness, not meanness or jollity, is the keynote to Aberdonian character, not so much lack of the graces or graciousness of existence as lack of colour in either of these. And this is almost inevitable for anyone passing his nights and days in The Silver City by the Sea. It is comparable to passing one's existence in a refrigerator. Aberdeen is built, largely and incredibly, of one of the most enduring and indestructible and appalling building-materials in use on our planet – grey granite.

It has a flinty shine when new – a grey glimmer like a morning North Sea, a cold steeliness that chills the heart. Even with weathering it acquires no gracious softness, it is merely starkly grim and uncompromising. The architect may plan and build as he will with this material – with its variant, white granite, he may rear the curvetting spires and swooping curlecues and looping whirlimagigs of Marischal College – and not escape that sense of one calamitously in jail. Not only are there no furbelows possible in this

architecture, there is amid it, continually, the uneasy sense
that you may not rest here, you may not lounge, you cannot
stand still and watch the world go by . . . Else presently the
warders will come and move you on.

To know that feeling in its full intensity the investigator
must disregard the publicity posters and visit Aberdeen in
November. Whatever the weather as his train crossed from
Kincardineshire into Aberdeenshire, he will arrive at
Aberdeen Station in sleet. Not falling sleet or drifting sleet,
but *blown* sleet – blown with an infernal and unescapable
persistence from all points of the compass, from the
stretches of the harbour, from the Duthie Park, down
Market Street. And through this steely pelt he will see
the tower and lour and savage grimace of the grey granite all
about him, curdling his nerve centres even as the sleet
curdles his extremities. If he holds by Guild Street and
Market Street up to the pride of Aberdeen, Union Street,
he will discover how really vocal this materialisation of an
Eskimo's vision of hell may become. Aberdeen is, without
exception, the most exasperatingly noisy city in the world.
Paris is bad – but one accepts Paris, it is free, it is
anarchistic, the cabmen are trying to kill each other – a
praiseworthy pursuit – and Citröens were made by devils in
hell and manned by chauffeurs from purgatory – and it is all
very amusing. But Aberdeen is not amusing in its epitome,
Union Street. This street is paved with granite blocks, and
over these, through the sleeting downpour, trams rattle,
buses thud, and (unescapable) four large iron-wheeled
drays hauled by Clydesdale horses are being drawn at
break-neck speed. There is no amusement in the thought
of the drivers being killed: you can see in each gaunt, drawn
face that the driver is doing it not for pleasure or the fun of
life or because he is joyously and righteously drunk – he is
doing it to support a wife, five children, a blind grandmother, and a sister in the Aberdeen Infirmary.

Aberdeen is the cleanest city in Britain: it makes you long

for good, wholesome dirt, littered roadways and ramshackle buildings leaning in all directions, projecting warm
brown sins and rich smutty reds through an enticing, grimy
smile. Union Street has as much warmth in its face as a
dowager duchess asked to contribute to the Red International Relief. If you escape the trams and the drays and the
inferno where Market Street debouches on Union Street,
and hold west up Union Street, you will have the feeling of
one caught in a corridor of the hills. To right and left tower
the cliffs, scrubbed, immaculate and unforgiving. Where
Union Terrace breaks in upon Union Street there is an
attempt at a public Garden. But the flowers come up and
take one glance at the lour of the solicitors' offices which
man Union Terrace, and scramble back into the earth
again, seeking the Antipodes.

Union Terrace is beset with statues: the advocates stroll
to their windows from plodding through briefs for the
Sheriff Court and look out on King Edward to the right,
Robert Burns in the middle and William Wallace to the left.
Aberdeen may be forgiven much because of those statues.
For her flinty granitic heart was moved to wisdom when she
commissioned them, giving their subjects that due proportion and appearance which they bore in history: King
Edward is merely vulgar, Burns pathetic and Wallace
heroic. The investigator may do worse than consider the
Wallace with care: round the plinth are written quotations
from his speeches to the Army of the Commons of Scotland; lounging upon the plinth, yawning and bored (even in
the sleet) are the tired and the old and the unemployed of
Aberdeen in great number. Wallace fascinates them, you
would say. He belongs to a past they dare not achieve, they
have come to such horrific future as he never visioned.

In his right hand is a great sword; his outflung left hand
points – to the nearby bulk, copola'd and gilded, of His
Majesty's Theatre. But I think the gesture is unwarranted,
for it is an excellent theatre, there are folk and institutions

in Aberdeen far more worthy of gesture and sword. One wonders if the slum landlords of Correction Wynd or the Gallowgate, emerging from their cars to make their way to the padded fauteuils of His Majesty's, ever cast an uneasy glance at the great Guardian.

Probably not – unless some socialist orator is holding forth from the plinth. It is a favourite place of the orator, the communist orator for preference. Unemployed Aberdeen chews tobacco and listens vaguely and smokes vague cigarettes, and you can hear the orator at a great distance, the thin Aberdonian voice in the thin Aberdonian patois – full of long *ee's*, and conversions of *wh's* into *f's* . . . Agitationally, in spite its unemployed, Aberdeen sleeps these days. A friend of mine once led a procession of the unemployed; the mounted police charged: and when they had passed my friend was found clinging far up in the branches of a tree. This is the reality that has succeeded those visions of the barricade that vexed young folk of my ilk in the War-time days: days that distance covers with a fine glamour, when the mob broke up the peace-time meeting in the Music Hall addressed by Ramsay MacDonald: and a party of them made to storm the platform: and a socialist pugilist pacified them, asking for a single representative to come up: and one belligerent young man ascended: and demanded to be led to Ramsay: and the socialist pugilist agreed: and took the young man behind the scenes and socked him in the jaw; and came dragging back the body as an exhibition of what Ramsay did to interrupters . . . Or another meeting, with locked doors, which a company of the Gordon Highlanders attempted to storm: and broke down the upper half of the door, and climbed in one by one: and as they descended were met by a solemn, six-foot pacifist with the limbs of an aurochs and hands like hams: who solemnly and pitifully knocked each one unconscious: and then revived them and carried them upstairs to the meeting, on the soldiers' tearful promise that they *would* be good . . .

Or the founding of the Aberdeen Soviet when the news of the Bolshevik Revolution came through from Russia; and how I and a cub reporter from another paper attended the foundation meeting; and were elected to the Soviet Council, forgetting we were pressmen; and spent perspiring minutes with our chief reporters afterwards, explaining that we could not report the meeting being ourselves good sovietists . . . *O tempora! O mores!*

Remote as the banners of the Army of the Commons. Yet (and to presume that the sleet is over, and you are now in your overcoat) if you turn rightwards from Wallace into that grouping and festering of mean streets that lie behind and beyond the Infirmary, surely it is impossible that these things have passed? There are odd little shops here, with revolutionary journals for sale? Instead, odd little shops which sell stockings and shirts and such-like necessitous intimacies on the hire-purchase system: and sue with great savagery the improvident purchasers. Fifteen years ago that young cub-reporter who, with myself, had been elected to the Aberdeen Soviet – we were so young and full of dreams we could not sleep o'nights. We prowled Aberdeen all the hours of the night, seeking not amorous adventure, but talking the moon into morning about jolly and heartsome and splendid things: life, death, the Revolution and the great green-cheeseness of the moon . . . And the years went by, and I journeyed afar; and garnered a little in experience, including a keen distaste for that snarling cry of the machine-gun which sends a man clawing earthwards on his belly; and twelve years went by and I came again to Aberdeen; and for curiosity I wandered into its police court one morning; and a shameful woman had purchased knickers from the owner of a little chain of shops; and had neglected her payments, and was now being sued, poor proletarian with her red-chapped hands and her wrinkled, terrified face, and her poor, shifting eyes and her stammering voice . . . I turned away my eyes and felt unreasonably sick. But the voice of the owner of the chain of shops brought back my attention as he spoke from the witness-box. And he was—.

With me the investigator turns to a thing more pleasant – Allenvale Cemetery, where the dead of Aberdeen lie in serried lines under immense granitic monuments. They move one to a wondering horror. Granite, grey granite, in birth, in puberty, adolescence, grey granite encasing the bridal room, grey granite the rooms of blear-eyed old age. And even in death they are not divided . . . Lower middle-class Aberdeen comes here of a Sunday in its Sunday blue suit and yellow boots and dickie and bowler: and parades, and admires the monuments, and goes back to Aberdeen high tea.

High tea in Aberdeen is like no other meal on earth. It is the meal of the day, the meal par excellence, and the tired come home to it ravenous, driven by the granite streets, hounded in for energy to stoke against that menace. Tea is drunk with the meal, and the order of it is this: First, one eats a plateful of sausages and eggs and mashed potatoes; then a second plateful to keep down the first. Eating, one assists the second plateful to its final home by mouthfuls of oatacke spread with butter. Then you eat oatcake with cheese. Then there are scones. Then cookies. Then it is really time to begin on tea – tea and bread and butter and crumpets and toasted rolls and cakes. Then some Dundee cake. Then – about half-past past seven – someone shakes you out of the coma into which you have fallen and asks you persuasively if you wouldn't like another cup of tea and just *one* more egg and sausage . . .

And all night long, on top of this supper and one of those immense Aberdonian beds which appear to be made of knotted ship's cable, the investigator, through and trans-cending the howl of the November sleet-wind, will hear the lorries and the drays, in platoons, clattering up and down Market Street. They do it for no reason or purpose, except to keep you awake. And in the morning when you descend with a grey face and an aching head, they provide you with an immense Aberdeen breakfast; and if you halt and gasp somewhere through the third course they send for the manager who comes and questions you gravely as to why you don't like the food? – should he send for a doctor?

I'm presuming the investigator has taken a room in one of the hotels in Market Street. They are very good and cheap and never advertise, and this is their free advertisement in return for their unostentatious virtues. And their windows look out on Aberdeen Harbour, a wide, dull stretch round which I can never wander these days without a vague feeling that all is not well with the harbour, there is a definite something missing in the ships and shipping. And then I remember: the War-time camouflage when the ships rode bravely bespattered in painted zig-zags, and all kinds of odd people came wandering across the North Sea and were landed at Aberdeen from those pantomime vessels. M. Krassin was deported from England by way of Aberdeen and I attempted to interview him as he boarded his boat: he had a little beard and a twisted nose; and I spoke to him in halting Russian and he said kindly that he spoke English when he was allowed to – only he wasn't. And as I came away from that abortive interview I saw a soldier walking along the quays, an elderly man, a sergeant, in full equipment, with rifle and steel helmet. And he stopped and looked into the water, thoughtfully, and laid aside the rifle and helmet, and jumped into the water. There he swam to and fro for a little and some loafers threw him a rope and dragged him out. He shook himself, large, solemn, like a great dog, picked up the rifle and helmet, and departed towards the station without saying a word . . .

Twice weekly in the summer season the London boat comes into Aberdeen, and twice weekly departs. The Aberdonians are an emotional people: they assemble in great multitudes on the quay where the London boat is leaving. As the syrens hoot they begin to cheer and wave handkerchiefs. About a tenth of the two hundred waving from the shore have friends or relatives on board. The rest are there moved by a curious pity. I have seen an Aberdeen woman in tears as she waved towards the departing boat, though she knew not a soul on board. Some are even more enthusiastic. They pursue the boat from quay to quay, bridge to bridge, waving and weeping, till they can pursue no further. The passengers stand and wave and cheer in return, then light cigars and stroke their tartan ties and tell how they climbed up Lochin-y-Gair.

Leftwards, Footdee sleeps with silent shipyards and factories these days, with great rusting cranes lifting their unmoving chains high in the air, and long cobbled walks silent and nerveless enough. A kind of palsy has fallen here, the investigator will note: the trawlers still come in of a morning in long sweeping lines, with laden creels for the Fish Market, but Footdee smells ill even these salt mornings, even this stinging November morning when the wind has veered a point and it has forgotten to sleet. This assuredly is the morning to survey the Beach.

The Beach, it is at once evident, was constructed by a cretin brought up under the tuition of an imaginative, unreliable, but high-spirited gorilla. Behind it stretch the Links: in front of it, the North Sea. Its buttressed walls rise and swoop with a care admirable for the gambollings of the lesser anthropoids, if somewhat at variance with the needs of a more normal populace. To your right is the Amusements Park; here the gorilla relaxed and scratched and was momentarily human, for here is a lovely scenic railways. The investigator, turning from the horror of the North Sea and the equal horror of the Beach, concludes that if he lived in Aberdeen he would spend his days on that scenic railway.

But this is Aberdeen by day. Aberdeen by night is a

different city, thronged with a more subtle, a different folk. The watching granite relaxes on the façades of the great grey buildings, in the manners and customs of the folk in the streets. At eight o'clock on Friday night all Aberdeen assembles and parades in Union Street; and here the investigator stands aside and views with care the high cheek-bones in the brachycephalic heads of the males, that singularly dis-harmonic head that is so singularly Aberdonian. The proletarian wears a cap with a long check peak, the petit bourgeois wears the regulation bowler hat, the bourgeois walks bareheaded, for he is in plusfours and his domed bald head is browned with the suns of the Links. There is an endless flow and unflow of the thin Aberdeen speech. But the bourgeois speaks English, and, strangely, speaks it successfully, acquiring depths and rhythm as he mislays the false, pale vowels and slurred consonants of his city. The women wear clothes indistinguishable from those of Paris or New York. But a strange fate haunts the Aberdonian woman. She cannot walk. Some go by with a duck-like waddle, some prance on squattering toes, some slouch with laggard steps. It is the granite side-walks responsible, the investigator concludes, as the hours fade and the throngs fade with them, and down over the Town Hall the clocktowers tell it is one o'clock.

But for prostitutes, policemen, and journalists Union Street is deserted now. With a sough and a sigh the nightwind, edged as with a knife, is blowing along Union Terrace: King Edward stands freezing, bald-headed: down in the station a train chugs remotely, with a flying shower of sparks. In the glare of the night lights the tramlines swoop down towards Market Street like great snakes: in a remote shop-front a policeman is flashing his lamp. A young man in a slouch hat goes by, yawning: the *Journal* has been put to bed. Two girls consult the investigator on his needs for the night. He is regretful, with another engagement. They intimate, drifting away, a profound conviction in his illegitimacy. So to bed.

In the days when I first knew Aberdeen two names fascinated me – St Machar and Kittybrewster. They lie at points remotely one from the other, the St Machar Cathedral and the Kittybrewster district, but these the investigator (who has now purchased a fresh supply of woolly underwear) may not miss. St Machar's Cathedral, they tell us, was builded first in the fourteenth century – there are still scraps of fourteenth-century architecture there. But towards the close of the seventeenth century the central tower fell in and smashed and demolished greatly chancel and transept, transforming the building from an active agency in dissemination of a cultural aberration to a seemly haunt for the archeologist. St Machar sleeps through it all undisturbed. But from youth the notion persists in my mind that he turns in uneasy remembrance now and again of the days when he and Kitty Brewster—.

Nor can any tell where Kitty lies. Perhaps beneath the smoke and soot and thundering trains of the Goods Station, lying, like good King Olaf, or Arthur in Avalon, waiting till they call her again and she wake and come forth and free the world. Dreaming below that clatter of an industrialism gone mad, Kitty must yet hear on the early mart mornings sounds more familiar and loved – the lowing of the great cattle herds they drive to the sales there – smell, smell back through the centuries that odour of dust and dung and cowishness that maybe haunted the hills when she and Machar—.

But this is incredible romance. From earliest times Aberdeen has engaged itself in eschewing romance. Hardly had Kitty and St Machar died in each other's arms (after a wild night's orgy on the Beach scenic railway) than Romance blew her trumpets through Aberdeen. It was the year 1411, and Donald of the Isles, gaunt, Highland and hairy, was nearing the city with an army of northland raiders. The citizens ran and busked themselves, piled into the tramcars at Castlegate and poured out in their thousands to contest the march of Donald. They met him at Harlaw, a misty morning, when the dew was white as hoar or grey granite on the whins, and arrayed themselves in long, dour ranks of spearmen against the usual Highland tactic. Donald flung forward the clansmen in sweeping lines of attack: Aberdeen stood fast through a long and bloody day and at night Donald marched back the remnants of his forces into the hills. This was a great turn of the tide in Scots history – and Aberdeen wrought it.

It was a city that remained incurably and gloriously anti-Highland. Stout business men from Mannofield and Cults may nowadays send their children to the High School in kilts and bonnets: in ancient times they would as soon have thought of sending them forth into the world in dishclouts and tompions. In the '45 the rest of Scotland might go Prince Charlie mad: Aberdeen stared out from its granite doorways with a dour startlement, then turned its back on the whole ill business. Freedom, the winds of romance, the crying of banners marching south – not for it, not for the flinty souls who matched their flinty dwellings. So instead it aided and abetted the men of Hanover, it feted and feasted the dour butcher Cumberland returning from Culloden field, and made him a guest of the Provost at No. 13 in the Guestrow – and there it stands unto this day to tell you if I lie.

But it is under orders for demolition – great sections of the older streets and wynds stand condemned, streets and wynds with antique names that move the antiquarian to suitable regrets when he considers their fate – the Upper Kirkgate, the Nether Kirkgate, the Gallowgate, the Guestrow. But I have no such regrets. Those gates to kirks and gallows: you think of a foetid sixteenth century stench and the staring mobs watching some poor, tormented hind dragged out to the Gallows in Market Square – and you turn, with relief and a new resolve, to face the glinting, flinting structures that tower new-built up Union Street.

For if you cannot come to terms with the grey granite, you must come to an understanding or else escape into Golf and the Conservative Club, if you have the suitable status, or into pub-crawling and the drinking of Red Biddies, that curious Aberdonian stimulant, if you are of the plebs. The understanding is no easy thing. One detests Aberdeen with the detestation of a thwarted lover. It is the one haunting and exasperatingly lovable city in Scotland – its fascination as unescapable as its shining mail.

But is there need to escape? There are moments when I think of it as the essential – something to be apprehended and in its apprehension to uncover new countries of stark and glowing wonder, something lighted and shining with a fine flame, cold and amber and gold, behind the flinty cliffs of Union Street, the flinty cheekbones of the disharmonic faces that press about you in an Aberdeen tram. I prefer to think that the bitterly underpaid and wet and sogging fisherman stumping up from the Fish Market after a night on the reel and drummle of the tides has apprehended that granite quality and made of it, warmed and kindly, his life quality . . . The investigator looks after him with a warmth and interest in the grey of the sleeting November morning as he peers from the stalactited window of his hotel bedroom and then turns to consult a train time-table.

As for the women of Aberdeen . . . it is strange the vagrant associations the mind hinges on this word and that. About half of the women of Aberdeen appear to rejoice in the name of Grizel – and rejoice with justness, for my saner self tells me it is a lovely and incisive name. But for some strange reason I can never hear it pronounced without thinking of a polar bear eating an Eskimo.

And that is all about Aberdeen.

Literary Lights

ONE OF THE MOST praiseworthy – praiseworthy in its entertainment value – efforts of the critic has always been his attempt to leviate himself out of himself by the ingenuous method of hauling with great passion upon his own bootlaces. In the words of Mr Alan Porter 'The critic, before he sets down a word, must beat himself on the head and ask a hundred times, each time more bitterly and searchingly, "And is it true? Is it true?" He must analyse his judgement and make sure that it is nowhere stained or tinted with the blood of his heart. And he must search out a table of values from which he can be certain that he has left nothing unconsidered. If, after all these precautions and torments, he is unable to deliver a true judgement, then fate has been too strong for him; he was never meant to be a critic.'

The present writer was assuredly never meant to be a critic. He has attempted no feats of manipulative surgery upon either his personality or his judgement. He confesses with no shame that the dicta of criticism laid down by Mr Porter appear to him analogous to the chest-beating posturings of a righteous baboon prior to its robbing an orchard. Flippancy apart, the researches of Bekhterev and Pavlov should have disposed once and for all of such archaic beliefs as the possibility of inhibiting a reflex by incantation. Indeed, it did not require reflexological research (of which the average critic has never heard – or, if he has, imagines it has something to do with the torturing of dogs and Mr Bernard Shaw) to dispose of this nonsense regarding 'heart' and 'head'. To commit hari-kari may be

an admirable and hygienic exercise, but is an operation
seldom survived by even the remoter portions of the extra-
intestinal anatomy.

Far more serious doubts assail the non-professional critic
when he enters upon the study of such a subject as (reputed) Scots letters. If he enters this great library from the
open air, not through an underground passage from the
book-lined gloom of a study, the piles of stacked volumes
are dismaying in their colour and size and plentitude. Only
here and there does he recognise a name or a title; the
books tower to dim ceilings, are piled in great strata, have
the dust of the last few years gathered yet thickly enough
upon them. How may he pass judgement? The books he
has missed – the books he has never read! What relative
importance have the few names and titles in his memory to
the hidden values in this great library?

For, in the pressing multitudes of reputedly Scots books
which pour from the presses, there may have been a new
Melville, a new Typee, a Scots Joyce, a Scots Proust?
Nothing impossible in any of those suppositions. The book
may have appeared, it failed to be noticed, (as hundreds of
good books have failed to be noted,) it was poorly adver-
tised, had inadequate publicity, was overshadowed by the
simultaneous publication of a great name – and moulders
now its representative copies in two or three libraries while
the remainder of the stock – not even 'remaindered' – has
returned to the printer for repulping. There is nothing to
say that this has not happened very often.

Even if the critic passes a judgement with some fair
knowledge of the factors – how of the unpublished books?
There may be manuscripts circulating the publishers' offices that sing a new, clear splendid note in letters – sing it
so loudly that no publisher's reader can abide the beat of
the music in his ears . . . This is not only possible, but very
probable. It was as true of the past as it is of the present,
though both gods and machines were of a different order

three hundred years ago. Yet even then it is possible that poets dwarfing Shakespeare remained unpublished and unplayed for lack of suitable influences, suitable patronage; and their manuscripts, with the wisdom and delight of the shining minds that begat them, have long mouldered to dust.

The new and unknown Scots writer facing the publishing, printing world has the usual chances and mischances to face in a greater measure than his English compeer. Firstly, in almost every case, he must seek publication in London. Scots publishers are surely amongst the sorriest things that enter hell: their publicity methods are as antique as their format, their houses are generally staffed by those who in Bengali circles would write after their names, and as their chief qualification, 'failed B.A.' (or slightly worse, 'M.A. (St. Andrews)'). He must consign his manuscript to alien publishers and the consideration of largely alien readers.

For, however the average Scots writer believes himself Anglicised, his reaction upon the minds of the intelligent English reader (especially of the professional reader) is curiously similar to that produced by the English poems of Dr Rabindranath Tagore. The prose – or verse – is impeccably correct, the vocabulary is rich and adequate, the English is severe, serene . . . But unfortunately it is not English. The English reader is haunted by a sense of something foreign stumbling and hesitating behind this smooth façade of adequate technique: it is as though the writer did not *write* himself, but *translated* himself.

Often the Scots writer is quite unaware of this essential foreignness in his work; more often, seeking an adequate word or phrase he hears an echo in an alien tongue that would adorn his meaning with a richness, a clarity and a conciseness impossible in orthodox English. That echo is from Braid Scots, from that variation of the Anglo-Saxon speech which was the tongue of the great Scots civilisation, the tongue adopted by the basic Pictish strain in Scotland as its chief literary tool.

Further, it is still in most Scots communities, (in one or other Anglicised modification,) the speech of bed and board and street and plough, the speech of emotional ecstasy and emotional stress. But it is not genteel. It is to the bourgeois of Scotland coarse and low and common and loutish, a matter for laughter, well enough for hinds and the like, but for the genteel to be quoted in vocal inverted commas. It is a thing rigorously elided from their serious intercourse – not only with the English, but among themselves. It is seriously believed by such stratum of the Scots populace to be an inadequate and pitiful and blunted implement, so that Mr Eric Linklater delivers *ex cathedra* judgement upon it as 'inadequate to deal with the finer shades of emotion'.

But for the truly Scots writer it remains a real and a haunting thing, even while he tries his best to forget its existence and to write as a good Englishman. In this lies his tragedy. He has to *learn* to write in English: he is like a Chinese scholar spending the best years of his life in the mystic mazes of the pictographs, and emerging so exhausted from the travail that originality of research or experiment with his new tool is denied him. Consequently, the free and anarchistic experimentations of the progressive members of a free and homogeneous literary cultus are denied him. Nearly every Scots writer of the past writing in orthodox English has been not only incurably second-rate, but incurably behind the times. The Scots discovery of photographic realism in novel-writing, for example – I refer to *Hatter's Castle*, not the very different *House with the Green Shutters* – post-dated the great French and English realists some thirty or forty years. But to the Scot Dr Cronin's work appeared a very new and terrifying and fascinating thing indeed; to the English public, astounding that anything faintly savouring of accuracy, photographic or otherwise, should come out of Scotland, it was equally amazing. At such rate of progress among the Anglo-Scots one may guess that in another fifty years or so a Scots Virginia Woolf will astound the Scottish scene, a Scots James Joyce electrify it. To expect contemporary experimentation from the Anglo-Scots themselves appears equivalent to expecting a Central African savage in possession of a Birmingham kite to prove capable of inventing a helicopter.

Consciousness of this inferiority of cultural position within the English tradition is a very definite thing among the younger generation of Anglo-Scots writers of today. Their most characteristic organ, *The Modern Scot*, is a constant reiteration of protest. Owned and edited by one of those genial Englishmen in search of a revolution who have added to the gaiety of nations from Ireland to Uganda, *The Modern Scot* has set itself, strictly within the English tradition, to out-English the English. As one who on a lonely road doth walk with fear and dread, very conscious of the frightful fiend who close behind doth tread, it marches always a full yard ahead of extremist English opinion – casting the while an anxious backward glance. It decries the children of 'naturalism' with a praiseworthy but unnatural passion, championing in their place, with a commendable care for pathology, the idiot offspring begat on the modern literary scene in such numbers from the incestuous unions of Strindberg and Dr Freud. It is eclectic to quite an obscure degree, is incapable of an article that does not quote either Proust or Paul Einzig, and raises an approving voice in praise of the joyous, if infantile taur-omachic obsessions of Mr Roy Campbell. Its motif-note, indeed, is literary Fascism – to the unimpassioned, if astounded, eye it would seem as if all the Fascist under-graduates of Scotland these days were hastening, in pim-ples and a passion for sophistication, to relieve themselves of a diarrhoetic Johnsonese in the appropriate privy of *The Modern Scot*. The entire being of the periodical, however, is rather an exhibitory, or sanitary, exercise, than a contributing factor towards authentic experimentation.

With a few exceptions presently to be noted, there is not the remotest reason why the majority of modern Scots writers should be considered Scots at all. The protagonists of the Scots literary Renaissance deny this. They hold, for example, that Norman Douglas or Compton Mackenzie, though they write in English and deal with un-Scottish themes, have nevertheless an essential Scottishness which differentiates them from the native English writer. In exactly the same manner, so had Joseph Conrad an essential Polishness. But few (except for the purpose of exchanging diplomatic courtesies) pretend that Conrad was a Polish writer, to be judged as a Pole. He wrote brilliantly and strangely and beautifully in English; so does Mr Norman Douglas, so does Mr Cunninghame Graham. Mention of the latter is peculiarly to the point. Mr Graham has, I believe, a large modicum of Spanish blood in his veins, he writes much of Spanish or Spanish-American subjects, and his word-manipulation is most certainly not of the English orthodox. But we have still to hear of Spain acclaiming him one of her great essayists.

The admirable plays of Dr James Bridie – such as *Tobias and the Angel* or the unforgettable *Jonah and the Whale* – have been hailed in Scotland as examples of modern Scots drama. They are excellent examples – but not of Scots drama. They are examples of how an Englishman, hailing from Scotshire, can write excellent plays. Mr Edwin Muir writes poems of great loveliness; so does Mr Roy Campbell; both are of Scots origin: ergo, great Scots poetry. Dumas père had negro blood in his veins and wrote excellent romances in French: ergo, great negro romance.

That such a position is untenable is obvious. Modern Scotland, the Gaels included, is a nation almost entirely lacking a Scottish literary output. There are innumerable versifiers, ranging from Dr Charles Murray downwards to

Mr WH Hamilton (he of the eldritch glamour); there are hardly more than two poets; and there is no novelist at all. To be oneself a provincial or an alien and to write a book in which the characters infect one's literary medium with a tincture of dialect is not to assist in the creation or continuation of a separate national literature – else Eden Philpotts proves the great, un-English soul of Dartmoor and Tennyson in *The Northern Farmer* was advocating Home Rule for Yorkshire. The chief Literary Lights which modern Scotland claims to light up the scene of her night are in reality no more than the commendable writers of the interesting English county of Scotshire.

Let us consider Mrs Naomi Mitchison. She is the one writer of the 'historical' novel in modern English who commands respect and enthusiasm. Her pages are aglow with a fine essence of apprehended light. *The Conquered* and *Black Sparta* light up the human spirit very vividly and truly. And they are in no sense Scots books though written by a Scotswoman. Their author once wrote that had she had the command of Scots speech possessed by Lewis Grassic Gibbon she would have written her Spartan books (at least) in Scots. Had she done so they would undoubtedly have been worse novels – but they *would* have been Scots books by a Scots writer, just as the worst of Finnish peasant studies *are* Finnish peasant studies, infinitesimal by the side of Dostoieffski or Tolstoi, but un-Russian in language and content.

Another writer hailed as a great Scots novelist is Mr Neil Gunn. The acclamation is mistaken. Mr Gunn is a brilliant novelist from Scotshire who chooses his home county as the scene of his tales. His technique is almost unique among the writers of Scotshire in its effortless efficiency: he moulds beauty in unforgettable phrases – there are things in *The Lost Glen* and *Sun Circle* comparable to the best in the imaginative literature of any school or country. He has probably scarcely yet set out on his scaling of the heights . . . But they are not the heights of Scots literature; they are not even the pedestrian levels. More in Gunn than in any other contemporary Anglo-Scot (with the exception, perhaps, of George Blake, in a very different category from Gunn, and the finest of the Anglo-Scots realists) the reader seems to sense the haunting foreignness in an orthodox English; he is the greatest loss to itself Scottish literature has suffered in this century. Had his language been Gaelic or Scots there is no doubt of the space or place he would have occupied in even such short study as this. Writing in orthodox English, he is merely a brilliantly unorthodox Englishman.

Once again, a writer who has been hailed as distinctively Scots, Mrs Willa Muir. So far she has written only two novels – *Imagined Corners* and *Mrs Ritchie* – and both show a depth and distinction, a sheer and splendidly un-womanly power which stir even the most jaded of enthusiasms. They suffer, perhaps, from the author's learnings and erudition-gatherings in the dull hag-forests of the German psycho-analysts, just as Neil Gunn's *Sun Circle* suffers from a crude and out-dated concept of history and the historical pro-cesses. But that psychoanalyst obsession is the common leprosy over all contemporary European imaginative litera-ture, and Mrs Muir's strength of spirit and true integrity of vision may yet transcend it. She has promise of becoming a great artist. But a great English artist. The fact that she is Scots herself and deals with Scots scenes and Scots char-acters is (to drive home the point ad nauseam) entirely irrelevant from the point of view of Scots literature: if she were a modern Mexican writing in Spanish and her scene was Mexico and her peasants spoke bastardised Nahuatl, would we call it a triumph of Aztec letters?

Mr John Buchan has been called the Dean of Scots letters. Mr Buchan writes mildly exhilarating romances in the vein of the late Rider Haggard (though without either Haggard's magnificent poetic flair or his imaginative

grasp), commendable essays on a variety of topics, uninspired if competent biographies of Sir Walter Scott, the
Marquis of Montrose, and the like distinguished cadaver-
litter on the ancient Scottish scene. He writes it all in a
competent, skilful and depressing English: when his characters talk Scots they do it in suitable inverted commas: and
such characters as do talk Scots are always the simple, the
proletarian, the slightly ludicrous characters.

Mr Buchan represents no more than the great, sound,
bourgeois heart of Scotshire. He has written nothing which
has the least connection with Scots literature except a few
pieces of verse – if verse *has* any connection with literature.
In compiling *The Northern Muse*, however, a representative
anthology of Scots 'Vernacular' poetry, he turned aside
from other pursuits to render a real service to what might
have been his native literary language. Yet even in that
service he could envisage Braid Scots as being only a
'vernacular', the tongue of *a home-reared slave*.

Mrs Catherine Carswell is among the most interesting of
the Anglo-Scots. Her *Life of Robert Burns* was one of the
most unique and innocently mendacious studies of the
subject ever attempted; her *Savage Pilgrimage* (which met
such a sad fate in the teeth of the enraged Mr Middleton
Murry) contributed as little to our knowledge of DH
Lawrence as it contributed greatly to our knowledge of
its author. With such a personality and philosophy much
more may be heard of Catherine Carswell: that the philosophy of her school appears a strange and repulsive one, as
strange an aberration of the human spirit as history has ever
known, merely adds a pathological to a genuine literary
interest in her development. Scots letters represses its
death-rattle to wave her on with a regretful relief.

Prior to writing *Hatter's Castle, Three Loves*, and *Grand
Canary* Dr AJ Cronin descended five hundred collieries on
tours of inspection. As a consequence he is notable for a kind
of inky immensity, and an interestingly Latinised barbarisa-

tion of the English language. While *Hatter's Castle* had a Scots scene its characters were gnomes from the sooty deeps of the less salubrious regions of myth: though acclaimed as great and realistic portraits. In *Three Loves* Dr Cronin showed a disposition to prove uneasy on the Scottish scene; in *Grand Canary* he escaped it entirely, taking his place (probably a permanent place) among the English writers of an order comparable to Miss Mannin or Mr Gilbert Frankau. He is also the author of a history of aneurism.

Sir James George Frazer, a Scotsman by birth, is the author of the immense *Golden Bough*, a collection of anthropological studies. The author's methods of correlation have been as crude and unregulated as his industry and the cultivation of his erudition have been immense. The confusion of savage and primitive states of culture commenced by Tylor and his school has been carried to excess in the works of Sir JG Frazer. From the point of view of the social historian attempting to disentangle the story of man's coming and growth upon this planet he is one of the most calamitous phenomena in modern research: he has smashed in the ruin of pre-history with a coal-hammer, collected every brick disclosed when the dust settled on the débris, and then labelled the exhibits with the assiduous industry of a literary ant. His pleasing literary style in that labelling is in orthodox English.

Mr Eric Linklater is a lost Norseman with a disposition to go Berserk amidst the unfamiliar trappings of literary civilisation. This disposition came to a head in *The Men of Ness*, a story of the vikings and their raids into the regions of stern guffawdom and unpronunciability. It is a pity that this disposition should be let loose by the author of *Juan in America*, – in the genre of Mark Twain's *Tramp Abroad*, and one of the most acute and amusing picaresque studies ever perpetrated by the literary farceur. It would be even more regrettable if Mr Linklater hampered his genius by an uneasy adherence to a so-called Scots literary Renaissance.[1]

Miss Muriel Stuart is one of the very few great poets writing in non-experimental English. She has a comprehension and a lyric beauty almost unknown to this English day: the deep passion of her poems in *Christ at Carnival* shines the more finely in that they lack the ornate imagery of Francis Thompson. One of the most magic lines in a memory prolific in the waste amusement of collecting magic lines (as is the present writer's) is her '*A thin hail ravened against the doors of dark*'. Miss Stuart, of Scots origin, has been hailed as a great Scots poet, She is as little Scots as Dante.

Yet Miss Stuart's genius brings us at last to consideration of the two solitary lights in modern Scots Literature. They rise from men who are writers in both Scots and in English – very prolific and controversial writers, men occupied with politics and economic questions, poets in the sense that life, not editors or anthologists, demand of them their poetry. But for the fact that this paper has been devoted largely to an argument that should have needed no enforcing, the work of these two would have occupied almost all the space under such heading as Literary Lights. One of these two is Hugh MacDiarmid and the other Lewis Spence.

MacDiarmid's poetry in Braid Scots came upon a world which had grown accustomed to the belief that written Scots was a vehicle for the more flat-footed sentiments of the bothy only; it came upon a world pale and jaded with the breathing and rebreathing in the same room of the same stagnant air of orthodox English. He demonstrated, richly and completely, and continues to demonstrate, the flexibility and the loveliness of that alien variation of the Anglo-Saxon speech which is Braid Scots. The first of MacDiarmid that the present writer encountered was something which still lingers in his mind (unreasonably, considering the magnificent *To Circumjack Cencrastus* or the sweeping majesty of the *Hymns to Lenin*):

Ae weet forenicht i' the yow-trummle
   I saw yon antrim thing,
A watergaw wi' its chitterin' licht
   Ayont the on-ding;
An' I thocht o' the last wild look ye gied
   Afore ye dee'd!

There was nae reek i' the laverock's hoose
   That nicht – an' nane i' mine;
But I hae thocht o' that foolish licht
   Ever sin' syne;
An' I think that maybe at last I ken
   What your look meant then.

This is probably, in Mr MacDiarmid's own view, no more than light versification. But it is certainly not English versification; the prisoner behind the polished walls has escaped and engaged himself in the moulding of a curious façade. Mr MacDiarmid, like all great poets, has his in and out moments – some of them disastrous moments; his care to set this planet aright has laid waste some of his finest poems – but, working in that medium of Braid Scots which he calls synthetic Scots, he has brought Scots language into print again as a herald in tabard, not the cap-and-bells clown of romantic versification.

Of an entirely different order, but a genius no less genuine, is Mr Spence in his Scots poetry. To show the width and sweep of Braid Scots from MacDiarmid to Spence, it is necessary to quote only:

Time that has dinged doun castels and hie toures,
And cast great crouns like tinsel in the fire,
That halds his hand for palace nor for byre,
Stands sweir at this, the oe of Venus's boures,
Not Time himself can dwell withouten floures,
Though aiks maun fa' the rose shall bide entire;
So sall this diamant of a queen's desire
Outflourish all the stanes that Time devours.

How far these two are isolated phenomena, how far the precursors of a definite school of Scots literature is still uncertain: they have their imitators in full measure: in William Soutar the Elijah of MacDiarmid may yet have an Elisha. When, if ever, the majority of Scots poets – not versifiers – begin to use Braid Scots as a medium that dream of a Scots literary renaissance may tread the *via terrena* of fulfilment, enriching (in company with orthodox English) the literary heritage of that language of Cosmopolis towards which the whole creation moves.

An experiment of quite a different order from MacDiarmid's writing in synthetic Scots, or Spence's in deliberate excavation in the richness of the antique Scots vocabularies, may be noted here. As already stated, there is no novelist (or, indeed prose writer), worthy of the name who is writing in Braid Scots. The technique of Lewis Grassic Gibbon in his trilogy *A Scots Quair* – of which only Parts I and II, *Sunset Song* and *Cloud Howe*, have yet been published – is to mould the English language into the rhythms and cadences of Scots spoken speech, and to inject into the English vocabulary such minimum number of words from Braid Scots as that remodelling requires. His scene so far has been a comparatively uncrowded and simple one – the countryside and village of modern Scotland. Whether his technique is adequate to compass and express the life of an industrialised Scots town in all its complexity is yet to be demonstrated; whether his peculiar style may not become either intolerably mannered or degenerate, in the fashion of Joyce, into the unfortunate unintelligibilities of a literary second childhood, is also in question.

For the Gaels, one cannot do better than quote James Barke, the author of *The World his Pillow* and *The Wild MacRaes*, and himself a remarkable Anglo-Gael:

'In Scotland today there exists no body of Gaelic culture. In the realms of imaginative literature – in fiction and drama – there is little or no original work in evidence;

and what does exist is of poor quality and vitiated by a spineless sentimentality.

'In verse alone the modern Gaelic writer would seem to find a suitable medium for expression – Donald Sinclair (died recently); Duncan Johnston of Islay; John MacFadyen. MacFadyen, I believe, has it. But here too the output is small and fragmentary and, in quality, perhaps best compared to the Poet's Corner of the provincial press.

'There is no one today in any way approaching the stature of the great Gaelic poets: Alasdair MacMhaighistir Alasdair and Duncan Ban MacIntyre – or even Alexander MacDonald or Ewan MacColl.

'The reason for the poverty of contemporary Gaelic culture is not difficult to state.

'When the Young Pretender and his Highland forces were defeated on Culloden Moor in 1746, there followed a ruthless military occupation of the Highlands. The clan system was broken up and all forms of Gaelic culture were suppressed. The ownership of partly communal land passed into the hands of a small group of private individuals. The land was soon cleared of its human population. With the exception of a few impoverished crofting communities the native Gael became subservient to the dominant land-owning class.

'First military suppression and dictatorship, then economic suppression were the cause of the decay of the Gael and his native Gaelic culture. From the field of Culloden to the first National Government economic, and consequently racial, decay has continued steadily. In the modern capitalist state the Gael finds himself an anachronism – almost an extinct species. The few of them who are articulate turn, therefore, to a hopeless backward looking, backward longing. A decayed economic system, can produce only a decayed culture.

'The present attempts to revive this culture are necessarily doomed to failure. In its hey-day, Gaelic culture was surprisingly beautiful and vital. As part of Scotland's cultural heritage it will survive for its richness and beauty. But a people can no more live on the glories of the past than it can survive on the memories of its last meal.

'The death rattle of Gaelic culture may be amplified by all sorts of bodies and committees. They delude themselves, however, in thinking that by so doing so they are performing an act of resurrection . . .

'Fionn MacColla, in English, it may be noted, is far away the finest example of the Gaelic influence. In a very profound sense, his English is the finest Gaelic we have.'

Sic itur ad astra.

The Wrecker –
James Ramsay MacDonald

LANGUAGE, THAT 'perfected crying of apes and dogs' at which Anatole France professed a whimsical astonishment in its ability to debate the profoundities of metaphysics, has never been merely a technique of expression for Mr MacDonald. Very early he was snared in the ancient debate between Nominalist and Realist and very early (albeit unconscious of the fact) took sides in that ancient argument. He has never succeeded in penetrating behind words to thought: there is, indeed, no evidence that he ever attempted this awesome feat. Even in elementary manipulation of English one is conscious of a curious phenomenon: he is a clever, if rather unintelligent child, engaged in lifting sentences piecemeal from some super-abacus frame and arranging them in a genteel pattern. He is not engaged in displaying either James Ramsay MacDonald or his reactions of awe or hate or wonder or love towards that bright glimmer between the shades of sleep that we call the universe. He is merely engaged in genuflection at the shrine of Words:

'Away to the north, across the Firth, rose the pale blue hills of Sutherland and Ross: to the south lay the fertile farms of Morayshire sloping up through green wood and purple moorland into the blue tops of the Grampians, with the ruined Palace of Spynie in the mid-distance; to the east swept the sea, bordered by a wide stretch of yellow sand bending away into the horizon, with hills in the background, the whole stretching out in peaceful beauty which has won for it the name of the "Bay of Naples" . . .'

Note both the cleverness and the rigid adjectival conventionality: pale blue hills and fertile farms and peaceful beauty. It is the kind of thing that the dux in a little Scots school pens while the Dominie beams upon him (I know, having been such a dux myself, companioned by such a Dominie). It is pre-adolescent, it tells one nothing about either Mr MacDonald's countryside or about his feelings towards it. It is the kind of guidebook chatter which raises your ire against an unknown (and probably inoffensive) landscape.

So with that philosophy of Socialism which Mr MacDonald was wont to exfoliate in the days before, glancing downwards and backwards, he caught sight of the seemly shape his calves occupied inside the silk stockings of Court dress. Perhaps this Socialism had once a logic, as certainly it had once a fine, if anaemic, sincerity, a passionate pity if also an unimpassioned patience. In the mazes of Mr MacDonald's vocabulary it behaves like a calf in an amateurish slaughter-shed, dodging with frightened moos the impact of innumerable padded bludgeons:

'Biologically "the negation of the existing state of things", its "inevitable breaking up," its "momentary existence" is impossible. Here we find, as we find everywhere in the Marxian method, a lack of real guarantee (although there are many verbal guarantees) that change is progress. The biological view emphasises the possibilities of existing society as the mother of future societies, and regards idea and circumstance as the pair from which the new societies are to spring. It gives not only an explanation of the existing state of things, but of its giving birth to a future state of things. It also views every form of existence on its actual process of movement and therefore on its perishing – very different from perishable – side. It lays the very slightest emphasis on its "critical and revolutionary side", because it is mainly constructive and the idea of "clearing before building" is alien to its nature.'

This is a waste of wind and water, a seeping marshland under a fog. Note the power of the word 'biological' in the mind of Mr MacDonald. It means one of a dozen things, and means none of them for long. Firstly, it is pure Darwinism in operation. Then it is Weismannism. Then (for all we know to the contrary) it is the epitome of the benign convolutings of Tantric Buddhism. We catch a faint glimpse through yellow fogs of verbosity of an idea that the great lizards of the Mezozoic suffered no deep or terrible calamity with the coming of the ice-caps. Did the stegosaurus freeze in his swamps and pass from the world for ever? Not at all. The stegosaurus looked about him and said: 'The cold comes on apace. I must discard my scales and grow me some hair.' And this the good stegosaurus did, mislaying scales, claws, reptilian intestines and reptilian nature, and was presently a mammoth.

This – if ever he has possessed a view, not merely a vocabulary – is Mr MacDonald's view of the processes of biological evolution. *Cassell's Popular Educator*, he tells with pride, was 'his only university'. We may well believe the truth of this statement. That the great lords of the Mezozoic age did indeed die away completely and catastrophically, leaving to rise to greatness in the alien mammalian world their lesser and harried kin, not their own direct evolving descendants, is an elementary scrap of knowledge in which the good Cassell had perhaps no space to specialise. Yet lack of that knowledge has conditioned the being of what purports to be a 'scientific Socialism' – the creed which was presently foisted upon the British Labour Party, the creed which presently wrecked that party completely and disastrously.

In ascribing to Mr MacDonald responsibility for bringing about (soulfully, with a radio-wide slurring of consonants) that wreckage, one is, of course, personifying many tendencies and many obscure gospels in the movement itself. Yet this hazy inability to grasp at the flinty actualities of existence, personal or universal, is in so many ways characteristically Scots that to Mr MacDonald more than to any other may be ascribed the major share in this notable achievement. He is as representationally Scots in his approach to politics as the late Sir James Arthur Thomson was in his approach to biology, as Sir Arthur Keith is in his approach to ethnology. They are as three investigators commissioned to three minute and elaborate experiments in the weighing and sifting of chemical constituents: and they approach their tasks uniquely clad in boxing-gloves and blinkers.

In the case of Mr MacDonald, at least, it is both farcical and tragic to note how much his inability to penetrate below words is caused by the fact that the shape and setting of the words are racially unfamiliar to him. English remains for him a foreign language: its terms and expressions, its unique twists of technique, he has followed and charted laboriously, competently, and unintelligently. Yet, mazed in these pursuits, he has never learned to think like an Englishman, he has never comprehended what Englishmen thought, he has never comprehended essential meanings in English vocabularies or English minds. As a result, he has foisted antique Scotticisms upon quite alien essentials, misapprehended the meaning, origin and intention of a great social movement, and (in ultimate prideful pose) stood aside to watch that movement murdered . . .

He is supposed to have Norse blood in his veins. It is extremely likely. One of his biographers, a babbling lady greatly given to clothing her expressions in the raggedest of verbal reach-me-downs, tells us that 'his homeland is Morayshire, and Morayshire, north and east of the Grampians, breeds a race in which mingle the blood of the Highlanders and that of the Norse rovers from across the sea.' His grandmother, by whom he was brought up, 'had seen better days, and, even in the poorest circumstances, retained the demeanour of a gentlewoman, a natural grace and dignity of manner'. Oh God, oh Lossiemouth! 'There he made the acquaintance of some of the remarkable men of the country through Samuel Smiles' "Life of a Scottish Naturalist", Thomas Edwards of Banff, "Thomas Dick, the Thurso Baker" – geologist. Above all, Hugh Miller influenced him then. Hugh Miller's "Schools and Schoolmasters" was among the first books he bought. The watchmaker also lent him Scott and Dickens.'

He appears to have flourished greatly in the sipping of this pale scum from the surface of English letters. Young, handsome, genteel, he set out for London.

London for a while was unkind. It employed him as an invoice clerk in a City warehouse at a salary of 12/6 a week. We are assured that this was the foundation of his Socialism and that he never forgot those terrible days. The 1931 cuts in the pay of junior civil servants – cuts in many a case reducing purchasing power to a lower level than 12/6 a week – were authorised during a period of temporary amnesia.

It was 1888. Presently he became secretary to a Liberal Parliamentary candidate; presently he had joined the Social Democratic Federation. But the Federation had never heard of Samuel Smiles or the dignity of labour or the necessity (they stared, astounded Cockneys) for 'independent *thote*'. Soon their soullessness had vexed the young Mr MacDonald from the ranks. He joined the Fabians, and, about the same time, obtained a footing in journalism.

Meanwhile, Labour representations in the Liberal Party was moulting forth its discontents. Keir Hardie had arisen as the apostle of Independent Labour. The young Mac-Donald watched this development carefully. At the Bradford Conference of 1893 Keir Hardie was instrumental in founding the Independent Labour Party. A cautious year afterwards Mr MacDonald adhered to the new party.

It was the strangest of parties. Disgruntled Liberal intellectuals with Parliamentary leanings supported it; intelligent workmen supported it; sentimental anarchists supported it. It had all kinds of philosophies, all kinds of codes of action. Round the problems of the class war it revolved like a monkey in a cage, distrustful of the tail-nipping propensities of the central axle. In the election of 1895 it put forward twenty-eight candidates. Young Ramsay MacDonald stood for Southampton and was rejected with great unanimity, despite a voice already highly trained in the enunciation, terrifyingly, of those platitudinous nebulosities before which the simple Keir Hardie bowed his head, acknowledging MacDonald Labour's 'greatest intellectual asset'.

For a moment we may let temptation have its way, and turn to the lady biographer for a gem-cut paragraph. She is describing MacDonald of the Southampton election:

'If he appeared a knight in armour, he was hardly, for all his charm and intermittent humour, the glow of his vitality, the Merciful Knight. But at the right hour he met the right woman. A hand was laid upon him that softened the rigidity, mellowed and sweetened the vital strength.'

Predestined the hero of a novelette, Providence had not bungled in her choice. He travelled; he wrote disappovingly of the unstatesmanlike Boer War; and he had a weekend cottage at Chesham Bois. He was shedding the rougher cut

lines of his Scottishness, though the unique accent remained undiluted. Cultured, curving of moustache, he
looks out from the photographs of those days. The conviction of continuity of culture became fixed in his mind –
the mind which could lump 'Cromwell, Milton, Hampden,
Penn, Burke' as 'the best in the life of England'!

In 1900 the Labour Representation Committee came
into being – the embryo Labour Party which returned two
men to Parliament in the General Election of that year.
MacDonald was elected secretary of the new organisation,
and worked with a fine assiduity in building it up. In the
next election – that of 1906 – he had his reward in two
fashions – he himself was returned to Parliament by Leicester and twenty-eight other members of the Labour Party
were returned as well. Mr MacDonald became a skilled and
outstanding Parliamentarian; more important, he became
the chief theoretician of the Labour Party – of that group of
men which claimed, and with some justice, to represent the
true commons of Great Britain, the lowly, the oppressed,
the Cheated of the Sunlight, the bitter relicts of the savagery
of the Industrial Revolution. He organised publishing
ventures, issues of series of Socialist books and tracts; he
engaged and won the attention of a vast audience beyond
his immediate ken.

Three quotations from his published works:

'Socialism is no class movement. Socialism is a movement of opinion, not an organisation of status. It is not the
rule of the working class; it is the organisation of the
community.'

Surely it was very plain. The stegosaurus was on the
move, shedding its vertebrate spikes, abandoning its carnivorous diet, and realising, appalled, that hitherto its
constituent cells had been quite unorganised.

'History is a progression of social stages which have
preceded and succeeded each other like the unfolding of
life from the amoeba to the mammal, or from the bud to the

fruit. Today we are in the economic stage. Yesterday we were in the political stage. Tomorrow we shall be in the moral stage.'

It was all so plain. Peace to the Abbé Mendel and his discoveries of violent revolution, from stage to stage, within the sleek skin of evolution. Today was the economic stage: our fathers lived quite without economic organisation, subsisting on sea-kale and mushrooms. Despite this, they engaged in politics – an abandoned pursuit we have quite outgrown. Tomorrow our children will inherit the moral stage – both we and our fathers being entirely without morals . . . And the day after tomorrow the world would enter on a millennial dotage.

'Intelligence and morality indicate the goal by which the struggle to escape the existing purgatory is guided. Human evolution is a stretching out, not a being pushed forward.'

The much-tried stegosaurus, properly coaxed, would set about elongating its spine . . .

To describe the opinions in such quotations as sub-human maunderings may be natural: it is also profoundly unjust. The Lossiemouth dux was writing good essays: he could, it seems, have written them almost in his sleep, and then stood by with a solemn smirk on his face while the Dominie read them. The Dominie was the British Labour Movement; and it put down each essay and gazed at the writer with a fresh upstirring from the wells of awe . . .

Nevertheless, he was no more than the epitome of the movement itself. From 1906 until 1914 there were strikes and disputes and wage-cuts: there were folk who starved to death, folk who lived mean and desperate lives, phthistic children who gasped out their last breaths in the slums of the Duke of Westminster – but the great trade unions were powerful and comparatively rich. Conditions pressed not too bitterly on the great mass of labouring men and women. There was no direct and brutal tyranny, and this philosophy of slow and gradual and easy change, when no blood would be shed and little exertion would be required and the repentant lion would turn to a lamb, suited admirably the temper of the padded times. In Germany, the other country with a great and well-organised labour movement, Marxism, though not definitely repudiated, was watered down to innocuousness, the Day of Change remotely postponed to the era of Germany's grandchildren – those children who have now inherited Hitler.

Then the War came.

The Labour International fell (as Mr MacDonald no doubt said) like a house of cards. Labour leaders lined up in platoons before the War Ministries of their various countries not to protest against war, not to threaten sabotage, not to proclaim the General Strike: but to clamour for salaried positions. That unique internationalist, Mr HG Wells, erupted like an urgent geyser – 'every sword drawn against Germany is a sword drawn for peace'. (Stout, chubby elderly men in comfortable beds could hardly sleep o'nights for dreaming of the gleaming swords.) Mr Arthur Henderson became a Cabinet Minister. Miss Marie Corelli wrote a patriotic pamphlet of great richness and ferocity, *What can we do for England?*, and later was fined for hoarding sugar.

The way was clear for Mr Ramsay MacDonald. He was offered a place in the Cabinet by a muddled Government anxious to conciliate this dangerous Parliamentarian. But the Government did not realise that, Parliamentarian or no Parliamentarian, this Scots Labour Leader, predestined the hero of a novellete, could no more break through the Author's plot than one of his favourite amoeba could escape its jelly-film. He refused the offer, proclaimed his opposition to the War, and went into the wilderness, dark, tremendous, and Luciferian.

He was to acquire great kudos with this action. His sincerity in opposing the War is undoubted; his sincerity from those early days in the genteel poverty of Lossiemouth to these modern days as an animated exhibit at the Geological Museum is undoubted. But there can be little doubt that, like Lucifer, he gathered a unique satisfaction from his position – the dauntless tribune (as a Victorian 'historical' novelist would have seen him, in genteel toga and sidewhiskers) defying the tyrannical Senate and the brutalised plebs. And there can be as little doubt that (as ever) he quite failed to penetrate behind words to that vile reality that the War was. Addressing a conference in 1918 he spoke of the 'hot and bloody faces on the Somme, only fanned in death by the wings of the angel'. That tumult of fear and filth to Mr MacDonald was no more than excuse for manipulation of the shoddy platitudes of minor poetasters.

In 1917 came the two Russian Revolutions: the first a proper and praiseworthy revolution, the stegosaurus paring its claws and going out to grass; the second – Mr MacDonald looked on the second with an astounded, wurring disapproval. It was a quite different beast, not the old, friendly dinosaur at all – an aggressive, alien, froward beast, biologically unsound. In Great Britain a certain amount of sympathy was manifested for the brute by the Labour Movement. This Mr MacDonald set himself to combat. By 1918, when Leicester refused to re-elect him to Parliament, the battle between Reform and Revolution in the Independent Labour Party was in full swing. By 1920 the revolutionaries had suffered a severe defeat and Mr MacDonald, still in the wilderness, was building up afresh his war-shattered gospel of 'evolutionary Socialism'.

'The patriotism which expresses a share in common life felt and valued is of a totally different quality from that which expresses a share in common power. The latter is the patriotism that "is not enough", that issues in no fine national spirit, and no sane political judgement. It is a blinding pride, not an enlightening dignity. Therefore political education should begin by the cultivation of the tradition of the locality, and democratic government should be founded on the self-government of the local community. "My fathers' graves are there." '

What appeal had Lenin and the sovietism of the Third International compared with this clarion call to upbuild Socialism on the Parish Council heroisms of our fathers – our non-moral, non-economic, but bitterly political fathers?

'In ten years the work of the Bolshevist Government, freed from outside attacks and commanding the necessities of life, will bring Russia to where (and no further) five years of Labour Government in this country, backed by public opinion, would bring us; two years of Bolshevism in this country would bring us where Russia was a dozen years before the Revolution.'

That experiment in Labour Government was unfair. In the 1923 General Election, the Conservatives, though numerically superior to either Labour or Liberal representation, found themselves unable to secure Liberal support. Mr Ramsay MacDonald was summoned to Buckingham Palace; he emerged from it the first Labour Premier. Labour burst into loud pœans.

They were mistimed. Earnest colliers poring over their *Daily Herald* learned astounded of the inclusion of the good and Conservative Lord Chelmsford in the Cabinet. There were other as astonishing personalities. In the Labour Speech from the Throne, a vague Niagara of bubbling sonorosities, nothing of any moment was promised. This was but just anticipation. Nothing was done. The Merciful Knight engaged in nine months' elaborate skirmishing with the Liberals – the radical, undignified, uneasy Liberals pressing him forward to all kinds and manners of dangerous experiments with the economic structure of our island. Mr MacDonald foughht them back at every point: he would consent to the clipping of not a single claw on the stegosaurus' hooves. Dazed Conservatives realised that here was the most Conservative Government since Lord

Salisbury's; obstreperous Mesopotamians were bombed with great thoroughness by orders of the Under-Secretary for Air, the personal friend of the Premier, the pacifistic Mr Leach. The communists – much the same collection of irreligious, vigorous blasphemous Cockneys as Mr Mac-Donald had turned from in a frayed disgust in the eighteen-nineties – began to prove quite as obstreperous as the Mesopotamians. Unfortunately, they could not be bombed. What change was there in the stegosaurus, they cried – except that it ate more flesh? Labour cursed them gruffly, turning trusting eyes to its Premier. He would tell them how the best was really changing – he knew about it all, *he* knew, HE knew!

Unfortunately, he was rarely visible on the English horizon. He fled from conference to conference across the European scene; at rare intervals, returning to Parliament, he uttered profound appeals for national unity to save the peace of the world – a world injected with a trilling diapason of consonants and false vowels. In Court dress he displayed an exceptional leg. More and more it was becoming evident to him how necessary was the slow and gradual evolution of human society – retaining dignity, tradition, culture.

But evil men conspired. The communists had taken to appealing directly to soldiers on the subject of the stegosaurus. One of their propagandists was arrested. Labour – uneasy, moody Labour – rumbled in protest and Mr MacDonald, bestirred from his sane and logical immersements in conference-creation, was reminded that he was a Labour leader. He was prevailed on to have Campbell released. Thereat the Liberals, soured of his tactics, voted out the first Labour Government.

In the succeeding election the stegosaurus lost all sense of honour – a frightened and unsavoury beast. It produced the famous Red Letter, pleasingly forged in Berlin, and proving that Mr MacDonald took his orders from Moscow.

For a moment it seems that Mr MacDonald caught a glimpse of the reality of the beast he had played with and patted so long – the sterile and unlovely beast he had assured the Labour Movement was really a gentle female beast about to give birth to an unique offspring. Then the smashing defeat at the polls came and he abandoned beast and plebs for the wilderness of opposition. And never, during that period of opposition, did he look again on the horror of the dinosaur's countenance. It was merely a dream he had dreamt: the beast was a comely, if occasionally mistaken beast; and he would soon invite him to ride its back again.

Meanwhile wages sank. The hours of the miners were threatened. Labour, long unused to any other general action than the Parliamentary, sprouted a dangerous revolutionism. It proclaimed the General Strike. For Nine Days that strike paralysed and exhilarated Great Britain. There was a blowing up of a sudden comradeship, a sudden and astoundingly Marxian class-consciousness. The Government, appalled, determined to arrest the strike leaders. The strike leaders, appalled, determined to save their skins. They abandoned the strike and abandoned thousands of those they had called out to victimisation and intimidation. Mr MacDonald and Mr Baldwin exchanged courtesies and congratulations in the House of Commons, and sent out bulletins to the effect that the dinosaur was itself again.

Labour turned to Parliamentary organisation. As the year of the next General Election drew near it flung all its strength into securing a heavy Parliamentary representation – to secure that way to reform and change which Mr Ramsay MacDonald and his colleagues had preached it since the days of the L.R.C. Its hopes were not disappointed. It returned over two hundred and fifty members to Parliament; it returned Mr MacDonald to the premiership; in conjunction with the small and radical group of Liberal MPs he was free to display to the doubting Stalin – the abandoned, uncultured, unloquacious Stalin – how a Labour Government worked swift and efficient change the while a Godless Bolshevist one did no more than stumble doggedly forward in the dark.

The stegosaurus' health was far from sound: it complained of internal pains. Breathlessly each morning the Labour voter opened his *Daily Herald* to read the news of the beast's safe delivery in the skilful hands of its midwife, Ramsay MacDonald. But still the news delayed. Mr Mac-Donald instead began to issue bulletins – quite unexpected bulletins – about the beast. Copulation and pregnancy were indecencies foreign to the dinosaur's nature. It was a cultured, amiable and happy beast – but for those pains. It was the duty of all men and women of good will to pool their resources to save the health of this happy, innocent animal . . . Between whiles, as in 1924, he sped rapidly about the European scene. He crossed to America and held a conference with President Hoover. Still the dinosaur languished. Mr MacDonald laid before his colleagues of the Labour Cabinet his plan to reduce unemployed relief to provide fresh rations for the monster's table. He did this with wrung withers, but the bankers, the dinosaur's physicians, saw no other way to save its life . . .

One abandons dinosaur (a very real beast) and simile with regret. It may be admitted that MacDonald's colleagues, refusing to agree with this final onslaught on the standard of that dumb, patient puzzled horde that had elevated them to Parliamentary position, abandoned the beast with regret as well, in spite of the feeble flare of revolutionary zeal they displayed when their late leader appeared – still Premier – at the head of his 'National Government', backed by row on row of that enemy against which so long and so often he had swung his padded mace. But outside the House of Commons there arose a slow creaking and cracking and spiralling of dust – it was the Labour Movement crumbling to dust. At the 1931 General

Election, leading the combined Liberals and Conservatives, Mr Ramsay MacDonald completed his task of wreckage. On the morning of October the 29th, 1931, the country awoke to find that the pacifist of the War-time years had for once abandoned the padded bludgeon and smashed to atoms with a merciless blow that party and group which had raised him to power, which had followed him and his unique philosophy for a long twenty-five years.

The Labour Movement may win again to shadowy triumphs, but the spirit, the faith and the hope have gone from it. Time, impatient, has turned its back on new reechoings of those thunderous platitudes which once seemed to ring prophet-inspired from a MacDonald platform. New armies are rising, brutal and quick, determined, desperate, mutually destructive, communist and fascist. Mr Ramsay MacDonald has completed to perfection the task set him by the play of historic movements and blind economic forces. He still hastens from conference to conference, solemn and creased; his voice still rings out those rolling periods; he poses, one foot on the step of his aeroplane, for the pressing photographer—.

But there is a greyness and chill come upon it all. One realises that this is hardly a living human being at all, but a hollow simulacrum. One realises with a start of enlightenment that indeed there was never life here at all, it was a fantasy, a play of the jaded Victorian sense, a materialisation of some hazy lady novelist's dreams after reading Samuel Smiles as a bed book. Even so, there are moments when the presence touches raw nerves: this ghost delays so long on the boards of history, unhumorous, unappeasable. There is hardly a Scotsman alive who does not feel a shudder of amused shame as the rolling turgid voice, this evening or that, pours suddenly from his radio. We have, we Scots (all of us), too much of his quality in our hearts and souls.

Religion

DEFINITION IS THE BETTER part of dissertation. Before one sets to a sketch of Religion in Scotland it is well to state what Religion is not. It is not altruism, it is not awe, it is not the exercise of a super-conscious sense. It is not ethics; it is not morality. It is neither the evolution of primitive Fear into civilised Worship nor the deified apprehension of an extra-mundane Terror.

Instead, a Religion is no more than a corpus of archaic science. The origin of Religion was purely utilitarian. Primitives – the food-gatherers, the ancient folk of all the ancient world – knew no religion. Their few and scattered survivors in this and that tiny crinkle of our planet are as happily irreligious as our own remote ancestors. They are without gods or devils, worship or cities, sacrifices or kings, theologies or social classes. Man is naturally irreligious. Religion is no more fundamental to the human character than cancer is fundamental to the human brain.

Man in a Primitive condition is not Man Savage. Confusion of those two distinct cultural phases has led to the ludicrous condition of anthropology and ethnology at the present day – the confusion which produces such eminent Scotsmen as Sir Arthur Keith capable of asserting that racialism is the life-blood of progress. Of a like order and origin are the wordy 'theses' of the various psycho-analyst groups which follow Freud and Jung. Psycho-analysts are our modern supreme specialists in the art of slipshod research. A Viennese Jew has been haunted from early years by the desire (inhibited) to cut his father's throat. The psycho-analyst, excavating details of this laudable, but abortive intention, turns to such gigantic compendiums of irrelevantly-indexed myth and custom as Sir James G Frazer's *Golden Bough*. Therein he discovers that parricide was common to Bantu, Melanesian, aboriginal Australian. Ergo, common to primitives: ergo, a fundamental human trait . . . The fact that Bantus, Melanesians and Australians are not primitives, but savages, peoples who have absorbed religious and social details from alien cultures and transformed their economic organisation in harmony with that absorption is either unapprehended or dismissed as unimportant: and we reach back to smear the face of Natural Man with the filth of our own disease.

Particularly is this the case with regard to Religion; and particularly is the truly utilitarian nature of Religion manifested in that long life of three centuries which the Scots people led under the aegis of the Presbyterian churches.

Religion for the Scot was essentially a means of assuring himself life in the next world, health in this, prosperity, wealth, fruitful wombs and harvests. The Auld Kirk in Scotland is the greatest example of an armchair scientific Religion known to the world since the decay of the great State cults of Egypt and Mexico. In the case of all three countries the Gods were both unlovely and largely unloved; and in the case of all three definite discomforts of apparel and conduct were undergone in return for definite celestial favours manifested upon the terrestrial scene. One of those innumerable (and generally nauseating) pulpit stories illustrates this:

A town minister was on holiday in the country, and consented to act one Sabbath in place of the local incumbent. While he was robing himself in the vestry he was approached by some of the elders, farmers all, and tactfully desired to remember in his prayers a supplication for rain – there had been a considerable drouth. Accordingly, he ascended the pulpit, and in the course of the service prayed that 'the windows of Heaven might be opened to cheer the thirsty ground, and fulfil the earnest hopes of the husband-man'.

Scarcely had he finished than a flash of lightning was observed through the kirk windows. The growl of thunder followed; and in a few minutes such a downpour of rain as was speedily levelling to the ground the standing crops, and leaving the cornfields ruined and desolate. Ascribing this disastrous phenomenon [very reasonably] to the minister's prayer, one of the farmers remarked as he tramped away through the rain: 'That poor fool may be well enough in the town, but God Almighty! the sooner he's out of the country the better for everybody.'

Behind those couthy tales of ministers and kirks, beadles and elders, sessions and sextons, a system operated with a ruthless efficiency for three long centuries. In Scotland the human mind and the human body were in thrall to what the orthodox would call a reign of religion, what the Diffusionist historian recognises as the reign of a cultural aberration, what the political student might apprehend as a reign of terror. The fears and hopes of long-defunct Levantines, as set forth in the Christian Bible, were accepted as a code of conduct, as a science of life, and foisted upon the Scottish scene without mercy and greatly without favour. This is an attempt at impartial statement, not an expression of anti-Christianity. Had they been the codes of the Korân or the Rig-veda the scene would doubtlessly have been even more farcical objectively, if in subjective essence the same.

Late seventeenth and eighteenth century Scotland saw the domination of the code at its most rigorous. Not only was the Sunday (meticulously then, as still in the meeting-houses of the Free Kirk, misnamed the Sabbath) a day of rigid and inexorable piety, but the week-days as well were under the control and spying activities of kirk-session and

minister, beadle – and indeed any odd being with a desire
to vex the lives of his fellow-men. The Sunday in particular
was sanctified to an exclusive care with the rites and wraths
of the Scottish Huitzilopochtli – war-god and maize-god in
one. In the *Social Life of Scotland in the Eighteenth Century* a
slightly modernised cleric says of the kirk-officers, beadles
and deacons:

> There was not a place where one was free from their
> inquisitorial intrusion. They might enter any house
> and even pry into the rooms. In towns where the
> patrol of elders or deacons, beadle and officers, paced
> with solemnity the deserted causeway eagerly eyeing
> every door and window, craning their necks up every
> close and lane, the people slunk into the obscurity of
> shadows and kept hushed silence. So still, so empty
> were the streets on a Sunday night that no lamps were
> lighted, for no passengers passed by, or if they did
> they had no right to walk.

This was the state of affairs everywhere, not only in small
and obscure parishes. Elders and deacons were empowered
to visit where they liked, to assure themselves that families
were engaged in unsecular interests. If admittance were
refused them to a house they could (and very frequently
did) invoke the civil magistrates' aid for breaking in forcibly. They could impose innumerable fines and penalties.
The power of life and death was in the hands of this great
priesthood, the guardians and functionaries of the science.
A minute of the Edinburgh kirk-session (from *The King's
Pious Proclamation* (1727)) says:

> Taking into consideration that the Lord's Day is
> profaned by people standing in the streets, vaguing
> in the fields and gardens, as also by idly gazing out at
> windows, and children and apprentices playing in the

streets, warn parents and threaten to refer to the Civil Magistrates for punishment, also order each Session to take its turn in watching the streets on Sabbath, as has been the laudable custom of this city, and to visit each suspected house in each parish by elders and deacons, with beadle and officers, and after sermon, when the day is long, to pass through the streets and reprove such as transgress, and inform on such as do not refrain.

During the week the minister might notify any member of his congregation that he intended to visit him in his own house and hold a 'catechising' of his family. This 'catechising' consisted of a play of question and answer on knowledge of the Christian Scriptures, the Christian Code of the Good Life, and the Christian Code of Eternal Punishment. Everyone was questioned in rote – the master, the mistress, the children, and all the servants within the gates. Those who failed to answer according to the code might be rebuked or punished, according to the nature of the offence; those who failed to put in an appearance at those ceremonies of droned affirmation and incantation might be very bitterly prosecuted. Until well towards the nineties of last century the officials of the Scots priesthood were the real rulers of the Scots scene, they were Spartan ephors, largely elected by the people and keeping the people under a rigorous rule. And then the rank blossomings of Industrialism loosened their hold, weakened their status, and freed Scotland from the nightmare of their power.

It is obvious that any people under the rule of such rigorous and forbidding code – belief in a joyless but necessary agricultural God, belief in a joyless but necessary ceremonial ritual – would develop strange abnormalities of appearance and behaviour. It is evident in the ancient scene in Mexico, for example, where every year thousands of human beings were sacrificed to the Gods of the earth and rain, that a few more hundred years of evolution along the same lines would have wrought a biological deviation from the human norm: the ancient Mexicans, but for the fortunate arrival of Cortes, would have aberrated into a sub-species of *Homo Sapiens*. The same may be said of the Scots. Left alone and uninvaded, they might have passed entirely beyond the orbit of the normally human but for the coming of the Industrial Revolution. This brought Scotland its slums and its Glasgow, its great wens of ironworks and collieries upon the open face of the countryside; but its final efflorescence broke the power of the Church and released the Scot to a strange and terrible and lovely world, the world of science and scepticism and high belief and free valour – emerging into the sunlight of history from a ghoul-haunted cañon.

There is still a Church of Scotland – ostensibly more powerful then ever, having recently amalgamated with its great rival, the United Free Church. There are still innumerable ministers of the Kirk to be met with in the leafy manse walks, the crowded Edinburgh streets, the gatherings of conferences and associations and the like. There is still the trickle of the kirkward folk on a Sabbath morning in summer, when the peewits hold their unending plaint over the greening fields and the young boys linger and kick at the thistles by the wayside, and young girls step daintily down whinguarded paths and over the cow-dung pats by this and that gate. There is still the yearly Assembly of the Kirk in Edinburgh – the strangest of functions, with the High Commissioner some vague politican generally discreetly unintelligible and inevitably discreetly unintelligent; with elderly clergymen acclaiming War 'for the good of the nation', the sword the weapon of Christianity, the economic crisis an Apollyon to be moved by prayer. There are still old women and men who find sustenance and ease and comfort in the droned chantings of the risen God, in

symbolic cannibal feastings upon the body of the dead God
at time of Communion . . .

But it is little more now than a thin and tattered veil upon
the face of the Scottish scene. This ostensibly powerful
Kirk, twin-headed, is riven with the sorriest of all disputes –
a quarrel over meal and milk. For the old United Frees will
not give up their own ministers and kirks in favour of the
Auld Kirk ministers and kirks; nor vice versa. So in most
parishes there are still to be found two churches in close
proximity, staffed by ministers preaching exactly the same
doctrine, ministers preaching to congregations of twenty or
so in buildings erected to house a hundred. But the
ministers themselves – of manse and walk and street and
conference – are of strangely different quality and calibre to
those who manned the Kirk in the mid-eighteenth century.

There are few such pleasant people as the younger
ministers of Scotland. Pleasant is the one possible adjective. They are (the most of them) free-hearted and liberal,
mild socialists, men with pleasant wives who blush over the
books of such writers as myself, but read them nevertheless
and say pleasant things about the pleasant passages. But the
older generation differs from the younger very greatly. It
has run to girth and very often to grossness. It grins with
unloosened vest. Its congregation grins dourly in comprehension. It is, in the country parishes, the understood thing
that the middle-aged, genial minister generally 'sleeps with'
his housekeeper – a proceeding, I remember, which greatly
astonished my innocent youth, for why should a man like
the minister want to sleep with anyone when he had a big,
fine bed of his own? The most luscious of filthy tales (with
women the butt and object of each and the sex-act the
festering focal point) I have ever heard were from the lips of
a highly respected and reputable minister of the Church of
Scotland who still preaches to an exclusive congregation in
one of the Four Cities. The minister a minister at the
beginning of the present century had been greatly freed

from the fears and tabus that formerly inhered in the functioning of his office, but had obtained no such measure of mental freedom and enlightenment as his younger colleague of today.

And that kirkwards trickle of the folk is delusive as well. Here you behold not the fervid Presbyterian but the bored (if complacent) farmer and his wife attending a mild social function. They are going to church because there is nothing much else to be done on a Sunday; they can meet a neighbour there and ask him to supper; the wife will survey with some interest a neighbouring wife's hat or the advances yet another neighbour is making in exhibition of her stages of pregnancy. The old fires and the old fears are gone. Men and women sit and listen with a placid benignancy to sermons as varied in opinion and scope as are the political reaches between fascism and communism . . . and they are quite unstirred. It is something quite unconcerned with their everyday life of factory and field and hope and fear, it is something to amuse the wife and good for the children . . . Why good? They are vague.

And though some of those children reluctantly holding kirkwards, reluctantly seated in those unpadded pews and staring with desperate earnestness at the buzzing busyness of a fly seeking to escape through the panes of a glazed window, may indeed have strange fears and dark terrors upon them, fears that awaken them screaming in the nights with this horrific God thrusting them into sizzling pits of fire because of some minor lapse of the previous day, fears that make lonely wood walks a terror, every screech of an owl the cry of some devil or gnome from the pages of Christian myth, yet their numbers are probably few. It is still a terrible and a dreadful thing that the minds of a nation's youth should be twisted and debased by those ancient, obscene beliefs and restraints; yet, good democrats, we may rejoice that it is now only the minds of the minority – the intelligent minority – that so suffer. And they are growing up into habitation of a world that will presently look back upon even the emasculated rites of the Kirk of Scotland as insanely irrelevant to human affairs as the Black Mass.

Nor does the yearly General Assembly resemble (as once) the Sanhedrin of the Jews. To a large extent it is the excuse and occasion for much tea-drinking and the exchange of views on theological scholarship, rose-growing, and the meaner scandals. Its public speeches have an unexciting monotone of supplication and regret: the young are leaving the Kirk, how may they be reclaimed? The tides of irreligion and paganism are flooding in upon us: how may they be stayed? A similar tidal problem once confronted King Canute. It is recorded that he used denunciation with singular lack of success, and modern experience appears to verify the historical precedent. The pedestrian who pauses midway across a meadow and seeks to stay a charging bull by alternately denouncing its brutish appearance and calling upon it to forgo its essential bullishness is unlikely to survive the occasion for a sufficient length of time to draw up an unimpassioned monograph on the subject.

Occasionally (as has been noted) the Assembly abandons the pagans and turns to consideration of such pressing matters as unemployment, war, and the economic system. In the case of the first and the last it is, (very naturally and to some extent blamelessly, for it is the assembly of ministers of a State Religion) impotent. More diversity of talent and opinion greets the subject of war. Padded elderly gentlemen with cheerfully carmine cheeks and grey whiskers uphold the Sword as the Weapon of Righteousness, used aforetime by Scotland in defence of her liberties: may not Scotland need the Sword again? A sad commentary on the relation of the Assembly to contemporary military science lies in the fact that no opponent appears to have suggested the archaic character of the sword in modern warfare. Why not the Saw-Toothed Bayonet of Salvation? Why not the Gas of God? . . . Vexed from that humble impartiality which is his aim the investigator toys with a vision of the plump, rosy parson in the dirty grey pallor of a gas attack – Lewisite for preference. He sees the rosy cheeks cave in, the eyes start forth like those of a hamstrung pig, the mouth move vomiting as the gas bites into lung-tissues. He turns with a vagrant sigh from that vision: that sight in actuality would almost be worth another War.

That many of the old and the middle-aged of both sexes find comfort in the Kirk and its ceremonies is undeniable. And this brings us to a fine human essence in the relationship of Kirk and people that may not be abandoned on recognition of the archaic nature of the rites of Communion and the like. That comfort was and is sometimes very real. The bitterly toilworn and the bitterly oppressed have been often sustained and cheered and uplifted for the cheerless life of the day to day by the lovely poetry of the Bible, the kindly and just and angrily righteous things therein. They have found inspiration and hope in the sayings and denunciations of some Jewish prophet long powder and nothing, but one who, like them, had doubted life because of its ills and cried on something beyond himself to redress the sad balance of things, to feed the hungry and put down the oppressor. The humble and the poor have found the Kirk and kirk life not only a grinding and a mean oppressiveness, they have found (and find) ministers who are cheerful and helpful beings, with or without their theology, knowledgeable men in medicine and times of stress, champions against lairds and factors and such-like fauna. They have found in the kirk itself, in the blessed peace and ease of a two hours rest in the pews, listening to the only music they ever hear, refreshment and good feeling. If it has chastised the free and rebellious and wrought many bitter things upon the Scots spirit the Kirk has yet atoned in those little ways.

For they are little ways. A contented helot is not a
freeman; a bitterly-oppressed and poverty-stricken serf is
still a serf though you tell him tales in an idle hour and
bind his worse hurts and soothe his worse fears of night
and the dark that comes down on us all. The Kirk of
Scotland, the Religion of the Kirk of Scotland, on its
credit balance has done no more than that. It has tamed
and clipped and sometimes soothed: it has used the sword
often enough: after 1600 it was used upon the people of
Scotland themselves. Its policy and its code in the seventeenth and eighteenth centuries produced that Scot who
was our ancestor: the Scot who had mislaid original
thought for a dour debating of fine theological points,
who was more concerned to applaud the spirited conduct
of Elijah with the bears than to guard his own economic
freedom, who at twenty, married, looked on the clean
lusts and desires of the marriage bed as shameful and
disgusting things; who tormented in a pit of weariness his
young children, Sabbath on Sabbath, with the learning by
rote of dull and unintelligible theological chatter from a
book that can be as painfully wearying as it can be
painfully enthralling; who looked forward to 'catechisings'
with a clownish zest or a clownish fear; who mislaid beauty
and tenderness and love of skies and the happy life of
beasts and birds and children for the stern restraints, the
droning hymns and the superhuman endurances demanded of the attendants at Kirk service; whose social
life revolved round the comings and goings, sayings and
preachings, rebukings and praisings of priests who were
often dull and foolish and froward men, often good and
dull and bewildered men; who, a logician, passed a sinner
to the grave and therefore to hell and those zestful burn-
ings beloved of the Presbytery.

Naturally there were sceptics throughout that era, very
cautious but biting sceptics:

There was a Cameronian cat
  A-seeking for its prey,
Went ben the hoose and caught a moose
  Upon the Sabbath day.

The Elders, they were horrified
  And they were vexèd sair,
Sae straight they took that wicked cat
Afore the meenistair

The meenistair was sairly grieved
  And much displeased did say:
'Oh, bad perverted pussy-cat
  Tae break the Sabbath day!

'The Sabbath's been, frae days o'yore,
  An Institution:
Saw straichtway tak' this wicked cat
  Tae Execution!'

Release from the secular power of the Kirk, or secular enforcement of the Kirk's displeasure, had effects on the Scots similar to those that sunlight and wine might have on a prisoner emerging from long years in a dank cellar. Freedom had been forbidden him: he became the conscienceless anarchist in politics, in commerce, in private affairs. Love of women and the glorying in it had been forbidden him: the modern Scot, escaping that tabu, is still fascinated and horrified by sex. He has seen it swathed in dirty veils of phrase and sentiment so long that now he would expose it for the ludicrous and lewd and ridiculous thing he conceives it must be: Scots in conversation, Scots novelists in their books these modern days are full of details of sex and the sex-act, crude and insanitary details . . . They have escaped the tabu and sought the reality and stumbled into a midden on the way. An aphasia of the spirit has descended on the Scot so that he can see only the foul in a thing that is neither foul nor fair, that is jolly and necessary and amusing and thrilling and tremendous fun and a deadly bore and exhilarating to the point of making one sing and dreadful to the point of making one weep . . .

This is where the effects of Presbyterianism join issue with the effects of the other Religions which dwindlingly survived in Reformed Scotland. Catholicism was more mellow and colourful and poetic: it was also darker and older and more oppressed by even more ancient shames. It produced an attitude of mind more soft than the Presbyterian: and also infinitely more servile. Sex has always been a tabu and shameful thing to the Catholic mind, a thing to be *transmuted* – in the fashion of gathering a lovely lily from its cheerful dung and transmuting it into a glassy ornament for a sterile altar. Episcopalianism is in a different category. From the first it was more a matter of social status than of theological conviction; it was rather a grateful bourgeois acknowledgement of Anglicisation than dissent with regard to the methods of worshipping a God. A typical Episcopalian was Sir Walter Scott – shallow and sedulous, incurably second-rate, incapable (so had his spirit-stuff been moulded) of either delineating the essentials of human character or of apprehending the essentials of human motivation. The Episcopalian Church in Scotland gave to life and ritual mildly colourful trappings, a sober display: it avoided God with a shudder of genteel distaste.

The modern Free Church member is the ancient Presbyterian who has learned nothing and forgotten nothing. As certain unfortunate children abandon mental development at the cretinaceous age of eight, Free Church doctrine, essentially un-Christian, abandoned development with the coming of the Kelts. It is a strange and disgusting cult of antique fear and antique spite. It looks upon all the gracious and fine things of the human body – particularly the body of woman – with sickened abhorrence, it detests music and light and life and mirth, the God of its passionate conviction is a kind of immortal Peeping Tom, an unsleeping celestial sneak-thief, it seeks to cramp and distort the minds of the young much as the ancient Maya sought to mould the brain-stuff of *their* young by deforming the infants' heads with the aid of tightly-strapped slats of wood. As fantastically irrelevant to contemporary Scottish affairs as the appendix is to the human body, its elimination may be brought about rather by advances in social hygiene than by surgical operation.

Debating those elementary facts with regard to Religion in Scotland the present writer before this time has met with the surprising complaint: 'And what is going to happen now? What are you going to put in the place of Religion?' The question shows some confusion of mind. The present writer had no hand in bringing about the decay of Religion; nor, alas, is he likely to have any hand in planning its succession. That succession lies with great economic and historical movements now in being – movements which may bring to birth the strangest of progeny on which we may look aghast. Of the future of Religion ultimately the historian can have little doubt: he sees its coming in ancient times, in the world of the Simple Men, as a cortical abortion, a misapprehension of the functions and activities of nature interlarded and interwoven with attributes mistakenly applied to human rulers. He sees its passing from the human scene – even the Scots scene – in the processes of change, immutable and unstayable. But—

But there may be long delays in that passing. Another abortion of inactive brains – that of Fascism – looms over a tormented world, a creed of the *must* jungle brute, the cowardly degenerate who fears the fine steely glimmer of the open spaces of the heavens, the winds of change, the flow and cry of strange seas and stars in human conduct and human hope – who would drag men back into economic night, into slavery to the state, into slavery (all slaveries aid his purpose) to the archaic institutions of Religion. What has happened in

Italy and Germany may happen in Scotland. The various Scots nationalist parties have large elements of Fascism within them. There is now a definite Fascist Party. If ever such philosophy should reach to power then again we may see deserted streets of a Sabbath, crowded kirks, persecutions and little parish tyrannies, a Free Kirk ministers's millennial dream. If such should be the play of chance it is to be hoped that the historian (albeit himself on the way to the scaffold or the pillory) will look on the process with a cool dispassion, seeing it as no more than a temporary deviation, a thing that from its nature cannot endure. Man has survived this disease far too long either to perish in its last bout of fever or permanently retire into delirium tremens.

One sees rise ultimately (in that perfect state that is an ultimate necessity for human survival, for there is no sure half-way house between Utopia and extinction) in place of Religion – Nothing. To return to clinical similes, one does not seek to replace a fever by an attack of jaundice. One seeks the fields and night and the sound of the sea, the warmth of good talk and human companionship, love, wonder in the minute life of a water-drop, exultation in the wheeling Galaxy. All these fine things remain and are made the more gracious and serene and unthreatened as Religion passes. Passing, it takes with it nothing of the good – pity and hope and benevolence. Benevolence is as natural to Natural Man as hunger. It is an elementary thalamic state, a conditioned reflex of mental and physical health.

Yet, because men are not merely the victims, the hapless leaves storm-blown, of historic forces, but may guide if they cannot generate that storm, it might be well to glance at this last at those members of the various Scots priesthoods who affirm their liberalism, their belief in change, their faith that in a purified Christianity is the strait and undeniable way to that necessary Utopia. One cannot but believe that this is a delusion:

Thou, in the day that breaks thy prison,
   People, though these men take thy name,
And hail and hymn thee rearisen,
   Who made songs erewhile of thy shame,
Give thou not ear; for these are they
   Whose good day was thine evil day.

Set not thine hand upon their cross.
   Give not thy soul up sacrificed.
Change not the gold of faith for dross
   Of Christian creeds that spit on Christ.
Let not thy tree of freedom be
   Regrafted from that rotting tree.

But, if the investigator should stoop to point a moral, he would do so rather in the tale of the Laird of Udny's fool than in heroic rhyme. Of Jamie Fleeman, the reputed fool of the parish, many a tale is told; and the best is that which relates how, of all kirks in Scotland, Udny suffered the worst from sleepy congregations. Hardly had the sermon begun than heads began to nod. One Sunday the minister – a new minister – looked down in the course of his discourse and saw only one member of the congregation awake, and that Jamie Fleeman.

Halting his sermon the minister exclaimed: 'This sleeping in church is intolerable. There's only one man awake; and that man's a fool!' 'Ay, ay, minister, you're right there,' called up Jamie in reply. 'And if I hadn't been a fool I'd have been sleeping as well.'

Postlude by Hugh MacDiarmid

ENVOI

Scottish Jews comin' doon frae the mountains
Wi' the laws on their stany herts;
Minor prophets livin' i' the Factory Close
Or ahint the gasworks – fresh sterts?
Folk frae the Auld Testament are talkin'
O' Christ but I'm no' deceived.
Bearded men, cloakt wimmen, and in gloom
The gift o' Heaven's received.

Scottish Jews comin' doon frae the mountains,
Minor prophets frae vennel and wynd,
In weather as black as the Bible
I return again to my kind . . .

The Sauria in their ain way
Had muckle to commend them.
Fell fearsome craturs, it's a shame
That Nature had to end them.

And faith! few men aboot the day
But hae guid cause to speir
Why sicna auld impressive forms
Had to dee for them t'appear.

Sae aiblins wi' traditional Scots,
Covenanters and the lave,
Wha's grand auld gurly qualities
Deserve a better stave.

But they hung on – and still hing on—
Survivals frae an age lang dune.
Gin they'd deed a century syne
They'd whiles shine oot . . . like the mune!. . .

Away, away, to the mune and the devil
Wi' these muddlers, ditherers, ancient disputants,
Auld Lichts, wee Frees, Burnsians, London Scots!
Let them awa' like shadows at noon to their
  haunts!

To their clubs in Pall Mall wi' Elliot and Horne,
Skelton and Gilmour and Montrose and the lave
And a' the ither bats and ugsome affairs
That hae made Scotland sae lang a Gothic grave!

Peter Pan nae langer oor deity'll be
And oor boast an endless infantilism.
Away, wi' the auld superstitions. Let the sun up at last
And hurl a' sic spooks into their proper abysm.

II

Songs of Limbo

In Exile

Chill through the dull, white night
The bare trees shiver,
Where long, dead, crackling grasses stand
Along the river.

Strident the voice of frogs
In marshes by;
And from the far sand-dunes
A jackal's wailing cry.

A little wind moans low
Amongst the eaves,
And showers with sudden taps
Dead almond leaves.

Sleepless, I lie and hear
The mid-night call;
Hear the quick, breathless hush
Ere pattering rain-drops fall.

You in my thoughts the while,
Tender and dear:
With all the darkness warm and exquisite
Your Dream-Self near,

(When all the unhappy times
Are dead and gone:
Dream-lips I'll kiss no more, O Shadow Love!
But your dear own.)

Out of the darkness, softly shod, you come
With perfumed hair;
Hands that are warmly trembling to the touch,
And bosom bare.

And bending low (as once of old you did)
With slender grace,
Like dew to thirsting desert sands, I feel
Your kiss upon my face.

And know, when comes the first still glint of dawn,
Grey-barred and clear—
Your soul has crossed the sund'ring leagues of sea
And loved me here!

                                                   Ludd
                                          February, 1922

LINES WRITTEN IN A 'HAPPY-THOUGHTS' ALBUM
PRESENTED TO RÉ, AUGUST, 1923

Ye who come after, and with varied pens
Herein may write
Of she against whose living sun all praise
Is candle-light . . .

Heed that your lays be sweet, shapely and fair
Of laughter and of sunshine and of mirth:
Thyme-scented air
In sunsets still; whispers of wandering winds
On dew-starred grass;
Dusk-light and song and wheeling call of birds
Where grey clouds mass
Above the night-stilled Downs; or quiet streets
Mourn in the rain
And hearts are glad where music throbs and falls in
pangless pain . . .

And nights shed happy hours that Love shall keep
Long years to dream—
Till on the roofs, swift spear-like,
Falls a gleam,
While roses lift their pallid heads across the lawn
And strange and pure, Out of the reddening East,
Comes forth the dawn . . .
Paint cameos of delight, O shadow-friend
With gladdening hand,
Naught that has beauty, kissed of labour's love,
From this is banned.
Give of your best, and they who follow after,
Moved unto thought or tears or quiet laughter,
Will know you for a friend and gladlier go
Because of you:
(For even I have glimpsed in staggering lines
The Beautiful and True.)

And so with vision blurred and phrases vague
(Dear Ré!)
I write and pass and eke for better men
Make way.
May Art's own children, singers with splendid song,
Adorn these pages,
So that, going down the dim far years
To after ages—
(When winters come not, and the Golden Age
Is near;
When no tears fall, and undreamt Brotherhood
    Has cast out fear)—
Some musing girl with heart and eyes
Like yours,
(Turning these time-sered leaves, while all about)
Red Autumn moors
—Even as we knew them – stretch beneath the sun)
Grave-eyed, shall say:

'Sure, Love and friends and gracious days and fair
Blessed Lady Ré!'

Six Sonnets for Six Months

Mid Year 1926

To My Lady Wife

If I have given
Less than I've striven
    To give:
If I have spoken
In phrases broken
    That live:
The frail rhyme that faills
    Is mine,
The height that it scales
    Is thine.

I THE RAINBOW ROAD

Oh, happy are we who find not what we seek!
  Who follow dreams across the fringe of day,
Hearing Love's voices never, save when speak
  The echoes where she sang and passed that way;
Musing on lights at dusk – She there abode,
  Perchance, long gone? – Dim-borne, across the
    wind
We hear her feet upon the rainbow road;—

  Oh, happy we who seek and never find!
Satiety's sere years we have not known,

Nor Love grown stale, with pale and woeful face.
Never in nights we've heard the anguished moan
    Of weeping Love in hours of hopelessness:
Great God! We have not lived. – Of dreams we've
        sown
    And reaped but harvest-chaff of happiness.

II IN MEMORIAM, RAY MITCHELL
b. 13th February, 1926; d. 16th February, 1926

Now that we've made our sacrifice of mirth
    To agony, we'll seek respite from pain
In quiet places of the mourning earth,
    In the sea's song, in fall of autumn rain,

In sleep, in silence, in the call of sheep
    On windy moors, in shadows cloud-drifts weave
Above lone lochs, in firelight still and deep,
    In the red torch of bracken lit at eve,

In all that passes in the silent hours
    When gloaming comes, when from the mountain
        head
Where dawn was born amidst the opeing [*sic*] flow'rss
    The grey clouds bear the ashes of their Dead.—

Oh, find respite from pain, as one who hears
    The benediction of another's tears.

III MICHAEL

Out of the dusk he reached his hands to ours.
    Our hearts were his, he brought us Heav'n's clear
        light.
Unborn, he friended us. Through magic hours
    We heard his voice go singing down the night.

Child of Desire, his name a battle-cry!
    Red faith would kindle at his spirit's flame;—
We saw him lead the shouting legions by,
    Heard ring upon the years a selfless fame.

And one went down to anguished ways of pain
    For that our vision and our sad souls' dearth.
O Child of dreams! In lands unknown of men,
    Far from the troubled ways of travail'd earth,

Still lead the shining hosts! For not in vain
    You cleansed our hearts for Love's own Lovely
        birth.

IV AN OLD THEME
12th May, 1926

How slow the spring! Through the long winter nights
    We hear the whoom of hail on frozen heights.
How dream of May beside an ice-girt mere?—
    Yet Spring is near.

How slow the corn! No burgeoning of green
    Where eastward slope the bare, brown fields is
        seen.
How dream of harvest and the curlew's cry?—
    Yet Autumn's nigh.

How slow the dawn! Oh God, how long the night
    To hopeless hearts who pray the gift of light
How dream the day when even dreams enumb?—
    Yet Morn will come.

How slow the march of Right! Yet, unforgot,
    It tarries not.

V TO MY LADY RHEA

Grey-blue the sky: the sun shines here today:
  Out in the English fields it's May again,
Beauty a-burgeon from the winter's clay
  And white desire within the hearts of men.

I hear the crooning breakers homeward go
  Through the long mists as memories through years
Far to another shore. Oh, Spring winds, blow!
  Bear unto her my dreams, ye messengers!

There, where the spears of rain shine o'er the moor,
  There, where the cloud-ships sail the louring skies:
You'll know her by her voice, the ways of her,
  Her laughter, and the peace within her eyes.

And when you bring my message to her, lo!
  She'll smile through tears. She heard it long ago.

VI THE LOVERS
5th June, 1926

The thousand lamps of the stars shall be ours,
  And the wind's voice singing, and the sun's light,
Music of earth shall haunt our dreaming hours.
  We'll sleep and wake, turn in the kindly night,

Each unto each, and know the other there,
  And kiss in dreams, and sleep with even breath:
We've paid to peace in pain and sick despair,
  We've made to Life the sacrifice of Death.

We shall pass on: of those we shall forget
  In the press of years, in newer sadness.
Yet sometimes, when the lights of night are set,
  Then shall we remember them with gladness,—

For that they gave, and bring in tears again,
   The love that makes our hearts remember then.

Her Birthday, 1928
A Sonnet Ballad

Lord God, I would never have lived, these I would
    never have
         wed—
Why, agony, nakedness, pain, beauty, the brunt of
    being,
And ecstasy, surgent as song and redder than blood is
    red,
Desire with her eyes of flame and her eyes made void of
    seeing,
And laughter, ringing and ringing, out from the
    throat of a
         child,
And peace – ah! even the peace that is quieter and
    sweeter than
         night,
And the pity that cleanses and sears, weeping a world
    defiled,
And the tenderness swifter than thought, whiter than
    snow is
         white,

But that you came from the nestling flesh this day that
    saw your
         birth
I had walked the teeming streets of life, from dusty
    mart to
         mart,

Buying of dreams as a sick man buys, unheeding hope or
    dearth,—
I had never watched the homing birds go eastward
  with my
     heart.

Blow from the wide, wide seas for her, morning winds
    of the
     earth,
Kiss the lips that are mine to kiss, and heed that the
  night
     Depart.

Rhea, Remembered Suddenly

You know, I'd been so busy all the day,
 I'd hardly given a single thought to you,
(Except half-thoughts that bud and fade away
 As in the Spring the blackthorn blossoms do),
I'd been so busy planning out the years—
 Rivers to cross, and half the boats to make!
How this and that infernal venture steers!—
 I had forgot I planned them for your sake.

And then it came upon me, walking there
 That I'd forgot, that you were mine – and mine!
Your voice, your love, your laughter and your hair,
 And all the secret hours and every line

Of your sweet self. And lo, and suddenly,
 I heard the trumpets blow by Keats's sea!
       24th March, 1929

Vision

We who have seen it when the scented year
Fades, and the leaves are touched of Autumn's hand,
And, quieter than a dream of Summer days,
Death comes unto the russet, fruitful land:
When out against the windy skies of eve
A lap-wing wheels with wild and eery call,
And in the fir-wood's fern-strewn fortresses
    The sunset's shadows fall,

Thenceafter walk as those with eyes unsealed,
Knowing that we behold the Hand of Change
Made manifest; and far by utmost line
Of sky and sea and cliff and bracken range,
The Vision, touched, intangible, hath passed,
Setting a sign for eyes of gods and men:
That that which is shall fade and die and fall,
    And Springtide comes again!

Dear Invalid

God's sweet heart are you, dear. Unfortunate,
  Your tortured soul to Him is high redress
  For our grey world's begrudged happiness—
Your body's pain His stern heart incarnate.

But, being God, will surely give you rest,
   Be merciful, leave you to me at last,
   And peace is yours when all your pain is past:
My peace, my love, of loves the tenderest.

The sea shouts, through the dusk: a vespertine
   Sky-blossom from a cloud's high couch above
   Floats down in golden riot as a dove
Within the homeland dawn's intense serene!

Look now to landward: thence, a ruthless tide,
   The Night comes. Dearest, I am at your side.

Vimy Ridge
Seven Years After

Sleep on, poor fools, sleep on:
   The lush grass grows
Keen of strange foods and dews,
   And no man knows
   If darkness rained upon
   High hope or hope undone,—
Here, where the dawn-wind blows;
Sleep on, poor fools, sleep on.

Sleep on, poor fools, sleep on:
   Strong hearts that beat
Empulse the nameless weeds
   Beneath our feet:
   Such fruit the years have grown,
   Such harvest, redly sown!
Here, where the morn is sweet;

Sleep on, poor fools, sleep on.
Sleep on, poor fools, sleep on:
    Your bones have paved
Ways unto bloody wealth,
    And left enslaved
    Dreams that ye kissed alone,
    (How bright the cold stars shone!)
Here, where the East's gold-laved;
Ah, sleep, poor fools, sleep on!
Sleep on, poor fools, sleep on:
    Did ye not die
Even as the Son of Man?
    Grey Calvary!
    Save of the skies and dawn . . .
Here, where all strife's put by,
Christ's comrades, sleep, sleep on.

Renunciation

Dream-Love that we loved so! Love that we found
    Beside a shadowed stream:
Pass in the Night: For we who kissed your hair
    Follow a greater dream.

Dream-eyes that mirrored ours: Close petal
    Tender, with silent tears:
We may not steal the sunshine from your depths
    To light the lowering years.

Dream-lips we never kissed! . . . Nay, night's gone by—
    By wind and wave strong-borne
Cry wild across the mountains and the deeps
    The Trumpets of the Morn.

Her Birthday

Heart's gentleness and quiet dignity
  Have been on you bestowed in great largesse,
  With sadness, and mute Hope's nobility,
Soft laughter, chivalry, and tenderness.

Pass on, from height to height and strength to
    strength,
  Until that sacred hour, for which you strove,
  When, all ill past, you shall attain at length
Heart's Garden, pleasaunce of a deathless love!

This day stands as a lonely monument
  That marks the sunset on a faded age:
  A summit gained – but yet inapparent,
Unsensed: for calm is Life's high tutelage,

  And you, unknowing and unsentiment,
Shall come in this wise to your heritage.

Spartacus

O thou who lived for Freedom when the Night
  Had hardly yet begun: when light light
Blinded the eyes of men and dawntime seemed
  So far and faint, – a foolish dream half-dreamed!

Through the blind drift of days and ways forgot
   Thy name, thy purpose: these have faded not!
From out the darkling heavens of misty Time
   Clear is thy light, and like the Ocean's chime
Thy voice. Yea, clear as when unflinchingly
   Thou ledst the hordes of helotry to die
And fell in glorious fight, nor knew the day
   The creaking crosses fringed the Appian Way—

Sport of the winds, O ashes of the Strong!
   But down the aeons roars the helots song
Calling to battle. Long as on the shore
   The washing tides shall crumble cliff and nore
Remembered shalt thou be who dauntless gave
   Unto the world the lordship of the slave!

A Last Nightfall

Swiftly,
Out of the mystery of waters,
The spuming night-tide
Climbs;
Abruptly,
Far in the brown dusk-stillness
A village night-bell
Chimes;
Right
Overhead, through Heav'n's rent bars,
Night,
Like a bellying beast,
Hangs,
Fanged with stars.

Here,
Where the grey rocks shake,
And the homing breakers
Beat,
Fear
Hath fled before Death
And our salt-sad kisses,
Sweet!
Nigh
Is the tide, and Life's light
Put by:
As a candle quenched,
A ghost
Lost in the night.

Lost

In wonderment God stood amidst the throng
    Gathered on London's fringe this cold, wet night,
And listened, rapt, to its strange, woeful song,
    And passionate speech of one whose face shone bright

With rain and some soft inner light. The crowd
    Compelled to earn night's rest in this sad way
Saw not God's aged form, as, with head bow'd
    He heard sweet talk of love, of souls astray . . .

Soft-voiced, God asked, 'Whose message bring you,
    Sir?'
    When, waifs all fled, these two stood there alone.
'Whose message, Friend? Why,' cried the minister,
    'The Christ's!' And God said, 'Who is Christ?'

And blown
About the streets that night the voice of One
Cried terribly, 'My Son! . . . My only Son!'

Vignette

The land was drowned in drowsy scent, I mind,
Of clover, that last evening, and the hedge
Drooped in the glare: The river's eddies spun
And slept amidst the sedge.

Nothing we said, for we had naught to say:
Quietly you wept: the curlews called: the brown
Slow night came on: I stood with tearless eyes
And watched the sun go down.

Nostalgia
A Parody

Hot lemonade and sweaty beer!
In Cairo it's damned hot this year,
And mosquitoes whine around,
Big as beetles, I'll be bound,
Jabbing with great proboscides
In a manner which indeed is
Jolly rough on that poor blighter
Who's the present sweating writer.—
What would I give to leave this hell
For Camberwell, for Camberwell.

Oh, ginger-pop upon the lawn,
Oh, glistening sandwiches of brawn!
And empty bottles on the grass,
And boards that warn all who trespass—
And sense the fragrance sweet and still
From Sydenham to Dogkennel Hill,
(Though some prefer the smell, I ween
Of fish they fry at Camberwell Green!)

Oh, little flakes of sun that through
The leaves fall upon you and you;
The bits of paper round about,
Old Uncle's venerable gout,
And kiddies whooping down the slope
Half-strangled in their skipping-rope . . .

Purring policemen come and go
(Go and come, for all I know),
Mighty friends of me and you,
Sterterous, beauteous, blond and blue—
Oh, how sweet they are!
And then, see the view of stout Big Ben,
Blazing Thames and Wormwood Scrubbs,
Southwark's fair and stately pubs,—
And hear the silly little breeze
Chuckling in between the trees!

And now a great fat motor-bus,
Too feeble to run over us,
(And swearing in a way that you
Would never dream a bus would do)
Puffs by up the long, baking hill,
Then tops the rise, grunts on until,
Enveloped in a writhing haze
It seeks the cool sweet shady ways
That pass through glade and dene and dell,
To Ruskin's home – and Camberwell!

A Song of Limbo

Come back, the days that are dead
  Come back, the chances we missed
Come back, the loves that we lost
  Come back, the lips that we kissed

Come back, the wines that were good
  Come back, the friends who were strong
Come back, the music that beat as a heart
  Come back, the sunshine and song!

Come back! . . . And dreaming we hear—
  Though we know not the whence nor the whither—
Call as they called of old—
  Fortissimo, *Come hither*!

Rupert Brooke

Far-seem beyond the hard Euboean strand,
  A broken pearl upon the pulseless seas,
Sleeps Scyros, Lycomedes' sea-swept land,
  Where Pyrrhus first looked o'er the Sporades.

And one lies there who lived, in greyer days,
  His brief, love-dowered world in laughing-wise;
Who garnered wisdom through Youth's wilder ways
  And sought the truth in all his Paradise.

And when the spray-washed sun to Rome imparts
  A glamour rich as of her lordlier days,
The West Wind climbs the dusk: stands high; departs
  Full nightward, there to hush the Scyrote bays

With aerial joyance of the Heart of Hearts,
  And gold-throat music of mute Adonais.

Dawn Death

Even as a whimpering child,
  Newborn,
Frets at the gates of Life,
  (Dear, is it morn?)

So all night long the rain,
  In sleep,
Hath grieved the tired hours.
  I heard you weep.

Low, that I might not hear,
  Yet knew
Your head bowed in the gloom.
  (Or dreamt it you.)

That I may sleep again
  Stoop low:
And if you are not he,
  I will not know.

I had not thought your eyes
  So clear,

Nor dreamt your arms again
   Around me, dear.

Hark to the fairy bells,
   Forlorn,
Ring in the garden aisles.
   (Dear, is it morn?)

Christ

They shew the tourist now the crumbling hall
   Whence Christ was led:
 They point each resting-place
Whereon he sat and wept and gabbled prayers
Unto his childish God. Throughout a street
Are little tablets set against each wall:
   'Here Christ broke bread',
   'Here halted He a space',
'Here stood to jeer His Judges and betrayers',
'Here Jesus bathed His head . . . His hands . . . His
   feet.'

Dim legends blown down dim and blinded years!
   O starved and pallid Soul
 They've set to walk the road to Calvary
And fear its own grey shadows and its end—
Darkness and doubt and pain and stinging death!. . .
Not thus our comrade passed. The salt, slow tears
   Shed as the vespers toll
   At Christmastide, are tribute unto He
Who loved the People, was the harlot's friend,
And blessed a robber with his dying breath.

Song

That you will never find,
   Never again;
Not though you brave the snarling wind
   And the sleeting winter's rain,
Not though you storm the utmost heights
   And the reeling crags attain
That you will never find,
   Never again.

Not though a way you blaze
   In storm and pain;
Though your hate a throne may raze
   And fire the hearts of men,
Though the peoples follow your light
   And see as the blind are fain:
That you will never find,
   Never again.

For that's gone by and said,
   And the years arraign
The first sweet kiss of the first sweet maid
   And the cadenced words' refrain
As a path to a gate that is lost,
   In a night that is blurred in rain:
And the path you will never find,
   Never again.

Lenin: 1919

'His shadow lies on Europe!' – (Whisper low!)
'Turning the day to blackest night below,
A shadow whereneath hell-fires belch and glow:
   The shadow of a sword.'

Your shadow, little man. I see your eyes,
Steadfast and cold, unutterably wise,
Look westward where the ling'ring sunset dies
   By ridge and ford.

I hear your voice – A prayer or a command?—
Wild helot-laughter fills a darkened land,
And old dreams die, and princes outcast stand
   Disrobed, abhorred.

You move, and all the nations of the Earth,
Shuddering in pangs of agonising birth,
Cry to the skies through wrack of doom and dearth
   'How long, O Lord?'

How long? The years are sun-motes in your sight:
   '*It comes.*' And still by daylight and by night
Hangs sky-obscuring, making faint the light,
   The shadow of a sword.

The Unbeloved

Oh, happy we who find not what we seek!
   True love lies in the seeking! We have found
In place of love immortal things which speak
   Never of love, but love's exquisite sound,—
The whispering of tall trees beloved of her,—
   And of love's scent – her lilies on the sward.
Things manifold! Love's shadows tenderer
   Even than love's self! In such lies our reward!

For love returned's at best uncertain, frail:
   Love won is weaker far than love despaired,—
True love is power to long, to yearn, to fail!
   But love met half-way's fragile love; —prepared
For wan years of satiety; —to grow stale,
   A draggled thing, most wretched, stripped and bared!

At the Last

When the last hours shall tread with silent feet,
When the last dream-sad eventide shall fade,
When the last night shall veil its starry hosts:
   I shall be unafraid.

For lusts that longed, desires that dreamt not death—
I hear them wail upon the seaward wind:

And Hope that yearned, and Faith that mocked the
    years,
  Have left but ghosts behind.

Oh lips of Love! unkissed and clammy now!
Soiled with the crusted stains of dead desire:
Grey ashes fill the hands that held a heart,
  And embers strew the fire.

The dreams dawn-winged come creeping home at
    dusk,
Peace moans through the rain-brakes of Pain:
Yea, were the gift of God's own splendour wrought
  I should not live again.

Réponse

I

Could I not watch with thee one hour? Alas,
The chalice of fair fruitless hours that pass
Is void: not one remains to thee or me:
  I could not watch with thee.

II

For shall the dusk say what the day-break sighs?
Or noontide whisper what the stardawn cries?
Oh, heart, hear thou night's dirge: 'It cannot be':
  I could not watch with thee.

III

Beloved, hope there is none of recall;
The sea's heart throbs not of our love, and all
Our yesteryears drift deathward wearily:
　　I could not watch with thee.

IV

Though day smote gold the grey, foam-feathered
　　brine,
Though laughing spray-buds sped that hour of thine
Swift shoreward down the dawn in seeking me,
　　I could not watch with thee.

V

O mutual loves, O loves unpassionate!
Undying loves, love unreciprocate!
Unshaken by heart's mutability:
　　I could not watch with thee.

VI

And our love's voices? – what of these remain?
The sad, sweet thunder of the sea's slow rain—
And lisp of snow-flakes in a broken tree:
　　I could not watch with thee.

VII

Were then the hills stirred, shaken with our love?
When died my heart, was slain the sun's above?
Not so, for these were strong – O little we!
　　I could not watch with thee.

VIII

O sky and wind-wan waves! Dawns fleet and fair!
(To me were these not what to thee they were?)
O lost loves well-beloved and lost, set free:
    I could not watch with thee.

IX

Shall not thine hour suffice, O saddened one?
Give up: shake off thy burden: yield, have done
Strive thou no more to me-ward o'er the sea:
    I may not watch with thee.

Peace
To the Irene of Kramelis

I sought your face where mountains blind the skies
    White crag on ageless hill:
I found a slavering beast amidst the snows
    Crouching above its kill.

I sought your kiss upon the lips of Love,
    Your clasp within Love's hands:
I left drugged lust where Shame sits spectre-wise
    And Sorrow weeping stands.

I sought at dusk where years as idols sat
    Dreaming, and ghost-winds blew:
And Death came forth to guide my falt'ring feet,
    Unveiled, and lo! 'twas you.

The Communards of Paris

We shall not grieve, O splendid hearts of old!
When find we that for which ye dearly sought:
We labour in the Dawn; in blackest Night:
For this same Day full gloriously ye wrought.

From your red graves of treachery and woe
We hear the battle-song that stirred ye on:
And scaling the last barricade well know
Yours is the glory, Pioneers of Dawn!

The Romanticist

They took the thing I love
Horror and shuddering shame:
Twisted the flesh in rotting agonies,
Spattered in filth the mouth
    that called my name—
(Was not the soul the same?)
Still through the tattered garments
    of the earth
I saw her heart stand pure and clean
    and white:
Yet turned and fled, and hiding
    Far away,
Wept through the moaning night.

On the Murder of Karl Liebknecht and Rosa Luxembourg

They gathered a Hundred Splendid Souls,
The Gods of the Heart's Day-Dreams,
And pointed adown the Verge of Space:
'See! Where yon Planet gleams!
Go down to the struggling Sons of Men,
And teach Them all Ye know,
And guide their Feet to the only Path
From the surging Pit below.'

Each Splendid Soul with a gladsome Heart
To its mighty Task went forth:
Some to the East, and Some to the West,
And Some to the Snow-capped North,
And Some where the luscious Southern Flowers
Are kissed by the burning Sun,
And Some where the Plains in the Gloaming lie,
And Some where the Morn is dun.

And Two of the Hundred Splendid Souls
Went back but Yester-Eve:
The Road well-paved, the Beacon lit—
Comrades, ye need not grieve!
For the Ninety-and Eight shall marshall the Host
Ere the Night-Watch-Fires low burn,
And the longed-for Dawn shall glint our Spears,
And the Splendid Two return!

When God Died

God died one morn
As dawn sprang red,
And the sun arose
With flame-crowned head,
Nor aught of all its glory shed
Nor seemed to know
That God was dead.

And Earth glowed to the light
That dawn's pale fingers led
By rivulet and rill,
By curtain-shadowed bed,
By whitening seas whence night-spume fled:
Nor any gladness lost
Though God was dead.

A lark sang clear
Against the sky
Of the gracious things
That would never die,
Being born of song and Eternity,
Fashioned of no sick dreams
Nor sprung of any lie.

In olden walks night-chilled
The sea-breeze shook and said:
'Oh; bloom, ye flowers of dawn!
Of skies and waters fed:
For Time and Fate are meetly wed,

And winters come no more
Now God is dead.'

And the Cities' clamour rose,
And men for love and bread
Strove in the heats of day,
Strove until overhead
The arc-glares' light was sickly shed:
Nor any dreamt or knew
That God was dead.

But the forests whispered
Each eventide
And called by cliffs
Where the night-waves ride
With a star for lamp—
With a star for lamp and guide:
'The world is better
Since God has died.'

Nox Noctes

Philosophies and sad, hard hopes, and songs
Bitter of tears, of winds that weep and strive,
That promise slays not; nay, but sink and pass
In joy of being alive.

In warm, sweet dreams that in those stilly hours
Heart unto heart, we'll watch the firelight's glow
Die out; hear the night-wind a-whisper in the trees;
See the globed moon ride low

Above quiet fields of snaken silver grain;
Whilst, tide-travailled, the rock-barred, distant sea
Makes in a litany of beating surf,
A song for you and me . . .

Heart unto heart, lips prest on quivering lips:
The dreamer's dreams fulfilled, wrought, fashioned
    fair,
And lo! about us like the scents of Spring
The fragrance of your hair.

A Communist's Credo

Yesterday, yours; *Today* – it is a sea
  Where writhe and foam the tides of storm
    And shine
Mist-spume o'erhung; but in the still, stark
    Hours
Reading the stars, I know *Tomorrow* mine!

Dead Love

We part not, my dear and I
With bitter word Nor bitter sigh,
Only in heartache and amaze
Beneath th' untinted sky

Neither with tears not bitter grief;
At this, the falling of the leaf,

When all the purple hills ablaze
Have fired the vales:

Neither with strength nor weakness torn,
Neither in love's wild noon nor morn,
Neither in dark nor sunny days—
Only with wings a little shorn.

For when I looked within your eyes
(Once stranger than the strangest skies)
Far down through all the rayless ways
I came where your soul lies;

Which, facing me from that still goal,
Knew neither fear, nor joy, nor dole,
Only, as when the atheist prays,
Looked strange, a stranger-soul.

And gazing, saw your vision fill:
(What horror held mine eyes?) . . . And still
The world goes on; the sunlight plays
Across the bracken on the hill.

Had we but loved so that the fire
Our passion burned from out desire
Had made the shuddering ages' gaze
Blanch from the dreaded pyre—

'Some little might be left me yet,
Some little, when the dark days set
To bring me where the breaker sprays
And sun and sea forget.'

But it was otherwise, for me—
We sought to solve Love's mystery
And 'scape the fire; with reason raze
The platform of Eternity.

And now, a little scorched, we stand,
Explorers back from out that land.
Behind us gather dusks of days
Long gone; you stretch your hand.

Not unto me – but where the dawn
Will tinge the eastern roses blown
When fringed and far, the daylight strays
On pallid hedge and lawn . . .

May you find comfort there, not grief!
Though stray and faded by Love's leaf
Yet the wild purple hills ablaze
Fire the dark valleys far beneath.

Verses towards 'Knowles' Last Watch'

All day we watched from the coppice,
From the hillside ledge all day;
Above, the sky was torture-barred
And the rose-beds pallid lay.

Pallid with little sunshine,
For they are flowers o' the sun,
And droop in the weather-darkness
And weep when day is done—

But the honeysuckle' tendrils
Reached through the broken fence,
And dew-wet sprayed in the greyness
Remembered incense:

Pungent and strange and sweet,
Culled from the Soul of Earth,
Smells of the passing seasons,
Ephemereal change and dearth[*sic*].

So. And your thoughts then, Norla?
Nay, but none shall say;
Not even I who loved you,
Who knew each path and way

Of your soul; who held your heart in my hand
Knew every wave and beat,
Whose eyes grew dim at your voice-sound,
At the tread of your coming feet;

Who had looked, hands on your shoulders
(Smooth and straight and white,
Head like a drooping lily's head,
Hair red-gold in the light)

Under your long, curled lashes
That I thought must surely make
With weight of their God-wrought fairness
Thin cheeks and white brow ache.

Looked in the wide grey depths, and saw
Love that left me afraid . . .
Lest I lose it – as lose I did – and still
I mind the words you said:

(But that was long before)
'Love . . . there are many like me,
Strewn as stars on the night's-edge,
Thick as waves of the sea.'

'And suns mate not with little stars
(Lest their lights grow dim),
Nor tides with waves; and I would not have
Them say *She made of him*

Like to herself, nothing and naught.
She was our friend!' For so
Will the fearful and hating seeing you say
With truth . . . These things I know.

'Having nothing to give you, dear,
But a love unloved and unsought;
Soiled with the touch of brutish hands,
Squandered, pandered, bought . . .'

'Love, look not at me now . . .' Then you wept,
And the sun went down,
And the languid gloaming wrapped the moors
In a mantle grey and brown—

Dimming the sunset's edge in the bay;
And the ships on the far sky-line
Red-gold blurred into a waste of spray,
A glimmering lake of wine . . .

And a reef of stars to the Eastwards
Filtered a twinkling glow;
And the firwoods massed and gathered
And crept on the plains below

As a bellying beast. Against the light
Your face was wan and dim
And once you whispered 'Oh God! Oh God!
Say not that I loved not him!' . . .

Then I caught your hand in the chilling dusk
(The night-wind keened like a knife)
And kissed your tears, and loved them away
That hour – O heart of Life!—

But we loved! The days that sprang in its wake
Were stolen sweets of God
When we climb Love's silvern-sunshine hill
By ways and paths untrod.

Feet and mind and soul – burned one
Till the shivering sky
In cloud-wrack cowered from our passion's breath
(Three weeks that fleeted by),

Dream-memories of days that were dreams.
Yet even their shadows thrill . . .
The braes that were bracken-brindled
And the hollow in the hill:

That held as a jewel in its breast
The dim-reflecting lake;
Fringed with a golden thicket
A summer-flower'd broom-brake . . .

Where we sat in freshening mornings,
Or dived in the still water,
Or watched the ripples circle
A thrown stone's languid stir.

These I remember always:
Your silvern laughter's sound;
Your wet hair about your shoulders,
Astray, wind-whipp'd, unbound.

Breaths of being and doing:
Your kiss, a chord of your song;
The times when you poised to swim
And the sun came full and strong,

On your face, as you stood there, slim and straight,
Gracious and fair, and sweet,
A lily crowned with a crown of gold.
(The water lapped to your feet.)

To Billie on her Birthday

To whom is this day consecrate?—
Red-circled in the Book of Fate
In capitals immaculate?—
 To Billie!

Who is most wise and kind and sweet,
Who brings mankind about her feet—
Kneeling in adoration meet?—
 Why Billie!

Who feeds the hungry, tends the lame,
In storm and sunshine is the same?—
The wandering winds breathe but one name—
 'It's Billie!'

Who makes one glad to be her friend?—
Knowing whate'er the years may send
She'll stand and greet one at the end?—
 Why Billie!

To whom do we wish gracious days,
Flower-garlanded as summer ways,
And love, and joy, and peace, and praise?—
    To Billie!

Dust

I have drunk deeply of the ancient wine,
    Wandered a summer in the Sumer [*sic*] land,
Heard in the dusk the bells of Cretan kine
    And maidens' song across the Cnossan strand,
Seen, where the grotesque temples groped to God,
    The sculptor-scribe who carved the Runic plan
Of sunds and sames and serpents intertrod,
    On terraces of Toltec Yucatan.

I hear new voices down the English morn,
And alien laughter by the lakeland meres,
And altars reared to faiths undreamt, unborn,
    Far in the seed-time of the sleeping years,—

I see the Christ, an outcast, stand, forlorn,
    A dream, a tale, a wonderment of tears.

Song of a Going Forth
Written for the Hegira of the Evelpidae

Let us go forth and venture beyond the utmost plain!
Beyond the utmost beetling crag where wilting
    sunsets wane!
Beyond the dark, dour valleys where Silence keeps
    her reign:
  Let us go forth!

Let us go forth and leave behind the dead days and
    the old:
Into the biting gloaming winds, the darkness and the
    cold!
What lies below the starsheen, what do the
    dream-days hold?
  Let us go forth!

IOMEN! Is not Life itself a Caravan that goes
'Twixt Valleys lapt and slumb'rous through Hills of
    Bitter Snows?
Perchance the long, last dusk is near: the end draws
    nigh: who knows?
  Let us go forth!

Morven

Ayont the brig and up the brae
   The lichts glint ane an' twa
On the kin'ly hills o' Morven
   An' the shielin' in the snaw.

Alow oor feet the drifts are blawn,
   But hame's nae far awa',—
Hame in the hills o' Morven
   An' the shielin' in the snaw.

It's weet abüne, an' ower the dykes
   Fu' lood the cushants ca'
By the windy hills o' Morven
   An' the shielin' in the snaw.

The mirky nicht has little licht,
   But losh! the gangin's braw
Ower the auld grey hills o' Morven
   Tae the shielin' in the snaw.

Mony's the weary year sin' laist
   We saw the gloamin fa'
On the God-loved hills o' Morven
   An' the shielin' in the snaw.

Or ken't the canty, couthy fouk
   Wha's gear an' grum is sma';
The fouk wha bide in Morven
   In the shielin's in the snaw.

    Lost far ahint, forever tint,
      The touns an' stour an' a',—
    O! the miles are lichtsome, lassie,
      Tae the shielin' in the snaw!

The Photograph

And here they caught her likeness, quick and fair;
    Eyes that challenge from the sweet-set face
Framed in a cloud of crispt and dead black hair—
    Dear head, there's naught of grace
You have not caught and poised and prisoned there
    In the white neck above the white-fringed lace.

Your soul looks at me here 'neath far, strange skies
How caught they in that bright-lit, garish room
The wash and glide of old tides in your eyes
The play of sunshine and the dusktime's gloom?
The ways of stubborn truths and sad-glad lies,
Roads' ending, and the unclimbed hills that loom?

Subtly behind your head they painted dim
The wall, and set a faint and spraying glow,
As though you stood and breathed some even hymn
Against an olden altar's steadfast glow:
Nay, and what altar? Eros or Ares grim? . . .
(Surely I heard your laughter, dawn-sweet, low?)

Tearless

Just as the sunset gun
Leapt, and the white smoke spun
In the face of the dying sun,
   One came to say

A word that left me stand
Quiet; I moved my hand
To stay the blurring sand,
   Pallid and grey,

Circling; and when I had gone
Into my room alone,
I heard the still dunes moan
   As a hurt child may.

And through the foetid smells,
Where Cairo's night-voice swells,
By harlot's courts and hells
Rang suddenly the bells
   Near where she lay;

In a building cold as a tomb,
With age-old damp and gloom,
Not even an English room
   Wherein she lay;

Hewn like a deep brown square,
Empty and dank and bare,
With a small barred window's stare
    On the place she lay.

(But I hardly supposed she'd care,
Being tired, and resting there,
While about her the sweat-wet hair
    Like a crispt cloak lay.)

The curtains flapped and shook
In the night Nile-wind's rebuke,
And the shadows crept and forsook
    The place she lay

As the golden Eastern moon
Climbed, till its rays fell soon
Like sunlight in a swoon,
    On the place she lay . . .

She'd hated the dark of old:
From dusk I'd known her hold
My hand, till the dawntime called
    The birth of day.

Yet the moving creeper's shade
Wherethrough the moonlight sprayed,
Left her quite unafraid,
    Though all alone she lay:

Being Dead; Song ceased forever.

At Dusk

Within the splendour of that Summer's dawn,
(That wondrous, loved, remember'd still morn)
Could we have seen the rain-swept dusk to come
The weeping woods – Oh, Love! Could we have
  known!

Could we have seen the harvest – lightly sown:
Have seen the dying day – so gladly born:
Have searched each other's souls a little more,
Finding stark truth – Oh, Love! could we have
  known!

Could we have dreamt those gracious roses blown:
(Faded and scentless, petalless, forlorn),
Could we have thought warm hands so soon would
  grow
Weary and limp – Oh, Love! could we have known!

A wind sighs overhead; the old trees moan
With dripping branches; dead years dully scorn
Our little love; and, fruit of all their faith
This bitter dusk – Oh, Love! could we have known!

Rondel

Ere youth be dead we'll ride the road again,
  The winding windward ways of Sunstone men—
Under torn stars, a moon volcano red,
  Clangour of ringing storm on mountain head—
    Ere youth be dead.

Ere youth be dead we'll ship by saffron seas,
  By shoreless sands and lost Symplegades—
Where through in ancient years the Argo sped
  Behind the dove that flashed and dipped and lead—
    Ere youth be dead.

Ere youth be dead we'll dream their love and lust—
  The dead world's springtime in the blowing dust,
The crying voices of the summers fled—
  Drink Lethe's draught and feed on dreams for
    bread
    Ere youth be dead.

La Vie est brève

La vie est brève,—
  Un peu d'éspoir,
Un peu de rêve,—
  Et puis – bonsoir!

La vie est vaine,—
　　Un peu d'amour,
Un peu d'haine,—
　　Et puis, – bonjour!

Life's but seeming—
　　Hopes a few,
Twilight dreaming—
　　And then, adieu!

And vain as Fate,—
　　Oh, love go light
With a little of hate!—
　　And then, good-night!

On a Vernacular Society

The barbarians sat amidst the hills of Rome,
Sated with almonds and red Tuscan wine,
Their togas girt about their shaven legs,
Their clipt hair plastered down with unguents,
And all remembered home:
　　　　　　　　The reeking hut,
The redwood stockade and the auroch's lowe
Through Odin's land. They had forgot the tongue
Brought through the Alpine passes, yet all swore
Such rhyme and radiance Latin never knew.
They swore to this in Latin. And one rose,
An elder warrior, he, from Palatine,
And read a paper on the antique speech.
But few could understand, for much of it
Was in that ancient speech. Yet all did cheer.

Some wept, and soon their Latin quantities
Were blurred with wine and memory, till one
Uprose and swore that he would take the road
Back through the Alpine passes, home again,
If they would follow him. At this there fell
A silence of surprise. They looked askance
One on the other, and with upraised hands
Did indicate that in the speaker's skull
Some evil god disported with his brains.
So night came down. Each called his slave and went
Back through the streets of Rome to perfumed baths
And song and dance.
                  They heard the rain that night
Come sheeting from the north, and in their beds
Did turn in wakeful warmth and sleep again.

WH Smith
Glasgow Central

BOOKS NON SCANNED   11.99

                    TOTAL   11.99
Delta   11.99

Thank you for shopping at
WH Smith

14/02/01 11:46 Tn:217120 Ds:0220 1551 18

Save as you spend with

It's **FREE** to join - ask for more details.

III

Polychromata

He Who Seeks

MANY-COLOURED? It is one of the names of our little Cairo – Polychromata. She has many names, the Gift of the River, and nowhere do her colours flaunt as here, in the Khalig el Masri. Long the evenings I sat and puzzled till I knew the Khalig and Life for one. Key-colour to the kaleidoscope, master-note in the syncopation – it is Quest.

For what? Full bellies and purses, the laughter and love, woman and fame and fantasy . . . All the so-desired apples of that mirage-orchard that flourishes by the Dead Sea . . . Eh? A cynic? God mine! I am only a dragoman!

Happy he who finds not what he seeks – it is the oldest of axioms. But when the desperate seeker himself acknowledges it, he grows the wonder and the legend in the eyes of men. As, indeed, may yet the tale of Andrei Bal'mont and his quest . . .

But of course. And beer – English beer. I think the gods must drink of English beer in Olympus these days, when they have laid aside their bowler hats and the last so-bluff American has made his tip and gone. The little Simon first stocked it here, not by command of the Anglo-Saxon, but at wish of me, Anton Saloney, dragoman, guide, ex-colonel of horse in the army of Deniken, and one-time Professor of English Literature in the Gymnasium of Kazan.

The tale of Andrei? See, I have become a teller of tales – I have invented more so-scandalous royalties than ever the dynastic tables held, I had a madam-tourist in the tears this morning when I told of the suicide of Rameses II from the top of Kheops' Pyramid, because of the false love who jilted him – yet this tale of Andrei . . . I have loved and hated it, as must all men, felt the ache of it and the beauty of it. Yet it needs some subtle tale-smith as your sweet Morris to tell it. Indeed, I think the little Andrei himself was of the Hollow Land, a faery-knight and a faery-saint. . . .

Yet perhaps he was a Russian of the Russians, the Slav eternal. Perhaps he was Man himself.

Look, my friend, I once knew and talked with this Andrei, yet already to me he is half a myth, a figure on that painted gauze of legend that covers the face of the East. How shall I make him live in English eyes – he and his tale and his quest?

II

I met him twice in life. The first time was at Perekop, on the bridge of the Crimea, twenty-four hours before the Tovarishii stormed our lines and littered the seas with the wreckage of our armies. He was a captain, holding an outpost on the marshes, and I came on him the last inspection I made. He was alone, holding the outpost, for his men had deserted; he marched on the sentry-beat, rifle slung in his shoulders, head bare to the cutting wind, thoughts far in dreams . . . Long I remembered him.

He was a youth, a student, with the pale, dark-framed face of the Little Russian. He had come south to fight the Red Terror, even as thousands beyond Perekop had come south with the Sovyeti to fight the White Reaction. He was lighter of heart than I ever knew soldier in the shadow of defeat.

'The world is wide, and there are other dreams,' he said.

I waved him good-bye and went back to my squadron. In twenty-four hours I was riding to the coast and safety on a French destroyer. Of Andrei Bal'mont I saw nothing more, nor ever again expected to see.

Yet he also escaped. Somehow he cleared the rout, and drifted south across the bitter Crimea. Late in the hours of the second day he tramped through the whoom of a snow-storm, and so, half blinded, yet still with untroubled heart, came to Yalta and the sting of the sleet-wind from the Black Sea.

It was night-time as he made his way through the deserted streets on the outskirts. The snow whirled thickly about him, and not a light could he see in the harbour, though he heard the beating of the waves. Then he tripped and almost fell over something that lay in his path.

He lighted a match, and looked, and in the momentary radiance of the little flame saw the drift of the snow, saw the white glimmer of a face. Then the match went out. He lighted another, shielding it in his hand against the bitter wind-drive. Then he looked down at the girl who had been asleep in the snow.

She was dark and sweet and fair, even there, in that hour of storm and terror. She had a little hollow in her throat and the light gleamed in it, wonderfully.

'I have been sleeping,' she said, and rubbed her eyes like a child, then smiled up at him so that he loved her.

He bent to help her. 'If you stay here you will die. What is your name?'

'I am Natasha Grodine. I am refugee from the Sovyeti. In the darkness I twisted my ankle and lost my way. But now you have come and I am safe. You are—'

'I am Andrei Bal'mont,' he said, and lifted her in his arms. He could not see her face till her cheek touched his. The snowstorm had cleared, but in the overhead, thin and bitter, high up, screamed *veter*, the wail-wind of the Russian winter. And suddenly, so lost and desolate as they were, their lips met and they kissed each other with great glad-ness. In the night she wound her arms around his neck, and laughed a little, tremulously, pressed against his heart.

And to the little Andrei, bearing her to the sea-shore, it

was as if a light had sprung and flamed in the darkness. All his years he knew had been but prelude to the moment when Natasha's lips touched his. He stopped and bent and spoke in an urgent amazement.

'I love you.'

'My dear,' she whispered, and kissed him again.

III

And all that night, sheltered in a hut on the quays, he knew of her presence near him in the darkness, and the fragrance of her hair. And because of love and Natasha, life was sweet in his mouth. The kisses of love – so sweet they are in the shadow of death! Close-pressed for warmth, they sat and talked of the wonder of this which had come to them. Once Natasha fell asleep, and, hour after hour, unmoving, he sat and held her in his arms. Once she moved and whispered in sleep, and he soothed her as one might the tired child. Then he rose and looked out, and it was morning.

With that dawn they found a refugee ship putting out to Stamboul. Andrei carried Natasha aboard and paid their passage with the last of his French money. The ship was crowded, but shelter they made in the lee of a hatchway, and lay wrapped together in Andrei's greatcoat the while the white coasts rose and fell, and flickered and dimmed through the driving sleet. Misted were the eyes of Natasha looking back at the fading shore. Andrei kissed the little hollow in her throat; it had seemed to him that a man might die to kiss that place. But she turned to him and caught his hands, and suddenly was weeping.

'Oh, Andrei, I'm lost – lost and afraid. Russia I've lost and all its days and sunshine and kindliness and laughter. They seemed everlasting. I never thought they could pass and finish . . . My dear, my dear! Say you will always love me, that it won't pass and fade, that you'll never forget!'

And Andrei kissed her hands, and swore that never

would he cease to love her, that never would his love grow old and tame, that never would he forget the night and snow wherein he had found her. So he swore to keep time and fate and life itself at bay. . . .

Twenty miles out from Yalta, up out of the mists of dawn came a Soviet gunboat, shelling the refugee boat and signalling it to stop. Andrei and six others were in the uniform of the White Raiders. For them there would be none of the mercy.

Then Natasha planned to save them. She flung aside the coat of Andrei, and beckoned to the far side of the refugee boat as it slowed down. The soldiers must go over the side of the ship, and hide in the water till the search by the Tovarishii was over. When the Red sailors had gone, they could climb aboard again.

Andrei was last to slide down the rope to the buoys. To these the others already clung in the shadow of the ship. Death to remain aboard – death perhaps in the freezing waters. And then for a moment, it mattered nothing, for in that moment Natasha, as he clung there, bent and kissed him, and her lips were salt with tears . . .

Paddling and freezing in the lee of the refugee boat, Andrei heard a sudden shouting and confusion. Then one of the others by his side cried out and gestured. The scream of shell-fire woke the sea. From the west, dimly, he saw a great French cruiser steaming out of the sleet-storm to engage the gunboat.

'Look – the ship!' cried one of the men.

Andrei turned his head and also cried out. They had drifted many feet from the refugee boat, and, as they looked, it forged away with beating screw into the bank of fog that had crept out all morning from the coast. Into the same bank with guns flashing red went the cruiser half a mile to the left.

For a little they swam and paddled and shouted, deserted in that suddenly vacant sea, under the sting of the sleet.

Then one cried out and sank, and two others drifted away into the fog. Inside that fog the gun-fire had clamoured for a little, then ceased. Andrei and his two soldiers tied themselves upon their buoys and lashed the buoys together . . . It seemed to Andrei that only a moment had passed when, looking at the two beside him, he saw that they were dead.

Already, in the icy water, his own legs and the lower half of his body had grown numb. Then a strange warmth surged slowly, steadily, up through his frozen body, and when it came to his heart he knew he would be dead. He began to paddle again, desperately. He cried out, and sang, and shouted, to stay the menace creeping upon him from the waters. And then he was suddenly tired, so tired, and sleep more desirable than ever life had been. He ceased to struggle, and the grey waste of beaten water blurred in his eyes. Night.

And then a great light awoke on the sea and beckoned and beckoned. He knew it and rose and struggled again and cried 'Natasha!'

IV

He was picked up by an oil-carrier and taken to Stamboul. There, in hospital, raving, for two months he lay, and at the end of that time, weak and a pauper, came back again, with the Spring come, to the world of men and the memory of Natasha's lips.

But he came not back the same Andrei, I think. He had wandered in mist and dreams for many days. He came out to a world that had dimmed and blurred at the edges. One memory, one hunger of desire alone possessed him. So clear was that memory, clear and unforgotten his oath as he had held Natasha's hands. 'Always will I love you. Never shall I forget.'

You see him, dreamer and saint as I think he was, he who

had tasted of love and seen the so-awesome tenderness no man may ever awaken twice in the eyes of a woman. He set out to seek Natasha as once men went forth to seek the Holy Grail. Found – God mine! He would have peace, would kneel at Natasha's feet and lay his head in her hands, and sleep and sleep till the world died . . .

He set out to search in the nameless flotsam-drift heaped on the Golden Horn with the destruction of the last White Raid. He tramped from consulate to consulate, from shipping office to shipping office, through a drift and tangle of rumour and legend. For we of the last White Raid were already legendary. Now he would glimpse at some street-crossing men whom he had once known; one time he saw his own brother, an officer of the Imperial Army, selling fruit outside the Mosque Sophia. And to Andrei these men – even his own brother – were but the faintest shadows. Yet half-remembered faces rising up out of the street throngs would set his mind to ache and ache, seeking names and memories and associations. Had they known Natasha?

Sometimes, on gutter-ledge or wharf, he would fall asleep – for he was still the sick man – or into long trances when he sat unsleeping, yet unthinking, the mind fainting and fainting within him, crying 'Cease! Come and sleep!' And from such moments he would rouse with a passion of anger at himself, because of that memory of Natasha's face, her eyes so pitifully misted. . . .

But neither of her nor of the refugee ship in which they had sailed from Yalta could he find any trace. He had never known the name of the ship nor the name of its captain.

Yet day after day, working here and there for bread, sleeping only when the exhaustion came on him, he tramped the quays of the Golden Horn. In those miles of jetties his so intent white face must have become familiar. I think the story of his quest long followed after him in rumour and surmise. Because of that rumour, because of the ache of sympathy which every lost lover may stir, he was met with unbelievable kindness – that amazing kindliness of the kennels. He was helped by the stray and the waif with whom he would never have associated the pity of the Christ.

And one morning he awoke to find his spirit had fought his body and triumphed, and the health was returning to him again.

Out of the delirium into monomania? So, perhaps. But I think his face grew the more gentle, and the hunger went from his eyes, and there the dreams came back. Yet was he the passionate pilgrim, with his ache of quest. But all the winds and dawns and colours of life were his again, interpreting that ache even as they accentuated it.

And then, late one evening, when he stood on a quay watching a ship unload, a man cried out at sight of him, and swore in the Russian. In the smoke-blur that was Andrei's memory flamed the remembrance. The man was the captain of the refugee ship.

He stared and stood, and grew white, thinking Andrei a ghost. Then he talked. The refugee ship had left the swimmers and made its escape that it might not be blown out of the waters in the fight between the Soviet gunboat and the French cruiser. When presently the two warships, still shelling, had passed into the haze on the Crimean coast, the refugee ship lowered its boats and sought in the fog for the swimmers. But they were nowhere to be found.

'Natasha Grodine? I remember her; you carried her aboard at Yalta. After we came to Stamboul I heard she joined the ship of refugees that sailed to Jaffa, to the Russian colony in Palestine.'

v

He was the pauper, as I have said. But a Greek boat of the coasts took him for deckhand, and on that boat he drifted southwards, down the painted coast of the Levant, so magical in summer days, more magical still at night when the masts dipped against the stars and the forecastle tuned its guitars. He learned the ways of a ship and the lives and beliefs of the men who with him worked, and he entered their poor, stupid dreams, and forgave those dreamers of their kind who had driven him from Russia. Food was bad, and the captain the bully, but when the ship stagnated in semi-mutiny it was Andrei who made the peace and brought concord, and lured the ship south, ever in pursuit of his tireless quest.

So, in the midsummer, they came to Jaffa, and Andrei bade good-bye to the Greeks. They wept at parting with him, and cried farewells for long as he waved from the shore. Then he made his way to the shipping companies and set his enquiries afoot. A day later, when he came back to the quays, the Greek ship had gone.

He found no Russian in the town, but instead street-fighting between the so-brave Arabs and the immigrant Jews. For a day, stayed strangely by memory of Natasha, he forwent his quest and helped in the streets, carrying the wounded to safety, walking through rifle-fire unscathed and unafraid.

Then at length, from the Greek consul, he learned that six months before a party of the Russians had indeed come to Jaffa. But they had gone up to settle in Jerusalem, to live by the tourist trade.

So Andrei took the road to the north, working his way across the dusty tundras, through the brown mud villages, up to the green foothills. A week he stayed to help in the harvest of an orange grove, then set out again. And one nightfall, outside a convent of the Irish nuns, where he sat drinking milk and eating bread and goat cheese, he looked up and saw the black bulking of the mountains of Moab.

Because he never begged for money, but only food in return for work, he was a pauper as on the day when he left the Golden Horn in the Greek coaster. But now the mountains, in a moment of weakness, awed him. He went down to the railway, waited for another evening to come, climbed aboard a covered truck, and in the morning found himself in Jerusalem, in a land of greenery and sudden rain.

He went up to the city in that rain, with beating hope in his heart that here certainly was his quest to end. Yet where to begin?

Then, as he stood mazed in the streets of English Jerusalem, came that adventure that was yet to tell no tale of his hidden self to Andrei's heart. For he saw a girl go by – a white girl in the brown-skinned throngs. And at sight of her he stood suddenly sick at heart.

Then he awoke and cried out, and turned and ran down the street in the direction she had gone. But the crowds had swallowed her.

All that day, in a mad passion of fear and the remorse, he hunted the streets and stews of Jerusalem . . .

VI

He knelt, wearied, yet finding a little peace, in the Church of the Holy Sepulchre, in that little room where legend tells was the Christ laid when brought from the cross. Then he went out on the steps of the church and so again came face to face with the girl whom he had thought Natasha.

And it was not Natasha.

She drew aside, then stared at his white face, faltering a query in words which stayed him. For she spoke in the Russian, with just such voice as Natasha herself.

'I am not ill,' he answered, 'only I thought you one for whom I search. My name is Andrei Bal'mont, and I was of Deniken's raid. Have you ever heard of a Crimean refugee, a girl Natasha Grodine?'

At that she gave a cry, and caught his hands, and flushed and paled. 'Andrei Bal'mont! But I have heard of you. Oh, I have heard of you. I knew your dear Natasha in Stamboul and loved her. You are the captain who saved her in Yalta, and hid in the sea from the Soviet gunboat—'

'She is here – in Jerusalem?'

'But no – she went to Alexandria with an uncle she found in Stamboul . . . Andrei Bal'mont – oh, I have heard of you. Natasha remembers. She does not believe you dead . . .'

But she knew nothing of Natasha's address in Alexandria.

'Stay with us here, us Russians. We will help you, though we are so poor. Stay with us and write letters to Alexandria. There is a Colonel Saloney in Alexandria, he made the Refugee Committee, and may know where your Natasha is.'

He bent and kissed her hands. 'I cannot stay a day, little sister. For Natasha remembers and I remember.'

Then she wept a little, I think because of his youth and his dark saint's face. But he went out through the rain, up the dark alleys, and on the outskirts of Jerusalem turned south again.

VII

And of all that Odyssey that finally led him to Egypt I know only in outline – in the outline and surmise. Westwards and southwards he went, crossing the mountains of Moab on foot that second time, holding south by the jungle swamps of Ludd and so on and on, as the summer waxed, to the fringe of the desert. And, as he went, and the days passed into weeks and so to months, ever clear and shining, a pillar of light by night and a pillar of smoke by day, led his quest.

And he learned to know the stars of the beggar's night, and thirst and hunger and the sleep of exhaustion. Sunsets he would watch the Evening Star come out, in mornings would see it lead the sunrise up over the sands. He came to look for it as one looks for the face of a friend – the star that crowned his quest and led his feet.

On the wild highroads of Palestine and Transjordania none sought to harm him. He tramped them, a man invisibly shielded and guarded. Near Amman he joined a camel train, and went south and east, into the desert, to some Arab city of the wastes. From there he struck out north-west again, and, at the long length, five months after leaving Jerusalem, came to Kantara on the Suez. There, for a little, he was stayed, and, as on the Golden Horn, searched from ship to ship for work. The luck favoured him again, for on the third day he was taken on as stoker of a boat going to Alexandria.

He landed at Alexandria in November. No Russian consulate was left, nor Refugees' Committee any longer, so from house to house his searchings began anew. At night he slept in the kennels of the poor, for bread worked at the wharves an hour each day, unloading coal. At these wharves he heard by chance of me, 'English' Saloney, the hotel guide, and remembered the name the girl in Jerusalem had mentioned.

Brown and sinewy, desert-Arab in speech and appearance, I yet knew him on the instant that evening I found him awaiting me on the hotel steps. I took him to my room, gave him the food and clothes, and sat and listened to him and all the story of his quest from far-off Yalta.

'Grodine?' I said, 'I remember the name. And the old Committee records contain the address of every White Russian in Egypt. Your quest is ended, my friend.'

VIII

We looked up the books, and there was the entry: 'Lef Ilyavetch Grodine and niece Natasha, 12, Harun-Badrawi, Khalig-el-Masri, Le Caire.' Andrei Bal'mont stared at it as though it had been the writing of the Belshazzar's feast, then kissed me, and was suddenly gone from the room. I ran after him.

'But you will need money – I will lend you—'
'Little friend, leave me my last road.'
So he waved and went, and I never saw him again.

IX

Now has my story been as Andrei himself told it me. But hereafter is only the dream I built on the so few facts I sought out later that year. One man there was who saw him enter Cairo in the sunset, one who saw him pass over the Bulaq Bridge. And there was Aida ed-Dowlah, the cripple, who squatted in the shadow of a garden wall in the Khalig . . .

But of that tramp from Alexandria to the little Cairo and its Khalig of many colours – how shall we guess? Certain at last, at last on his final road, he went eastwards. But as he walked the night ways he saw with an ache and an amazement the stars less bright than of yore. And his feet were heavier, and the smell of the wind stung him not at all . . .

It was sunset when he came to Cairo and sought his way to the Khalig-el-Masri, through the throngs of Polychromata. Up there, perhaps, beyond Abbassieh, were the Red Hills crowned in fire, and he stopped and looked at them and looked back across all the days and roads he had traversed. And suddenly his eyes were blind with tears.

Sunset over Cairo . . .

Then, at length, out beyond the Khalig's colour and clamour, he came to the garden wall of a house, and looked, and suddenly stood still. For there, in the gloaming lowe of the garden, no dream, but sweet and real, stood Natasha herself, more dear and desirable than in all his memories.

He clenched his hands and choked back the cry that quivered up into his throat. He stood suddenly sick at heart.

Knowing nothing of his nearness, white and dim in the

fading light, she stretched out her hands, and he heard the sound of her tears, heard her whisper to the sunset his name . . .

Night and dreams and quest, Natasha herself – or a weeping girl in a garden?

He stood heart-wrung, his lips half-opened to call. Then, overhead, faintly, came out the Evening Star.

X

Half an hour afterwards, out from Cairo over the Bulaq Bridge, to the night and the high road and the sting of the wind, Andrei Bal'mont tramped forth again on his quest.

The Epic

I

BUT YOU ARE of the moderns, my friend, and therefore primitive. In the squatting-places of the dawn-men also was the telling the story. They honoured the stylist long before there was the written style. Art was of art, not of life. But to me the tale without theme, the poem without purpose – it is salt without meat. The theme is the man . . . God mine, as Connan proved!

Here, under the night-sky, above the Khalig, where once Connan sat and planned to snare the immortals – who may believe that all the tales are told? Our Cairo – she pens such plot and theme through every hour as makes of all recorded tale a ghostly script, a story writ in water.

Mother of aliens, alien to us all! Yet what city is like to her? In the scents and smells of her, her days and nights, colours and chance voices there are which wring the heart. Unreasonably. Unforgettably. Her very street-names cry in our ears like bugles: Ismailia, El Musky, El Manakh, Maghrabi, Sheikh Rihan. They ring beyond their meaning . . .

Surely no language like the English in which to tell the Cairene tale! I, Anton Saloney, who was Professor of the English Literature in Kazan Gymnasium – that before I became colonel in the army of Deniken and was set to wander the world for the good of the proletarii – say it. Only this wayward, featureless, fatherless tongue may sing our *Polis Polychrois*. Not even the Arabic, I think, comes near to the English for him who seeks to interpret Cairo's soul.

As Connan sought to do.

II

He came to Cairo, this Englishman – though I think he had perhaps the Irish blood – John Connan, early one July, when there were but few of the tourists and the khamsin blew every morning as a furnace back-blows upon a stoker. I met him outside the Hotel Continental and me he engaged as guide because I did not call him Mister nor say that I would take him to the place of the genuine antiques.

He was the wit. 'Russian? Good God! Do any survive outside Dostoievsky?' And he regarded me with amaze and sadness, then selected one driver of arabiych from the smellsome horde that surrounded us.

'We will go to the Pyramids,' he said. I assumed the surprise.

'Do they exist outside the little Hichens?'

Thereafter we became the more friendly, though he did not cease to yawn. He was a man whose soul and mind yawned; to me he reminded those bull-men of Assyria whose faces are curved and cruel, yet stamped with an awful weariness in their stone. Then I remembered the frontispiece of a little book.

'You are Connan the poet,' I said. 'I read your poems in Kazan.'

He closed his eyes and mimicked this book-English of mine – for I have never made to learn your speech argots.

'I was Connan the poet. But now I am Connan the lost. I write no poetry, because there is no poetry left in the world. I know, for I have heard men screaming on wire entanglements, and known a woman who sold her body and taunted the buyer.'

'These things have been,' I said. 'Always they have been. They are old as the world is old.'

'I also am old,' he said, 'and every minute I listen to moralists – especially moralists out of Dostoievsky – I age an hour.'

He followed me amidst the Pyramids, Kheops, Khefren, and Men-kaura, yawning. Only the Sphinx amused him. He said of it disrespectful things in that fashion I cannot imitate, with the humorous no-humour of the Englishman or American, comparing its face to that of a notable pugilist. The next fortnight I took him exploring the Cairene bazaars.

And slowly in that fortnight, in the hours we tramped the Khan Khalil or the Suq el Fahlamin – where the little artists of Europe pursue the local colour and the wood-workers of Egypt pursue their art – I came to know that his indifference was no pose. He was the sick man. Mentally. He wrote no poetry. He never read in books. Some thing in life there had been that blinded the windows of his soul. Perhaps that woman who had taunted the buyer.

Once he had been the poet of note in your English world. But that time was long past. He had written nothing for many years.

You must see him, a bull of a man, this Connan – great, with the black-blue hair and the blue eyes and ruddy face.

His was no bodily sickness. Never I learned the story of the wanderings that had brought him to Cairo or that thing which had shocked the assurance from his heart. Perhaps the woman I imagined was not all to the blame: such the idea that grew on me. Yet I liked him . . .

The English 'like!' So-English a word, the word of 'a-little-cold-love!'

He had been the ruthless individualist, with the little courage and the little splendour, one who could sing of passion but not of pity. And he had found no pity. He might have been a genius but that he was a brute.

III

And then, towards the ending of that fortnight, came the change upon him. He yawned not so much. He walked and looked with a stirred interest, a dawning wonder. All unknown to me, some Cairene colour there had been, piercing his darkness, and he had awakened. In a little while I saw in him grow, dimly at first, the purpose and desire.

For evening after evening he turned, though we were far in El Katal or El Fostat, and led back to this place where I had once brought him – here to this table in front of the café of Simon Papadrapoulnakophitos.

Then I understood that the Sharia Khalig had gripped him also, though I knew not to what ends, and I told him the history of it – this street young in Cairo, this street where once was a canal and may still be seen the tide-markings of the waters. Young though it be, it is somehow Cairo itself, and immemorably ancient, as though the city had awaited this street since the first of its years. If you sit long enough in the Khalig all Cairo will sometime pass by – boyar and beggar, brown man and black, and the men of the shades of white, and all the women of the history of the world, the vile and the fair and the pitiful. And you will hear the drifts of all speech and all passion, all hope and all desire if you sit and listen in the Street of All Egypt, that is older in soul than the Ramesids and so young that it rides the electric tram-car . . .

Perhaps I told him these things, perhaps I told him more. He listened, but the last night of the fortnight it was he who talked. And he invented a little child-game, as I thought it. We would sit and scrutinise the Khalig's throngs, looking for the face that symbolised the Khalig's – the soul of Cairo herself passing by.

'If we sit long enough we may – who knows? – look on Cairo herself. Eh, Colonel? And we'll know her at once. A face will rise from the crowd-drifts and haunt us, and be gone in a minute . . . And all our lives we'll remember that face.'

I took up the jest and played with it, for I also have been the poet. 'Why a woman? And what will she look like?'

'Could the Khalig or Cairo be anything else but a woman? Oh, she'll look a princess and a dream, fair and wild and dark and splendid, robed and crowned, with jewelled feet and jewelled hands. Age-old and very young, evil and dear and desirable, she'll go by . . . With the pride of all her days and all her blood and all the colours of Moquattam.'

But there had come on me the irritation. This bull-man unwearied I found I liked less. The Nietzsche, the fascist, the bolshevik – how may any one of them ever reach to the heart of a maid or a sunset? 'Perhaps like the Christ she will pass poor and despised, with hidden face, without splendour or sin, this Khalig's soul you dream.'

And I can still hear the roar of his bass laughter.

IV

For a week or the so I did not see him at all. He knew his Cairo by then, and could heed to himself. But I had to live and seek other employers.

Just then came another my way, and for some days I forgot Connan. He was the so-rich Egyptian millionaire, my new client, and had made much money putting the cattle into tins in Argentina. Now he had returned and built a great house in Heliopolis, and me he chartered to compile his family-tree. At the end of three days I had proved his descent from Akhnaton, Cleopatra, and de Lesseps, but he was still unsatisfied. Yet he paid well, so I took no ease, but spent another three days creating and allying his ancestors to Moses, Muhammud, and the Mamelukes. When I had run out of ancestors Semitic I remembered Solga Yon, the Tartar who burned the monks in Kiev. He was my own ancestor, but I take no pride in him. So I brought him on a raid into Egypt and married him into the millionaire's family, thereby ridding my family history of unpleasantness and adding fresh valour to the blood that had tinned the good bullocks of Argentina.

This work kept me away from the Khalig, and to the café of the little Simon I came not. But the evening I returned again, there, where you now sit, was Connan, great and black against the sunset like an Assyrian bull-god. He was very drunk.

'I will have beer,' I said, 'the English beer.'

He shook his head, calling me Fedor, for it was still his jest that I came out of Dostoievsky. 'A man who will drink beer in the Khalig will crack monkey-nuts on Mount Olympus.'

'It is a kindlier drink than the Greek brandy. I would drink but little of the good Simon's cellar, my friend.'

'I am very certainly drunk, Fedor. But it's a celebration.' He ordered the beer for me. 'For I am no longer homeless. I am a citizen of Cairo, and the rat-like Simon boards me by the month, brandy and all.'

He had rented a bare room in the Khalig and bought himself a table and chair and an Indian string-bed. Simon Papadrapoulnakophitos sent him his meals, and he spent his days in sleep and his nights in wandering the streets.

'Down in the Gozi quarter, my room, and above where the metal-smiths chink their tools in early dawn. High up it is, Colonel, and you can hear the rustle of Cairo awake and watch the morning come down the streets like – oh, like Wilde's girl with silver-sandalled feet. And the wind comes up from the early Nile, across the Cairene roofs . . . Must come and see me there. Sometime. Moralise to your heart's content, and I'll show you the ugliest nigger that ever salaamed outside a Beardsley grotesque.

'A decadent place, the Gozi.

'Rented the room from an old Jew who takes the precaution of being an absentee landlord. The house had canal-tidemarks on it still, is five storeys high, and rocks in the traffic. Like a tomb inside – a greasy tomb full of the unease of the unquiet dead – what a phrase! A warren where pallid things live like worms cut off from the sunlight. When I am not listening to the Khalig itself, I lie abed, up there in my garret, listening to the house – as God probably lies and listens to the attenuated whisperings of terrestrial life . . . When you come, look out for the stairs, Colonel. They're of stone and have no bannisters, and they sweat in the night-time.'

'How long are you to stay there?' I asked.

'Eh? Till I die or Simon's cellars empty.' He brooded for a little and was not drunk. The Khalig cried below us. I heard his voice come in the half-whisper. '. . . Or I turn poet again.'

So, only for a moment, then he moved his glass of brandy, and laughed his bass laugh, and was the ruddy animal.

'What a street! Even its ugliness is as no other. Should see the new *femme de chambre* in the Gozi house. She came three days ago – brings up my food from Simon's waiter and cleans out the room. A Sudanese I think she is, and as hideous as a harpy. Kinky and clumsy, with a plague-pitted face; a body and soul that have never evolved . . . Ugly as sin, though willing enough. Hangs round unnecessarily, as though she had something to say and had forgotten the way to say it.'

'A slave, perhaps,' I said. 'There are still slaves.'

'Are there?' He had forgotten me again. So intent did he sit that I turned to look at that which drew his eyes. But it was only the Khalig. Then he spoke again in the whisper.

'Oh, it'll come to me yet. Some day it'll come to me, and I'll write it all – stuff that'll blind and drown the Georgian poetasters!'

'Eh?' I said. 'What stuff?'

'God, man, haven't you eyes? The Khalig – the Epic of the Khalig!'

v

Next night, though I came here to the usual table, there was none of the Connan. Nor the night after that, nor the next. Perhaps he had gone from Cairo, grown wearied, I thought, or wandered in some other part of our Many-Coloured. I asked of him from the little Simon. He still sent the meals to the Gozi quarter, but himself had seen nothing of the Lord.

By this he did not refer to divine revelation, but to the Connan, whom he believed a noble, being English, and it being a proper thing for Englishmen to be lords. Just as we of Russia who are neither bolsheviki nor boyars are incomprehensible to English minds.

But the fourth evening the waiter told me a woman awaited me with a message. I went down to the Khalig and the woman who waited came out of shadow and gave me an envelope. Then I saw her face and knew she must be the Sudanese slave.

I turned my eyes quickly from that poor, hideous face, so alien and unlovely. She stood silent, looking at the Khalig, the while I broke open the envelope. It held an unsigned note.

'Come with the messenger, Colonel. I have something to show you.'

'This is from the Khawaja Connan?' I asked, not looking upon the face I knew was turned towards me. But she said nothing, and I raised my eyes to her. She was making motions with her fingers. As she did so, set in that so-grotesque masque of a face I saw her eyes, deep and brown and sad, infinitely patient and beautiful eyes. I made the foolish noises before I understood.

She was dumb.

VI

The Sudanese left me to climb alone, and in the darkness I found that the stairs did verily sweat, as Connan had made avow. The stairs were without the rail, and far down, as in a well, was the lamp of the street doorway. I spread my fingers against the wall and so climbed to the ultimate attic, where was Connan's room.

I knocked and went in, and Connan, sitting in his chair, wheeled round. For a moment I thought him again drunk. He sat with hair like the feathers, and his ruddy face as one sleepless. He read my thoughts and laughed aloud, and his laughter echoed down and down into the silence of the house. Not until I heard the echo had I ever noted how cruel was that laugh of his.

'Drunk as a mujik, Fedor. But not with brandy. There has never yet man drunk what I've been drinking.'

He waved his hand to the room, and then I saw. It was littered with the scrawled sheets of paper. On the table in front of Connan was the disordered pile and on the string-bed another. He thrust a bundle upon me.

'Sit down, man, sit down and read. Not all of it – it would take you hours. Only that. Read it.'

I sat on the bed with the pile of pages on my knee, and for the little while the so-dim light of the oil-lamp and the English script vexed me; also it was a chance page, and much had gone before. But almost at the once a line leapt to my eyes and rang in my brain. In the minute I had forgotten Connan and his room, and was far on the wings of Connan's genius.

For I had lied. He was the genius, and I knew that this century might never see his like. Once I was the Professor of English Literature, and I have read much in the language, but of nothing to compare with those sheets that lived and sang in the Connan's garret of the Gozi.

For it was the song of the Khalig he had written, the song of all Cairo, the song of Egypt and the world and the days unnumbered since first the brown Stone Men drifted their dusk hordes across the Nile. In the Khalig's colours and voices he had found the tale of all humanity and told it as I had never read it told before – not even in the songs of your Shelley. Of the daedal wars and love and death and the birth was his tale; sunset and morning and the travail of heat and the lash; the battle-song ringing across the waiting lines at dawn; the bridal song and the birth-night agony, and all the quests and fulfilments of men. All the voices that Cairo has ever known cried from his pages – the emir's voice and the voice of kings and the love-song of the slave outside his wattle hut . . . God mine! I can but remember it now as one remembers the faint chords of music once heard and lost . . .

And I sat and read on and on, till presently, out of the Khalig's colour and clamour I heard arise a new note, faint at first, but clearer growing till it dominated. And I understood with sudden flash of memory Connan's child-game at Simon's café. What I had read was but background and scene, and this was the Epic of the Khalig's soul – of her who was life and more than life, Purpose and Desire and Achievement. Out of the dreams and changing fantasies she came, veiled and singing, lonely and alien, she who was love divine itself – and yet had known no lover . . .

I knew of a great silence. I had finished the last page. I looked at Connan, great, a bull-god in the black shadows from the little lamp. But in the dimness his eyes were bright-shining.

'Well?'

'You are the genius, friend Connan,' I said, and could think of no more.

'Genius? I have achieved the impossible, Colonel.' His voice rang with the arrogance. 'I've done what every Cairene poet has dreamt of since the days of Kusún – found the Soul of the Khalig, as I swore I'd do. One by one I draw the veils from her face.' His cruel laughter boomed again. 'To her first bridal I bring the Spirit of the Khalig.'

I cannot explain it, but the strange shiver passed through me then. I made ready to go. 'If you do not rest and sleep you will have the breakdown.'

But he did not hear me. He had pulled more paper towards him and had begun to write, and when I said the good-night I might have been to him but one of the murmurs that ever haunted that room.

Then I passed down through the dank darkness, and so into the midnight Khalig, with the music of Connan's lines still ringing in my head. Out in the night-quietened way it was cool and sweet, and I stopped and looked up at the stars . . .

And suddenly a so-great desolation came on me, under those bright stars. For I could not doubt the truth of Connan's vision. Life – beauty and the splendour, blood and strife and colour – and nothing more. Pity and faith and hope – the foolish whispers drowned in the roar of the Khalig . . .

I remember standing with that foolish, wistful ache at heart, looking up at the light-glow from Connan's room.

VII

From dawn the next day I was followed and haunted by the premonition – the foolish thought uprising urgent and crying: This happens, this is Fear. It wheeled through the brain as I worked in a room of the millionaire's house at Heliopolis. Somehow its concern was Connan. All day it haunted me, and in the evening when I returned to change, before taking the millionaire and his family on a moonlight excursion to Gizeh and the tombs of their ancestors, I made the determination. I would go down the Khalig and call at the Gozi house.

But opposite the little Simon's I was seen and a letter brought to me. It had been awaiting me since mid-day.

I looked at the Connan's writing. 'For God's sake come to me. I am afraid.'

That shock that follows a premonition justified was mine. In ten minutes I was in the Gozi, had climbed the stair, and knocked on Connan's door.

He bade me come in, but in the dark doorway I stood hesitant, I remember, till he lit a match, and so the lamp, and we looked at each other . . . And I looked upon the face of a man who had seen terror.

His black-blue hair above the temples was patterned in crispgrey. I stared at that hair of his, and it seemed to me that the markings were in shape like the impress of fingers. Then I looked round the room. The papers were gone, but in a corner – there was none of the fireplace – were heaped great piles of charred pages.

'Yes, that's the Epic, that's the song of Cairo's soul that the world will never hear.'

I turned back to him. He laughed dreadfully and covered his face with his hands. So doing, his fingers covered the greyed lines on his hair, and I stood frozen with the understanding.

'God mine, but why?'

'Why? If I hadn't burned it, man, hadn't sent for you, I'd have gone mad. Do you hear?' He stood up and his voice rose to the scream. 'Mad. Look at me . . . God, say it – say I'm not mad! . . .'

And then, in the burst of remembered fear and horror, he told me of the happenings of the night and morning. He had written all through the night, leading the Epic triumphant to its triumphant conclusion, but with the coming of the dawn he had stopped, exhausted. The lightening of the East roused him a little. He went to the window, and opened it, and leaned out into the air. The false dawn had passed from the sky, and it was quiet as the first morning of creation. Down below, far off in the quarter, he heard the tinking tools of some Gozi smith. Something else also he heard, but thought it a delusion, and still leant there, leaning with closed eyes.

He had thought he heard a footstep. The delusion recurred. He opened his eyes and turned round . . .

'My God, don't look at me like that, Colonel! She was real, I tell you. She stood not three feet away from me, her arms outstretched – *The Spirit of the Khalig, the woman I had created!*'

He covered his face again, then jumped up and raved at my silence.

'She was real, I tell you, real. Veiled and unearthly, but real. I think I cried out, for I knew I was mad. And then, my God, she was in my arms, her arms around my neck, and we kissed each other, and there was such magic and wonder in her kiss as my Epic had never known . . . A ghost, a dream, a symbol – she kissed my lips, Colonel! – and called me the one lover for whom she had waited throughout the ages—'

I tried to laugh at him, but the laughter choked in my throat. He was staring blindly in front of him, and suddenly he broke into a whispered chant.

'*Oh my beloved, you for whom I have sought so long! So-*

*weary and never-ending they've seemed, the years in their
suns and shadows . . . Tonight, at midnight, I come to our
bridal.'*

'I think I fainted then. When I awoke the Khalig was
stirring below, and I was alone in the room.'

VIII

So, in that early dawn, he had taken the Epic of the Khalig,
the thing of beauty which he had created, and burned it.
Page by page he had burned it, then spent the rest of the day
fighting wave after wave of madness which rose up out of
his heart to engulf him.

But the exhaustion he had held off crept on him now. He
had sat down on the bed, and, while I talked, his head
began to nod in weariness.

I talked on, and he lay back with closed eyes. Of anything
and everything I talked, except poetry and the Khalig. I
talked of autumn and stars and his English fields, and smell
of ploughed lands, and kindly peasant song. Of all the
quiet, secure things I talked, and in a little I looked at him
and saw he was asleep.

I spoke on, dropping my voice to the whisper, then
stopped, and tip-toed over to him, and listened to his
breathing. Nature had come to his help and he was safe
from dream and delusion . . . I remember his face turned
from the light, and of how I thought it, in despite its cruelty
and wan strength, the face of a child, pitiful and
uncomprehending . . .

I closed the door of his room and crept down the stairs of
that unquiet house. The darkness moved as if alive. There
was no lamp and I had to feel for each step. In the entrance
doorway, in the radiance of the street, I stopped and
listened, hesitating, then shrugged at the foolishness which
had come upon me also.

For it had seemed to me that I heard, far in the depths of

the house, the sound of a woman weeping, desolately, as one in despair.

IX

The stuff of dreams we are! How might I have known – I who do not know even yet?

For the next morning Connan was discovered dead in his room. Somewhere near the midnight he had shot himself through the heart with the second chamber of his revolver.

In the doorway of his room, also shot through the heart, lay the Sudanese slave . . .

Accident? Coincidence? *God mine, she was clad in the bridal robes of a Cairene maid!*

The Road

I

SOME PROCESSION RELIGIOUS, I think. Ah no, the Warren strikers . . . And look – God mine, here in Cairo! – *a women's contingent*!

The first I have ever seen. Surely Jane Hatoun marches there, surely somewhere in that brown drift is her face and voice uplifted! Surely at the least she turns in dream, dreaming she hears the ring of feet on that Road she prophesied these thirty years ago!

Some friend of mine? Jane Hatoun? She was memory blowing down the night before ever the good *sovyeti* replaced in Kazan Gymnasium – if replaced him they have – the Professor of the English Literature who fled to join the Whites. A legend of the bazaars, a tale of the *harm* and *soq*,

embroidered and of the miracle-adorned, that Woman's
Deliverer who was once Jane Hatoun and walked your
English fields . . .

But the legend that stirred me to the aching wonder that
night I heard it in a room beyond Khan Khalil – stirred me
so that I wrote to England for the upturning of records, so
that even to Angora I wrote . . . What irony of fate that with
me alone, Anton Saloney, alien in race and sex, should rest
the full tale of the Prophet of Sharikhan! Powder and the
dust, and yet – and yet – I may never hear the discussion or
read the book on the women's regeneration, but I hear Jane
Hatoun's voice come ringing across the years.

II

This from your records English and those of the Egyptian
official: In the 1878 one Lutf Hatoun, a student, was
expelled from El-Azhar for the heretical beliefs and the
liberalism. He escaped but narrowly with his life. Yet he
was rich, an orphan, and had none of the ties, and reached
to Alexandria in the safety.

From there he sailed to France, and so to England, to
gather yet more of the foreign liberalism. Three months
after his arrival in London he married the English girl;
before the lapse of the eighteen months he and his wife were
dead, killed in the great train accident.

They left but one child, a daughter.

Such the ragged record of official fact upon which I, with
my letter from Angora, may weave the imaginings. She was
brought up, this child Jane Hatoun, by the aunt artistic and
advanced. There was the much talk and poetry and misty
idealism all through her early years. She was given the
education and the freedom beyond that decade even in
England.

The aunt, the artist, was member of some society of the
painters that may have been your Pre-Raphaelite Brother-

hood; she was friend of the Ruskin and Morris and the gentle rebels of those days. The New Age was nigh when all men would be free and kindly and happy, and all women not only the equals of men, but the goddesses to inspire . . . Except in the brown lands of the Nile, which had haunted Jane Hatoun from childhood – her father's country, where was still the untinged darkness, where women were the cattle-slaves and dolls, where the light Pre-Raphaelite had never shone.

In the breathless resolve that grew stronger and stronger with her adolescence, Jane Hatoun determined herself as the missionary to carry the gospel unique to Egypt. In England were many to guide the coming age, but she – she would go to Egypt, where were the none . . .

In the 1899 the aunt died. Six months later Jane Hatoun, aged twenty-one, with the little luggage and the great faith and the incomplete knowledge of Arabic, sailed for Alexandria, which her father had left in the flight twenty-two years before.

III

'She was tall and slender, yet with the full bosom and the eyes like the deer,' was one to write of her. The type forgotten – of heroic mould, large of limb, young and eager and unawakened. She had little evidence of the Egyptian blood, but colourful hair and the white skin whereneath would rise the quick blood. And of her is there one phrase written that is curiously illuminating. 'She had beautiful hands – kind hands. They were kinder than the mercy of God, her hands.'

And for background our Polychromata – brown and seething and sullen and vivid, aged and unwearied, veiled of face and soul.

She came alone, but with the letters of introduction to the notabilities, native and European. With the youthful-

ness and enthusiasm she set about her intention express of
seeking out the intelligent women of Cairo and holding
with them the meetings and discussions.

From the women of the *harîm* soon drifted strange
account of those talks. For she urged them to learn the
reading and writing, to demand the freedom and the
shedding of the *pûshî*, to organise the Women's League
of Al-Islam.

It sounds the teaching harmless and pitiful enough –
Freedom and the Alphabet. But to that Cairo it was the
gospel of blasphemy, and there grew the mutter of anger
against the English girl. It might have become the official
protest, have resulted in the closed door and the expulsion
from Egypt. But for the happening mysterious.

Jane Hatoun disappeared. In a night she disappeared.
Followed the questionings and searchings by native police,
but they were the searchings unavailing. She had been wont
to walk the bazaars and hovel-lanes unguarded and un-
attended . . . It was the quest regrettably hopeless.

IV

Sixty years of age, politician, schemer, a Muslim of the *Haj*,
and, had he had his way, a Muslim of the *Jihad*. Such Ali
Mabkhut esh-Shihada Bey, high in favour with the Khed-
ive, but uncertain friend of the English.

He was the strange hybrid, an Egyptian-Japanese. His
mother, of one of the few Muslim families in Japan, had
been brought to Egypt in the 1840 to implement some
primitive Pan-Islamic plotting of Holy War.

Old and with the shrivelled face and the beast eyes, a man
like a hyena, he lived in the barrack-palace of Sharikhan
upon the Nile. When Jane Hatoun first came to Cairo he
was in the Yemen, making the marriage in the rich Yâhya
clan, and from there he at length returned with his new
bride to those rooms in Sharikhan that had known the

many women, where I think the very air was choked with the murdered soul-stuff of women . . .

A week thereafter he heard of the English girl, but saw her not, and his *harîm* remained undisturbed, as was he himself. Until the one day when, coming from the visit to a friend in the Muski, they pointed to her passing in the street.

You understand, she was friendless and counsel-less in Cairo, and with the confidence and enthusiasm un-bounded. Presently was she receiving the invitations to visit a house on Nile-bank, the small house where lived two women Egyptian, widows, eager for the new knowledge. She was delighted, and made the many calls, and at length, one night after the long talk, was induced to sleep there. A servant promised to take a note to the hotel, telling the guest's whereabouts . . .

In the night that guest awoke with the stifling breath and the feet and hands bound in cloths. Across her face were also bound the cloths. Underneath was the motion of a boat on water, and overhead the dip and sway of a lateen sail. She was upon the Nile.

She sought to struggle, but a great hand stayed her, and she lay wide-eyed in the unquiet darkness. Then the boat stopped, and she was carried up the dark flights of water-steps till the lap of the Nile was lost. Through the many corridors with the unpainted walls she was borne, then into a room that with lights blazed, that hung sick with the smell of musk, that was strewn with the gorgeous rugs in the barbarian clamour of colours.

He who carried her was a giant negro, but she had the no eyes for him. On the divan sat one who smiled at her, who smiled the tigerish smile from withered, evil face the while her face and feet and hands were untied, who smiled while she stood blanched and horrified, who smiled even while her screams were echoing down those corridors of night.

V

For the week she was the creature demented, raving and weeping in that guarded room to which the Bey went daily. And then from terror and agony came merciful release. The screamings ceased to be heard in the nearby *harîm*. Instead, came the other sounds – sounds which smote the whispering groups to amulet-clutching silence. They were peal upon peal of laughter, laughter which rose and fell and never ceased, the laughter of the mad.

The Bey's visits ceased with abruptness and next day Zuria, the new wife from Yemen who for a season had been supplanted, overheard the conversation between Shihada and the head-eunuch, Abd-er-Rahmân – a negro who had for the beast-master of Sharikhan the strange love and the unclean devotion. The mad woman was to be gagged and flung into the Nile in a sack, as one drowns a dog.

But the day following came the change in Jane Hatoun. No longer was the wild laughter, but only the crooning and the muttered talk, and when Zuria, with the secret, vicious plan at heart, went and begged the life of the mad girl as a new slave, Shihada did not refuse. She who had been Jane Hatoun was taken from the painted room, given the corner of a couch in the *harîm*, and set to the menial tasks.

VI

Drudge and slave and butt of the *harîm* she became, as fear of her child-like insanity faded. Two of the women indeed befriended her, and those – so-strange our hearts! – Ayesha the Abyssinian and Namlah the Copt – the two who had posed as the widows in the little house on Nile-bank. Ayesha was dark and secret and of her friendliness made little show, but Namlah, when she could, tended the mad girl with the scared pity which presently waxed into the strange, adoring love.

But the most followed in the blind hate of Zuria – of her who could not forget that she had been robbed of her lord a month after marriage. Freed though she was from sight or touch of the Bey – he had the orthodox horror of the mad – Jane Hatoun's life was the unceasing persecution, the deliberate torment. There were the orders not understood but mercilessly punished, the setting of heart-breaking tasks, the blows and jeers – all the slow, evil cruelty of the idle and sex-obsessed.

At the first, in the visits from other Cairene *harîm*, it had been the custom to hide the mad Englishwoman away. But with the passing of time even that ceased, for there were none who dared betray the secrets of Sharikhan. And the chatter and coffee-drinking would interrupt the while the white slave of Zuria was made the exhibition and the mock.

'I saved her for our amusement – from the death of the drowned dog I saved her,' Zuria would repeat the many times, and not until the one afternoon in the late October, when the room was crowded and Jane Hatoun crouched at the feet of Shihada Bey's chief wife, did the miracle happen.

They saw the slave suddenly rise and confront Zuria. Suddenly, and for the first time, she spoke in the clear and ringing Arabic.

'From such death will none save you, O evil woman . . . Be silent, fool who has vexed my hours. Silence – and look!'

She flung her arm towards the deserted end of the room, where hung the heavy velvet curtain above the doorway. Aghast, silenced, they turned and stared.

And it seemed to them as they looked that upon that curtain was flung the sudden picture. Ever the darker grew the room and the picture ever the brighter, and when it stood clear and yet shaking and fading in the wind-movement of the curtain, there arose a moan of terror.

For the picture showed the water-steps of the palace at night, and a woman, naked and bound, being uplifted and flung into the water by the giant negro Abd-er-Rahmân.

Behind was the flicker of a lantern upon the dark Nile, and lighting the face of the woman whom death awaited.

And the face was the face of Zuria.

She screamed, falling forward on her hands, and at that the picture ceased and vanished. Above the grovelling thing at her feet stood Jane Hatoun, with the light unearthly in her eyes and hands outstretched to the terrified women.

'Look and believe, women of Egypt! By this sign shall you know me, the Prophetess of God!'

VII

Shihada Bey was not in Cairo. He had gone on the secret political mission to Turkey, leaving Abd-er-Rahmân in charge of Sharikhan. And, while all unconscious he plotted in Stamboul, from his zenana on the Nile there spread through women's Cairo the story amazing of the Prophetess of God.

No mere thaumaturgist, but the first woman Prophet of God, one whose message superseded Christ and Mohammed, one who arose to deliver the women of the world . . . Nightly to her came the revelations and each dawn she would chant account of them to the rapt and shivering audiences of the zenana. Not one of her audience could read or write, and no record but the fragmentary verbal survives.

'And the day shall come when our bodies shall be no more houses of shame but temples of the living God.'

'And Woman shall build a City, and its name shall be Freedom; and Man shall come against that City with a Torch, and its name shall be Lust; then woe to that City if it trust in walls, for it shall not endure . . .'

Yet she preached no war on men, but rather the flaming creed that was to purge love of cruelty and abomination for those who set their feet on the Way, *El Darb*, the Road of abstinence and sacrifice and selflessness . . .

El Darb – it haunted her teachings. Somewhere, attainable by a mystic Road, was an amazing, essayable happiness, life free and eager, life in the sunlight beyond the prisons of fear and cruelty . . . The Buddhist Seven-Fold path, the Aryan Way, and yet also a Road to be built and laid to the City of God.

And it was Woman whom she called to the paving of this Road, Woman not as the lover or mother of men but as that dispossessed half of humanity which has never asserted the individual existence. She called her to an Expedition, a nameless Venture, out in the open air and the starlight, she preached her a God scorned and denied of men, she preached her a soul and a splendid endeavour . . .

Abd-er-Rahmân, and his eunuchs, freed from their master's presence, kept but the careless watch. They were seldom seen, and from them was the Prophetess guarded and shielded, so that of these happenings – other than the increased number of visitors – they knew nothing. First of disciples, first to come forward from the ranks of those who merely looked and listened and feared, were Namlah and Ayesha. But there was the convert amazing almost as soon. Zuria, whose death the Prophetess's first curtain-picture had foreshown, became the Paul of the wild new faith!

From that one may guess that were things other than the ascetic Road in the teachings – the colourful, incoherent imaginings of the Eastern mystic, the startling, incomprehensible revelations, the phrases of magic and prophecy . . . No mere thaumaturgist, miracles were yet of the daily occurrence – the miracle-pictures of the *harîm*-curtain, the laying-on of hands – all those strange powers that lie with the spiritually over-stirred.

Such our nature, perhaps through the wild prophecies and miracles it was that her fame spread amidst the Muslim women and even into the quarters of the Greeks. She was not once betrayed, and presently the story ceased to be a story, became the secret cult and the kindled fire, awaiting

to blow out in flames of faith upon the winds of the
world . . .

And then over Cairo that November, out of the lairs of
the Black Warrens and the Khalig Canal, spread the
cholera plague.

VIII

When returning one night in secret from his political
mission, and bringing the secret guest, Shihada Bey entered the palace of Sharikhan he found a quarter of his
servants dead, including two women of the *harîm*. Of those
who still lived, half were smitten with the plague of the
fouled waters and Cairo no place for the wise man to tarry.

Tarry he did not, but fled to Alexandria. With the dawn
he was gone, but his secret guest remained still in hiding,
for entry into Egypt was forbidden Dirhem Ragheb.

Ah, you have heard of him – Ragheb Pasha, the Ghazi's
friend and confidant. Enemy of the Faith, the mullahs have
called him, him who has fought to destroy the creed of his
fathers, with all its tenets of black bestiality and sex-enslave-
ment. But this was the thirty years ago, and though member of
that society that was later to become the Young Turk, he was
not yet the ascetic and fanatic, but the young man with the
courtesy and the ready smile, the humour and impatience of
restraint and convention. He had the no illusions regarding
the Bey; they were but the temporary political allies.

He had a palace wing almost to himself, and passed the
days in the reading and smoking, till on the fourth afternoon of his coming he looked out on the great central
court, the *hôsh* of Sharikhan, and saw that which made him
drop his book in the wonder.

Pacing the *hôsh* was a woman, a girl of the English surely,
or his eyes lied, a girl tall and stately, with the eyes unearthly
and the little smile upon her lips. And after her, the pace
behind, two native women.

They were Zuria and Namlah, who had brought the Prophetess to walk in the open air after the hours of nursing and prayer in the palace. And as he gazed Ragheb saw the very beautiful happening – the English girl stop till the two native women were beside her, and put her arms about their shoulders, and point to the sunset. So, in that grouping they stood for the minute, so still and crowned with fire that he followed their gaze.

Seen through the opening of the *hôsh*, magically paved in rippling gold upon the Nile, lay a road that stretched from their feet to the sun.

IX

'I loved her from the first moment I saw her pass below me,' he was to write, and I have thought of him and that very sweet and ancient song in your language. 'I would have burned Sharikhan for her,' he says, the grey-headed confidant of Kemal . . .

But he did not burn Sharikhan. Instead, he waylaid her next evening she walked, and that time alone. She stopped and stared at him with the mysterious eyes, unafraid and unrealising. He stood bare-headed in front of her, and fumbled in his English.

'My lady, who are you?'

She put her hand to her forehead, still standing so and staring at him. She stammered the confused words, and then suddenly her face was suffused with blood, and she gave the low, wailing cry and would have fallen but for his arms. So holding her he was aware how fragile she was, but at his touch she struggled like the mad thing and sank to her knees.

He stood over her in the pity and the doubt, and something of the apprehension also, for he knew not that the eunuchs of the palace were but recovering from cholera, and none but women likely to interrupt them. And suddenly, he says, unknowing her story, he was blindly angry.

'By God, the Bey! You are no Muslim woman. He stole you, abducted you?'

She raised the frightened face from which the light unearthly had gone. It was the face of a child, remembering horror.

'Stay with me,' she whispered. 'Stay with me. You are my friend?'

X

The madness that had veiled from her the past had shivered away in an instant. Came back horror and remembrance and the understanding . . . And then sight of the kind and compassionate eyes of the one human being who seemed not alien.

That night she passed through the nightmare hours. One of the women was dying, and she found herself kneeling with the whole of the *harîm*, praying an insane ritual prayer through which revolved and returned some jargon of a Road, some means to salvation which she had preached in her madness. And when the woman, her eyes fixed in adoration on the Prophetess, gave the last gasp, Jane Hatoun found herself bending over the corpse and making upon it the mystic sign she had taught . . .

Almost that night her reason reeled again, in the smell and reek and the chanting, and there came on her a shuddering horror and disgust of the *harîm* women who seemed to be her especial disciples – the eager Zuria and the faithful Namlah.

But alone, early in the dawn, she managed to steal away from them to the room where hung the great curtain, and attempted unavailingly to summon upon it the images. Morning was breaking outside, and she unlatched the never-opened windows and watched the light come upon the Nile.

That day she had again the secret meeting with Ragheb. 'I swore I would take her away as she begged – to France, to England. Nor did I make any conditions. Oh, sometime, beyond the seas – for I was to abandon politics and country for her, my English Lady – perhaps then she would come to me.'

He made the arrangements for a boat to come from Bulaq and take them away next sunset. All over Cairo the cholera plague was receding, and there was the no difficulty.

But of the new conditions in Cairo another was aware, for that night there arrived at Sharikhan the messenger with the news that Shihada Bey was returning in twenty-four hours.

XI

All that momentous next day were the swift rain-showers upon the Nile, and – thing unprecedented in Cairo – a haze that almost blotted out the opposite bank. And within Sharikhan, in the *harîm* of Shihada, Jane Hatoun sat and listened to the dying Ayesha.

Sometimes she wandered in delirium, sometimes came out of dreams and recognised the Prophetess, and made the little struggles to remembrance, the pitiful confessions.

'The Road, the Road, O *khâtûn*! So little I have done, I have been weak. And the Way is steep and hard, the shining Way of Women. I have hardly trod it. Will God understand?'

Over and over again. And it seemed that not the miracles and the chantings, but vision of some wondrous Way of Life had lighted her dark, starved soul . . . Kneeling there, repulsion forgot, Jane Hatoun listened with the breaking heart.

And against the window the wonder of Cairene rain! . . . Rain that fell on the long fields and the pleasant lanes and the lamplit streets of the kindly towns, rain of the lost England to which Ragheb would take her . . .

'I found her at sunset waiting on the water-steps, as we had planned. She was transformed to wonder, with flushed cheeks and breathless laughter. She hardly seemed to see me, but pointed across the Nile.

'I looked. It was our boat.'

XII

They started and fell apart, and Ragheb turned with pistol gleaming in his hand. But from the shadows came no eunuch, but only the Coptic slave-woman – the hysterical woman who stared and then fell on her knee and caught the skirt of Jane Hatoun.

'Oh, leave us not, us who are your children, us to whom you have brought the Faith – leave us not, O *khâtûn!*'

Ragheb caught the stem of the boat, and steadied it, and turned with outstretched hand. But Namlah clung to the Prophetess with the courage of desperation. 'Ayesha is dying and calls for you, she who is passing from the Road. She calls your blessing—'

'I thrust her aside. "Quick, into the boat. We can be at Bulaq before darkness. And then the road to the sea!"

'But from my English lady came the strange, strangled sob, and she looked at me wildly, and drew back with the strange words.

' "Go you, go you. Haste, for the Bey comes, and already Abd-er-Rahmân has seen you speak with me."

'I stared at her and did not understand. The shadows grew deep upon the waters. And then my English lady raised the slave-woman and stood with her arms around her, and looked at me with tormented eyes. And these are the words she said, as I remember them:

' "Oh, I cannot come!" And suddenly she wept, and spoke my name, which she had never done. "So easy to escape – my heart is breaking to come with you! Love and you – there was never woman who heard such call but went. Oh, I am only the mad Prophetess still, I think, and these women have followed and believed in me, and how may I desert them?"

'I pleaded with her, but she did not seem to hear. The boatmen, frightened at nearness to Sharikhan, kept calling from the water-steps. And then I saw come again on my English lady's face the unearthly light.

' "Forget me, Dirhem, I have never been. Yet beyond the Road I would have loved – more than life I would have loved you!"

'And then for the quick moment she kissed me, me who had never known of her love, and so was gone.

'I never saw her again.'

XIII

What happened with the return of Shihada is the dim and tangled tale, the swift confused falling of last sands heard in darkness. Perhaps he looked upon Jane Hatoun again, and the beast-desires stirred in him. Perhaps he had heard from Abd-er-Rahmân of the meetings with Dirhem Ragheb and the flight of the latter. At the least, there occurred in that *harîm* room the scene unprecedented. Zuria, in defence of the Prophetess, struck with the knife at Shihada, and while the Bey grappled with her Jane Hatoun picked that knife from the floor and drove it through his hyena-heart . . .

They stripped and bound the two women, the eunuchs, and carried them down to the water-steps, obeying Abd-er-Rahmân, who had loved Shihada, who had become the raving madman with no thought of the morrow and its explanations. Behind them they clanged to the great door above the water-steps, and thereon beat the demented women the while murder was done in the rain and darkness.

But through that door they heard Jane Hatoun crying courage to Zuria, crying that the sunset Road was theirs. And then they heard her singing by the waters, in the alien tongue and the unknown words. Struggling and splash, a single sharp cry, wild and agonised. And then the singing ceased for ever.

XIV

But in the women's legends of Cairo Jane Hatoun perished not that night at the hands of the eunuchs. She escaped upon the water and the darkness, and some day – surely from that Avalon where Arthur dreams, and sleeps the Danish king – she will come again and preach the faith that is to deliver the women of the world . . .

And who may say that she will not?

A Volcano in the Moon

I

THAT GLOW ABOVE the Khalig? It is the moon-rise. And the so-sudden hush? Always is there this hush at the moon-rise. I think our Polychromata turns nightly and looks with startled eyes at that mysteriousness growing to being above the Khalig walls.

A lovers' night and a lovers' moon! But no moon in the world like our Cairo's . . . Tonight they'll be questing the skies from Palais de Koubbah, but perhaps with me alone, Anton Saloney, who once watched human faith and hope and hate battle amidst those crater-mountains the many hundred thousand miles away – battle in the cause splendid beyond their own guessing, in days when the Great Shadow still lay black across the world – perhaps with me alone, the spectator, remains the memory vivid and so-shining.

Our Cairene moon – she has had the lovers other than those who kiss beneath her light! Not least of them Gellion and Freligrath – Gellion who died of the broken heart because of her, Freligrath who in his last hour must have sat at his study window and peered at that glow in the wonder and the doubt . . .

II

In dim days before the War, when I was professor of the English Literature in the Gymnasium of far Kazan, Thibaut Gellion, coming to Cairo, took to the study of the moon.

He was an astronomer with the small private means, the Gellion, a Frenchman of Frenchmen. To Egypt he came because of the health of Mme Gellion and because the clear skies would suit the adventurings of his nights. In the little the great telescope brought from the Ardennes threatened the stars from an observatory built on the roof of a house in Palais de Koubbah, and in the less while, absorbed, Gellion had forgotten madame. He forgot her often. For she said of the stars that doubtlessly they were leaves in a book of which le bon Dieu was author . . . but the first page gave her to yawn. Unlike was the little Flore, their daughter, who, knowing not God out-moded, had the childish passion for the skies.

He had but few friends in the astronomical world, the little Gellion. Cantankerous, he was the born heretic, the champion of the lost cause and the wild surmise. Yet of the strict and impartial. His enthusiasm for his heresy of the moment was but equalled by his severity in the sifting of evidence that appeared to support that heresy. As result, he never substantiated the single belief of importance, nor had ever the illusion of so doing – until the year before his death.

After three months of the moon-study in Cairo – in France he had been the Martian, a champion of the good canals – he entered into correspondence with the Bavarian herr professor, August Freligrath, and with him, though for all Germans he had the loathing, became fast friends. Herr Freligrath was of the greatest of selenographers and had long been supporter of the heretical belief that volcanic life was not extinct upon the moon . . . I am the layman, and all the learned journals of Europe wherein they fight these battles are to me the journals closed. But of Freligrath's belief Thibaut Gellion in Cairo became the supporter enthusiastic. Both had conviction of the play of gases from the volcano in Schroter's Valley (low down there, to the right, above the moon North Pole), but their evidence and photographic records went unaccepted . . . There was not enough of the evidence, nor was it strong enough, and like Gellion, Freligrath was of himself the severest critic.

In winter of the nineteen-thirteen the Bavarian professor – he was the widower – came to Cairo with his son, Friedrich, a boy of fifteen. Gellion and his guest passed their days and nights in the Koubbah observatory, and the kindly Mme Gellion, who had even less respect for national animosities than she had for stars, took to her heart the boy Friedrich. He said of the star-study that it did not interest him, being hurtful to the back of the neck, and these two were the pagans disrespectful in a house of sky-worshippers.

He was the boy quick and certain and planful. Upon sight of Flore and the Nile he loved both, and never forgot either. Flore was the year younger. Dispossessed of the observatory, she took Friedrich the adventures through the bazaars, into the forbidden Black Warrens, to the far Caliphs' Tombs, to the Ghizeh stones. They were of the young and light-hearted, yet the children of scientists both.

'When I'm grown up,' said Flore, who was a dusky child of the southland French, with the tanned cheeks and the steady eyes even then, 'I'll be as Mme Curie. But an astronomer. In America, at Mount Wilson observatory. And discover many stars.' She had the after-thought. 'Then I'll marry Herr Friedrich, and he can do my calculations because he's so good at maths.'

They sat by the Nile, far from Koubbah, while she said this. It was the March day on the seaward-making waters, with Bulaq Bridge in the distance and the world at their feet. Athwart the sunshine spattered and drifted the occasional rain-shower. Long was Friedrich to remember Flore sitting there. But he struggled with the honesty he also possessed.

'You'll be an astronomer, but I – I'll be an engineer.' His second love, the Nile, drew him. 'I'll come to Cairo and build aqueducts and dams to drain and flush the streets each morning. And make an end of dirt and disease and cholera in those beastly Black Warrens.'

She drew the little away from him, being very woman in spite of her youth and her stars. And if you think of their love as childish you understand them not at all. 'But how can we live at Mount Wilson, then?'

He was miserable, but honest still, and you see him, the tow-headed German boy with the puzzled blue eyes, looking from Flore to the Nile. He made the halting confession. 'I do not know.'

There was the silence when his world cracked, then a movement, and a tanned cheek against his. 'Perhaps Koubbah will do for my telescope.' She sighed a little, abandoning Mount Wilson. 'And I'll love to come and look at your dams.'

'And I at your stars,' he said, and kissed her. A shadow fell on them and the sunshine was suddenly obscured. Flore jumped to her feet.

'We'll have to run. Look at the water glimmering under Bulaq Bridge. There's a storm coming down the Nile.'

III

Six months later, when the War broke out, the Freligraths were back again in Bavaria. The Gellions were at Alexandria, having moved there for the hot weather, and on the first ship that would take him Thibaut Gellion, patriot, was hasting across the troubled Mediterranean of those days to the help of his France. On the day he sailed Flore's mind was troubled with the terrible imagining.

'My father, if you met Herr Freligrath or – or Friedrich – what would you do?'

'Shoot the animal,' he said, and did not smile.

So dim those days – God mine, we may hardly believe them! Least of all that insanity of the hate and vituperation which cloaked Europe like the miasma. None of us escaped its poison. Not even the science, experimental science, most selfless and international of things, was free. All over the world in the scientific journals rose the wild accusation and the foolish challenge . . . In that lunatic world a German could write the article, in the responsible science gazette, accusing the English of mathematical inability or the deliberate falsifying of their biological experiments – and be believed! Of such cases were many, and of their class were the war-writings of Thibaut Gellion.

He found himself in France too old for the soldiering. While he pestered the ministries for employment he furnished the French gazettes with articles on the dishonesty and stupidity of the German astronomers. At the last he even published an attack on Herr Freligrath as the liar and cheat.

No frontier is barrier to hate, and in Bavaria that article was read by August Freligrath, friend and colleague of Liebknecht, one of the two public men of Germany who had tried to keep the peace.

IV

At the length, in the nineteen-eighteen, December, Thibaut Gellion, hospital-worker, returned to Cairo to find his wife dead and Flore, up-grown and of the strange, still holding the house in Koubbah with the aid of her nurse, Mathilde.

Almost the physical wreck came back the little Gellion, and but slowly could his mind turn to the skies and the forgotten stars. He sat amazed and furious in the Koubbah house over the terms of peace and the re-admittance of the German animals to the councils of civilisation.

But he might not long resist the lure of his observatory. Flore, who in the years of his absence had made of herself the competent selenographer, became again his assistant. She found her father one strangely altered. There were the long periods when he was the student, quick and sceptical, but those broken by the dark spells when mind and soul seemed to forsake his body. It was as though some shadow wavered across his days – the shadow to her incomprehensible. Unanticipated, mysterious, it would fall and darken even his happiest hour.

Spite all her pity and all her horror, Flore had looked on the War with clear eyes. It was the stupidity; and now it was over, and one might hope and dream again. A week after the return of her father she wrote a letter to Friedrich Freligrath, sending him the greetings and remembrances. I think her heart went with that letter, that shy, wistful calling of the boy's name across the gulf of four nightmare years.

The letter was never answered.

V

On some infrequent portions of the dark side of the moon is not always the darkness. In the drunken tilt and libration of the satellite as it swings around our world come the occasions when one at the powerful telescope may glimpse uncharted lands ere these swing back again into the darkness for the long periods.

In survey of that shadow-land Thibaut Gellion sought to find his old self – as Flore sought forgetfulness of the wound to her young, proud heart. Hour by hour, in the full-moon glow, they would chart and photograph and sketch.

Then presently the happening unexpected – the night when her father, with the amazement in his voice, called Flore to the telescope, and in the little observatory of Koubbah were the strained hours of watching and the hasty erection of camera apparatus. Next night was the same, the while the telescope eye hung above a minute edge of the lunar disc, where the dazzling whiteness of day on the moon fell sheerly off into utter darkness and a snow of stars. On that edge of disc was a crater-mountain, uncharted and little observed. It tilted sunwards, and also almost full to the earth, and far within its towering walls was a drifting smudge like the smoke from a cigarette.

They were looking across the lifeless wastes at the first active volcano indisputable upon the moon.

VI

So Gellion was convinced, for, unlike the volcanoes he had once suspected in the Schroter's Valley, it was evidently a crater in the eruption violent and continuous. Yet to the proof of its existence in the astronomical world were the difficulties most desperate. There was no measuring its depths of crater-wall in the position he had seen it, and not for the uncertain period of months would that tract of the lunar land be again observable. Lying inside that borderland where were to be considered conditions and contingencies such as might well dishearten even the super-mathematician, the crater could be but seldom viewed from the earth, and even then at the different angles and power because of the approach and recession of the moon-floor. In the most moon-observations it would be altogether beyond telescopic range . . .

Yet – to prove its existence and prophesy its reappearance would be to crown his life-work.

I can but glimpse the task enormous of the little Gellion. Later was I to make of the matter the study that I might understand a little. But that is still the little.

Yet, after the stupendous toil of a month, he completed the task of compiling a chart of periodicity – the times when the volcano inside the crater might be seen at its full and no other explanation of the smudge-phenomenon be possible.

In that month of intensive calculation and rejection occurred still the hours when the shadow mysterious fell upon him and he was approachable by none but Flore. But such moods grew the rarer with the nearing of success, and he finished his thesis with the conclusion that once in the five months the volcano-glow of the lunar crater would be clear to earthly eyes.

VII

The day after that first momentous observation I had had with Flore the encounter in the bazaars. It was Ramadan, and we were both the strayed and foolish spectators of a procession Muslim. For the little it seemed that El Azhar was to cut our throats for reasons religious, but Flore, white-clad and slim like the boy, and unafraid, stood smiling and whistling the little tune, and I spoke in the Arabic with the big voice. So they allowed us to pass and we made the acquaintance.

'I have to thank you, M. le colonel.'

I made the protest. 'But it was you who saved us. The Muslim – they believe a whistling woman to be possessed of a devil.'

She had the entrancing laughter of the grave-eyed. 'So I would have been if they had touched me.'

So I became the occasional visitor at Koubbah, was once – greatest of favours – allowed to look through the telescope, and was many times lectured by the little Gellion on the subject of star-charts and German iniquity.

Flore had but the few friends in Cairo – she had been of the too-busied with her stars – and I took her to the amusement and relaxation she would have denied herself. Then, for the little, she would forget moon and craters and her father's moods and that unanswered letter, and be merely the girl, with the laughter and the teasing and the enchantment.

She had the love for music and the dance and the pretty clothes, and to me, the romantic, there seemed but the one way in which these could ever unite and mingle with her passion for the stars. Once, in the half-jest, as we sat in the scraping of violins in a house above the Nile, I asked her when that would be.

Is there anything quite so tragic as the bitter laughter of youth? She turned away, that I might not see her eyes.

'Oh – when the Nile runs back through Bulaq Bridge!' she said.

VIII

He was the Frenchman, Gellion. On the eve of publication of his discovery, which, if verified, would change the face and nature of the science selenography, he delayed that publication, remembering his one-time colleague, Freligrath of Bavaria. Forgetful of all that had passed, he despatched his calculations to Bavaria and invited verification of the phenomenon before it was made known to the European societies. The time for the second full-observation of the crater was now near.

But August Freligrath, who had gone through a war and

two revolutions, who had once rescued his son with an Ebert-signed pardon the while that son, young and a rebel, stood facing a firing-squad, was the changed man also. He had been shocked and embittered by the Four Years and their aftermath, and there lingered with him memory of that article which Gellion had written in the far days of the nineteen-fifteen.

Yet he was honest. When the letter came from Cairo he was already the sick man dying as a result of privations suffered in political prisons. But he began the study close and intent of that section of moon-surface where Gellion believed he had made the epochal discovery. On the night of the full-observation he sat the long hours at his telescope in spite the remonstrances of Friedrich.

And within Gellion's crater were only the black and steady shadows of no light . . .

All next day August Freligrath sat at his desk, writing as in the fever. A week later, in the German astronomical journal, appeared under his signature the savagely-satirical account of the Gellion claim and his own disproval of it.

'The romantic French amateur, like the poor, is always with us. To suggest – as undoubtedly M. Gellion himself would do were he investigating the claims of a "Bosche" – that he is either liar or cheat is possibly to exaggerate. Rather is it a case of mistaken devotion. With so strong a gift for self-deception and undisciplined enthusiasm astrology, not astronomy, would seem to call M. Gellion.'

IX

That journal came to the Gellions already dismayed and uncomprehending. They also had looked in a crater-well of blackness and on no smudge of gases from the volcano they believed existed.

To Flore's father, in spite his pugnacity, the article of Freligrath's was as death-blow. He shrank from it, very small and pitiful and suddenly aggressive not at all. I went to see him, ill in bed, and he lay with the closed eyes and moving lips. Within the week he was dead.

He was buried next day, for it was the summer, and of stifling heat. I came back to the little house in Palais de Koubbah, to one who did not weep but stood with clenched fists and stormy eyes.

'Oh God, those Bosches, those German swine! Father was right always, and I wrong . . . Oh, Anton, my friend, I am so lost . . .'

And she wept a little then, so proud and angry and desolate, and of the comfort I had none. Instead, my friend, I stood shamed in front of her – shamed that I was a man and with all men responsible for those twin deserts we make and call by the names of war and peace . . .

I walked home from Palais de Koubbah that evening. Near Zeitoun the moon came up, and I stopped and stared at it and lighted the pipe, with about me on the white road the shadows like the dancing ghosts. And there came on me with force of vivid revelation a fantastic thought—

The adventure-soul in man – the sum of its selfless achievements was as that volcano in the moon, the flaring light, the beacon in the wastes. And perhaps, like that volcano, it also was doomed to cease and pass, was already flickering to extinguishment before vanishing for ever in some final night of war and hate.

X

Unexpectedly the new development. I went one night to Palais de Koubbah and found a cold, pale Flore with eyes of a stranger. She had the story for me. Friedrich Freligrath was in Cairo. He had called at the Gellion house and been refused the admittance. Then he had written a letter and enclosed with it a sheet of paper in another hand.

In hesitant French, set out in the ornate German script,

the letter. 'I tried to see you, but the good Mathilde would not even know me. My dear, it is surely a mistake. I had no part in the disagreements of my father and M. Gellion.

'A month ago the Egyptian Government set a European competitive examination for a constructional engineer. In spite of my deplorable youthfulness, I have been selected to build those aqueducts I promised, and which you said you would love to see. May I come and look at your stars? . . .'

His father had been found dead at his study window three weeks before, and the sheet of paper enclosed held the beginnings of a letter found amongst Herr Freligrath's papers. It had probably been the last thing written by the Bavarian astronomer.

I spelt out the German. It was the note addressed to Thibaut Gellion . . . They had both, perhaps, been too hasty. There was a mistake in the calculations; they had not allowed for . . .

They had not allowed for death, for there the letter ended.

XI

Secretly I noted the address of the young Freligrath. He lived in Abbassieh, and next evening I went to see him and to him explain myself. He sat and stared at me, then laughed and passed his fingers through the up-standing, tow-coloured hair he had retained from boyhood. He was the personable young man, planful and eager still, but with the surface-flippancy of his generation.

'So I am the son of a murderer, eh? And the little Flore a chauvinist? What a world! Have a drink?'

We spoke in the French for a while, for I have little German. Then we made the discovery. He was the enthusiast of the language English, as I am. Some far-uncle of his it was, he told me, who translated your Tennyson into the so-exquisite German.

Thereafter we spoke the English and were presently the interested acquaintances. I took him with me to see our Polychromata by night, and here, in the Khalig, in the seat where you now sit, introduced him to the little Simon and his so-surprising English beer. And then I heard details that filled out the troubled Gellion-Freligrath story.

'That letter you speak of – I never saw it. Bavaria was too busied with bayonets those days to pay much heed to its mails.'

I told him that in the next moon was another night of the full-observation, and that this time Flore Gellion was confident of proving the volcano's existence. He shook his head.

'Her father's calculations are correct enough – so far as they go. Either his premises were wrong, or he forgot some integral fact. I know. Mathematics is my hobby also, and I spent the voyage from Europe in checking my father's copy of the Gellion periodicity-chart. It is absolutely correct. She'll see no volcano.'

'But the uncompleted letter of Herr Freligrath?'

He shrugged. 'I do not know, and what he believed we will never know. In his later years he worked and thought like a man half-blinded in a shadow, my father – the mountain-shadow of the War.'

XII

With but the short space of time for the task Flore, whatever startled ache of memory Friedrich's arrival in Cairo had awakened, flung herself into the checking of the Gellion calculations. To speak of my meeting with Freligrath I could find no opportunity.

But I learned that nowhere in the calculations of her father was the mistake to be found. They must have been built on the false assumptions basically. Yet that was impossible, else how could she have shared the telescopic illusion?

The matter of the uncompleted letter of August Freligrath worried her, though she pretended to scorn it. What had they not allowed for, the German and her father?

Once she and Friedrich met, in the Sharia Kamil, coming face to face and knowing each other at the once. I heard of the chance meeting from Friedrich, for of it Flore made no mention.

'She looked me through, and then passed on.' He laughed; laughter was his cloak. But presently he was angry. 'Yet she is Flore Gellion and I Friedrich Freligrath spite our fathers and all the years of blood and hate. What have we to do with those weary animosities? I tell you there was the half-moment, before she cut me, when I could have taken her and kissed her, and she kissed me. I saw it in her eyes . . . And then the Shadow.'

He forgot his laughter-cloak, this pleasant young man, and I saw the Spartacist of Bavaria. 'Curse their mean and dirty little nationalisms, their petty spites and their petty patriotisms! Curse the infernal moon and all its volcanoes! What have we to do with their lunatic astronomical past, dead Gellion and dead Freligrath?'

'Some day, being dead, the future may demand that of *your* past,' I said. But he paid no heed. Instead, stood staring at the sky in the kind of desperation.

Overhead, like a portent, hung the sickle moon.

XIII

From moon-rise on the calculated night Flore Gellion sat the long hours in the observatory, looking up under her eye-shades through the light-flooded glass of the giant lens. She sat in a little saddle below the telescope, and in the observatory was the dead silence but for the ticking of the clockwork which synchronised the movements of the telescope with the minute motion of the lunar disc. I sat and looked at her, or wandered to the uncurtained portion of the glass roof and stared up, foolishly, at the full moon. Sometimes Flore brought the great camera into play and I helped with the changing of slides. At moon-set I went down and brought up the coffee Mathilde had made. Flore had come from the telescope. She sat at a little table, her hands covering her eyes.

'Only tired, Anton.' There was the break in her voice. 'And my eyes.'

'And the volcano?'

'Look and see. Quick, for the disc is beginning to fade.'

Our Cairene moon – she sails the sky the mystery and wonder to the naked eye. No less the mystery of her strange lands which start to being under the telescope. In the little was the blur gone from my eyes and that unearthly landscape lay below me, etched in ink, under its pitiless day.

Upstanding full in the centre of the lens, its outer sides clothed in the dazzle of sunshine, I looked for the first time upon the fateful Gellion crater.

XIV

Here, where I had promised to meet him, Friedrich was awaiting me the following night, and I made no greetings but answered the question in his eyes.

'There is no volcano. Flore herself could see no trace of activity, and the photographs show none.'

There came on his face the pity and something of the dismay. But I think it was no selfish dismay. 'I had hoped, after all . . . I spent the better part of last night, rechecking the chart and trying to find some omission. If only I were an astronomer! . . . Did you look?'

'I looked. Tundra and rock and the blazing daylight and the mountain-shadows. Shadows like the spattered drops of night. It is a world of shadow.'

There was the silence, and then suddenly his quick

breathing. I looked up and found him staring at me. 'My God, of course it is!'

'It is?—'

But he was on his feet. 'The seasonal orbit-roll! Why didn't they think – but they were blinded in shadows themselves! . . . Or did my father guess it before he died? Eh? *The shadow, man, the mountain-shadow!*'

And he was gone.

XV

I spent the next three days with a tourist-party down in Helwanles-Bains, and came back to Cairo in the evening and the tiredness. It was late and I was about to make the undress, when I was told of the messenger newly come for me.

I went down and found it the good Mathilde, grumbling and indignant.

'You are to come with me, mon colonel. So mademoiselle will have it.'

I made the reflection that youth knows not of tiredness. 'She is ill?'

The old Frenchwoman was of the very indignant. 'Sick of the mind, I think,' and sat opposite me in the taxi which had brought her, saying nothing more.

She showed me up into that moon-showered observatory, with its clocks and instruments, and I knew the telescope in action by the ceaseless tick. But the saddle-seat was unoccupied. There were no lights, nothing but the play of shadows, yet in those shadows the murmur of voices that puzzled me.

Then the electric light came on, and Flore was in front of me, and from the seat behind her rose someone else. She stood as if to conceal this other from my gaze, but I took her shoulders and put her aside, and looked.

It was Friedrich Freligrath.

And then, while I stared from the one to the other, they were the embarrassed children till Flore's arm was in mine. She pulled me to the telescope seat and sat me in it.

'Look, colonel.'

It was the same lunar landscape, the same crater into which I had looked. But in the crater-mouth, in place of the inked shadow, was a fainter blackness, and presently, as I looked, I caught my breath at that wonderful sight and knew something of the awe and fear.

For the shadow moved and changed, and suddenly lightened and lightened till it was almost a glow, there, in the wild lands a quarter of a million miles away. I swung round to look at those two behind me, and then back again to peer across the gulfs at that amazing flicker of the gas-clouds.

And then Friedrich's hand was on my shoulder, and he was explaining.

'It was the shadow of the crater-walls M. Gellion did not take into account. He found it impossible to measure the depths of those walls, and then must have forgotten them as a factor – the gradual encroaching of their shadow, in a circular tilt, upon the crater itself. But for that omission the chart of periodicity is correct. The night you and Flore watched, that volcano was moving there, but it lay in the shadow of its own crater-walls. With the passing of the lunar year the acceleration of the shadow is swifter than the tilt of the moon-floor . . . Oh, I'm the astronomer, colonel! I've been absorbing lunar lore through the pores of my skin during the last seventy hours!'

'And how—?' I asked, and then stopped, for I knew.

'Friedrich had inspiration when he heard you talk of the shadows. He went home, estimated a depth of crater-wall, allowed for the shadow, and amended my father's calculations . . . Oh, the pity of it that they should never know! Last time Herr Freligrath and my father held their observations – if they had delayed two days they would have seen

the volcano. This time it was not observable until four days
after the originally-calculated date.' She was silent, then
laughed the little, but with tears in her eyes and her hands
outstretched to the German enemy, making the question to
which she should have known the answer. 'My dear, you've
surpassed us all! How did you do it – you whom astronomy
always so bored?'

XVI

I walked home again that night, for it was too late to find the
vehicle and my tiredness was gone. Flore and Friedrich
came part of the way with me, talking of the Gellion-
Freligrath discovery which they were to publish. At parting
they laughed and kissed me, being both impulsive children
of the Frankish blood, and whether they ever went home
that night to further scandalise the good Mathilde or else
walked the roads singing and planning the storming of the
stars, I do not know. But I remember that as I heard their
glad young voices crying au revoir down the white moonlight, there came to me the whimsical memory. Surely the
Nile was running back through Bulaq Bridge this night!

Then I forgot those lovers re-discovered; they faded from
my mind, cyphers and symbols in a story yet untold, an
adventure uncompleted. For I found myself on that stretch
of Zeitoun road where, but the short month before, I had
stood in the silence under the moon, alone with my vision
of human futility.

And then I knew that I had dreamed. While the truth
remains a passion even in the darkened and wounded mind
of a Gellion or Freligrath, while passion itself flowers forth
in a Friedrich a bloom that is other than desire, there is no
night that may ever blind the flame that lights the wastes.

There are only the shadows that pass.

The Life and Death
of Elia Constantinidos

I

PULL IN THE DECK-CHAIR here, my friend. So. Now we can sit and watch our Nile slip past, and pity the poor Cairenes this sultry noon . . . Eh, a book even this holiday jaunt to Barrage! The light one, I trust – of the mystery and pursuit and villain-exposure? Many of such I myself read, hoping that in one at last will the villain triumph . . .

Campanella! God mine, it is thirty years since I read him, since I too walked the City of the Sun. In Russia; surely in the dawn of time! Campanella . . . Perhaps they were his streets that Elia glimpsed; perhaps in those pages long-forgotten lies interpretation for another dreamer who saw the Ghosts of Sunland.

Ghosts? The unquiet dead who mow and moan across the astral planes? Not such were they who haunted Elia from that first vision on the Asian hill to the last dark hour of all. Not such are they with whom – who knows? – perhaps this hour, the exile gone home, he walks the City of the Sun!

II

And his tale: Three years younger than our century, Elia, born in Samos, of the dark Ionian stock that has watched the nations pass and re-pass to the Asian shore, the processions phantasmagoric, since the days of Homer. He was the unwanted child, the child indeed unexpected and inexplicable. His mother, the strange, irritating woman who all her life had loved solitude, who would even linger in the night-fields to find that wonder of silence, made the no explanations at his birth, for she was dead. So also, for the little, it seemed that Elia would not live.

But live he did, and was normal but for the one ailment which vexed his early years and the Island doctors. This was some complication of the blood-pressure, resulting at the irregular intervals in the violent and erratic functioning of the heart. Here, when in Cairo many years later, my friend the Dr Adrian tested that heart, and was by it the much and morbidly intrigued . . .

From no such intriguement did Constantinidos *papakes* suffer. The brute farmer, desperately delving a livelihood from the land, with already the adequate family, and soured by the loss of his wife, Elia remained to him the unwanted and mysterious interloper. With such the atmosphere in that little farm of the Samian slopes, where from dawn to dusk was the unending toil, it was miracle that interloper survived childhood.

At the age of five or six he was working on the vinelands or tending the goats on the hills. At night he slept in a small room shared by his three brothers. The bed held but three – a jeering three, and the little Elia's couch was a heap of sacking. By dawn he would be out of doors again, trudging on errands to the village or driving the flock out to the hill-pastures.

And in that environment he grew into a boyhood the living refutation of the philosophies determinist. He had been born with some unquenchable well of friendliness and wonder – those the gifts that all his life he was to give the world – in his heart. From the later Elia I was to know I can build the mind-picture of that Samian boy of six – slight, and pale, with the shock of the matted dark hair, the broad brow and girl's mouth, the stare of friendly eyes. Not once, I think, in the desperate wrongs and bullyings of those early years, did he apprehend cruelty as conscious cruelty; always the puzzlement, never the resentment, followed the tears of pain in those eyes of his . . . Once, in the moment of discernment, his father cursed him for those his 'fey' eyes.

And then came the first of those happenings that were to interweave throughout his life like the threads of gold in the cloak of frieze. He was seven years of age, had spent the day in the vine-plots, and was tramping home in the sunset. It had been the day of desperate toil and heat, and his boy's head and body were alike the throbbing ache. But something in that sunset he was so long to remember caught even then his stare of attention. 'It was so quiet I thought it waited for me,' he was to tell.

So, for a moment, then, the thing unknown since early childhood, came the sudden sick giddiness. He fell to his knees and lay against a bank, gasping, the blood throbbing in his ears. In his pain he covered his ears with his hands, raised his head a little, and then, seeing, gave a cry of wonder that he yet heard but as a whisper.

For, below his feet, from that hill that looked out to the mainland and was called the Asian hill, was a Samos and sea other than he had ever known. Where the village had sprawled a moment before now swept up to sparkling points a great building of glittering walls, and far in the haze of the sunset in Asia the light struck fire from another such shining structure. Where had straggled the rows of vine-poles were marshalled now against the fervent sky line on line of giant trees, unknown. And upon the wind the smell of those trees came to him, and the smell was as of flowers.

He sat and stared. He was not afraid, only wondering, and then, for the swift moment of the utter conviction that shone and passed upon his soul, he knew that he had seen those trees before, had lain beneath them some other sunset and watched the great birds go wheeling into the gloaming of the Asian coast . . .

There was not a sound, but he became aware that he was not alone. He turned his head and beside him saw standing, very still and intent and grave against the unearthly silence and the horizontal limnings of the sunset, a naked boy.

So close was he that Elia could see the flex of muscles in his neck as he moved his head. That head was crowned with flowers, and, taller than Elia, he stood with one hand resting manfully on an unclad hip and the other shading his eyes. There was about him a still friendliness, a companionship, miraculous when allied to that strange beauty of sun-painted skin and crowned valour of head. So, dimly apprehending, the little Elia gazed at him, the moment of the coloured and wonderful silence.

And then, I think for the first and last time in his life, he knew fear. All the dark tales of the Islands and the Asian shores, the debased imaginings and superstitions, clamoured suddenly in his boy-mind. It was a devil who stood beside him, a *phantasma*, a ghost. He crossed himself, tried to cry out, tried to stand up.

And at that the naked lad wheeled round on him with lowered head and sheen of body, and in the so-doing became a mist, a nothingness, leaving a scared and remorseful Greek boy who sat the long hour to stare at the brown-roofed village and later find his way home through a palpitating darkness.

III

Nor, strangely, did memory of that fantastic vision die. It crept with Elia up through the years. Alone in the darkness, he would lie awake and think of it. Out in the fields, in the moments of supreme weariness, bright as ever in remembrance it would return to him. And once or twice, in the times of vivid happiness and laughter – for even were these in that resented childhood of his – it would seem to him that in a moment he would look again on Sunland, that see it indeed he did, dimly, through the shaken boughs of scented trees . . .

These are his words, and I try to follow, watching that Greek lad grow up amidst his vines and goats and the sunsets vision-bringing of the Asian hill. In the little time, as it seemed, his brothers were men, broad of shoulder, quarrelsome still, capable of the much wine-drinking and the sniggering tale. Elia remained the drudge, silenter than when a child, yet quiet, I think, with a quietness that invited no fresh imposition of drudgery. From those eyes that his father held 'fey' something of the wonder had perhaps faded and had come the puzzlement. For all through the years and that silence of his, the friendliness in him stilled but unchanged, grew the questioning: Why?

Drunkenness, blows, cruelty; the seeking of shelter and stifling sleep when the night was a velvet miracle; shame of nakedness; filth of body when the sea cried its loveliness through each dawn; fear of solitude; patriotism and hate; unwanted fatherhood; worship of an incomprehensible and unlovely God; toil and toil from dawn to dusk that toil and toil might be repeated . . . The list unending. These things – why were they?

And here the difference. Not as you and I and the hundreds other in the young revolt did he question these things or their like. The no hatred and rebellion moved him. Only the aching wonder, the fantastic disbelief . . . Life was not so, could not be so. It was some trick, some play of shadows, some foolish dream from which he and the world would presently awake.

And northwards and eastwards throughout those cumulating years clamoured the great, unmeaning guns of the European War. Under their clamour two of his brothers vanished to Athens and the army. The third betook himself to the other side of the island as a fisherman. Was left Elia alone on the little farm with the dour, greying man who drank the more now and seldom spoke a word to the son he hated.

Came an autumn with the guns the dying clamour and
Elia seventeen years of age. Constantinidos *papakes* had
developed the rheumatism and might not move, and in the
week of the great Island fair it was Elia who loaded the
year's produce into the clumsy waggon and with that
waggon journeyed miles away, to the sea-board town of
Vathy. He had been there but once before, and that at the
age of eight, and in the evening of the first day of the fair he
wandered the streets like a traveller astounded from the
planet Mars . . .

She beckoned to him from a doorway in a side-street,
and he stopped and stared at her, at her youth, her eyes
unabashed, her painted lips. He knew nothing of women,
had hardly ever seen a girl of his own age. The most
innocent, perhaps, of any in that city, he looked at her,
and then, at sight of that smile, I think his dark boy's face
lighted and lighted with the friendliness that was his. He
went towards her and she took his hands and suddenly he
found himself trembling on the verge of speech and wonder
unquestioning.

IV

In the dawn he awoke, in the very first of the light, and the
silence which wrapped all Vathy seemed a threatening thing
in that fetid room. There was splash of early sun through
the grimed window that overlooked the sea. Slowly, unbelievingly, he turned his eyes from the room to one who
slept beside him . . .

In the sick remembrance he crept out of bed, somehow
crossed the room, seized the window-catch and flung it
open. The sea-air smote his face like a blow. With that
current of wind came the sudden giddiness, the gripping at
his heart. He gasped, stood swaying and blinking; gripped
the window-ledge . . .

The unclean room with its peeling walls and gaudy eikon

had vanished. Out from a great embrasure that was not a window but a wide sweep of loggia, battled in stone, he looked upon the sunrise and the sea. Behind arched a great room with painted ceiling and the flutter of white draperies around a bed that swung in the morning air. And beside him, unheeding his nearness, standing together in the morning swordfall of sunlight, was the boy of the Asian hill and one other.

The boy of the Asian hill – but the boy no longer. Straight and golden and splendid in the morning of manhood he stood, the seabreeze in his hair, his arm about his companion. And then, as Elia watched, the unknown companion turned half-round in that embrace, glancing up with drowsy eyes into the face of him who held her. And at sight of her and that look on her face, at that white radiance of unshielded loveliness and drowsy tenderness, a moan quivered from the lips of Elia. He sank to his knees: the picture wavered and blurred before his eyes. Yet, for the stayed moment, was one detail vivid – he who had been the boy of the Asian hill swinging round till he stood plain-seen . . .

And then Elia laid his face in his hands and wept, there, in the fetid room of the harlot, with the sea-air blowing upon him.

For it was his own face he had looked upon.

v

He went home from Vathy, a boy still living the memory of a dream. But the shadows came swift across it. Within a fortnight of his return the conscript officers came down from Smyrna upon the village, read the long and puzzling proclamation, and marched away Elia and a score of others for training to fight the Turks.

All over Greece that year swept the wave of jingo patri-otism. Greece was to grow an empire – again! to hold again in its length and breadth the ancient coast which the dreamy Ionians had colonised. In the great camp on Chios it was an exultant and singing conscript army of which Elia found himself part – Elia with the friendly, questioning eyes and puzzled brow.

For there were things of that life that wrung his soul with the pain of their beauty: reveille shrilling down each clean, sweet morning, the song and laughter and the beat of many feet upon the march, the stark, dark hours of sentry-go. Things that lived though past and dead, shining things. But there were others.

I think they waked in him his first anger – the guns, the bayonets, all the clownish apparatus of the mass-murder. Insanities impossible, yet insanities insistent, the hideous nightmare shadows that darkened sunlight from march and camp. They could not be, they were but the horrific imaginings. And yet—

But neither disentanglement of impressions nor rebellion was he ever to achieve on Chios. For within six weeks he and the thousands of other conscripts, the long lines of the half-trained columns with shining new English guns, had landed at Smyrna and were marching up through Asia Minor to that battle-line that beckoned and thundered in the east beyond Manissa.

And as they marched ever nearer, and the rattling of great windows quivered in that remote sky, Elia was to tell me how the singing presently died. Then the happening inexplicable. For he found that it was he himself who restarted the singing, and the others who followed his voice. The strange white happiness came on him in the midst of the aching horror of surmise that held all the column.

'You see,' he was to tell me, 'I knew it could not be real. Life could not be as mad as that. There was something other than death and mutilation to which we were marching. There was something splendid behind those hills.'

And then came down the rains.

Through miles of warm downpour they marched. But they were never to reach the expected battle-line. For that afternoon Kemal Pasha smote the flimsy Greek lines as with a great fist, and the columns of reinforcements found themselves like bewildered ships breasting the westward pouring tides of rout. They halted and flung up hasty entrenchments throughout the night, and in the dawn the Anatolians attacked.

He was never to remember that day nor its happenings. Not even of shadow-land was it. But later he was to be told of it, and the reason of the decoration pinned on his tunic. For they told him that he sang throughout each wave of attack, fought with the mad fury, took over a sector of line when all the officers were dead or deserted, and held that sector with a few hundred amazed and stimulated men till they were in danger of being surrounded. And a madness came on his men as well. For they too sang throughout those beating hours of attack and counter-attack, and singing, led by Elia, marched off through the dusk of that day, an undefeated rearguard.

The Greek army poured towards the sea and Smyrna, and fighting and retreating behind came Elia and his company. Communications were lost, and but for the hasty confirmation of Elia as their commander they had no instructions. Late the second afternoon, the Turks close behind, they marched into Smyrna – Smyrna expectant of massacre and looting, with streets blocked by terrified crowds pressing down to the ships and safety. Here and there a fugitive stopped to scream taunts and execrations at the staggering, blood-weary company that Elia led.

And then, in that black hour, weak for loss of sleep, swaying forward under pressure of a will that was not his own, there happened again to the Samian boy – he was little more – that thing which he had twice known since child-hood – the gripping sensation about his heart, the beating of blood in his ears. He reeled but did not fall; instead, found himself marching on, his feet passing and re-passing without his volition. The blood-pressure eased from his ears and now there shrilled and shrilled in them music stirring as a trumpet heard at night.

No Smyrna street he trod. Instead, was the glassy way, half-shadowed in sunset, half the strange blaze of light. The way thronged and cheering it was, and down the opening lane of that throng – men and women, flower-crowned and cheering, golden and kind and glorious – he was marching. Behind, amidst that voiced exultation, came on his company – explorers from the outer wastes of the universe, an expedition returned from deeds that men would sing forever. And beside Elia marched one whom he knew, one whom he had seen as boy and youth, one who turned calm, searching eyes to left and right.

Then, the glimpsed moment, Elia saw for whom he searched. She stood a little apart, sweet and fair, serene on her lips the little smile. And there happened in that visioned wonder the wonderful thing. For across the ways, not on the glorious being who marched beside Elia, *but on him, himself*, fell her eyes, and in their depths he saw leap swift pity and compassion . . .

The picture of a moment, all this. His little company saw Elia's hand go to his eyes, saw him half halt and turn back. He was in Smyrna, in the raining darkness. Behind, on some hill, raved the nearing guns of the Anatolians.

VI

They took him to Athens, and the story of his fight in the rear of the retreating army – the story of heroism in those dark weeks of shame and black defeat – thrilled through all Greece. He was decorated, confirmed *archegos* in the army, discreetly and hastily taught to read and write, – and given the training of new gangs of recruits from the Peloponnesus.

These things happened to him without his consent and barely with his understanding. He found himself in a new life that included the possession of a man-servant and the obligation to drink much wine and seek amorous adventure. With the smiling, puzzled friendliness, he took those gifts in his hands and looked at them . . . To train men to kill each other for the no need or reason, to drink when he did not thirst, to seek love of women as alternate narcotic and stimulant . . . It was the idle fantasy, and from it the young and popular Captain Constantinidos turned with the impatient sigh to the upbuilding of that strange, dreaming faith evolved in a night in Smyrna.

Somewhere, somewhere if he searched, awaited him his *moira*, his fortune; somewhere was explanation to shadow and sun-dream. Somewhere, in the world of reality, friend and lover, awaited *kore loukophotos*, the maid of the dusk . . .

With that staggering simplicity that was of his soul-stuff he did the simple and obvious thing. He deserted – though he never paused to think of it as desertion. He dismissed his servant, laid aside his uniform, and clad himself in some other clothes he had bought. Then he went down to the Piraeus, walked aboard a ship, and asked for work. By some chance the ship, about to sail, lacked its full complement of crew, and he was engaged at once.

He knew nothing of the ship's destination. Friendly, obedient, with that still, dark face and the stare of questioning eyes, he set about learning the tasks of the common sailor. It was the unseaworthy cargo-boat he had boarded, and as it lurched southwards across the Mediterranean an unwonted contentment came on him. His search had begun.

He left the boat at Alexandria in the same unconsidered indifference in which he had boarded it. He came into Egypt, alien, unafraid, unthinking, still that wondering peasant boy of the Asian hill. In the railway station he bought a ticket, found a train leaving for Cairo, climbed

into it, and by the end of the journey looked out and saw the
Pyramids marching up against the reddened desert of
evening.

VII

All that night he wandered Cairo, turning south at Bab el
Hadid, down Clot Bey, and so, going eastward, till he came
to the Khalig. Through the hours, till after one o'clock in the
morning, he stood under an archway and watched the
throngs go by. Some night of festa it had been, and faces
innumerable lifted and sank continuously from darkness
into the glare of the lamps – faces he searched in a wondering
wistfulness. Then, crossing a deserted Khalig, he set out
again on his nameless search. Down through dark lanes
towards the Suk el Nahassin he must have wandered in those
still hours, under lighted balconies and shuttered windows,
later in the ghostly radiance of flowering stars, seen far up, as
from the bottom of a canyon. Drifts of singing and drowsy
voices came to him, belated travellers, the fewer and fewer
with the wearing of the night, slipped past him in that silvered
darkness. Once he stood a long while and listened to the
baying of dogs in one of the khans – an eerie crying of
desolation that made him shiver, though he knew not
why. And once he heard a lost child weeping, and sought
it through a maze of alleys, till he lost himself and emerged a
long time afterwards to see the stars paling over Citadel.

In the silence of our Cairene false dawn he turned back
towards the Khalig. Long lines of donkeys were passing
through it to the early marts. An occasional native, wrapped
and hooded, for the morning was chill, hastened by. Elia sat
down under the archway, waiting for the day. High up
above his head waved already the tentative banners of the
sunlight, but the Khalig itself was still in shadow.

Perhaps he slept then, for he started to knowledge of the
warmth of day and the sound of approaching footsteps. He

raised his head and looked out, the sun blinding his eyes a moment. Then he leapt to his feet.

For the footsteps were those of that girl who had looked her pity at him across the faery streets of Sunland Smyrna.

She, and no other. Down the Khalig she came, the sun a radiance about her head, unveiled, ungarbed, herself the morning, dreams in her eyes. Lightly she came, unconscious of that look of his that was a prayer. And then in a moment he had cleared the archway shadow and stood in front of her. The Khalig flickered to his gaze; he closed his eyes, reached out and seized her hands . . .

There was a startled ejaculation, a tugging, a whimper of fear. He opened his eyes – and looked down on the frightened face of the harlot of Vathy.

VIII

He had found his fortune. Only then, I think, did he see for an instant, and for the first time, his dreams and puzzlements as but the idle stupidities – awoke to the world that men called sanity and looked about him – the impossible, fantastic world that made of his love a woman of the streets.

They were married within a week at the Greek Consulate – the frightened, haggard-faced woman and the Samian boy with the dark, puzzled eyes which she too thought 'fey'.

'But you do not understand,' she had protested tearfully. 'I am – I am—'

Dazed, aching of heart, he had yet kissed her, with wonder for her tears and the face marred by things unspeakable. 'You are Kalo whom I love,' he said, with a sick amazement at his own words.

Late that night, when they sat alone together, she said a wonderful thing that yet seemed to stab him to the heart.

'I saw you once again after that morning in Vathy. In Smyrna, before I came to Egypt. It was the night the Turks took the city.'

He turned towards her, a lost child, weariness in his face. 'Oh, I am tired.'

And then, at sight of the pity and compassion leap in her eyes, he stared a moment and knelt weeping beside her.

IX

With their little store of money they rented a flat of three rooms in a narrow alley-way off the Khalig. Then Elia set to the desperate search for work. He laboured as a road-sweeper, as a water-carrier, finally for a little while as an extra waiter at the café of Simon.

So it was he came into my life the brief while, in the brief moments in the night-lighted Khalig to stand beside me and tell me, because of the bond of friendliness and trust that a chance word had forged, this story of his fairy hauntings.

Lost, fantastically tragic, perhaps I could have helped him, perhaps friended him. But to me, who stand aside and listen and look, he was then only a voice, a tale, another colour in our city many-coloured. Intrigued, insincere, I remember that when he had finished I evolved, for my own amusement, and in the glow self-commendatory, the explanation airy and poetic.

'Perhaps they are of the real world, those your Sun-Ghosts' – *Phantasmata toi helioi* he had called them – 'and you and I and the little Kalo but the vain imaginings, the dark, sad dreams of the People of the Sun . . .'

And then I stopped. For he had turned his eyes on me and behind their puzzled friendliness I saw that which shamed me, the glib romantic, to silence.

X

So I knew him, and he was gone, finding at length the more permanent work in a Greek printer's. The long hours of work they were, from which each evening he would return to Kalo Constantinidos and the little flat. And what doubts of himself and his own persistent disbelief, what stilled puzzlements each day brought to his eyes – how shall we know?

Yet his impossible simplicity suffered no change. He rescued from the street and the tormenting of the gang of urchins a half-crazed negro who had once been a cook. Him he installed as servant in the tiny flat, and was repaid by Salih ibn Muslih with the adoration and the jealous worship – the jealousy that extended even to Kalo.

But Kalo was happy. Always to her I think Elia remained the wonderful, inexplicable lover, so that even when he brought home the crazy negro she protested with but the half-heart and indifference. Life, life that had been the long nightmare since she fled from starvation to the painted houses of Vathy, of Smyrna, of Cairo – it blossomed now the scented hours, like a flower transplanted.

And Elia? Even when he held her in his arms did the look of puzzlement go from his eyes? He who knew neither fear nor regret – did her fear of the old negro seem to him the thing unreal? Her little human frailties of temper and desire – were those to him the shadowing of the sun?

I do not know, only look back across the years and see them there, in those little rooms in that little street, amongst the neighbours Syrian and Greek, inquisitive and friendly; Kalo by the open window, her hand to her eyes, awaiting her Samian boy come up the street each evening . . .

That the picture, and for background the twisted body and crazed mutterings of the negro, ibn Muslih.

XI

Then the happening horrific, of which were never the full details known. Late afternoon a woman who lived in the flat below that of Elia and Kalo thought she heard come from overhead a scream, the sound of scuffling. She listened, but heard no more, and thought herself deluded. Then an odd apprehension touched her. She climbed up to the other flat and knocked at the door. Thereat was again the stirring, the sound of struggle, and then scream on scream that was suddenly stayed by the sound of a blow . . .

There were men in the building; they ran and brought gendarmes, and a great crowd collected. They battered in the door of the Constantinidos flat, and there, amidst the litter of the struggle, stood in horror till one went forward and covered that pitiful thing whose singing they had heard the few hours before.

At that moment a shout arose from the street. 'From the back window! He escapes from the back window!'

The negro, stained knife in hand, had been seen descending the fire-escape. He made a crazed gesture of defiance and fled up an alley-way of warehouses, the mob at his heels.

Then, even while those who had broken into the Constantinidos flat stood there in the helplessness, they heard a voice raised in surprise, and turned about. In the doorway, with friendly, questioning eyes, stood Elia.

They parted and made way for him, and, wondering, he went forward . . .

XII

The crowd ran ibn Muslih to earth in a bottle-necked cul-de-sac. At that neck, worked up into the dervish rage, he stood and defied them, knife in hand.

Someone flung a stone and the negro reeled under a shower of missiles which followed that first one. Three gendarmes ran back for their carbines. And then the crowd was flung to left and right, and another madman, Elia

Constantinidos, with the white face and blazing eyes, fronted ibn Muslih.

Bleeding, defiant, the negro looked up. Over him swept the swift change. At sight of Elia he gave a low wail and covered his face with his hands. The knife slithered to the ground. Elia crouched like a beast to spring, and the mob waited with panting breath.

Then the happening inexplicable. Elia was seen to reel, to grip his head as one in pain, and then walk forward towards ibn Muslih with outstretched hands. Behind him they yelled his danger, and at that shout he wheeled round.

'It is only ibn Muslih. My friend, ibn Muslih . . .'

For a moment amazement held the mob. Then a growl of horror and anger rose. Someone shouted a foul taunt, a fouler accusation. A stone hurtled through the air and glanced from Elia's forehead. But he heeded it not. Fronting them, there had come on his face the light unearthly. He flung out a sudden arm, and words incomprehensible as those of that last cry on the Hill of Crucifixion rang in the ears of their stayed anger.

'*Why, it is we – we who are the People of the Sun! Those others – look, look, they are but shadows!*'

A panting gendarme, newly on the scene, an Egyptian recruit who knew nothing of the circumstances except that here was a desperado at bay, knelt down, steadied his carbine on his knee, and fired . . . He gave a grunt of satisfaction.

The mad light went from the eyes of the Greek desperado. He coughed, looked round with puzzled gaze, pressed his hand to his chest, and then crumpled and fell at the feet of the glaring ibn Muslih.

XIII

And that is the tale of Elia Constantinidos, whose name to this day is the abomination and the hateful thing in the quarters of the Khalig.

But I – I heard of it and wept. What last fantastic vision did he see when he faced ibn Muslih? How transformed, in what strange picture-images did that last scene rise? And who are they – what dreams of life attainable, splendid, unshadowed – those who all his life haunted him?

We question and wonder and forget, like men in sleep. For not Elia alone, but all men they haunt. Under the many names and through the many faiths they pass, immortal, undying, the shining ghosts we glimpse and remember in wonder and weeping, as the faces of dead children are remembered.

Cockcrow

I

EH? THAT? Only the crowing of a Lemnos rooster! From the fowl-run behind this café it comes – the fowl-run of the little Simon.

You had not suspected in him the tastes bucolic? In our Cairene evenings I think he wanders out there and dreams of a farm in Lemnos – he who would die of the broken heart if he forsook the Khalig's colours and call! . . .

The challenge absurd in the sunlight – but in the dawn – how of the haunting it is! Haunting, I think, with the memories not our own, the stored race-remembrances innumerable since first the jungle-fowl was tamed and that challenge of the morning heard in an Indian hut. What agonies and waitings has it not ended, what vigils and prayers! That drowsy clamour – surely it is in all memories, vivid and unforgettable, for at least the one night that would never pass, for at least one stretch of the dark, still hours!

That morning so many years ago, my friend – think how it must have shrilled above the hills of Jerusalem!

II

If you walk the Shari' Abbassieh today you will see the house of Lucius Ravelston stand shuttered and dusty in the sunshine, with its little garden deserted. Last we heard of him, the Ravelston, he was in Hadramaut, on expedition in search of the lost sand-cities of the proto-Semites. In days when that garden knew him he would stride to and fro with the hasting guest by his side, discussing the languages international and the inhabitability of the moon and the character of Marco Polo; of all such things he would discuss with the naïve fervour that another devotes to the scandal or the politics . . .

The guest would pant beside him for the little, then give up with a laugh, and sit to watch his host, pipe-smoking, trample the flower-beds in the heat of exposition.

More nearly the seven than the six feet in height, a giant, with the rapt stare of grey eyes under knit brows and the strange brown hair like silk. He had an athlete's body that Phidias would have loved, though of Hellas the good Aristotle would perhaps have baulked at his mind.

Indeed, this would have been but reciprocal, for the good Aristotle he regarded with the detestation utmost. Giant and genius, he was yet something of a child, and men dead and dust three thousand years he could love or detest with as much fervour as though they wrote in the journals contemporary.

'A snippety suburban mind – the mind of a fossil-collecting curate.'

'But I have heard of him as the Father of the Sciences,' I would say, and so bring upon myself recital of Aristotelian fatuities, the while the drowsy cluckings would cease in the native fowl-run beyond the garden, and the good sun, talked from the sky, went down behind the Red Hills . . .

He was the crusader essential, hating all neat, unorigi-native minds which look on life with the cold, conservative calm. Not yet the forty years of age, he had been surgeon in the great war of Europe, the leader of a Polar Expedition, the assistant of Knut Hammssen in that Odyssey through the Gobi Desert. From such exploits of the heroic he had settled down in Cairo to study the scourge cancer. In laboratory and study they fight the last crusades.

Research-worker, student, he yet waged the wars un-ending in journal and congress and popular press. Enemies in battalions he loved, though there were occasions when he would forget the date of a battle, going into lengthy abstractions as a mystic into a trance. These were escapes to the super-normal, when some thought would suddenly fructify in his mind and he would wipe the dust of tragedy and comedy and friendship from his hands, and retreat to the barred room and the microscope and the notes and the lamp-lit table for the days or weeks on end . . .

My friend, Dr Adrian the gynæcologist, also knew him and loved him.

'An anachronism, fifty years behind the times, Ravelston. In the Huxley-Haeckel tradition. Last of the warrior-sa-vants. Science has more triumphs and heroes than ever, but Ravelston's the last of her champions to go out into the arena and defy embattled Stupidity. Pity. They lent colour to life, the giants.'

'They brought fire from heaven, if I remember,' I said. 'But I do not think he is the last. There will always be giants.'

Coming from the house called Daybreak, we were pas-sing through Abbassich late in the night, and stood looking up at the flare of light from the room of Ravelston. Adrian laughed.

'The Titan, eh? There was also a vulture in the story, wasn't there? We must warn Lucius!'

III

That autumn the giant went to England, to London, to see to the publication of a book – not the such book as you might write, my friend, needing no supervision, but the production marvellous and intricate, with the diagrams and the changing print and the chemic symbols much-strewn to confusion and despair of printer. Adrian and I made the call occasional at the Abbassieh house and saw to its ordering. It was the place pleasant, and we spent many hours of ease in the great library, or drank the good Ravelston's wine under the lime-trees in his garden.

Behind he had left, in the rough, the great work on which he had been engaged since coming to Cairo. Though only in first draft, Adrian had promised to read this treatise and contribute to it the preface. He would groan aloud over calligraphy and contractions, yet read on in fascination. Once or twice he interviewed clients of the giant, and of one of those interviews told me. The man was a Greek who had suffered from the internal pain diagnosed by his own doctor as a cancer tumour. Under treatment of Ravelston he had been made well and whole again in a month.

'A month! Unless it was a mere fluke, colonel, Ravelston's in the process of perfecting a treatment for cancer that'll wipe it from the face of the earth . . . Beyond the dreams of Lister.'

We would smoke and make the meditation, and discuss the absent Ravelston. Of his private life we knew nothing.

'He has no private life, no private ambition. He's a Republican of your Plato, colonel, a Samurai out of Wells . . . Marry? He'd forget a woman in a fortnight – unless she developed *sarcomata*!'

Ravelston cabled the date of his return, and I found the Dr Adrian, Cairo's leading gynæcologist, with sleeves rolled up, and the scurry of native servants, flapping a negligent duster around the library. ' "Prepare the house,"

eh? Must be bringing home a shipload of zoological specimens.'

It was the afternoon when the boat-train was due from
Alexandria. 'It is his jest,' I said. 'Or perhaps he brings the
tourist friend.'

'God forbid,' said Adrian, and then we heard a taxicab
come in the sharia below and the sound of a key in the door.
Then Ravelston's voice upraised.

'Adrian! Saloney! . . . Hell, what a dust!'

We went out and waved to him from the landing. He
stood in the doorway, in the winter sunshine, and beyond,
in the street, seemed the fight in progress between the
native porters and a mountain of trunks. These things, and
then—

Simultaneously we saw her. She stood not in the belt of
sunshine, but in the mote-sprayed darkness within the
door. I made the bow ineffective and Adrian the fumble-
ment for the collar of his shirt.

'Pamela – Dr Adrian and Colonel Anton Saloney. You
people, this is my wife.'

IV

She called him never by his first name, but sometimes
'Ravelston' and sometimes 'Stealthy Terror', – the first
because it was fashionable so to address a husband, the
second because of some secret jest they shared together.
She ransacked the Abbassieh house from top to bottom,
and had shaken from it such showers of dust as seemed
to warrant the eviction of the Sahara itself. The roof of
one wing was cut away and installed with a special glass
that interrupts not the violet ray, and for this novelty
she was the excited child, as indeed was Ravelston
himself.

'He has sun-bathing on the brain,' said Adrian. 'God
knows why – unless it's to admire the pretty Pamela . . .

Done without it all his life and now he pretends it's essential to health, whereas it's merely a craze and fashion.'

'You do not like Mrs Ravelston?'

'I don't,' he said, with the curtness. 'Lucius was a Samurai, and now – Good Lord, look what he's becoming!'

And indeed I also, with the amazement and pity, watched transformation of the giant from research worker and world-enthusiast into lover and follower. He planned and rode the excursions with her, the while library and laboratory remained locked and neglected, took her to innumerable balls and festas, humoured her in the whims and desires most wayward and foolish. She declared a passion for the language Russian, and determination to learn it, and I was hired to teach such accent as Ravelston himself possessed not.

She was the pupil impossible – would lie deep in her chair and yawn, or look from the window and comment on the passers-by, or remark on my appearance or her own with a frankness startling.

'Why don't you trim that nice brown beard of yours, colonel? . . . All right, then. Sorry. Where were we? . . . "*Smeyat'cia, posmeyat'cia* – to laugh." . . . But how can they? Laughing in Russian must require a surgical operation. Stealthy Terror would laugh well in Russian.' Would drop the book and clasp her hands about her knees. 'Why have you never married, colonel?'

She would smile sleepily because of the sun-bathing, and stretch like a cat, with the winking of golden eyes.

Beautiful? But no. She had the nose too short and the upper lip too long. Yet the charm that is beyond proportions and measurements – the careless, insolent mouth that was somehow like the mouth of Ravelston himself, and eyes very deeply lashed and wonderful, and the sheen of hair, cut like a boy's, and very dark and fine. Beside Ravelston, she looked on occasion like his son.

She tired very quickly of the Russian, and the lessons in it ceased. She tired of the sun-bathing, and I think her first quarrel with Ravelston was over that tiring. Thereafter she carried it out infrequently, as a boring duty . . . 'She would tire of the glories of heaven and yawn in the faces of the Archangels,' Adrian would growl.

Light, irresponsible, blindly selfish, insolently cold and insolently passionate, she seemed no more fit mate for Ravelston than a woman of the Warrens. She was daughter of his publisher, and early on his visit to London they had made the acquaintance. Ravelston I believed she had married as the new 'thrill', the new and unprecedented experience – because of his stature and his reputation and that otherness of his – the otherness that now, alas, seemed to have vanished. She had an endless craving for change, for thrill and glitter and running laughter, for the dance and the perfumes, the admiration and the adoration. Anything that savoured of study or the weariness of toil was 'horrible'. All that was enemy of the good time and the careless hour was 'horrible'.

And yet – I could not dislike her. Perhaps because of beauty of gesture and attitude, and the ring of her boy-laughter and that bright scorn she had of things; perhaps because once or twice in her I glimpsed a dark fierceness that might have been her soul, imprisoned and lost, beneath the shifting play of moods that was her life.

v

One morning, near five o'clock, coming from the all-night dance at the Mess Artillery, they overtook Dr Adrian and me, and gave us a lift to the house in Abbassieh. We sat the four of us hunched together in Ravelston's little car, and the dawn was in the sky into which we raced. Pamela looked tired, and as we turned into the garden-way of the house I saw that she was asleep. The garden was dim and scented, and through it the giant carried her indoors.

And then, suddenly, a cockerel in the native fowl-run next door flapped and crowed with piercing loudness. Pamela awoke with the cry of terror, struggled in Ravelston's arms so that he halted, and then stared from the one to the other of us in slow realisation. But in her eyes was still terror.

We laughed at her, and then stood of the awkward and embarrassed, for she laid her head against Ravelston's shoulder and wept with an intensity in her amazing. Adrian and I would have gone, but that the giant motioned to us to follow. In the downstairs room he switched on the lights, and set Pamela in a chair, and knelt beside her. She stared into his face with the colour slowly coming back to her own.

And it was then, in that moment of the overstrung, that she told us.

She had been a child of twelve in the last years of the War, in the London suburb, in some area unfortunate traversed again and again by the German air-raiders. Often was the screaming of sirens and the falling of bombs, and her child-nerves played on by inexplicable terrors, her sleep shattered in sudden hurryings to and fro . . .

And then came a morning that she might not forget. There was the usual alarm and she and her brother, a child of three, were hurried out to hide in a garden-shed, the safest refuge. The nurse left them there the moment the while she ran back for clothes, and in that moment, looking out, Pamela saw the night flash and flash again. She cried out to the nurse, and then in terror ran after her in the direction of the house. Half-way across the garden she heard her brother call her name, and turned, confused and remembering. In that moment came catastrophe. She was flung to the ground by the explosion which wiped out the shed, and the darkness rained splinters of stone and wood around her. She picked herself up, bruised and

bleeding, and through the squalling scolding from a nearby chicken-run heard a cock which crowed unceasingly,
unendingly, above the clamour . . .

'Ravelston, I heard him scream – I know I did – and I
can't ever forget . . . and that crowing. Oh, I was a coward,
a coward! I killed him. He had that lost-boy stare you have
when you sit and think . . . Oh, beastly coward!'

He laughed at her, the giant. 'You could have done
nothing. You're brave even to remember it. Tired now.
Carry you to bed?'

Adrian and I, forgotten, went out into the morning
without the promised refreshments. The laboratory and
all the other windows but for one, far up, shone dark as
dead eyes.

'What do you think of her now – and this story?' I said.

'Hysteria. Explains a little and doesn't help a jot.' We
passed out of range of that lighted window. 'Poor Ravelston! Titan and Pandora – complete with vulture!'

'Eh?' I said, and would have made remarks regarding the
mythology confused, but that he went on:

'Um. You didn't know, of course. There's cancer in her
family – *carcinomata*. Hereditary. She doesn't know it
herself, but Ravelston did when he married her.'

VI

Here, it seemed to me – I who cannot help finding story and
plot in every life I look on – were elements enough of the
drama. Ravelston, with that secret upon him, with his
unsurpassed knowledge of the stages of the cancer-march,
turning in desperation from the rigour and slowness of
impersonal research to the sunbathing and each other of
the swift, glib cures; Pamela, insolent, selfish, young,
looking forward to years of pleasure and amusement –
all that she craved – all unconscious that the most frightful
and agonising of diseases lay like a beast awaiting her . . .

But Nature has little stage-sense. She can make of apparent tragedy the thing ludicrous and meaningless, of comedy the thing horrifying. So at the house in Abbassieh. One morning Pamela complained of the unwellness, and the symptoms described to Ravelston. With fear upon him, he made the no-examination himself, but sent for Adrian. An X-ray apparatus was brought from Citadel Hospital, the many photographs taken, and Adrian made the searching examination. Then he went away with the apparatus and in the evening returned to them.

'Mrs Ravelston has a magnificent constitution. There is nothing more wrong with her than a passing ailment.'

'Eh?' said Ravelston, and leapt from his chair. Then abruptly he was gone from the room. Adrian was left alone with Pamela, cigarette-smoking, undisturbed, but sitting considering him, chin in hand.

'What was Ravelston fussing about, doctor? What did he and you expect?'

He had never liked her, and it seemed to him then that the truth might sober her. In a moment he was telling her of the suspicions and the facts, and in that moment regretting it.

'. . . Expected I'd develop cancer? Nice. Married me knowing it? – Thought I'd be a convenient subject-study, I suppose? I'll remember *that*.'

Adrian stared at her in amazed anger. She nodded to him the insolent dismissal. 'That's all, doctor. You can send in your bill.'

VII

More and more rapidly with the passing of the weeks, the lives of those two began to split apart. Ravelston, relieved, exultant, rid of that immediate personal fear, turned again to laboratory and desk. He grew again to the habit of shutting himself up for the hours and days at a stretch, immersed in the matters that to Pamela were the incomprehensible unpleasantnesses.

Conscious of his defection from the round of inane pleasure and sight-seeing, he would on occasion burst from laboratory or study to the rooms of Pamela, caress her – and then vanish again in a banging of doors, leaving, I think, one who sat breathless and with singing heart. But so only for the moment.

If Adrian might not, I at the least could comprehend something of the startled anger and resentment that followed his revelation. A freak . . . A 'study'. . . . Even with the cooling of first anger – anger that to her generation is the thing crude and clownish – she forgot not at all. Indeed, the changed behaviour of Ravelston was constant reminder. She had expected, I imagine, that Ravelston would always comport himself as in the days of the honeymoon, with his work relegated to a secondary place. She had expected that Prometheus would continue to bring fire from heaven, but only – in the phrase of Adrian, who disliked her so – 'to provide her with a damn little foot-warmer'.

Instead, there were now the moments, in chance meetings and at meal-times, when he stared at her as though she were a stranger. The 'freak' had ceased to be freakish, the 'subject' had refused to be satisfactorily cancerous, in disobedience to the expectations of heredity . . . She had ceased to interest.

So, knowing that she lied, she must have told herself the many times, and so, in the mixture of boredom and pique, and with that urgency to grasp from life all that it might offer in sensation, she turned to the gaudy glitter of the European season, to the dancings and the gatherings, the gossipings and philanderings, the motor-excursions and the flowering acquaintanceships; finally, to the growing amusement and interest in Andreeius de Bruyn.

VIII

I met them the one afternoon outside the Continental Hotel, where I awaited a client. I had been the dragoman to him a month before, and from his car he nodded to me a mocking salutation.

'Afternoon, St Peter!'

This was his crude jest because of an incident during that month that would smell none the sweeter for the telling. There had been keys in the incident, and I had saved him from the slit throat, and a Muslim woman from the attentions of one who imagined he was honouring a 'native'. It was the incident he had done better to forget.

Before I might reply, she who sat by his side turned her head, and recognised me, and laughed.

'Hello, colonel! *Kak vi' pazhivaicte?* Oh, and – *pocmesyaietc'ie!*'

To her and the Russian horrible I smiled then, as she commanded. Perhaps there had been other than an expression pleased on my face at sight of her with De Bruyn. She whispered something to him, and they laughed at me, and the car shot away . . . De Bruyn!

He was the young Dutchman with the much money and the less perception of responsibility to life than possesses a mayfly. Villains have gone from life as they have from literature, and perhaps De Bruyn was no more evil than was Ravelston, his antitype. Like Pamela, it was merely that the gross selfishness that is in all of us, the thing instinctive, had never known the repression or the transmutation. Wants and desires were things to be purchased or cajoled, never to be forgone. In Cairo he had already organised the orgies and excursions and fantastic entertainments innumerable. In his handsome face he had eyes which they said could hold and fascinate any woman . . . To me they were the bright, shifting eyes of one morally unborn.

That excursion of theirs I witnessed had not been the

first. Alike her insolence and selfishness, and perhaps also her fearlessness, fascinated De Bruyn. He laid the cold-blooded siege, without concealment of desire or intention, as is the fashion of the philanderer modern. From Pamela Ravelston was at first the amusement, and then the some-thing else that was still a mocking thing, that mocked even when at last she found herself in his arms . . . Love or hate, Lucius or Andreeius – what did it matter, so long as boredom was cheated?

As casually as that, and yet quite irrevocably, she must have come to her decision and sat down and wrote the letter which she sent to Ravelston from the Ghezireh ball.

IX

Early in that morning of her writing, I was walking home, all of the meditative way from the Koubbah observatory. In Abbassieh I saw a light in the room of Ravelston, and there came on me the sudden resolve, I would acquaint him with the D Bruyn matter, for in those chill hours it loomed to me with the appearance serious.

I went round to the back of the house, through the garden, and pressed the bell that sounded in his room alone. Hardly had I ceased but there came the noise of footsteps, and Ravelston, gigantic, towered in the doorway dimness.

'Saloney!' He gave a strange laugh. 'I thought – but never mind what I thought. Come in.' He banged the door behind me and gripped my arm. 'Come up here. I've something to show you.'

He led me up the stairs of the back, and then, on the landing that led to his study, had the new resolve. 'Not here. Further up, first.'

On that other landing he opened the door and switched on lights and stared round the room. Then laughed again.

'Look, Saloney! She was here yesterday. Everything here

is hers. There's not a thing but's known her touch. Eh? And she's slept in that bed; I've heard her singing up here, going to bed at midnight . . . Remember the way she had of singing – with that little hoarseness? And of sitting with clasped knees? Eh?'

He bent down and very gently and deliberately picked up a chair. And then he went suddenly berserk-mad. He hurled the chair at the great dressing-glass and brought it smashing to the floor, and then set about deliberately wrecking the room. I stood in the helplessness and watched, and when he had finished the place looked, strewn with the torn and trampled draperies, like a murdered girl. Once I tried to stay him.

'But why—?'

'Come away, colonel. Out of it! Unclean, this place. Come down below and have a drink.'

Below he poured out the whisky and tossed me a letter. While I read it he walked up and down, his hands twitching. In face and voice was that flare of mirth that is the anger of his kind.

'Good letter, eh? "Not being either a dragoman or a doctor, I'm tired of Abbassieh; not being either a cancerous freak or a beastly disease you're evidently tired of me." Who told her about the cancer? Never mind . . . A little adultery for amusement, eh? Who's this De Bruyn?'

I told him. 'A lover? A dirty little lover and her days and nights spent planning dirty little caressings and kissings . . . while I've been working. I've been made fool and cuckold because I could not play – the lap-dog! She expected me to give up for her the world, my work, the things that are me . . . For a little loving and mating!'

And suddenly he stopped in front of me and laughed – a laugh of the genuine amusement and relief.

'Lord, why didn't I see? I've been blind as a mole! Oh, not only to this dirty little intrigue. To fact. Loving and mating, begetting and desiring – those, or the life without

flambeaux or kindliness, of work unending, with nothing
but the surety that some day the swamps will be cleared
away . . .'

He was walking to and fro again, but no longer in the
anger. Rather was it the exultation.

'I know. See it only now. My work's been going to pieces.
One can't have both; one must choose. Warmth and light and
caresses and the safe places – or loneliness and vision . . .'

His eyes were shining now. It was the Ravelston of the
garden-talks, lost and forgotten those many months, and I
thrilled to meeting with him again. I stood up and seized his
hand.

'But you are right. You will press on to the greater work
alone.'

He laughed in the ringing confidence, and then dropped
my hand and wheeled to the window with lightning swift-
ness. Upon the garden lay the dawn. Again shrilled out that
sound that had startled us, and at its repetition he swung
round upon me, gigantic, with horror on his face.

'My God, if she's scared – alone – with that fool! . . .
What rubbish you've been talking, Saloney! Rubbish!
There wasn't a soul to the world till I found Pam! The
future's trust to me – guerdon and promise. And I neglected and forgot her . . . Lost her now, I who could have
kept her mine, could have made her true and clear and fine
as a sword, could have tramped with her desert and star-
field . . . Work! She was light to my clumsy groping, and
I've lost her—'

But I had heard another sound through the hushed
morning. I caught his sleeve.

'Listen!' I said.

X

De Bruyn and Pamela, you must understand, had planned
to arrive at Alexandria, where was De Bruyn's yacht, early

in the forenoon. They danced till as late as three o'clock at
the ball on Ghezireh Island. Then Pamela sent off the letter
to Ravelston by a native messenger, and they went out to
the car which had been awaiting them.

De Bruyn came flushed with the wine and dancing, and
as he wrapped the rugs about Pamela he was of the over-
affectionate. This she told him, with her usual fearless
insolence, and he sat beside her sulkily, driving out of
Cairo.

But he was the skilled driver, steering with reckless care,
and in the little they were clear even of the grey mud
suburbs and the stars were the splendour above them.
Pamela Ravelston yawned, and sank deep in rugs, and
presently was asleep.

For an hour the great racer fled westwards, along the
Alexandrian road. Then De Bruyn suddenly swore, and the
car bumped and shuddered and fell to the crawl. They were
in the midst of a village, shuttered and sleeping, and the
roadway was pitted with uneven holes.

The searchlight rays of the headlamps shook and made
the standstill. For a moment, amongst the narrow lanes
branching from the roadway, the noise of the car was
deafening.

'Curse it. Puncture,' said De Bruyn. 'Stay there, Pam.
No need for you to get down.'

Pamela stirred sleepily and murmured something the
while he got out and fumbled with the lamps. Above the
silent, mud-walled village the sky glimmered amethyst in
the false dawn.

And then from a mud-hut near at hand a child began to
cry, and shrill and clear, awakened by the noise of the car,
misled by the false light in the sky, a cock crew and others
throughout the village took up the call till De Bruyn lifted a
dawn-greyed face, and laughed and swore.

'Those infernal birds! They would wake the dead. Eh?'

And as he stared in amazement at one who sat and wept

there in the flickering light, and then sprang to vivid life, and swore at him, and made the unreasonable demand, he did not know that that clamour about them had indeed awakened the dead.

XI

'What?' said Ravelston.

But I was looking out of the window as the great car of De Bruyn halted in front of the house, its noise deafening. Out of it leapt someone in a whirl of the dance-draperies, someone whose key slotted urgently in the street-door, who came up the stairs with flying feet.

'Ravelston . . . Old Stealthy Terror . . . I've come back . . .' White-faced, but the scared and shivering repentant not at all, she stood in front of him. Neither fear nor regret had brought her back, but remembrance of that lover with the lost-boy stare. 'Oh, I've been such a fool! Dirty and a coward . . . My dear, I forgot!'

'We both forgot,' he said, and took her in his arms – those arms in which perhaps she is sleeping tonight in some desert of the Hadramaut.

But I turned away and went down to the street. As I opened the door, De Bruyn, starting up his car, glanced at me with the wry, white smile.

'Morning, St Peter.'

And then I had a sudden sense of the moment dramatic, of the story told and re-told the many times, in the many ways.

'Poor Judas,' I said.

Gift of the River

I

KEITH LANDWARD SEEN in Athens? And you have heard
of Landward? Read of him in the *Egyptian Gazette*? . . . The
story scandalous, no doubt.

An abduction charge initiated by the Greek Institution?
And with the hastiness dropped, though it was sufficient to
bring about the ostracism of Landward and his unwed
victim – if one may ostracise those who walk unaware of
both laws and law-givers!

To Landward I think a marriage ceremony would have
seemed the gross sacrilege . . .

Eh? But how? . . . Let me tease you for moral, my friend,
you who are young, the realist declared – though where was
ever yet realist who dipped pen in the inks of reality? I,
Anton Saloney, the much and foolishly over-read, have met
him never!

Love – is desire; possession – satiety. Are not these the
axioms realist?

Yet Heloise walks a garden still, and tonight – who knows
the agony of Abelard under these stars? Who knows the face
of Paolo in the Khalig throngs? Yet I have seen him pass. I
have seen in a Nileward window the light set by one who
waits and weeps Leander – dust and legend those three
thousand years!

Polychromata – the City of Many Colours. But there is
the one colour that abides and changes not. Gift of the
River is our Cairo, and what gifts but the miraculous does
the Nile bring? Who may say, knowing Keith Landward

and his tale, knowing romance and miracle for the children of faith and necessity, that even Hero waits in vain?

II

And his tale fantastic which I have pieced together – it begins as indeed no tale should begin, when Joan Landward died in the Nile house beyond Bulaq Bridge.

She had spent a bare five months in Cairo, brought here for health, and for portrait you must make imagining of one with the dark hair and the grey eyes and the white cheeks stained with bright blood-ovals. As though painted on the pallor of her skin were those ovals.

Keith Landward, the husband, brought her here in the late November, and I took them the explorations of the bazaars. She had in those explorations the much delight. Life she found continually the wonder and delight . . . Laughing, she would cough and stop, and the bright blood-ovals flame in her cheeks, and Landward's eyes leap to her in startled fear. It was, you understand, hers the lung-wasting that had brought them to Egypt.

'Insane climate. Treacherous,' he would storm, with that the startled look still in his eyes. 'Dr Adrian says so. We'll go back to Majorca.'

'Not yet. Not until the Spring. I'm in love with Colonel Saloney's Cairo – *and* the Nile. So's Steadfast. Bark yes, Steadfast. Do it in Esperanto!'

She had the dog, the little, solemn, thick-coated beast called Steadfast, and to him she had taught the many little solemn tricks. In the narrow, high-walled garden of their house, with the watersteps leading down to the River, she would prevail on Steadfast to make the evolutions ludicrous, culminating in the absurdity of 'the fairy dance', for my delectation, and on her never did the exquisite funniness of those pall. Landward, laughing and scowling, would shake her shoulders.

'Stop it, Joan! You'll exhaust yourself.'

'Sorry, but it's Steadfast to blame.' Seated, she would lean back against Landward's hands and look up into his face with just the such solemnity of tenderness as was in the eyes of the dog looking up at her. So-sitting, she would reach her arms round his neck, her fingers twisting in his hair in the mock-cruel caress, and be very still.

'Listen to the River!'

She loved the Nile, and I think listened much to it in that garden the while she worked and translated with Landward. He was the linguist, the master of many tongues – never have I known anyone master of so many – and the language-study was his life-work. It was his the dream to build up a scientific international language – not one of the so-easy elisions and evasions, but a tongue founded on the broad evolutions of human speech, a flexible, synthetic World-Speech that would presently be taught the earth over . . .

He was a Scotsman of the far Western Islands, of that Celtic fringe that is now denied by your historians. Dark as Joan herself, quick and emotional and subtle, he worked not in the plodding, but in sudden flares of the inspiration and enthusiasm. But that men turn now from the romantic leisure as from childhood's toys, he might have been poet or painter of the twilight melancholy. The poet, I think, for words, the power and beauty and terror of words, could move him as stars or music another. His Joan and his World-Speech – those his two loves, grown inextricably the one.

'There won't be a frontier or a fort in Europe fifty years after we've finished,' he would declaim, and she would look at him with shining eyes. Swift herself in the learning of languages, this dream of the World-Speech had grown as vivid for her as for Landward.

But presently he was in difficulties. The framework of the World-Speech was already planned, but how to garb it in the living flesh?

'Accent – intonation – some common denominator of word-rhythm and music . . . Damn it, Joan, it's an impasse. Take another twenty years of work . . . Oh, curse all fools since the Tower of Babel!'

And he got up, tramping to and fro in one of his sudden rages. Then her silence, the fact that she did not laugh at him as usual, brought his gaze to her. She sat very still, with eyes closed.

'*Joan*!'

Fear for her haunted his life, though he hid it even from himself, except at such moments. She roused and looked up at him.

'What? . . . Oh Keith, my dear, don't look like that! I'm ever so well. Only lazy . . . And this accent-business won't take twenty years: nor twenty months. You'll find it long before then – I'll find it myself! . . .' Her arms round his neck, the solemnity in her eyes as he bent over her. 'Lazy this afternoon, my dear. And the sound of the River—'

That night, lying wakeful in the darkness over this matter of the World-Speech accent, he heard Joan cough and turn restlessly and the sound of her hand come out to seek him . . . He sat up in panic and turned on the lights, for the hand had ceased to seek and the noise of the River below had suddenly grown to the noise of a torrent.

III

That shining room in the crematorium of Al Fostat – always shall I remember the smell of the mimosa wreaths that blinded the white coffin, and the still, dark face of Landward, and that strange burial-service of your Church, at the once so-beautiful and grotesque . . . Then the Dr Adrian and I, with the uneasiness of what might happen if we left him, drove back with Keith Landward to the house above the Nile.

He went with us in silence, but suddenly, in the garden of

the house, at sight of the solemn little dog Steadfast padding to and fro, burst into one of the rages that with him
were temperamental.

'That infernal dog – can't have it here. Interrupt my work
. . . Must go on with my work. Do you hear? . . . Take it
away, Saloney. Eh? Anywhere you like. What the devil does
it matter to me? Never want to see it again.' He raised his
voice. 'Ibrahim! That fool Ibrahim – why hasn't he set my
table out here? Does he think this is a national fête?'

He darted into the house, there was presently the sound
of cursing and commotion, and he appeared again, driving
the scared and laden Ibrahim Garas, his Egyptian servant.

'Down there. In the usual place. And take away that
other chair – *that* chair, you fool! . . . Anything you two
want? Eh? Oh yes. Good-bye.'

IV

The little dog trotted beside us, making the heart-breaking
whine, and to me he was a worry, for Landward in such
mood might order him to be drowned. Adrian had no place
to keep him, nor had I.

Then I remembered my friends, the Freligraths, and that
they perhaps could help. After parting with Adrian I took
the electric train out to Koubbah, and at the domed house
of the Freligraths waited in a downstairs room for her who
had been Flore Gellion to descend from immersions
astronomical.

'Anton my friend! Ages since you came to see me. And
who is this?'

The little beast Steadfast whined up at her with pricked
ears, and then dropped his head again. I made the explanations.

'*Quelle honte*! But of course he may stay here.' She knelt
and encircled him in her arms. 'It is but right, since your
mistress is with the stars, is she not? . . . Stay to tea, my

colonel. I've delayed for Friedrich, but cannot wait longer. Ribaddi in Rome and I are doing the Venus transit together, just after sunset.'

Already was that sunset near and I bidding farewell, when we heard the car of Friedrich Freligrath, the Nile engineer, coming from Cairo. He came in the haste and we waited for him.

'Am I very late, Flore? Hello, colonel! . . . Gods, what's this? A doormat?'

He made the embrace of Flore, and the little beast Steadfast growled at him, but without spirit. Still standing, Friedrich drank tea.

'Going, colonel? If you'll wait a minute I'll drive you back. I've to go into Cairo again, Flore – there has been an accident a little way up-river. That was what delayed me. One of our launches ran into a crowded Greek pleasure-boat and spilled half the passengers into the Nile.'

v

Keith Landward sat in his garden and listened to the sound of the River.

That first agony of desolation – the awakening agony of a wound realised which had led to the violent scene in the presence of Adrian and myself – had passed. He sat now and looked down the future, the corridors of the days and nights he would tramp alone, without hope or heroism, vision or God. These things he had left behind in Al Fostat with the ashes of Joan.

He closed his eyes, and the dull ache passed from these to his heart. Agony had done its utmost, and now was merely tiredness unutterable with him; that, and the sound of the River.

And suddenly, listening there, a verse of your Swinburne's, that he had not read or thought of for the many years, came into his mind.

From too much love of living,
From hope and fear set free,
We thank with brief thanksgiving
Whatever gods may be,

That no life lives forever,
That dead men rise up never,
That even the weariest river
Winds somewhere safe to sea.

'Even the weariest river . . .' He looked round about him in slow amazement. The ache passed from his mind. *Why had he not thought of that before?*

He thrust aside the pages which had once spelt vision and achievement but seemed now petrification of the idle and inane chatter. Very calmly and deliberately he walked up the garden and into the house. His revolver required cleaning, and he took it out to the balcony of carved mushrabiyeh work that overhung the Nile, and sat there smoking and cleaning with the River below him.

Both fear and agony had fallen from him. It was the very lovely evening. Waiting for the sunset, the River was the hushed blue expectancy, except where a launch that went by against the further shore clove the water in a furrow of gold.

'That is lovely,' he said to himself.

His senses were sharp and vivid as never before. He finished loading the revolver and laid it aside, and sat, head in hands, thinking of all the beautiful things he had ever known. Sunsets and sunrises and ripple of water; music heard at night; a naked bather in a Majorca cove; Joan; her laughter; singing; the beauty of words . . .

Below him and the balcony was the continual whisper, the whisper and the sigh.

'The River . . . How she loved it! Tired. It called her.'

He raised his head. The sunset was raining darkness over Cairo. Below him the River flushed and paled and dimmed.

He picked up the revolver and twirled its barrel, set the hammer – and dropped it clattering to his feet.

In the lower rooms Ibrahim had switched on the electric lights, and their radiance was flung upon the Nile. But it was beyond that radiance, the thing he had seen. He closed his eyes in the unbelief, opened them again, and then—

Out of the darkness it swirled into the light, going seawards, rising and falling on the slow current, a thing white and unmistakable.

It was the body of a woman.

VI

From the Dr Adrian, met on his rounds the next day, I heard of the happening at the Landward house.

'Keith saw her from his balcony, ran downstairs, jumped in, and pulled her ashore . . . Must have cost him a vile expenditure of temper! A girl of seventeen or eighteen, unconscious, but alive. She had banged herself somehow. Hair clotted with blood at the base of the skull . . . Another casualty of that pleasure-boat accident.'

'Of it I have heard,' I said. 'She has been identified?'

'Not yet, though that won't be any difficulty. I've supplied descriptions to the Police, the Greek consulate, and the Nile people. Greek quite certainly. Spoke a few words of it this morning, and apparently doesn't know any other language . . . Some dialect of the Islands, Landward says, and very pure . . . Yes, said that! Thank the Lord, in one way, the poor girl was nearly drowned. Her intrusion has jolted Landward into one of those towering rages of his – and I was afraid of something else.'

'She has told her name?'

'Not yet. The pure Greek stream is – or was this morning – only a tricklet. Too exhausted to do anything but sleep. Probably been reclaimed and taken away by now.' He mused a little. 'Something wrong with her eyes, I think.

Eh? Oh, white and gold – like a Greek out of Wilde. Or a *koré* of the vases.'

VII

But neither that day nor the next came anyone to identify Landward's salvage. The captain of the pleasure-boat, interviewed, swore that all the people flung overboard in the River accident had been rescued by himself or the launch. He was the man shifty and untrustworthy, and frightened that he might earn a reputation for the reckless handling of his boat.

'Obviously a liar,' said Adrian. 'Don't suppose he had the faintest idea how many passengers were on his precious boat. It was a three hours' jaunt up and down the River.'

'There are no relatives – the police have no information?'

'No, that's the devil of it. The girl must have been friendless. Meanwhile Landward's going about like a roaring multi-lingual lion. Went along to the Greek consulate yesterday and kicked up Hades. Swears his work's interrupted and disorganised . . . Hope it's only his work. I went out on that balcony this morning, looking for him, and found this lying on the floor.'

He displayed the revolver, of which, and other things, I was afterwards to hear from Landward himself the full tale.

'And that's not the worst of it. I thought there was something funny about the girl's eyes. That blow on the head's responsible, of course . . . She doesn't remember any of the happenings before the accident. Doesn't remember even her own name. Pass in time, naturally. Amnesia never lasts.'

VIII

To Keith Landward he made presently the suggestion.

'There is, of course, a Greek Institution for the destitute. She can be handed over to that.'

'Eh? Paupers' home? No, she can stay here till she's better; if she wants to.'

And with this the ungracious and unreasonable invitation – for she was as yet unable fully to understand the situation – the nameless Greek girl stayed on at the Nile house. Adrian has the sardonic wit. That day, when he decided the girl should be taken out of doors, he called Landward from the book-strewn balcony to which the latter had retreated on hearing the garden was about to be invaded.

'She'll have to be carried to the garden. As you carried her up you may as well take her down. She might object to Ibrahim.'

'He swore, but went up the stairs to her room and knocked at the door,' Adrian was to relate to me. 'I was climbing up from below and heard and saw most of the comic incident. I know a little Greek. She called out "Who is it?" and Landward replied "It is I" – a statement possible in Greek, but just as idiotic as in English. Her voice came back – surprised and amused, I thought – "Oh, come in. I am almost ready." In he went . . . to come striding out again in an instant, banging the door. You see, the Egyptian women-servants had taken up some clothes a minute or two before, and Landward, going in, found his protégée in quite an unnecessary state of negligée.'

'It was an accident.'

'Oh, innocent enough, I imagine; but a bit surprising, seeing she tucks herself up to the chin even when speaking to her medical adviser. Anyhow, she wasn't in the least embarrassed when he did carry her down. Doesn't seem in the least aware of the upset to the Landward regime. She's the confidence of an infant, or –' He shrugged.

'Eh?'

'Quite. A friendless Greek girl in Cairo – starvation and worse send scores south from Smyrna and the Archipelago each winter. This memory-obscuring may be a fairy-tale. One never knows ... If it is, she must envisage the situation as one of heaven-sent opportunity. Poor thing!'

IX

Next day I called at the Nile house – I who had not been there since the funeral of Joan Landward – and in the garden saw the sight unexpected. Under the great green umbrella Keith Landward sat with table and books. In a chair beside him, the much-wrapped and with the yellow-gold flame of hair, was a girl. Landward's face was lighted and eager. He was alternately listening with the devotion and writing with the rapidity. At sound of the door closing they looked round and Landward, with the no-appearance of cordiality, made the brusque introduction.

I know a little of the ancient speech – which is to the modern Romaic as Virgil to the twitterings of the little d'Annunzio – and that it seemed to me would have been the fitting speech for her. And then I had the surprise. For, though with accent and quantities unfamiliar, it was verily almost in the ancient tongue that she spoke.

'You see, I have no name.'

I cannot hope to convey to you the ring and beauty of those words she spoke. I stood and stared at her with the mists of strange questioning and wonder rising in my mind. Somewhere, somewhere—

And then I knew. A figure on a vase I had once seen, made when the world was young, in the dawn of Europe. Even to line of nose and forehead so beloved by Athenian craftsmen, she was that figure. I groped for name and memory, and, unembarrassed under my rude stare, she smiled with slow-widening eyes.

Eyes like sunflowers. And suddenly I heard myself speak.

'I think it should be Kora,' I said, with the utter conviction that in a moment was gone, leaving me foolish and

embarrassed. The wonderful eyes budded a question, but
Landward broke in with impatience.

'Eh? What's that? Kora? It'll do as well as any other,
won't it? Must have a name . . . And now we'll get on – if
you'll excuse us, Saloney.'

X

With enthusiasm Landward set to the teaching of English
to his River-salvage, though for other reasons his interest
had first awakened in her. They had both accepted my
christening, and neither was embarrassed by the fact that as
yet she possessed no surname.

One afternoon I collided with the hurrying and book-
laden figure in Esbekieh. It was Landward, happy, with the
face of a boy.

'. . . Intonation – that was the root difficulty of the
World-Speech. But I believe I've fixed it in phonetics at
last. Kora has just the requisite tone and accent . . . Natural
enough. Greek is the oldest and purest of the Aryan
dialects, and in what ever out-of-the-way spot of the Archipelago she or her people originated the spoken tongue
must remain amazingly archaic.'

'The mind-obscuring – the amnesia – it is going?' I
asked.

'Eh? No, I don't think so.' He shrugged aside this
triviality. 'I haven't asked. I've been too busy.'

He had accepted her as an accent and intonation, not as
an individual. Compilation of the World-Speech again
obscured his every horizon. Kora could now walk to and
from the garden unaided. She was still clad in the absurd
Egyptian clothes. Unless questioned, she never spoke to
Landward in his long spells of work, but would sit under
the green umbrella, head to one side, apparently lost in day-
dreams.

And then, a thing disturbing to the contentment of toil

and achievement, he was conscious in himself of a vague uneasiness, of vague, unworded questions whenever he raised his head and met those sunflower eyes fixed upon him. Drugged with work, living betwixt sleep and wakefulness, as he knew himself – what when he awoke?

XI

And then into their garden came the official from the Greek Institution.

He was a young-old man, the American-cultured Greek, and was shown to Landward, under the green umbrella, at the moment when the latter sat alone.

'You are the Mister Landward?' he asked in the American English.

'I am,' snapped the linguist, in the Romaic, and for the moment this seemed to disconcert the young-old man. But he made the quick recovery. He was directed to enquire into the conditions under which a young Greek girl was living in the house. The circumstances of her rescue were well known to the Institution. But there had been rumours. Was or was not this girl living with him as his mistress?

Landward had listened in the daze, and now sat staring his dazement. The young-old man became confidential and made the greasy smile . . . The girl was, no doubt, a stray from some unlicensed house, and there need be no difficulty. Between friends. Providing she was not being forcibly detained. And even then, if it was certain there would be no scandal—

Landward had looked beyond him. The American Greek turned round. The girl was coming down the garden towards them.

If he had had any hesitations with Landward, he had none with Kora, presuming her to be what Adrian had suspected. She stared at him with wondering eyes as he made the easy greeting in Romaic, and then, pulling out his notebook, put the coarse questions.

But at even the first of these the rapidly-fraying temper of Landward, until then held marvellously in one, snapped. Like the most of those who toil for the ultimate brotherhood of all men, he was one with the intense prejudices and dislikes; amongst these, his hatred of nasal Americanisms. Questions apart, the Greek's accent had already undone him, and for Landward to seize him abruptly and ungently, rush him to the garden-gate, tear that open, and kick out into the dust and the street the young-old convert to trans-Atlantic acumen and intonation was the work of a moment . . . He returned to find a wondering Kora awaiting him.

'You are very hot.' She considered him gravely, brought out a scrap of handkerchief, and, with the air absorbed, dabbed his forehead. Then:

'But what did he mean? How does it concern him? Of course we live together. Though at night—'

She shook her head, of the puzzled, her eyes raised to him. Then the puzzlement slowly faded and remote amongst the cornflowers came hurrying, strange lights . . . Landward turned his head away.

'There are such men,' he said, lamely, avoiding her eyes, shamed by that white innocence.

He went away on the pretended business, but returned to the garden that evening, tramping to and fro for hours. The evil chatter of the Helleno-American should have stirred him to disgust alone, but now, in the agony of self-hatred and remorse, he shuddered away from the thoughts suddenly uncovered in his mind . . . My God, and Joan – Joan who had taken the light from the world – she had not been dead two weeks. . . .

In the bright moonlight of his room, long after the rest of the house was quiet, he undressed, trying not to hear that haunting song of the River below his window.

Somewhere, out of the swift, strange dream, near to the dawn, he awoke, and as the realisation came to him it seemed that the noise of the River below grew to the sound of a torrent.

In his arms, very fast asleep as a child might sleep, one arm around his neck, a shoulder white to the moon-dazzle, lay the girl Kora.

XII

That morning I awoke to the free and lazy day. I had no clients. At the Freligrath house the fortnight before had occurred that happening eternally miraculous, and I went out to Koubbah to make the call. Flore Freligrath, the very young and modern mother, I discovered hard at work in her study, with Thibaut August asleep in a portable cot and the dog Steadfast outstretched in the boredom upon the floor. At sight of me he leapt up with the whine.

After I had admired the sleeper, doubtlessly miraculous but hardly of himself admirable, I found the solemn little dog attempting to follow me from the room.

'I am afraid Thibaut August and I bore him,' said Flore. 'He has never displayed those tricks of which you spoke.'

'He is the lover steadfast,' I said, and patted him, and took my leave. But I did not return to Cairo; instead, tramped to the hut of Mogara, and there remained the little while, and then struck across the roads and so presently the dusty Cairene streets to the house of Landward on Nile bank.

I did not go through the house, for the garden gate hung loose, and by it I went in, half-expecting to see under the green umbrella heads dark and golden bent in collaboration over the type-scripts of the World-Speech.

But Keith Landward sat alone, and as I crossed the garden to him he raised the livid face. I stopped. It was the face of a man horrified and self-tortured. He spoke in a whisper, as though I had been standing there for hours.

'Saloney, how is it a Greek drab from the River can have the face of a saint?'

'I do not—' I began, and then understood at the once, glancing to the house and then back at his face.

Adrian had been right.

Beyond the garden gate came the sudden snuffling and low whine. We both looked round. In the opening, padding into view, was the little dog Steadfast.

He had followed me from the Koubbah observatory, you understand. I did not care to look at Landward. And then we heard the other little sound and looked towards the house.

Down the path was coming the girl Kora, and at sight of her Landward sprang to his feet and flamed red and swore aloud.

'By God, but *that* I won't stand!'

XIII

She had been rummaging in the room of his dead wife and wore the red frock, absurd and yet becoming to her white Greek beauty, in which I had last seen clad the dark slenderness of Joan Landward. She halted in front of us, pleased and unembarrassed, and smiled at us with the sunflower eyes, and spread the short skirts for our inspection.

'Like my frock?'

Landward swallowed, made to answer, and in that moment something hurtled past us like the animated ball from the catapult.

It was the little dog Steadfast. He had gone suddenly mad, was barking and sobbing in the delirium of joy. Again and again he leapt to lick the hands of the girl, then spun round in the dizzying circles, then rolled in the abasement at her feet. She looked down at him in the lighted wonder.

'It is the frock—' I began, and then stopped.

The little beast had reared himself up, in the culminating pride of performance, and at that her delighted laughter rang clear.

'*Look, look, the fairy dance!*'

XIV

In two strides he was beside her, his face ashen, the face of one whose sanity toppled, his eyes the blaze.

' "The fairy dance" – where did you hear that, where?'

She stared up at him, lips quivering, eyes suddenly clouded and frightened. In their depths struggled effort at that memory neither of them were ever again to seek. She put her hand to her head and stammered in the little broken English.

'I . . . Oh, once . . . Steadfast . . . I do not know.'

Then fear and questioning went from her eyes. Compassion came there. In the moment she was in his arms.

'*Keith . . . Oh, Keith, my dear, don't look like that!*'

XV

Somehow I was out of that garden; I have forgotten how I went; they did not hear me go. In his arms, her fingers twining in his hair in the mock-cruel caress . . . My friend, I am no realist. I fled: such coward as he who looked on Kora in Eleusis.

East is West

I

SEE TO THE dip and play of them above Heliopolis! They are like birds, despite the good Mogara . . . The fighting machines, I think.

Incongruous over Cairo – those aeroplanes? They outrage the atmosphere Eastern? But why? Was not Daedalus of the East – of Crete and the Crete prehellenic at that? Was it into La Manche so-admired that the first of the aeroaut martyrs fell? . . . Yours the geography unreliable, my friend. The Icarian Sea lies not in Western Europe!

East is East and West is West – it is the heresy pitiful, the concept pre-Copernician. Those the fighting-birds of steel: they were made in your England – and are numbered with symbols evolved in the East two thousand years ago; your aeronauts – they bear on their tunics the winged crests of ancient Egypt!

For East is West and West is East; they merge and flow and are the compass-points of a dream. And the little jingo men who walk the world, lifting here the banner Nordic and there the flag Mongolian – in the white hands that raise the banner is the blood of cannibals pre-Aryan, the banner itself is a-flutter with symbols obscene first painted in the jungle-towns of Cambodia; the little Jap is a White, a mongrel Ainu, and salutes on his flag the design first graved on the ancient stones of Cuzco! . . .

Then of race or culture-barriers I would recognise none? God mine, I can recognise nothing else! Like Simon Mogara, like all of us, my life is fenced about with tribe-taboos, my ears deafened with the whining rhymes of cultures troglodyte! Like Simon—

II

But I will tell you of Mogara the while we sit and watch the aeroplanes. And the tourists haughty who pass us by this dusty Abbassieh roadway will think us tramps or the Europeans gone native!

Mogara. It is almost four years ago since I first met him, the one evening in January. I had gone to live in Heliopolis that I might be near my clients of the hotels, and that day had spent the many and wearying hours indoors, in the Cairo Museum, explaining to a party indifferent and irreverent the unauthentic history of King Oonas. Returned at sunset, I set out to walk across the sands towards Helmieh, so that I might meet the evening wind.

I remember that evening very well. There was a thin ghost-play of lightning on the horizon and presently a little wind stirring to whorling puffs the tops of the sand-hillocks. I had stopped to light the pipe in a miniature nullah and from that climbed out, and so came abruptly on Mogara, the silhouette.

'Good-evening,' I said in the uncertainty.

He also spoke in the accent un-English. 'Good-evening.' He wheeled slowly on his heels till almost he faced me. Then: 'Would you mind stepping aside – or falling flat? The wind's just coming behind you and I'm going to launch her.'

I stepped aside in the hurriedness and some bewilderment. A little film of mist-powder came drifting over the tundra. Mogara raised his arms and flung a glittering bird into the air.

For a moment it swayed perilously, as if about to fall. Then came a little click and sputter, and with the flapping of great wings the fowl amazing soared upwards. So, for perhaps the hundred yards, it soared, in the long curve towards Cairo. Then, unaccountably – for the wings beat quickly as ever – it began to fall, but backwards, and towards us, like a boomerang. Mogara ran forward and I followed him. The bird slipped down into his arms the moment I came to his side.

'This bird,' I said, 'it is—'

He turned on me the face deep-scowling in thought, and with the little start I realised that he was no European. It was a face of the heavy and even bronze, with thin nose, straight brows and lips, and with the startling disfigurement of two long-healed scars stamped darkly from right eye to ear. For the little we looked at each other, and then he smiled slowly.

'It is, God willing, an ornithopter.'

III

I grew to know him well and made the occasional visits to his hut in Zeitoun. It was little more than the hut, being an American bungalow set in a little garden. The one half of it he used as workshop and study, the other he slept in and therein cooked the much of eggs and rice, being inexpert in the preparation of foods more ambitious.

'Flying? There has been no flying yet. Aeroplanes are not flying-machines. They're structures of cambered planes juggling with artificially-created currents of air. The aeroplane is a mistake – no true forerunner of the flying-machine. Like the pterodactyl, it's only a tentative air-experiment, destined to die childless . . .'

'And this,' I would say, pointing to the bird-winged model, with its little petrol engine and gleam of aluminium, boat-shaped body, 'this the ornithopter – presently it will fly?'

He would scowl and laugh at that, then jump to his feet and stride to the window and watch a flight of desert-making birds. 'Damn it, colonel, it flies already. You've seen it. Only –' he would peer upwards unfriendlily at the dots that were birds – 'it doesn't keep flying. There's something—'

There was something, some law of the flight insoluble, which brought his models to ground after every first hundred yards or so, albeit the wings still beat. Model after model he had tried out. In itself the tremendous achievement, he had solved the initial difficulty of the ornithopter – the building of wings strong, yet flexible, capable of the under-sweep and the poising blow, capable of lifting the machine into air. But in the air it refused to stay.

He would expound these things to me, the child in matters aeronautic, with the great logic and clarity, and in the swing of exposition would a strange thing occur. His voice would lose its mechanic staccato and acquire an alien lilt and rhythm. Once, in the midst of such converse, he pulled himself up and laughed.

'Did you notice that – the half-caste sing-song? Funny. And quite ineradicable.'

He had the genuine, impersonal amusement in these traits betrayed by his own personality. But it was the same half-sardonic, half-impatient amusement which personalities always stirred in him. He had none of the half-breed's resentments or enthusiastic championings – 'perhaps because I'm a quarter-breed. The snarling of the bleached and the coloured go over my head. People don't count. Aeronautics is my job.'

He was of the lesser breeds intermingled enough. His grandfather, a Goanese half-caste, had settled down in Jaffa after wanderings dim and inexplicable. There, as the orange-merchant, he had flourished, acquired a Cretan wife, and, in the course of time and nature, a son. This son, exported to France for education, married, and returned to Jaffa after the several years with a Parisian lady who took life as a jest and the circles orange-growing by storm . . . Such Mogara family-history and social advancement till the appearance of the little Simon.

His appearance seemed to his father the event retrogressive. The Parisian lady, true to character, found him the oddity amusing. They had expected the child who would show no trace of the Goanese grandfather. Instead, they found themselves parents to an atavistic little infant who might have been a Hindu undiluted. As soon as he was old enough his father, in the some disgust, exiled him to school and university in Lyons, where colour is little bar and they of the skins dark-pigmented accounted amongst God's creatures.

He was twenty-nine years of age that evening I encountered him on the Helmieh sands. In that interval from the Jaffa days he had become the French citizen, had during the War served in a French air regiment and acquired the high Legion decoration, had succeeded to and sold the business orange-exporting on the death of his father and mother, had travelled to America—

Of those the American days I heard only in disjointed, sardonic outline. Early after the War, dissatisfied with aeroplanes, he had set about experimenting with helicopter-models, and, abandoning that second stage, with flexible gliders and winged kites. He might have remained in France to this day but for the lack of readily-procurable apparatus in that country immediately after its exhausting triumph. The experimenter's needs drove him to America to work and study.

There he found himself, to his own amusement, treated as servant and inferior. Even from other experimenters and aeronauts was the occasional jibe at the 'nigger birdman'. Settled in a new town built on the aircraft trade, he went out one night and found the streets in the excitement and turmoil. The usual story had spread of the negro and white woman. Presently was the negro, also as usual, dragged out of jail by the crowd and lynched. Ensued a kind of anti-colour pogrom . . .

Mogara brought out of that turmoil the scarred face and a week in hospital. A citizen of France, apologies were made through stiff consular representations and an indemnity offered . . . I can see the light of amusement flicker on that brooding brown face as he lay in hospital and heard of the indemnity.

For he was as completely indifferent to revenge as to reconciliation. Mankind I think he envisaged largely as the straying packs of parti-coloured puppies, baying unaccountably at the moon and indulging in the dog-squabbles equally unaccountable. Amidst all this canine pride and uproar his the 'job' to find a corner obscure and pacific where he could build an ornithopter that flew . . .

I remember making the interjection.

'But for whom, then, do you work – for whom add to the sum of knowledge? If such is humanity, why seek to build this flying machine?'

'For my own private pride, I suppose . . . To visit the moon and see what all the howling's about.' He shrugged. 'How should I know? . . . Anyhow, I decided against returning even to France, and came to Egypt instead, where there are other browny men in charge. Being the shade they are I calculated they'd probably neither hinder nor mutilate me, nor look askance at my feet.'

'Your feet?'

He grinned, the scars creasing in dark serrations on his cheek. 'Yes. You see, I have the half-caste's passion for yellow boots.'

So, with such jest indifferent, to switch to other matters. I remember he told me these things at his garden-entrance on the Zeitoun road one evening, the while we smoked a parting pipe. When he had ceased speaking there was the little clatter and cloud of white dust far up the road towards Cairo, and I watched it idly.

They were the man and girl on horseback, and as they cantered near I drew a breath of admiration. The man young, of the thirty-forties, with the soldier's shoulders, the cold, narrow face with clean-cut features, the cold stare of blue eyes. But the girl – like her companion of the English, like him result of that fineness of breeding and the much nursery-scrubbing that has made the English aristocrat. And the something – as so often in the feminine of that type, and so seldom in the masculine – it had brought to flower in her: the beauty indefinable as the grace of a lily. Very young, bare-headed with the shock of the tidily-untidy hair, slim and upright and with easy hands she rode, head a little thrown back. As she went by her eyes passed over us in the momentary scrutiny, distant, indifferent, impersonal – and bored.

So they passed into the evening, and I, who love types and so seldom find them, had the sting of gratification. These the English, the Aryans ultra-bred, dominant, blood-proud, apart. How apart from all the lesser breeds, they of the pigmentation, 'without the Law'!

I glanced at Mogara in the little shame for my own thoughts. And then I saw that he had scarcely noted the passing of the riders. He was staring up into the sky at the inevitable flight of sunset-winging birds.

IV

All next day he worked on a new modification of the keel of his model, and about five of the afternoon went out across the ranges beyond Helmieh to test it anew. For a little, near the original mound where I had found him, perhaps, he stood awaiting the coming of the wind. Deep in thought and the calculation of mathematical minutiæ he saw the sand-heaps at length begin to puff, and, setting a dial, launched the bird-machine into the air. It beat upwards with stiffer motion than formerly. A clatter of stones behind him drew his scowling attention. He glanced over his shoulder.

Not a dozen feet away a bare-headed girl sat on horse-back, her eyes fixed on the flight of the ornithopter. So only for the moment he noted, then his attention also went back to the model. It flew perhaps two yards further than usual, then commenced its usual boomerang descent.

He swore, ran forward and caught it, and heard behind him the amazed intake of breath. The girl had dismounted, and as he turned with the bird-machine in his arms her eyes were very bright with excitement.

'Oh . . . sorry if I'm spying. But that was wonderful!'

'It was rotten,' he said, neither graciously nor ungraciously, but with complete indifference to either her apologies or applause. Undiscouraged, she came nearer, her horse following with down-bent, snuffling head.

'But why? It's an ornithopter, and it flew. Real flying, not just aeroplane gliding . . . And my brother argues we'll never have ornithopters – never anything more than a lopsided helicopter or so. Wish he could have seen that! It wasn't a secret test, was it?'

He had been aware of a slight surprise at meeting someone who knew the difference between an ornithopter and a helicopter. Now, still with the absent-minded scowl, but half-heeding her presence, he answered the question.

'No. Why should it be?'

'I thought all experiments did these things secretly and then pestered Governments.' This with the flippancy, but then a return to excitement. 'I say! Most thrilling thing I've seen in this boring country – most thrilling thing I've ever seen, I think . . . Do you know the old Frost ornithopter in the London Science? Is yours on the same principle?'

'If you've seen the Frost—' He was launched the more successfully than ever had been his model. He set the bird-machine on the ground, demonstrating its build and principal departures from the Frost model. He brought out the pencil and scrap of paper and dashed off lines of the calculations dizzying and algebraic.

The girl remained undizzied. Still holding the bridle she knelt down in the interest, and the horse extended over her shoulder the inquisitive head . . . They must have made the amusing grouping there on the sands.

She had flown many times in aeroplanes, had the English Aero Club's pilot certificate, had, like himself, an obsession that the aeroplane was traitor to aviation and that Romance which had lured men to the conquest of the skies since the days of Cretan Daedalus.

'It wasn't for the sake of a world of super-engined kites that Icarus and Egremont and Lilenthial died. But real flying . . . And you won't sell your model to any Government, or make it a war machine?'

'Good Lord, no.'

'Good man!'

He saw a hand stretched out towards him, and stared at it. His thoughts came hurtling down from rarefied heights like an aeroplane disabled. He found himself kneeling side by side not with a pleasant voice and a disembodied enthusiasm, but an English girl . . .

That stare and silence of his drew her eyes. So, for a little, they looked at each other in the mutual wonder: the girl, white and gold, radiant and aloof even in excitement; Mogara, lithe and slight, with the slightness un-European, the dark, scarred face, the scowl of thin-pencilled brows . . . He saw the girl's eyes widen, and at that, with a sardonic little laugh, he was on his feet.

'Yes, I'm a native. But you're quite safe.'

And then, dimly, indifferently, he realised that he had made a mistake. The girl's eyes looked through him as she too rose to her feet.

He had ceased to exist.

V

At nine o'clock that evening, passing down the Sharia Kamil, my eyes fell on the small car unmistakable. It was the yellow runabout, the property of my friend the Dr Adrian, and it stood in front of a little open-air café with many tables. At one of those tables, deep in the usual self-game with dominoes, sat Adrian himself.

This is to him relief and narcotic in one, this game played with the great seriousness. To me recurred the wonder whimsical: Is he ever victor – and over whom? . . . He looked up and saw me and swept aside the pieces.

'Hello, colonel. Haven't seen you for ages. Sit down and gossip. How's Heliopolis?'

'It is the place dry,' I said, and at that he ordered me the wine. Then:

'Seen anything of the Melforts there? Cousins of mine – air-people, newly come from Malta?'

'I did not know you possessed the cousins,' I said. He grinned and yawned, having passed the toilsome day.

'Knowledge that was never kept from me, unfortunately. I was forced to punch the aristocratic Melfort nose quite early in my career.' He was reminiscent. 'And was getting as good as I gave till Joyce, in a pinafore and a white wrath, separated us with a shower of stones and pelted us impartially . . . Murderous little pacifist.'

He expounded the brief and irreverent family history the while I drank the wine. These Melforts were the remote cousins only: the grandmother of Adrian had been sister of the grandfather of Reginald and Joyce Melfort.

'But we come from the same county town, you see, and there's been a kind of family friendship – patronising on both sides – kept going for three generations. The Adrians have been the medical and impoverished branch; they've assisted new Melforts into the world and signed their certificates of departure for the next during the last seventy

years or so. Know more of Melfort history than the Melforts themselves, who've only passed on the high lights to
their descendants.' He chuckled as at some secret jest.
'Grandfather Melfort went out to Jamaica, raised rum and a
great deal of money, and returned to perpetuate a military
and gentlemanly stock. Put his son into the army, and
grandson Reginald followed in his father's footsteps . . . It
was he whose nose I punched.

'Not a bad chap really, I suppose. Only – he never had a
chance. Born in India and reared on the usual pap. A
Nordic snub-man with highly-scrubbed virtues and a disposition to pronounce what as hwaw. Transferred to the
Air Force during the War and is a squadron leader or
something now. Has taken the latest wonder of science and
made of it a means for forming fours in the air and
inspecting engines to see if they're properly shaved . . .
That kind.'

He broke off, as in conversation he so often did, to refute
his own exaggerations. 'No. That's damned unfair. A very
good airman, I believe. Straight as a die, efficient, proud of
the Service, an excellent example of the breeding of an
aristocrat in three generations . . . Let's be unfair. Impartiality's too much of a strain. He has less imagination than a
wombat, and the colour, caste and class prejudices of a
tabu-ridden Brahmin. In his secret soul he believes the
Anglo-Saxon saheb evolved from a special type of ape
which always cleaned its teeth in the morning and even
in the early Miocene wore badges of rank on its fur . . . I've
been invited to dinner in ten days' time, and if Reginald
and I don't quarrel and bandy authorities and sneers, it'll
be the first occasion since the nose-punching episode. Joyce
had better stand by with an armful of stones.'

'She is the sister?'

'Occasionally. When she remembers. Keeps house nom-
inally for Reginald: keeps him on tenterhooks actually.
Modern and un-modern. A romantic's idealisation of

English womanhood in appearance – she'd delight your eyes, Saloney – and in mind a quattrocento adventurer, mystic and mountain-storming. Flies aeroplanes and innumerable outrageous opinions, waxes hot over all kinds of unexpected things and cold over everything which her appearance warrants . . . By the seven goats of Egypt – Hi!'

He leapt from his chair with the beaming face and the startling shout, and seized the arm of a passer-by – the man bareheaded, absorbed, chest-clasping the large and ungainly parcel. Thus assaulted, the stranger dropped the parcel – which split, grocery-disgorging – and turned scowlingly upon Adrian. Almost immediately vanished the scowl.

'God, the doctor of Chaumont!'

'Air-ambulance 30Q!'

They fell to the hand-shaking, the enquiries innumerable, the laughter of men who had shared the war-episode unforgettable. Adrian turned to make the introduction, but I forestalled him.

'I am acquainted,' I said, 'with M. Mogara.'

VI

For four days after his meeting with the unknown girl on the sands, and with the little Adrian and myself in the Sharia Kamil, Mogara kept to his workshop, fitting the new keel to his ornithopter. On the fourth evening he tramped out beyond Helmieh again to put his modification to test. As usual, he walked in the study brown, and so almost dashed his head against horse and rider – both of which had been regarding his approach for over a mile.

It was the girl, and she surveyed him insolently. 'What is your name, Mr – Native?'

He was in a good humour, expecting better results from his model. He twinkled at her sardonically. 'Mogara – memsaheb . . . And my grandfather was a Goanese.'

She flushed angrily. 'He may have been a Chinese albino for all I care. You are very much concerned with your family history, M. Mogara. Hasn't it ever struck you that it may be boring to others? Or your role of the dark and dangerous male the other evening – wasn't it rather cowardly?'

He was sardonically undisturbed. 'No doubt I'm both a bore and a coward. Meantime my job's not psycho-analysis but amateur aeronautics.'

'Of course it is! And since the tests aren't secret why mayn't I come and watch them? Why have you kept away from the trial-ground these last three evenings? Can't you see that I want to learn, that it's your ornithopter I'm interested in, not you, you—'

He stared at her. It was the one appeal which could have touched him. On his face, dark and scarred, she saw a scowling wonder. A slow smile followed. Then:

' "Blithering ass" are the words you want . . . I'm sorry.' He held out a tentative hand. 'If—'

Her fingers touched his. They regarded each other gravely for a moment, laughed together; then Joyce Melfort dismounted, sat down, clasped her hands about her knees, and watched . . .

You must figure her so, evening after evening. For the meetings went on. Almost every evening she rode across the sands to find Mogara, with some new modification imposed upon his model, waiting for the sunset wind.

And presently, in between times of the test-flying and the calculations abstruse, they would find themselves deep in talk – talk that ranged away from aeronautics and back to it and away again. She found his mind the encyclopædia of sheer fact, the mind of the scientist, a little warped, almost passionless but for that the desire and pursuit of knowledge; hers was to him revelation of how knowledge may be transmuted to idealism and hope and purpose . . .

Except a sardonic scepticism for all enthusiasms nationalist and religious he had the no-philosophy of life. She made him see all human existence in the terms of high Adventure – the Adventure scarce begun, the struggle from the slime to the stars. *Per ardua ad astra*. Every scrap of new knowledge was equipment for that Adventure; every man who fought the beast in himself and the anti-christ many-guised, who kept the honest ledgers and the open mind, who knew the ache of wonder and a desire beyond fulfil-ment – he fought in the spear-head of the Adventure . . .

And Mogara, his model half-forgotten, would brood and listen till he too glimpsed faith and belief in that Republic in the skies which lies beyond our shadowed uncertainties, which sometimes seems but a generation away.

Sometimes, as they talked, they would lift their heads and see the wheel and glitter of the Squadron Leader Melfort's aeroplanes practising dusk landings at Heliopolis.

VII

'A nigger chappie with a bee in his bonnet and one of those helicopter-thingummys. He's been at it for months, they say, practising out on the sands beyond Helmieh. Saw him myself last night when I went up to do a spot of night-flying.'

Joyce Melfort came riding against the sunset of the tenth day since her first encounter with Mogara. Fragments from the chatter at her brother's table the previous evening rode with her, like buzzing gnats . . . She had been coldly angry, then wondering and amused. Now, with an amazement, she found herself angry again.

From far across the sands Mogara waved to her, absent-mindedly. As she rode towards him the buzzing of an aeroplane engine grew loud overhead. She glanced up-wards, saw one of the machines of her brother's squadron dip towards her and Mogara as though they were the bombing target, and then rise and wheel back towards Heliopolis.

'Now that that anachronism's gone—'

She reined in, dismounted, and stood watching in silence. Mogara clicked out the wings of the much-tried model, set revolving the little dial and pointer in its heart, and then launched the contrivance into the air.

He did not stop to watch its progress, but turned round towards her with the now not-infrequent smile. ' "Hope springs eternal—" ' he patted the neck of her nuzzling mount. '– If you're not bored with the performance by now, I think your horse must be . . . Eh?'

She had caught his arm in the painful grip. 'Quick! Look!'

Mogara wheeled round and stared skywards, stared at a flapping-winged model which neither failed nor descended, which rose and rose with steady purr of miniature engine and then began to wheel overhead in great circles . . .

Its inventor gulped, swore inadequately, and then found Joyce Melfort's hands gripping his, shaking them up and down.

'Why, you've won, you've won!' She glanced up for reassurance and then executed a little dance. 'My dear man, can't you realise it? Waken up! Aren't you glad? . . .'

Her voice died away. There came in her eyes the terror and expectation. Unaccountably in his arms, she saw his scarred face terrifyingly close. So, the moment she would remember forever, and then, kissed by him, there awoke in her something like a dream forgotten . . . That – then they were apart, and she had slashed him across the face with her riding-whip.

He staggered a little under her blow, and then, in a queer silence, not looking at her, brought out a handkerchief, and dabbed at the blood-pringling weal which flushed angrily on his unscarred cheek. He lowered the scrap of linen, looking at it in a kind of wonder, and at that Joyce Melfort's stricken remorse found voice.

'Oh, I'm sorry . . . I was a beast. But you shouldn't—'

He smiled at her, without a hint of mockery, with dull eyes. He was very quiet – dazedly quiet.

'I know I shouldn't. That was the only possible reply.' He turned away uncertainly, fumbling with the handkerchief. 'And now you'd better go.'

He expected to hear the sound of her footsteps going towards the horse. Instead, there was complete silence. He glanced round again. She stood where he had kissed her, in her eyes an angry flame of courage and resolution. She began to speak.

'Listen: I'm sorry – because I hit you. Not because you kissed me. Why shouldn't you?' Her voice quivered a little, but her eyes were very unwavering. 'I – I wanted you to.'

They stared at each other. Overhead, absurdly, and in the circles drawing gradually earthwards, wheeled the un-heeded ornithopter model. Mogara shook his head . . .

She found herself listening to an impossible renunciation from an impossible lover, the while the darkness came flowing across the sands.

'. . . You're splendid to have said that. But tomorrow – and the next day – it'll sound impossible. To you it sounds half-impossible even now . . . English – and I'm a mongrel. Your people—' He seemed to forget what he had intended to say. His voice trailed off. He shrugged, and held out his hand, and was oddly shy, and stammered for the first time since she had known him.

'Thanks for you – for it.' Her limp fingers touched his. They smiled at each other strainedly. 'This isn't anything, you know. We aren't anything. And there's still your Adventure. For both of us. Always there's the Adventure . . .'

She found herself mounted and riding towards Helio-polis. A hundred yards away she looked back and saw Mogara snatch a magic bird out of the darkness, like a boy playing with a dream.

VIII

And less than a dream was it presently to seem to him. In the Zeitoun hut he sat and stared at the ornithopter model. Successful. He had won. Successful.

He went to a mirror and saw the ghostly reflection of his own face, scarred on both cheeks . . . So it had actually happened.

He began, mechanically, to prepare a meal. What was it he had said? The Adventure: still the Adventure . . . Aeronautics not enough now. Something to follow and believe in. *She* believed in it . . .

He heard the galloping horse stop at his garden-gate; heard hasting footsteps come up to the open door of the hut. For a moment a figure was dim against the night-dimness, and then Joyce Melfort was in the room.

They stood facing each other. He saw her breast rise and fall, breathing as might one who had run a race.

'M. Mogara – did you or did you not kiss me out there?'

He nodded whitely. Thereat she gave a sigh, and suddenly collapsed, limply, happily, into a chair.

'Then that's all right. Because you'll have to marry me now, in spite of my deplorable ancestors. Where can I throw my hat?' She jumped up in expostulation. 'My dear, whoever told you that was the way to cook a sausage?'

She knelt over the sputtering oil-stove, and, so kneeling, wheeled round and laughed up at him. 'Poor brother Reginald! . . .' She stopped to make mirthful appraisement of her finger-nails. She was incoherently light-hearted. 'Knew as soon as I got home that he knew. That was *his* machine that came bombing us this afternoon. He'd heard about us – came down to spy, my dear . . . Was waiting for me, he and Adrian – they'd been quarrelling – and oh! what does it matter what he said? I felt too sick to notice much till Adrian broke in with a kind of shout. "Who? *Simon Mogara?*" Stared from one to other of us and then laughed and laughed, and then grew white and furious. "*Nigger?* Why, damn your impudence—!" and it all came out, and so did I, and made for the stables, leaving Reggie like a ghost and Adrian shouting wishes to you . . . What an evening! Who'd have guessed it? Who ever? And now—'

His queer, frozen silence made her glance up. In a moment she was beside him. 'Why, why – Simon! . . .'

IX

It was some time before either of them stirred from that position wherein she had told her eager secret amazing. Smell of burning sausage roused Joyce. She broke away and danced to the oil-stove, and Mogara, released from necessity to hold her in his arms, sank down into the chair she had vacated and stared at his yellow boots as though they were the footwear unbelievable . . .

An hour later, on parting under the stars at the garden-gate, he heard her gay answer to his question come out of the dimness: 'Why, soon as ever, dear!' Dimly from her saddle she bent towards him to give him the ghostly kiss. Then had the whimsical thought and laughed a grave little laugh.

'But our children – whatever'll they be citizens of?'

Her hand, warm and assured, in his, he stood and looked up at her, and beyond her at the stars, at the years he saw with their difficulties and disillusionments and perhaps the bitter shames for her to face. But in his voice she heard only the tenderness as he answered with the jest that was more than jest, that would surely cry its promise through all their lives.

'Why – the Republic in the skies!'

X

For East is West and West is East and the little fascistic German blesses as the Aryan symbol exclusive the swastika they worshipped in the Temples of Chichen-Stza . . . Eh? You see, the good Adrian, until provoked beyond endurance, had held it as a dark and mirthful secret that the Melfort grandmother, wealth-bringing, had been a 'white mulatto' of Jamaica.

Vernal

I

NOON AND APRIL and eighty-four in the shade! Who would dream it, here in the Khalig-el-Masri, that the Spring is in our northern lands, and the wind and the rain? . . . Grey clouds and shadows and the whoop-whoop-whoop of birds in mist, and the calling of lost sheep. God mine, how today the Volga must be crying through the willows! There are boatmen singing there, and the dance of the waters, and all the earth coming so green . . .

And nowhere such foolish ache of heart as mine in Cairo!

How does it stir us so, here where Spring is a day and a night, more fugitive than a dream? No mere season, surely, but the mood universal that comes every year to cry of things undone and unachieved . . . Eh? Oh, the lips unkissed and the poems unwritten and the mountains unscaled and the sins unforgiven and the hearts unfrozen . . . We stir from the so-dreamless sleep of the day-to-day and wake and stare – even here in Cairo where the Spring is as a girl who passes with hasting feet and urgent eyes . . . As once I saw her pass.

Beat on the table for the little Simon, my friend, and I – God mine, if only I may forget my Volga and the willows! –

will tell you the story that for me still haunts each Cairene Spring.

II

In the beginning was God, and He created James Freeman. And James Freeman served Him all the days of his life . . .

This is not blasphemy. It is paraphrase on the wording quaint of that English Bible wherein I sought to master style in the Gymnasium of Kazan. So of himself always I think believed James Freeman. Long before we met here in Polychromata, and watched the little drama unfold to that evening in Spring, was he assured of the standing with his God. Since childhood had that standing been certain below his feet.

Of your English sects I know but little, and that little from Dickens and Trollope and the casual mention and the tale without footnotes – as told me it was by Norla and the Dr Adrian, and ultimately James Freeman himself. But it seems he was born of parents who early designed him a priest, and themselves held by the faith of some church that conforms not to your national belief. This in the English provincial town where was smoke and glare of furnaces night and day to furnish the so-ready similes for the hell of the conforming wicked.

When I met him he was tall and thick-browed, with the white hair and stooping shoulders and the rasp of voice. He had the face that seemed to me as the face of a lion – if one might think of the lion that had forsaken the meat for other food – perhaps because the meat had disagreed with him . . .

But that is the description unfair. He was of a type outside my comprehension and love – surely the priest-type that goes fast from the world. Since the age of twenty he had preached and believed the ancient, cruel God of sacrifice and supplication and the bitter codes. By the age

of twenty-five he had had the church of his own, and in the
glare of those furnaces, himself already twisted and bitter
and white-earnest, preached salvation and damnation in
name of his God.

And then, in that twenty-fifth year, he had loved and
desired and married.

How comes love to such as those? I think it moved and
shook him, and perhaps he was the lion he had forgone, and
there were the nights of stars and the scents of the veldt
when the world and its sins fell from him, and he and his
mate were alone and splendid under splendid skies . . .
Surely, surely. And then –

I think he came out of the love ecstasy in the sudden –
looked at himself, and through the strange, distorting
mirrors of his beliefs saw himself one unclean and lustful,
a sinner in the jargon of his creed. Perhaps in a night his
restraints and tabus came back on him again. And with
them must have come that harshness of demeanour and
expression bred of his own repressions and tortured inhibitions . . . To one who had known him only the lover he
became the cold and affrighting fanatic.

She must have lived in the hell he was incapable of
imagining, spite his furnaces and sin-creed. Of her kind
there have been the pitiful many. They have gone uncom-
plaining and unrecorded to the dead: but for their slow fate
was not Mary Freeman.

I never knew her, and to me she is but a dream. But I
think of her as one awakened to wonder and desire, and
then starved. For nearly the six years she endured that life –
or had it ceased to be the endurance till there came re-
awakening and the call of the stars again? They had the
child, the girl of five, Norla, and perhaps that tie had held
her. They lived in your London by then, in some suburb
where was church of their sect.

And suddenly, without the note or notification, she was
gone. The mystery was not the mystery for long. Near at

hand had lived the political, a Russian, and artist, and he was gone also.

It was the Spring, in March, and Freeman met her leaving by the gate of his house, and singing a little song. He spoke to her and she said strange words, not looking at him. 'I am going out to seek the Spring.'

He turned and looked after her, I think, in a moment of astonishment, and watched her out of sight. Nor did she ever return.

III

She wrote to him from the south of France, asking that she might be divorced and so marry the Russian. Again, at the end of a year, she wrote, the pitiful letter saying that the Russian was dead. To neither letter was reply sent by James Freeman. He brought his sister to rear his child and barred out into the night that pitiful face that surely came to haunt him after the second letter.

He became preacher of the savage purity, persecutor of the poor outcasts of the streets. Throughout the War he preached a God of Battles tied to the gun-carriages, and in the after-War ecstasy of self-flagellation your London took him to its heart. He addressed the great demonstrations, organised the violent crusades. From denouncing the sins of the age in the little, unknown church he was invited as preacher in your cathedrals and made the divine doctor and given a great church.

But he was already an old man. The bitterness had overflowed from his heart to his body. There came on him the chronic rheumatism and he was ordered to the sun and South France by the so-assiduous doctors.

But to go to the South France he refused with a surprising outbreak of violence. He handed over the great London church to the substitute, and came to Egypt, to Helwan, and later to Cairo.

With him he brought his daughter Norla.

IV

I may never think of the Spring but I remember Norla
Freeman; I may never read in your little gazettes of the
modern woman who lacks the seemly dullness and virtues
but I think of this English girl. For she was refutation of all
the printed spite of us of the superseded generation. Cold
and stark and vivid . . . And yet the Spring!

My friend Dr Adrian took me to the Pension Avallaire
and made the introductions between us. She sat in the
garden, in a dream, when we came upon her. She had that
red hair known to the old painters and it was the sudden
flame of colour against the Pension greenery.

'Miss Freeman, this is Colonel Anton Saloney, of the
Russian White Army and the Republic of Plato.'

This is the good Adrian's jest, because that I am unmarried and hold belief in men yet upbuilding the ultimate
wise state.

'I am from Utopia myself.' She was tall and slender,
standing so, red-crowned, with the serene purity of laughter in opal eyes. She sighed. 'Dr Adrian will have explained
to you. My father is an invalid and can't take me round
Cairo. I –' she considered the garden '– sketch. My father
insists that someone should go with me, and Dr Adrian
suggested you.'

She had an aloofness that puzzled me, but that later I was
to know so well. Defence it was she had erected – she who
found sunsets of more interest than souls – against that
world of meaningless enthusiasm and denunciation and
hysteria in which she had been reared.

'I shall be of the honoured,' I said, 'if you think me
suitable.'

Then was the sudden smile again and the peep of
friendliness.

'I like you. Will you come and talk to my father?'

I followed her to where Dr Freeman sat on the balcony of

his room, with below it the garden of Esbekiyeh and the sunshine and the changing colours of our Cairo. He peered at me from beneath the heavy brows. He did not offer to shake the hands. I was only a dragoman.

She turned to leave us, then bent over her father, adjusting the cushions, and in that so-simple action I had a sudden glimpse of vivid strength and certitude of character, the reality like the current below the surface-serene river. The Dr Freeman looked after her and then spoke in the pulpit voice.

'Dr Adrian tells me you are reliable, which is not the case with natives. Are you a gentleman?'

I made him the bow. 'My ancestors have cut throats for nine centuries.'

He crouched in his chair, the old priest with twinging bones, humourless and cold, considering me. 'You will be required to select the places fit for Miss Freeman to visit. I do not wish her to see the filthy and unclean sights of Cairo. Understand? Nor to make chance acquaintances amongst strangers or your friends. You will remember that you are my employee and hers.'

I, the ex-Professor of the English Literature, have withstood much of this, my friend, and also have built my defence. I take refuge in irrelevant conjecture and fantasy . . . That daughter of his – surely I had seen her the many times before?

Out in the garden of the Pension she waved me the au revoir. And suddenly I remembered.

One might see her face in a hundred prints and pictures. For so, the girl unawakened, the Lady of Serenity, is portrayed on the ikons the Sitt Miriam, the Virgin Mary of the Coptic Church.

v

You must bear that picture of her, my friend: early dawn in the northland Spring. Never the bird-song or the morning wind or the flying clouds yet had she known; she did not dream that a soul may flame splendid as never a sunrise.

Between us came very quickly the friendship. For was I not of the Republic of Plato and a dragoman to boot? Not that she made consideration of these things. Cairo was hers, and all its sights and colours and sounds, and the funny Russian to make the occasional jest and order the taxi and row the boat and see to the provided lunch.

'But you have . . . talent,' I said, that first morning I took her to the Gamaliyeh bazaar, and was allowed to look in her book of sketches. They were the pencillings and the charcoal work, tentative touchings and limnings, and they caught the breath. Yet I had been to say the something else before I looked closer. She knew it and the smile peeped from her eyes.

'But not "genius", Colonel Saloney?'

'Some day that will come.'

She meditated a subject, eager and young and alien and wonderful against that brownness and flame of savage colour, where the traders come with spices from the Red Sea lands and Arabia, and the camels droop in the long rows, and the air is sick with the smell of attar of roses. Then: 'If it doesn't come now, it never will . . . That woman there, with the yellow skin and the jade ear-rings! Do you think she would allow me?'

I looked and saw a painted woman of the streets. 'I think a camelier would be the better.'

So one was found and posed and sketched, and she forgot the woman. Then we were threading the bazaars to the next view of interest, the next face that caught her attention, the next vivid glimpse of blue nowhere as in Cairo stand and threaten and then faint and crumble in the yellow haze of sun.

In the next days I took her to the Khan Khalil, to the restaurant in the Muski, to Old Cairo and the sleeping walls of Citadel. At Citadel it was, while she sat and sketched and

I smoked the pipe that she uncovered for me a little history-chapter of that life that seemed to run with such swift serenity: the battle with her father before she could take the drawing lessons, before she could attend the colleges and lectures. They had fought this battle to an end, and she had won.

I took her to my Pyramids one morning, when they stood against the dawn, lonely, and with the mournful beauty, impressive not at all, but infinitely sad. I took her to the Museum one afternoon, and watched her stand amidst the bright flight of pigeons like one out of Plato or an old Greek myth. One afternoon I rowed her out from the bank of Dubara, down past el Roda, to a place in the afternoon sunlight where were the long reeds standing sentinel, and the water of the crystal clarity, and presently sunset amber upon all Cairo.

'It is as though the world were listening,' she said, and listened herself, like a child. And then, very far and remote in that silence, as though we were in the valley of Avalon, came on the Nile a nameless under-murmur.

'What is it, Colonel Anton?'

'Cairo,' I said. 'Life.'

We turned down-stream, past the island, to the right bank, where the lines of houses amidst the water-lanes lifted in broken serration red against the sunset. I rowed the boat to the bank, to the shed of the Greek who leased it – a cousin of the little Simon, and also of the incredible surname Papadrapoulnakophitos – and in a little we were walking up from the water-front through a street that had been of the so-silent three hours before.

But it was silent no longer, and I suddenly understood, and hurried the English girl who would have loitered. There were faces everywhere, seeming to have no bodies: faces in doorways, grey faces in windows, faces in apathetic groupings from which came the apathetic calling and twitter . . .

Women's faces – there were only women, women of all ages and surely all nations – painted faces with dead eyes, and in all that street not a stir or a breath of air, but only the high, unreal voices and the dead laughter that comes from far back in the throat.

'Colonel Anton – all these women – we must come here again. What is this place?'

I looked at her and saw the answer to her own question dawn in horror and disgust in her eyes. I said nothing, and in silence we passed up through that street of shame.

VI

The last day of my engagement by the Dr Freeman, Norla and I and the sketch-book spent far by the Bab-el-Futtuh. We returned early to the Muski, to have the tea together as the parting feast, and in the old arabiyeh would have passed down the street to a restaurant we had before used, when opposite a new café we heard the sound of a violin. Thereat Norla stopped the arabiyeh and turned to me with the eager eyes.

'That music, Colonel Anton – Can we go there?'

'But of course,' I said, though with secret doubts. Yet it was the last day and there could come but little harm . . .

So presently we were seated at the little table, in the packed restaurant, with the honey-cakes and Norla pouring tea, and the stout Egyptian women of the freed harems sitting near us, and the little Jew-men of the blue serge and yellow boots. Here and there was a Greek and once I saw an American. The band at the far end played with the raggedness.

'I hope that violinist plays again,' said Norla, and hardly had she spoken but the tanking of the piano ceased and the violinist stood up in the little hush.

I recognised him at once, and me also he recognised and smiled at, with his eyes straying to her who sat beside me.

Then he began to play. As often, he was now making the improvisations, the little tunes that presently faded and altered, the ripple and the cadence and the strum . . . He flung his gifts in our faces with the same carelessness that he flung himself in the face of life.

Alexandr Sergeyvich, who called himself Utrá – of the Morning. Thirty years of age, ex-aristo, revolutionist, anarchist. He had shed the name older in Russia even than mine, had at the age of eighteen written a successful opera, had in the civil war hoisted the Black Flag of Anarchy and held a country the size of Scotland against all comers – White, Green, and Red – for the full three months. Then he had passed to the Sovyeti, to Lunacharsky and the Department of Education and Culture, and the planning of a gigantic Palace of Music and the writing of the revolutionary song-cycle. But his anarchism was of the soul, and there was no discipline that might tame him. Within two years he was making his way from Russia while the Cheka watched the ports for his arrest. He and his violin had thenceafter wandered most of south-Europe before he came to Cairo and greeted me one day in the Muski . . . He had once been a student of mine in the English lectures at far Kazan.

Black of hair and eyes, with the brown face and the long, swift smile, and tall and slender . . . Alexandr of the Morning, dreamer of dreams, born out of his due time . . .

I awoke from the reverie and was suddenly conscious of one who sat beside me, stirred and transformed. I had glimpse of white face and rapt eyes, and then followed her look. Alexandr Sergeyvich, his eyes fixed on our table in a look that shocked me to realisation, was playing as never before I had heard him play.

He was playing my Volga and its willows and the shouting waters in the sun. Life in the morning he was playing, life running swift and sweet, and its call ringing and ringing like far laughter. He was playing that life that never was but always may be, love young and eternal and with ecstasy unquenched, love with shining feet and unbraided hair . . .

He had finished and stood beside us. He had threaded the tables without the hesitation or doubt.

'Miss Freeman,' I said, 'this is M. Utrá.'

She looked up at him. Dawning in her opal eyes was that which I had never seen before. They made none of the conventional greetings, but looked at each other in the white wonder.

'It was glorious,' she whispered. 'I never knew life could be like that.'

He spoke in the half-whisper also. 'Nor did I,' he said.

VII

In a week's time, while I was tramping the Ghizeh sands or helping the stout lady tourist to surmount the steps of Kheops Pyramid, Alexandr Sergeyvich, a little worried over the proprieties – he, the leader of the Black Bands! – was kissing the hands of his Norla in the garden of the Pension Avallaire.

'If you'll take me to your father, I will ask his permission.'

'Oh, my dear! . . .' And then the gravity. For they had met three times already, and after the third meeting he had written to her. 'That letter of yours – about all the happenings since you were a boy, and – and other women . . . What is the past to me? I'm not an auditor.'

'You are divine,' he said, very humbly. And then, with his shattering earnestness: 'When will you marry me?'

'Whenever you like. But there's my father – he's an invalid still . . . And I love him also.'

He had been the gentleman before he was the anarchist. Which of them was it that kissed her hands then? 'I shall write to your father and explain everything.'

And the next day this he did. He was a Russian of the revolution, you will remember. He told the Dr Freeman of his love for Norla and his desire to marry her, he told of whom he was, of his life, his sins, his poverty. He wrote of those things with the starkness and simplicity of a Gladkov – that simplicity that leaves even the liberal of the older generation shocked and agape; he wrote with that devastating earnestness that was of his soul-fibre, and made none of the decorous attempts to gloss . . .

To the Dr Freeman, the preacher of purity crusades in London, it must have seemed as though he had received a letter from a polite and regretful fiend. He read it at breakfast, in the private room, and Norla was startled at the pallor on his face. He tried to get up, and made the unsuccessful attempts, with the rheumatism twinging his bones.

'This Russian anarchist and seducer' – he glared across the table with cruel eyes – 'how long have you known him?'

She herself was to tell me of this conversation, and the little lie she told then to shield me. 'A week. I met him by chance when I was separated from Colonel Saloney.'

He raved at her. 'You will not see him again, do you hear? Whatever the loose blood you inherit from your mother, I'll see that it's held in check.'

Once she would have kept the serene silence. But it was a new Norla whom Alexandr Sergeyvich was evoking.

'I will see him when I choose.'

He choked, with empurpling face. He made another effort to rise, then sank back with the groan. Their eyes met. In a moment, contrite, she was kneeling beside him.

'Daddy – I didn't mean that . . . Let me help.'

And this he suffered her. I think he believed he had won, and that night he wrote to Alexandr Sergeyvich the letter which I will not quote. There is an obscenity of suspicion which goes with the dark old sacrifice-cults.

But while he wrote Norla also was writing. She had sat the long while in self-struggle, remembering that half-promise given to her father. But the old standards and the old allegiances – they were fading from her like the garments of gossamer.

Across in the Esbekiyeh Gardens was a dance and the scraping of violins. A night in mid-March it was, with the Cairene scents and the Cairene lights. But in the air the premonition of the something else that brought to her heart the sharp, sweet ache.

Far away, through miles and miles of your English lanes, the Spring was burgeoning that night.

VIII

At two o'clock next day, in response to the letter she had sent me, I was at the Pension Avallaire, and in a quarter of an hour, with the Dr Freeman's consent, we were driving to the Nile in a taxi.

She had found it urgent to be rowed down to el Roda again, to make the final reed-sketches.

'We will go to the other place for a boat,' I said, with troubled remembrance of that street that led to the wharf of Simon's cousin.

She shook her head. 'I wrote reserving a boat – to the Papadrapoulnakophitos man.' She twinkled the opal eyes. 'His name covered three lines on the envelope.' But she was grave. 'Colonel, I want to tell you . . .'

And so of the whole business I was told. I sat in the stunned silence, and also a little of the horror, for am I not of my generation? Utrá, the Black Anarchist – and this English girl!

'What are you to do?' I asked. We were on the Nile by then, and I was rowing up-river. She shaded her eyes with her hand, looking into the heat-haze by left bank.

She did not answer my question. Suddenly were the little flags of excitement waving in her cheeks. 'Turn in by that jetty, please.'

Unthinking, I drew up by a line of green timbers. In the

moment someone was in the boat, and it rocking under his weight. While I stared at Alexandr Sergeyvich bending to the swift kiss of the English girl I made realisation of a story-plot in which I figured as the false clue.

IX

'This is unfair to me, Alexandr Sergeyvich,' I said.

I had rowed them up-river, and they sat opposite me in that still place where once Norla had listened to the call of Cairo. It was she who answered.

'There is nothing unfair, Colonel Anton. For you didn't know. You can tell my father as soon as we go back. By then Sashka and I will have decided.'

'Sashka!' How had she come to that name already? And then I saw on his face, as he looked at her, that which stilled forever some of the doubts that had tormented me.

'We'll marry,' he said, 'if you can love such fool as I am. I'll write saleable songs and music, I'll work myself to a shadow for you. And I know we'll win.'

She trailed her hand in the water, not looking at him, but across at the sun above Moqattam. 'And your anarchism and your dreams and your faith in freedom – you'll give up all these?'

He set his face and looked at her not either. 'All these.'

She turned to him very swiftly. 'You'll give up nothing for me. My dear, do you think I don't love you for your dreams as well? You'll put them in music that'll shake the world yet – and I'll paint them in pictures that'll light it forever! . . . Remember that thing you played in the Muski café? We'll live like that, you and I, and never grow old!'

'Listen!' I said.

They turned their faces towards me in surprise. And then, far away, from some hidden cote, it echoed down the river again – that calling that Solomon heard these four thousand years ago in the hills of Palestine and set forever in magic words.

A rainbow sprang and vanished against the shores of el Roda. Trailingly went by the thin curtain of rain. Behind the hills was already the disc of the sun, half-hidden.

I turned the boat and we drifted down the Nile between the tinted shores. Never-ceasing in that sunset silence was the calling of doves. Norla and Sashka had ceased to whisper, and sat hand in hand. And then Norla spoke in the serene voice that yet held a golden tremor.

'Colonel Anton, will you go back to the Pension Avallaire and tell my father not to worry? I am going with Sashka.'

I stared in the stupefaction. 'But you cannot have the consulate marriage for many days . . .'

Over Bulaq hung already the evening star. Already were the ghosts of shadows. And through them, answer to me, Norla Freeman's laughter, very low and tender.

And then, in the helplessness, I understood. They had passed beyond the hold and restraint of me or anyone. The world and wonder was theirs to-night . . .

The jetty. I pulled in, and in the moment we were on shore, walking up through that street where once I had hurried Norla. Towards the river was coming an arabiyeh, and we drew aside to let it pass.

But it did not pass. There came the sudden order in English, the groan of pain, and the Dr Freeman was in the street beside us.

x

The false clue, you understand, had not misled him. From the first he had doubted Norla's story of the sudden necessity of the reed-sketch, and with the passing of the day his doubts had increased. After we had gone from the Pension Avallaire he had driven to Sashka's address, and, finding the Russian so-abominable neither there nor at his café, directed his arabiyeh to the boat-shed of Simon's cousin. They had had difficulty in finding the street of approach, and the anger of his passenger had but seemed to increase the stupidity of the driver.

Of those things we learnt afterwards, but at the moment we stood and stared at him in that twilight street – I, at least, in consternation. He stood the moment in silence, leaning on the heavy stick, looking from one to the other of us, with for background the loitering, weary-faced women crowding in doorway and at window.

'So you have been for a "final sketch" – you and the Russian "gentleman"? And who is this?'

Norla was white-faced, but she spoke in the voice as quiet as his. 'This is Alexandr Utrá, whom I am going to marry.'

'Another Russian "gentleman"?' He glared at her malignantly and then made the foul sneer, standing there with quivering hand upon his stick.

'M'sieu'—'

Sashka with the smouldering eyes confronting him. And then the Dr Freeman gave evidence of that passion that seethed in him. He lifted his stick and struck with it, blindly, savagely . . .

For a moment was the foolish scrimmage in the street strangely hushed. Then I was holding the Dr Freeman's wrist the while he raved at us and in the eyes of Sashka glowed murder.

'My God, my God!'

I thought it the moan of pain and released his wrist. He was staring up the street, and we followed his gaze. Even the eyes in the dim faces that backgrounded him turned to follow it. And in the street, though the Dr Freeman was shivering as one in an ague, was nothing.

I caught his arm to support him. Some current seemed to shiver through me. And then I saw.

Down the street, emerged from a middle house, was coming a woman, fair and young and with red-coiled hair.

With noiseless feet she came, looking neither to the left nor right, but ahead, with shining eyes, and for the wonderful moment I could smell the fragrance of the primrose pinned at her throat. With hasting feet, clad in the trailing dress, she went by, down to the shadows and the glow of the Nile, and as she passed I heard on her lips the murmur of a little song . . .

'*Mary!*'

We lifted Dr Freeman into the arabiyeh, and then Norla was shaking my shoulder.

'What was he looking at? . . . Colonel Anton, you're dazed as well. What did he see come down the street?'

I looked, as one coming out of sleep, at the dimming Nile, at Sashka, at Norla, at the crowding faces.

'I think it was the Spring,' I said.

XI

I shall not tell you of the talk I had the next evening with an old priest very broken and frightened, nor of the little gathering a fortnight later at the Presbyterian Church, where Alexandr Sergeyvich Utrá was married by the father of the bride to a Norla who bore the great bunch of English primroses, and stood with shining eyes, there, surely at the Gate of Spring . . .

But within twelve hours of that happening in the street of shame I had gone back there, making enquiries at the middle house on the right side of the street. For the little they would give me no answer, those women with the dead eyes, and I was turning away, when one in the doorway leaned and whispered to me.

'Yes, there was one who died in this house yesterday. In the evening, at sunset.' There came the high, toneless laughter from far back in her throat. 'An Englishwoman. We called her the Sitt Miriam.'

Daybreak

I

THE LITTLE CLUSTER of bell-flowers – From Scotland? But it has travelled far! I may smell it? . . . God mine, it is heather!

It cloaks your mountains in purple this time of year, does it not? Never have I seen it before; but I have smelt this smell. I have smelt it blowing on a wind from those mountains I have never trod, a breath of that autumn I have never known . . .

Eh? In imagination? But no, in the reality – I, Anton Saloney, here in our Cairo, almost the year ago today.

II

And the tale begins, if I must tell it, neither here in Egypt nor in that Kazan where I was Professor of the English Literature before I became White soldier, refugee, and dragoman. It begins in the far Scotland that sent you the heather, with Roger Mantell on the autumn walking-tour up through your Urals.

He was the young journalist in London, this Roger, and very poor, as is proper for the journalist. Something of your own height and appearance he had, with that brown-ness of the hair and eyes that indistinguishes the English-man, and a certain far-awayness of outlook that made of him the not too-good journalist. History was his passion, and he had taken the walking-tour to plan the writing of a book. This book was to refute the foolish Spengler – him who believes all history goes in cycles, like the mad dog chasing its tail.

And one night-time, very late, passing through a village amongst those hills, he heard a girl singing a peasant song – so sweet and strange and beautiful in the dark that he halted and listened. And the song was this:

> Oh, the memory an' the ache
> 　They have stown the heart fra me,
> And there's heather on the hills
> 　In my ain countree.

All next day, though many miles away, he found memory of singer and song haunting him. So pressing was it that he turned about and went back to lay this ghostly thing. Outside the village school he heard the voice again.

Then, in the growing amazement at himself, he rented a room at the village inn, in three days obtained introduction to his singer, and within the week, though his history had not progressed even in the draft beyond so-hairy Eoan-thropus, was planning nothing of greater import than to steal the singer from her hills.

Her father had been the village schoolmaster and she was teacher of the school. And because he had been a poet this dead father of hers had called her Dawn. To watch her stand against the sunrise, as many a morning she did when they tramped the hills together and the mists were rising, caught the amazement ever again in the throat of Roger. Slight and slim and dark and quick, this singer of the hills, with clear eyes, grey and grave, but with the little twinkle-light deep down in them. She had the pale, clear skin with the faint blood-flush. She detested the poor Spengler and could run like a deer.

Indeed, though one who had lived in the hills all her life, she was of the most modern – one of that woman's miracle-generation that knows nothing of the reserves and hesitations and tantalisations. She had the body of a gracious boy and the mind of an eager Greek.

If Roger first loved her for her voice, I think she loved him at first sight, protectingly, because of that far-awayness of his look. Under painted skies, children in a world transformed, they walked that autumn. Roger had been the unawakened tourist, but Dawn took him out into mornings of wonder when, in the silence, he would hear the sun come audibly up from the east, hear the earth stir and move as from its sleep. Or into fervid noons, to lie on a mountainside and listen to the drowsy under-song of bees rising and falling on the never-coming wind. And the brown night would creep over this land of Dawn's as one very ancient who went home from toil . . .

It seemed to him that she had deeper kinship with those things than he would ever fathom. 'I don't believe you are human at all,' he said to her once. 'You're out of the hills and the sunrise.'

She laughed at him, and then was grave, in that fashion that somehow had power to wring his heart absurdly. 'I never remember my mother. She died when I was born. And my father was always lost in his books. I carried all my desperate wrongs and fears to the hills.' She sat with cheek in hand and looked across the sun-hazed valleys. 'I think they love me, those hills, almost as much as I love them.'

'How can they help it?' said Roger, her lover.

III

In the little time they were deciding when they would marry and how many children they would have, and whether it would be better to wait until Roger made the thousand a year or only the eight hundred. Not till there was security and certainty were they to mate . . . At the least, that was Roger's planning, and Dawn, this so-amazing Greek boy who was more than the boy, sat and looked at him and her hills, I think perhaps with the twinkle-tapers lighting her grey eyes.

For he had come in the first months of the autumn. Day by day it deepened around them. Purple grew the mountains and under the long heats of day climbed to heaven in a shimmering blaze. Out of the earth rose all the songs of fruition and ending, and that second week there was a moon that came and never seemed to set. They could not keep their beds, these two, but stole out to meet each other in the white radiant wonder.

Till one night – this but the guess-work of mine – they kissed each other and in their kiss was already a wild regret. The hours are on wings, on wings! beat the shadows that were night-birds. Now, now! beat their own hearts . . . Perhaps Dawn held him at arm's length, and laughed at him with the little breathlessness. 'But, Roger! . . . A thousand a year!'

And then, whatever his answer, in some such hour of the earth-magic they came to their decision.

One night, under a moon that trembled on the wane, but waited for them still, they climbed together up into the hills and the radiance and not a bird that called in the shadows but was their friend, and there was none of the need to say good-night.

IV

But no moons endure forever, and presently Dawn was with Roger in a little flat in London and those days on the hills dimmed till they were of a dream.

I have never seen your London or known its life, but it seems they went to live there in the season of the fogs which rise from a blind little river amidst the streets. They began their life in a half-twilight, with the million under-murmurs of other life a still roar about them. In the morning Roger was gone to the office of his gazette; often he did not return until midnight. For many weeks they would see each other only at night-time, each wearied and a little tired . . .

And in the little was the amazement, I think, and silent tears shed in the darkness that love could ever tarnish so. For they came to look on each other searchingly, even on the wild occasion angrily – Dawn to see her dreamer of the hills visionary and unpractical, immersed in his book and the refutations of cyclic catastrophe, irritable over the refractory phrase or the inadequate reference. And to Roger it sometimes seemed that he was tied, by all un-reasonable bounds, to a boy quickly bored and swift to anger, one whose eyes could light with other than mirth, one whose laughter could ring cruel and very clear . . .

But these are of the things inevitable? They are not the less heart-breaking. Sometime, both knew, they would come to the adjustments and live with lesser friction. They would, in their English phrase, 'settle down'. But the ache in the dark of love, a thing so-shining, to look forward to the settle-down!

Yet was that never to be, for a day came when they looked at each other in unbelief and the settle-down fled out into the blinded streets and romance rang her bugles for them again. The great secret was theirs, theirs partner-ship in the abiding mystery . . .

But who am I to speak of it or understand? We of the unmarried are emotionally unborn, even though, wistfully, we catch a glimpse of understanding. This child of theirs was to be – oh, that hero that every child may be! – a captain of the hosts of the morning, Dawn and Roger in one, doer and dreamer, one who was to confound all erring Germans and bear the torch of vision yet another league up the Defile through which march the hosts that have climbed from the beast.

And they named him, and dreamt of him and hoped for him, and the months fell away, into spring warming Lon-don, into the summer, till there came the day when Dawn must pass through her hours of agony and Roger doubt his vision of history. For there arose the complications and the bringing of a surgeon . . .

In the end was the child born dead, and for the little it seemed that Dawn herself would die.

V

But she lived, returning to life wan and a stranger from a desolate land. She must bear no more children, nor must she stay the winter in England, the doctors said.

Roger – a Roger grown practical at the last – took her north to the brief summer-autumn of her hills. So soon as he could leave her he went back to London again. In a week he was sending her the news that he had found a gazette willing to send him abroad for a year, to Egypt, to act as the correspondent and write a series-impressions of Cairo and the Nile-country.

VI

So they came to our Polychromata, those two. On the voyage Dawn grew again the Greek boy, and her laughter came back, and the little twinkle that changed and yet abided in her grey eyes. They came from the ship at Alexandria and found a *pension* at Kubbah. From there they set to the search for a house.

At the length, up on Nile bank to the north of Gezireh Island, they came one afternoon on that at sight of which Dawn cried 'Oh Roger!' in the tone that stirred in him always a memoried cry from a day of agony. They stopped and looked at the desired possession, and laughed eagerly, and kissed like the children they were.

For that was the supreme wonder of their days – their love that had flamed anew. As never before it flamed. But the burning is the wrong simile. It burgeoned and blossomed, strange and sweet, not the love of the first early days nor yet the compassionate passion of the dark London time. It was something that made of their first wild desire a childish greed, of the settle-down necessity a humour and a fantasy . . .

They surveyed the empty house by Nile bank and went back to Kubbah in the apprehension that it would be gone by morning. But the next day they found the agent, rented 'La maison Saniosu', and engaged two Egyptian servants. It jutted out upon the Nile, the house, old and of crumbling stone, mantled with a brown creeper that reached down its tendrils to the water. It was two storeys in height and had a high-walled garden also skirted by the Nile.

They had taken it furnished, so after a few necessary purchases in the bazaars, and in the intervals of Roger writing the so-masterly series-impressions, they had but to debate a new name for it.

Above the door was its name carved – Maison Saniosu.

'Let's call it Sans-Sous and be done,' said Roger. And this, because they were very young and very poor and very happy, was a great jest, and almost on that name they decided.

But one morning – a morning early in October – happened that which solved the so-urgent matter. In their room Dawn was the first to awake. Upon the window was the urgent tapping of a twig and she looked out on the wonder of a Nile daybreak. Presently she awakened Roger and they sat side by side watching in the sky the silver that changed to amber and so to copper and then into the blind flush of azure.

They had been awakened by the first of the seasonal morning winds that brings the end of the khamsin time, but that they did not know until later. Only that unexpected wind had brought to Dawn an inspiration.

'I know – name for our house! Was there ever such suitable name!'

Roger stared at her. 'What?'

'Why, Daybreak.'

He made the teasing of her. 'But that is your own name. It is Dawn.' Then he laughed, and there were words in your English Bible that he remembered, very wonderful and beautiful words:

' "*Until the day break and the shadows flee away—*" '

VII

I met them first in the mid-November, in front of the Sphinx, when Dawn was posing it and her Roger and an Egyptian dragoman for the photograph. I also had come to photograph it for a client I had.

Roger apologised for his Philistine wife who insisted that he and the dragoman should stand beside the Riddle of the Sands. I made her the bow.

'I think she is wise,' I said, 'for this is no Riddle, but only a foolish vanity in stone. If I might I would have madame in my photograph with the Sphinx.'

I have that photograph still, with the little madame, slight and sweet and brave, standing beside that owlish carving of the foolish dead. Then I helped them catch the donkeys which had strayed and we went to Mena House and drank the much-needed tea, for the donkey-catching had been a task of the mirth and great speed.

From the first I think their liking was for me as mine for them. Presently, when we had ceased to laugh at memory of a donkey which had raced Roger for almost a mile, they were telling me of the house called Daybreak and that sudden wind from the Nile that now tapped their window each morning.

'It is a *green* wind,' said the little madame, and paused in the doubt of my understanding.

'I know,' I said. 'It is of the Delta crops and harvesting. Yet few know it for a green wind.'

'I am a peasant myself,' she said. 'Is that why?'

I looked at her and wove the fantasy. 'You are of the most ancient race, I think. Of the brunet race that held the Mediterranean lands long before there was Celt or Saxon or Slav. They are not of the history-books: they passed north and south into bleaker lands before history opened. But perhaps there was one of them, some far-father of yours, who once tilled the Delta lands and woke to that green wind. Perhaps it is a memory that has come to you across ten thousand years.'

'That is a wonderful thought,' said Dawn, and looked at her Roger.

'I will steal it for an article,' said Roger, and there was the laughter amongst us:

VIII

In the little I was a frequent visitor at the house called Daybreak. I talked of the Nile and the little Cairo and gave to Roger good copy for his London gazette. Soon to both of them I was the close friend, and knew this tale of theirs I have told you, even as they knew mine. When I told Roger of those Four Years which ended for me in the storming of Perekop by the Sovyet heroes – heroes they were, though my enemies – I remember the long silence that fell.

'That is life,' he said. 'And it seems blind chance and aimlessness . . . But there's something behind it greater than a dark malignancy. Though that malignancy is real enough. Perhaps in ancient Egypt they saw it, the Dark Shadow, and built the Sphinx and Pyramids to ward it off.'

'And this other thing,' I said. 'What is it?'

'Oh, something equally nameless and untheological. It has led us up through the dark Defile of history, has turned in many guises to help again and again the stragglers and the lost in their hour of utmost despair. It will lead us to the sunrise yet.'

'That Daybreak the poor Spenglers have never visioned,' I jested at him, though I loved his faith. We heard the singing of Dawn inside the house. 'And the little madame is its prophet.'

He laughed and was a poet. 'She was made in secret when the Dark Gods slept!'

Never since Kazan had I known such friendship as those nights when the little madame and I would sit and talk under our Cairene moon, with the bulking of Bulaq beyond the garden wall and the far wail of native song in our ears. Sometimes was Roger with us, but often indoors, working on the so-great book that was not in the contract with his London gazette – the book that was to bring him reputation and money. I brought the violin to that garden, and Dawn would sing for me peasants' songs that left me homesick for my Volga lands – though they were songs of that Scotland I have never seen. Once she sang that verse which had halted Roger in the hills, and I have forgotten it never:

> Oh, the memory an' the ache
> > They have stown the heart fra me,
> And there's heather on the hills
> > In my ain countree.

But of course I loved her. From the first moment I think I loved her. And with Roger also I was in love. They were to me the surety of my dreams. I loved them as one loves those dream-children, keen and beautiful, who will people our happy world a thousand years after we are dead.

IX

And then, in the February, there came the horror into their lives.

At the first I did not understand their silences and strangeness. I said to myself that I was the too-frequent visitor – what need had these lovers of such alien as myself? For a little there was the bitterness with me, and I stayed away from the house called Daybreak, going there not at all until the passing of two weeks. When next I went it was to endure their reproach and in the eyes of the little madame a hurt puzzlement.

'You have tired of us? Why have you stayed away?'

I kissed her hand. 'But I had thought you tired of me,' I said, and blundered over words which I desired not to say. 'There seemed the difference the last time I came . . .'

Then was there the silence, though Roger broke it with a sudden laugh and talk of indifferent matter. His eyes were the eyes of a sick animal. And when presently we were alone he went to the window, and looked blindly out on the sunlight and the Nile, then turned and told me.

And then, God mine! I also knew the sudden sickness of mind, and had no word to say because of the horror of the thing.

For another child was coming, and, as they had been told, Dawn could never live through such a thing again.

X

I proposed the committee of doctors which may deal with such cases, but Dawn, modern of moderns though she was, would have none of it. For she could talk of these things, being my friend and of her miracle-generation.

'I think – oh, I don't know, but it would be cheating.'

'But this is the absurd fatalism,' I pleaded, as Roger also had pleaded. The little twinkle set its lights in her grave eyes.

'Anton, my dear, was it absurd fatalism that led you to fight a hopeless fight in your White army? . . . And have you lost – even yet?'

That was in the garden of Daybreak, in the late March, and we were silent as she leant on the wall and looked down on the hastening waters. She had a sudden idle thought.

'Oh, that morning wind from the Delta – it does not blow now.'

'Eh?' I said. 'The wind? It will not come again for many months.'

XI

I procured for them Dr Adrian, the English gynaecologist, who is my friend. Dawn liked him, for he is the droll, but to Roger he talked with a grave face, for he had from London the particulars of the case when the other child had died. The little madame must know no unhappiness or worry. Also, she must leave Cairo.

For the summer months drew on. They blazed their strong heat that summer as never before, I think. Yet Dawn, even when Roger at this would have written to his London gazette and made the resignation, refused. They would stay on at Daybreak. On the little madame was the Cairene spell – that spell which makes of a chance house and garden in this strange city more homely than home.

But never so long a summer . . . A tent was set in the garden, and through those long days of white warmth we watched Dawn with the stealthiness of criminals who fear their gaze may be detected. So she told us; laughing, but with the wistfulness. I doubt if Roger comforted her; it was she who gave the comfort. For him it was to start out of even the happiest moment into the blank silence when terror walked his brain and looked from his eyes. And from that would he be awakened with her arms about him, and her teasing tenderness . . . Then I would stride away, with the sick fear upon me also.

God mine, it was pitiful, heart-breaking.

But I set out to be the droll, even as did Adrian – he who has said that no gynaecologist can be anything but gynae-colatrist – in his visits to the house called Daybreak. We sought to weave the conspiracy, we three – the conspiracy to keep afar the malignant shadow of which Roger had talked. Presently the Egyptian servants also understood and were in that conspiracy. With the ending of the khamsin-time I organised many of the late afternoon excursions – to the Barrage, to Heliopolis, to the desert, borrowing a car from Adrian to take them to those places.

One afternoon in late September I took them to Abu Zabal. For mile on mile we went into that brown country, where stand in sleep the white-washed villages under their smoke-pencillings, and there is no other colour at all, but only the white and black. We had tea as a picnic, making it under the lee of a ruined dyke in the sunset. It was such sunset as seemed to fire the world.

'It is the Ragnarok,' I said, and Dawn poured sand on Roger, who was lazy and lay flatwise, to make him sit up and look at it.

'I've seen a Grampians sunset like that,' he said.

The little madame caught her breath. She began to speak in a whisper.

'It's autumn there now. Oh, my hills, my dear hills! Can't you see them and smell them, Roger, climbing purple into the sunset? And hear the curlews crying down the glen?'

We said nothing, and then we saw that she was weeping – desolately, with uncovered face, she who had been so brave.

And the time drew ever nearer like a black wall of sand.

XII

There came a night when Roger Mantell and I tramped that garden through hours that seemed never-ending. The cruel aloofness of the yellow stars and the whispering Nile! And it seemed to me then, as I think to Roger himself, that the dream of his history was false, that alone and unfriended man wandered amidst the cold immensities of space and time . . . Beside and above us, against the southwards sky, were the lights of the house called Daybreak.

To and fro, hour on hour, I walked Roger, and talked to him of the stars. I remember I stood pointing out to him Alpha in Centaur when Lesdiguières, the French colleague of Adrian, called him from the garden-door.

For Adrian was not there. That night of all nights he was in Alexandria, and, though we had sent the telegram for him, would not be back until the morning. Lesdiguières, good and careful, but of the old school and the old fashion – it seemed but a moment when I next heard him calling me. But it must have been longer, for in the east were the ghost-limnings of the day.

'The child – born alive, yes. A boy, and of the complications none. But the girl' – and I knew he meant the little madame – 'is exhausted. She will not see the day, I think. She is calling for you.'

I shall not tell you, my friend, of that so-close room – the windows Lesdiguières had closed against the night miasmas – nor the smells of the antiseptics, nor the stout French nurse who was presently gone out of the room with the doctor. I knelt and kissed the hand of the little madame – so-tired, a child herself, lying there, Roger's arm under her head. She was sinking very quickly, dying of exhaustion. But as I rose to go she whispered 'Stay.'

I looked at Roger, but for me he had no eyes. I turned to the closed window and saw in the sky a pallor that waned and flushed and spread. And there came in my mind then, into that silence a bitter memory – the words Roger had quoted the day they named their house.

'*Until the day break and the shadows flee away—*'

Suddenly there was the rustling sound and I looked round. The little madame had sat urgently up in the arms of her lover, her eyes shining.

'Roger, Roger, look – the hills!'

And then upon the window I heard a little tapping. I wheeled to it and saw the urgent twig beating upon the pane. It was the first of the Delta winds. Of sudden impulse I undid the catch and flung the window open to the Nile daybreak . . .

And then I heard from Roger the little cry of wonder.

For suddenly, borne on that first Nile wind, out of the dawn the room was flooded with a nameless scent, and it seemed to me a moment I stood in a great valley, and up the grey slopes climbed the dawn, and as it climbed those hill-slopes mantled a misting purple . . .

A moment the thing was, in a strange, sweet silence, and then gone. I turned and looked at Roger's white face.

'My God!' he whispered. 'Did you smell it? *It was heather*!'

We looked at the little madame lying silent in his arms. I thought her dead, and then, while we stared, we saw she was asleep.

XIII

And she lived, coming out of that health-giving sleep with no memory of the morning happenings. In the spring Roger took her and his son away from Cairo and Egypt, back to her hills, for he was by then the great man because of his book. And me she kissed farewell – me, the dragoman! – and there was a mist in her clear eyes . . .

But Adrian when he came that morning: 'You saved her life,' he said to me, while we three stood in the garden and the little Dawn slept in the room above the Nile. 'It was the Delta morning wind that did it – the change in the temperature, you know. That fool Lesdiguiéres must have half-suffocated her.'

Yet until prevail the years that make all things dim will it seem to Roger and me that once, in an hour of desperate need, we were granted glimpse of the kindlier, nameless

thing that verily shines and abides behind all the blind ways
and destinies of Nature.

It is Written

I

FIRST SUNSET AFTER Ramadan! Our Cairo is painting
herself in the red tonight – that is the phrase, is it not? . . .
Hark to the drumming with which the little Muslim celebrates the reprieve of his stomach!

Eh? The religion vigorous – Islam? It is a withered tree
that creaks and falls; this shouting and show is but the last
wind in its branches. Nor falls it alone. In all the Forest of
Faith is a rending and overthrow. The specialised creed and
the specialised god – what plants amazing and monstrous
they will seem to the future generations who excavate them
from the strata carboniferous!

Yet they pass not alone, I think. The Disciples Twelve,
the priests and worshippers – in their company passes even
the Thirteenth Disciple – the infidel who feared and
doubted and disbelieved. Doubt and devoutness, faith
and fear – they pass in a drift of twigs and leaves on that
slow wind that beats through the dying Forest. And in their
place—?

How should I know? Perhaps there comes the era of God
Himself, creedless and testamentless, without priest or
shrine, triumphant slowly amidst the darkness – as once
Godfrey Steyn glimpsed him in the eyes and speech of an
unbeliever.

II

Steyn! It was an evening in May when I first met him. I had passed through the dusty drooping of trees in the garden Esbekiyeh when on the side-walk, near to the little café, I was hailed by name. I turned and saw my friend, the Dr Adrian, seated at a little table, intent on the game of dominoes. But it was not the usual self-game he played. He had the opponent.

'Oh, Colonel. I've been waiting for you to pass. Knew you'd come this way sooner or later. Here's someone who wants to know you. Mr Steyn: Colonel Saloney.'

I made the bow and at that Adrian's companion also rose and bowed, and smiled with an absent friendliness. He had the hair too long and the face too pale, and for a little I thought him one of Adrian's patients. His face I seemed to know and made the rude and puzzled consideration of it. This he endured without embarrassment. And indeed I may have stared not so long as I thought before I remembered his prototype. He had such face as one sees in the portraits of your little Shelley – comely and kindly and the face of youth, yet not weak at all.

He might have been thirty years of age. He had the soft brown hair like silk, and the eyes that were also a shade of brown. His voice in conversation was the voice very clear and accentless – this perhaps because he was a trained elocutionist, and sought to conceal the fact.

'Won't you sit down, Colonel Saloney? And have a drink?'

I murmured the thanks. Adrian, sweeping the dominoes-game to himself, grinned. 'Mr Steyn is a parson, Colonel, so you'll have to forgive him his lemonade.'

The brown eyes twinkled. 'My constitution, not my profession, you'll have to forgive, you know. I've no objection to wine – except being forced to drink it. Makes me sick . . . Colonel, Dr Adrian has been telling me about you.

Oh, lots to your credit! Have you any important engagements during the next few weeks?'

I was a little disappointed and bored . . . So he was the tourist and wished me to show him Cairo and expound the Sphinx and crawl the pyramid-tunnels in his company. 'None of importance.'

He cupped the lean, pale face in a brown hand. 'That's good, if I may say so. Because I want you to act as my guide and general assistant on an archeological expedition to the Wadi Faregh.'

'Faregh?' I shook my head. 'That is the bare stretch of the hills fifty miles west of the Pyramids? But I know nothing of it. And I am no archaeologist, whatever the good Adrian may have been saying . . . Faregh? But surely there are no remains there?'

Adrian glanced up the sardonic moment from his game, but said nothing. Godfrey Steyn sipped the sickly lemonade and turned on me again his charming smile.

'Doesn't matter though you aren't an archaeologist. I'm not, either. Nor though you've never been to Wadi Faregh. I want someone who knows the country and people generally, and can organise a small expedition for me. I'm going out to Faregh to look for the tomb of one Polyorthes, a Hellenised Egyptian who was buried there seventeen hundred years ago.'

I was a little intrigued. 'The tomb of importance? There were but bare burials, seldom with either mummification or inscription, so late as that. And even of such tombs in the Wadi Faregh I have never heard.'

He was silent for the little, looking out into the street. His face changed from the face of the polite and gracious youth to that of the fanatic, the enthusiast. He spoke with a quietness of voice that stilled me.

'I have almost certain evidence that this Polyorthes was buried in Faregh, and that buried with him is a document, a Lost Testament, in the handwriting of our Saviour Himself.'

III

This he actually believed. The while Adrian, sardonic and indifferent, immersed himself in the game of dominoes, and I, a little uncomfortable, drank of the wine he had ordered me, this priest with the face Shelleyan proceeded to relate the story that was in reality the thirteen years autobiography.

I may summarise it for you with brevity, though indeed was the original brief enough. Too brief in places, so that I had difficulty in comprehending the chemic structure of a personality at once fantastically medieval and pleasantly modern.

For both these things was Steyn, he who had landed at Basrah as the clergyman-missionary in March of the nineteen-fourteen. Twenty years of age, newly out from England, the mystic that was the essential part of him a little overlaid by the muscular Christian of the theological college, he had stood on the hotel verandah that first afternoon and watched the mirage-sway of the jungle-walls across the Shatt-el-Arab. Within twenty months there came rolling up against those walls another mirage, and he stood and stared at it aghast . . .

The boy Shelley in a world of Anarchs, he saw evil and cruelty, crowned and robed and acclaimed in an incense of blood, stalk the Mesopotamian days and nights. As an Army clergyman he went through the campaigns of sunglare and horror, fighting not Turks, but something greater than these – belief in that dark Consciousness now unleashed and triumphant across all the world. Belief in it would make of him a cheat and impostor; disbelief – to deny the evidence of his senses . . .

That mind medieval of his is outside your comprehension – as once so completely outside Gillyflower Arnold's. But I think he endured the agony Gethsemane-like. God – the all-powerful, the all-good, the creator – a super-ape bending in amusement over the foetid scum that writhed and fought on this rotting mud-ball that was his creation . . .

He was but one of many in those years startled to some such horrific vision. And, like the many, he refused that vision. Somewhere was explanation, somewhere recoverable that faith in goodness which was more necessary to his existence than sunlight or food. Meantime, work.

It was the after-war years by then, and he fled from his own thoughts into relief-work amidst the refugees and refuse scattered in the Anatolian hinterlands – the straying tribes war-uprooted, the starving thousands who drifted over mountains and deserts without country or home or mandatory power to own them: Chaldeans, Armenians, unprosperous Jews, Nestorians.

And amongst these latter it was, in the nineteen-twenty-five, that he made that discovery which was to lead him to Egypt and the Wadi Faregh.

He had been sick with fever, and was nursed by monks, some half-dozen of whom still inhabited the portion of a ruined Nestorian monastery in the mountains beyond Lake Van. Once had it been a great monastery-citadel, the sanctuary of Christians Asiatic; now, ruined by centuries of war and earthquake, it remained half-forgotten by the world beyond the encircling mountains. Towards the end of his convalescence Steyn had proof of the local earthquake force when throughout a night the ground heaved under his bed and the ancient buildings creaked and groaned.

Next morning, assisting the monks in re-building the living-quarters damaged in the tremor, he came on the centuries-lost library of the monastery, and, amidst its earthquake-uncovered scrolls, of which he was made temporary curator, the writings of a fifth-century monk, one Nicolaos of Corinth.

Those writings formed the beginning of the monastery

record, diversified with moralisings and rebuttals of heresy. Steyn spent many curious hours deciphering the monkish Greek and trying to reach at meanings in fears and formulæ long dead – even to him. And then, somewhere near the end of the entries in the hand of Nicolaos, he came on these words:

> But of those who have corrupted our faith with the teachings of the heathen Mani, it is told that Polyorthes, the Egyptian, he who lived within the life-time of his own false prophet, bore with him for many years a writing which the Manichaeans believed to be in the hand of Christ Himself. And this document they told, in their heretical blasphemy, revealed teachings other than those recorded by the Fathers – teachings which would yet be made known to men in an age when the world was ripe to receive them. But Polyorthes, the Christian Manichaean, disappeared, and was heard of no more, neither he nor the false testament.

IV

To you or me this might have seemed but the curious reference to an ancient fiction. But it lighted the life of Godfrey Steyn as might the personal revelation. He abandoned all his work – there were a score of American missions to tend to his refugees by then – and set out to search for other records regarding Polyorthes, the ancient Egyptian with the Greek name that was perhaps the nickname, him who had been the Christian Manichaean.

His researches led him to Trebizond, to the lines of ancient monasteries fringing the south Black Sea, to Merv, into Soviet Russia, where the tovarishi, with much courtesy and irreverence, believing him to be an atheistic historian, made free of every ecclesiastical document in their possession. And in eighteen months, pieced together from a score of sources, he had the full record of the fate of Egyptian Polyorthes. The Manichaean had died in his native land, in a solitary house in the Egyptian hills: undoubtedly the Wadi Faregh. Together with 'an heretical script' he had been buried in a secret tomb by two negro slaves who subsequently disappeared . . .

'And that is why I have come to Egypt. If archeological remains are unknown in the Wadi Faregh, so much the better. It'll never have attracted grave-robbers. For I believe that lost script to be the Last Testament of Christ Himself.'

Before that fantastic faith I might have known my objections trivial. 'But even if the tomb exists – Surely there is no mention anywhere else of Christ Himself having written anything? I know nothing of your Christian Mysteries, but is not the complete doctrine revealed in the New Testament – complete and final, as miraculously made known to the Council of Nicaea?'

He laughed aloud, the pleasant modern who could so suddenly replace the medieval mystic. 'For one who knows nothing of the "Mysteries", colonel, you're too ingenuous! . . .' His eyes shone Shelleyan again. 'Nicaea and the New Testament final? They've left unexplained that which God's Messenger came to explain and justify – the *conscious* cruelty and darkness which rules the universe, against which the forces of light and pity fight so feebly. If God be God, how do these things persist?'

I am no theologian. I made the bewildered shrug. 'Perhaps they are the character-tests in the purpose inscrutable. Perhaps resultant on the workings of impersonal natural forces.'

'And my agony and despair of those years – my groping after that God without whom sanity is impossible? What impersonal natural force is that resultant on? . . . Character-tests? Purposes moulding us? These ancient lies! Three million lie and rot in France and what meaning had their tortured deaths? To what betterment did agony mould each individual of them?'

To that I had no answer. It was the thing outside my mental range. But there began to stir in me a wondering imagining.

'An authentic message from Christ Himself! That would be wonderful!'

I had hardly known I spoke aloud till I saw their faces, Steyn's and Adrian's, turned on me. Then Steyn held out his hand.

'And you will come with me to Faregh?'

'I will come,' I said.

v

Within a week, fifty miles away from Cairo, we were setting up our encampment on the lower spurs of the Wadi Faregh. I had engaged five labourers – one to act as cook – for our little expedition and had obtained from the Ministry of the Interior the permits necessary and the good map of the ordnance survey. So equipped, we had journeyed out to those hills to seek the tomb of the lost Egyptian.

Above, and curving away into the west, stretched the limestone ridges, rowelled here and there by the sudden nullahs which we were to explore. They were cloaked in a thin growth of bush and desert-grass that June. South of our encampment an ancient well still yielded water – perhaps it had yielded water to Polyorthes and his slaves seventeen hundred years before.

Crowning the western foothills, hill-climbing a little, was the thin row of date-palms, and the second evening of our arrival Steyn and I sat at the door of our tent and watched those palms stencil their unquiet shapes against the coming of the sunset.

So sitting, Steyn began to quote from that Ave of

Rossetti's – the lines very beautiful in that stillness and flowing light under the hand of darkness.

> Mind'st thou not (when June's heavy breath
> Warmed the long days in Nazareth,)
> That eve thou didst go forth to give
> Thy flowers some drink that they might live
> One faint night more amid the sands?
> Far off the trees were as pale wands
> Against the fervid sky—

They moved me strangely, those words, and that picture of the Virgin, in some such setting as the night-threatened Faregh, going forth to revelation of her miraculous destiny. Moved me as beauty may always move me. For I have been too much the romantic to be ever the conscientious Not-Knower. I am not more remote from the Old Believer than I am from the English or German agnostic – him who sees all anthropomorphism as merely the ridiculous garbing of idealism in an extra-terrestrial brain and heart and lips and lungs gigantic.

To believe that a human maid once bore into the world an incarnation of the Consciousness which set the Galaxy in the sky and may hear the undersong of life in the world within the electron! To believe such thing, to have proof of it! A message from that strange prophet, human or divine, who still for all of us stands the figure sky-whelming at the gateway of all spiritual endeavour that has meaning . . .

The darkness came striding from the desert over the shoulder of the Wadi. Steyn had finished his quotation. He leant forward and shaded his eyes, and I followed his gaze. Betwixt two palms, far off, minute, something moved.

'What is it?'

And so into our encampment strolled Gillyflower Arnold, geologist, atheist, and lawn tennis champion.

VI

'I'm a stray female,' she said, 'but you needn't bother to light a lantern for me. My camp? Over there, half a mile beyond that hog-back. I'm prospecting for oil – Government commission.'

Thus, succinctly, our visitor, the while I offered her a campstool and Steyn bent to the lighting of a lantern. Beyond, at a little distance, was the singing of our labourers about their fire, and now it was almost complete darkness.

'You are of an expedition?' I said.

She sat down, removed from her face the tortoise-shell glasses, and rubbed her eyes. Her voice had the accent faint, but to me easily recognisable – I who have assisted at the pyramidal priming and mal-education archaeological of so much transatlantic femininity. 'I *am* the expedition – or at least, I lead it. Myself, an Egyptian surveyor, and three servants.'

I made the noises of apology, and at these Steyn and the girl chuckled together, and at that moment the lantern flared up.

She was indeed but the merest girl, no middle-aged and mosquito-salted explorer, as her voice had seemed to warrant. In the dusty breeches, puttees, and boots she sat; but her shirt was dusty not at all and very unmasculine, the fine silk shirt. Bare-headed, her hair in lamplight and sunlight alike had that blue raven-wing sheen I had met only once before in Egypt – such hair as possessed the little madame who once lived at Daybreak House. But her eyebrows were almost fair, very fine brows, of one line of tinting, like the brows of a Japanese.

She had a face thin and humorous, redeemed from severity by the girlish curve of chin, even as it was denied beauty by the spectacles American and absurd. She sat cross-legged, cigarette-smoking, and nodded an easy acknowledgment of our introductions. She talked about

herself and her work without apologies, because her work
seemed to her the most important thing on earth.

A mineralogist, she was already apparently of such note
as to be sent out to Egypt by an important American
company to consult the Government with regard to exploring and mapping the putative oil-centres in the Ba-
haira. To such good effect had she carried out those
consultations that the Cairene Government had fitted
out an expedition for her and sent her to the Wadi Faregh
for preliminary investigations.

'Of course, oil shouldn't be a matter for exploitation by
any single company. Or any single Government. But what's
one to do, seeing we're such fools we haven't got a world
board of control yet? . . . And my people are the sanest and
cleanest of the lot. I'll see the World Board hasn't a rotten
mess to take over in Egypt. Great work, you know. The
world's fuel is growing scarcer every year.' She laughed. 'So
in depressed moments I dramatise the business and pre-
figure myself fighting silence and primordial darkness, the
last Ice Age and the extinction of the human species! . . .
You people – archaeologists? I'm afraid you'll find the
Wadi disappointing.'

It was Steyn who answered her. He gave a little laugh and
looked away from us, out into the night, which was moonless but the soft splendour of starshine.

'Archaeologists? No. We also have come to fight the
Darkness.'

VII

Each evening of the days that followed it became the
custom for Gillyflower Arnold to visit our camp or we
hers. The latter was the more common occurrence, for the
leader of the oil expedition had brought net and rackets into
the desert and nightly, up to the time of our arrival, had
insisted on impressing her stout surveyor as partner for the

mystic gambollings of tennis. Except in the infrequently-ordered doubles, he now escaped these objectionable activities, as I did, and we and the massed camps would sit and watch Gillyflower Arnold and Godfrey Steyn executing the manœuvres agile and enthusiastic. Steyn was discovered as a player extraordinarily good; and, occasionally beaten, Gillyflower would stand and marvel at him.

It was as though she had discovered a Stone Age shaman making the miraculous breaks on a billiard table.

Palæolithic indeed was the cultural period in which she placed him. 'Medieval? My dear man, you're pre-Adamic. This worship of light and fear of darkness – it's the mumbo-jumbo of the carrion caves. Saints and ministers! And in the twentieth century too!'

'Even in the twentieth century – when a young woman comes five thousand miles to dig in the earth for weapons to fight that same Darkness! Do you think it's any the less real because you call it Cosmic Chance or something equally nebulous?'

'My *dear* shaman! You're not in the pits of Neanderthal now! Why personify the thing? What good has belief in gods ever done? Isn't our job in this age plain enough – to bring order and decency into human life for the first time and bring adventure back?'

I left them, both flushed and arguing but good-tempered, and walked away into the starlight to smoke a pipe alone on a Faregh brow, with below me the murmur of their young voices. And beyond the hills and sands – Cairo – Egypt – the world that had known so many creeds and faiths, where the young have sat and talked and debated through the million evenings, loving and hating and questioning the gods who shine and pass . . .

But indeed, when I had gone up to my hill-brow and pipe, there had fallen the quieter spell on them – these two with the philosophies apparently irreconcilable. You imagine Steyn sitting there, facing her, talking, with for background the dusking desert, and Gillyflower Arnold bending on both the finely-pencilled brows . . .

He did not argue then: merely told her of the world and life as he had seen it, the necessity of a guiding Consciousness to account for his own consciousness . . . And then the blood and agony of the rotting migrant-treks in the Anatolian hinterlands, the butchery and cruelty of the War, evil exultant under the shams of plenty and peace, evil that crawls in the shape of vile and loathsome disease and unmeaning suffering and torture through all Life . . . Darkness. Everywhere the hand of a Consciousness, surely – but a Consciousness that, without explanation, was surely vile.

'You are fair and wise and brave and eager,' he said, 'and do you think that is equipment enough to believe in the triumph of the Adventure which you see all life to be? A natural law might kill or crush you – but what of the Darkness that may maim and torture you horribly, that may wipe the cleanest and most selfless of your work from all record as a slate is wiped clean, that may even vilify the fairest things of your memory till that memory disgusts the world? . . . For all those things have been.'

'I never thought of it that way,' she confessed. And then: 'Oh, but I won't believe it! It's only a horrible dream . . . Even if it were true, how would the finding of this lost script help?'

'Don't you see – Christ, the Messenger, the Captain of the Adventure – *He* knew what He came to lead men against, He must have known why Darkness, the stark denial of God's Godhead, so prevailed . . . The script – it must be explanation and plan of campaign in one, the Lost Message of the Christ!'

She sat and looked at him with scornful, troubled eyes. Reared in a dogma of unbelief as stern and uncompromising as any Calvinist's creed, she felt her no-faith crumbling and dissolving even as the world of the ancient materialist has crumbled and dissolved into the unchartable atom-swirl of the modern physicist . . . Words and symbols and dreams – and yet – and yet –

'Christ – the Great Captain . . . Of course it's only dramatisation – hero personification of the Adventure's essence. But splendid enough, Steyn! Thrilling to think we may have had a Leader, Someone who saw the beginning and the end!'

He looked at her, glad – and a little startled, I think. For perhaps his world was also blurring and losing outline a little. That heroic explorer-spirit in which she saw life and the universe – it blew now and then as a sharp, keen wind amidst the cloudy veils of his mysticism. And in its blowing he would glimpse with a strange amaze and fear a Christ he had never dreamt . . .

VIII

There was no oil in the Wadi Faregh.

So Gillyflower Arnold informed me, one dusty noon we met, each accompanied by a labourer, in a nullah of the Wadi.

'I'm packing up in a day or so and reporting back to Cairo. There isn't a drop in the whole range.'

'Nor a god-script either, I fear.'

She laughed and then frowned. 'I haven't seen a trace of anything that looked like a tomb. How's Mr Steyn?'

'He is in bed with the touch of fever,' I said. And added: 'He takes this failure to heart.'

We looked at each other in some helplessness, for somehow he had grown the mutual charge. With the passing of day on day of fruitless excavation and exploration, the strain on him had begun to show. His face thinned, and the charming smile and boyish laughter were the less frequent. At first Gillyflower Arnold and her tennis-games had had the power to bring him out of his trances of brooding, as had her laughter and irreverence and American exuberance. But of late he had shown the disposition to avoid her encampment, or, when there, to avoid anything but the talk most trivial . . .

He had fallen in love with her, as was almost inevitable. But there was the something more than belief in the hopelessness of his love that made him avoid her presence. And that thing it seemed to me was fear – fear that after all he had followed only an ancient fiction, that no script had ever existed, that his very vision of life was false. He had outlived and out-faced his belief in the divinity of that consciousness which ruled the universe, but either to out-face the scorn and pity of Gillyflower Arnold or to go forth into the stark deserts of atheism were the thoughts from which he shuddered away.

Yet I did not care to think what would happen when the oil expedition had left the Wadi.

And then next day Gillyflower Arnold discovered the tomb of Polyorthes.

IX

She became visible at half-past two in the afternoon, on the brow of the hill, waving, an excited silhouette. She cupped her hands and called, 'Bring your people and pick-axes. I've discovered a passage that looks like a tomb-entrance . . .'

Yet when we reached the ridge beside her she regarded Steyn doubtfully. 'You can't come like that.'

He was newly up from his bed, the fever still upon him, staggering, white-faced. He laughed.

'Do you think anything can hurt me *now*?'

She stared at him, seemed about to say something, changed her mind, shrugged, and turned and led the way.

On the extreme western edge of the Wadi a precipice-shelf that faced the desert; at the foot of it still standing the gleaming apparatus of the oil-boring; three feet away, the rock-covering crumbled aside by the drum of the apparatus, the partially-uncovered mouth of a brick-walled passage . . .

At half-past three Godfrey Steyn and I, having had cleared from the entrance the fallen rubble of rock, pushed a lantern in front of us and crawled into the passage.

X

We crept sweating in the foul air, but the passage was of the shortest. Within eighteen feet of the entrance, it emerged upon a rock-hewn chamber, plain and undecorated, dry and cool. Set in the midst of that chamber was the rock kist – a great stone box on which rested the unhinged lid of stone.

We seized that lid, and, panting, lifted it aside. Then I held up the lantern.

A mummy-coffin of the simplest: for a moment the wood still smelt fresh. Upon it inscriptions in the Persian and the Greek, the latter of which I read and remembered, and will always remember:

> Polyorthes, the traveller, son of Thi-Hetep: I, who pass to the darkness, yet have seen the light of Ormuzd: I, whom the Prophet Mani blessed at Ctesiphon in the names of the Christ and the Buddha: To any who in after years follow a tale and rumour and find these bones let them seek that which is written even in the darkness of Ahriman.

Within the coffin: An unmummified body which fell to flaking shreds and brown bones even as we looked at it. Under the head of that body a roll of what might have been either parchment or papyrus – a roll that crumbled like an ash and rose in the little puff of dust . . .

XI

She came across to our encampment at sunset, went into Steyn's tent, and emerged from it a moment later.

'Steyn – where is he?'

He had fainted outside the rock-tomb where we had left the Manichaean Polyorthes and his unread script. We had had him carried to the camp, and then Gillyflower Arnold had gone back to the precipice-shelf to see to the re-sealing of the tomb.

Now I stared at her in surprise. 'He was there but the short time ago. Tossing in fever. I looked in.'

'He's gone.'

I went to his tent, pulled aside the flap, and looked in. Then I had the sudden thought. I began to search. Gilly-flower Arnold stood in the doorway and I heard her quick breathing.

'Anything missing?'

I turned and nodded. She clenched her hands.

'Not—?'

We stood outside and looked at the familiar fall of the Wadi evening. It was very silent and very desolate. Suddenly Gillyflower Arnold began to speak in a quick, high voice.

'Darkness . . . Perhaps he was right after all, colonel; perhaps there's something . . . Oh, it's a lie, it's a lie, anyway. Cowardly even if true . . .' She laughed a little hysterically, then shook my shoulder. 'What are we standing here for? We should be searching. We must find him.'

I do not know how long we searched amidst those reddened hill-slopes and sudden valleys. It seemed that we called and clambered and stumbled for hours, though it may have been only a few minutes. Once Gillyflower Arnold stopped and laughed and looked at me queerly.

' "Seek in the darkness of Ahriman—" ' wasn't that the phrase . . .?' She became rigid. 'There. Look.'

He sat bowed of shoulders like the Rodin Thinker, his face in shadow, the night almost upon him. He moved his hands, and in those hands something glinted and flashed red as with blood.

XII

'Wait!'

The other searcher was gone from my side. Steyn half-started to his feet, and in that moment the revolver was snatched from his hand and sent hurtling down the hill-slope. Dazed, he faced in the half-darkness a raging accuser.

'Coward! You beastly coward! Christ – the Captain – do you think He came in triumph or that He won? Do you think He lost because He seemed to lose, do you think He's lost now because a mouldy script has crumbled to dust? Had He no terrors of the Darkness to face, foes to out-fight, that He might leave select campaign instructions to you? . . . You coward! Deserter!'

He was motionless. She made a despairing gesture. The passion in her voice was very near to tears.

'Steyn – listen! Can't you see, don't you understand? It is God who fights to reclaim the world! What does it matter the fable we accept or reject? Perhaps the old stories are all wrong, perhaps it was God, not Satan, who was overthrown in the beginning of time . . . Wonderful to think – Christ – you – I – *we're the champions of the dethroned God!* . . . That lost script – it's written wherever there's pity and courage in the world . . . Oh, my dear, help me . . .'

He seemed like a man emerging from a trance. He stared at her, then reached out and caught the hands extended to him.

'Why, I've been blind! . . . Oh God . . . Gillyflower! . . .'

XIII

I turned about and walked away, and left them there with the coming starshine. I climbed to a Faregh brow, and sat and smoked the pipe, with below me the murmur of their young voices. And beyond the hills and sands – Cairo – Egypt – the world that has known so many creeds and faiths, where the young have sat and talked and debated through a million evenings, loving and hating and questioning the gods who shine and pass . . .

Yet perhaps indeed scripts and gods, faiths and fears – they matter nothing if the Message that is written endures.

The Passage of the Dawn

I

WHAT IS IT? A camel-train with *bersim*, I think . . . Unpleasant? He smells not sweetly, the camel . . . You have startled the driver; he thought us *jinni*, perhaps!

That tinkling? You did not notice it as they passed? It requires the distance for effect. To have your heart rise in your throat you must hear it ring across dusk miles of desert – or as Oliver Gault once heard it beyond the fairy mountains of Mesheen.

Sit here in this doorstep and rest, my friend. Young men should dream their loves at night, not wander the streets of Cairo with the middle-aged and prosy Russian! Even though it is your last Egyptian night, and tomorrow await you sea and ship and weeks wherein your Cairene days and I will fade to the merest names – and even those of uncertain orthography!

. . . Very soon the morning now. See that greyness above the roofs? In an hour we will go down past 'Abbas Pasha and stir the little Simon to provide a last Greek breakfast in the Khalig. Meantime—

Eh? Gault? Mesheen? I had forgotten both till that camel went by. In the self-defence I have forgotten . . . Weeks now since I went out to that desert-house of his – coward and fool that I am!

But I will go again: this very morning I will go! Somehow I will find the courage . . . Oh, dreamer of dreams, fantastic fool though I am – who knows, who knows—?

. . . Bear with me a little, my friend. A camel's bell – that it should stir one so! Yet perhaps this very night in Abu Zabal another heard it go by – one who may find forgetfulness never, unless – unless—

II

And for beginnings of all this strange haunting of three lives is to go back across a year and eight hundred miles of desert to the last outpost of the company Trans-Saharan Transport. A stifling night of February, far beyond Kufra, in the regions where the oases ceased and the raiding Tuareg of Air and Tibesti came but seldom. And in his tent, on the edge of the encampment, Oliver Gault, the sick and fevered surveyor, hating his work, his companions, his life.

'Mosquitoes crawling battalions deep on my face, and my stomach rotten with fever. I was at the last stage: I'd have broken down before morning. Next tent that infernal Caprotti was jerking out a tune on a sand-clogged gramophone – the needle seemed to be playing round and round on my brain-tracks. Air thick as soup, and yet cold . . . And that greasy blaze of stars!'

So to me he was to describe that place, in the uncouth jargon that is the modern English colloquial – the speech-debasement from which is yet smitten the occasional vivid phrase . . .

The year before that I had known him in Cairo. Slight, quick, restless, with the strange flare of light in pale eyes, the mouth unevenly cut, and a face tanned almost negro-black: Oliver Gault. He was then in negotiation with Trans-Saharan Transport for the post of desert surveyor. This was the new American company, proposing, after the planning of routes and roads, to run the constant caravans of caterpillar automobiles throughout Sahara, linking in trade and travel Cairo to Air, Algiers to Timbuctoo . . . The project florid and magnificent, and one that had fired the quick imagination of Gault, though he would speak of it in the humour as twisted as his mouth.

'In a year we'll have the Tuareg talking through his nose, dancing to jazz and uplift, and holding Monkeyville trials . . . Nothing can withstand the progress of nasalisation.'

Young though he was, he had already reputation as Saharan explorer and geologist. With Hassanein Bey he shared credit for first traversement of the stony deserts – though this credit he would claim for himself, and jeer the Bey from the field . . . Not the gentleman, you understand, either in birth or outlook. But I think the gentleman passes from the world. Up in his place rise the Gaults, cruel and crude, restless of outlook, tenacious of purpose, without honour and without faith – yet stirred by the gleam occasional of a new vision and a new selflessness that no knighthood of the world has ever known . . .

But that new vision is still but a mirage-picture in the dusk. From Gault that evening he was to describe it was more remote than belief in the articles thirty-nine of your Church. He was the man frantic with fatigue and disgust, his nerves frayed to twisted rags by the months of self-overwork and discomfort and monotony.

'I think I'd have gone mad in a minute – I was reaching for my Webley to go out and settle the hash of either

Caprotti or his gramophone when I heard our sentry shouting a challenge, and an angel of God, disguised as a Sudanese and smelling like a cholera epidemic, came clumping into the camp on a camel. All the way from Kufra. He'd brought the mail-bag – three letters . . . I opened the single personal one, read it, and gave a croak. Like an overcome bull-frog . . . And then I was laughing and crying, in hysterics, the pages slipping and falling from my heat-rawed hands and being picked up and being lost again . . .'

The father whom he had hated – the war profitmaker in England whom he had regarded always with the savage contempt, even before the days of the final quarrel, whose life of safety and security his own aching restlessness and bitter no-content had despised – was dead.

'I found myself chanting an insane sing-song – "Saved from hell, saved from hell!" And then I grew calmer. Hell – of my own choosing. Whatever for? *Whatever* for? Why hadn't I stayed in England and wallowed in war-profits? . . . And then I was scrambling for my boots and weeping and singing again. Sand and dirt and discomfort, prickly heat and Baghdad boils and potted meat – finished and done with! The world waiting there in the east – if I didn't die first! – the world where I could laze and laze and laze . . . bathe and bathe and bathe . . . spend and spend and spend . . . live like a lord . . . sleep like a hog . . . go clad in sin and shining raiment . . . drink of life like a fly in a tumbler! . . .

'And women – oh, my God, were there still women with white, white skins, and would any of them be alive when I got back?

'They must have thought me a raving lunatic, the road-men. In an hour I'd chucked my billet, handed over the road-survey to little Savraut – who did foolish things and tried to stop me with a revolver, not knowing that I was a soul reprieved. Then I grabbed the camel, some food and

water, and was on the way to Kufra before midnight . . .
Reached it in three days. Rode most of them delirious, I
think, with an insane conviction that the world in the east
was a mirage that I must overtake.

'A mile from the first oasis the camel gave a ping like a
clock-work toy with the works gone wonk, and doubled up.
I staggered into Kufra just ahead of the sunset.'

III

Six weeks later, all unconscious of that happening, in the
last days of Spring and the season tourist, I was preparing
for myself a short holiday. Three weeks on the beach at
Mustapha I planned, where none would question me as to
whether the good antiques of Frankfort were genuine or
your Mr Wells an incarnation of Akhnaton . . . I had saved
a little money, you understand, and was sick of Cairo, the
Mediterranean calling me like a pleasant friend a year
neglected.

And then one morning I was handed the letter brought
by a messenger over-night. I opened it, recognised the
handwriting, and read:

DEAR SALONEY,
Come and talk to me. I learnt the other night that you
were still in Cairo. I myself have been here a month
and a half, but I'm going to Alexandria next week –
thank God! for I'm very bored.
Any time this afternoon if you can manage it.
OLIVER GAULT

I stared at the notepaper in stupefaction. Oliver Gault –
whom I had believed to be in the Sahara beyond Siwa – he
was in Cairo and staying at Shepheard's Hotel!

I had no commissions to carry out, and no engagements
that afternoon. So, in the some curiosity, I dressed myself

in tourist drill and sun-helmet, playing the little game that I was the English tripper arrived for the hasty week in Cairo. In the taxi I rode to Shepheard's, speaking to the driver in the loud and inaccurate French, as only an Englishman may speak. At the entrance, where I had the many times waited for custom amongst other dragomans, I handed the card and was shown to the cool lounge to await the coming of Gault.

He was taking the bath, they told me, in the tone respectful, as was proper to my bad French and the cut of my drill. It was the room deserted and I leant back in my seat and closed my eyes and heard the sound of the little waves come racing up the beach at Mustapha . . .

'Anton!' In the voice of the amazement, the voice half-choked. 'Oh, Anton Kyrilovich!'

IV

I opened my eyes at that. As one confronted by a ghost I sat staring, myself white-faced I think, as she was. Then I came to my feet and stood at attention and kissed her hands.

'*Princess!*'

She looked round the room the swift moment, then flung her arms about my neck and kissed me. Then laughed, and wrung my hands, and for the little we stood breathless. Slowly the colour came back to her face and to her lips the amused smile – amusement at herself and me.

'Anton! I thought you dead or a gay commissar all these years! . . . In Cairo for nine of them? And since we met – oh, I don't want to remember how long!'

'Twelve years,' I said, and tried to smile. We Russians have learnt to smile at much which is unamusing. We sat down and looked at each other, I and she who had been the Princess Pelagueya Bourrin . . .

Of those far days in Kazan, when I was still Professor of the English Literature in the Gymnasium and – though this you may find hard to believe! – without suspicion that in twelve years' time I would be the middle-aged dragoman sitting on a Cairene doorstep at dawn – of those there is no need for you to know. She was the girl of eighteen then, and I, though the mere professor, had yet the personal dreams, for I came of a family as old and noble as hers – we could still consider that of importance, we whom the soldier-groom Budenni was to sweep from South Russia as so many vermin!

So distant in the years from that quiet room at Shep-heard's. . . .

She was changed unbelievably – and yet hardly at all! – she whom I had always found strange pleasure in addres-sing by the formal title. And of this my princess – even now I do not know the colour of her hair and eyes. I think they are both that black that is on occasion the brown: when the sun comes on them. In unexpected lights and moments the sun comes on the hair and eyes of Pelagueya . . .

Short-cut hair; in the absurd, short skirts, the dress of white over-stamped with the whorls of gold; with still that clear pallor of brow and cheek that is Russian, and the smooth out-jut of cheek-bones, and the long, sweet fall of lips . . . Unchanged, except that the sunlight in her eyes brought the different picture: Like Spring sun on a Ural river when the ice lies frozen beneath.

'Of course you look older, Anton. But handsome as ever, Oh, Anton Kyrilovich, it's so long since I saw a man blush! and with a beard – I hardly knew you a moment because of that beard.'

The beard was safe topic. 'All Russians are bearded – outside Russia. Without it I would not have been the refugee authentic, nor the guide interesting.'

Of my profession for nine years I told a little. There came the swift pity and anger in her face.

'A dragoman! How horrible! If we had known, we might have helped – at least at first. But they said you were killed at Perekop. Some other Saloney, of course. We escaped to France and lived – I will not tell you how we lived. Then Boris went back to Russia secretly three years ago, and was arrested and shot. That broke father's heart. He died and left hardly a son – Poor father!

'And then, on that awful strip of coast – Oh, Anton, you escaped much by becoming a dragoman! – I began two years as companion, teacher, nursery-maid. Once I loved children . . . Amongst nouveaux riches, Brazilians, French bourgeois . . . Why isn't there a revolution in France? *We* at least had pleasant manners!

'And then this January—'

She had looked one night at the pearl necklace she had hoarded, and all the pleasant life forgone – the life of ease and consideration, laughter and gay song and cultured voices – had cried in her ears to take the mad risks. She had gone to Paris, had had the orgy of purchasing pretty clothes. Then south to Marseilles and so a passage to Egypt.

'But why Egypt?'

'They said the bigger and more brilliant Brazilians came here. I came after them, Anton, to sell myself as advantageously as possible . . . I'm glad he's not a Brazilian, though.'

She had looked away whilst she was speaking, but now she turned her head directly towards me again, the little spot of blood flaming below each cheekbone, but with the cool irony still in her eyes.

'I'm glad to have seen you again, just once, Anton. It's been the final and artistic touch. You see, I'm leaving Cairo in a week's time as the mistress of a millionaire.'

'Pelagueya!' And then, at sight of the laughter still in her eyes: 'You are joking.'

The laughter was suddenly gone. 'Joking! Anton, I'd have sold myself to a Jew from the ghetto – if he'd had money. Shameless? You haven't known those last two years

– condescension and mean rooms and the life of a servant.
The nursery-maid emigrée, the pauper princess! . . .
Rather than face that again I'd go back to Russia and turn
tovarish. But I'm to do neither. And my millionaire's not a
Jew. Of the canaille, of course, but rather amusing . . .
Especially now that he hates me.'

'Hates you?'

She laughed. 'It was comic. He explained that of course
he had no romantic love, that I was, in fact, just something
he wanted and could afford. Nevertheless, he offered
marriage. I told him that the price was too small and that
in Russia we Bourrins did not wed with the gutter . . . How
easy to sting the vanity of those animals! He's accepted my
counter-proposal, but every moment I think he swears that
I'll pay to the uttermost for that acceptance . . . The
bargaining instinct, I suppose. We've had the terms and
endurance of the association drawn up by a lawyer!'

She clasped her hands round her knees, the defiance
leaping in her eyes. 'Shocked, Anton? But me – Oh, I'm to
have the things that haven't been mine for years except as
desperate luxuries: money and laziness, leisure; clean food,
clean hands, and long, long bathes; books and jewels and
pretty clothes. Clothes! The loveliness of clothes, Anton! If
I could only take you upstairs and show you the things I've
been buying!'

I found my voice strange and high-pitched.

'And the price?'

She suddenly wrung her hands. I thought she was going
to weep.

'The price! What cowards you are – men! Liars and
cowards and cheats, weak and emotional! Greedy liars,
greedy cheats! . . . If I came to share your dragoman's room
would I not pay the same price?'

I had nothing to say to that, nor looked at her, the
princess who had strayed from a fairy story into the legend
of Gomorrah. And then her hand on mine.

'I didn't mean that. Or I did. Oh, Anton, it's too late. If this was 1917 and Kazan and yours wasn't a dragoman's room . . . All our faiths were futilities, and before I grow old – oh, my friend, I must *live!*'

She withdrew her hand, laughed again a little unsteadily, and sought for her cigarette-case. Then she passed with lighted match, and the amused scorn flickered on her lips.

'The exhibit. Here comes my millionaire.'

I did not look over my shoulder, hearing the footsteps approach. I sat with a grip on myself, trying to believe that all our faiths had not been futilities, our codes cowardice. And then she spoke, in English, in the insolent drawl.

'This is a countryman of mine, Mr Millionaire. Mr Oliver Gault: Colonel Anton Saloney.'

v

I can still hear her gay laugh, the trifle breathless, as she glanced from one to other of us, and learnt that I had come to Shepheard's to meet him.

'Then I will leave you,' and, with the smile to me and the nod patronising to Gault, she was gone. I had stood up, but Gault turned a casual back to her nod and looked out through the window. He was clad in the soft and expensive flannels, the clothes well-chosen and seemly, but for one detail. This was a tie of the vivid red, and, still in the dazement of his revelation as Pelagueya's millionaire, I stared at it foolishly.

'Why do you wear that?'

He turned his sun-blackened face and grinned at me, twistedly. 'Oh, to show my kinship with Budenni! . . . Coming upstairs?'

And there, upstairs in the suite gorgeous, I sat and listened to him, with all the time at back of my mind the thought: This is Pelagueya's millionaire. But I made the no interruptions or denunciations heroic . . . It was the very evil and unkind dream I was dreaming, and through it all I heard forgetfulness and the Mediterranean calling on the beaches of Mustapha.

'. . . And only a month since I rode into Kufra, Saloney. Like a bad nightmare badly remembered. Lord, how the mosquitoes must be mourning my passing!'

'How have you passed this six weeks?' I asked.

He grinned and sprawled in a chair. 'In bed, largely. Clad in silk. Look at these socks . . . God bless my parental profiteer and his forgiving last testament . . . A little man comes and shaves me each morning, and another finds my braces, and three bring my boots – one to each boot and one with the laces. They'd fetch a palanquin and carry me down to lunch, if I asked for it.' He yawned suddenly and jumped to his feet and swore.

'And I'm bored, Saloney – oh, fed to the teeth! Dances and outings and chatter and opera – Lord, that opera! I've escaped to heaven from hell – St Peter himself shook hands with me on arrival: I think it was St Peter, though it may have been the manager – and the harping and the company celestial bores me. Or is it only Cairo – your Polychromata? I'd rather live in a damn dye-factory . . .'

He prowled to and fro, restlessly. 'The peasant in the palace, the Zulu in Versailles – the unimpressed Zulu. Is it that, or do we just outgrow these things, along with wigs and patches and gibbets and powder . . .' He stopped and grinned again, his face the satyr's. 'Anyhow, there's one thing we don't outgrow. Still that.' He stared at me a sudden curiosity. 'Are you in love with this Princess Pelagueya, colonel?'

How the sea was calling out beyond Pharillon!

'Told you of our relations – our prospective relations? She has! . . . And the price? I'll see she pays it. By God, I'll see to that!'

But not even in a dream – I made to rise. 'This is the beastliness.'

He caught my arm. 'Oh, sit down, colonel. Beastliness? Of course I'm a beast – a starved beast, a beast hungry for beauty and tenderness. What else is there to grope after? And I'm to buy it, and in a week . . . To think I might have been still in Sahara!'

I could not hate him, even in a dream; they are the kind beyond hate, those. He sat down and yawned again, and stretched.

'Sahara . . . the old company. Wonder where they are, little Savraut and Caprotti and Ba Daghshar and the rest? Somewhere north of the Mesheen massif . . . Pity that infernal détour was necessary.'

He seemed to await the question. He began to scatter cigarette ash on the gorgeous carpet in the idle illustration.

'Mesheen. A mountain block beyond Kufra. Lies north to south thirty or forty miles. Block in several senses. Terra incognita and absolutely impassable – a wilderness of closed gulleys. Every nullah we tried ended in a cul-de-sac. There's no pass at all through the massif and the road'll have to wheel up north by a long détour to carry on towards Air. We searched for days . . .'

He dropped his cigarette and absent-mindedly ground it into the floriferous carpet. 'Funny thing happened there. We hadn't a single camel with us, the range seemed uninhabited – couldn't be inhabited. No oases anywhere near at hand. And yet – one night, at the other side of the impassable walls, I heard a camel's bell.'

The ice-flare in his eyes. 'Clear and distinct – and no possible camel-train could be there. Later I heard a yarn amongst the Arabs of the road-gang that a pass through the mountains had once existed . . . An old chap told me of it – some crazy legend of a *Madhiq el Fiqr*, with guarded entrance, that traversed Mesheen from east to west.'

'*Madhiq el Fiqr?*' I sought in the inadequate English and Arabic vocabularies of my mind for translation. 'The Passage of the Dawn?'

'Eh? . . . That funny Russian twist! Morning Pass I called it. You're the better poet.' There came on his dark face the sudden, strange dreaming look. 'The Corridor of the Morning – the Passage of the Dawn!'

He leapt to his feet, and swore. 'Gods, almost I thought myself back there! Waken up, Saloney. A drink to celebrate my beatification?'

VI

Next day I went to Alexandria. Behind, in Shepheard's, the Princess Pelagueya Bourrin, descendant of boyars, prepared to consummate her bargain with Oliver Gault.

There was no shame between them, you understand, no embarrassment and no pretence of affection. Rather the reverse. They were each conscious of a bright, sharp enmity. Pelagueya made no concealment of her scorn, nor Gault of the fact that for that scorn she would pay dearly. As he had paid.

'A heavy price, Mr Millionaire,' she had said, when they came out together from the office of the shocked and amazed little lawyer in the Sharia el Manakh.

'It is worth it,' he had answered, looking at her, the derisive grin for once vanishing from his twisted mouth. And at that look, so far from love, somehow not lust, she had shivered a little.

But there is no courage like to that of their generation – the generation to which the gods are foolishness and the codes and restraints but maunderings of dull dotards. They cry for life without veils or reticences, and face it without veils themselves. In that last week Pelagueya and Gault evolved a strange friendliness – mocking on her part, sardonic on his, though they would meet but seldom, and then as casual acquaintances.

On the Monday they were to go together to Alexandria, where Gault had already bought a house. But on the

Saturday he came to her with the proposal that this plan should be altered. There was an old Turkish castle out in Abu Zabal which he had once seen. An acquaintance had told him it was lately renovated, and to let. If the Princess Bourrin was agreeable, they would go there, instead of Alexandria, for the first few weeks.

'But why? We'll be very bored. It's on the edge of the desert, isn't it?'

'That's the chief attraction. I want to get out of a comfortable bed each morning and make faces at the Sahara.'

She laughed at that, for once unguardedly. 'Yes, I think I can make the concession.'

He called for her early on the Monday afternoon, bringing the great touring car. Her luggage was loaded into it, and together they drove out of Cairo. She lighted a cigarette, and sat watching him for a little, then made a request. Could she drive?

'Why not?' he said, and relinquished the seat to her. The car ran through the long afternoon into the Egyptian country. Once he looked at her with the twisted grin.

'Honeymoon.'

'Canaille.'

It was nearly two hours before he spoke again. 'Five miles now.'

Now they came to a slope where the road zig-zagged ruttily and steeply away beneath them. Little stones pattered on the wind-screen. Out of a field by the side of the road a heavy cart, the single-poled, wooden-wheeled, was being drawn by oxen. Two boys in charge stared up at the nearing car and beat the indifferent beasts. Their shouts came up the evening.

Gault looked at Pelagueya, saw the puckering of her brows, the tinge of colour mount to each cheekbone. He hesitated only a second.

'Shall I—?'

He leant over, slipped his right arm under her left, put both hands over hers, and grinned at the road. A wisp of her short hair clouded his eyes an irritable moment. He felt her fingers strain under the pressure of his . . .

It was a difficult moment. The oxen laboured aside, clumsily, up the steep mud-bank sheered the off-side wheels of the car. Then, with a breath-catching swerve, they were on the road again, with the sunset-reddened incline sloping away before them.

It was as if that sunset would never die. In front and behind the road glowed in gold and red. Under the dim clumps of date-plams fled painted shadows. Gault's hands still remained on the wheel, and to Pelagueya it seemed that in a moment she would weep.

Then she heard him speak, jerkily.

'Look here, that contract . . . You'll be all right, but you needn't— We'll go back to Cairo.'

They glanced at each other, whitely, queerly, strangers trapped by wonder. The car sped on. Then, the fairy princess, she turned her face to him.

'Do you know you've never kissed me? . . . And it's only three miles to Abu Zabal.'

VII

They spent two halcyon and amazing months in the old Turkish castle, the while the summer waxed. They talked the sun out of the sky each day and never lost interest in the talking. They had waited all their lives to talk to each other.

'We'll buy a yacht and go drowsing through the Mediterranean. To Greece. To Crete. South through the Red Sea to India – Java – Sumatra . . . Wander together forever, princess . . . Was there ever a man so lucky as I am?'

They sat listening that evening to a nightingale that sang in the cypress grove at the end of the garden. And Gault, listening, was aware that his love had already changed from a romantic passion to something akin to a vivid pain.

'When are you going to marry me, Pelagueya? Sometime? Why not now? I'll make Saloney persuade you when he comes tomorrow.'

But on the morrow, when I came to kiss the hand of my lost princess, she would not be persuaded by me either.

'Some time. When we know each other.'

He swore at that. 'Don't you know me by now? Every secret of body and soul?'

She laughed and kissed him, gaily. 'You English boy!'

But that afternoon Gault was restless, and together we tramped into the village, leaving Pelagueya sitting in the shade of the cypress grove. Coming back at sunset we could still see her there. And suddenly he was talking to me with a strange passion.

'Lord, Saloney, what fools we are! Wanting even when we've the world in our hands! Wanting something we cannot name . . . Pelagueya – God, she's wonder itself, life and love and God to me. And yet – and yet – sometimes I feel I could sell my soul for the gift of an hour's sheer unhappiness! What is it, Saloney, what is it? Marriage – the world's sanction we've forgone and she refuses . . . Is it that?'

We were within hearing of Pelagueya by then, and she waved to us. He knelt beside her and laid his head in her lap.

'On edge today, princess – like a fool! Don't go away, Saloney. I shan't make more love in public than I can help. Sit down and listen for our nightingale.'

That velvet silence of the Egyptian evening closed in on us. Suddenly Gault started and cursed, and moved his head restlessly. Pelagueya put her arms around his neck, silencing him, and we listened.

From far across the tundra it came, on the Cairo road, sweet and remote, a faint music growing clearer and clearer, then fading into the gathering dusk – the tinkling of a camel's bell.

VIII

Next morning he came into Cairo with me, and it was late in the day before he returned to Pelagueya in Abu Zabal. At the first look at the flame in his eyes she shivered. But he caught her hands, like a man in desperation.

'Pelagueya, will you come into Cairo and marry me tomorrow?'

She shook her head, smiling with trembling lips. He laughed queerly, brought something from his pocket, and tore it into little scraps. Then, looking away from her, he spoke.

'I've been into the offices of Trans-Saharan Transport. They've a caravan leaving Sollum in four days, and I'm going with it – paying part of the expenses, on a special expedition. I've been commissioned to make a detailed investigation of the Mesheen massif.'

'I knew,' she said, and smiled at him, weeping.

'You knew? But how? . . . Have you tired of me, then! . . . I'm a fool. Don't cry, princess . . . What have I done!'

'Tired of you? Oh my dear! . . . Of course you must go. And I'll wait for you, and perhaps—'

He was holding her close, the old ice-flame in his eyes. 'You'll marry me when I come back? Fairy and reward! . . . It's that infernal mountain range that's worried me. Mesheen. I'm to find the pass I know lies through it – the Passage of the Dawn. Little Savraut and Caprotti are to be detached to assist. Be back again inside six months . . . And then—'

IX

Within six months he was dead, killed in a manner very horrible by a raiding band of the Tuareg of Air, he and two others of the special expedition which was exploring the mountain passes of Mesheen.

Pelagueya sent me news of it from the castle at Abu Zabal

to which she had returned after the passing of the hot season. I went out to her, and she greeted me with the old, kind smile and the easy talk, till we stood together near that cypress grove. And then, suddenly, she broke down.

'Oh, Anton Kyrilovich! I sent him back there. Did I do right after all? I could have married him; perhaps I could have kept him—'

She wrung her hands, staring across the tundra. 'Only – there was something else. Always – haunting him. And I loved him so. He could never hear a camel's bell go by but he remembered.' She turned to me with groping hands. 'My friend, my friend, what took him back there? What was it that I could not give him, that was not mine to give?'

And then she gripped my hand and stood rigid.

'Oh, listen!'

There are many camel-trains go by Abu Zabal. From far across the tundra, as once before I had heard it, it came, sweet and faint, growing clearer and clearer, then fading till it died remote on the Cairo road.

And suddenly, for the moment vivid, it seemed to me that I understood that aching restlessness that had driven Gault to his death in Mesheen, that Pelagueya herself had shared when she let him go. As in a vision, I saw again that room at Shepheard's, the dreaming look on a dark, still face—

The Passage of the Dawn! All his life he had sought for it – and who does not share that search? Somewhere, we dream, beyond the twilights of love and hate, ease and unease, there is the morning. Somewhere, beyond the mountain-walls, there is wonder and the morning.

(And this is the last of the Saloney stories.)

IV

One Man with a Dream

A Stele from Atlantis

'ASSES,' SAID THE archaeologist, rather heatedly, 'are constantly asking that question: What is the good of archaeology? "Good!" If you'd even as much imagination as a cocaine-sodden louse—'

The young man suggested, mildly, that the archaeologist was mixing his fauna badly. His suggestion was waved aside.

'If I'd like to mix some people in lime and bury them in the Death Pit at Ur. "Good!" What d'you want us to do? Dig up the bones of the Anakim and grind them to powder for manure? Find out how the Ancient Egyptians cured their warts? Practical results! If ever archaeology produces a practical result it ought to be suppressed . . . Same as was that infernal exhibit Ayscough brought from Crete.'

The young man seemed about to make another remark. I forestalled him. 'Ayscough? What's happened to him? Haven't heard of him for years.'

'Nor ever likely to hear again – at least as an archaeologist. Happened to him? How the devil should I know? Mouldering in some insanitary hole or another on the Continent: he scooted out of England at the double. Serve him right – shouldn't have mixed up Edgar Wallace with archaeology. Murdering swine!'

'Eh? Murdering? Surely that's going it pretty strong?' I suggested. 'I know he hadn't the best of reputations, but . . .'

'But you weren't present at that Kensington gathering when he exhibited the brown cylinder, were you? No. So you know nothing about him.'

'Tell us,' suggested the young man.

With a bored smile the archaeologist regarded him; reflected; stretched back in his chair. 'Well, why not? Can't cause much trouble now: you haven't enough intelligence for it to trouble *you*. Never met a "practical man" yet who was troubled by anything but his own lack of brain . . . Well—

'Two years ago now. I'd just returned from some sultry work digging up the ancient Maya. Dusty work. Got into a bath on my arrival in London and spent about a week there. In the midst of my ablutions came Ayscough's note inviting me to the Sunday gathering in his Kensington flat.

'I had met him once or twice before at dinner and the like. Didn't know much about him, except that he'd the ability to make my spine crawl with distaste. Man like an Assyrian bull, black-bearded and red-lipped and with a boom of a voice. A swashbuckler and quack; he had that reputation. Also, he'd the reputation of being a genius into the bargain. He kept the archaeological world buzzing. If all his finds were spectacular, half at least of them were genuine. And he'd a most extraordinary nose for questing out relics in places other people had passed over again and again.

'Crete and Cretan history were his specialities . . . (Know anything about them? *You* wouldn't. Thank God the rest of us went to school . . .)

'Well, made up my mind to go to Ayscough's. Nothing better to do that Sunday. Arrived to find quite a hefty tea-fight on. A score or so of archaeologists and their women. Prowling about very bored looking, or saying unkind things about Genesis. (Don't see the reference? *You* wouldn't.) Rolland from Egypt there; Crain, who was also a Cretan authority; Melfort, whom I'd last heard of in Peru . . . I attached myself to Rolland, whom I knew well enough, and who was sitting as far away from our host as he could get.

' "Hullo! Roped you in as well?" I said.

'He scowled. "Roped us all in. Wonder what the damn cheap-jack's got up his sleeve this time?"

'I quoted from the invitation letter issued to all of us. "A discovery bearing on the lost civilisation of Atlantis—"

'Rolland was unreproducible for a second or so; he ended his tirade. ". . . Atlantis be drowned!"

' "Precisely," I agreed. "If there ever was a continent there, we owe the Atlantic a debt of gratitude for extinguishing the most boring race of idiots that has ever vexed posterity . . . Hello! is *this* the discovery?"

'She'd glided into the room while I'd been talking to Rolland – a woman like a panther. Lovely, I suppose. But she smelt *musk* to me as she did her jungle-slither to Ayscough's side. Rolland scowled at her.

' "That's the Cretan wife."

'I remembered then. I'd heard of her before – ran across an old copy of an English newspaper in Mexico City, with the sensationalette headlined "The Ayscough Romance". (Don't remember it? Can't help that. Do I look like an official of the Pullman Course?) Ayscough had gone out to Crete to undertake excavation in an out-of-the-way district. He'd taken his wife with him, pretty little Nellie Ayscough, whom I didn't know at all, but whom it was said he'd treated none too well . . . Said that in private, of course. The newspaper account had had no mention of it . . . Well, six months after their arrival in Crete a treasure-thief had broken into the Ayscough camp, murdered Mrs Ayscough in her hut, and escaped unidentified.

'Aina Paroulos, a Greek woman doctor living near by, had been summoned, but Nellie Ayscough died within a few minutes of the attack . . . The newspaper "romance", of course, had arisen from the fact that, just before leaving Crete to return with his finds, Ayscough had married Mlle Paroulos . . .

'All that I remembered, standing dawdling with a cup of lukewarm tea in Ayscough's drawing-room, and listening to the unchivalrous remarks that Rolland was making *sotto voce*, about "The Cretan woman".

' "My God! To see that slithering native in Nellie Ayscough's place!"

'I didn't feel very excited about it, though I myself hate overgrown cats outside Zoo cages. But Rolland had known Nellie Ayscough, and couldn't forget her.

'. . . "Nice little thing. Like a primrose, somehow. You didn't know her? Interesting voice – it used to develop the most remarkable and charming little sing-song when she was excited over anything—"

'I interrupted him then. "Sh! The Body's going to be brought out of the bag."

'Our host had moved into the centre of the room. Now he was booming at us. "I think we're all here. Aina, will you bring in the exhibits?"

'The panther did a neat glissade from the room. We settled down to look as credulous as possible, though Rolland began to whistle through his teeth, drearily, and not low enough, "Tell me the old, old story".

'Ayscough scowled at him like a bad-tempered bull. Said nothing, however. Instead, collected a small table and planked it in the centre of the room. Waited. Hadn't long to wait. In a minute Aina Ayscough was back, carrying a faded brown clay cylinder. Behind followed two servants – one with an ordinary dictaphone, the other carrying a thing like a gramophone suffering from elephantiasis. All three articles were placed on the table. Then the servants left the room, and the woman stepped back to Ayscough's side.

'He'd lost his scowl. Nothing he liked better than a chance to afflict a private gathering as though it were an audience in the Albert Hall. Quack he might be, but – lots of confidence in his own quackeries, I thought, watching him.

' "Ladies and gentlemen, I will be brief, as this is only a preliminary demonstration. Suffice to say that this stele, this clay cylinder, was excavated by my workmen on the very day that has such tragic memories for me. It lay, indeed, newly extracted from the copper box in which it had been discovered, in the very room where my wife was sitting when murdered. A little prior to that I had examined it and made out a scratched inscription on the rim – any of you may see it now – in archaic Ionian: *A speaking-tube brought from Atlantis by me, Kleon of Knossos.*

‘ "Further examination convinced me that in "speaking-tube" I had made no mis-translation. From the rifle-whorls inside the cylinder I am convinced that not only is this a relic of Atlantis, that continent concerning which there has been so much dispute, but the relic of a high Atlantean civilisation. I believe it is something equivalent to a modern gramophone record, and that, mounted on a proper recording instrument, it would speak to us in the voice recorded on its clay thousands of years ago."

‘Something to that effect he boomed out, for all the world like a pedantic Assyrian bull-man. But impressive, all the same. After all, we were archaeologists. I found myself craning to have a better look at the thing. Infernal nonsense, no doubt; still—

‘George Ayscough was enjoying himself and the little stir he had created. He looked us over, almost benevolently, and then opened a panel in the side of the thing that looked like a gramophone gone wrong. Inside there was a glimpse of two brass rods. Ayscough picked up the clay cylinder, mounted it on the brass rods, and closed the aperture.

‘ "Such an instrument – that which is here on the table beside me – I think I have perfected. Owing to the fragile nature of the clay stele, no actual recording had yet been attempted from it. Quite likely the process will gradually disintegrate it. However, any words omitted will be taken down by the dictaphone, thus retaining for future study the message, doubtlessly in an unknown tongue, from Atlantis.’

‘There was a perfect rustle of stretching necks. I whispered to Rolland: "What do you suppose it’ll say?"

' "Sing 'What are the sad waves saying?' in Atlantean, of course."

'But he was as impressed as any of us. Quite evidently Ayscough himself regarded the moment as the crown of his career. The Cretan woman stood like a stroked cat, sensual, immobile. Looked as though she would purr in a minute.

'But she didn't.

'The apparatus creaked a little as Ayscough turned the out-jutting handle and released a spring. We held our breaths.

'There came a click of mechanism engaging, a smooth purr, dead silence. Then, with startling suddenness – blood-freezing thing it was – there rang out from the body of the squat recording instrument the sound of a woman's scream – a sing-song babble of words:

' "Oh, my God, George! You – you and that woman Paroulos! I tell you I've borne enough; I won't stand more of it! . . . George! You're mad! Don't point that at me—"

'Then came the sound of a recorded revolver shot – and a splintering jar inside the instrument as the clay cylinder from Atlantis crumbled into a thousand flakes.

'Eh? What? Explanation? *You* would want that. What do you think I am – Old Moore, or a Commissioner for the Education of Feeble-Minded Adolescents? . . . Ring for a drink, somebody.'

The Woman of Leadenhall Street

(*During excavations for the foundations of Lloyds' new building in Leadenhall Street there was unearthed the skull of England's oldest inhabitant – a female of a sub-*

human species which perished long before the arrival of
Homo Sapiens.)

I

REMOTE ON THE dark forest fringes there rose the belling
of great deer.

The woman stirred a little at that distant sound. A
momentary breath of consciousness blew upon the grey
thought-track of her mind, then ceased and passed. The
fogs of exhaustion descended again. Her body relaxed
limply into the cobalt clay of the hillside, and the cloud
of insects, startled upwards in an angry buzz, hung a bare
second in insectile hesitation, and then drooped earthward
with a smooth drone.

The belling ceased. But for the hum of the insects it was a
silent world under the steady, zenith-ward climb of the sun.

A colourful world – matted and veiled, arabesqued and
sentinelled with the patterns and pillars of a surgent vegetal
life. Around the two hills, louring naked, squat and asym-
metrical in the light of the early sun, the tidal lagoons
stretched league on league; above them drifted a thin grey
scum of mist in the heat. Unending tracts of marsh,
spreading east and south, red and russet, waving tall, brittle
grasses in the breath of a ghostly breeze that had meandered
far from the estuary mouth, hemmed and horizoned those
lagoons. Land and near-land still cowered as a dun and
tenebrous background, in spite of the coming of the sun
and the pastel tintings of broom and furze. But below the
changing veils of heat-haze the lagoons drowsed in an azure
blue that sometimes deepened to violet, in pools and far
recesses to indigo, farther up-river to a flowing placidity of
grey, broad and shallow, reed-isleted.

Beyond that, the cane-brakes; beyond those, a serrated
row of trees that was the forest's vanguard – the forest that
pushed steadily south and west, resisted by the cane-brake,

but ever encroaching as the banks grew firm with the loads of shale and sand and black loam that the river brought from its uplands. Till in time, perhaps marsh and lagoon would contract and retreat, eastward, seaward, leaving the two dominant hills naked no longer above a forested plain . . .

The marsh-reeds stirred at the foot of the hill where the woman lay. A sudden squeal rent the quiet air, crescendoed agonisingly, evoked a chorus of similar cries. Lean, hirsute, short snouts and tails uplifted, a drove of wild swine broke out of the reeds and came scurrying up the hill from the mud-bath of the shallows. All but one of their number; screeching still, that unfortunate receded backwards, un-accountably, into the sky-blue waters.

The woman started again – started almost into sitting posture on the clayey hillside. She smelt and heard im-minent danger. She strove to rise, dragged at an unhelpful right leg, almost dropped that Thing grasped so tightly in her gnarled left hand. Then she subsided and cowered into the clay as the waving line of snouts swept into view.

They swept up and past her, splitting to right and left of the island that was herself. Up and up they went, over the hill, the chorus of their outraged cries growing in intensity as they crossed the slopes and then plunged marshwards once more. Dizzy and weak, body and head and eyelids red-smeared with clay, the woman sat rocking backwards and forwards, attempting to bring to a standstill the waver-ing world before her eyes. Her tongue lay hot and parched in her mouth, and she peered about for means to slake that immediate need. Not for long was there need to search. The clay was pitted with miniature pools from a recent rainfall. One was not a yard distant across the slope. Moaning faintly, she wriggled towards it.

Drinking with protruded, distended lips, she halted midway to sigh a wordless satisfaction. She sat back on her haunches, peering over her shoulder, her ears pricking abruptly like those of a carnivore.

Only the crying of a curlew.

Squatting in the hot sunshine, licking her lips, she rubbed at her matted eyelashes in sudden irritation. Her mind, poor and slow and dim, groped for means to soothe two pressing pains – the hunger that gnawed at her stomach with dull, persistent teeth; and the wincing scars ripping her body from shoulder to loin, loin to heel in red serration. They stung and quivered agonisingly in the strength of the increasing day, those scars, and she crouched again in an effort to shield them from the sun-glare. At that, a waving, tenebrous corona, the mosquitoes sang shrilly above her head.

She pushed forward a torn and aching leg, not scarred, but lacerated. She thought back uncertainly across dun deserts of memory. The scars – they had come to her that morning, far up an arm of the lagoons, as she forced her way through the waiting spikes of the giant thorn-brake, her eyes ever on the Twin Hills of the South. She had plunged and fought and scrambled through the brake, breathlessly, eagerly, those hills before her eyes in the changing dawn-light. Unheeding the sting of pricked and torn flesh, chattering, fey, she had at length fought clear of the barbed green entanglements, abandoning in their midst even the ancient hatchet that had once been Yellow Face's. The Place at last – there, with its Twin Hills!

Incontinently, sheer on the verge of the marsh as she stared and ran, she had stumbled into the midst of a pack of carrion-beasts trotting up towards the thorn-brake. They had broken from about her in a scurrying scramble, a confusion of snapping jaws and flying brushes. She had waved the beasts aside and then heard their growlings, receding not at all, but following her. She had glanced back.

Following her indeed they had been, though at first with caution, as was the nature of carrion-beasts. She had hastened on, looking back every now and then at her

fan-shaped escort. Haste had undone her, for the beasts
had gathered courage. Leading the pack, brush erect, head
erect, fangs bared, trotted a great brindled brute – in a trot
that every now and then would change to a snapping
experimental rush at her heels. And presently, realisation
and terror upon her, she had forgotten Place and Hills and
was slipping and stumbling and racing madly from tussock
to tussock, with the carrion-beast pack, trotting and growl-
ing no longer, but baying and streaming like the wind, in
hot pursuit . . .

The woman nodded, half-drowsing, reclining against the
hillside. Her lips fell apart in drooling reminiscence. She
had out-manœuvred the pack. When she took to the water
they had halted and scrabbled and splashed on the muddy
mere, snapping one at the other, or sitting down, tongues
lolling out, watching her with pricked, mocking ears. So she
had won clear of them, swimming slowly from islet to islet
of the lagoon wherein the morning tide was rising. The
saltiness of the water had touched her wounds to agony,
but, almost before she was aware of the fact, she was
swimming in the shadow of the nearer hill. Marsh and
reeds and ferns uprose again. It was as she gained her feet
and went wading and wandering hillwards amid them, that
that great sharp sliver of an unknown stone, edged to a
keenness unknown of hatchets, had torn the jagged rent in
her right leg. Then the hillside and unconsciousness . . .

The Place!

The mosquitoes buzzed upwards again in chorused
protest. Ceasing to squat, the woman abruptly dragged
herself erect, red-smeared, grotesque, her head hanging
forward from her shoulders, knees bent and rachitic as were
the limbs of all her people. Her hand went again to her eyes,
and into those eyes, as she peered round at the forsaken
world under the blaze of the sun, there crept an inarticu-
late, dumb misery, a wordless questioning that strove to
attain to words, to question herself.

The Place in the South! Here at last, through the lands of peril, she had attained to it. The Shining Stone was still fast-gripped in her hand. And – why did the magic delay?

Upright, for a moment she stood, dully questioning. Then, dizzy again, squatted and stared, holding her head, hearing and seeing nothing in the land of the deserted lagoons but the far crying of the curlews and the rising of the heat-fog. The Shining Stone—

II

She tried to follow up the matter, to realise that fear and that hope that had led her south, that had been with her while she stood and stared around. But, as ever, any effort at concentration was an ache and a pain to the poor, brutish brain behind the sloping forehead. She moaned softly, closing her eyes, and sat and drowsed, presently awakening from that to stare at the dancing of the midges over a nearby pool and to play with a handful of loose, pliable clay. It was soft and slimy and agreeable. She made noises of satisfaction, teasing and moulding the handful left-handedly. Then her brow corrugated again. She abandoned the play and again, arm across her forehead, peered east at the marshes, north at the dark forest-fringe. The Place – it was surely the Place.

For always this Place and the memory of it – memory of a memory, here forgotten and lost utterly, there cherished as a little fire borne to and fro in all the chances of hunting and mating and begetting – had haunted the Folk, up there in their slow wanderings through the wild lands of the North. It was a thing that a mother, squatting under the lee of a great boulder or in the heart of a leaf-strewn thicket in the famine time, would remember, and break from her soothing croon to remember, pithecanthropic eyes ailing and querulous. It was a thing that would catch the night-time camp-circle of the hunters to silence or a wild chattering. It was a thing of which she had first heard awedly, yet believingly for all that. It was the first tale she had ever heard . . .

She lay back against the clayey hillside. Lying so, with the sun almost overhead and her shadow dwindling, she did not think of that first tale as a tale or a sequence of words. She thought in picture-images, feeble and dim and but faintly related one to the other – yet here and there etched sharply and vividly, or coloured with accuracy and beauty. Pictures of actions and gesticulations, looks and glances and gestures – by these she sought down through that almost voiceless corridor of the past. Speech she hardly knew of. They had known, none of them, much of it in the forests of the North: except in times of famine or over-pressing fear, when one or other in some Folk-group would burst into wild storms of wailing or the mouthing of unintelligible noises that would end in the rage of madness. Then the Folk would scatter and run, and gather at a safe distance to scold and abuse the madman, or pelt him away from the squatting-place with showers of sticks and stones.

But that first time.

Far in the North: though she did not think of it as north. About them: the bush country of that flat, fertile land, here and there interspersed with great, grass-grown hummocks that were often hollow and porous, though none but beasts laired in their interiors. Country alive with small, killable vermin it had been, and free from the incursions of the large carrion-beasts. But north of it, horizon-hemming, marched a Forest, black, immense, and terrifying – a Forest the Folk never dared enter because of the Fear that dwelt therein. They never stirred to the ingress or exit of any living thing, those vast avenues and mazes, yet Fear and Death dwelt in the heart of them. So the Folk knew; so in childhood they had learned in pictures in the eyes of their elders. And if a night were still, windless and rainless, looking out from the clan squatting-place one would glimpse reflections of the

Fear upon the sky, hunting through the night. One moment that night sky would be velvet black or softly powdered with starshine; the next it would fill and float and whoom with the circling of a gigantic flame in the bowels of the Forest . . .

The most of the Folk, indeed, had never known it for a flame. It was Fear, bright and terrible, in its northern terrain. But the woman of the Hill had known. Once, as the night fell, she herself, lost far up the bracken-garmented breast of an eastwards mountain-range, had looked down through an opening in the Forest and stared with frightened eyes, seeing the Fear circling ceaselessly round and round a huge, saucer-shaped depression in the earth. It fell and flamed and rose again as the night came on, and she had crouched and looked.

But that first time.

That also had been at evening: an evening on the verge of the cold season, with the driving of windy gusts against the great break-wind that shielded the squatting-place. The smoke had been drifting south in a flame-shot glow, and Yellow Face, crouching hands on hips, had peered into that south in the trail of the smoke, in his eyes the look of a sick monkey, his lips moving and mowing foolishly. The red and black hummocks of the near bush-land, lichen-spangled, were darkling into fantastic, frightsome shapes in the coming of night; but still he had looked, and then began to gesture the while they stared at him with pricked ears.

They had just eaten – a pig killed by Yellow Face that day, the while the beast rooted and fed amid one of the patches of edible grass that every season grew the more scarce and un-nourishing. Yellow Face had killed it with his great hatchet of gleaming stone – that hatchet like to none other possessed in the squatting-places of the Folk. He had brought back the pig and handfuls of the edible grass to his Folk-family, and they had fed to their full on the fire-charred flesh, and then sat and drowsed until his actions and the sounds from his shrivelled lips aroused them.

Even she herself, she remembered, had eaten, small though she was and her wants and hungers often forgotten. With hands pressed to her stomach she had sat in the comfort of the fire-radiance, glad of it, afraid to creep into the dark nest of interlaced boughs where she passed her nights; for there always it seemed that the Fear from the Forest drew nearer. With the rest she had pricked her ears and stared at Yellow Face, while one of his sons, her brother Thin Leg, had leant forward with a stick in his hands and poked the fire into a cloudy shower of sparks, then into a concave-sheeted cobalt blaze. Yellow Face had swung round on them, his sloping, hirsute brow corrugating angrily at being thus interrupted. And Thin Leg had grimaced and dropped the stick.

III

Thin Leg. Now, lying on the sun-warmed slope of the Hill, collecting these pictured memories in an effort to trace the necessity that had brought her to this Place in the South, the book of memory slipped awry and showered her mind with paged portraits of Thin Leg: dim crayon traceries, childhood remembrances of that brother of hers, child like herself, downy, fleet, and agile enough despite his underdeveloped body. Friendly generally, in the warm days, scampering in the sunlight within hail of their mother; one quick to mimic and slow to work at the gathering of the edible grass . . . Thin Leg, upright and almost as tall as Yellow Face, dripping in the blood of a beast he had killed – a horned beast from the great black herds that roamed the eastern country where the bush failed and the llanos stretched in the face of the sunrise . . . Thin Leg, a silhouette against the dark Forest, the firelight on shoulders and buttocks, staring northwards at the Fear, frightened of it, like all of them, yet fascinated also . . . Thin Leg of the pantomimed adventures and braveries . . . Thin Leg that night of mating . . .

She saw that last picture etched in chrome-red, looking at it impersonally now, seeing her own reluctances and hesitations as she had followed out the ritual of mimic struggle that was unvarying when a brother mated with a sister. The Folk had squatted around the fire, clapping their hairy hands, swaying rhythmically, ululating the mating cry. And suddenly terror and horror, mimic not at all, had come upon her, as though Thin Leg were himself the Fear from the Forest. She had known that the thing was forbidden, could not be, and had turned and fled through the bushes, hearing the crackling pursuit of Thin Leg, hearing his panting breath; squirming and turning. Then his hand upon her shoulder—

IV

But that first time.

Yellow Face and his excitement! Standing absurd, the Shining Stone that usually hung from about his neck clenched in one gnarled hand, he had gestured and whimpered towards the south, the foam-spume gathering on his lips. And Thin Leg had mowed and motioned behind the bent back of the old man – derisive motions, as Yellow Face's arms flailed the air like the wings of the Flying Beast . . .

Many years after that speech of Yellow Face's it had been when she caught her one and only glimpse of a Flying Beast. They had grown scarcer and scarcer, these monsters; not for generations had one of their kind been seen, though the tale of them persisted. And then, mated with Thin Leg, the original camp-fire long lost behind in distance of years and miles, she had seen the beast from a grotto-mouth in the Chilterns. Evening was coming down, and she and Thin Leg had heard the droning buzz, like the buzz of a great dragon-fly, far up against the sunset. They had cowered in the semi-darkness of the grotto, looking at each other, chill and apprehensive, Thin Leg with the hatchet that had once been Yellow Face's fast-gripped in his hand. Then they had crept to the grotto-mouth, and there, in the fading autumn light, watched the wheel and glitter and burnished hesitation of the great skyey monster that had come from the west. With beating wings it had swayed away northwards through the autumn sky, into the cold light of the coming starshine. So it had vanished, and she had never seen it again, nor any of its kind.

Then Thin Leg, standing at that grotto-mouth, had begun to gesticulate and mouth at her in a fashion reminiscent of their father, Yellow Face. Not understanding, she had laughed at him, and, angered, he had struck her across the mouth, pointing after the Flying Beast, chattering ever the more quickly and excitedly till some purport of his meaning was borne to her. No beast, no bird, the Thing they had seen. It was – it was a Fear. Once there had been many of them, swooping from the skies, the Beasts of the Sun . . . So Yellow Face had told him . . .

v

But that first time.

Dreamer and visionary – though the woman on the Hill did not think of him in these terms, had never so thought of him – Yellow Face had been, one striving desperately in that twilight of speech and intelligence to transmit mysterious tidings transmitted to himself from countless ancestors. Tidings slipping from the world and sub-human memory, they were – tidings of enormous import that that chattering pithecanthrope sought to convey to his hearers in the sunset of his world. And somehow, one or the other a moment, he had awed them to understanding. She herself, startled, puzzled, scared, had peered at the pictures he evoked . . .

To the South – in the South somewhere was the Place of Good Life. There, a place of Twin Hills, long lost in the southern fastnesses, was the home ancestral of the Folk-clans. No belly-hunger had been there, neither threat of cold nor fear, nor prowling beasts of the night – for those who bore the Shining Stones . . .

It had wavered and snapped then, that picture-film from the brain of Yellow Face. It had slipped and shattered in a misty fusion of unrelated images. Then, knit and kneaded by the force of his will, had uprisen to clarity again. He was telling a story, some mythic memory of antique weal: In the South, in the Place, had been warmth and safety, no night, pictures, pictures – the magic of the Shining Stones . . .

He had passed into unintelligibility again, the fire-glow uplighting his gestured excitement, the Shining Stone on its string of deer-gut upheld to the sky. Round and flat and mysterious it was, strangely scrawled and scratched, the magic Stone. Few of them had ever examined it at close quarters, for Yellow Face defended it with the fanaticism of faith. It was magic and wonder and with it, in the Place of Twin Hills, life, free and safe and lovely, might yet be his.

VI

But Yellow Face had died, and his dream of a wild adventure in quest of the Place in the South had remained unfulfilled. Yet, from other wandering groups of the Folk who hunted south of the Forest of Fear, came also a drift and tangle of rumour and legend regarding the Place and the happenings there at the world's beginning. A great and happy Place indeed it had been, made magical by the multitudes of Shining Stones therein. And life had been free and great, without fear of beasts or hunger, until – so the picture-tale had passed down uncountable generations of refugees – the coming of the Black Danger from the skies.

The Black Danger. But what it had been no one knew or might convey to another, except some shadow of its memoried frightfulness. Worse than death by fire or hunger or the teeth of wild beasts it had been. For the Black Danger, in the Place in the South, had smitten the world from the sky.

So the tale and half-tale had strayed and risen and fallen and been forgotten and yet remembered again. Sometimes even she herself would brood upon it – in long summer noons when there had been plentiful food-gathering, and the reek of charred meat was yet in the air, and her children played and squabbled in the warm mud of some lake-mere, and Thin Leg slept and slept with his spear by his side, turning and grunting and sometimes crying out in nightmare. The Black Danger from the skies that had smitten the happy Place in the South: perhaps the Flying Beasts had brought it. For had not Flying Beasts been plentiful also in the long ago? . . . Yet, if in the Place there had been so many of the magic Shining Stones, how did it come that they had not warded off the Black Danger?

So, on the verge of a thought-synthesis, she had sometimes pondered, looking at the Stone which had been Yellow Face's as it rose and fell on the brown breast of the sleeping Thin Leg. But such occasions were rare enough. Hunger and beast-raids and the terror of nights and the crying of children pressed into almost every waking hour of her life. Children—

They had died quickly and often up there in the scrubland south of the Forest of Fear. The wail of birth and the sigh of death were sometimes separated by but an hour, sometimes a season, seldom more than a year. She had had many children: the first had grown to the height of her own thigh, and him she had discovered drowned in a marsh near the squatting-place. The second had vanished that winter when the land lay white with snow week on week, and the Folk-groups had fled eastwards from the roaming packs of carrion-beasts. The worst of winters that had been, and the straying groups, forced to a reluctant, snarling co-operation, had built great bomas of tree-trunks and thorns on the top of a hill, and lighted fires inside the stockade-circle, and fought off the carrion-beasts for night after night. Until at length the spring had come again.

But the scrub-land, year on year, grew ever the more dense, the edible grass ever scarcer. And the herds of beasts increased and multiplied, finding that country congenial, as did none of the thinning clans of the Folk. And sometimes there would creep into the eyes of Thin Leg that ailing, querulous look his woman had known in the eyes of Yellow Face. Clutching the Shining Stone, he would peer into the South and mouth and mow unintelligibly . . .

For with him, as with his father, the legend of the Place was undying. It was at once refuge of thought and torture of thought in the dim saga of his life. He had grown the butt of alien camp-fires because of that obsession of his – his dream of the safety and security awaiting him, and him alone, if he journeyed to the Place in the South with the Shining Stone. But he had never dared break away from the horde and adventure south. The unknown lands were lands of terror; greatest terror of all their loneliness. And though others might hearken to his dream and believe in it, yet the horror of the Black Danger that had come upon the Place was remembered also. And none but himself bore a Shining Stone and might journey under protection of its magic. And action and initiative had dwindled to a little fire in the midst of a great grey fluff of lethargy in the minds of the Folk.

Until the coming of that spring.

VII

It had brought torrential rains after an unusually mild winter. For weeks great glistening sheets of water had swept across the tender greenery of the awakening earth as the trees put forth their foliage. The Folk had crouched hunger-stricken in their dripping squatting-places, watching the blinded country in which it was impossible to follow game, gnawing hungrily at stray scraps of carrion, in the night-watches seeing above the bending trees the circling glow of the Fear in the Forest.

Till one morning that glow had spread across the whole sky. Then, in the depths of the Forest, had risen roar on thunderous roar, as if a great beast cried aloud in pain; and suddenly the sky had begun to vomit a rain of mud and stones across the dripping scrub-lands. After that followed a deluge of flaming cinders; and then they saw that the Forest was on fire.

They had fled southwards, such as survived. Days afterwards, the rains descending again, they had looked back and seen the great Forest as a black-edged wound against the northern sky. Game had grown scarce and the carrion-beasts an ever-pressing menace; but a worse terror came. For out of the charred Forest, threading its paths of smouldering jungle from their unknown habitat in the north, there descended through the rains pack on pack of giant bears, white, immense; and relentless in their hunting of the Folk. They had killed Thin Leg, two of them, and devoured him before the eyes of the woman who had been his sister and mate. He had screamed and screamed terribly, and the beasts, eating him, had not killed him immediately, but, their paws upon him, had torn at his body hungrily, yet with a certain deliberation . . .

They had gone at last, and the woman had climbed down from the rocky eminence where she had taken refuge, and had searched among the bones as the night was falling. In

the last glimmer of light she had found it, the Shining
Stone, polished and scratched anew, and she had lifted it
from the grisly heap and fled with it, sobbingly, yet with a
strange, exultant stirring at heart, southwards at last.

VIII

East, south, and west, the packs of white bears at their
heels, the Folk had fled into the lowlands beyond Charn-
wood Forest, and then taken to the hills again. Her own kin
lost, she herself, clutching the Shining Stone, remembered
the tale of its magic! In the South, in the Place of Twin
Hills, were food and safety and light and warmth for they of
the Shining Stone.

Summer ablow over the jungle wastes, flowering yellow
and green as she still pressed south. Waste lands for leagues
she would thread, sometimes through long miles of the
edible grass ripening to maturity on the slopes of some lost
valley. Sometimes, at some river estuary where a drunken
sprawl of giant rock-shapes lurched out against the sky, she
would see another of the circling Flames and hear the
whoom and roar of it as she fled steadily southward. Once,
north of the Chilterns, a night of rain and cold, she had
entered a great cave-place as the afternoon was waning, and
had seen multitudes of the Folk, with strange skins upon
them and in strange, contorted attitudes, lying dead upon
the floor. She had not realised them dead, for the face of
each was comely and fair. Then she saw that from each
mouth the tongue lolled forth black and shrivelled. At that
she had ceased her calling to them, though her voice went
echoing and echoing on, disturbing flights of bats. And at
that terror had come upon her, and she had turned and fled
from that place.

And once, holding still that midway route between
sunset and sunrise, she had followed for two long days
the winding track of a great ribbed beast – a track which

swept the dizzy edges of hills and plunged into slumbering glens and wound a dripping way through the very bowels of the mountains. Naked, with drooping shoulders and flying hair, she had trudged on and on under the scorching sun through wide desert spaces, a lonely figure clutching still the magic Shining Stone, peering out beneath ragged brows at the undulating wastes of jungle in the south.

Lost far behind her lay the country of the Folk. Yet one sunrise she awoke to the sound of voices. She had crept from beneath the bush of her night-shelter at that sound, and stood poised to flee. Near at hand a rock, rounded like a tree, but greater and taller than any tree, reared its head far up into the morning heavens. And upon its summit bodiless voices sang and wailed, dreadful and sweet, in the coming of the morning wind. Strange, crumbling images looked out from the shining rock-walls at the rising of the sun. And about the base of that rock lay scattered the bones of ancient men.

And once, one night in a cavern in the Chilterns, she had lain and watched, hour on hour, the up-springing of long lines of fire in the east. Next day she had looked for the coming of the Folk-clans from that direction. But instead it had been the fire which had advanced with the dawn, and then she had seen that it was another of the circling Flames that had exploded and was devouring the neighbouring lands . . .

And at long last, she had looked from a forest edge and seen them standing against the dawnlight, huge and pale and golden, the Twin Hills of the Place. Out from the Vale of St Albans she had seen them in a morning mirage, and had followed them, and found them, the Shining Stone and its magic guiding her, defender and surety of her faith—

IX

What was that?

She had been drowsing again. Now, starting awake, she

looked about her, and saw the sun low in the sky and the
northern forest afire with its light. She brushed the haze of
pain and exhaustion from her eyes and turned them on that
commotion that had broken out at the foot of the Hill. She
gave a grunt and tried to rise.

Her scarred leg refused to move.

Her screamings died away. The great white bear shook
himself, and now, snuffling at her tracks, ascended the hill,
gigantic, dripping. She turned her head and looked wildly
around the sun-hazed lagoons, looked across at that other
Hill shining in the afternoon light, and then dropped her
head upon her left arm and thrust her right far out, and
relaxed every bone in her body and sank forever into a pit of
silence and forgetfulness – she and the dream that Life had
dreamt of her species in an idle moment of geological time.

X

From her right hand the Shining Stone rolled out a little,
and spun a little, and fell. Last of its kind above the surface
of the earth, brought back to that Place after long wanderings, the dying sunlight caught it up and looked at it and
spun it into the clay again. Wrapped and forgotten in the
wild lagoons, under the heaped earthworks and crumbled
masonries of the Black Danger, lay the world that had
worshipped it with an inane faith till Nature wearied of that
world and stamped upon it, and blotted it out utterly, it,
and all its hopes and desires and prides.

But even so, last survivor, arrogant yet in its claim, it
seemed to fling back the sunshine, with worn, bevelled
edges encircling that picture of him who slew the dragon –
that another dragon might rise and lay waste the cities of the
earth.

One Man with a Dream

One man with a dream, at pleasure
Shall go forth and conquer a crown—

I

BOOM!

Hardly had the distant reverberations ceased before the sunset wind blew in the greenery of the city palms. It was as if Cairo sighed audibly. Day was officially dead. Crowned in red, squatting in the colours of the west, the Moquattam Hills peered down, perhaps to glimpse a miraculous moment on the surface of the Nile.

The Nile flowed red like a river of blood.

Rejeb ibn Saud, squatting in the Bulaq hut by the Nile bank, looked at his wrist-watch, at the face of the unconscious boy on the string-bed, at the fall of light on Gezireh across the river. But for one insistent whisper, the startling sunset was now a thing woven of silence.

'The sea! The sea!'

Song of the homing Nile! Gathering, hastening to fulfilment and freedom, joining its thousand voices, all the yearnings of its leagues of desert wandering, in that passionately whispered under-cry: 'The sea!'

All that afternoon the cry had haunted him. Now, as the boy on the bed tossed and moaned, ibn Saud shook himself, stood up, and bent over the bed.

'Son Hassan . . .'

The hut door opened of a sudden. Out of the sunset glare, into the dimness of the hut, Sayyiya, ibn Saud's sister-in-law, entered. She was a Sudanese, young, full-faced, thick-lipped. At the tall figure of ibn Saud she glanced inquiringly, then also went to the bed and bent over it. The boy Hassan seemed scarce to breathe.

'In an hour we shall know, master.'

'In an hour I shall not be here.' The man looked away from the string-bed. The chill on his heart had chilled his voice. Even at that moment, only by an effort could he keep from listening to the insistent whisper of the river.

'You go to the Khan Khalil to lead the Jihad? It is to-night?'

Ibn Saud nodded. It was tonight. An hour after the fall of darkness the Warren hordes, poured into the Khan il Khalil, were to be mustered and armed. Police and gendarmes, half of them active adherents of the insurrection, would have withdrawn from all western and central Cairo. The two native regiments had been seduced from allegiance to the puppet Nationalist Government: were enthusiastically for the rising: themselves awaited only the signal from the Khan il Khalil, the lighting of the torch.

And it would be lit. That was to be Rejeb ibn Saud's part. Golden-tongued, first in popularity of the rising's masters, he was to be the last to address the brown battalions in the Khan. For them he was to strike fire to the torch that would, ere another morning, light the flames of vengeance and revolution across the European city from Bulaq to Heliopolis.

The song of the Nile – of a sudden he knew why it had so haunted. Such the cry – of fulfilment, of freedom attained – that would tonight rise on the welling tide of the Black Warrens, from thousands of throats, from all the pitiful Cohorts of the Lost, the Cheated of the Sunlight . . .

'Master, if you come not back—'

Ibn Saud started. In his cold ecstasy he had forgotten the hut, Sayyiya, even Hassan.

'That is with God. But if Hassan – Listen, woman. You will come to me at the Khan. When the change, one way or another has passed upon my son, come to the Shoemakers' Bazaar, by the south side of the Khan, and send word to me. You will find your way?'

'I will come.'

Something in her glance touched him, stirred him from his abstraction.

'The time has been weary for you since Edei died, Sayyiya. If I live through this night—'

Suddenly the woman was crouching at his feet on the mud floor. Passionately, scaredly, she caught at the long cloak he had wrapped about him.

'Master – Rejeb . . . Those English whom you lead against tonight – they are ever strong, ever wary. If you die, what will happen to Hassan and to me? Master—'

Ibn Saud's cold eyes blazed. He flung the woman from him, flung open the hut door. Beyond, seen from the elevation of the Bulaq bank, the Cairene roofs lay chequered in shadows.

'And what of the folk – our brothers, our sisters – who die out there in their hovels and hunger? Thousands every year.' He blazed with the sudden, white-hot anger of the fanatic. 'What matters your miserable life – Hassan's – mine – if we can show the sun to those who rot their lives away in the kennels of the Warrens? We miserable "natives" – unclean things with unclean souls – tonight we shall light such a candle in Egypt as no man—'

He halted abruptly. The fire fell from him. Speaking in Arabic, he had yet thought in a famous alien phrase. Under his dark skin spread a slow flush. Without further speech he bent and kissed his son, and then walked out of the hut into the wine-red gloaming.

Sayyiya crouched dazed upon the floor. Then a sound disturbed her. From the throat of the boy Hassan came a strange, strangled moan.

The small, wasted body tossed for a little, then lay very still.

II

Darkness was still an hour distant. European Cairo thronged her streets, cried her wares, wore her gayest frocks, set forth on evening excursions to Saqqara and the Sphinx. John Caldon, seated on the terrace of the Continental, awoke from a sunset dream and turned towards his brother-in-law, Robert Sidgwick.

'Eh?'

'. . . the edge of a volcano.'

'Where?'

'There.' Sidgwick waved his hand to the brown driftage in the street below them. 'The political situation's the worst it has been for months. The Cairenes have been propaganda'ed for months by Nationalist extremists. Trade and employment are bad. The native quarters are seething.'

'Very proper of them.'

Caldon smiled into the lighting of a cigarette. An artist, he was making a westward world-tour from England. Together with his wife and daughter, he had arrived from India, *via* Suez, only the day before. Sidgwick's statement left him unimpressed. He had never yet encountered a white man, settled amongst brown, who was not living on the edge of a volcano. It was the correct place to live, just as it was the correct thing for a volcano to seethe pleasingly upon occasion.

Sidgwick had the monologue habit. Through the quiet air and the blue cloud from his own cigarette Caldon caught at a number of phrases.

'This damn self-government foolishness began it all . . . Treat a native as a native.'

'Why not as a human being?'

'That's what we've done here. Look at the result.'

Caldon was boredly ironical. 'Self-government – with an army of occupation! An alarum-clock with the alarum taken away!'

'It's advisable – if you give it to a native . . . Take it my sister's never told you about young Thomas O'Donnell?'

Caldon shook his head. Sidgwick nodded, without pleasantness.

'Well, the telling won't hurt you. He was a half-caste – an Irish-Sudanese, of all grotesque mixtures. His father had had him sent to a school in Alexandria; some kind of irrigation engineer out here the father was, and pious to boot. He died when his son was seventeen, leaving instructions for the latter to be sent to a theological college in England to train as a missionary. All very right and proper. To England young Thomas O'Donnell came. To Bleckingham.'

Caldon, with some little show of interest, nodded. Sidgwick resumed.

'You know – though your people didn't settle in Bleckingham till about a year after the time of O'Donnell – the lost tribes the Theological College spates over the countryside to tea and tennis on spare afternoons? One of these tennis-do's I met O'Donnell. He was a tall, personable nigger – not black, of course. Cream-colour. But it wouldn't have worried me in those days if charcoal had made a white mark on him. He was interesting. I liked him, invited him to tea. Clare Lily was young also, in those days, you'll have to remember.'

'Why?' A tinge of red had come on the artist's cheekbones.

'Oh, Caesar's wife is stainless enough,' hastily. 'But a young girl hardly knows herself – or the stuff she handles. Had it been a white man, of course . . .

'Yes, Clare Lily became fairly intimate with O'Donnell. Flirted with him, no doubt. Mother was then the same invalid as you knew; I was supposed to be my sister's protector. But I suffered from attempting the assimilation of indigestible theories on the brotherhood of man. I admired O'Donnell. Oh, he fascinated.'

The light all down the Sharia Kamil had softened. Caldon sat rigid. It was Sidgwick who dreamt now.

'The outcome of it all was what I'd expect now. O'Donnell and Clare Lily went picnicking on Bewlay Tor . . . The nigger attempted to act according to his nature. Clare Lily's screams saved her – attracted some students mountaineering. O'Donnell went berserk amongst them. You see, he wasn't a white man.'

'What happened to him?'

'God knows. He didn't wait to be hoofed out of the College. They traced him as far as Southampton, where it was supposed he'd managed to get a job on board some ship . . . Hallo, here's Clare. Good Lord, what's the—'

A woman was running up the steps from the taxi which had stopped below the terrace – a woman with a white, scared face. Behind her, weeping, came trailingly the ayah of Caldon's daughter.

'Jack, Jack! Oh, my God . . . Clare Lily – we lost her down in the bazaars, in the horrible Warrens. Jack – they stoned us when we tried to find her . . .'

III

Never had it all seemed so secure.

But Rejeb ibn Saud, far out of the direct route from Bulaq to the Khan il Khalil, and striding down the Maghrabi with his 'aba pulled close about his face, saw signs enough that were not of the olden times. Few native vendors were about; no desert folk, sightseers of the sightseers from foreign lands, lingered by the hotels. Here and there, making way for the strolling foreigner, some dark Arab face would grow the darker.

Ibn Saud had sudden vision: Fire in the Maghrabi,

massacre and loot; the screamings of rape, crackle of rifle fire, knives in brown hands . . .

In three hours – at the most.

Ibn Saud half stopped in his stride; the Maghrabi blurred before his eyes. Slave of the faith which had bound him these many years, he was yet compounded of so many warring hopes and pities that his imagination could suddenly sway him, to gladness or to despair, from a long mapped-out path . . . The Green Republic of Islam – attained through murder most foul and bloody – was it justified?

A stout Frenchman and his wife moved off the sidewalk in order to pass the crazed native who had suddenly stopped in their path, muttering. Looking curiously back at him, they saw him move on slowly, dully, with bent head.

So, with none of his former pace and purposefulness, he went, in a little turning northwards into the deeper dusk of the Sharia Kamil. The whimsical intent that had originally led him to diverge through the European quarter still drew him on, but he followed it in a brooding daze. At the entrance to the bookshop of Zarkeilo he was jarred with realisation of his quest.

Nevertheless, he entered, and, disregarding the assistant's question, passed down into the interior of the shop to the section that housed Continental editions of English fiction and verse. With an almost feverish eagerness he began to scan the titles. About, the walls were here and there decorated with sham antiques – bronzes, paintings of Coptic Virgins, and the like. To a small red volume ibn Saud at length outreached an unsteady hand.

Rememberingly he turned the leaves. Ten years since this book had lain in his hands, but he had remembered it – remembered because of those lines which haunted him, which had inspired him since, a homeless vagrant, he had landed at Suez to his dream of Egyptian Renaissance, to the years of toil and persecution in which he had built up this night's insurrection . . . With their music and their magic, undimmed from of olden time, the words leapt at him from the printed page:

> One man with a dream, at pleasure
>> Shall go forth and conquer a crown;
> And three with a new song's measure
>> Shall trample a kingdom down.

Rejeb ibn Saud replaced the book, straightened, stood upright with shining eyes. Doubts fell from him. Outside, in the night, his dream went forth to conquer . . .

His eyes fell on a sham antique crucifix. Last of the gloaming light upon it, the tortured Christ fell forward from the cross. Upon his head, each carven point a-glitter, shone the crown of thorns.

IV

'Stone her! Stone her!'

Nightfall; in the fastnesses of the native quarter – the maze of the streets that radiate around the eastern sector of the Sharia el Muski; a girl running – a child of nine, English, with a flushed, scared face; behind, peltingly, laughingly, dirt and stone hurling, a horde of native children.

Such adults as were about turned amused glances to follow the chase. The hunt was up!

Ibn Saud halted and watched. Nearer drew the child, casting terrified glances to right and left. Then she caught his eye. Straight as an arrow towards him she came, clutched his cloak, and clung to him, panting.

The pursuing children surrounded them. One, a ragged hunchback, caught at the girl's dress. Ibn Saud spoke.

'Let be.'

'Why? She is English. We are to kill them all tonight.'

Hate and curiosity in their eyes, the children drew closer. Two loafers joined them, and one addressed ibn Saud.

'It is so, brother. Let the children have their sport. Who are you to stop it?'

'I am ibn Saud.'

At that name the children, cruel no longer, but shy and worshipping, drew away. The loafers, whose hatred of the English had apparently not induced in them any desire to join the army of the insurrection in the Khan il Khalil, slunk aside. Ibn Saud touched the girl's head. She had lost her hat.

'How did this happen?' he asked in English.

'Mother and nurse took me to the bazaars. I saw a shop I liked, and went into it. It had lots of doors. Perhaps I came out at the wrong one. When I did I couldn't see either mother or nurse. Then I walked and walked. And those children struck me and cried things and chased me. I ran. Then I saw you.'

Thus, succinctly, the little maid. Ibn Saud stared down at her, a wonder in his eyes.

'But why did you think I would help you?'

The girl raised clear, confident eyes. 'Oh, I knew you would because – because you are different.'

An odd flush came on the face of the insurrectionist. He stood thoughtful. Folly, in any case. He was only saving the child for—

Oh, inevitable. He glanced impatiently round the dusking street. Then:

'What is your name?'

'Clare Lily.'

He stood very still and then bent and stared into her face. For so long did he remain in that posture that the child's lips began to quiver. As in a dream ibn Saud heard himself question her.

'Where is your mother staying in Cairo?'

'At the Continental. If I could get a taxi—' She was calm

and methodical and very grown-up now. Ibn Saud took her hand.

'Come.'

He hurried. Through a maze of odoriferous alleys and walled-in corridors – the kennels of the Cheated of the Sunlight – he led her till on the dusk blazed a long sword of light. It was the Sharia el Muski, strangely bereft of traffic. With difficulty ibn Saud found an *'arabiyeh*. When directed to take the child to the Continental, the driver blankly refused. Not tonight. Then ibn Saud drew aside the folds of his head-dress, and spoke his name, and the driver saluted to head and heart. In Cairo that night that name was more powerful than the Prophet's.

What would it be by dawn?

'Thank you very much.' The earnest eyes of the child looked up into ibn Saud's dark face. With a sudden thought: 'Please, what is your name? – so that I can tell mother.'

Child though she was, she was never to forget him, standing there in the lamplight as he answered her:

'I am Thomas O'Donnell.'

v

Brugh! Boom! Brugh!

In a great square space, ringed about by the bulking of the bazaars, three bonfires burned, shedding a red light on the massing hundreds of the Black Warrens. Against the Khalil wall was upraised a giant platform. At the other side of the square, curious, antique, a thing of the ages and with the passion of all Man's sweated travail in its beat, was mounted a gigantic drum. Out into the night and the lowe, over the heads of the massing insurrectionists, over the hastening chains of Cairenes converging on the Khan from alley and gutter, its challenge boomed, menacing, stifled, a gathering frenzy.

Already, eastwards and northwards, curtains of scouting insurrectionists, awaiting the final word, hung as self-deputed guards upon the heart of the revolt. But there was little need of guard. The gendarme had laid aside his uniform, kept his rifle, and was now mingling with the mobs of the Khan il Khalil. The petty official, long European-clad, was in burnous and kuftan, uplifting his voice in the wail of chanting which ever and anon rose to drown even the clamour of the drum. Spearhead of the revolt, the Cairene Labour Union massed its scores of rail and tramway strikers.

The hour was at hand.

'Brothers—'

From amidst the notables on the platform, one had stepped forth. High and dim above the Cheated of the Sunlight he upraised his hand.

Es-Saif of El Azhar. An echo and an interpretation of the savage drumming, his voice beat over the silenced square. He had the marvellous elocutionary powers of the trained native, the passion of the fanatic, the gift of welding a mob into a Jihad.

Presently, at the words rained upon them, long Eastern wails of approbation began to arise. Other speakers followed Es-Saif. The great bonfires, heaped anew, splashed the throngs and the grisly walls with ruddy colour. Quicker began to beat the blood in heart and head. Clearer and louder arose the pack bayings of applause.

Jammed in the midst of the vast concourse below the platform, Rejeb ibn Saud stood listening to the voices of his lieutenants. As if deafness had crept upon him, they sounded incredibly remote . . .

Clare Lily! Dream-child, clear-eyed and unspoilt. By now she would be safe. And tomorrow, somewhere amidst charred beams and smoking rafters, he might stumble over her bones . . .

Surely the square and the bodies around him steamed

with heat? What was Es-Saif saying? 'Our starved children who have died, who have cried in the darkness and held out their dying hands—'

Children crying in the darkness . . . What was all history but a record of that? Hundreds, this night. Clare Lily weeping in terror, the terror-filled mites of the Warrens, Hassan . . .

'Ibn Saud!'

In a long lane that was closing behind him, a man had forced his way from the foot of the giant platform.

'We thought you lost or captured. We would have torn down your prison with our bare hands. Come, it is near your time to speak.'

He spoke in the commanding voice of a worshipping disciple, and then turned back towards the platform. Through the opening throng ibn Saud followed him . . . Near his time. In a few minutes now he would stand forth on that platform and fire the blood-lust in the maddened horde whose lusts he had trained and nourished all these years.

He found himself climbing to the platform. Dim hands guided him on either side, faces, red-lit, grotesque, profiled and vanished in the bonfires' glare. Abayyad was speaking now. At sight of ibn Saud, Es-Saif leapt up, and kissed him and led him to a seat, wondering a little at his lack of greeting, and the brooding intentness of the dark, still face.

Wave upon wave, a sea of faces below him. As one looking out upon his kingdom ibn Saud stood a moment, and suddenly his eyes blazed, aweing to silence the murmured questionings of Es-Saif.

Clare Lily – Hassan – all the children of the Warrens and of all the warring races of men – *With them lay the world*. Not with his generation – white and brown alike, they had failed. Yet he and his faith – a faith builded on an ancient wrong in the long-dead years – had sown hatred in the hearts of the Warren children against Clare Lily and her kind. He had sought to poison the unguessable future that was not his: he sought to murder it now in death for the hearts and hands that might save the world, might win a wide path through all the tangles of breed and creed and race, reach even to that dream that might yet be no dream – the Brotherhood of Man . . .

Below him the mist that was the mustering insurrection quivered. What was that?

He stared across to the far side of the Khan. Through the throngs, from the direction of the Shoemakers' Bazaar, a Sudanese was slowly forcing his way towards the platform. With the force of an utter certainty, Rejeb ibn Saud knew him for what he was.

He was Sayyiya's messenger.

VI

Abayyad's voice rose and fell in penultimate peroration. Behind him, ibn Saud, watching the approach of the messenger, stood with a sudden fire alight in his chilled heart.

For the sake of that his vision of the World of Youth, he would stake all on Chance and the mercy of God. If Sayyiya's note told of Hassan's recovery, he would violate every enthusiasm of his life in the Warrens, would speak peace to the mobs, cry on them to desist, preach to them the vision of the world that had arisen before his eyes. So, if there was a God, if he had but spared Hassan, he would speak . . .

The lights in the Khan il Khalil flung a glow upon the heavens. Ibn Saud looked up. Beyond the glow, clear and cold, shone the stars. Infinitely remote, infinitely impersonal . . .

Clare Lily – Hassan – the saving of the near and dear to one – how pitiful!

'Ibn Saud! Ibn Saud!'

The shouting of his name beat in his ears. Urgently upon his sleeve he felt the hand of Es-Saif. Abayyad had finished. Following the shout, upon the Khan fell a vast hush, broken only by the sound of a throaty breathing as Sayyiya's messenger reached the platform.

Ibn Saud took the note that was handed up to him, unfolded it, and read.

VII

Then a strange thing happened. About him, on the platform of the insurrectionists, they heard him. Ibn Saud laughed – a low, clear laugh, and glanced up again at the stars.

Infinitely remote.

The note slipped from his hand. To the edge of the platform he stepped forward and spoke.

For a full minute, sonorous, golden, the voice beloved of the dim brown multitudes of the Warrens rang clear. Then, obscuring it, began to rise murmurs of astonishment, counter-murmurs for silence. The stillness that had held the massed insurrection vanished. The crowds wavered and shook.

'Traitor!'

A single voice spoke from the heart of the mob. A hundred voices took it up, a hundred others – those of ibn Saud's personal following – shouted to drown the word. Pandemonium broke loose. Men screamed and argued, and over the whole Khan swung and wavered the hand of an incredible fear.

'Infidel! Englishman!'

Face distorted, Abayyad sprang forward upon ibn Saud. As at the touch of frost, the hand of that fear stilled for a moment the tumult below.

In that moment Abayyad, with gleaming knife, struck home.

Ibn Saud shook him off. Crowned and infinitely humble, he outreached both arms in a benediction, ancient and immemorial . . .

With a roar as of the sea, the hordes rose in a wave and poured upon the platform.

VIII

Es-Saif wanders an exile in the land of the Senussi. The secret history of that night in the Cairene Warrens – that night which saw the insurrection fall like a house of cards in the wreckage of the stormed platform of the Khan, which saw the rebel battalions, heart-broken and in despair, break up and scatter to hut and hovel – is as dim to him as to any who heard the traitorous speech for which Rejeb ibn Saud paid with his life.

Yet from the platform Es-Saif salved a curious relic – the crumpled note sent by Sayyiya to the leader of the insurrection. Reading it, who can guess the dream for which ibn Saud cheated himself of his bargain with God, or what crown he went forth to conquer?

'To my master, Rejeb ibn Saud. The mercy of God the Compassionate be with you. Thy son Hassan died at the fall of darkness – SAYYIYA.'

For Ten's Sake

I

IT WAS Easter Day.

Under the feet of the watcher on the Hill of Burial the earth suddenly shook, quivered for a moment as might one in a nightmare, and then slowly subsided.

Mevr, the Hell-Gate of the East, lying asleep in the afternoon heat, scarcely stirred from its siesta; since its foundation in the days of Asoka as a meeting place of the Central Asian caravans it had known the shocks of minor earthquakes. Like an obscene, sated animal it sprawled under the vacant grey eyes of the watcher. The heat-haze shimmered above it; northwards, its streets straggled towards the dim bulking of the Kablurz Beg; westwards, across the dun tundra, wound the white track to Persia and far Iraq; eastwards, another caravan route vanished on the horizon towards Baluchistan.

As so many streams they seemed, these roads; streams flowing into the dark cesspool of Mevr and emerging from it – cleansed. Behind, in the City of the Plain, the caravans left their floating scum to fester and reek under the brassy noonday sky, under the sickened stars, under the seemingly endless patience of God . . .

The vacantness vanished from the eyes of the watcher: they blazed with the hatred of the fanatic, the monomaniac. A tall, gaunt figure, he rose from beside the dark mound where he had been crouching, and outreached thin, clutching hands.

'How long, O Lord?'

So, for a moment, he stood, threateningly, weird in his shabby black, a prophet of wrath above Mevr. Then the dullness returned to his eyes; his glance grew wandering and fell on the mound at his feet. Suddenly he dropped to his knees; in his throat came a dry sob.

'Oh, Dick, Dick! Mevr might have spared at least you . . . Janet it took, me it will take, but you— Oh, my son! . . .'

Farther up the Hill of Burial two grave robbers, Abdul Khaled and Osman the Nameless, had also been squatting on their haunches and looking down on Mevr. The cry of the man below reached their ears and they peered down at his black-coated figure. Then Osman (who was nameless in that, being a Turk, he was known merely by a contraction of Osmanli) spat expressively and contemptuously.

'It is the Englishman, the mad hakim, making prayers by the grave of his son.'

Abdul grunted. He was a soured man, for their day's work had so far disgorged nothing of value – not even a skeleton hand bearing a ring. In'sh allah! the greed of relatives these days was growing to unbelievable bounds, so poorly were kindred disposed of. The mad hakim did not interest him, except professionally.

'The grave of this son of his may contain some trifle of value,' he suggested.

The Nameless One shook his head. 'No unbeliever buries even a brooch with his dead. Did we not but yesterday spend two hours over the resting place of that accursed Russian pig – may his bones poison the jackals who have since doubtlessly come to scrape them, seeing we did not fill in the pit! – and find nothing?' He rose up wearily, a burly brute, bestial faced, with squinting, red-rimmed little eyes. 'We'll seek a night's lodging at Miriam's. Eh?'

The fat Abdul had uttered a sudden gasp of pain. Now, clutching at his side, he rolled over on the turf. Then he tore something from the dirty djibbeh which enveloped him and flung it a yard or so away. Osman saw hit the ground a small green viper, yellow underneath upturned, broken-backed, writhing.

'Allah! It is the end.' Abdul began to beat the ground with his feet and suddenly composed himself and drew a knife from his belt, for it is better to die by the bite of steel than the slow virus of the green-backed viper. Osman tore away the knife.

'Wait. I will call the hakim.' Forthwith, waving his arms, he shouted down the hill to the far, black-coated figure. In a little the latter stirred, stood upright. Down the windless air was borne Osman's shout.

'Haste, effendi. My brother has been bit of the yellow scorpion!'

For a moment the old man, who had once been Richard Southcote, MD, stared up at the gesticulating Turk. Then returned to his eyes the same light as had been there when he had risen and threatened Mevr. He laughed, laughed aloud, ringingly, unemotionally, so that Osman dropped his arms and stared, and presently saw the hakim deliberately turn his back and walk down the hill towards Mevr. From the ground Abdul groaned.

'Give me the knife, Nameless.'

The bestial-faced Turk stared down at his fellow-scoundrel. His hands began to shake. Then, abruptly, he dropped by Abdul's side and tore away the stained djibbeh. His intention was evident. Abdul shrank away.

'Fool! Not that! It is death!'

The Turk's great hands gripped him. 'Peace! I drink worse poison every day in the Street of Ten!'

With that, he bent his trembling lips towards the little oozing incision on the brown hide of Abdul the graverobber.

II

As the mad hakim entered Mevr from the Hill of Burial, the foetid city began to stir to life. In a narrow alley beggars squabbled querulously, stealing the chance alms dropped amongst their blind. The old man passed unseeingly amidst the sprawl of diseased, wasted bodies. In front he heard a shouting and commotion and the beat of a little drum. Coming to the great bazaar of the Suq es Iraq he was in the midst of a familiar scene.

A caravan – lines of laden, dusty camels and thirstily vociferous drivers – had newly arrived from Bokhara. The dust arose in clouds, babel of many tongues filled the air. From the nearby streets the vile things which had once been women were already flocking into the Suq. They mingled with the caravan drivers. One, a ragged harpy with a shrill voice, Southcote saw wheedling at a black-bearded came-lier, already drunk and sitting, cup of arrack in hand. Suddenly, with an insane ferocity, the ruffian leapt to his feet and smote the woman a blow that cracked her jaw. She fell with a scream of pain, and wild guffaws of merriment broke out. Loudest of all laughed the two Persian gen-darmes who patrolled the bazaar. The camelier stared vacuously down at the woman . . . It was, set against its background of heat and dust, a scene that might have been filched from hell.

The old man looked about him with smouldering eyes. Slowly he made his way towards the centre of Mevr. Presently he found himself passing by the entrance to that which stank in the nostrils of even the City of the Plain – the entrance to the vile Street of Ten, a loathsome resort of thieves and murderers, where were practised unnameable vices of which even Mevr talked under breath, where no gendarme had ever dared patrol, where of a morning the knifed and rifled bodies of the night's victims were flung out into the reeking gutters of sunrise, whence, two years before to a day, young Dick Southcote had been brought, a bruised and lifeless and dreadful thing, to his father's house.

As Southcote passed there stood by the entrance to the Street of Ten two whom he – and, indeed, all Mevr – knew by repute. One, pock-marked, lithe, white-clad, was a murderer who killed openly, with bravado, who sold the services of his knife to any who sought them; the other, Selim of Damascus, was a spy of the desert robbers, warning them of unarmed caravans, sharing in the loot of massacred trains.

Yet in Mevr they went scatheless. No gendarme dared lay hands on those whom, it was openly rumoured, the Governor himself had hired upon occasion. Indolently, insolently, they lounged in the hot afternoon sunshine. About them, from the cotes near by, pigeons wheeled with a blue flirr of wings.

Two horsemen, Europeans both, came trotting past the entrance to the Street of Ten. To the lounging scoundrels they nodded, under the pigeon-cloud ducked. Then in front of them, disappearing up a side street, they caught a glimpse of the bent figure of Southcote.

'The old man has been visiting his son's grave.' It was the short, burly man who spoke. He was the German Consul, not long transferred from Alexandria, but finding Mevr congenial and reminiscent of East African days.

'Then he has been visiting the foulest spot in Mevr.' The thin, debauched-looking Greek in white ducks who was known as 'Mitri' called himself a doctor, and had a reputation so unsavoury that the German raised amused eyebrows at his remark, looked after Southcote with a twisted grin. 'Poor fool! And to think, Herr Consul, that that crazed Englishman had once a European reputation!'

'So?' The German was indifferent. He had pulled out his watch, looked at it, and was now mopping his moist forehead. 'Twixt his horse's ears 'Mitri' was surveying Mevr with the owlishness of one unsoberly reminiscent.

'European. He was "Earthquake" Southcote. In Italy and Syria he spent years in seismological studies, was decorated by the English Society, and was famous. These things I know, for I learned them from his son.'

'Ah yes, the son.' The German, newcomer though he was, had heard something of the Southcote story. 'And how came this – Academician and his son to Mevr?'

'Because this place is in the Central Asian earthquake belt. The Doctor Southcote came to study it, and brought his wife and son, who was a boy of eighteen. The wife died of malaria six months after they came. Though a scientist, the old Southcote was a Calvinist with a God waiting round the corner ready to be unpleasant. In such manner he took the death of his wife. Six months after that, when his son was killed, he became a madman and now abides in Mevr he knows not why.'

'You knew him once?'

'Mitri' stared unwinkingly ahead. 'I knew the son. Pfuu! . . . Me the old Southcote looked on as a native, and hated me on some Old Testament authority; me he considered an evil influence on his son.'

The German chuckled greasily. 'Mitri' abruptly reined up his pony. They had come to the Midan. The Greek pointed leftwards.

'You will be late for your festa, Herr Consul. And the Governor's desires are his belly's.'

'Auf wiedersehen.'

'Auf wiedersehen.'

'Mitri' slowly rode down the rightward wall of the Midan. An 'evil influence'? He?

Something dreadful came in his face. Then, with a twisted grin, he looked down at his shaking hands – the hands which had strangled the life from out Dick Southcote.

III

Coming towards the tumble-down native house which he and Janet had furnished three years before, the mad hakim encountered Ahmed, the water-seller and scavenger. The latter was slinking along in the gutter in his usual fashion. Though it was late in the day, his bleared eyes were of a habit fixed on the ground, for from the pockets of such numerous drunkards as speckled the early morning gutters of Mevr he gathered the wherewithal to augment his scanty legitimate earnings. At the old Englishman's approach he glanced up swiftly and shiftily. Dull, tortured eyes met dull, evil ones. Upon his thigh Ahmed made with two crossed fingers an obscure sign – the age-old sign wherewith the East wards off the evil eye.

Southcote's face twitched unhumorously. Ahmed was well known to him. He paused in the doorway and looked after the scavenger, broodingly. Impersonated in the foul carrion-grubber was Mevr itself . . .

Entering from the street, he made his way to the room which was study, laboratory, and dispensary in one. The dingy walls showed streaked with a steamy damp, the furniture was ragged and thick with dust, for, beyond seeing to meals, the old Iraqi woman who acted as house-keeper did nothing. Southcote laid aside his hat, sank into a chair by the window, and there, upright and still, sat staring bleakly and unseeingly. Minutes went by. On a ledge of the window which tunnelled the thick wall a golden-eyed lizard flittered to and fro. The house was utterly quiet.

Presently Southcote moved. Under his heel something crunched. He glanced down and saw that the floor was strewn with broken glass. Then, catching a glimpse of a broken photoframe under the table, he bent, gaspingly, and picked it up. It was a photograph of Dick, shaken from a ledge by the recent tremor.

Beside it, flung to the floor by the same cause, was a small, black-bound book. That Southcote let lie. With thin, unsteady fingers he smoothed the crumpled cardboard of the photograph. From a narrow, slatted window the sun-light streamed in and dappled the pictured face of the boy who lay beneath the mound on the Hill of Burial. Over the youth and freshness and the gladness in the young eyes the mad hakim sat and yearned, as a thousand times he had done. Dick, the strong, the light-hearted, his murdered boy . . .

Two years to a day since the murdered lad had been carried into this very room: two years to a day since that black morning when something inside his brain had seemed to crack as he called down God's vengeance on the City of the Plain. Certain of its coming, certain of the doom that would fall on Mevr, he had ever since waited, his hatred of the foul place growing upon him month by month so that he shunned the native populace and the moving scum of the caravans, refusing help to the hurt even when they came to his door begging it. Never dependent on practice for a livelihood, he avoided even the few whites of Mevr because of that otherness of purpose for which he knew that God had designed him.

Once, when Kuchik Khan was sweeping down from the north with his army raised on Soviet gold, it had seemed to Southcote – unconsciously grown Eastern, un-European, a fanatic at once egotistic and sublimely selfless – that the hour was nigh, that in fire and rapine was God about to cleanse the earth of Mevr as once before He had cleansed the world with the sword of Tamerlane. But Kuchik's army had melted away, and Mevr breathed again, and Southcote, with vacant, staring eyes, had climbed the Hill of Burial and looked to the skies and prayed for even such patience as God's own . . .

But now, sitting with the crumpled photograph in his hand, an aching misery came upon him. He was only the mad hakim, dreaming a dreadful vengeance, living an insane hope. Of Dick was left nothing more than the captured beauty of his pictured face.

Upon that face he had never noted – as any stranger would at once have done – the heavy, sensual mouth, the contraction about the eyes which, spite the youthfulness of the latter, spelt viciousness. To the father they were the eyes of murdered hope, staring unavailingly, in a black world that knew not retribution.

It was the first moment of doubt within Southcote's last two years, and, in the instant of it, the ground shook under his feet. Upon the floor the little pieces of glass danced: the walls groaned ominously: a cup fell and smashed.

It was the second tremor within an hour.

IV

Into the eyes of the mad hakim had come an unwonted interest. Now he laid aside the photograph and rose to his feet. From the table he picked up a box of matches, made his way from the still quivering room, turned to the left, descended a flight of stone stairs. On a landing some eight feet below ground-level he stopped by the entrance to a small doorway and lit a candle which stood on a stone ledge.

The door opened easily at his touch. The candle lit up the smaller cellar of the house. In one corner was a chair and table; in the centre of the room an instrument embedded in the floor, held down by iron clamps, and rearing itself up, a cluster of thin glass rods, to a graded aluminium dial and pointer.

The Southcote Seismometer is a scientific toy, a mathematician's dream gone astray in the realisation. In seismological works its possibilities are constantly referred to and its absolute unreliability demonstrated. As an instrument the purpose of which is accurately to gauge and foretell a many hours distant earthquake it is recognised as a magnificent failure.

Yet there, in front of the old man in that stifling cellar in Mevr, was that seismologist's dream, the Improved Southcote, standing as it had been left on the day of its first installation, exactly two years before.

Candle in hand, Southcote approached it. Every day – single surviving habit of the one-time scientist – he came down into the cellar to clean the mechanism and make readings. Mevr, situated as it was, seldom failed to register some forthcoming or passing tremor. On the twelve gradations of the dial the pointer more often than not hovered between zero and one.

Southcote flecked some dust from off the instrument, and then bent to read it.

The pointer quivered above nine.

V

For a moment, after his first amazed start, the old man was merely the scientist, calm and deft. He tested the apparatus, searching for flaws, altered gauges, diminished the mercury pressure in one of the long glass rods, and then changed back again to normal. Promptly, with the last move, the pointer swung again to nine. Then it began to creep up the dial towards ten . . .

And then, equally suddenly, the scientist died in Richard Southcote. Realisation smote him like a breath of fire. Back to his eyes flashed their uncanny glow, only with it was now triumphant assurance as well.

Mevr was doomed!

In less than an hour, uprising out of the earth, its fate, swift and awful, would leap upon it. Richard Southcote's prayers had been answered, his faith and his patience justified. Far in the bowels of the earth an awful force, more stupendous than that of the San Francisco earthquake, was minute by minute gathering to rise and smite and utterly blot out in torrents of falling masonry and crashing landslides the Hell Gate of the East.

VI

Quietly the mad hakim left the cellar and went to the room above. There his preparations were simple. Alone of Mevr had he been warned, alone knew of the impending doom. And from the Hill of Burial he would watch, as, ah God! how often had he watched and prayed, that doom overtake it.

He picked up his hat, glanced round the bare, dismal room, and turned, God's witness as he knew himself, to leave the house and Mevr forever. Then his eye fell on the book which had lain on the floor beside the photograph of his son.

It had been Jenny's Bible. He picked it up, mechanically seeking to re-set it in its shattered binding, to smooth its soiled edges. As he did so, with a strange deliberation it opened in his hands.

'Peradventure there be fifty righteous men within the city. Wilt Thou also destroy and not spare the place for the fifty righteous men that are therein?

'. . . And He said, I will not destroy it for ten's sake.'

Outside, through the drifting heat-waves, came the droning purr that was the voice of Mevr; within his house the mad hakim stood and re-read of the mercy promised to another City of the Plain.

'. . . And He said, I will not destroy it for ten's sake.'

If there should be ten righteous men in Mevr—

Suddenly Southcote's ringing laughter cracked the silence. The Bible, hurled against the wall, showered the floor with flimsy leaves . . .

Underfoot, in Mevr, and for the third time that afternoon, the ground shook.

VII

It was near sunset. Out of the east the massing clouds drove swiftly towards the City of the Plain. A thin wind blew.

Through the deserted Suq es Iraq a mule clattered. Its rider was an old man with smouldering eyes. Squatting in an alley-way were two beggars, and one of them leant out to peer after the rider.

'God! Saw you the mad hakim? His face—'

'I see only the sky,' said the other, uneasily. 'There is death in it.'

Upon the foulness of Mevr, in its brutal pleasures and its jaded voices, began to descend some such feeling. A strange quiet held the city. And overhead, steadily, unwonted storm-clouds massed.

Hastening from the doomed city to the Hill of Burial, the

mad hakim looked down the street towards the Southern
Gate and saw it thronged with the stalls of the afternoon's
chaffering. The way was blocked.

Southcote pulled up his mule. One other way out of the
city remained for him to take – through the street unvisited
and loathed, the place where his son had been murdered.
Was it not fitting that he should pass through there?

At the thought he shuddered and turned his mule. Then
he glanced up at the sky. He must hasten.

Right down through the narrow opening he drove his
mount, betwixt open cesspools, under the evil lower of
overhanging, crumbling balconies. And then, above his head,
in Persian in the Arab script, he read an ancient inscription:

The Street of Ten

VIII

What was that! Some dim association of the numbers
clashed in, his mind. He half halted the mule, and the
beast, clumsily, swung to one side—

'Curse you!'

The mad hakim looked down. Almost under the mule's
feet sprawled a naked brown child. Its mouth was open, its
eyes pierced upwards a surprised terror . . . Came a stamping of unshod feet in the dust, a lean arm outreached, and
the brown mite whisked away. Ahmed the scavenger,
weeping salvage in his arms, and cursing with the resource-
ful obscenity of the East, glared up at Southcote.

Dazedly the old man met his eyes. Within his brain, as at
the stroke of a bell, he heard some voice count.

'*One!*'

The mule plunged on. The street twisted leftwards. On
the sidewalk a man and woman moved lurchingly.

An everyday sight in the tainted city; some woman of the
streets leading a victim to her house. Yet, passing, it

seemed to the mad hakim that somewhere, before, he had seen those two—

An unnameable impulse made him look back. The man was the black-bearded camelier of the Suq es Iraq: the woman, she whom Southcote had seen him fell to the ground. Came the ruffian's shamed voice:

'Courage, little sister. I will not leave you.'

And again, within Southcote, spoke an unknown voice: '*Two*!'

With the mad hakim rode some haunting presence. Up to the sky he looked again. The sun had vanished. The overhead wind was a thin scream. A lowering greyness had fallen on Mevr. Far thunder rumbled. From the path of the mule a strange group arose and staggered aside.

It was a man, bent almost double under the inert body of another. Southcote pulled his beast up, heard a voice that was not his own question:

'What ails the man?'

From under the weight of the Turk, Abdul the grave-robber looked up at the Englishman with red-rimmed eyes.

'He is my brother. I was stung of a viper. You would not come when he cried your help on the Hill of Burial. He sucked the poison from my wound. Now he dies.'

Haggardly the old doctor stared. Within him, ever since entering the vile stew where his son had been murdered, had arisen an awful doubt. Now it clamoured in his brain. Ahmed, the camelier, these grave-robbers—

Crash! went the thunder. For a moment, blindingly, a dagger of fire quivered down the Street of Ten. Southcote's terrified mule bucked and clawed at the air . . .

IX

When he came to himself he seemed to be peering through a red mist. In his back was a terrible pain. He tried to move and lay unmoving.

The red mist cleared. A crowd of faces were peering down at him. The mule had flung him violently against a great corner stone.

He tried to moisten his lips; failed; made a desperate effort to sit up; lay still . . . And then, yet seeing clearly, hearing distinctly, he understood.

Paralysis. Death.

And upon his tortured brain at the thought, wearily, there came great peace.

X

In Damascus, twenty-three years before, a querulous old man had died, cursing the son who had disgraced his name, and who stood by his bedside, dry-eyed and scornful, to the last. In life the old man had availed little; in death he left a memory that had consequences unguessable.

Through the crowd Selim of Damascus pushed his way and knelt by the side of the mad hakim, and gathered him in his arms. As he strained to lift the limp body, one touched him on the shoulder.

'I will take his feet, brother.'

It was Ali, the murderer-bravo.

'For he is old, Selim.'

Together they lifted him. Homeless themselves, they looked around them doubtfully. Then a woman's voice called near by.

'In here.'

In the doorway of a house of shame stood a weary-faced woman, beckoning. Overhead the thunder rumbled as Selim and Ali bore the body of Southcote into the dark entrance of the house of Miriam the harlot. She guided them down a corridor into a large room where, on a bed, another woman lay moaning and fever-flushed. The heat of the place was stifling.

At a table a man was pouring a dose from a medicine bottle. He looked up. Miriam nodded.

'I bring another, "Mitri". He was thrown by his mule.'

She motioned to the two men. Southcote they laid on a pile of rags which did duty as another bed. Miriam knelt behind him and raised his head. 'Mitri' came across the room, halted suddenly, stood swaying unsteadily.

'My God! Southcote!'

So, for a minute, 'Mitri' standing as if petrified, Selim and Ali lingering in the doorway, the harlot kneeling, weary-faced. Then, drunkenly, 'Mitri' spoke.

'Do you know who this is, Miriam? – The father of Anah's seducer; the father of the thief who ruined the daughter whom you reared to be other than you are; the father of the man who made your daughter – that.' He pointed to the wasted woman upon the bed, and ceased, and swayed a little upon his feet.

Outside the lightning flashed. Miriam looked up with weary, unchanging eyes.

'I know it is the mad hakim – the father of Dick, whom you killed because always have you loved Anah and I prayed you to do it. But our hate helped nothing, friend. Anah dies, remembering only the dead lover whom she tried to save . . . You must help this old man. And God will judge.'

By the side of the Englishman 'Mitri' knelt unsteadily. As he did so the old eyes opened, and slowly from them a tear trickled down the still face.

XI

A living soul in a dead body he had lain, the while blinding revelation came upon him. Dick, the son for whom he had cursed Mevr – Dick, a seducer and thief; Dick, righteously killed by the drunken 'Mitri' . . .

For a little, listening to their voices, that alone had been upon him, and bitter as death was the taste of the knowledge. And then, printed as in letters of fire across his vision, he saw the passage in Jenny's Bible.

'Peradventure there be fifty righteous men within the city. Wilt Thou also destroy and not spare the place for the fifty righteous men that are therein?

'. . . And He said, I will not destroy it for ten's sake.'

Blindly, blasphemously, he had rejected what was surely a command. Righteousness? Who were the righteous? Who, in the shadow-show of life, might lift him a light whereby to judge and condemn his fellows? Yet he, vengeful and hating, had done so, the while the harlot and the thief, the drunkard and the murderer, reached to unguessed heights of pity and forgiveness, heroism and shamed kindliness . . .

Righteousness? As a silver thread he saw it now, winding through the lusts and cruelties, the filth and crime of every life in Mevr. And of Hope and Faith and Charity was it woven. Before him he saw the scavenger, the two graverobbers, the camelier, the murderer and the thief, 'Mitri', Miriam, Anah – those in whom, unguessed of him, had lain the seeds of righteousness – passing in the vomiting doom of Mevr, the doom of which he alone had been warned, the doom he was helpless now to avert . . .

Was that God's will? Up at 'Mitri' he stared, and remembered that voice which had counted within himself as he witnessed the unguessed heroisms of the Street of Ten. Surely he heard it speak again . . .

Kneeling beside him, they saw the sweat start out on his forehead, heard him breathe as one in a nightmare, saw the glare in his eyes. Then, with an awful effort, he sat upright, heedless of their attempt to restrain him. His head swam.

For an awful fear had suddenly gripped him. Was his vision false? By some new law other than that which had doomed the Cities of the Plain could righteousness indeed be reckoned?

Aloud, in the stifling room – desperately, with sudden inspiration – he began to count. Ten righteous . . . From Ahmed the scavenger to the murderer of his son . . .

. . . *If there should be but Ten* . . .

And there were but NINE.

Again, peering round the dusking room, he counted. Then, in the shadows about the doorway, between Ali the murderer and Selim the thief, he saw stand for a moment One whom he had never known. One with bleeding hands and feet and hidden face.

A quarter of an hour later the bells of warning clanged out over Mevr, and from house to house the watchmen cried the message brought to the Governor from a brothel in the slums. Out into the safety of the plains and the falling dusk of that Easter Day, just as the first tremors of doom shook the City of the Plain, streamed the multitudes of fugitives.

And through the multitudes a murderer and a thief, two of those reckoned in the sum of the righteous Ten, carried Southcote to safety.

Roads to Freedom

Pity is a rebel passion. It caused a man to become a convict and played a strange part in his road to freedom.

THREE HOURS HAD passed since his escape.

It had been entirely unpremeditated. The gang had been returning at mid-day from the quarry. A bank of summer mist had drifted across the moor. The gang emerged from the quarry ravine into the light, tenuous curtain of vapour.

The two warders shouted to the convicts to close up. A wind stirred the mist as they cleared it. Then one of the warders swore and shouted to his companion.

The little, thin-faced convict in the rear file had vanished.

Three hours ago. The tolling of the prison bell had ceased. The siren had ceased to hoot by the great entrance gate. The mist had cleared from the purple of moor and hill. Three good miles away from the quarry, half-way up the side of the Tor, Clayton lay on a ledge, sick with self-disgust the while he watched the pursuit close in on him.

As he deserved. Lord, of all the hopeless, snuffling, sentimental half-wits temporarily at large.

He was all but exhausted. Prison had not hardened his frail city body and the first desperate dash through broom and gorse had torn great ragged v's in his coarse canvas clothes. There had been rain earlier in the day, and he was mud-smeared from head to foot as result of convulsive undulatings across an exposed potato field. His feet, what with wading in a stream to delay pursuit in case the hounds were put on his track, were simmering damply inside his thick, unpleasant boots. He lay with a little trickle of blood oozing from his lips. He had always had a bad lung.

Oh, *what* an infernal fool!

For at the moment of his escape he had struck away in the opposite direction from the Tor. He'd had no intention of making the prison landmark. From others he'd learned how almost every escaping convict made that mistake. Its slopes invited a fugitive. Similarly, unfortunately, they invited pursuit. On notification of an escape prison lorries at once swept out to the Tor, encircling it and disgorging parties of warders, and none had ever been known to pass through the Tor cordons into the wild country beyond, which was indeed the best point of escape – once attained.

So, outside the belt of mist into which he'd seen the rest of the gang clump heavily, he'd crept and crawled and fled pantingly across open spaces to further clumps of cover, southwards, in the direction of the scattered Bewlay village farms. In the hot summer weather, with a heat-haze over all the land, he had been conscious that his small, yellow-brown self would seem little more than a flitting shadow to the casual observer. And in the direction of Bewlay lay possibilities of further concealment, hiding until the coming of night, and a burglary in pursuit of clothes.

So he had planned, the hooting of the siren still in his ears, resting for a breathing space in the shadow of a field-rick of hay. Almost, for a moment, he'd forgotten planning altogether, burying his face in that new-cut hay, drinking in the smell and the savour and the free, wild cleanness of it. Free . . . A bee had fallen out of a clump of clover beside him and hummed about him for a moment and, following it, he'd raised his eyes and seen – opportunity.

The sound of the warning gun crackled over moor and field from the prison at that moment. The old man was halted, leaning on his stick, his face turned in the direction of the sound, his lips fallen slightly apart, slowly fumbling one the other in a ruminating toothlessness.

He stood not five yards away from the field-rick.

For a moment Clayton had lain rigid, watching the old farm labourer who was obviously past working age, who was obviously almost senile and certainly incapable of making any resistance to a sudden attack. No need to hurt him much. Grab him and throw him. Off with his jacket and trousers. Tie his hands and feet with one of the straw ropes from the rick. Shove him under a swathe of hay and then clear out by Bewlay.

Just one little rush. The deaf old ears'll never hear you coming over the grass. Won't hurt the old man. Be discovered before night. Easy. Splendid chance.

And then the old man, unwitting any other presence in the field, had turned about and made his slow way across

the second hay-crop towards Bewlay, unharmed and un-
pursued.

For, even while his reason argued the comparative harm-
lessness of his attack upon the old man, the would-be
attacker's imagination had, as ever, broken loose . . .
Shock. Heart failure. The old body crumpling to stillness
under his hands. Or buried in the hay, moaning and
twisting, the old face turning grey, turning black, all his
days and nights of fields and freshness and earth-smells
ended in a pain-stabbed darkness of suffocation . . . Can't
do it. God, can't do that . . .

On the slopes of the Tor, Clayton, panting, lay and
watched his pursuers and remembered the moment, and
snarled at the memory. Why hadn't he? White-livered
skunk! Choking the life out of someone else – wasn't it
the way of the world? Never learn sense? Weep for the
warder's adenoids in the punishment-cell next . . .

And then that next encounter after creeping from the field
where he'd seen the old man.

He'd come upon the woman by chance – or rather, upon
evidences of her nearness. The Bewlay stream broadened
and hesitated into a half-lake, half-estuary just beyond the
hay-fields, and then twisted southwards on its journey to
the sea. In the line of approach from the hay-field it was
fringed with poplars and willows, and, after a rapid rush
across the high-road to the shelter of the poplars, he'd
climbed a fence and made his way amid the tree trunks,
very thirsty, smelling the hot, summer flow of water.
Hadn't seen or heard a soul. Till he'd pushed through
the last of the willows and almost stumbled over the neat
pile of clothes by the brink of the estuary.

He'd started back at sight of them, and crouched by a
bush and looked round. Not a sound. And then, away over
towards the other shore, he'd heard a rhythmic splash, had
glimpsed a head and arm and shoulder. A swimmer,

making the other bank in lazy, enjoyable stokes. The sunshine glinted from his wet shoulder.

But Clayton had looked again at the clothes, looked back towards the swimmer, whistled to himself.

They were a woman's clothes.

He'd found himself grinning at them – planning, deciding, remembering. Clothes and paraphernalia of some walking tourist – pack, skirt, jumper, shoes, stockings, beret, oddments. Large enough shoes – some bouncing modern female hiker attracted to a quiet dip. Fit him all right. Best disguise possible. Last time—

Crouching by his bush, remembering that last time with a catch of breath. Years ago, after a night of amateur theatricals. Had played some woman part or other well enough. Rita had sat in the front row and clapped his performance. Then, at the end, they'd challenged him to walk down the street and accost a policeman and ask him the time and the whereabouts of a quiet, inexpensive lodging for a respectable female . . . And he'd done it. Towering policeman, fatherly and courteously jovial. Had almost spoiled the business by insisting on himself conveying the inquirer to the lodging . . . How Rita had laughed, listening to his account of it, hands on his shoulders, weak little, haughty little face upturned to his . . . With a different look from that last time he'd seen her through the fog of the court-room, staring at him in hysteric dismay the while he confessed to the forging of a cheque Rita's own neat little hand had forged. That terrified face of hers – Lord, what lies it had urged him to!

He'd jerked himself back from that unnecessary memory in sudden awareness that he ought to be donning the woman tourist's outfit. No time to lose.

The flashing arm of the bather caught his attention. She had turned about and was making her way back. Hurry then, she'll soon be here. Safe as houses to steal them. She'll spend a good hour looking for them, and another hour hiding by the side of the road in her bathing dress, waiting to hail some passing woman for rescue . . . He'd found himself biting his lips in desperation at his own apathy. Hurry, you fool!

And instead; staring at that nearing flash of shoulder, with a groan he'd again found himself in the grin of that inane, sentimental self who haunted his existence – the self who had ruined him, brought him to prison, spoilt his chances in the hay-field. The woman – a walking tourist attracted to a quiet and unpremeditated dip in this lonely place – the chances were ten to one she had no bathing dress at all. Gone in for a nude and sensible swim. Enjoying it there in the sun. And then back to the bank, shake herself, feel thirty years younger than when she'd entered the water, look round for her clothes . . . Hunting through the wood. Getting cold. Hiding. And search parties out all over the countryside – warders first, and gangs of yokels and village toughs out beating the woods for a lark . . . Rare sport when they found her. Round in a grinning semicircle. Slow, clownish starings and guffaws, and she—

She had been quite close by then, the swimmer, and, a little sick, casting a glance of hatred at her, he'd turned round and stumbled away back through the trees to the high-road, another chance lost.

Now he lay on Bewlay Tor in the late afternoon sunshine with the cordons of searchers closing in on him, beating the heath as they might for any other vermin.

There had been nothing else for him to do but make the Tor, what with the time he had lost in the hay-field and the wood. His plan lay in waiting till the cordon tightened, creeping stealthily through it in its thinnest part, and making west in search of a third chance of safety and disguise.

The third chance. By God, he wouldn't be such a fool as miss *it*, whatever the consequences to others.

But in what direction to make a bolt? He peered through the heat-haze. Far down in the north-west glinted the pools of the wild Tor hinterland. In that direction, surely.

A crawling brown lizard against the purple brown of the Tor, he began to make his way across and down the slopes. Half-an-hour went by. By then he was half-way down the north-westwards shoulder. His immediate objective became plainer to him. A wide, shallow gully, in winter probably a roaring torrent but now a long, clayey scar, swept diagonally down to the foot of the hill. It was completely without cover, unlike the surrounding slopes.

And up either side of it, closing in upon it and then spreading out again, were coming two parties of warders – three on its left and two on its right. To the gully itself they were paying no attention. It was an impossible hiding-place.

It was also the colour of the hideous uniform in which Clayton was clad.

In another five minutes he had wriggled into it and along its clayey course. Here and there a small stone cast a long shadow in the afternoon light, and Clayton lay with his face in one of those shadows while the three leftwards searchers trudged past, one of them indeed pausing on the brink a moment to stare vacantly in the direction of Clayton's stone. When their retreating footsteps told him he still remained undiscovered, he crawled a few yards further down the dried stream-bed.

There were still the two warders to the right. But nothing to fear from them, if he played 'possum a minute longer. One minute and they'd be past and he'd have broken the cordon.

The heat-haze shimmered. Suddenly Clayton became aware of a sound near him.

Chin resting on the clay, he looked. Within a couple of yards of him a rabbit, its neck caught in a wire snare, stared at him with oval, wet eyes. It had backed the full length of the snare, and the wire had already bitten deep in its flesh. It was its scream he had heard.

They lay and looked at each other. And suddenly, digging his hands into the soil in a passionate effort at self-restraint, Clayton himself could have screamed. His reason shouted his folly and then was choked to silence in the rising tide of the old emotion. He forgot the warders, passing now almost opposite. He forgot everything in a blind passion of pity.

He found himself leaping to his feet, scrambling to the side of the crouching captive, seizing it, prying loose from its neck the murderous garotte.

The rabbit screamed in an agony of fear. There came a shout from the right.

Rabbit in his hands, Clayton crouched half-erect and looked.

Oh, my God!

Ten yards away the two warders met his gaze. He turned his back upon them and waited, still with the trembling rabbit clasped against him.

Half-an-hour later the last five searchers met in two parties at the far side of the Tor.

'Who was that down there in the gully after we passed? We heard an infernal screeching.'

'Eh? Oh, that old poacher from Bewlay. He'd been snaring rabbits and wasn't anxious to recognise us. Turned his back on us when we called to him. Not another soul about. Guess 998 never made the Tor at all.'

First and Last Woman

ALL DAY AND EVENING I had held eastwards across an unfamiliar tundra country that had the appearance of having once suffered a bombardment of enormous meteorites. A full spring moon, flushed and wonderful, rode in the sky, when, lifting my eyes, I saw the shadowy cliff-edges of a giant plateau uprising a few hundred yards in front of me. Almost at the same instant I became aware of her, and halted with clumsy stealth.

'Good evening.'

The First Woman I had seen for five hundred years was regarding me curiously.

'Good evening.' I groped for my hat, and then remembered I had none. Probably such articles existed now only in museums. If there were museums.

The First Woman did not move.

'Eighteenth century, aren't you?' she queried.

'No, twentieth.'

'Oh, yes, I heard about you. Suspended animation in a vault they excavated, wasn't it?'

'Something like that.'

'Interesting.'

The moonlight scintillated up and down the barrels of the gun-like apparatus whereon the First Woman leaned. Behind her, what I had taken for a plateau was the massing of strangely fronded trees into a giant forest that towered black to the stars. Far to the east, over the place where London had once been, a hazy new cluster shimmered in the Milky Way. It was the Aerial City from which I had escaped that day.

A little wind blew from the dim forest depths, and stirred the First Woman's hair. Her face was in shadow, and she was strangely garbed.

'How is it,' I asked, 'that you speak English?'

'Oh, we all learn some of the dead languages.' Her voice was oddly mechanical, without inflection or accent. 'I took English and Magyar. Being the last, I was allowed to choose as I liked.'

'The last?' Much blood-loss in fighting my way that afternoon through a brake of giant, sentient thorns had made me weak, and I leant against a rock that jutted out near at hand. 'Last what?'

'The Last Woman, of course. They aren't going to manufacture any more.'

'*Manufacture*—?'

A ghostly recrudescence of twentieth-century shame-facedness in the discussion of such matters – even with a woman whose existence outside my own sick fancy something at the back of my mind still debated – came upon me. Some different twist of meaning that the word now had, doubtlessly . . .

'Haven't you learned *that* yet?' The First Woman moved her head so that the moonlight shone full upon her face. In her icy grey-green eyes was unbelieving disgust. 'Do you think that children are still . . . *born?*'

I stared at her. The very loathing incredulity of her query carried appalling conviction. She was real. She had said . . . I covered my face with hands that shook.

'Then – then—'

Could that be why the beings of Aerial City had seemed to me so machine-like, so unhuman – even in their cruelty? Oh! impossible!

'Why, of course.'

The First Woman began to explain in a voice reminiscent of a smooth, finely-geared gramophone. Behind her, from the forest, a crackling sound, as of a gigantic body being slowly levered over dead bracken, broke out, and then died away in stealthy rustlings. The First Woman regarded me with expressionless eyes.

'No single human being alive today has been *born*. No human being has for over a hundred years. Long before that it was possible in the laboratories to build up exact reproductions of the lower forms of life, but Professor Tzerik, the negro Commissioner of the Mrxocken Institute in Uganda, was the first to manufacture a really satisfactory synthetic child. It is said to have taken him over seven years,

but in those days laboratory apparatus was still unbelievably primitive. At present the International Child-Factory in
Sumatra can turn out new humans, when called upon by
the Life-Control Council, at less than a fortnight's notice.'

The First Woman paused a moment, scanning the sky,
and by the better light I saw she was garbed as an Egyptian
maid might have been in the years of Ramessids. Her body
was slim and graciously curved.

'With the creation of the Unborn, women all over the
world revolted, and refused any longer to undergo unprofitable and unnecessary torture, like the lower animals.
Besides, in time it was made criminal by law; for, as the
years went on, the Unborn grew to dominate the earth, and
the helot-classes, in whom only base desires continued to
exist, were gradually exterminated . . .'

Far overhead, above the grotesquely-massing trees, a reef
of stars paled in the moon's splendour. The Pleiades had
changed not at all. Somehow the fact was strangely com-
forting. I heard myself question the First Woman.

'Then why produce more human beings in your laboratories? Surely you have the secret of lasting life?'

She did not answer, but stared intently eastwards over
my shoulder. I turned to look. Beyond the bush-strewn,
rocky track I had crossed lay the rolling veldt, dusk, and
still, and moonlit. Nothing there. But in the stillness of the
night I heard a strange sound, steadily drawing nearer.

'*Sirroo! Sirroo!*'

Abruptly the First Woman caught up a cloak from the
ground, flung it over the bright-gleaming barrels of the
mechanism in front of her, and, signing me to do the like,
crouched with covered face. I slipped down in the shadow
of the rock, and peered up into the sky.

Now the sound, though I could see no cause for it, filled
the night – a sound like that of the incoming surf on a rocky
shore. Then I saw. Momentarily the sky above me was
blotted and blacked out by the passage of an enormous

flying-machine – one that beat the air with wings as might an eagle. It wheeled and dipped above the place where we crouched, hovered uncertainly, and then passed on over the forest.

'An ornithopter!'

'Yes.' The First Woman uncovered her face, looked after it, and then surveyed me indifferently. 'But what were you asking? Why are more human beings manufactured? Because people get worn in time, of course, and it is easier to create children than build up the tissues of worn old men. Why should we? Life and Death are merely different arrangements of matter, and the extinction that the old animal-humans so dreaded never existed. Now, all the life-forms we use for foods are also laboratory products, and the atom-cells of a man who has passed to so-called death are often re-grouped and re-vivified in some new body.'

'Why did you hide from the ornithopter?' I inquired, listening to its far-off, fading beat in the night-stillness.

'I did not hide. No doubt you crossed one of the television plateaux this afternoon and it was searching for you.'

I thought this out. It was puzzling. The First Woman's eyes were inscrutable.

'Then you did it to save me? Why?'

'Because I wanted to ask you something.' She leant forward interested, and yet cautious, as might a woman of the dead years towards a fanged and uncleanly carnivore. 'Tell me, is it true that in your age men and women used to put their mouths together and call it love?'

The fantastic query oddly stirred my anger. 'Yes, lovers did so.' My anger vanished. Far back in the dim gulf of years I remembered times—

'But it was . . . abominable. Had you no sanitary laws then?'

'I suppose not.' I looked at her helplessly, wondering how many of the words she used possessed the same meaning in her mind and mine. 'And were you – made in Sumatra?'

The crackling sound in the forest had come to hesitant life again. A pungent, strange odour drifted down the still air. Vaguely disquieted, I looked across into the jungle maze, and then back at the First Woman. It seemed to me that in the white radiance of the moon her expression had subtly changed. She spoke:

'Do you want to live?'

'Live?' I stared at her apathetically. 'I don't know.'

'The Born always did.' For one who was but a synthetic parody of human kind, her voice was strangely touched with bitterness. 'Listen, and then it would be well for you to go. This is why I am the Last Woman. There is a story about me. Two of the laboratory assistants in Sumatra – a man and a woman – were once seen to put their lips together. They both came from some barbarian valley in the Northland, and were actually said to have been *born*. After I was placed in the First Nurseries it was rumoured that they were my – what is the word? – oh, parents. So they were put to the Lethal Death, and it was decreed that no more of the female types should be created. Ever as I grew up I was carefully watched to see if I had any traits of the Born, and because of little things – emotions which I had foolishly learned and practised in imitation of the old animal humans – it was decided that I had.' Her laughter – musical, cold, soulless – rang out contemptuously. 'As if I were such as you! Have we one thing in common? I saved you to convince myself.'

Fleecy-edged rain-clouds had sailed across the face of the moon as the First Woman talked, and the sleeping forest near us seemed to move and stretch uneasily in dreams. Dimly only did I follow her nightmare story, for I had fallen to thinking of those others – fashioned like her! – who had given men vision and high comradeship and love that had been a shining splendour since the childhood of the world.

Fantastic fulfilment of the centuries! Nothing of that which in women we had thought immutable and eternal – neither mother-love, nor mercy, nor tenderness – survived here. They had all been illusions – pitiful houses of sand builded by men on the stormy shores of Time . . .

'And why,' I said, 'did you ask me if I wanted to live?'

Weariness in her voice. 'Because you will not live long if you stay here. You saw the ornithopter? It was not looking for me. For three years now I have been isolated here, herding the giant synthetic snails they make for food across the forest in Farnboru.' She touched the gun-like muzzles beside her. 'You see the Ejector here? It is my only protection when they come at night, smelling one through the trees. This morning I threw away the last gas-cylinders, and all afternoon I have been hiding from the ornithopter which brings fresh supplies. Now do you understand?'

The stealthy movements in the jungle undergrowth seemed momentarily to hush. I rose to my feet, very close to the First Woman, and stared down at her.

'You mean to be killed? Why?'

Now the moon was sinking, even as, far away by the Aerial City, the thin grey fingers of the morning were touching the sky. But as I spoke the moonlight slanted full upon us again through a rift in the clouds. The First Woman held out an uncertain hand.

'Because I'm tired of it all.' There was something like wistfulness in her cold eyes. 'In those funny old things called books I've read that in your age, when two people went apart for a long time, they used to shake hands. Will you—?'

I took her hand. She was very near, and the dew upon her hair made it seem bound with a fragile silver net. A ghost ache of memory stirred within me again. I had known another with just such unforgettable eyes . . .

With a little sob, the First Woman looked up at me from my arms. In her eyes was dawning a dazed wonder. She hid her face.

'Then the story was true?'

Through the tree-trunks I became aware that the forest was teeming with crawling horrible Things each twice the size of a camel. From the rocky plain on the other side, other ghoulish abominations crawled in towards us. There was no escape.

Sudden conviction came upon me. I touched the First Woman's hair, and even as I did so the nauseating breath of one of the nearing monsters blew upon us in yellow spume.

'One of our old barbarian poets once said we are such stuff as dreams are made of. And this isn't real, you know. Can't be. We'll awaken soon . . . don't cry.'

And somewhere, far above the eastern marshes, a night-bird wheeled and wailed against the promise of the dawn.

The Lost Constituent

MIRZA MALIK BERKHU was born in the hut of a Nestorian silver-smith in Mu'adhan in the year of Our Lord 1200. Ten years after his birth he was sold as a slave to the Janissaries Regiment of the Pultow . . .

This is no tale of mine, you understand, but one transcribed and edited from the wordy chronicles of Neesan Nerses, sometime Nestorian Bishop of a long-vanished diocese in the Persian hills north of Sar-i-Mil. It is one of the earliest and shortest of his tales – those fabulous pseudo-histories leavened with ingenuous moralisings little to modern taste or the point generally. Living in an un-literary century – he began writing about the year 1245 in the Gregorian calendar, though twelve years earlier according to his Julian reckoning – he had no competitors to fear, and in his darkness of medieval ignorance knew nothing of

the vivid phrase or the startling opening. No living reader
but would skip the first three thousand words and fifty years
of narrative to reach Baghdad of the year AD 1250, on a
morning of the second date-harvest.

A city colourful enough that morning, as the Bishop
paints it: banner-hung, crowded and prosperous, with its
sheen of lacquered minarets and gilded towers, its Tigris a
rippling scimitar in the sunlight. Half the palace guards had
ridden out an hour before sunrise to bring the conqueror in
from his camp beyond the Western Gate. They had ridden
out, stout young men who had never known war, with
much beating of drums and clanging of gongs, to the
amusement of an irreverent populace already thronging
the streets. The shouted advice and aspersions of the
Baghdadese the Bishop records with unclerical zest, but
the passage is best left untranslated, especially as it delays
both the action of the story and the passage of the sleek and
sulky guards. Men with grievances, the guards. They had
ceased to count. They were out of favour, forsooth, because
that unquiet fool Mirza Berkhu was returning from one of
his wearisome victories.

Their private thoughts they appear to have kept to
themselves, however, the while their captain spoke a long
address of welcome to Berkhu at the head of his dusty and
saturnine troops. Berkhu himself greeted the address with a
sardonic grin. In chain-armour, six feet in height, mounted
on a black Arab, his nose under the peak of his Christian hat
looking more beaked and aggressive than ever, he rode
beside the captain under the archway of the Western Gate.
And there indeed he half-halted.

'What's this smell?'

The guards' captain smiled sourly. 'Roses,' he said.

Rose-scent it was. The Baghdadese had surpassed themselves in preparation for the return of their hero. They had
had camel-trains of roses brought from the surrounding
suburbs, and with great blossoms, white, yellow, red, had

hung River Street in scented curtains. Berkhu was almost startled, though he recovered quickly enough, and thereafter for nearly àn hour rode forward between parallel banks of screamed approbation and showering favours, till his horse and armour were smothered with roses. Once he glanced up towards the gleaming heights of the Citadel – the palace where, as boy-slave to an entire regiment, he had been lucky to steal as much as three hours' sleep a night . . . But God! how he had slept! Never such sleep as then!

Black faces, brown faces, small wizened yellow faces, even – those last the faces of little Hun traders from the remote north. So, amidst a kingdom of uplifted faces, rode Mirza Malik Berkhu, First General of the Caliphate, a Minister of the Divan, a poet, a heretic, and a notorious lover and wine-bibber. Fresh from the slaughter of raiders on the borders of Turkestan he came, and at either saddle-horn dripped a dozen severed heads: heads of hideous raiders whose kin would yet very terribly avenge them. But of that Berkhu suspected nothing. Nor would he have cared greatly had he done so.

Hideous heads. They might give thanks to God they were freed from the necessity of embarrassing their owners. Dead. They who had been quick now very slow. What had happened to them?

And, staring down at the trunkless dead, for the first time in his life he found himself thinking of life. He had been too busy living ever to think of it before. Living – since those days as the slave-boy in Citadel . . . Weariness and sleep, thirst and satiety, dust and boredom – unceasingly, unendingly. Life; his life. All life? Nothing else in it? Or had he mislaid some ingredient that might have transformed the whole to a thing like – like a bugle-cry in a camp at morning?

Sound without earache? . . .

So, the bored General in fantastic speculation, he rides through the streets of Baghdad and the lengthy prosings of

Neesan Nerses, who arrogates to himself considerable knowledge of the happenings inside Berkhu's head, and approves them not at all. They were, one gathers, wrong-headed.

The palace gates: Fanfare of trumpets, the carpet of state, dismounted procession. And there, within the great rooms, remote in that building like a worm remote in the wood-work of a cabinet, says Nerses, Berkhu came into the presence of the Caliph. A little, dried-up man, white-faced, the Caliph, and as Berkhu prostrated himself with clash of chain-armour he sat a long while considering his general. And Berkhu knew himself very near to death, and grinned sardonically in his beard, considering the floor under his nose. He had become too popular and well-loved in Bagh-dad. Besides, the mullahs had been at their work against the heretic.

Presently the Worm-King spoke, and at his words guards and pages, saints and sinners, dwarfs and diviners who enlivened the lighter hours of Muhammud's successor, withdrew. Then Berkhu heard himself addressed.

'Rise, General.'

So they faced each other. The Caliph was blunt.

'I had no need of this victory or campaign. The populace forced it on me. Nor have I any need of you. So you do not return to your army.'

Berkhu laughed. It was characteristic of him, this un-seemly levity, says Nerses. 'Not even my head?'

Now those two had once been friends – long before, in the days when a gallop across the sands and the strife of spears was like wine in the mouths of their youth. And they peered at each other in that dusk and scented room, and the Caliph sighed.

'O Malik, we've come far, you and I, since those morning rides to Baqubah. What have they given you, all those years that have passed since then?'

'Fools to fight and much weariness to endure,' said the

heretic General, and also was blunt. 'But not so much as they have given you.'

The dried-up little man who ruled Islam nodded. 'That is true. Now the weary should rest. For me there is none, but for you—'

And again he considered him, and Berkhu thought amusedly of the dripping heads waiting outside on his saddle-bow. But that memory of the Baqubah rides had disturbed the Caliph's intention.

'You will retire to your palace and garden on Tigris-bank. There you will remain until I give you leave to come forth.'

Thus the little Worm-King, looking in Berkhu's mocking eyes. Then the General made another prostration, rose, and passed from that room – passed, indeed, from all the colourful life of Baghdad, and for ten long years, in macabre pursuit of life's own secret, was remote from it as the dead.

II

But that pursuit began not at once. The first few months of exile merely accentuated his boredom – though Nerses gives it a more theological name – to an agony almost unendurable. Wearied though he had been of camp and field, his army and command, never had he known such weariness as that endured, day on day, in the great blue-painted rooms of the Tigris-bank palace. They were set with gilded screens of fine mushrabiyeh work, those rooms, hung with Persian cloths, their floors mosaic'd by the cunning hands of Shiraz workmen. In one of them multitudes of chryselephantine statuettes, idols of pagan gods and spoil of a raid on raiders of the Hindu Tiger King, stood to peer unholily from floriated niche and lacquered pedestal upon the flowing of the Tigris. Fountains sprayed in the inner courts – fountains in eternal cannonade of besieging legions of lilies through the early summer and of roses and mimosa in the intenser heats. The garden-scents haunted Berkhu even in the remotest cellars to which he betook himself.

But he also wearied of wine very quickly. He wearied of the innumerable palace women, their squabblings and their lusts. In his library, unrolling from their scrolled silver cylinders the tales and romaunts of Arab imagination, he found no surcease. Rest from himself – there was none. What rest indeed had any man ever found from himself except in the blind restlessness of youth?

So for three months, while in Baghdad the indignation and curiosity over his dismissal began to die out. Within six months, his army dispersed to the limits of Irak, he was forgotten as hero and conqueror. Over-clouding that once burnished reputation arose another.

The heretic General was engaged in sorcery.

III

It was a common enough pursuit in that age and country and the word covered a multitude of darksome activities. What led Berkhu into his quest of the life-essence Bishop Nerses – who at this point mysteriously abandons the narrative and involves himself in an entirely irrelevant denunciation of the Latin Rite – only hints at in a belated and hurried aside. It was a devil-inspired memory of the dripping heads that had hung from his saddle-bow and the aching speculations they had aroused.

Life, this burden and weariness of days and years – yet if a man could re-live it deliberately might he not search out some secret certainty and splendour to light the years as with a torch? If youth came twice . . .

Slowly the hope kindled. At first his studies were little more than an amusement – a bored amusement. He had a great Riverwards room sealed to his own exclusive use, and there immersed himself in such Satanic literature as was then available; and might never have passed beyond such harmless whiling away of time but for the fact that a Greek slave from Istambul, newly come into his possession, discovered himself a chemist of some little note and considerable pretension.

Instantly he was impressed into the service of Berkhu's private room, absolved from all other duties, and promised his freedom when, by creation or rejuvenation, they had run to earth the life-formula.

Abiogenesis was as favourite a dream of the pseudo-savant of that time as it is of his successor of this. The Greek's private opinions are not recorded. Probably they were highly sceptical. Nevertheless, he taught to Berkhu all he knew, and, having been wrung dry, found himself relegated to the position of sweeper-up and bottle-washer the while his amazing pupil went on into mysteries the Greek had never essayed – not even with the aid of the still-unproven algebra.

Days swept seaward on the southern flow of the Tigris, according to the poetical but unastronomical bishop. Weeks followed them into months, into years, and remote, unapproachable in his palacewing, Mirza Malik Berkhu, once the first soldier of Islam, still climbed and adventured unceasingly amidst the ghoul-haunted slopes of sorcery.

What he had begun as an amusement, a relaxation, had become an obsession – a fact which tempts Nerses into a lengthy disquisition, unnecessarily Freudian, on the psychology of the Devil. The quest of youth, the life-essence, the life-formula, had beckoned him through experiment after experiment. Gradually the immense treasure accumulated during forty years of campaigning was largely dissipated, though the Tigris-bank palace continued to house some hundred women, guards, slaves, and parasites unclassifiable. The Greek assistant had died and his place been taken in rotation by innumerable other, drawn to Baghdad by rumour of fabulous reward. One by one they had been tested, found wanting, and dismissed – renegade mullahs, shamans from the far North, even, according to Nerses, Buddhist priests from remote Tibet. Their promises and formulae wilted under performance, for, however otherwise changed, Berkhu remained disconcertingly practical even in his sorcery.

He had had an immense furnace installed in the room of the chryselephantine statuettes – heat being a natural corollary of hellish studies, according to his chronicler – and appears to have gathered together a laboratory equipment of tanks and test-tubes and coolers extraordinary enough for his day. He had progressed from his first crude experimentings with the bones and blood of this, that and the next animal to the attempting of more complex syntheses. The furnace would whoom, the retorts bubble reddishly, and the sorcerer and his assistant of the moment pore over charts and diagrams the while some new concoction – the brain of a slave, the poison-sac of a cobra, poppy-essence, mandragora – seethed to an odoriferous spume. Then would come the testing of its efficacy: Berkhu had strong belief in testing the results on his assistants, and the emetics of the time, much in demand after each test, were crude and forcible. It was seldom an assistant stayed for a second experiment.

But Berkhu went on undiscouraged, through list after list of unhygienic recipes, the mildest ingredients of which seem to have been the livers of wolves and the hearts of bats. Until that phase passed also. The ingredients fined down. The sorcerer General was on the track of the simple, elemental things, amazed that he should have neglected them.

He had great bouquets of flowers brought to him for dissection. The laboratory was turned into a hothouse for the forcing and observation of innumerable seeds which sprang overnight, strangely manured, into sudden plants. And these, in turn, were culled and ground and pounded into nauseous mixtures which sometimes maddened and sometimes slew . . . And still the secret eluded him.

Yet, looking back over his experiments, a strange conviction grew upon him. Again and again, by a score of different routes, he had neared success in manufacture of the life-essence – but for the discovery of a single constituent. Mysterious, unnamed, unsegregated, this lost ingredient slipped betwixt the bars of formulas and tests. Again and again . . .

In research a forerunner of the moderns, he abandoned his furnace. He had a new laboratory built on the roof of his palace. There, in the blaze of the sun, great crystals were erected to concentrate light into pools of wine and water and oil and liquids unnamable. Sometimes the wavering gleams from the palace roof would scare the strayed stranger in Baghdad's streets at night, the while Berkhu experimented with the radiance of the full moon.

And still the secret eluded him.

And outside Baghdad advanced the Mongols.

IV

But Berkhu was deeper in the devil's toils than ever, says Nerses. He cared nothing for Mongols, but only for his search. A long-forgotten figure began to appear in the streets of Baghdad, to wander the heat and dust and din of the daytime bazaars, the soqs of the cameliers who came from the Gulf of Ormuz with pearls and sandalwood and outrageous travellers' tales, the quarters of the Persian poets, the kennels of the Somali dervish-troupes. At night the drowsy mullah would start at sight of that wanderer on the floor of his mosque, some ghaffir shrink into his doorway at sight of that beaked, thin nose and sardonic, searching eyes. The heretic General had abandoned his palace roof and gone out into the world in quest of the lost constituent.

If neither in blood nor bones, drugs nor scents nor sunshine lay the secret towards which he had struggled by so many roads, might not the ultimate bridge to it, this last evanescent ingredient, abide in some creed or phrase or stanza, all unwitting its own power?

But neither in fable nor fantasy, incantation nor dogma, the droning of the mullahs or the screamed revelations of epileptic dervishes could he find a clue. Nor by purchase of Christian scripts and long poring over the forgotten creed of his childhood did he find it. For, as Nerses sententiously points out, he sought not life eternal but youth on earth. His was the quest not of the humble heart but the golden grain – to recapture the years of the slave-boy in Citadel and with that as beginning upbuild a life full, perfect, un-haunted by a mysterious weariness and frustration.

And then a dreadful fear came on him and all one night he tramped the palace roof-spaces in agony – albeit a questioning, sardonic agony still. How if the lost constitu-ents of the life-essence he sought and the life he had lived were the same? He himself – perhaps it was he who was at fault . . . .

He fell to a night-long examination of himself, under the circling stars, with far lights twinkling meaninglessly on the Persian hills and once or twice vexing him from his in-quisition. What did he himself lack that the life-essence eluded him? Except youth, he had everything: Courage, strength, passion, ardour even yet, wit, fantasy, invention. Love he had known, hate he had known, fear, exaltation, hope . . . Everything. What dream or desire in the minds of men had not been his?

Women?

Next morning he abandoned his hermit-existence. He emerged into the life of the palace again – a procedure which struck the palace with the amazement due to a divine advent – had his principal wife garotted, the rooms cleansed of her lovers and favourites. Then, in this last pursuit of the lost constituent, he indulged in such debauch as the palace had never known even in its heyday. He clad himself in fine robes again, feasted on delicate foods and wines, and sent out his steward to the slave-market to purchase women. There was less selection than of old, but they brought him gorgeous creatures still – white Circassians, damask-skinned Persians, dusky and sly and spirited women of the mountains. And in their arms, in wine and laughter and song Berkhu still searched unavailingly for the golden grain.

And the Mongols drew ever nearer.

v

They were battering at the gates. They brought up great Chinese bombards and hurled jagged rocks into the city. Their battering-rams clove in the Western Gate and they poured in and swept the Janissaries back. Then the Worm-King, roused from his half-life in the Citadel, fled across the Tigris and across the desert. Mutinous, disordered, the Janissaries made but a half-hearted defence against the attacks of the yellow plainsmen. Then, in that hour of desperation, says Nerses, the populace remembered one who would surely save them, one who had been the Lion of Irak, greatest of generals.

Their shouting filled the streets below his palace and he awoke from a long meditation and went to the wall-parapet and looked down. At that the shouts redoubled. 'Berkhu! Berkhu! The Mongols – save us!'

And Nerses tells that they swarmed into the palace, kneeling in desperation and entreating him, and slowly, coming out of his dream, he listened and understood.

'The Mongols at the gates! God, why was I not told? Go back, you scum, go back and hold them. I'll follow!'

He drove them from the palace, all except a young captain of Janissaries who stayed to guide him. Then he turned and shouted for his attendants. But the palace had emptied overnight. Men and women, lovers, lackeys and favourites, they had fled across the Tigris in the wake of the Worm-King. All except one old woman, toothless and bent. She heard his shouting and came, bringing him food and clothes and armour. The Janissaries' captain had vanished down a corridor to watch from a window the swarming tumult by the Western Gate. And as Berkhu buckled on his chain-mail with the help of shrivelled hands his heart rose high and singing within him. He glanced at the face of the woman and dimly, hurriedly, tried to remember that aged, rheumy face.

'I do not remember you,' he said, snatching the scimitar from her hand.

She raised her head and looked at him, and, strangely halted, he stared back.

He remembered her then. He had thought her long dead. She was a Caucasian slave, the first woman he had ever possessed . . . . Years before, in the dawn of time. How she had hated him, how loved! That he recalled, and himself of those days, and suddenly, says Nerses, some sealed and secret chamber seemed to crumble within his heart.

'Do you remember those years, Saith? I –' he heard himself, an unwonted liar, with amazement – 'have forgotten them never, nor all the wonder you gave me then—'

The Janissaries' captain was at his elbow. 'My lord, my lord, the defence is broken again!'

Half-blinded, the old General found himself with the young man at the palace gate. There he had sudden thought and gripped the Janissary's arm. 'See to her – that old woman who tended me.'

The Janissaries' captain stared. 'What old woman? *It was some young maid.*'

Then the tumult of the street-fighting came up towards them, and Berkhu rode towards it, wondering, and took command of the flying Janissaries, and hurled the Mongols back. But behind, at three different points, their horns were blowing and the fires rising. Twice was the Western Gate cleared only to glut again with the ingress of fresh hordes, and Berkhu knew that he and the city were doomed. He drew his cavalry together and charged once more, still brooding, and then, says Nerses, in that final mêlée some realisation seemed to come upon him. He half-wheeled round, the old Lion of the River, back towards his palace, as though some secret amazing was revealed to him at long last. He shouted incomprehensible words.

'O God, the lost constituent!'

And then the charge of the invaders swept over him, and the Mongols slew him and planted his head on the Western Gate. And they took Baghdad and slaughtered therein for many days.

The Floods of Spring

IN THE LIBRARY of the Monastery of Mevr one turns the crinkled pages of the *Chronicles of Neesan Nerses* with careful fingers, lest presently those pages crumble into so many handfuls of dust. They are bound with rotting sinews, there are dark stains across the last third of them, perhaps the blood of some lost Nestorian priest; one corner of the bundle has been scorched with fire – a relic, that, of the Turkish invasion that depopulated Alarlu long after Bishop Nerses had ceased to rule and write there, looking out on the Persian hills from the high tower of his thirteenth-century diocese. And out of those ancient pages the eye brings sudden phrases unexpectedly homely or inexplicably alien, for the Bishop mingled in a cheerful amalgam record of Alarlu's life and Mongol morals, Nestorian rites and denunciations of the Roman Church, beggars' tales and Persian legends. All was grist to his mill and he wrote with an omnivorous disregard of plausibility and stylistic criteria that in happier times might have earned his writings fame and fortune from many a groaning printing-press.

But it was not until my second week in the Monastery library, bending in some weariness over the long, looping scrawl of the Nestorian script, that I came on this tale of Zeia and Romi which I have called the Floods of Spring. It bears no title at all in the Bishop's record. The sheets on which it is written lie crumpled betwixt a treatise on goat-breeding and a dissertation on demonology – and whether this is their appropriate placing by the Bishop himself, or but the chance cataloguing of later ages, I found it impossible to guess. The story had been begun and left off several times. On the margin of the first page, indeed, is scrawled, as thought in irritation: 'But surely this was only a dream that came to us at Bushu . . .'

One visions the Bishop hesitating above his script, frowning at it in indecision the while the daylight waned from the hills of Alarlu. Dream or delusion – how else explain that double avatar and immolation in the ruined lands of the Bushu Nestorians?

II

It was 1262. The Mongols had gone, leaving Baghdad smoking and desolate, and its few surviving inhabitants free to creep starving from well and cellar to gaze on that desolation. Gone also, never to return, in the company of his Mongol friend and lover, was the Bishop's only son. Winter closed in on the upland plateau of Alarlu, kept by its Nestorian farmers, and Nerses retreated to his high tower and his writings the while the cold grew more intense, though across the waste lands of Iraq the sun heats burned fierce and vivid still. Out of that burning desolation, penetrating up even to the Bishop in his tower, came presently rumours and tales of the mangled world the Mongols had left behind. Amima Nerses came back one day from buzzard-shooting in the foothills, her bow slung across her back, on her pony a dying woman who still clasped the skeleton of a child in her arms. She had had no food, the woman, for many days; there was no food to be found in the plains, nor any prospects of it, for not only had the Mongols destroyed the crops – they had broken down the ancient irrigation system, smashed in the dams and flooded the cornlands . . . The Bishop heard the story, fed the woman, saw her die, and went back to his tower to write that fierce pacifist diatribe which reads as incongruous to his century as a treatise on psychoanalysis. The plains and their horrors – thank God for Alarlu and the safety of his Nestorians!

But there were others of his creed remote in those plains. They had heard of him, though he not of them, and journeying across a land of famine and murder, they arrived at Alarlu late on a raining night in January.

Amima, bursting into the Bishop's room, brought the news of them.

'Six of them – marshmen from some place on the Euphrates called Bushu. They have already eaten three ducks and all today's loaves.'

'We must not be inhospitable,' reproved the Bishop, 'seeing especially that they are of our Faith.'

'It was only with the eye of faith I could grasp that my loaves had gone so quickly,' said Amima, flippantly. 'Their leader, Kalaitha, is now mourning over a marrow-bone and Mesopotamia. He prays that you will see him.'

So the Bishop went down to the great room where the brazier burned and the six Nestorian tribesmen sat at meat. They were tall, gaunt men, members of a Christian pocket in a kink of the Moslem Euphrates country, and their leader, the white-bearded Kalaitha, laying aside the marrow-bone reluctantly, rose and kissed Nerses' hand and explained his mission.

'The Mongols came, burning and killing and breaking

down the dams. So we fled to the marshes and there hid until they had gone. But our priest fled not, and him they killed. Now we have returned to our homes, and are a people lost, being without a priest.'

'Have you repaired your dams?' asked the Bishop.

'No,' said Kalaitha, 'for a madness of sloth has fallen upon our people, being without a priest. So we six elders—'

The six, abandoning for the time a tribe mysteriously beyond their control, had journeyed to Amarah, seeking to induce the Nestorian Bishop there to send them a priest. But the Bishop was fled. Scared and horrified at the sights of the maddened country through which they passed, Kalaitha and his companions had yet ascended the Tigris to Baghdad, in quest of *its* Bishop. But the Bishop was dead. Turning southwards again one of them had halted and pointed to the far loom of the Persian hills.

'There, it is said, a Christian Bishop rules in the mountains. The Mongols may have spared him. He will give us a priest.'

And now here in the mountains they were. Nerses was unsympathetic.

'It is an engineer rather than a priest you want,' he told them, disregarding Kalaitha's shocked look, 'seeing you have not yet repaired your dams . . . And I have no priest to give you. There is none other here but my chaplain.' He thought for a moment. 'Who rules now at Bushu in your absence?' he asked Kalaitha.

The delegation glanced one at the other with an odd unease. Nor did Kalaitha seem more assured than his followers.

'It is the no-rule of Zeia.'

'No-rule? Zeia?'

'He is a stranger who came to us from the marshes. He makes no claim to rule, yet the people follow him, though he speaks of our customs as folly. He laughed at this mission of ours in search of a priest.'

'Then he is a man of sense,' said the Bishop. 'See now to this. Return to Bushu and take to Zeia my message that he himself is to journey up here to me in Alarlu, where I myself will question him and ordain him as the priest you lack.'

Two of the delegation grinned. Kalaitha stroked his grey beard and shook his head.

'He will refuse.'

'Refuse!' It was a century when Christians did not balk at a Bishop's commands.

'So he will do. For it is he who has led the people into the madness of sloth, preaching – he and his woman Romi – that the earth is for the pleasure of our lives, not our lives for the slavement of the earth. Also, he says of priests that they must be either children or fools, or more often both.'

This lunatic-sceptic of the marshes sounded not uninteresting, thought the Bishop. He walked the room, meditating the matter, watched the marshmen. It was a difficult matter.

'Tomorrow I will decide what to do for you. Meantime, you shall stay here and eat.'

'We have been much an-hungered crossing the plains,' agreed the grey-bearded Kalaitha, brightening. 'Our stomachs being saddened by memory of Bushu, whose people are without a priest.

III

Half that night the Bishop walked the room of his tower, listening to the late winter rain sweeping over Alarlu. A mission of folly if he went on it, yet – escape from these rooms haunted by remembrances of his lost son . . .

In the morning he called up Amima as she was mounting her pony in the courtyard, preparatory to riding out on her usual rounds of the plateau boundaries.

'My child, almost you rule Alarlu as it is. Could you and Eidon, the chaplain, heed to it between you for a month?'

'For a year, if need be,' said Amima, thoughtlessly. And then was startled. 'But you—'

'I am going down to the plains with Kalaitha and his men to see to this madness in Bushu.'

IV

He has left but scanty record of that journey across the ruined lands to the southern Euphrates. I think they took the eastern road, skirting Baghdad. At least, the Bishop comments on the plentitude of game in the Persian foot-hills, and, later, of a man who was reputed to rear serpents in a hidden farm near Baqubah, and sell their eggs at profit. Almost, one can believe, he felt inclined to abandon his mission and turn aside to investigate the activities of this unorthodox poultry-farmer. Near Eik a band of robbers rode out and assailed the Nestorians, and the Bishop shot two of them with arrows from the Mongol bow his son had brought to Alarlu. Kalaitha's companions fought valiantly, putting the attackers to flight, but Kalaitha vanished and was later found hidden in a nullah, combing his beard thoughtfully, peering from behind a tussock of grass, and declaring that courage went from a people that lacked a priest.

'It is better to lack a priest than to lack life,' said Nerses dryly.

'So declares Zeia,' said Kalaitha, shocked.

'I will have somewhat to say to this Zeia when we come to Bushu,' promised the Bishop, taking the lead again.

And at length, after venturings bloody and fantastic enough from our view-point, but so commonplace to the age and country that the Bishop but notes them in passing, they forded the Tigris at a spot somewhere below the modern Kut, crossed the lands between the two rivers, and late one evening reached the eastern banks of the Euphrates. Beyond the River was a brown, dusk land,

and even in that dim light it was possible to see on the far bank the heaped and crumbling ledges where once the dam of Bushu had stored the River waters at time of flood. Now the River ran shallow and muddy, too low in its bed to reach the dam-points even had they been operable . . . Nerses' party had been sighted by the Nestorians of Bushu, and presently a round, flat-bottomed bellum was being poled across the River towards them. But the Bishop's attention was elsewhere, held by an unusual phenomenon in that treeless land.

'What is there?' he asked, pointing beyond the dam ruins and the brown cluster of huts huddling beyond the dam. Against the evening's encroachment on the remote marshes to which the Nestorians had fled at the Mongol invasion a little gathering of plumed titans watched the coming of darkness.

'It is the Last Grove, my lord,' said the grey-bearded Kalaitha, indifferently. He rubbed his stomach, and watched the languid approach of the bellum with impatience. 'Surely it will be they have prepared a kid to feast us.'

'Last Grove?' queried the Bishop. 'Of what?'

'Of the Ancient Garden,' said Kalaitha. 'So were we told in the days when we were a people that lacked not a priest.'

v

Next morning the Bishop rose from his bed in the guest-hut at the first coming of the light. Bushu still slept. A little unplanned grouping of huts, odoriferous and insanitary enough, one imagines, even in the white wonder and stillness of the morning. But the Bishop tells nothing of that: he lived in an unfinicky age. Wearied no longer, for he had taken no part in Kalaitha's feast and retired early to the guest-hut on the previous evening, he walked to the verge of the village. A marsh bird wheeled over his head. Around, in the lush grass, fed straying goats and kids. Bushu lay before him, with its flood-ruined lands. Behind, in the sunrise, was the soft sweep of the Euphrates waters.

Now the Bishop saw that there had been two dams – the main-feed from the River and the long storage-dam. Midway the latter, a half-submerged islet, had stood the Last Grove. Then the Mongol guran had descended on Bushu, smashed in the river flood-gates and the gates of the feed-dam, allowed their cumulated waters to pour into the storage-trench, and seen the ancient banks of the latter melt and crumble in an avalanche of mud.

So it must have been. Now, viewed from this lower side, the bottom of the storage-dam was but a wide swathe of grass encircling the shining tamarisks of the Last Grove – a swathe of vivid greenness in those landscape browns and greys that were as yet unstirred by the black loam prickings of re-cultivation.

All this the Bishop noted, and then he saw something else – a woman coming towards him from the direction of the tamarisks. She walked dreaming, with unbound hair – a free, sweet walk, says the Bishop. Presumably, unlikely though it seemed, there was some bathing-place beyond the grove which accounted for her lack of costume. He would have retired discreetly enough, but that it was too late. She had raised her head and seen him. She came forward, embarrassed not at all. She stood in front of him, smiling at him – smiling down at him, as he realised with a little shock, from her great height.

'You are the priest from the mountains?'

Her voice seemed to the Bishop as sweet and alien to a Nestorian woman as her walk. He had thought her young, but now he was uncertain – uncertain as he was of the colour of her eyes and skin and hair – the magnificent mane, this, garmenting her deep-breasted beauty not ineffectively. Young eyes, gay eyes – and yet within them a heart-breaking tiredness . . . He tells how he shook himself to sternness.

'I am the Bishop Nerses. Is it customary for the women of Bushu to greet strangers – so?'

'Custom?' The great eyes opened puzzledly. Then lighted with the sun in them. The woman laughed. 'I do not know.'

He had an inspiration. 'You are the woman Romi – the wife of Zeia?'

'I am Romi – for so was the child called who slept and slept in my arms and would not wake.' There was no gaiety at all in her eyes for a moment, but only tiredness. 'As for Zeia, he also sleeps.' She sighed and laughed in a breath. 'He was always a laggard.'

She turned away from him lightly. Her action had the discourtesy of a child's. He stared after her frowningly, and then for a moment suffered from a brief hallucination. Almost he started forward with a cry—

That walk of hers – it had been his wife's. So the mother of Amima had once walked, and no other woman in the world.

VI

Three hours later, goes on the Bishop, a score or so of the Bushu Nestorians, headed by the grey-bearded Kalaitha, gathered on a riverward space outside the village to listen to him. This was the purpose of the gathering, Kalaitha told him, and Nerses regarded the unauthentic venerableness of the headman in some perplexity.

'But what am I to tell them?' he asked.

'That I do not know, my lord. For we are a people without a priest.'

There was little help to be had from this bending reed, the Bishop decided, and looked upon the gathering without enthusiasm. Less than a score out of a village population of over three hundred!

'Where are the others?' he asked Kalaitha.

'They would not come,' said the headman, 'being busied eating or sleeping or lying in the sun.'

The sun-bathers were everywhere obvious. They trooped in pairs towards the tamarisks of the Last Grove, or lay, like beasts themselves, among the somnolent goats of the herbage stretches; reclining in the shallows of the River, their voices came down to the gathering. It was indeed madness that had come upon Bushu.

Then, as the Bishop looked round him with dark brows, two figures emerged from the huts and approached him.

One was the woman Romi, clad now in an incongruous brown cotton garment. The other was a man, gigantic, bearded, with tousled hair and garments that appeared to have been assumed in the utmost absent-mindedness. As he walked he rubbed his eyes and yawned. In sight of the gathering he stopped, regarded it surprisedly, and then, followed by Romi, walked to the front of it, inspected the Bishop with lighted curiosity, and sat down. Romi sank beside him, deep-breasted mate of a sleepy Titan. The Bishop stared at the two of them, startled. For a moment he had seen flicker in the giant's face the likeness of his own son's . . . Was this a fever that was coming upon him?

He addressed the somnolent gathering.

'Your headman came to the hills, seeking me, that I might provide you with a priest. I think he did ill in the venture. Priests do not grow on the Persian hills, even as they do not grow by Euphrates, for the plucking. Moreover, it were better to have seen to the rebuilding of the dams. How have you managed to live since your return from the marshes?'

A sleepy voice said: 'We had stores of grain hidden under the huts which the Mongols did not find.'

'And when you have eaten this stored grain – what then?'

There was silence – an undisturbed silence. The Nestorians sat and stared with bovine eyes. Romi, dreaming, looked into the bright sunlight. Zeia appeared on the point of falling asleep again. And Nerses tells that he felt anger stir within him.

'Have I come to address those bereft of their senses?' He pointed to the man beside Romi. 'You, Zeia, you have misled this people. Why?'

The giant started, yawned, stared, spoke drowsily.

'The spring comes again, O priestman. So we two heard, and came also.'

'And is not the spring the time of labour? Is there not ploughing and planting to be done, lest famine comes?'

'So we two also believed in the foolish dream we dreamt. But there are better dreams. There is sleeping and love and the sound of birds; there is noon and sun and cool grass wherein to lie when the wind comes through the trees; there are stars and the coming of the moon to watch.' He raised great grey eyes upon the Bishop.

'Ours is the older dream.'

Then the Bishop knew it was a sorcerer with whom he dealt, for under the stare of those eyes strange dreamings arose in his own brain. He crossed himself.

Romi laughed. And, laughing, Nerses saw that she wept.

VII

It was February. The Bishop walked up to the ruined dyke and considered the brown flow of the Euphrates. In a month at most the floods would come, would go roaring down to the Shatt el Arab, leaving the River at its usual level, the dam empty, Bushu doomed to starvation – if this madness still persisted among the people.

Now Nerses was no stranger, in the readings of his Church's fortunes, to the vagaries of Abelites, Abrahammen and the like. Every catastrophe brought them wailing and naked across the face of whatever land catastrophe fell upon. And, sooner or later, time gathered and destroyed them, even if their fellow-men gave them welcome and tolerance. So it would be with this Zeia and Romi, the bringers of madness to Bushu.

But when? And whence had those bringers come?

Kalaitha, questioned as to their origins, had told a simple enough story. They had been encountered in the marshes. They had come walking out of those marshes, naked and yawning, one morning while the refugees from Bushu were debating the safety of returning to their ruined village. Then a woman had recognised Zeia.

'He is my cousin whom I have not seen for years – my cousin Zeia from Shim'un.'

Shim'un was another Nestorian community, far down the River. Undoubtedly Zeia and the woman were fugitives, and still dazed, for Zeia had neither denied nor admitted the relationship. Instead, he had waved aside those crowding about him.

'We return, for the way is open again.'

But Romi had knelt and fondled an abandoned child, one whose mother was dead and itself close to death from starvation. And Zeia, impatiently, had waited while Romi lifted the child and bore it with her. Together they had held eastward, and, moved by a strange instinct, the Bushu tribesmen had followed.

Nor had the instinct been at fault. Bushu they had found deserted and the Mongols gone . . .

And soon it was like to lie deserted again, the Bishop reflected. Here before another spring would be famine and death, here, where a sorcerer lunatic of the marshes had outfaced and outfought a Christian priest. Unless—

Nerses turned from the River dyke and went down to the village. And that evening he commenced his campaign.

From hut to hut he went, taking with him Kalaitha as secular authority. To each individual he gave the command that on the morrow he was to join the others, with spade and mattock, by the verge of the ruined feed-dam an hour after sunrise.

The Bishop, as he tells, had expected resistance, if not point-blank denial of his authority. But opposition was of the feeblest. Toil was engrained in the natures of these peasants, and, sun-weary of their lunacy, they had but required the voice of decision to rate them out of it. By midnight of that February day in the year 1262 the cowed Nestorians of Bushu were pledged, one and all, to attend the dam-construction of the morning.

But for two exceptions. The hut of Romi and Zeia had been found empty.

'They walk often in the night hours,' explained Kalaitha, and would have ended with his unvarying formula but that Nerses interrupted him hastily.

'And ye have been unable to prevent them, being a people without a priest. Let be. The mad go unconscripted, even in such times of stress.'

But, falling asleep an hour later in the village guest-hut, the Bishop heard a sound that made him rise and look through the hide-shielded cavity that was the window. It was the time of the moonrise, a still hour of fleeting shadows and the dance of pale ghosts on that Euphrates land. And the sound drew nearer, and the Bishop saw the cause of it.

It was Zeia and Romi returning from their mysterious midnight excursion. Naked, crowned with flowers, their voices lifted in a low song that had neither words nor melody, yet it seemed to Nerses that he had heard it often, that so the winds sang round Alarlu, that he had heard it in the laughter and agony of many men. And with that song and the singers was a companying terror that made the Bishop reach back into the darkness by his bed, in quest of the Mongol bow.

Behind the singers stalked a lion – a great, black-maned brute of the swamps. The eyes in its swaying head glowed in the moonlight. And, as it walked, a slobbering chant came from its hanging jaws.

Then, on the verge of the village, Romi turned about and spoke to the beast. And it lifted its head as though listening to her, then turned about and padded away into the dimness.

So they came and passed, the two sorcerers and the beast, and the Bishop closed his eyes and crossed himself – and then looked again on the pallid moonlight and wondered if he had but dreamt.

VIII

Dawn – a spring dawn, fervid and eager, as though it were the soul of Irak herself in swift expectation of seed-time and the coming of the tiller. But all over the land where there was already famine the dams stood as heaps of rubble and charred beams, the soil lay waste and untouched, for there was no grain for food, far less for seed. Except, the Bishop noted grimly, at Bushu.

Seed here in plenty – but was there time now in which to plant it and ensure its fructification by the River?

The mainfeed-dam was a jumble as though a great Titan had trodden down all its landward bank. The locks which had connected it with the Euphrates lay buried under some fifty tons of shale and sand. The deep channels of the main distributaries had been smeared into faint traceries by the flood unloosed by the wrecking Mongols five months before . . . And the spring floods were not more than a fortnight distant.

'If only I were an engineer!' the Bishop groaned, and for the first time in his life regretted many hours spent in poring over the esoteric cults of the ages. Better he had kept to Archimedes. 'Who tended the dams before the Mongols came?' he questioned Kalaitha.

The headman brought forward two men – stolid, unenterprising labourers. They had indeed done no more than tend the old-time irrigation system. They had shored and delved and repaired with diligence enough, perhaps, but theoretic questionings of pressure and resistance had vexed their lives but little. The dams had functioned from time immemorial – or rather, from the time of that first Sargon to whom the Bishop, in another text, refers with unintentional humour as an 'ancient devil'. But Sargon's engineers were long dead, and in their place a Nestorian Bishop who was an authority on the Latin Rite and the Buddhist penetration of Fusang had to grope out method and formulæ for himself.

A third of the Bushu tribesmen he set to planting, a third to redigging the distributaries. The remainder was impounded for the heart-breaking task of clearing the feed-dam.

All that day they laboured, and Nerses, surveying their work in the evening, saw that they had made little or no impression upon the ruins. His heart sank as he thought of the short time they had before the floods came.

Next morning he withdrew half of the workers from the distributaries and joined them to the squads labouring in the dam. It blazed a red heat that day. Far off, as the afternoon drew on, Romi and Zeia were seen to stroll from the village towards the green coolness of the Last Grove. A little growl of anger went up, but the Bishop stayed it.

'Do ye grudge the demented their diversions?'

There was laughter at that – a shout of laughter that for some reason fell to a shamed silence as they watched that unhasting twain against the trees in the bright weather. Reasonlessly, Nerses felt the shame no less his. He doffed his robe then, to the wonder of Kalaitha, and joined in the task of filling with earth the great skin sacks which toiling ant-trains of women and children bore upwards to the rim of the dam. Unhasting as Romi or Zeia the sun passed across the heavens. But at nightfall half the rubbish had been cleared from the floor of the dam.

They toiled until after sunset. Then, setting a guard upon the place, the Bishop went to bed, and in the early hours of next dawn was back at the excavations. There the guard greeted him with unlooked-for news. A boat going down the Euphrates in the night hours had hailed the Nestorians with the news that the floods were earlier this year, owing to the intense heat of those spring days. The snows were already melting in the Armenian mountains.

'How long does that give us?' the guard had called to the River sailors.

'Two days, O unbelievers.'

IX

Two days – and still half the dam to clear and the River lock to unearth.

They began work in search of that lock. The massive gates lay smashed and buried, as has been said, under many tons of sand. At length, and with care, they were unearthed and brought to the surface – they, together with an ancient implement of copper and the skeleton of a girl. Some time in the ancient days a blood-sacrifice had taken place here. But the Bishop, for once, was in no mood for archaeological enthusings.

'We must have timber for new lock-gates.'

'There is no timber to be found in this land,' said Kalaitha.

Nerses pointed to the shining standards of the Ancient Grove. 'Is there not wood there?'

Kalaitha blanched. 'The Ancient Grove stood untrodden for generations until the Mongols burst the dam. Nor would we harm it now. For it is the last of the ancient Holy Places, as we were told in days when we lacked not a priest.'

'Then ye were told lies,' said the Bishop shortly. 'Call the village carpenters.'

So they were called and assembled and the Bishop put himself at their head and descended on the Grove. It was but the tiniest plantation, as he discovered, unremarkable but for its lack of rotting timber. Counting the tree-rings as each tree was hewn down, Nerses was confirmed in his belief that the grove's antiquity was but a fable. Less than a hundred years had elapsed since the trees were planted . . . He counted again, and a little chill of fear came upon him. *Less than two score years had passed, yet Kalaitha and others spoke of the Grove as unaltered since their childhood.*

x

Late afternoon. The Ancient Grove was a treeless desolation. Looking down from the banks of the main dam the Bishop could see the heaped tangle of splinters and boughs he and the carpenters had left behind. The axes, gripped in terror-taut hands, had ceased to ring there. Ceased also was that demented wailing – like the crying of lost and tortured children – which had burst on their ears in the early hours after noon.

But memory of it, as they worked to bind the tree-trunks together in the form of a new lock-gate, was with Nerses and the others still. They had paused and listened to it with blanched faces, seen in the blaze of sunlight the running figures of Romi and Zeia disappear in the tangle of the Ancient Grove, heard the wailing die to a moaning whimper that yet seemed to go on and on, far down the Euphrates country . . . Silence since then. And now another sunset was near.

Suddenly the Bishop became aware of Kalaitha and the carpenters, halted in their tasks, staring at the River.

'What ails you?' he asked the headman, and then saw himself.

The Euphrates mid-channel stream was flowing brown with silt. Far up the ruined cornlands of the River a giant beast with crested head roared and quested southwards. This was the signal of his coming, and, unused to such signal, the Bishop stared a moment appalled.

'The flood – it is coming?' he demanded, and then, as Kalaitha and the others bent guiltily to work, realised that they had but seized an opportunity to rest their aching muscles.

'Always is there a day's warning,' said Kalaitha. 'It will not come until noon tomorrow.'

XI

Two hours later exhausted Bushu went to bed in the darkness. Before them, in the Bishop's calculation, was some three hours' toil next morning ere they clove a way through the Euphrates' bank and laid a new channel to the new lock-gates. Little time to spare, but time enough.

A sickle moon came out and rode the sky that night, and in the air, says Nerses, there was a moistness he had never met before in the ancient lowlands. Despite the ache of all his bones from days of unaccustomed toil, he could not sleep, and lay wakeful for long in the dimness, in uneased tiredness. Near the time of the moonset he fell into an uneasy doze and was startled out of that by the murmur of voices near the guest-hut. As once before he raised the hide-curtain of that window, and, as once before, saw Romi and Zeia alone together in the night.

'It will be here before the dawn – quicker than they have ever known it come.' It was Zeia's voice. 'This ancient folly it will sweep away – it and the priestman. We did not dream this spring.'

So the Bishop heard, then a lower murmur of voices, then, amazed, he saw that the woman Romi was weeping.

'O my children, my children! Toil and war and death, toil and death and famine – and how may our coming end them! We are no more than a dream they dare not dream

. . . The priest is right. They would starve and die if they followed us. We must rouse the sleepers.'

'Rouse them? It would not help. In a moment it will be darkness.'

And Romi's voice: 'That is no bar to us.'

Zeia's laughter belled across the moonlight. Then the Bishop saw Romi's hands upon his shoulders.

'So once before you laughed, at the dream of another spring which passed . . . And some time – oh, some time our dream will come again, no dream, for us and all the world. But now—'

They stood and looked at each other in the waning moonlight. Then Zeia laughed his drowsy laugh again, and nodded, and hand in hand they turned about and passed out of sight, hastening. Of what had they talked?

And then, suddenly, in the dawn darkness, realisation burst upon the Bishop. The spring floods!

XII

He dragged on his robe, tore open the door of the guest-hut, ran up the village street and began to beat upon the door of Kalaitha's house. But already the watchers of the dam, standing in the dim radiance of the time between moonset and sunrise, had heard afar off a low murmur that grew to a throaty baying, that grew to the roar of a thousand wolves in pack-cry. They knew the sound for what it was, and cried their fear, and fled undecidedly towards the village. And, running, they met – or dreamt they met – two figures, naked, gigantic, racing from Bushu towards the abandoned dam.

They crossed themselves, the dam's guardians, and yelled, bursting into the village and adding fresh confusion to that already created by Nerses' eviction of Kalaitha from his bed, and Kalaitha's voiced conviction that he was being assaulted by robbers. Then, disentangling recognitions, the

awakened Nestorians of Bushu heard the news brought
thus pantingly. A groan of despair arose.

'Too late!'

Another cry followed: 'The sorcerers bewitched us from
our work. Where are they?'

'Zeia!'

'The harlot Romi!'

'Kill them!'

They broke down the doors of the alien hut. It was
empty. In the eastern sky a pallid, tentative hand touched
the blinds of darkness. The Bishop at length made his voice
heard above the uproar.

'Who will come with me to the dam?'

'Too late!'

Now from Bushu itself they could hear the sound of the
coming flood, and, slowly, the hand poised in the heavens
drew wider the curtain of the day. With that filtering of light
a strayed damguardian came stumbling into the village
street.

'The sorcerers – the dam!'

The cry brought silence. The Nestorians wheeled Riverwards and looked.

Against the promise of the sunrise, in the dimness that
was almost dawn, two Titans laboured upon the ridges of
the dam. Under their hands the black wall to the River
melted away to right and left in showering curtains of sand-
spume even as the Bishop watched. And the howl of the
nearing flood rose and rose.

They saw it then. The dark Euphrates banks glowed grey
in a reeling tide of suds, and in that moment the dam-
channel miraculously cleared clove through to the River! A
boiling yellow torrent of water poised, hesitated, whelmed
leftwards, burst through the new lock-gates, flooded and
spun and mounted till it brimmed the dam.

Then the gates closed and the surplus of water swirled
outwards to the Euphrates.

XIII

'The sorcerers . . .'

The words rose in a long sigh. The boiling flood had come and gone. Now dam and channel alike glimmered lifeless in the light of dawn.

A man near the Bishop gripped his arm and pointed.

The morning had hesitated still in the sky, strangely. Then, slowly out of darkness, that grey shape like a clenched hand grew to clarity again. From its midst a long red beam of sunlight traversed the sky, quivered, hesitated, acquired hilt and guard, became a sword, and twice, gigantic, arc'ed across the sky.

Nerses crossed himself and prayed, his mind a tumult. And when he raised his head again day had come upon the land.

Thermopylæ

I

TO SEE THE FACE that launched a thousand ships peep from below a poke-bonnet at a street-corner confessional induces a sense of shock that speedily passes into irritation. Such face, you feel, no doubt had once its appropriate function and setting; but in the twentieth century it is fantastic. Horatius kept his bridge well enough for the purpose of inspiring later ages to juvenile recitation; re-incarnated as a gangster with a machine-gun in a Chicagoan alley he loses charm. Leonidas and his Spartans, holding liberty and Thermopylæ against the hosts of Asia, were heroes, but—

And you stand, a strayed tourist in the unfrequented warrens of Cairo, and stare at that wall and inscription in the Sharia el Ghoraib.

It rises high, this street-wall that girds the rear of some ancient khan. It glimmers dour and brown and unremarkable, all the length of it – except at this one spot. For here, from a distance of three feet upwards, the dried mud is pitted and flaked as though, in its liquid state, it had been pelted with pebbles. Below those marks of an incomprehensible hail-storm, a great red stain is a dull blotch in the sun-shimmer, and carved into that blotch, in letters Greek and gigantic, is the single word

ΘΕΡΜΟΠΥΛΑΙ

You stare at it and transliterate Thermopylæ; you go closer and see a line of smaller lettering. A quotation – a familiar enough quotation.

A misascribed quotation.

Who really spoke it? You wander back in thought to forgotten pages of a forgotten history-lesson. Of course! Not Rhizos – whoever he was – but Dienekes of Sparta when they told him the Persian arrow-hail would darken the sun . . .

Fantastic thing to find inscribed on the wall of a Cairene khan!

II

It stood a wall still uninscribed that night seventeen years ago when the weavers of Selitsa – over thirty of them, men, women, and children, clinging to pathetic and parlous packages wherein were shrouded their dismembered looms – tumbled out of the Alexandria train into the dark inhospitality of Cairo Central Station.

'Are you all here?' roared Georgios Londos, a trifle

mechanically, when they grouped round him outside the station gates. They chorussed a tired and optimistic yes. Londos ran his eye over them, scratched his head, considered the flowing darknesses and jaundiced lightnings that were Cairo, and seemed a little at a loss.

'Then – we're here, then.'

Here indeed at last they were – Sina, with his wife and mother and two daughters; the Latas; the Vasos; the little thin widower with a single son and a name like a battle-cry, Kolocrotoni; these, the others, and the two who were the group's actual, if unnominated, leaders, little Trikoupi and the giant Londos. Here in Cairo at last . . .

'What shall we do now, Big Londos?' piped ten-years-old Rhizos Trikoupi from the side of his father, Elia. He voiced the silent questionings of the party.

The giant of Selitsa yawned, ear-achingly, and found solution in the yawn. His silhouette vanished, materialising to view again as a dim recumbency.

'We'll sleep. I haven't had a wink since we left Dourale . . .'

III

There was no moon that night, but presently the coming of a fine frostiness of stars. In that starlight the Greek weavers huddled in an uneasy rhythm of sleep beneath the bland bass snorings of giant Londos.

The winter nights are cold in Cairo – as you may have noticed from the terrace of the Continental. And long – when you lie on damp cobble-stones and your body exudes heat and inhales rheumatism in enthusiastic accord with some mystic law of physics. Young Rhizos Trikoupi was never to forget the feel of those cobblestones under his insufficiently-padded hip: it was so bad he thought the cobbles must ache almost as much as he did . . .

A late train chugged out of Cairo. He raised himself on

his elbow and watched its wavering comet-tail of sparks
grow dim and disappear. Perhaps on board it was some
Greek returning to Greece – Cairo to Alexandria, Alexandria by unending discomforts of the trading boat to Dourale, Dourale to – perhaps someone on board that train
would even journey up from Dourale to Mother Selitsa in
the eparchy of Oitylos!

Once Spartic of the Spartans, Selitsa town. But its
weaving community had fallen on evil days and were near
to starving when Londos, a lumbering Moses, knocked
from door to door and at each delivered his ultimatum.

'Stay here – and starve; abroad – we may eat. Greece buys
but the goods of the American machines; Mother Selitsa has
no need of us – but she's sent our reputation abroad. Such
cloths as ours still sell well in Egypt. Let us go there.'

And here the most of them were – the last of their money
gone in fares for their varied and uneaseful journeyings –
sleeping on the Cairene cobble-stones, waiting for the
dawn.

Rhizos laid his head down again, and again sought sleep.
But, with a pallor upon the stars, the night had grown
colder than ever. He found young Kolocrotoni awake near
him, and they conversed in whispers, looking at a sky that
grew darker and darker in the moment before morning, and
then was suddenly a flaunt, all along the flat roof-spaces,
with the blown streamers of a host of crimson banners. The
boys stared raptly, the cold forgotten.

'When we've beds,' averred young Kolocrotoni, cautiously, 'it mayn't be so bad to live here.'

Rhizos remembered giant Londos's promise. 'Our
Mother has a fortune waiting us here.'

IV

And then—

Were this still no more than prelude I might sing you a

very pretty Odyssey indeed of the wanderings of those Selitsa weavers in search of a place in Cairo wherein to lay their heads. Penniless, full of hope, and much be-cursed by the Greek consul, Londos and Elia Trikoupi tramped the streets while the other males guarded the women and looms and grew hungry and thirsty and were evicted by carbine'd gendarmes now from one squatting-place, now another. For Cairo declared itself overcrowded and poverty-stricken already. 'Go back to Selitsa,' said Cairo, literally and in effect. Whereat Londos, an uncultured man, cursed it forcibly. 'We'll stay in Cairo and set up our looms,' said he, 'on a midden – if need be.'

Not that they might not have found employment. But they had learnt, they and generations before them, tenacity in the bitter Peloponnesus. They were determined, with an altogether regrettable archaic obstinacy, to erect their own looms, not to work for others. They found an archway under which they were allowed to camp, and there endured existence for three days until on the third midnight giant Londos returned to them in some excitement and shot the sleepers out of sleep, and some of them nearly out of their wits, with his shout:

'I've found it!'

Dazed and drowsy, they packed up and set out after him, tramping through the dark Cairene streets for hours, a grotesque procession enough. Until beyond the Bab el Zuweiya, and at the foot of the Sharia el Ghoraib, Londos halted and pointed. And the place to which he had brought them was the cul-de-sac wherein the sharia terminated, a waste space of half an acre amid the high walls of the surrounding khans. Once it had been a rubbish depository, but had been long abandoned for even that purpose. Yet still from the ancient buried offal arose a sickening odour.

It troubled even the nostrils of the gentle Elia Trikoupi, no æsthete. 'Has it not – a little perfume?' he asked, turning diffident eyes on the giant. Whereat Londos's immense laugh boomed out over the sleeping Warrens, startlingly. The other Greeks took it up. They stood and rocked with laughter in that Cairene midnight, hungry, forsaken, light-hearted. The giant of Selitsa wiped his eyes.

'Little Perfume – what a name for our midden! You have christened it, Elia!'

v

They set to building sheds on the edge of it next day – the waste and odoriferous piece of land claimed by no one, the seeming haunt of half the pariah dogs and all the amorous cats of Cairo. They tramped to the edge of the town, to Nile-bank, to the Greek quarter, begging, borrowing and stealing stray pieces of timber and canvas. They delved out foundations at the edge of the waste – the smells that arose were dreadful – and drew up the huts at an angle fronting towards the Sharia el Ghoraib. In three days the huts were almost habitable. And then Londos procured a slab of wood and a piece of charcoal and, grinningly, scrawled a legend on the slab, and nailed it up above the angle hut:

Little Perfume

They were on an island, the Selitsa settlers – an exceedingly dry island. There was no water nearer at hand than that in the public fountain at the far end of the Sharia el Ghoraib, From this fountain water had to be fetched – a task which fell to the children, for the older settlers from Selitsa, men and women, betook themselves to the looms as soon as these were erected. On an advance of yarn and silk they set to weaving the mantles that had already won them reputation in Egypt, and the straggling, hourly procession of children making towards the fountain would hear the thump and boom, rise and fall, behind them in every hut of Little Perfume.

It seemed to them the only friendly sound in Cairo. The sharia looked on them sourly, and at the fountain itself they would find the Arab hosts marshalled to give battle – children who threw stones and dirt, and spat with some venom. Ring-leader of this Asiatic opposition was a small, ferocious and underclad girl whose favourite amusement was to drop dust-bricks into the fountain just prior to the arrival of Rhizos and his companions. Rhizos bided his opportunity, found it one afternoon, dropped his bucket, pursued the damsel, tucked her head under his arm in a business-like if unchivalrous fashion, and proceeded to punch her with great heartiness . . . But such satisfactions were few enough, and wilted in retrospect on the painful return march to Little Perfume, with small arms aching and small back breaking and the conviction deep in one's heart that some meddler had elongated the sharia in one's absence . . .

That was in late winter and for a time the locality was endurable. But the summer drew on. Desperately engrossed as they were in the attempt to find an opening for their wares in the Egyptian markets, the Selitsa settlers had borne with their strangely-odoured habitat uncomplainingly. They rose with the first blink of daylight, into those fervid Cairene mornings when the air is unthinkably pure and the day for an hour has the hesitating loveliness of a lovely woman, and cooked their scanty breakfasts and set to work at their looms. They ceased not even at the failing of the light, but took to the coarser work under the glimmer of great tallow candles, giant Londos and the gentle Elia leading in feats of endurance, Sometimes it was midnight before the humming of the looms would cease, and Londos, a little unsteady, would lumber out of doors to look up at the splendour of the Cairene moon and chuckle tiredly as he caught the glitter of moonlight on the notice-board of the settlement.

But the summer drew on, and with it each morning arose

from the waste of Little Perfume, as though a foul beast hibernated underfoot, a malodorous breath of a vileness unendurable. With it came clouds of mosquitoes – insects rare enough in Cairo – and hordes of flies. By midday the ancient dunghill had a faint mist. In a fortnight two of the Greek children were dead and half of the community was sick in bed.

The evening of the day on which they buried the children Londos stalked to the door of the hut where Trikoupi leant pallidly over his loom and little Rhizos knelt by the heap of sacking on which his mother slept uneasily.

'Come out, Elia.'

So Elia went out, and waited. Londos strode up and down in the evening light, debating with himself, once stopping and throwing out his arms hopelessly. Then he halted in front of the gentle Trikoupi.

'There is only one thing we can do, Elia.'

'Leave Little Perfume?' Elia had guessed this was coming.

'No, remove it.' Londos pointed to the waste hillock towering away behind the huts. 'We must shift that, and quickly.'

Trikoupi stared at him as though he had gone mad. 'Remove it? But how? And where?'

Londos indicated the lowering of the Moqattam Hills in the sunset. 'There. It is two miles away, beyond the town boundaries.'

'But move this hill – It is a month's work for scores of men.'

Londos nodded. 'And we must do it in a fortnight – if our children are to live.'

VI

They did it. It turned in the telling of later years into an epic of struggle, a thing of heroism and great feats, intermingled with shouted laughter. The fatigue and horror and weariness the years came to cover with the tapestry of legend: how Londos, stripped to a breech-clout, dug and excavated and filled every one of the sacks and baskets for four days on end, the while the others bore them on their two-mile journey – Londos, gigantic, unsleeping, pausing now and then to drink the coffee brought him, and vomit up that coffee at the next nest of dreadful stenches and even more dreadful refuse his shovel uncovered; how the gentle Trikoupi bore loads without ceasing, day or night, till he was found walking in his sleep, a babbling automaton; how the women, laughed at and pelted by the Cairenes, bore load for load with the men; how three died in that Iliad – one of them, the Vasos mother, by the pits beyond the walls – and there was no time to bury their corpses; how the police descended on the excavators and gave them a time-limit in which to finish the work; how in desperation the weaver Gemadios went to Citadel in the dark hours of one night and stole a great English Army hand-cart, and worked with it for two days (doing feats in the removal of offal) and then returned it, the theft still undiscovered; how—

They did it. It was cleared at last. The burning Cairene sunshine smote down on ragged floors, once the floors of some Mameluke's palace, perhaps, in the days of Cairo's greatness. Underneath those floors was plentitude of bricks and stonework. And the odours died and passed, and the weavers, men and women, reeled to their huts and flung themselves down beside their looms and slept and slept, and woke and groaned with aching muscles, and slept again.

Little Rhizos Trikoupi, staggering to the fountain alone that night with an endrapement of pitchers, found seated on the coping the ferocious little female whose head he had once punched. She sat and regarded him without apparent hostility. He disregarded her, ostentatiously.

But as he lifted up the laden jars she came to his side.

'I'll help,' she said, friendly of voice.

She bore a jar to the confines of Little Perfume. There

she set it down and smiled at Rhizos. 'My name is Zara,' she said, inconsequently. Then told him disastrous tidings, casually. 'They are not to allow any more of your people to carry water from the fountain to the Place of Stinks.'

VII

It was a crushing blow. Londos and Elia Trikoupi went and argued with the ward-masters. But they refused to be moved. All of them except Muslih, a Nationalist and father of that advanced feminist Zara, were quite openly hostile to the Greeks. The fountain was intended to supply the streets which surrounded it, not such carrion-grubbers as might settle in abandoned middens . . .

That evening Londos himself, bidding the children stay at home, went for water with two great buckets. He came back hatless and bleeding, but grinning, with a jeering, stone-pelting crowd behind him. But the buckets were full. He put them down, emptied them into the settlement's jars, and started out again. By the fountain-coping three men still lay and groaned where he had left them. He refilled the buckets.

But next morning Rhizos and young Kolocrotoni, scouting, came back to tell that there was a policeman on guard at the fountain. Giant Londos swore at that information and scratched his head. It was one thing to crack the cranium of the stray and obstreperous Cairene, another to do the same to a gendarme. The Greeks collected to debate the matter, Elia Trikoupi, dust-covered from exploring the uncovered floors of Little Perfume, arriving last.

'Abandon Little Perfume now we will not,' swore Londos. 'Not though we have to carry water from the Nile itself. Those lawyers! Elia, we'll rear that son of yours to be one and defend our interests. Then we may drink in peace.'

'We may drink before that,' said Trikoupi, gently. 'If you will all come with me—'

They went with him. He led them to the middle of the waste of Little Perfume. In the ground was a circular depression filled with earth and building rubbish. Londos stared at it and then embraced Trikoupi.

'A well – once a well. And we'll make it one again.' He threw off his coat, groaned like a bull at an ache that leapt to fiery being between his shoulder-blades, and called for a spade. 'This will clinch for ever our right. We can start building. We can start making gardens.' He sighed, almost regretfully. 'The great tale of Little Perfume is over.'

VIII

But indeed, could he have known it, they had lived no more than its prelude. Almost unnoticed, yet weaving assiduously into the web and woof of Cairene life stray threads of story-plot from Little Perfume, the War years passed over Egypt. Demand for the products of the looms that had once hummed in Selitsa grew in volume and value. Nor did the aftermath bring any slump. The settlers flourished.

Yet out of its profits the little community succeeded in banking scarcely a piastre. Replacing the saving instinct of generations a new habit had grown upon the weavers – the enrichment and embellishment of Little Perfume. Its gardens grew famous throughout the Warrens. They even planted trees – quick-growing Australian trees procured by Rhizos Trikoupi when he learnt of those plants in botany lessons. A great shed, built of mudbricks, airy and cool and flat-roofed, gradually rose to being in the centre of the one-time rubbish depository. This was the communal loom-shed. Round it, one by one, were built the houses of the weavers – twelve houses with much space and garden-room. Those houses at night were lighted no longer by candles, but by electricity. The long-tapped well brought water to each . . . Londos, gigantic still, but bulkier, slower, than of yore, would sometimes walk away down the Sharia el Ghoraib and then wheel round abruptly, in order to shock himself into fresh surprise over the miracle of Little Perfume. He would stand and stare at it fascinatedly, and so was standing one evening in October when young Rhizos Trikoupi, the law-student returning from his studies in Cairo, hailed him as he came down the sharia.

'Dreaming again, *papakes*?'

'Eh?' The giant started. 'Ah, you, Rhizos. And how much have you learned today?' He chuckled. 'Apart from the shape of the ear of Zara Muslih, I mean.'

Rhizos coloured a trifle, and attractively. Daily, almost, he and Zara, both students at the University, travelled into Cairo together. Her father, the fervid progressive and friend of the Greeks, had determined to give her such education as would shock her mother and every other veiled woman east of the Bab el Zuweiya . . . She had certainly lovely ears.

Londos chuckled again, clapping an ungentle hand on the law-student's shoulder.

'And why not? But remember you are our Samson, and there must be no Delilahs.'

'There are no Philistines,' said Rhizos, tolerantly, and then nodded back towards the Sharia el Ghoraib, the street which had stood decaying ever since that midnight when the Selitsa settlers passed through it to the conquest of the ancient offal-heap. 'At least, not nearer than the sharia! What is happening there?'

'Eh? Oh, the house-breaking in the upper half?' Londos shrugged indifferently, his eyes on the night-shadowed peace of Little Perfume. 'Its owner following our lead at last – it has taken him ten years. Clearing away the huts and building houses, I hear. Site-prices are soaring high in Cairo.'

IX

Cairo, indeed, was advancing in Westernisation in great strides. Site-prices had doubled and trebled since the War.

New buildings were springing up in every ward of the ancient city of the Mamelukes. Nor were effects unforeseen and numerous enough slow to erupt from all that causal activity. Title-deeds and land-rights were everywhere being questioned and overhauled, claim and counter-claim jostled one the other in every lawyer's office. And presently, from the midst of this maelstrom of modernisation, a long wave reached out and burst like a thunder-clap against the shores of Little Perfume.

Twenty-four hours after that talk with Londos, Rhizos returned to find his father, the giant, Vasos, and old Sina in anxious consultation over a long tri-lingual typescript. They cried out their relief at sight of him, and Londos handed over the document.

'It was wise to train this son of yours, Elia,' he said, and wiped his forehead. '*He* will deal with it.'

Rhizos took the crinkling sheets of paper and sat down and read them, and presently was aware of a deafening, sickening beat of blood around his own ears.

It was a notice to the effect that the site-property of El Ghoraib, 'commonly known as Little Perfume', was required by its owner for building purposes, and that the Greek squatters at present in occupation must vacate it within a month's time.

X

The Greeks took the case to the courts, Rhizos engaging a lawyer on behalf of the settlement. But even with this development Londos and the older weavers refused to treat the claim seriously.

'An owner for Little Perfume?' said Londos. 'It must be the man in the moon. Or of a certainty a lunatic.'

He proved less unharmful. They caught their first glimpse of him as the case was being tried – a *rentier*, a Parisian Egyptian of the new generation, suave, sleek, and bored. His lawyers submitted the claim with a casualness which was deceptive. It covered certainty. El Ghoraib, together with the near-by Sharia el Ghoraib, had been the property of the Falih family from time immemorial. The title-deeds were impeccable.

'Why did you not evict the squatters before?' demanded the Greeks' lawyer.

Falih smiled. 'Because until recently I'd forgotten El Ghoraib's existence.' He added coolly: 'And I make no claim on the squatters now, provided they leave the site undamaged.'

It was as heartless a case as had come within his province, said the Egyptian judge in a curt summary. Nevertheless, there could be no disputing the claim of Falih.

Judgment was entered accordingly, and Londos and Trikoupi, acting for the settlers, allowed to appeal.

The appeal was quashed.

XI

The news was brought to Little Perfume. Giant Londos, shrunken, rheumatism-crippled, stared from Rhizos to his father, then around the circle gathered to hear the news – all old men, bent with toil at their looms. Rhizos could not meet that stricken look in the eyes of the giant whose labours in clearing the rubbish-waste were already legendary.

'But – it means we go out of here as we came! It is impossible,' said Londos, and burst into tears . . . The old men sat silent, but Rhizos slipped out of the gathering and walked the Cairene evening in a red passion of anger. He found himself at length outside the door of the Muslih house, at the other end of the Sharia el Ghoraib. It was a familiar enough door to him and in a moment it was closing behind him the while he made his way to the room where Zara sat over books and lecture-notes. At sight of him she rose eagerly.

'The appeal?'

He laughed. 'Quashed. Falih can evict us when he chooses.'

She kindled from his own anger. 'It's a shame – oh, a damned shame! Those old men and women who have worked such a miracle . . . Can't they claim compensation?'

'They can take away nothing but the looms they brought. We're liable to prosecution if we damage the very houses we've built.'

She looked at him in helpless pity. 'Surely something can be done? If only that Bill were passed in the Chamber!'

'What Bill?' he asked, indifferently.

He had been too busy heeding to the court cases to know of outside events that might affect them. He listened half-unlistening, until meaning of what she was saying penetrated the cloud of his anger.

'A Bill enforcing value-compensation for improved sites – to become law as soon as passed! That would mean Falih would never dare evict us from Little Perfume. It would cost him too much . . . But when will it pass?'

'They are fighting it, my father says, but it is bound to pass. When? Within the next week or so, perhaps.'

'Too late. If only—'

He began to walk up and down the room, Zara looking at him. He stopped and stared at her, absently. They had each the same thought.

'If we could keep off Falih till then—'

XII

That was on the Monday. Next day the Greeks of Little Perfume received a notice from Falih's agent to vacate the site within twenty-four hours.

They made no attempt to comply. Instead, Rhizos went and argued with the agents. Reluctantly, those agents extended the time-limit another forty-eight hours. But they were insistent that at the end of that period the site be left vacant. Later in the day they sent a note curtailing the extra forty-eight hours to twenty-four. The growth of support for the new Bill in the Chamber had alarmed Falih.

Meantime, Rhizos organised the inhabitants of Little Perfume. At a meeting they voted him to control the situation, with young Kolocrotoni his assistant. Then they retired to uneasy beds, wondering what the next day would bring.

It brought Falih's bailiffs, four of them, knocking at the door of Trikoupi's house. The Greeks gathered round the arrivals quickly enough, while a crowd of curious Egyptians flocked in from the far end of the sharia. Nor were they hostile to the Greeks, those Egyptians. The Greeks had won their place. Here were thieves come to dispossess them . . . The bailiffs grew angry and frightened, beating upon Trikoupi's door. The gentle Elia opened it.

'This house must be cleared,' said the leader. He motioned forward one of the others. 'Carry out the furniture.'

Londos, who had been waiting for this, as instructed by the absent Rhizos, rose from a chair. They saw a tipsy giant behind a table littered with full and empty bottles. 'Drink first,' he invited, swayingly. 'Drink to our leaving this place of stinks. Sit down and drink.'

The bailiffs hesitated, but a growl came from the crowd pressing round the open door. Falih's men sat down and, not unwillingly, filled glasses from the bottles indicated . . .

They passed down the Sharia el Ghoraib late that evening in two arabiyehs hired by Rhizos; they passed down it drunk and roisterous and singing improper songs. They had fallen mysteriously asleep after the first drinks, had slept until afternoon and had awakened to be again forcibly regaled with draughts of the potent Greek brandy . . . Listening to their drunken brawling receding into the evening, Rhizos turned to Zara, who had come to see the day's *dénouement*. She was flushed and laughing at the strategem's success, and he stared at the shapeliness of her ears.

'We've won the first skirmish, but tomorrow—' and his face grew dark.

She suddenly kissed him. 'Luck for tomorrow!' And was gone, leaving him staring after her breathlessly, with flushed face.

XIII

Tomorrow—

The papers bore news of the Bill. It had passed, after a fierce struggle, into the Egyptian equivalent of the committee stage. From there it had still to emerge, still to receive the King's sanction. Rhizos read the news from the sheets of *El Ahram*, he and young Kolocrotoni together.

'Falih's men will return long before then,' said Kolocrotoni.

'They'll return today,' said Rhizos, 'unless we go to them instead.' He had already planned his next move. Within half an hour, after canvassing from house to house in Little Perfume, he went down into Cairo with notes to the value of three thousand piastres in his wallet. Of what he accomplished on that journey he never told. But he returned with an empty wallet and Falih's agents did not come that day. Falih himself, indeed, had gone to Alexandria.

But Rhizos knew it was only a respite, that to buy off subsidiary agents was not to buy off Falih's lawyers. He read the news about the Bill with growing anxiety. There were difficulties in the committee stage.

'It's hopeless to wait for it,' said Kolocrotoni, dark and young and fierce. They stood together in the sunset, looking at Little Perfume from Londos' ancient stance at the mouth of the sharia. 'Better that we leave it so that this Falih will wish it were a midden again.'

'How?' asked Rhizos.

'Burn it, blow it up.'

'Blow it up? Where are you to get the explosives?'

Kolocrotoni laughed. 'That would be easy.' And he told of a warehouse in Cairo where arms were stored before being smuggled through to the Senussi. 'It is from there that the Nationalist students get their arms.'

'Could we?' asked Rhizos.

Kolocrotoni stared. He had hardly meant to be taken so seriously. 'Revolvers?'

'Yes.' Young Trikoupi seemed to be calculating rapidly. 'Or automatics. Thirteen revolvers and ammunition.'

XIV

Now, as I've told, there was only one street which led into the square of Little Perfume. Down this street the next morning came a body of men, labourers and carpenters. With them was Falih's own lawyer. Gemadios's youngest son brought to the Greeks news of the invaders' approach. Giant Londos, bending over the garden-patch in front of his house, with a great hose in his hand, nodded.

The lawyer halted his host, glanced at Londos, and then walked past him. Or rather, he prepared to do so.

'I would not pass,' said Londos, in friendly tone. And added, as an anxious afterthought, 'This is the first time I have used a garden hose and I am still inexpert.'

The little lawyer turned on him angrily, and at that moment was lifted off his feet by a stream of water hitting him in the chest. He rolled out of Londos's garden, rose, and was promptly knocked down again. The hose appeared to have gone mad in the hands of Londos. He stabbed a beam of water to and fro amid the heads of the lawyer's following. They broke and ran for the sharia, and, running, found themselves objects of suspicion to the Egyptians of the sharia's hovels.

Cries rose: 'Who are they?'

The answering cry came quickly. 'Thieves! Stop them!'

Thereat, apparently in a passion for justice, the Sharia el Ghoraib emptied a multitude of pursuers and assailants upon the followers of Falih's lawyer. They were pelted with refuse, kicked, cuffed, and finally driven ignominiously from the street. The little lawyer, beyond the reach of the last missile, turned and shouted. Zara Muslih, standing listening at the door of her father's house, heard him and went up through the laughing, excited street towards Little Perfume. Beyond the inhabited quarter, towards where the sharia terminated in the strange settlement of the Selitsa weavers, she found Rhizos Trikoupi staring up and down the two hundred yards of high, blank-faced street-wall.

'The lawyer has gone for the police.'

Rhizos nodded. 'I expected he would. But he'll take some time to change his clothes and get there. By then the police chief will be having his siesta. They'll not dare to disturb him very early in the afternoon. When they do, the lawyer will find that my father has arrived simultaneously with himself, lodging a counter-complaint of assault and damage.'

Zara's eyes sparkled. 'This is generalship. Oh, splendid!' Then her face fell. 'But how long can you keep it up – playing them off by tricks?'

'This is the last of the tricks.'

'And father says the King is almost bound to sign the Bill the day after tomorrow.'

Rhizos's eyes turned to the high, ravine-like walls about them. 'We shall keep Little Perfume until then.'

And then some realisation came to Zara of what he intended. She stared at him, sick at heart. 'But – it will be the gendarmes who will come tomorrow.'

He nodded. 'I know. And you must not come again until – after. Not down into Little Perfume, I mean. I don't want other people implicated or arrested.'

'Am I "other people"?'

He could smile at that. 'Always, for me. Apart and adorable, my dear.'

But her momentary flippancy had passed. 'Oh, it'll be madness.' Her eyes widened. 'And it's not just a scuffle you intend. *That* is why Kolocrotoni has been buying revolvers – I heard of it . . . Rhizos – you who've always hated fighting and laughed at the dark little melodramatics of history!'

His look almost frightened her. 'Do you think I haven't hated the trickeries and treacheries of the last few days? Do you think I don't hate the dirty little pantomime we're staging now? But I'd rather mime in the dark than crawl like a coward in the sunlight.' He shuddered and passed his hands across his eyes. His voice fell to a dull flatness. 'And there'll be no fighting. Look here, Zara, I must go back.'

They touched hands, not looking at each other. She did not kiss him this time. Her eyes were suddenly blind with tears.

xv

That evening the Greeks – thirteen of them, young men between the ages of eighteen and thirty, and all unmarried – moved out from Little Perfume with pickaxes and shovels, and, a hundred yards along the Sharia el Ghoraib, began to dig up the roadway. It was very quiet, in that hushed Cairene semi-darkness, and Rhizos Trikoupi, with knit brows and a tape-line, went from side to side of the street, measuring and calculating. It might have seemed to the casual onlooker like an ordinary gang of street workmen but for the silence that went with its operations. Young men from the representative families of the settlement – Kolo-crotoni, Vasos, Sina, the two young Latas, Gemadios, Zalakosta and the others – they dug and hewed through the dried mud and were presently excavating the ancient paving-stones. From behind them there was silence also in all the locked and shuttered houses of Little Perfume. Even the looms had ceased to hum.

For a battle had been fought there over the paper Rhizos had prepared and forced the Greek householders – his father among them – to sign. This was a document dis-owning Rhizos and his followers as 'young hotheads' whom the elders of the community were unable to restrain. Little Perfume, it declared, entirely dissociated itself from them.

'I will not sign it,' swore Londos, in bed with rheuma-tism, and groaning as he stirred indignantly. But, like all the others, sign he did at last, and held Rhizos's hand, peering up into his face. 'If only I could come with you!'

'You'll be less bored in bed, *papakes*,' Rhizos assured him lightly. 'Probably we'll all catch damnable colds. But our bluff will keep them off for a time – and they can only give a few of us a week or so in prison when it's over.'

But midnight saw a barricade, business-like enough and breast-high, spanning the sharia from side to side. Then, leaving the Latas, armed with cudgels, to look after it, Rhizos and his companions went back and slept in Little Perfume, a sleep that was broken in early dawn by one of the Latas coming panting to the door of the Trikoupi house with the news that Falih's lawyer was approaching with his gang of labourers. Evidently he expected to take the set-tlement by surprise.

Rhizos dressed hurriedly and went to the barricade. With the lawyer he saw two Egyptian policemen.

The party was evidently staggered at sight of the barri-cade. What happened then is not quite clear. For a little, while his young men ran up, Rhizos stood and parleyed with the lawyer, the gendarmes at first laughing and then losing their tempers in the quick, Egyptian way. One of them unslung his carbine – it was in the days when they still carried carbines – and, levelling it at Rhizos, ordered him to start demolishing the barricade. For answer Kolocrotoni, looking over the barricade, at some distance from Rhizos, called out:

'Drop that carbine!'

The gendarme looked up and found himself covered by a dozen revolvers. His carbine clattered to the ground. At the order of Kolocrotoni the other policeman also disarmed. Sina climbed over the barricade, and, in the midst of a queer silence, went and collected the weapons. Then he returned and the two parties looked at each other undecidedly. Suddenly the first gendarme turned round and hastened down the Sharia el Ghoraib. His companion trudged stolidly after him. Falih's lawyer, after a moment of hesitation, followed suit, his gang behind him in straggling retreat. The young Greeks at the barricade avoided each others' eyes and beat their hands together in the chill morning air. Somewhere a cock began to crow, shrilly.

At ten o'clock a policeman came down the sharia, surveyed the barricade and its defenders, and then retired. Kolocrotoni brought Rhizos a cup of coffee, and while the latter drank it, himself mounted to the highest point of the defences and watched. Suddenly he drew a breath like a long sigh.

'Here they come.'

XVI

How far those thirteen young Greeks had imagined the affair would go it is impossible to say. In the subsequent inquiry the police affirmed that the Greeks fired the first shot. There can, at least, be little doubt that the police at the beginning made no attempt to shoot. The squad of twenty men marched to within ten yards or so of the barricade, and Rhizos called them to halt. For answer the officer in command ostentatiously turned his back on the barricade, ordered his men to club their carbines and charge, himself turned round again – and came forward at a rapid run, swinging a loaded stick in his hand.

The attackers were greeted with a hail of stones. Carbine and revolver shots rang out. The officer pitched forward into the dust, and for a moment the policemen wavered. But only for a moment. They came on again. And then Rhizos committed himself openly. He leant over the barricade and shot three of them in rapid succession. Thereat the survivors broke and ran. The Greeks did not fire, but glanced, white-faced, at their leader. Rhizos, white himself, calmly ejected the spent rounds from his revolver, and reloaded it.

Then, with a glance down the empty sharia, he climbed the barricade and inspected the four uniformed figures lying in the dust. The officer and one other were dead. Two of them lived, one with a broken arm, the other with his skull slightly grazed. Rhizos bandaged the last one, helped the man with the wounded arm to his feet, and pointed down the sharia. Holding to the wall, like a sick dog, the policeman shambled out of sight. Rhizos was turning in perplexity to the other bodies when his companions called to him urgently . . . He gained shelter just as the rifle-fire opened.

None of the defenders had any experience of warfare, and it says much for the skill with which the barricade was constructed that in the first few minutes only two of them were killed. Kolocrotoni was shot through the shoulder. Rhizos, calling to the others to keep their places, crawled to him and bandaged him. Presently the rifle-fire ceased for a moment, but after another abortive charge opened again . . .

By evening there were eight Greeks, including Rhizos, left alive. In spite of threats and entreaties on the part of those who held the barricade, non-combatants – the gentle Elia among them – crawled out from Little Perfume and took away the bodies of the dead. But with the evening the gendarmes withdrew (in futile search of a way over the khan walls, as was afterwards told), the stretch of street in front of the barricade was left deserted, and, staring at each other unbelievingly, the young men ate the food brought them from Little Perfume.

It was dreadful in those evening hours. Rhizos had two bonfires lighted at a distance of fifty yards or so down the sharia, so that there might be no surprise attack. A tarpaulin had been brought from the settlement and erected behind the barricade in the form of a hut, and what dark thoughts assailed the outlaws till they dropped exhausted in its shelter no one will ever know. But long after midnight some of them awoke and heard Rhizos, alone wakeful and guarding the barricade, singing in a strange, shrill voice snatches of a song they had never heard before. It was a frightening thing to hear in the listening silence of the sharia, and Kolocrotoni prevailed on him to go and lie down. Utterly weary, he swayed to the shelter, staggered – and was asleep before Kolocrotoni's arm caught him and lowered him to the ground.

Near three in the morning, eluding somehow the police-picket at the upper end of the Sharia Ghoraib, Zara Muslih reached the barricade and whispered the news to Kolocrotoni: the Bill was to be signed and issued in the morning. The story of the affray in the Warrens had hastened the signing.

'And you must all get away at once,' she urged. 'Throw up rope-ladders over the khan walls.'

Kolocrotoni shook his head. 'We cannot leave here until the Bill is definitely signed, Rhizos says. If we abandon the barricade now the police may be in possession of Little Perfume before morning.'

'Rhizos – he doesn't know what he's done! You people were in a searchlight of sympathy before he started this resistance – no one has a scrap of pity for you now . . . Oh, tell him I *must* see him!'

The young Greek shook his head again, looking at her with narrowed eyes. 'He's asleep. This isn't a woman's business.'

A moment they looked at each other, Kolocrotoni implacable, Zara desperately pleading. Then she glanced at that tragic barricade for the last time, and went back through the dying light of the bonfires and never saw either Rhizos or Kolocrotoni again.

For at starset, in the lowering darkness that precedes the Egyptian morning, they shook Rhizos awake. The police were approaching again, and in considerable force. He started up as he felt their hands on his shoulder, and looked at them, Kolocrotoni and the younger Latas, remotely, alertly.

'*What is it? The Persians?*'

They stared at him, stumblingly attempting to follow strange rhythms and accentuations in his speech. 'It's the gendarmes,' said Kolocrotoni. 'And we'll hardly be able to make them out. There's not a gleam of sun yet.'

Rhizos laughed, jumping to his feet, speaking again in words they barely understood – albeit they might have been direct answer to Zara's passionate denunciation . . . Then he shuddered and passed his hands across his eyes, as though awakening from an inner sleep.

'What is it? What have I been saying? I had a dream . . . The gendarmes?'

Far down the sharia came the steady tramp of disciplined feet.

XVII

They sent an armoured car against it eventually, that flimsy erection behind which a dwindling band of Greeks defied the hosts of the Orient. It crashed through, indifferently, half an hour after the promulgation of the Bill, and it was then that Rhizos and Kolocrotoni were killed. Three of the defenders, Sina and the two Latas, escaped back into Little Perfume, their ammunition exhausted. There they managed to scale the khan walls and were seen never again in Cairo. But before they went they told the tale of those last few hours . . .

The historian pauses, his theme in diminuendo, himself standing in the bright Cairene sunshine, lost in fantastic speculation as he sees again that misascribed quotation graved below the word *OEPMOIIYLAI* on the dusty wall of the Sharia el Ghoraib:

So much the better. We shall fight in the shade.
— RHIZOS OF SPARTA

A Footnote to History

I

OF ALL THE voluminous chronicles of Neesan Nerses which lie still unedited and untranscribed in the archives of the Monastery of Mevr, one caught my attention and held it so that I went back to it again and again, savouring its flavour, puzzling over it, this footnote to those fabulous annals of a fabulous century. Through that recorded clamour of war, controversy and wild adventure, with background unceasingly the arrow-hail of the Mongol bowmen, it sings with the sweet, bitter voice of the pipes of spring, unforgotten in a haunted wilderness. As I think Bishop Nerses himself could never forget, looking out at evening from the palace windows of that long-vanished diocese of his above the hills of Persia.

For his diocese of Alarlu is as vanished as his century and Nestorian Mevr, kindly, indifferent, stacks the records of the lost historian in crumbling confusion with unread medicinal tracts, treatises on mountain devils, horoscopes, monkish diaries and the like. From the heights of Mevr you can see far off at dawn the glint of the hills amidst which Nerses ruled that pocket of Christian Assyrians so long ago – those hills across which his son came riding that afternoon in the year 1260, across which he watched that son ride out again and vanish for ever before the passing of another nine months.

1259: Twice that year the Bishop rode out at the head of the Assyrians and beat off marauding stragglers from Hulagu's army. All one night he lay and watched across the desert, from an eyrie in the hills, the flames of Baghdad light the sky. For men who were devils were ravening there, as he knew, and with heavy heart he went back to his fortress-palace in the dawn – to hold early Mass and tend the sick and superintend the clipping of goats and ache for news of his son.

And presently his daughter Amima – sixteen years of age, with her mother's flaming darkness of hair and eyes – came treading through the byres, seeking him out and storming at him because he had neglected to change from his night-soaked riding-gear. The Bishop smiled at her, guiltily.

'I forgot. I was thinking of the goats,' he confessed.

Amima stamped a small foot.

'A goat never forgotten – yes. You were thinking of Hormizd.' And then softened, perhaps at sight of the misery in Nerses' eyes. 'There's no news of him? What kept you out on the hills all night?'

'The barbarians have fired Baghdad,' said the Bishop, 'and Hormizd was in the Khalif's guard.'

'Then Hormizd is safe,' averred Amima, flippantly, 'for he said before he went that the horses of the Khalif's guard were chosen for their fleetness in running away . . . He'll be here tomorrow.'

But tomorrow passed, weeks and months went by, and no news came of Hormizd, the Christian mercenary. And, as he tells, what had been a vivid pain settled to a dull ache in the heart of Nerses, and more and more in spare hours he shut himself up in his watch-room above the palace, penning his record of the times from the varied information that ebbed up to Alarlu with wandering mercenaries, starving pilgrims, Arab brigands, lost Moslem mullahs – the flotsam and jetsam of a continent in travail with history. He built up those records, I think, as a barrier against that ache, and Amima rode the Assyrian boundaries and kept the peace, as he realised with a dull gratitude. And Hulagu swept north again, he and the loot of Persia and Iraq, and Paschal brought one white morning its driving snows to the Persian hills, and through those snows—

Amima saw the coming of them, went out, accosted them, came racing back on her Arab pony. Up the ringing stairs to Nerses' tower she ran and burst in on the Bishop deep in his *magnum opus*, that laboured dissertation on the Latin Rite which lies unread and unreadable to this day.

'Father!' she panted, and sank at his feet and shook him. 'Hormizd has returned!'

'Hormizd?' He stared at her, for a moment unable to associate the name with anyone he had ever known, as he tells. Then he got to his feet, trembling. 'Hormizd—'

Hormizd and no other – tattered as a beggar, minus his gay silver helmet, his chain-mail hanging in ragged links from his shoulders, but his eyes as restless and eager as ever. He was waiting in the central courtyard, he and his companion, and Nerses heard his laugh as he went down the stairs. Then, at sight of his father, the laughter went from the Christian mercenary's face. He knelt for the Bishop's blessing and then was in Nerses' arms the while the Persian wolf-hounds clamoured around the two of them, and Amima, booted, spurred, the small warden of Alarlu's marches, confronted Hormizd's fellow-rider – a pallid-skinned giant, bearded and moustached as were no southern men, clad in leather, with a great horn bow slung at his back.

'You are a Mongol?' she demanded, staring up at the tip of the bow above the immense shoulders.

The giant glanced at her gravely, indifferently, stroking his beard. 'I am a chief of the Outer Hordes.'

'A heathen?'

'Leave be, Amima,' said the Bishop, loosening his arms from about his son, while Hormizd scowled at his sister and turned to the giant, the eager impatience passing from his face into such look as made Nerses catch breath.

'Father, this is my brother from the horse-tail hordes whom I have brought to the refuge of Alarlu.'

II

All that night the snowstorm raged, and the Assyrian herdsmen drove the goats into the byres, and kindled at Nerses' orders a great flambeau of pitch-soaked wood to flame on the palace roof, a guide to the lost and perishing in the wastes beyond Alarlu. But in the great guest-room, with the brazier's glow ruddy upon the whorling inscriptions of the ancient walls, none thought of sleep for many hours the while the story of Hormizd's adventurings in the plain was told, now by Hormizd himself, now by his giant blood-brother.

In stumbling Persian, beard in hand, staring at the brazier, the giant. 'I am Gezir Noyan, from the Plains of the Outer Wastes. We dwell on the edge of the world, far to the north. In the long seasons there is no darkness in our nights, and up in the great rivers at dawn the ice-islands clash as they go north over the edge of the world . . .'

One's imagination touches in that scene in the Alarlu

guest-room, though Nerses' record attempts no such limnings: Hormizd, despoiled of his battered armour, lying full-
length on a goatskin rug, his eyes on this pagan blood-
brother of his; the brazier's light jerking from dour neutrality of tint wide red-specked patches on the leather jerkin
of the giant himself; Amima kneeling with chin hand-
cupped. Nerses himself that brazier which burned seven
centuries ago probably showed robed and bearded, en-
sconced in his high chair, his long, curling black hair
already streaked with grey, his eyes wandering continually
to the face of his son . . .

And the tale of Gezir Noyan:

'Now the spring came and with it messengers from the
Great Horde, the yellow men who had brought us into
alliance in the time of the Khakan Genjis. The horse-tail
banners were out and the great khan going south to the
conquest of the followers of the Foul Prophet. So I gathered my bowmen and rode to join them.

'Beyond Kara Kum we marshalled and news was
brought that Persia lay undefended. So Hulagu led us west
and south, leaving a little force to vex the Persian borders
from the north. And one morning the breath came pantingly in our throats and men fell and died. For we had come
to the great poison desert of Kizil Kum.

'And this for eighteen days, with no taste of water and
drinking the milk and blood of mares, we crossed, holding
to the south-east and bursting at length on the green plains.
Merv Hulagu fell upon and devoured and I plundered with
the others, yet was sickened with slaughter after the first
two days. So I withdrew my gurans from the city, and
would have marched north again, abandoning the horse-
tails, but that Hulagu sent a cloud of spearmen to stop the
way, and for the time we surrendered and consented to
march with him again.

'And we came to Baghdad, dragging with the Hordes
great bombards from Khita which hurled rocks and levelled

the walls. Of that tale you have heard. On the third morning of the fighting I reached the gates of the Citadel and there found the horse-tail standards had already broken through, despite the desperation of such of the Khalif's guard as had not fled with their master across the river.

'And in a corner of the great courtyard, half-choked with smoke, while Hulagu's Mongols smote off the heads of the dead and wounded guards and flung them into carts to be taken to build the great skull-pyramid without the city, I came on five of the yellow men attacking this my brother Hormizd. He was singing and laughing as he smote down one Mongol after the other, and they drew back, as they had reason to do, and shouted for bowmen to shoot him from a distance. But in that moment he staggered and fell and I saw that he had a great leg-wound. The attackers shouted and made at him again. But I put them aside.'

'Why?' It was Amima's clear young voice in the semi-darkness. 'How was Hormizd more to you than any other stranger whom your barbarians were murdering?'

Hormizd jerked to angry attention in the brazier-glow. 'How can a woman understand?'

'Nor can I understand.' The giant's face turned from one to the other of them. 'More? I do not know. But I knew him for my friend. So I bandaged him and bore him out of the burning citadel, and prevailed on a flying citizen with a mule to carry him out of Baghdad to some place of safety where he might recover—'

But it was Hormizd's turn to interrupt, leaping to his feet.

'God, with what tongue of a colic-stricken camel is he afflicted! Heed not this tale, my father, else in a moment will it appear that it was I who saved *his* life, not he mine. Now listen to the truth of it—'

And Hormizd's truth was indeed a jewel with different facets from Gezir Noyan's. There had been no casual, unhindered rescue of Hormizd in the blazing courtyard of the Citadel. Instead, Gezir had killed two of the attackers and held the others at bay till some of his own men from the Outer Wastes came to his aid. With their company he had made his way out of the Citadel, carrying the wounded man, fighting every inch of the path, for the news of this attempted rescue of a guardsman had spread, and Hulagu's orders were being defied. And this casual tale of finding a citizen with a mule – it had been done only after a long period of desperate search, through streets swarming with plunderers who not infrequently had heard rumours of the rescue and sought to stop it. Then, finally, on the outskirts of the city, Gezir had indeed prevailed on a fleeing refugee to carry away the wounded guardsman, while he himself turned back to face the wrath of Hulagu—

'And what happened then?' questioned the Bishop, while the whoom of the snowstorm came to them from outside the palace of Alarlu.

'Ask not of him, else will he say that the Khakan embraced him and wept on his shoulder in admiration. This happened: He was overpowered by the foul horse-tails, dragged to the great square next morning where Hulagu sat sharing out the plunder among the Hordes, and there accused of saving the life of an enemy. And Hulagu ordered that he should be impaled upon the walls, and he was hurried away to the western gate, and there would have been tortured and slain but that Hulagu heard that the men of the Outer Wastes would revolt again if this was done. So he sent a fresh order that Gezir was merely to be stripped of his rank and titles, enslaved, clad as a woman, and given in chains and under stripes the foulest tasks of a camp-follower.'

Even Amima stirred a little at that. But Gezir Noyan merely smiled into his beard, though his face twitched a little.

'It was a just sentence. Indeed, a merciful one. I had saved an enemy from the pyramid of skulls.'

So, reviled, spat upon, avoided by his own followers from the Outer Wastes, he had been set to the vilest tasks in the great Mongol army which still lingered amid the smoking ruins of Baghdad. Till one day in the litter of the horse-lines, raising his head he had seen a man limp past, and had thought little of it, bending to his task again. Then the limping leg had passed once more and a little sack had been dropped into his hands. He had concealed it without attracting notice and in the moonlit squalor of the slaves' quarters opened it that night, discovering it to contain a small file and a stabbing-knife.

For Hormizd, guided out to Baghdad's suburb of Baqubah – still intact, having fortunately made no resistance to the invaders – had lain recovering from his hurts and wondering as to the name and fate of his rescuer. So soon as he could he had had enquiries made through Assyrian merchants trading in the Mongol camp. And at last he had learned the full facts. The stranger who had befriended him, whose memory and face haunted him, was a man degraded and ruined, doomed to the foulest tasks in the Mongol camp.

And, hearing the news, Hormizd had cursed his wounded leg and lain making wild plannings. Winter was coming on and the march of the Hordes back to their plains about to begin. How to rescue the giant?

A plan came to the Christian mercenary. So soon as he could walk again he had one of the Assyrian merchants engage him as a camel-driver in bearing provisions into the encampment of Hulagu's army. Once within the lines, stretching mile on mile to the north of Baghdad's ruins, he had sought out the degraded chief of the Outer Wastes and left with him that tool and weapon which Gezir uncovered in the moonlight. Next day the camel-driver had passed near the giant again, dropping him a little bag of food, and the giant had raised his eyes and recognised the other and whispered a promise to have his irons filed through in readiness for escape before another nightfall.

So he might have done, and Hormizd conveyed him safely outside the Mongol lines. But next morning Hulagu's army had begun its long northwards trek. On its flank, among a medley of other followers, rode Hormizd on his stolen camel; in its centre, his chains filed almost to breaking-point, trudged Gezir Noyan. Under the shadow of the Alarlu plateau they had passed, the Hordes, and Hormizd had glanced up longingly at the far heights where a band of rescuers might have been gathered to make a sudden descent on the straggling army with the horse-tail standards. But there were other means of escape to hand.

The Horde of the Outer Wastes, sullen and mutinous, still held to the great army, but many of its members no longer avoided their disgraced chief. But for the terrible vengeance Hulagu would exact should he discover any of them attempting to free Gezir they would have had little hesitation in striking off his chains. And at length, again obtaining direct contact with Gezir in a pass of the mountains, Hormizd had put their hesitations to use.

Under the lee of the Kablurz Beg one stormy night the giant succeeded in filing through his chains and creeping to the limits of the camp. There, at the point guarded by his own following, he was given a horse and leather coat, a bow and the vowed devotion of that following, and passed out into the night. And in the night beyond the light of the camp-fires was awaiting him that stranger for whom he had suffered so much, the stranger who in turn had sought to defeat an army for his sake.

'Where now, brother?' Hormizd had asked, when they had kissed. 'Your followers say they will still receive you as chief in your own land. Let us ride there.' And he had turned his mount round towards the northern passes.

But Gezir had caught his arm. 'That journey is one of months and you would ride with a wound half-healed. It

would be death. Also' – as Hormizd laughed at this prophecy – 'there would be no safety for me in the north. I
would live in Persia henceforth. Let us ride to your home in
this Alarlu of which you have told me. It is near?'

'Very near,' said Hormizd. 'Yet—' Then he had turned
about slowly, with a last glance at the stars above the
northern mountains, and stretched his hand to Gezir in
the darkness, and guided him back on the road to Alarlu.

III

That winter of 1259 lasted scarcely a month in the Persian
hills. Presently the spring was with them at Alarlu, the grass
green in pasturage for the great herds of goats, the snows
melting and waving their feathery bands of vapour down over
the deserts of ruined Iraq. Bishop Nerses rode at the chase,
trying out the Mongol bow of horn, and once, far up towards
the Kablurz Beg, slaying a lion with it, as he tells with some
pride. He had a multitude of duties in that dawning of the hot
weather – marriages, baptisms, riding the marches and
beyond to find out what government, if any, he would have
to treat with in the interests of his Nestorians; judging,
meditating, escaping Amima's candid eye and tongue when
he had forgotten to change from a soiled robe; continuing his
great work on the Latin Rite. But he was not too busied to
watch the fortunes of his son Hormizd and the barbarian
chief Gezir, nor slow to apprehend that since their coming to
Alarlu each played a rôle for the benefit of the other. Lovers at
first sight they had been, inseparable and passionate friends
they had grown, yet both hid their inmost thoughts and
desires with such skill that neither suspected the other. But
Nerses, uninterfering, friendly to both, watched the tragi-
comedy played with a tightening of his heart-strings.

Hormizd – Hormizd, still young, son of a wayward
peasant mother, brother of Amima whom the Assyrian
community regarded with mingled pride and horror – he

was a prisoner in Alarlu, feeding on dreams that he might forget the horizon-beckoning realities. Stupendous dreams he would recite to his father in that watch-tower above the Persian hills – a mission to Rome; a league of Nestorian bands throughout Kharismia to seize the land and defy Mongol and Moslem alike; manufacture of that fire-powder which the Mongols had brought against Baghdad . . . Nerses would sit and look at him and listen to him, while the Latin Rite went unconfounded, and remember his own youth. There were wider lands than those beyond the deserts to explore, as he tells he might have told that son of his: the wonder countries of meditation and contemplation, of knowledge and, belief and faith. But he kept the knowledge to himself because the spring was crying out there on the hills and he remembered his own youth.

And his dreamings, it was soon obvious, Hormizd himself regarded as but dreamings, not to be mentioned in the hearing of the grave Gezir. For not only was Alarlu the only safe refuge for the latter, but it seemed he had settled contentedly enough in that refuge. He was, indeed, a warrior and wanderer only by necessity. He averred a grave interest in all things Persian, in goats and olives and camels and the cultivation of millet, a fondness for palm-wine – that wine which had earned for the Nestorians of Alarlu the worst of reputations among the surrounding Moslems. He made proposals for the breeding of other horses than hill-ponies, for manuring the fields with the dust of powdered bones in that fashion of agriculture which the Mongols had learned in the conquest of Kin. Except in the matter of Christian observances he played the part of the Alarlu-born Nestorian to perfection.

And Hormizd, putting away his dreams with his battered armour, tried to model himself in like pattern, blindly unapprehensive that Gezir Noyan in his secret soul loathed the life of the Persian hills with such loathing as few exiles had ever brought to those hills.

He hated the endless rise and fall, heat-haze and mirage-sway, glister of distant desert and undistant sandstorm which made up the scenic phenomena of the land he had adopted for the sake of Hormizd, believing Hormizd would perish on the journey to the north, or in that north grow weary for his native Alarlu. He hated the braziers and scented woods, the bell-ringing, the spiced dishes, the bright, fervid air and unending heat. Inside the palace walls he went with the air of a proud, trapped animal. The wide and stream-flecked plains, bright with tamarisks, the long, unending nights of the northern summers haunted him night and day, says Bishop Nerses, with a lover's memory and a lover's passion.

But he never talked of them except in moments of self-forgetfulness, and then to Nerses alone, in the watch-room above the palace to which he would sometimes climb to tell of the gods of his people, of the great Northern trinity of Esegé Malan, Mandiu, Hotogov Mailgan – gods from belief in whom the tolerant Bishop made but little attempt to convert him. Squatting in that tower of Nerses, the giant, great beard in hand, would pass from memories of the gods to memories of their worshippers, to tell of the land of freezing colds and great herds, the winding tracks of tribal migration across unending snows, the far roaring of the sea northwards, in winter, at the world's end, when the banners of the Golden Roan waved in the midnight sky. Sick with nostalgia, he would tell of those things . . . Until they would hear ringing steps come up the stairs and Hormizd would burst in upon them, seeking his brother, and the giant would cease his tale the while those two looked at each other like the fools and the lovers they were . . .

Then they would go down the stairs together and Amima, chance-met, would still her singing to scornful silence at the sight of the detested pagan. And the Bishop, with the threads of the tangled skein ready to his hands to untangle, with vision of a Hormizd lost to him for ever, would bury his face in those hands in an agony of indecision.

IV

And then one of Hulagu's lieutenants took a hand in the matter.

In Baqubah he heard of Alarlu, as the Bishop tells, and the odd little community of Assyrians that had sheltered there from time immemorial, tolerated as peaceful subjects by the Khalifs. But peacefulness in his subjects held no appeal for the Mongol. So he sent an embassy up into the hills and they encountered on the lower slopes a shepherd whom they questioned. He answered them civilly, and turned, offering to guide them. Then, in sport, one of them shot him through the back with a barbed arrow, and they left him screaming in a pool of blood and rode casually up the hill roads till they came to Nerses' palace.

The Bishop came down from his manuscripts to receive them. There were some half-dozen in the embassy, true Mongols, not such strangers as Gezir Noyan, and their thin moustaches drooped across flat, yellow faces. Their demands were brief and casual and their leader spoke them in a sing-song chatter, looking round the crowded courtyard as he spoke. Half the Alarlu herds and fifty virgins under the age of sixteen were to be driven down to Baqubah at once . . . The spokesman broke off and, still with an expressionless face, reached out, gripped Amima by the shoulder, and swung her into the hollow of his arm.

'This maid can stand surety for the other forty-nine. See to the orders of the governor, slave.' And he turned away, preparing to mount, while the rest of the Mongols, after a hungry glance around, were already in their saddles.

For a moment the Bishop and his followers alike were speechless. But only for a moment. A roar of indignation arose, someone strode past the Bishop and next moment

Amima was reeling away, freed, while her captor dropped, still expressionless, and Gezir Noyan unclenched a bruised fist . . .

The other Mongols were dragged from their horses and disarmed, and the Bishop held an anxious conference with Gazir and the elders of the community. Release those men they must, else the Hordes would come up from Baqubah and destroy them utterly.

But while they sat in debate they heard a wild shouting and a sudden, piercing shriek of grief from the courtyard. They rushed outside and found confronting the Mongol embassy Hormizd Nerses with the body of a dead Nestorian in his arms. It was the shepherd whom the Mongols had shot and whom Hormizd, out hunting, had come upon just before he died . . .

The cries of rage died down. All looked at the Bishop, waiting for him to speak. Amima hid her face. And Nerses, as he tells, braced himself to pronounce the dreadful words.

'Let these men be taken outside the courtyard and shot to death with arrows.'

It was done. Nerses heard the thudding of the arrowheads as he climbed uncertainly to his room. And Alarlu cleaned its hunting spears and all through two long nights the smithy furnaces flared the while Gezir Noyan, a skilled maker of arrow-heads to fit the short bow, beat out bolts to arm the Assyrian bowmen against the coming invasion.

Come it did, more quickly than they expected, though not in such force. The news from Alarlu appears to have reached Baghdad at the very moment of the recall of Hulagu's lieutenant. He had no time to send a strong expedition against the Christians in the hills, but on the northwards march detached a complete guran, eight hundred strong, with orders to raze Alarlu to the ground, pile the heads of the men in a pyramid, and drive the women out in the wake of the Mongol army. With them, dragging it across the desert, the guran took a bombard, one of the terrible engines brought from China.

Amima was the first of the Nestorians to take the field. She was down in the plains, in the first lightening of that morning, on a ride in search of buzzard. Two Mongol scouts rode round a shoulder of the foothills. One, failing to see in Amima a woman and fit matter for other diversion, hurled a javelin. Amima ducked, avoided it neatly, and raced her pony up through the gorges to Alarlu. There she turned round her panting mount a moment and saw the Mongol guran a moving blotch like the shadow of a sand-storm upon the desert – a shadow that rapidly neared the foothills.

Now, Gezir Noyan, tells the Bishop, was that early dawn engaged at the head of the gorge in planting a new millet patch on which Alarlu was to try out the Kin notions of manuring. The Bishop's daughter came pelting across the patch on her pony, glanced over her shoulder, glanced impatiently at the giant and his two Nestorian helpers.

'Back to Alarlu! The Mongols are in the foothills.'

Gezir dropped his implement and ran to the edge of the gorge instead. There he saw the Mongol guran, with the remembered horse-tail banner of Chépé, already beginning the climb to Alarlu. It would reach the plateau long before defenders came from the palace. Gezir turned to the Nestorians.

'We have hunting spears. We must hold them until Hormizd brings your brothers.'

Two miles away, while Hormizd shouted and mustered the Christian levies, while Amima rounded up stragglers from outlying fields, while Bishop Nerses, as he tells, struggled absent-mindedly to fit a coat of chain-mail over the robes in which he had just celebrated Mass – they heard an appalling sound. It was the Chinese bombard.

Halted half-way up the gorge the Mongol captain, stand-ing impatient witness of the fight waged on the dawn skyline between his advance guard and a handful of Christians, had had the piece levelled and fired. Spinning clumsily in its flight, the great stone ball fell in the midst of the attacking Mongols, rose again, killed one of the Nestorians, narrowly missed the head of Gezir Noyan, and ricocheted into the new millet-patch. With a roar of laughter the attacking Mongols who had survived the descent of the bombard's projectile flung themselves upon the two surviving defenders of Alarlu's Thermopylæ, and a moment later when the racing Hormizd and his levies burst in view of the millet-patch they found it already aswarm with yellow plainsmen . . .

Three times the Nestorians charged and three times were beaten back. Then suddenly a thunderous explosion shook the hills. A bright light rose and flared like a geyser. The Mongol guran turned back on itself in wild confusion, and Hormizd rallied his men and charged again . . .

Bishop Nerses, galloping across the plateau a few minutes later at the head of reinforcements, abruptly halted those reinforcements and pointed. Like the battle-figures on a wind-shaken tapestry, remote and unreal against the fervour of the sunrise above the darkness of the Alarlu gorges, the remnants of the Mongol guran were already streaming down the hillside in wild rout. The blowing up of the bombard had both killed their captain and shattered the morale of the attackers. Behind them, slaughtering without mercy, went Hormizd and his levies.

But at the foot of the gorge Hormizd abandoned both the pursuit and his followers and rode back at breathless speed to Alarlu, with sudden memory upon him of Gezir Noyan. Beyond the lip of the plateau, wending towards the palace, he came upon a procession of Nestorian wounded. And in a litter in the midst of that procession, unconscious, hacked and bleeding from a dozen wounds, lay the giant of the Outer Hordes.

V

For a little it seemed to the Bishop impossible that the man could live. Nevertheless, he had Gezir borne to his room in the palace and his wounds cleansed and bandaged. Then he drove out the stricken and helpless Hormizd and summoned a Nestorian woman to act as nurse.

But this order was unexpectedly countermanded. Next morning, when Gezir regained consciousness, he stared over the Bishop's shoulder in surprise at the Bishop's assistant.

'It is not seemly that your daughter should tend me.'

'It is not seemly that a heathen should die in Alarlu palace,' said Amima, also addressing her father. Nerses, as he tells, stared from one to the other of them in some bewilderment.

Hormizd found himself as a pariah in the great house. Only by stealth could he obtain converse with Gezir alone, as he complained to his father.

'You are better, my brother? Amima heeds to you?'

Gezir would groan and toss. 'As though I were a sick calf . . . And a heathen calf at that. God of the Golden Roan, if I could but see the skies again!'

VI

Summer aflame over Alarlu, deepening into the wild russets of autumn Persia, with the millet standing dark brown and parched, ripe for harvest. They set to gathering the olives – a great crop that year, and one that sold at price in the famished towns of Iraq. Gezir Noyan still lingered in his sick-room, progressing but slowly, all unaware the remarkable result his illness was producing outside the range of that room.

For Hormizd, robbed of his companionship, yet tied by his presence to Alarlu and its lands, had begun to discover in his blood something of which he had never before been aware – that aching land-love inherited from generations of hillmen-peasants, that love which could lure Neesan Nerses from the most absorbing of travellers' tales, the most clamorous point of a theological treatise, out to the wonder of burgeoning or corn-laden fields, of ripe orchards of olives. Hormizd discovered it with characteristic enthusiasm.

'The fool I have been, my father! I who longed to wander in far lands when I might have gathered olives in Alarlu! I'll never take armour or bow again unless other raiders come against us. Gezir and I will make this the granary of Persia.'

He set to work as a peasant in the fields, stealing indoors occasionally, much begrimed, and wary of discovery by Amima who was as irreverent towards his land-love as all his other passions, to talk enthusiastically in Gezir's room. And the black-bearded giant would listen and assent, then turn his face to the stone wall, as though seeking sleep . . .

The olives had been gathered and the tiny flails were pounding the millet in Alarlu village when Gezir's relapse took place. All one night he raved in delirium, crying out in his old passion of homesickness for the wind-swept plains of the north, held down and tended by the scared Hormizd, summoned to Amima's assistance . . . They did not wake the Bishop and by morning the giant was quiet again. Out on his usual early ride Nerses came on his son staring northwards towards the dim bulking of the Kablurz Beg. Only then did he learn of the happenings of the night, and Hormizd broke off abruptly, clenching his hands.

'Prisoner! Why did he never tell me he so hated Alarlu? I thought him a contented guest . . . If he should die here, far from those lands he loves—'

He laughed strangely. His hands were shaking. And because this love of a man for a man was something that the Bishop knew in the bitter silence of his own experience, he looked at his son and ached for him, saying nothing.

'Amima quietened him, at the last. He saw her while he raved in the devil-fever and thought her some woman of his Horde.'

The Bishop started a little at that. 'And what did Amima do?'

'She kissed him and made pretence to be that woman, and he fell asleep in her arms.'

VII

It seemed that night had been the turning-point. Thereafter Gezir began to mend rapidly. Soon the bandages about his great limbs could be dispensed with, and, propped by servants, he could totter out to the sunshine of the courtyard. Thereat the Bishop, with a sigh of relief, closeted himself with a wandering Buddhist monk from far Cambodia and for a week, as he tells, forgot Alarlu and all its problems in debate of the life of Sakya Muni and its likeness to the later incarnation of another Master. Then, with the departure of his guest, he descended from his tower one afternoon and came on an unexpected idyll, and at the sight thereof stood as surprised as many a father before and after him. And the sight was his daughter Amima in the arms of the pagan giant of the Outer Hordes, standing together under the sun-awning of the inner court.

For a moment he disbelieved his eyes and then, as he tells with a touch of sad whimsy, he saw that the two were not kissing each other, as would surely have been seemly. They were deep in debate. Amima in her giant's arms had not ceased to be Amima.

'But you are a heathen, a worshipper of devils,' she was saying, and Gezir Noyan was frowning at her perplexedly.

'I worship the same trinity as yourself, though under different names. And your Isho – who is he but Uha Soldong, the Golden Roan of heaven, though with us no helpless babe? He rides the skies in our northern lands, Amima . . . What thing have I done now?'

'You have blasphemed,' she said, and put his hands away, and turned from him into the palace. Yet, going, she glanced back at him, secretly, anxiously, as the Bishop noted. Gezir stared after her, smiling . . .

He started as he heard the footsteps of Nerses, and for a moment they looked at each other. Then Amima's father also smiled.

'I think Alarlu will have none of those gods of yours, unless you worship them under the names it knows – though those names may be but names.'

At that invitation and acceptance of himself the giant flushed a little, tugging at his beard. 'Of those names you will teach me, father of Amima.' He turned and looked out over the Persian lands with such contented glance as the Bishop of Alarlu had never yet seen on his face. 'For even home is called by many names.'

VIII

Bishop Nerses sat long in his tower in idle, happy thought that evening, watching the sunset colours turn to darkness and that darkness pale in the coming of the star-rise. So the skein had unravelled itself, Gezir and Hormizd alike had found content by ways unforeseen, and Alarlu would keep them . . . He turned to his scripts light-heartedly.

And, while he sat and wrote, his son Hormizd, grown strangely self-absorbed of late, was riding back through the starlight from a two-days' expedition into the plains . . .

Nerses heard the sound of his arrival, heard him hand his pony to a palace servant. But he did not ascend to the tower immediately. It was nearly an hour later, as the Bishop noted by the notchings of his candles, before footsteps came up the stairway and Hormizd asked permission to enter. Behind him bulked the giant.

'Father, I've come to pray that you give me leave to go from Alarlu again – with my brother Gezir.'

'Go?' The Bishop stared at him, and knew at once what he meant, knew at once that this was no planning of a casual expedition. 'Leave Alarlu? But you've loved it of late.'

Hormizd laughed with a strange gaiety, avoiding his father's eyes. 'That was but a passing fancy – and oh! there are other lands to see before a man dies. There isn't a Mongol guran on all the borders, the road to the north is clear, and Gezir and I would take it – back to his people in the Outer Wastes.'

And then, his face as pale as death, Gezir Noyan made a despairing gesture as Neesan Nerses' eyes turned on him.

'This is no plotting of mine, Bishop Nerses. I have told Hormizd he will die if he never again sees Persia – for there will be no returning. And I – I have no desire to go. I have grown to love – Alarlu.'

Hormizd's laughter rang out.

'Listen to him, my father! So he still dares affirm to us, who know his hunger for the northern lands, who've heard him raving of them in dreams – dreams wherein he mistook my sister Amima herself for some lost love of his!' The giant started. Hormizd turned from both of them, and Nerses saw his hands shaking again. 'I die? I've always longed to cross the deserts to the wild lands. It is I as well who would die here in the littleness of Alarlu, as my father knows, who will give us leave to go. . . . And then – the road to the skies where rides your Golden Roan, my brother!'

'Ah yes, the Golden Roan,' said Gezir, dully.

IX

The whole of Alarlu palace and village turned out the evening of their departure, and Nerses saw already on the trees the dark, bitter green of winter. And, amazed and stricken, yet with pain stifled in exhaustion, he watched the two young men. Amima alone was absent from the throng of farewell-makers.

Two baggage-mules, loaded with the provisions and weapons the travellers were to use on their thousand-miles journey into the darkness of Asia, were brought out. Gezir Noyan, gigantic and alien again in leather jerkin and hauberk, more pallid than ever, knelt for the Bishop's blessing, and stood up, and looked round about him half-desperately.

'The Lady Amima—' he began, and stopped, with words stuck in his throat, looking down at her father.

And the Bishop tried again, knowing the uselessness of his urgings. 'Then why leave her? Hormizd is doing this only to pleasure you. Tell him you do not want to go.'

The giant shook his head and turned away. 'Already I have told him, but he laughs the louder each time, believing me a liar for his sake. Were that all, I could stay, but – do I not know this son of yours? There is joy and fever in his blood to see far lands, and I go with him, for he is my brother.'

The crowding Nestorians drew back. Then Hormizd knelt also for blessing, and stood up, and embraced his father, both knowing they would never meet again. And Hormizd swung into his saddle and bent from it his gaily helmeted head.

'I'll come back again – if ever the deserts and years will give me passage, my father.' He laughed with stricken face. 'Think of me sometimes in those northern lands – here, when the olives ripen in autumn.'

'But there's no need to go. Gezir would stay. He would marry Amima—'

Hormizd laughed again, turning his face from his father's. 'He is a prince of liars and a prince of brothers. He would swear for my sake that the burning pains of hell were pleasant and agreeable. Amima? He has pined this year with memory of some woman of the north – her of whom he raved in dreams.' His horse leapt forward under the touch of sudden spurs. 'Ready, my brother?'

And when next Bishop Nerses raised his head he saw the darkness come raining from the east over the deserted hills.

x

One pauses above the last crinkled leaves of the ancient script to hear far across the centuries that remote piping of resentment and bitter pain in hearts long powder and nothing on the winds of forgotten days; to watch those two who had ridden into Alarlu nine months before ride out again, following and misjudging each other in a passionate obstinacy of love; to start in sudden, puzzled wonder, as did Bishop Nerses himself that night at the words spoken to him by Amima when she climbed to him in his tower.

'Fools? They were wise at last, each for the other, as only lovers might be.' She hid her face and then looked out into the starred silence, her breath coming in a sob. 'Oh, I *knew*, my father, I who loved them both. Always I knew, even while I hoped . . . Each sick at heart himself and wise for the other – *for to the end it was Gezir's Hormizd who was the real Hormizd, Hormizd's Gezir the real Gezir.*'

V

The Glamour of Gold

The Glamour of Gold
and the Givers of Life

I

IF MAN THE ARTIST and Man the Agriculturist have lengthy histories and pre-histories, it is certain that Man the Explorer has an even greater antiquity. His antiquity extends far back beyond his humanity to the distant wanderings of the common ape-stock which fathered such divergent near-humans as the Peking Man of China, Pithecanthropus of Java, the great-jawed Heidelberg man of Germany. Exploration is among the most ancient of urges, nor need we assume that even in the pre-human days of humanity it was always exploration in search of more pleasant foods and pleasing shelters. Curiosity was a continual urge, even though only that spasmodic and uncontinued curiosity that a modern man may study in the antics of the monkey-cage. Beyond the next forest, the next line of hills, went a dim reasoning, *there might be something new*.

Twenty or thirty thousand years ago the great ice barriers of the Fourth Glacial Age began to break down all over the northern half of the Old World. The Ice retreated from Europe and Asia, leaving the great Russian plains seeping swamps, breaking down the Central Asian mountain-and-snow-ring in which it is possible that Man himself had attained (sheltered in that nook from the glacial rigours) his humanity. It was the Spring-time of the world, and different groups of men set out on slow wanderings, millennium on millennium, to the ultimate homes of racial differentiation. They were probably medium-sized, browny, indeterminate beings, those early forerunners who turned their backs on each other and set out to found the various races of mankind. Neither the bleached pallor of the White, the curled hair and flattened face of the Black, the yellowness and eye-folding of the Mongol were yet in evidence. Climate and mutation were to play their parts in effecting those changes that are now so obtrusive to our eyes: Man the Early Explorer in his explorations was to father all the racial prides and fond prejudices of Modern Man.

That Early Man appears to have approximated very closely indeed to the Natural Man of Rousseau and the Encyclopædists; indeed, the Natural Man of Rousseau was no chance imagining of a dreaming sage (as is so often supposed), but a personification of the qualities of the last surviving groups of early men discovered by civilised Europe – the primitives of America. He was cultureless, houseless, godless; he had no devils, no classes, no agriculture, no clothes, no domestic animals. He was merely an animal, and not unrare on this planet in that he was also a toolusing animal. And, to judge by the evidences from the scarce Primitive groupings which until lately survived in this and that corner of the world, he was on the whole a happy and kindly animal, easily amused, a singer and hunter, unoppressed by strange fears, unstirred by strange hopes. The Golden Age was for long a reality on our planet: the first explorers who wandered west into Europe, east into China, south into Africa, were of the very stuff of the wistful dreamings of poets in the cities of civilisation a long twenty thousand years later.

In Europe Cro-Magnard and Magdalenian man hunted the horse and the bison through long ages, painted great pictures, led dangerous and happy lives, generation on generation, in a great artistic flowering of the human spirit in a world slowly recovering from the Ice Age rigours. South and around the Mediterranean were folk of like blood and quality: their rock-paintings astound the modern traveller in the nullahs of the Sahara. But gradually a period of desiccation set in. Slowly the forested, swampy Sahara grew arid and brittle. Ungulates and carnivores drifted eastwards along the Mediterranean coasts with that shrinkage of the verdure of North Africa. With them went the happy-go-lucky tribes of Early Man, hunters and fishers. So doing, they came at last to the banks of the lower Nile.

The Nile resisted the desiccation. Year after year, most uniquely flowing of rivers, it brought down the warm equatorial waters to generate the seeds of the plants along its shores. Wild barley grew along those shores in great natural fields, sprang to greenness, ripened, fell to the ground to be revived again, surely and certainly, on a fixed, unwavering day, by the next year's floods. It was a process profoundly and plainly impressed on the mind of the Primitive who had come hunting into that region: in no other region could the process have been so plainly impressed. He found the barley easy and succulent food. And at last one of his number, long afterwards deified as Osiris, the First King-Irrigator, was moved to assist the processes of the river, to dig a channel to further stretches of land for the river to fertilise, to inaugurate the first attempt at basin-agriculture.

So, suddenly, man became an agriculturist, storing the surplus of the seeds for next year's flood-sowing, creating architecture in building sheds for that storage, creating villages and so towns and so civilisation in the necessity to carry out those operations communally. So classes came into the world with the differentiation of men into Kings (Chief Irrigators), Priests (Followers and Tenders and Interpreters of the Kings) – and Plebs (the Labourers at the Sowing and Reaping). In a few hundred years there came into being on our planet – and at the time on no other portion of it than the Nile basin – civilisation: not slowly evolved from barbarism as barbarism was once supposed in its turn to have sprung from savagery, but a direct transition from the life of wandering, carefree Natural Man.

Now, godless and devil-less though he had been, Natural Man like all other animals had always sought to avoid death, and had reasoned that the cause of death was the loss of blood, that blood itself, in fact, was Life. Consequently, long before the coming of civilisation, he had in various parts of the world greatly prized objects and materials the colour of blood – red carnelian and the like. He had prized the cowrie-shell as an amulet because of its life-giving shape – its obvious similarities in shape to the portal of mammalian birth. He had traded in such objects over wide areas, and valued them greatly.

With the coming of civilisation, with the swift rise of gods and the study of death and decomposure, that search for life-givers became intensified if also diversified. Green was now looked upon as a Giver of Life – any object of green – because of its likeness to the life-giving corn. Jade and malachite were searched for and valued accordingly. So was gold the colour of the sun which warmed and ripened the crops – a great Life-Giver. With the surplus of energy and population that agriculture created the ancient Nilotic kings sent out their captains and mariners far and near in quest of those seemingly necessary things.

Exploration of the world was launched again – exploration not originally for trade or conquest or the seizing of rich lands: but for amulets against death and misfortune, precious metals which would ensure the wearer long health and earthly immortality, residence in a happy eternity of terrestrial bliss.

II

The urge of this irrational quest for irrational Givers of Life spread civilisation abroad the Old World. The exploring miners and traders and exploiters of Egypt carried agriculture, its banes and blessings, to Sumer, to Syria, to Crete. There the autochthonous primitives, learning practice and theory, in their turn erected altars to strange gods, upbuilt their characteristic civilisations, quested like their mentors the Egyptians out and abroad the unknown lands for gold and pearls, jade and amber. Sumer carried the seeds of civilisation into India, rearing Mohenjo-Daro and its attendant glories, into Central Asia and from there engrafting the tree of Chinese civilisation. So with Crete, civilising the Mediterranean basin and the Greek lands, penetrating remotely to Spain, and from there to Britain. Civilisation fathered the first deliberate exploration, exploration in its turn fathered the great divergent and diverging cultures of the ancient world.

But gradually the irrational element in the quest died out. Gold came to be prized not as a magic metal, a mystic Giver of Life, but (owing to its scarcity) assuming direct and ascendant values over other commodities as a means of exchange and therefore of definite social wealth. In a measure this was mere transmutation of the original idea of gold – a transmutation which still holds the world in thrall. But it was of definite consequence. The fantastic element in the quest lapsed, or, as the poets of the succeeding Greek and Roman civilisations saw it, the Silver Age which had succeeded the Golden Age in its turn departed, to be followed by the Iron Age of brute exploitation and conquest, the ages which produced the warring armies of Assyria and the throat-cutting raids abroad Europe of the early Greeks and Celts. And, just as the value of gold was transmuted in men's minds, its direct and urgently personal-appealing importance to some measure lapsed. Sargon sought territory rather than the metals within it: he sought subject peoples and subject cornlands. So with Alexander the Great, so with most of the great military conquerors.

Encouraging their merchants to trade afar, the Mesopotamian and Mediterranean civilisations had already, by the close of the last millennium before Christ, fairly definite knowledge of many countries outside the range of their own political sway. Pytheas, a Greek trader from Marsala, had sailed up the coasts of Spain, circumnavigated Britain, and voyaged to a remote Thule which was perhaps Iceland, more probably Norway. The Greek Alexander (the trader, not the king), had coasted Southern Asia remotely to Hanoi. The east coast of Africa had been definitely explored as far south as Dar-es-Salaam: perhaps even further, for Herodotus has a story of an expedition despatched by the Egyptian Pharaoh Necho which circumnavigated Africa, taking several years to do so, keeping close to the coasts, landing and planting crops, awaiting their ripening, and pushing on till finally it came to the Pillars of Hercules, and so at last the Mediterranean. Two at least of these three great journeys were journeys in the interests of trade, colonisation, land-seizing.

Necho's expedition is perhaps the exception. It brings us to other exceptions which still dwindlingly survived. In 500 BC Himilco the Carthaginian visited the West Coast of Europe, perhaps touched on Ireland, and then penetrated far out into the Atlantic – attaining the Sargasso Sea, as some think. He could hardly have done so in quest of definite spoil. Here and there in the drabness of the records other attempts erupt into notice – inexplicable attempts upon this and that point of the compass from the view of the new commercialist orientation of exploration.

For the explanation of such attempts it is necessary to glance again at those first beginnings of all civilisations in the Valley of the Nile. As we have seen, the First God was the deified King-Irrigator. Dying, he yet lived in his successor; and also, in the hazy theological metaphysics of those days, individually and personally, in remote lands of the sun. For he was a Child of the Sun and his flesh might not put on corruption.

So arose the idea of immortality, a play and a counterplay

of thought and surmise upon a very prosaic happening. Assembling for the first time in villages, men no longer, as did their primitive progenitors, left their dead to decompose where they fell. They carried the bodies remotely from the villages to the sandy Western bank of the Nile and thrust them into holes, kings, commons, priests, heaping the sand well upon them.

But it was a peculiar burial-place. The hot Egyptian sands did not, as sands in burial elsewhere, decompose the body. Instead, they preserved it uniquely. Astounded Egyptians carrying their dead there would find that hungry jackals had been at work and had torn out corpses and partially devoured them. This was understandable enough, but not (for hunters accustomed to seeing the decay of death) the state of the cadavers. The dead Egyptians looked almost as in life, dead hardly at all, surely in a sleep, surely awaiting the coming of some fresh life . . .

To ensure that life yet more fully – that mystic life in some unnameable land – mummification, tomb-building, was introduced, and spread everywhere in the tracks of the Archaic Civilisation. With that diffusion – to Europe, to Asia, remotely into Africa – spread the myths and legends that went with the practice, legend of a mythic land in the West (originally the Nile *West* Bank) where the happy dead lived a new life, free and immortal,

> the island-valley of Avilion,
> Where falls not hail, or rain, or any snow,
> Nor ever wind blows loudly.

The idea and belief took root in theology, in folklore, as the Garden of the Hesperides, the Fortunate Isles, Valhalla, Wineland, the Land of Gold. And it was regarded not as a distant land in the skies, not in exact essence the Heaven or Hades of the various mythologies, but as a definite terrestrial paradise. Generally its direction was adscripted to the

West. As geographical knowledge enlarged it receded more quickly and quickly into the Atlantic. Sometimes, though seldom, the East found it its home, what with the tales that came to Europe of the magic Spice Islands – inextricably confused with the Fortunate Isles though indeed they were but the East Indies.

So again the irrational element had come into exploration, the quest for a land of geographical fantasy, a land of Youth and Fortune and Gold.

III

Men being of the lowly clay they are, concerned with food and mating and the begetting of children, drowsing by chimney corners, yawning in peace in long summer days, worshipping with benignant incomprehension the incomprehensible Gods, that Quest of the Fortunate Isles was never in itself in any age a deep and passionate racial urge. At the most it was the main motif in a number of exploring lives, it gave hope and fear and a dim uncertainty to the far land and sea-wanderings of many men in the days before Christ. A man set out on a new trade route in the hope, as a remote ambition, of finding the Golden Land of Youth. If he failed en route he might at least fill his pouch with good terrestrial treasure by the way.

The origin of the belief and quest, as we have seen, was a fantastic misapprehension of the action of Nature in a matter of human burial. But, spreading through the Mediterranean, throughout all Europe, interweaving with fresh by-products of religious and theological fancy, it acquired a surer belief to foundation it. That belief was built on vague race memories of the world that once had been – that world of Early Man which those first civilisations (even while they enjoyed the fruits of civilisation) looked back on regretfully as the vanished Golden Age when good King Cronos reigned in heaven and Zeus the warlike usurper was still inapparent. Some fragment of that ancient world, went the poet's misty dream, might still survive – far off under the setting of the sun . . .

The fourth and fifth Christian centuries saw the over-throw of the Roman Empire. Europe was plunged into political and cultural anarchy; trade languished as did imagination; exploration as motif or desire vanished from the European scene. Slowly a version of Christianity, garnished with many an odd notion from the older reli-gions, spread abroad Europe; slowly the kingdoms and principalities of the Middle Ages took more or less perma-nent shape; slowly the great trading, exploring, debating class came into prominence – the middle class. Men read the ancients in a new-found leisure, speculated in mon-asteries and the great guild towns, carried the seeds of those speculations from the Mediterranean to the Baltic. Popula-tions grew at considerable pace: in the less kindly agricul-tural regions the press of population was the root cause of the unending moving and raiding and colonising of the first Christian millennium. That spread of population was to father the Crusades, with which this record is unconcerned. But also it was an urge to find new ways of trade: it begat anew the desire for geographical exploration: it begat the long line of earth-conquerors who were to subjugate the earth.

And in the medley of reasons that have urged European explorers abroad the planet since that year AD 1000 – desire for loot, for fame, for fun – the quest of the Fortunate Isles, sometimes deliberate, sometimes unapprehended, has moulded innumerable lives and journeys and voyages. Until the beginning of the present century one may trace it as a thin vein of unauthentic gold in all the grey fabric of geographical adventure. And in the lives of at least Nine of the great representative Earth-Conquerors its influence was predominant; and with them is this chronicle.

It was a quest curiously mixed and – by the time of the

last of the Nine – transmuted. Yet Leif Ericsson and Fridtjof Nansen, separated by a space of nine hundred years, both quested the unattainable same. They did it under different names and guises: the essence remained. Marco Polo alone belongs to this record not so much because of the influence of the quest upon his life as the influence of his life upon the quest. Columbus and Cabeza de Vaca were seekers of the Fortunate Isles naked and unashamed in intention; Magellan's search was darker and colder, his Fortunate Isles the isles of clove and nutmegs, but the urge to their attainment drawn from Columbus's; Vitus Bering slowly and unwilling sought the same fleeting land in the fogs of the North Pacific; Mungo Park pursued it inland, with a cold fire, to its abiding place by the bank of an unknown river, Richard Burton (who would have laughed the imputation of the quest to scorn) sought the same Debatable Land in Harar, in Arabia, in the Lakes that give birth to the Nile; Nansen quested it, disguised as 'knowledge of a mathematical point' towards the utmost Pole.

How that quest interwove in their lives and thoughts and actions, was acknowledged, repudiated, foregone, but yet was the principal thing in the lives of those Nine; how the sought-for Land of Youth sometimes betook itself to strange shapes, to the likeness of the City of God, to the likeness of a mental refuge from a half-integrated self, to the likeness of the realm of icy knowledge: is the theme of this book.

In all its changings – from a definite Island in a definite sea to a definite standpoint in human thought – it remained and remains *terra incognita*, the Unknown Land; and it may be said truly that the lives of those Nine, all of whom were great and successful explorers, are all in a fashion tragic epics. So in a fashion is all human life. But tragedy itself has no part in that belief in the happy Fortunate Isles which dominated the lives of those Nine who were representative

of so many men: it was glamour gloriously unescapable.
Leif at Brattalid, Burton at Aden, Mungo Park in Peebles,
Bering toil-worn on the Yenisei, Magellan glowering east-
wards from Goa:

> Whether at feast or fight was he
> He heard the noise of a nameless sea
> On an undiscovered isle.

Mungo Park Attains the Niger
and Passes Timbuctoo

I

IN THAT HASTING conquest of the earth's surface which
began in the eleventh century and continued campaign on
campaign till to our remoter vision the surface of the planet
seems tracked like a spider-web, interior Africa for long
remained uninvaded. Before Columbus, the Portuguese in
the service of Henry the Navigator had coasted the Western
shores slow year on year, each year penetrating a little
further south along those coasts that they named 'of Guinea' and 'of Gold'. They traded with the shoreward natives,
fought them, stole them, shipped great numbers of them to
Portugal as slaves. They noted how below a certain line of
the coast – the mouth of the Gambia – the Africans changed
from indeterminate brown to black – they passed beyond
the region of the Arabised Moor and came to the territories
of the true Negroes. And at last, after long years of sailing
and debating that have mention elsewhere in this record,
they rounded the Cape of Good Hope, attained Zanzibar,
and made the passage to India.

They were followed by the ships of other maritime nations – the Dutch, the Spaniards, the English. The former landed in South Africa and took to an adolescent plundering and planting that in maturity evolved its colonisation. The Portuguese, from Angola, penetrated far to South-Central Africa, and erected strange 'kingdoms' in indefinite localities before the close of the seventeenth century – kingdoms which presently crumbled to dust with the decay of the Portuguese power at home. Africa remained in its great northward bulking, despite those incursions from river and coast, an unknown country.

Deep in the heart of that unknown country Europe had long been apprised of the rumour of the Niger, a great river draining the forests and mountains, a river rivalling the Nile, a river on the banks of which stood fabulous Timbuctoo.

Rumour of this river had haunted the Mediterranean lands from earliest historic times. The Egyptians of late Dynastic days had sent an expedition in search of it – an expedition which actually appears to have reached the Niger's banks somewhere in the region of Lake Chad. With the coming of the outbreak of Islam upon the world communication or dream of communication with that distant river was cut apart – until the Arabs themselves evolved light and learning in travel and geographical curiosities. In advance of those curiosities mixed drifts of Libyan-Berber-Arabs crossed the Sahara in the ninth century and came in contact with the barbaric Negro states of the Archaic culture on the upper waters of the Niger. From that contact presently arose the great Negroid kingdoms of Songhay and Bornu, to astound the Arab geographers who came exploring south from Morocco in the eleventh and twelfth centuries.

Strangely, discovering the Niger, those geographers remained in considerable uncertainty regarding two matters of ancient debate. Where did it rise? – In the Nile, according to the map of Ibn Mohammed al Idrisi, published in 1153; in Unknown Land, according to Ibn Batuta, most famous of the Arabs, who paid a visit to Timbuctoo in 1353. Where did it set? – in the Atlantic, according to al Idrisi; in the 'sands of the interior' according to Ibn Batuta.

But, with the slave raidings of Portuguese, French, and English down the West African coast in the seventeenth and eighteenth centuries, that coast became so well known and mapped that it seemed no longer possible to assume that an unknown river, of such immensity as the Niger in debouchure, had its outlet on the Atlantic. All the great river mouths – the Gambia, the Congo – were known. Could the Congo be the Niger under another name?

In 1778 the English African Association was formed under the presidency of Sir Joseph Banks for the encouragement of the Scientific Exploration of Africa.

Within five years of its foundation the Association had despatched three explorers into Africa in pursuit of the Niger. The first, Ledyard, an American marine, had some idea of tackling the problem from Libya. But he died in Cairo ere his mission was well begun. Lucas, the second man selected, had once been a slave in Morocco. He proposed to travel to the Niger country across the Sahara, and actually set out on that mission from Tripoli. But, after five days travel, he turned back his caravan, having come into collision with 'revolting Arabs' (he referred to their political activities). The next selection of the Association was Major Houghton, fort-major at Goree, where the great French aerodrome is now built, a man of singular courage and address, in the phrase of the time, and well acquainted with Arabic.

Houghton's venture progressed further than that of either Ledyard or Lucas. With assistance and co-operation from a white slaver on the Gambia, one Dr Laidley of Pisania, Houghton passed through the negro 'kingdoms' of Woolli, Kasson, and Kaarta. Beyond Kaarta was Ludamar, a 'kingdom' of half-breed Arabs – 'Moors' as they were dubbed in the nomenclature of the times. Jarra was the border town and Houghton wrote from there his last and characteristic letter to Laidley five hundred miles away:

> Major Houghton's compliments to Dr Laidley; is in good health, on his way to Timbuctoo; robbed of all his goods by Kend Bular's son.

With this last cryptic message, Houghton disappeared into Ludamar, was again robbed, crawled on his hands and knees to a Moorish village, was there refused food, and either allowed to starve to death or knocked on the head and his body dragged into the woods.

News of the catastrophe filtered down to the coast with the slave caravans, and Laidley sent it on to the African Association in London. The third venture had not been lucky. Banks and the others looked about for someone to take the place of the unfortunate Houghton.

II

The remarkable individual chosen for that fourth attempt upon the Niger had been born in a Scottish farmhouse near Selkirk in 1771. He was one of thirteen children, his father a peasant-farmer, his mother a handsome and competent woman of that exclusive and surprising breed which tills the land in Scotland. It was a family neither very poor nor affluent: they kept one servant, the Parks, though sight of the small whinstone house of Fowlshiels might lead the modern investigator to doubt the fact. Mungo's father was deeply religious, a stern and dour man; his mother appears intellectually to have been of a like barrenness, if fecund physically. Mungo's brothers and sisters were ordinary and kindly and uninspired folk. He himself, through the play of innumerable small chances, grew up differently to his strange destiny precipitated by the death of Houghton in far-off Ludamar.

He was a tall and handsome and shy youth, with brown hair and a small mouth, and a very pious mind. His shyness is the thing most frequently commented on in his early days: it persisted, but little modified, all through his life. That modification was the assumption of an appearance of extreme coldness and reserve. Mungo below that mask was possibly such a warring civil insurrection as we may never penetrate and chart.

He was educated at the Grammar School at Selkirk, a very competent and model scholar, one who read books and books and still more books as he tramped the muddy Scots roads evening and morning in search of the much-prized Scots education. He read much of the Border poetry of that time, novels and religious tracts, and very early seems to have been moved by the wonder of plants and plant-life. It was possibly this incipient passion for botany that moulded his whole life in the ultimate shape it took. He refused the Church and elected to study medicine, to the great disappointment of his parents.

This was in 1786. He was apprenticed to a neighbouring practitioner, in the fashion of those days, and rode the district in company with his master, dosing the ailing and assisting at unique and bloody operations. He seems to have acquired no great love of his profession; but he was a difficult youth either to know or to love. By 1789, when he went to Edinburgh to matriculate, he appears almost as mature as he ever became – coldly devout in the Presbyterian fashion, self-centred, controlled, occasionally very eager with friends and kindly with the unfortunate.

But even when he was a full and formal doctor, he seems to have paused in doubt of the next step. He was only twenty-one years of age, but considered that he was wasting his own time and the Lord's very seriously in not settling down to a profession – his own profession or some other.

He confided those doubts to a friend of his brother-in-law, James Dickson. So doing, he made yet another contact with an outpost of destiny.

Sir Joseph Banks, a man of many concerns and projects, was interested in the dour young Scot, sympathised with his unwillingness to spend his life in the dreariness of a Scottish general practitioner's round, and at last found him more congenial occupation. This was to act as surgeon on an East Indiaman, the *Worcester*, sailing for Bencoolen in Sumatra.

Mungo sailed with the ship into a year of which we know little or nothing. He seems to have enjoyed the voyage and to have botanised considerably in Sumatra. He wrote a paper for the Linnean Society describing eight new and hitherto unchristened fishes. He spent sweating hours in the fo'c'sle, doctoring the ills of the sailors with a cool dispassion, long nights staring at the homeward stars as the *Worcester* at last turned about to seek England. They rounded the Cape of Good Hope in good weather, and he saw for long weeks, dark in the east, the bulking of that strangest of continents vexing his horizon. Wonder – the explorer's wonder – awoke in him. What lay within? What man of his colour would first attain the gates of Golden Timbuctoo? . . . Perhaps, like Hanno, he looked out on that distant shore some night and saw its fires lighting up the darkness.

The *Worcester* reached England. Mungo, paid off and unemployed, took up residence with his brother-in-law in London and looked about him for work. More determinedly than ever, he was not to become a general practitioner. On the other hand, long sea-voyaging wearied him excessively. It was an impasse.

It was an impasse which the news of Houghton's death, received by the English African Association, speedily ended. The Association, comfortably unfrightened (as it well might be) at the fates which had befallen its various explorers, determined to despatch yet another in search of the Niger's source and outlet; and it looked around for a suitable person – 'educated and trustworthy' – to take up the task.

Mungo's name was again brought to the attention of Sir Joseph Banks by the indefatigable brother-in-law. Sir Joseph remembered. Sir Joseph was interested. He spoke to his fellow-members of the African Association.

Mr Park sounded suitable.

Mr Park was summoned to an interview. He was cool and eager and respectful, a young man with a face still faintly browned by the suns of Sumatra. There was nothing he would like better than to take up the search for the Niger, he declared, 'for the unravelling of the secrets of those strange lands profoundly fascinated me'.

He was formally commissioned, and sailed for Africa in May 1795, directed, in his own words

on landing in Africa to pass on to the River Niger, either by way of Bambouk, or by such other route as should be found most convenient. That I should ascertain the course, and, if possible, the rise and termination of that river. That I should use my utmost exertions to visit the principal towns or cities in its neighbourhood, particularly Timbuctoo and Boussa; and that I should be afterwards at liberty to return to Europe, either by the way of the Gambia, or by such other route as, under all the then existing circumstances of my situation and prospects, should appear to me most advisable.

III

Mungo's first meeting with Africa in speech and person was at Jillifri, a port on the northern bank of the Gambia. Here his ship put in to trade in beeswax and ivory, and here he began to collect his information regarding that inland country through which he purposed to travel in search of the legendary Niger.

It was a country of small negro and pseudo-negro kingdoms, some pagan, some recently Islamised. Coastwards, the prevalent and prevailing negro type was the Mandingo, heavy, tall men, good traders, 'a mild, sociable and pleasing people'. Their chief magistrate was the 'caid', their tribal conferences were 'palavers' – a word which showed an antique Portuguese influence. They cultivated maize and rice and cotton, exported slaves, taxed alien slavers, and were in general a barbaric people slowly moving from their ancient orientation in contact with the Europeans.

Interspersed with them were the warlike Jaloffs, an aristocracy on horseback, Moors in Mungo's phraseology, and the wild hinterlands Negroes, the Feloops, unsociable souls who cut the throats of slavers and lived in remote jungles. These Feloops, we may guess (for in this later day they have been long merged in other groupings) were the original Golden Age Negroes moved to those unrestraints of conduct and ethic which contact with the cultured has ever wrought in primitive men.

It was a swampy, wet and uncertain land that which lay into the sunrise, Mungo gathered. And he would do well to learn Mandingo, the lingua franca, before he adventured its unknown perils.

He had now reached Pisania, last Gambia station of the white slave-traders, and put up at the residence of Laidley, the obscure medico and slaver-philanthropist who had befriended Houghton. The Gambia was close at hand; so were the rains. Disregarding both, the solemn young Scotsman sat down, hour on hour, with word-lists and native teachers, to plod through the mysteries of Mandingo.

Slavers would come and look at the young man, and tell him tales of the interior; he disregarded most of these with a placid suspicion. He was indifferent to the slaver's trade but distrustful of his veracity. By the end of July he considered himself equipped for the journey ahead, and would have set out then but that he caught a chill while observing, genteelly, an eclipse of the moon. Next day he was down with fever.

For three weary months this fever kept him prostrate. The rains – the tremendous gushing rains of the African coast had come on, swashing across the Gambia, burying all activity in their silvery pelt. The Gambia rose and rose, and Mungo found little sleep o' nights in the chorusing of the African frogs. He took the matter with a cool, priggish philosophy: he was at least being inoculated against the fevers of the interior.

Slowly the fever abated. He resumed his studies of Mandingo, and questioned Laidley on the obtaining of servants and horses. Laidley – he liked Mungo – very obligingly loaned him a young Negro slave, Demba, a cheerful and happy and garrulous individual, who was promised his freedom on Mungo's safe return to the coast; also, he hired for the young Scotsman's use an older native, one Johnson, who had been a West Indian slave and appears to have learned little to strengthen either his morale or morals in the plantations of English Jamaica. Asses to carry Mungo's small quantity of luggage and trade-goods were purchased, as well as a 'small and hardy horse' to bear Mungo himself into the dark interior of Africa.

At last his fever had passed. He felt well and strong again. On the 2nd of December, 1795, he set out eastwards accompanied by Laidley and two other white slavers. Besides these was a small caravan – two negro merchants, Johnson, Demba, and a couple of interior natives returning to their homes from working on the Gambia. Mungo carried with him on the horse an 'umbrella, a pocket sextant, a thermometer, two compasses, and a few changes of linen'.

That night they reached an inland village, Jindey. Here they slept, and here, the next morning, the three white men bade Mungo good-bye, never expecting to see him again. Several miraculous chances were to disprove their expectations. But we gather from Mungo's chronicle that for a moment he himself felt very young and dispirited and lonely as he watched those men of his own blood and breed turn about and ride into the westwards forest. He looked about him at the broad, dark, alien faces, thick-lipped, round-eyed, of the strange people among whom he had come, and felt no lightening of heart. Then – already in his mind a faint bugle-call the very name – he remembered the Niger, and rode briskly forward.

IV

He was now in the 'kingdom' of Walli. Walli, at its frontier, proceeded to tax him heavily. Seeing that the tax-gatherers were in too great number to be shot down or ridden down, the young Scotsman submitted to the imposition, and rode on. It was a flat and fertile land. But jungle waved in the south; forward were great stretches of forest.

Three days of riding amidst little villages brought them out of Walli into Woolli. No one as yet had hindered Mungo greatly, or helped him either. He was still in lands close to the coast, and the white man a phenomenon looked upon without astounded gape. On the 5th of December, however, he reached Medina, the capital of Woolli, a sunshine land, with the mudbuilt 'city' set amidst wooded hills and gentle declivities. Here he was hospitably entertained by the negro 'king', one Jatta, who had previously entertained Houghton. Houghton's name, indeed, was constantly on the negro's lips. Did Mungo know what had happened to Houghton? Mungo shook his head at this rhetorical remark: he desired information. He had it. Houghton had been murdered by the Moors!

Mungo tried to look as shocked and surprised as possible. He was always scrupulously polite and respectful in his dealings with African potentates. Jatta regarded him with a sorrowful eye, and said it was evident that nothing would stop him. He would pray for the white man.

On the 8th, still in Woolli, and still travelling undisturbed, Mungo and his small caravan, considerably scratched and jaded, arrived at a town that is famous in story and controversy. It was Kolor: out of that town Mungo was to bring the first account to Europe of a negro ritual to enrich our vocabulary. Kolor was the home of Mumbo-Jumbo. When the goodman of Kolor arrived at the conclusion that one of his wives was in need of correction he did not hale her before the magistrates or hit her in the jaw: he proceeded outside the village gates where hung a suit made from the bark of a tree. Getting within this suit and closing down the visor of the mask, the negro would wait until the fall of dusk and then enter the village, uttering loud cries. Hearing these, the entire population would assemble around the village bentang – a tree in the midst of each plaza. Orations and singings would take place: finally, Mumbo-Jumbo would point to the recalcitrant female for whom, she unknowing, all this ritual had been prepared, and would have her dragged to his feet. Then he would beat her unmercifully with a stick amidst the loud rejoicings of all the other women.

Mungo appears to have been a personal witness of this custom in operation. He regarded it with genteel disapproval and resumed his journey. Soon he had passed beyond the last stretches of country trodden by white men – except by the unfortunate Houghton, the news of whose fate continued to haunt his track. Crossing the borders of Woolli and Bondou, he found himself, beyond the village of Koojar, on the verge of a great forest, the true African jungle. The trees towered tall and dark green, a seemingly impenetrable wall. Wild beasts and bandits

lorded over this tract in disgusting harmony. Mungo's
servants, tremblingly, sacrificed to the gods of ways and
means, and Mungo pushed the caravan forward into the
treey depths.

For two days they traversed this unkindly region at
considerable speed, still holding due east, feasting at this
hospitable village, fasting at another. In places Mungo
found himself an object of enthusiastic regard; in others
– such as in the village encountered towards midday of the
19th of that month – he was persecuted by the ravenous
curiosities stirred in the African breast at sight of the young
alien from Scotland. Women manifested an astounded
amaze and a desire to ascertain whether or not Mungo
could be really human in those portions of his anatomy
which the other sex regarded as of paramount proof.
Mungo, gasping, mounted his horse and fled in horror,
followed by his grinning caravan.

So far, so gently. But these days of peaceful penetration
were numbered. The forests ceased. Fertile cultivated land
appeared with ant-gangs of slaves at work in the fields.
Crossing the Falemè river, they reached Fatteconda, the
capital of Bondou. This was Foulah domain, not Negro,
land of the browny men from the Saharan fringe. Some of
these invaders, surprisingly, seem to have shed their Mohammedanism in their southwards progress: Bondou's
ruler, Almani, was a pagan. He was also a thief. An hour
after Mungo's arrival in the capital, he was summoned to
court.

Court proved to be in an open field. Almani questioned
the traveller suspiciously: why did he wander so far afield, if
not to acquire gold and Givers of Life? Out of curiosity, said
Mungo. Almani sniffed suspiciously, and dismissed him till
next day.

That next day brought disaster. Again interviewing the
unauthentic monarch, that individual indicated that he
would consider Mungo's new blue coat, with brass but-

tons, a suitable gift. Boiling with inward rage, but outwardly preserving a calm appearance, Mungo took the garment off and handed it over. Noblesse oblige. Almani, somewhat shamefaced, said that Mungo could now proceed out of Bondou duty-free.

After an interview of somewhat embarrassing intimacy with several of Almani's harem, Mungo rode out of Fatteconda with his escort on the morning of the 22nd. It was again a land of bandits, nearing the borders of Bondou and Kajaaga. The heat beat down with restless intensity, and Mungo sweated under his beaver tile. It grew too hot for daylight marching. They halted at a village, waiting for moonrise.

With the rising of the moon they set out eastward through the forests. Beasts howled and the long moonbeams danced and played down remote corridors of the trees. Dawn brought the borders of Kajaaga, and midday of Christmas Eve brought them to Joag in that state.

Joag evinced the first definite marks of African hostility. As Mungo rested under the bentang tree of the town plaza that night a band of horsemen came seeking him. They had been sent by Batcheri, King of Kajaaga, an indignant monarch. Why had Mungo not visited him at his capital, Maana? Mungo replied that he had had no time. All night he and the raiders argued around the bentang tree. Finally, losing patience, the horsemen seized his luggage, broke it open, stole what goods they desired, and departed with the dawn.

All next day Mungo sat hungry under the bentang tree, wondering what would happen next. He had still some gold and amber concealed on his person, but dare not reveal the fact in case the horsemen of Batcheri should return and relieve him of those valuables as well. His attendants were very thoroughly frightened. But towards night an old woman gave them food, and with the coming of that night came further succour.

This was in the person of a nephew of the king of Kasson, the next native state through which Mungo must pass in his quest for the Niger. This minor royalty had been visiting in Kajaaga, and heard of Mungo's plight. He was polite and assiduous. Let Mungo accompany him to Kasson, that civilised state, and all would be well.

Thankfully, Mungo accepted the invitation. Next morning, after sacrificing a cock to the denizens of the jungle, the joint expedition set out from Joag through the healthiest and most fertile African country that Mungo had yet seen. The forests towered green and tenebrous far in the hills of the north. But the lowlands were closely cultivated and nearing harvest. Far off they caught a glimpse of the Senegal. This they must cross to enter Kasson.

v

They forded the Senegal. The horses were seized and hurled over a cliff and bade to swim to the promised land. The nephew of the king of Kasson kept a hospitable eye on Mungo during the crossing. But his hospitality was of base metal. No sooner had they landed in Kasson than he demanded a present. Mungo, probably feeling politely murderous, handed over 'fourteen shillingsworth of amber and some tobacco'.

The nearest town was Teesee. Here dwelt the father of Mungo's 'deliverer', a negro of the name of Tiggity Sego. He was a sour ancient. Regarding Mungo with a dull eye, he dismissed him without demanding a present. Mungo hoped to push on unmolested.

He was mistaken. Borrowing Mungo's horse, Tiggity's son rode off on a mission to the north. For eight days, wearied, Mungo, though unmolested, wandered the streets of Teesee, mud-walled, heat-smitten, in the throes of a war-scare. War was about to burst on and around all this grouping of little kingdoms. Pagan Teesee lived in fear of

the nearby 'Moors' of Foota-Torra and Gadumah: while
Mungo was there Foota Torra sent an embassy with the
demand that Teesee acknowledge the Prophet: otherwise
Foota Torra would come down and exterminate the unbelievers. With a touching unanimity the inhabitants
promptly declared their conversion to the tenets of Islam.

At length Tiggity Sego's son returned from his wanderings, bringing Mungo's horse. Mungo prepared to depart,
as unostentatiously as possible, from Teesee. The ruling
powers demanded again, and indignantly, where were his
manners? Falling upon his luggage, they gutted the bundles. Plus the similar robbery which had taken place in
Kajaaga, three-quarters of the young Scot's original bag-
gage had now disappeared.

But even yet he was not disheartened; cold, calm, priggish and composed, he rode out from Teesee with his
following and held on for several days through Kasson.
At a village, Soolo, he encountered a negro slave-trader
who was in debt to Laidley in Pisania, and who had been
instructed to pay the debt to Mungo. This he was proceeding to do readily enough when more of the minor royalties
of Kasson appeared on the scene and demanded that
Mungo ride at once to the capital, Kooniakary. Distrust-
fully, he collected his small caravan. What new robbery was
to take place?

Demba Sego Jalla, however, proved unexpectedly honest, a happy prince but for the fact that he had scarcely set
eyes on Mungo than he began to ask if the latter knew what
had happened to Houghton – Mungo was more than tired
of Houghton by now. He replied that he knew of the latter's
fate. Blearily and kindly, the king dismissed the explorer.

His forward route lay through Kaarta. But Kaarta was
about to engage in war with a yet more distant principality,
Bambarra – Bambarra where Mungo now heard the Great
River itself was to be seen. The king advised Mungo to
avoid the war-threatened lands and hold north by Foola-

doo. This he determined to do, and returned to Soolo to collect the debt from the slave-trader and refresh himself before attempting the trackless north-eastwards lands.

On the 1st of February word came from the king that the route into Kaarta was still practicable, and Mungo could travel that way if he chose. He did choose. Mounting his horse, and accompanied now only by Demba the slave and Johnson the servant, he rode across a tributary of the Senegal and found himself on the disturbed Kaartan borders. Streams of fugitives were pouring into Kasson, for Bambarra, as usual, was expected to win in the coming war with Kaarta.

It was a land of hills, matted with vegetation, sparsely, so that they reminded Mungo, with a sudden qualm of homesickness, of his own Border country. Beyond those hills lay a stretch of desert. This they succeeded in crossing in one night, halting at a watering hole and being hospitably entertained by some shepherds. Hospitality was not general. At the next village, Feesurah, the landlord overcharged him outrageously: surprisingly, he was supported in this outrage by Mungo's own slave and servant. Cold and imperturbable Mungo surveyed the situation, paid the exorbitant charges, and pressed on westwards through more forested country. Becoming separated from his attendants while all three were berry-picking, he met a ludicrous adventure. This was in the persons of two mounted blacks, encountered in a forest track, men who had never before set eyes on a white man. They uttered moans of horror, covered their eyes, put spurs to their horses, and galloped away.

Rejoining his companions, Mungo rode on and came to a wide plain in the midst of which, in mud and stench, squatted Kemmoo, the capital of war-threatened Kaarta. Its ruler was the Desi Koorabarri, a heroic warrior and a kindly soul. This unusual combination of qualities listened to Mungo, thought it nothing unusual that an intelligent man should want to view far lands, promised him every support in his venture, and dismissed him with presents. Rather staggered, Mungo slept the night in Kemmoo, and in the morning sent his pistols to the Desi as a return present.

The black king acknowledged them and sent back an escort to help Mungo reach the borders of Ludamar, the northwards kingdom of the Moors. There Houghton had been killed, a dangerous and fanatical land. But war had now broken out between Kaarta and Bambarra, and it was impossible to press on directly into the latter country.

The young Scot rode northwards with his escort through Lotus-land; here the lotus berry was gathered as a commercial product. He tasted it and found it mildly appetising. But all the while his mind was vexed with a disquieting question: how would the Moors of Ludamar greet his mission?

VI

He came to Funingkedy, the last of the Kaartan towns to the east. Already he was passing beyond the round-shaped negro huts, walled with stakes. Funingkedy had a 'Moorish' appearance. It lived in constant terror of raids from the horsemen of the north. Mungo halted here a day and night while a caravan gathered to proceed to Ludamar.

It was resolved to travel at night to evade the bandits. In great fright and at great speed the strange convoy stumbled northwards, hour after hour, Mungo and Demba and Johnson at the tail of it. At daybreak on the 18th of February rocky hills came through the mists and began to serrate all the north. It was a land of streams, with wild horses disporting by the banks. Under those hills showed a walled town. Unhalting, the scared caravan pressed on; at noon Mungo entered his first Moorish town, Jarra.

Laidley had given him an order for money on a slaver

who dwelt even as distantly as this. The slaver received Mungo and his blacks kindly: he was the only soul in Jarra who did so. They were stared at aggressively by the haughty horsemen who clattered through the streets. The negroes, here a subservient, helot populace, could lend them no aid. Mungo sent off a present to the ruler of Ludamar, the Emir Ali, asking permission to skirt through the border-lands down into Bambarra.

A fortnight went by – a fortnight of black looks from the Moors and frightened looks from the blacks. Both Demba and Johnson made it clear to Mungo that they would refuse to adventure forth into Ludamar. At last one of the Emir Ali's slaves arrived to guide Mungo on his way eastward. At that Demba relented, and joined forces with his master.

They had gained the southern fringe of the Sahara, waste sandy land wherein they made but slow and heat-hazed progress for several days. Infrequent villages would erupt upon the horizon – villages where the travellers were stared at askance by the negroes. The first of March brought the considerable Moorish town of Deena. Here Mungo lodged with a scared if hospitable black; but soon the news of his arrival had spread abroad. The Moors came flocking in droves to gaze on the Christian, to spit at him; finally, they broke open his luggage, stole what they desired, and departed.

Mungo resolved to escape in the early dawn. He and Demba fled eastwards through a misty morning wherein lions howled. Day brought heat and thirst and a long stretch of parched ground. Once they halted and would have ventured a near-by well but that, even nearer, they heard the cough of a lion apparently as thirsty as themselves. They slept that night, uneasily, in a hut of some Foulah shepherds.

But next day, as they swung south towards Bambarra, forest came again, interspersed with cultivated land. Here for three days they journeyed unmolested, Mungo noting with a cool interest the effect of the passing of a cloud of locusts and the equally surprising effects produced by the native manufacture of gunpowder. They came to the village of Dallu, and rested there the night. It was almost the last town in Ludamar, and Mungo confident that he would now escape from the land of the Moors, robbed, indeed, but unharmed.

But even while he sat so thinking a band of Moors entered the hut. They were a party of the Emir Ali's horsemen, sent to fetch him to the Moorish capital, Benowm, there to gratify the curiosity of Ali's wife, Fatima, who had never yet gazed upon that horrific animal, the Christian.

VII

This was disaster, and Mungo knew it. He begged to be left alone, he offered all his goods to the Moors, he must have seemed – that moment while his mask dropped a very young and frightened alien indeed. The Moors soothed him, sardonically. Ali wished him well: but Fatima also wished to see him.

Back along the dusty roads to Deena, where he had been maltreated a few days before. Here a son of Ali's was in residence. This son, a genuine foretaste of the father, interviewed them, threatened them, and so frightened them that that night Demba attempted to escape. He was frustrated and thrust back into the hut. Mungo slept with a cool wisdom.

Next day they reached Benowm in the Southern Sahara – no town of Arabs, but a great encampment of black tents. Benowm gave a yell of surprise at the appearance of Mungo, abandoned all its worldly goods and flocked to follow him. He was led to the presence of the Emir Ali, a venerable scoundrel who looked on him coldly and then determined on an acute psychological test. It was evident that the Christian was starving. Good. Christians ate pigs. Also good. A pig was brought and offered to Mungo, in the hope that he would eat it and thus openly prove his uncleanness.

Suavely, Mungo declined the gift, affirming that pork was abhorrent to his palate. Somewhat dashed, Ali considered a moment and was then struck by a bright notion. He commanded that the pig be loosed in the hope that it would attack Mungo.

Instead, carefully excepting Mungo, the pig attacked everyone within range. It was secured and led captive away. So were Mungo and Demba to a hut where all night the guards kept thrusting in their faces torches of lighted grass to see that their captives were still unfled. They were given a little food and water, and slept uneasily.

Next morning they were led to a hut. Here Mungo was commanded to take off his clothes so that the Moors might examine them. They were especially amazed at the appearance of his feet. They had expected extremities departing from the true Moorish norm of *homo sapiens*. Obsequiously, Mungo disrobed and re-robed through a long, stifling day. Night brought little rest. The pig of the previous venture had been tethered to the ridge-pole of the hut. All the hut lay in sleep. But in the dark Mungo awoke with the consciousness that someone was creeping upon him. Thereon he jumped to his feet. Discovered, the intruder turned to flee. Fleeing, he stumbled over Demba and pitched head-foremost on the pro-Christian pig. The pig yelled and then bit the Moor in the arm. Pandemonium ensued, only dying down as dawn neared.

Day succeeded day of maddening captivity. Ali would neither release him nor promise a date of release until Fatima arrived. Bored and hungry, Mungo stared out at the life of unbearable Benowm and dreamed of the Niger and templed Timbuctoo, and listened to the plaints of Demba. Ali had messengers take away all his possessions except one compass which he managed to secrete on his person. Not contented with that, the Emir decided to put the talents of the Christian to direct use. He appointed him court barber and ordered him to shave the head of one of the harem boys. Slyly, Mungo nicked the young Moor's head till the blood gushed. He was at once relegated to the lists of the unemployed. But the captivity went on.

Page on page in his chronicle tells of that strange arid life in the sands that fringe the Sahara. Fever struck him and he crept out to the coolness of a grove of trees. The Moors pursued him and threatened to shoot him unless he returned at once to the stifling hut. He returned. Health came back with a break in the weather. The break brought a deputation from Ali's harem – a deputation of giggling women wishing to inspect Mungo's genital organ, to see whether or not Christians were mere uncircumcised pagans. With a dour geniality the priggish young Scot said that he would be pleased to give an ample demonstration to one of the number (pointing to the prettiest) if the others departed. The women laughed, and went away laughing, sending him a gift of meal and milk . . . Women of Africa favoured Mungo.

He was taken on a round of the harems. The women treated him to coffee, sniffs, and looks of amazement. Bored with his company, the riders of Ludamar, returning from the visit, used him for impotent target practice: they poised the young intruder in the middle of an open space and whirled about him, lance-brandishing. He endured it all with a stony face. When would he be released?

Two travellers, Moslem merchants, came to Benowm. They had acquired tolerance in their wanderings. Lodged in the same hut as Mungo, they watched him starve and imparted information to him. Timbuctoo? Mungo could never journey there. The inhabitants were the most fanatical of all the Southern Sahara, and would assuredly cut his throat. As for the Niger, the Joliba, he would come on that in the lands of Bambarra.

It seemed to Mungo in those sweating days that never would he obtain his release to make that attempt. But the warlike events in the south affected Ludamar. News came that Mansong, king of (for Mungo) the still unknown state of Bambarra, was about to invade Ali's principality. That venerable scoundrel was stirred to considerable fright. He gave order for the camp at Benowm to be struck and a move made northwards, to another site, Bubaker. Arriving there through the dust and smell of desert travelling, Mungo at last was introduced into the presence of the woman responsible for his captivity.

Queen Fatima proved fat, respectable, comfortable and cretinaceous. She looked on Mungo with an affected disgust, then relented slightly, and, as a compensation for the maltreatment of the past two months, presented him with a bowl of milk. Unbelievably, it seems he felt gratitude. But it waned in the ensuing days. Bubaker was an even more disastrous place than unbearable Benowm. It was now the middle of the hot season. Water was very scarce. Night and day the wells and the troughs surrounding them were besieged by hordes of maddened cattle trampling each other in search of the precious fluid. The Moors, by scrupulous rationing, had enough to drink: their rationing scheme did not include comforts for the Christian or his slave. Demba and Mungo gasped with parched throats through long hours. Did Demba attempt to approach the wells, he was beaten off. They begged a little water now and then from the slaves of the Moors.

Mungo entered into long periods of delirium, seeing in dreams the placid waters of Yarrow, sweet and grey and crystal-clear, and himself go scrambling down its banks from the grey homely lour of the biggings of Fowlshiels – down and down to drink there and lave there and forget the dream of the Great River he sought. Sobbing, he would come from sleep in the stifling dark, alone, a captive, in the hot dark only the tormented breath of his slave-boy, Demba.

One midnight, the fever upon him, he resolved to try his own fortune at the wells. They lay at a distance of about half a mile from the city of black tents. He set out, staggering with weariness. It was pitch dark, moonless, with a shimmer of stars. Beyond the woods he stood in doubt, and then was guided towards the wells by the lowing of the heat-maddened thirsty cattle. Even at this hour the shepherds were toiling there, filling the troughs in the light of great torches. By that the approach of the Christian was descried. The Moors paused in curiosity to hear his request, and then drove him away with curses and abuse.

But Mungo had sharpened his spirit to a steel-like point on humiliation and insult. Beaten away from one well, he would try another. So the thirsting hours wore on, with the dawn near. At last he came to a well where an old man and two boys drew the water. Hearing his request, the old man readily acceded and drew him up a bucket of water. Mungo was about to take it in his hands, when superstition suddenly overcame the old Moor's kindness. He recollected that this was a Christian, and his touch polluting. Turning round, he poured the water into a nearby trough, where three cows already drank, and indicated to Mungo that he could share with these beasts.

So the son of Mungo Park of Fowlshiels, that cold prim youth who had landed neatly clad and composed on the Gambia beaches six months before, knelt down in rags and filth among the kine, and drank and slobbered in their trough, crying with delight and fever as he drank.

But now the worst of the hot season was waning. Winds arose and whirled the desert sands icily about the encampment. Clouds came flooding up from the south, dimming the flare of the midday sky, and with them, presently, the flow of sheet-lightning unending upon the African horizon. The rainy season was near at hand. To Mungo this presented a new terror. The Moors were accustomed to retreat further out into the desert to escape the rains of the jungle belt. Would they take him with them?

But a fortunate accident prevented this. The Desi, the heroic king of Kaarta, having beaten the Bambarrans and his own rebels, threatened Jarra, the frontier town on the Ludamar-Kaarta line. In Jarra were several hundred refugee and rebel Kaartans. They sent an embassy to the Emir Ali to hire a couple of hundred of his horsemen as mercenaries with which to assail the Desi, and Ali resolved to set out and treat with them in person. If only he would take his Christian captive as far as Jarra . . .

Mungo begged the intercession of Queen Fatima. Surprisingly, intercede she did. Some of his clothes were returned to him, together with his horse, saddle and bridle. Then he and Demba were ordered to accompany Ali on his southwards march.

It was the 26th of May when the cavalcade set out from Bubaker. Mungo was worn to a mere shadow: but now a monomaniac, the Niger and the thought of reaching it haunted his days and nights, dispelling the knowledge of the little vexations of the hour. Even the news brought to him the first night they camped – that Ali had stolen Demba and had sent him back to Bubaker – moved him only a little. He swore to himself to obtain Demba's redemption when he had found the Niger. Till then . . .

Jarra was entered on the 2nd of June, and Mungo made his way to the house of the slave-merchant. Here he obtained food and apparently some money. He sat down to plot an escape from Ali.

Events aided him. The Desi of Kaarta was on the march against Ludamar, his army unafar from Jarra. Ali promptly mislaid his warlike intentions and retreated hastily up country again. Apparently he had forgotten Mungo's existence. Now was the time to escape and prosecute his search to the south-east.

Johnson promised to accompany him.

VIII

On the forenoon of the 27th the Jarran sentinels gave the alarm: the enemy were descried from the walls. Wiltingly Jarra evacuated. Mungo and Johnson rode out east through a crowded confusion of flying negroes. The heat was intense and great dust-clouds overhung the perspiring flight of the fugitives. The Moors had long before ridden north.

For two days, east and south-east, that flight appears to have pursued a breakneck speed along the borders of northern Ludamar. Then the tempo slackened. The Desi would not penetrate thus far. Mungo was in the best of spirits. Now it seemed that he had definitely escaped the detested Ali. Resting at a village, Queira, he took stock of his position, and gathered information on the best routes into Bambarra.

But that afternoon – the 1st of July – he was apprised that he was still unforgotten of Ali. A party of Moors rode into Queira, questioning the inhabitants as to his whereabouts. The inhabitants seem to have lied magnificently. Very well, said the Moors, they would seek out the Christian tomorrow. Yawning, they went to bed.

Mungo, in a sweat of fear, gathered together his scanty wardrobe, waiting till stillness fell on Queira. That was towards morning. In the grey chill of the false dawn Johnson came and whispered that the Moors were asleep. He himself refused to accompany Mungo, but rendered this last service. So they parted, Mungo riding east. He never saw or heard of Johnson again.

Beyond the watering-place of Queira he was recognised by some shepherds. These set up a loud howl of distaste. Mungo rode on with a beating heart. Presently he heard behind him a loud cry to halt, and looked back. Three mounted Moors were pursuing him. This was the end: he was the captive of Ali's men.

Surprisingly, it proved quite otherwise. The three Moors seized his bundle of clothes, inspected it, stole the cloak, clapped spurs to their horses, and rode away. They were merely engaged in a little private robbery. Mungo beat his jaded mount to some pace and rode away again.

East-south-east all that day he rode through a desolate land of sand and cactus-clumps. Here and there he saw herds of goats feeding, but dared not approach, lest he be apprehended by the Moorish shepherds. By afternoon he was fainting for lack of water; he dismounted from his horse, unsaddled the beast with a curious compassion, and clapped it on the flank to encourage it to desert him. There was no need for it to perish as well as himself. Then he fainted.

When he came to the cold night air had revived him; the horse stood patiently near at hand. Refreshed, he saddled the beast again, but did not mount it. Instead, driving it before him, he stumbled on through the night.

That night was to prove one of the most terrifying in the journey. Alone, lost and unaided in the heart of Africa, suffering agonies from thirst and hunger, chance guided his steps so that he did not stray in the usual circle but held his route still evenly. Yet in the pitch darkness he could see hardly a hand's-breadth in front of his face; his horse was almost as weak as himself. Thunder growled overhead and once he imagined he heard the patter of coming rain. He raised his face, with open mouth, to the skies. Instantly his mouth was filled with sand: it was a sandstorm.

Late that night real rain came. He tore off his clothes and spread them to soak and wrung off the water into his mouth. Blessedly refreshed, he clad himself and tramped forward again.

At midnight avoiding a village he found himself in thin forested country again, descending some trail he could hardly see. A slow dawn filtered down through the tree-tops: he heard the croaking of frogs at a near-by pool and sought out that pool and drank and climbed a tree to spy out the land. Far in the south-east he saw a pillar of smoke.

About noon he came to it, a Foulah village where he obtained some food and sleep. But presently, outside the walls of his hut, he heard some of the villagers planning to tie him up and send him to Ali. At that he made his way out of the village, sleep weighing so heavily on his eyelids that he could hardly see the forest track ahead of him. Riding a few miles, he dismounted, lay down under a tree, and was instantly asleep again. Roused from that by two Foulahs who imagined he had overslept the afternoon prayer, he yawned at them hazily, mounted the weary horse, and held on south-east again.

The Sahara fringe was left behind. It was country thinly wooded, deep in lush grass. Presently a forest-track led Mungo's horse to a pool beside which he determined, foodless though he was, to pass the night. Mosquitoes came in multitudes to sting him; hyenas snarled about his encampment; far off a lion roared. But the young Scot, lost, forsaken, exhausted, slept the sleep of the tired.

Riding next forenoon, desperately hungry, he achieved the passage of some low, hilly country and came to a village where Foulahs entertained him hospitably. He was now on the borders of Bambarra. Dense woods sheltered those borders. Towards twilight he mounted and rode towards them. Narrowly escaping a roving band of blacks, he held on in search of a pool beside which he might sleep. About midnight he came on such a pool, and spent an uneasy night beside it, continually disturbed by the wurring circling of a band of wolves.

Dawn found him, weary and haggard, pressing down the dense forest tracks towards Bambarra. Somewhere in those early hours he passed from Ludamar into Bambarra at last. Early forenoon brought him to a high-walled town, Wawra, where the headman, once a Gambia slaver, had considerable respect for the white men. He entertained Mungo hospitably, expecting presents in return. Mungo blandly left him in the expectation, eating and resting through a long and blessed day of ease.

In Bambarra: and the Niger flows through Bambarra.

IX

The slaver dismissed him, shortly, from Wawra next morning, and he rode to a village called Dingyee, where he found a Foulah ancient willing to be hospitable in return for a definite favour. This was a cropping of Mungo's hair. With the hair in his possession, the Foulah planned to pound it to a paste, eat it, and thus acquire the wisdom of the white men. They exchanged food and hair, mutually gleeful, and Mungo pressed on to the next village, Wassiboo. Probably the Foulah died in convulsions.

Beyond Wassiboo was a dense forest, trackless, impossible to attempt without guides. Mungo halted for several days, assisting the villagers in their tasks, easily treated and carrying himself with a polite ease. By then he was beginning to recover his outward equanimity after the horrors of Benowm and Bubaker.

On the 12th of July a small caravan of Kaartans, bound for the capital of Bambarra, offered to guide the white man through the forest. It was a journey of several days' duration. In between patches of the great ocean of trees were tracts of fertile land, surrounding small and hospitable villages. But as they drew nearer to the Bambarran capital the land grew less fertile, the inhabitants less welcoming. Also, Mungo's horse staggered wearily in the rear of the Kaartans' caravan. Bored, they finally gave him up and pressed on themselves.

Wet weather had come, a foretaste of the great seasonal rains of interior Africa. Squelching through the mud, driving his horse, on the forenoon of the 19th of July Mungo met his first slave-caravan, coming from Sego,

Bambarra's capital, and bound for Morocco, five months' march across the Sahara. He turned cold, sickened eyes from the appearance of the shackled slaves, and went on his way, unmolested.

Sometimes, in this and that haggard little village, he hungered, refused all sustenance but a drink of water. But now he looked too poor to rob, and, that apart, was apparently in the midst of a pagan people, who, outside the normal press of living, had no particular desire to rob anyone. The white man passed before their busied gaze, strange as a unicorn, and they stopped and stared a little in surprise, giggled and then let him go. Not in the whole course of his journey did he encounter savages: he never penetrated to the wild cannibal kingdoms of Benin far down the Niger.

But now Bambarra was coming very close. The inhabitants were becoming cultured, citified folk. They grinned at sight of Mungo, ragged, shoeless, plodding behind his gaunt mount. Wits offered to purchase the beast as a zoo curiosity. Mungo declined meekly, pressing on south-east.

He arrived at a village towards the end of July in company with two shamefaced negro travellers – shamefaced in that they must travel with this white scarecrow. That night Mungo, what of the news he heard, could hardly sleep. Morning found him with his horse already saddled, impatiently awaiting the opening of the village gates. Out of these he rode in company with the negroes, shortly afterwards overtaking the Kaartans who had deserted him earlier on the trail. Somewhat ashamed of themselves, these refugees now promised to introduce him to Mansong, the king of Bambarra, as soon as they arrived at the capital, Sego.

The road led by the verge of a marsh, though beyond that and all around the country was trim and well cultivated. Presently one of the negroes beside the Scotsman pointed ahead – see the water!

Mungo looked, gasped, took a long breath, the first of his European kind to see the sight. There, 'broad as the Thames at Westminster', *and flowing to the east*, was the Niger.

X

It was one of the greatest feats in exploration he had accomplished, but he was impatient to accomplish more. Flowing to the east – then did the great river indeed lose itself in the sands of the interior? And where, along its banks, stood the Golden City, Timbuctoo? He resolved to seek an audience with the King of Bambarra, obtain – somehow, by some miraculous chance – supplies from him, purchase a canoe, and set off down the Great River.

He descended to the water-front at Sego. Mansong was reputed to live on the southern bank. Ferries plied continually from one shore to the other, but Mungo was refused passage for the excellent reason that he had no money to pay it – money he found to be cowrie-shells. He sat down and waited patiently, the Kaartans having disappeared.

Presently a messenger arrived from Mansong. He had heard of the coming of the white man with a superstitious disquiet. Not under any circumstances must Mungo cross the river without permission.

Weary and again dispirited, Mungo sought out a village further up the bank. The day he spent in hunger and sunglare, without food or water. But at night an old peasant woman took compassion on him, invited him into her hut, fed him with fish, gave him a bed, and sang him to sleep – one of the great and nameless heroines of all time had she her just due, for her feat was equivalent to that of an English or American villager inviting a ragged and scrofulous negro to share a single-roomed cabin. For three days Mungo waited in her hut, sending messages to Mansong, imploring help.

On the forenoon of the 22nd of July, a messenger arrived from the king. Provided that Mungo would set about leaving the neighbourhood of Bambarra, here was a present for him. Mungo opened the bag which contained the present, and found five thousand cowries.

It was a sum sufficient to take him well on his road back to the coast. But he planned quite otherwise. Purchasing some food, he set off eastwards along Niger-bank.

It was rich and well-cultivated land, the inhabitants busy and indifferent to his passage, Bambarran negroes, pagan and practical. But two days later he reached Sansanding, a considerable riverine port, with Moors, mosques and mulishness. The Moors assembled to threaten Mungo, to demand that he acknowledge the Prophet, and to watch him eat raw eggs. He endured the threats with a still, dour face, declined to either acknowledge or repudiate the Prophet, and let it be known that the story that white men lived exclusively on human flesh and raw eggs had been somewhat exaggerated. Finally, the negro headman rescued him from his tormentors and saw him on his way along Niger-bank.

Four days of constant though slow progress brought him to the village of Modiboo. The countryside through which he had passed was renowned lion-country: on one occasion he and his horse, both too tired to attempt escape, passed within a few feet of a couchant lion. The woods that fringed the Niger from Sego onwards thinned out around Modiboo. The Niger had broadened greatly, he saw, fed by the swamps and invisible streams. Midway the river were islets where the herdsmen pastured their cattle without fear of raiding lions.

But Modiboo itself was the beginning of the end of his exploration. Waking the morning after his arrival there, he found himself ill with fever: the swamp-mosquitoes had stung him greatly. Modiboo's headman, looking on him in alarm, refused to give him shelter a further night. Reeling with fever and weakness, Mungo and his horse both, they set out for the nearest village, Kea.

En route, the horse collapsed. Mungo removed its bridle and saddle, patted it, left a tussock of grass in front of it, and went on through the dim forest tracks, fever-hazed, completely alone.

Kea refused him shelter. He found a boat which took him diagonally across the river to the utmost town, Silla, that he was to see that year. Beyond Silla, into a dim haze of names and lands flowed the Great River, past Timbuctoo the sought, into the lands of the Houssa, into man-eating Maniana . . . So he heard, sitting in a leaking hut in Silla. But he himself, he realised, was incapable of further journeying. Meagre though he considered the information he could bear back to the African Company, much though those unseen mysteries of the Lower River beckoned him on, he must turn and make the coast.

XI

It was the 30th of July. He had himself rowed across the Niger, gained the northern bank, and set out on his return tramp to the coast five hundred miles away, himself ragged, shoeless, weak with fever, in his possession only a few thousand cowries which would not act as currency beyond the boundaries of Bambarra.

And now even within Bambarra he found enemies arising. The Moorish shereefs who acted as Mansong's counsellors in Sego had prevailed on him to believe that the white man was a spy. Hearing that he had turned about and was retracing his footsteps, Mansong gave orders that he should be arrested. Strangely, his subjects showed no particular eagerness to arrest the polite and obsequious beggar. They avoided him, cursed him from their doors, but let him pass.

He had recovered his horse, tended and revived by a village headman; but the beast proved more a care than a help. Continuously the rains streamed from a grey African sky. His fever mounted and lessened and sometimes departed for a day or so, only to return with greater virulence. Holding north of Sego and avoiding Bambarran officialdom as much as possible, he tried to work out an essayable route to the coast.

By way of Ludamar he could not venture; the Kaartan borders were still disturbed; southwards, across the Niger, was the kingdom of Kong, a land of mountains, impossible because of language and other difficulties. He must attempt a passage along Niger-bank as far as possible, then strike on westwards through Manding and Fooladoo.

Begging at villages en route – here repulsed, here kindly entertained – he pressed on through the rains. His fever lessened. By mid-August he was deep in the land of the Niger floods – great tracts of country seasonally swamped by the burst banks of the Niger. At Koolikorro he earned a night's keep by writing charms for the headman on a board. This the headman washed from the board into a calabash, and drank down with many prayers. He probably needed them. Everywhere Mungo now halted the natives warned him it was impossible to escape the Niger floods in this season. He must halt a good three months ere they subsided.

But he could not halt. He was without food, clothing other than the rags he wore, or money – for the Bambarran cowries had long been spent. Still the rains held on. But for a while, towards the third week in August, he found himself dragging his weary horse through high and hilly country, pleasant to the touch after the squelch and slither of the flooded lowlands. Here, at Kooma, a lost Utopian valley of refugee blacks, he was kindly entertained and pressed on westwards with a gladder heart.

His gladness was premature. That day he was halted by a
gang of robbers, stripped, robbed of everything he possessed but his hat and a pair of trousers, and so left
'completely abandoned, naked and alone; surrounded by
savage animals and men still more savage'.

XII

At that moment, so he tells in his *Travels*, he saw growing
near at hand a small flower. Could God, who reared this
flower for his own delight in the wilderness, abandon to
perish of hunger a creature made in His own image? God
could and did. The bones of slave caravans were raddled in
uncountable tracks from the heart of Africa to the utmost
seas. But to Mungo the rhetorical question had only one
reply: surely not!

Refreshed, he pushed on to the next village. There he
met with a kindly reception. The headman promised to
attempt the capture of the robbers. Mungo thanked him
and hasted on into the west.

A week later, while he rested at a hunger-stricken village,
two messengers overtook him. They drove in front of them
the horse; on its back was loaded some of the scanty
belongings which had been stolen from him. Mungo gazed
at the horse forlornly. It was more an encumbrance than an
aid, he feared. His fear was justified. Next morning it fell
down a well and took the united efforts of the villagers to
retrieve it. Disgusted, he presented the beast to the village
headman, obtained a spear and sandals in exchange, and
resumed his journey to the coast.

The rains had resumed their seemingly endless pelt, the
country swam in front of his eyes, a surge of green vegetable
life, rain washed. He twisted his ankle and rested starving
days in the village of Nemacoo. Slightly recovered, he
plodded on again. But relief was near at hand. Crossing
the slopes of a mountain he came to a town, Kamalia, a

centre of the slave trade and also a centre of gold-mining. Here he fell in with a slaver, Karfa Taura, who was preparing an expedition to the coast. If Mungo chose to delay his departure till the next year, and would pay to Karfa the price of a slave when they reached the coast, Karfa in return would feed him and lodge him and bear him with the Gambia-wards caravan.

XIII

With a cold serenity the haggard young alien tendered his thanks and acceptance.

Mungo never forgot that kindness of Karfa's. In all his subsequent dealings with the slavers, in all his subsequent comments on slavery, that memory lingers, sometimes uneasily, at the back of his mind. He was weak and shelterless and indeed had developed fever again. Karfa nursed him, fed him, gave him a hut for his own use, and in general acted the Good Samaritan.

Meantime, and slowly through the dripping weather, the caravan bound for the distant Gambia began to assemble. Recovering from his fever Mungo went and inspected arrivals. Sometimes he was hailed and recognised by pitiful slaves who had been haughty freemen far to the north in those days when he journeyed through Kasson and Kaarta.

Mid-December came. The rains ceased. A dry and parching seasonal wind blew from the north-east. Mungo gradually recovered his strength, watching the flames of the grass-burning light the night-time sky. Soon impatience succeeded lethargy. Still the days dragged by. They faded into weeks. Would the caravan never start for the coast?

Yet this at length, on the 19th of April, 1797, the caravan did, a total of 73 human beings. Many of the slaves had been in irons for years, awaiting this move. Africa gossiped; Africa yawned; even on this march it insisted on halting every few miles to fire muskets and make speeches. Politely impatient, Mungo plodded in the rear.

Soon they came to the border of a great wilderness, the wilderness of Jallonkadoo. Within it for a stretch of several days there would be no villages for rest or shelter. Having dawdled so far, Karfa's caravan now decided on a forced march. It plunged into the wilderness at breakneck speed.

Perspiring as he limped along in his fraying sandals, the cold young Scot looked about him, seeing no wilderness, but well-wooded land of hill and glen alive with game. It had remained unsettled because of tribal wars. That night they camped in a place where wild beasts prowled, making the night hideous. Next day at noon a hive of wild bees attacked the caravan and put it to flight over a wide area. One of the slaves, a woman, proved recalcitrant and Mungo listened with sickened heart to the sound of the lash on her bee-stung flesh.

Still the wilderness continued, in spite of forced marching. The woman again proving recalcitrant, or incapable of keeping up with the march, was stripped and left to be devoured by wild beasts. Pressing on through great thickets of bamboo the caravan arrived at a village, Sooseeta, having crossed the Jallonkadoo at its narrowest point, a distance of a hundred miles.

Jallonka, the 'kingdom' through which they were now travelling, was the home and abiding place of great bands of bandits. Avoiding these by stealth and stratagem, the caravan crept on towards the coast. On the 30th of April they reached the village of Tinkingtang. Ahead rose mountains, serrating all the western sky.

Next day they crossed those mountains. Now they were in lands not unremote from the coast, and Mungo began to feel again a stir of cold joy in his heart. If he could only last the pace of the march!

More mountains and craggy trails, the slaves groaning under their burdens. But on the 12th of May they crossed the Falemè river, south of a point where Mungo on his eastern journey had crossed it long months before. They were now in fertile, well-cultivated land, under better governance than Jallonka, Negro-land, far south of the Arab and his afflictions. A new wilderness, Tenda, a ragged stretch of forests and bamboo-clumps, was crossed without casualties, if with feet-aching weariness. Town after town, where white men had been heard of and this poor, strayed specimen (he was generally taken for a half-breed Moor, however) occasioned little surprise. Village on village while the west drew steadily nearer. At last, on the 1st of June, 1797, Mungo Park lifted his face and looked on the Gambia again. It was eighteen months since he had last seen it.

XIV

They came to the capital of Woolli, Medina, on the 4th of June. Here it was that Mungo had been so hospitably entertained by the ancient chief, Jatta, in the course of his outward journey. Jatta, the explorer heard, was ill, but the caravan pressed on before he could make inquiries. Probably he had little urge – as always human beings meant little to the young Scot. On the sixth Jindey was reached, on the ninth Tendacunda, a village close to that Pisania from where Mungo had commenced his journey.

Here he heard the news and gossip of the coast. Neither Demba nor Johnson had returned. Everywhere it was presumed that Mungo himself had perished in the interior. The natives stared at him unbelievingly: this could not be the white youth of eighteen months before. Nor, indeed, was it.

Next day one of the white traders at Pisania rode through the woods to greet Mungo, and he himself mounted a horse again and took his way to the coast, to white faces and food and clothes and the blessedness of a razor again – astounding Karfa, when shaved, with his appearance of a 'mere boy'. Laidley paid the sum Mungo had agreed with Karfa in distant Kamalia, and Mungo waited anxiously for a ship to take him home.

But it was no season of ships: no ships were expected for several months. Fortune proved kind, however, an American slaver, the *Charlestown*, appeared on the Gambia, and Mungo shipped a passage via the West Indies.

The ship sailed on the 17th of June, slave-laden. It was leaky and rotten. Soon the ship doctor was down with fever and Mungo had to take over his work. They halted long weeks at Goree, up the coast, under the broiling autumnal suns, awaiting provisions and new shipments of slaves, Mungo staring a sick distaste at the heat-hazed African shore.

Yet at length the *Charlestown* turned from it, putting out across a sullen Atlantic. Steadily the ship leaked. Slaves were brought up to man the pumps. Mungo toiled in a hell of disease and filth and fever. In the neighbourhood of the West Indies it became obvious that the ship would never make America. They put into Antigua.

Here Mungo disembarked and found a ship to take him to England. He reached it on the 22nd of December, after an absence of two years and seven months of such journeying as few had ever encompassed.

Shivering in the cold blow of the winter winds, he arrived in London in a sleeting dawn and went to walk in the gardens of the British Museum till the day should lighten and he could search out acquaintances. So walking, he was met by his own brother-in-law, Dickson – the same who had procured him his commission to search for the Niger.

Dickson stared as though at a ghost.

The African Association was to stare in similar fashion. All presumed him to have perished. Rumour of his travels and discoveries spread abroad London, Mungo himself closeted with the Association members and drawing up a hasty abstract of his journeys. It was published and his full account awaited with some eagerness. He went to Scotland to write it.

So he came back to the farmhouse where he had been born, and found changes enough there, a strange place to one whose eyes were still blinded with the sun-shimmer of the Niger country. He could not forget that even a day, even while he was falling in love with Ailie Anderson, the daughter of that general practitioner to whom he had been apprenticed. He would write his travels, marry Ailie, get him a new commission to seek out the Niger's source, find Timbuctoo, and live happily ever after.

XV

So he planned, but his plans went agley in many ways. His *Travels* were published, much read, much discussed, much attacked – principally by the Abolitionists. Then, and gradually, he was forgotten. The Government had more pressing business on hand than equip for the Niger the kind of expedition that the cold, haughty Scotsman demanded. He turned from them, sick at heart, to seek out work as a doctor in his native Scotland.

He had married his Ailie: they remained lovers and friends all their short married life. They moved to Peebles, where Mungo practised his profession, and was wearied to the verge of insanity, riding the barren hills attending the ills of the ploughmen and crofters. He had made friends with that writer who was then Mr Walter Scott, and with him at least found a suitable companionship to discourse unendingly the questions of the Niger: where did it rise, what was its outlet: where stood Timbuctoo?

Tormented by a dyspepsia – the result of many a horrific African meal – bored and disgusted with an uncongenial profession, he endured a long five years. Slowly the dream of again seeking the Niger faded from his mind. Then events awoke it. Presently it was no dream, but an intention and a plan.

The British Government had awakened to the advantages that might accrue to British trade with a survey of the West Coast interior. Mungo was summoned to London and questioned as to whether he would captain such an expedition. He replied that he would.

Innumerable delays followed. But gradually the expedition's personnel was assembled: Mungo himself to command, his brother-in-law, Alexander Anderson, to act as lieutenant, and a Scots acquaintance, George Scott, to be general assistant. They would sail for Goree, enlist there a guard from the British garrison, strike across country to the Niger at Sego, build a fleet of boats, and sail the Niger to its outlet – either into the Atlantic itself or into the sands of the interior.

On the 30th of January, 1805, again in quest of the Niger, he and his companions sailed from Southampton.

XVI

From the first this second and more ambitious expedition met with halts and disasters. The ship took nearly a month and a half to make the Cape Verde Islands from Portsmouth. Here Mungo and his companions landed and purchased a great number of asses to serve as pack-animals. Then they sailed for Goree.

There soldiers to the number of thirty-five were enlisted, enticed to the service by the offer of double pay and discharge from the army at the end of the Expedition. Two sailors came from the *Squirrel* frigate – future boat-builders for the fleet which Mungo was to sail down the Niger. An artillery officer, Martyn, also volunteered. Captain Mungo Park, tall and cool and cold, had the expedition embarked for Kayee on the Gambia.

But here another long delay took place while they attempted to enlist native aid. Laidley was dead at Pisania; the free blacks, for some reason that Mungo could not fathom, were chary this season venturing the interior. Nevertheless, he succeeded in enlisting the services of a Mandingo 'priest', Isaaco, to act as his guide, and on the 26th of April the expedition set out on its march, a long array of donkeys and soldiers in stifling red coats – soldiers who jested blithely as they tramped forward into the waiting east.

Mungo planned to reach the Niger by much the same route as he had taken in returning from it ten years before. This he believed he could do in six weeks or so. But now, with the approach of the rainy season, the weather grew ever more hot, the air more stifling as the soldiers plodded white-faced down the forest-tracks. Theirs was not the stuff to make explorers, poorly fed, of indifferent physique, like all of the English working class of their day. Presently two men fell ill of dysentery: Mungo came to a swift decision, a decision that was to rule all his subsequent ruthlessness on the march. He had the men abandoned at a village and pressed on.

They passed through Medina, while the weather still retained its sultry stillness. On the 29th of May, reaching the village of Badoo, Mungo halted to write his last letters before he should reach the Niger. In those letters he told of the complete health of the expedition, their luck and happiness so far, and his conviction that they would reach the Niger in less than a month. . . . Some of the statements in the letters are deliberate falsehoods, some – true or false – now read with a pitiful flavour of old tragedy. It seems as though Mungo turned his face against the obvious facts louring behind the rain-clouds in the east.

For beyond Badoo they found the forests wilting under the great tornadoes that heralded the seasonal rains. Long before then the expedition should have passed through that countryside, attaining the shelter of Bambarra. Instead, they tramped down wind-blown forest-paths into early June, when the hesitating rain finally came. It came in long swathes of water athwart the dripping lines of men and animals.

Presently the paths were tracks of mud. Soldiers began to fall out in the increase of fever and dysentery. Mungo had them left at this village and that, and pressed on, aided by Scott and his brother-in-law, Anderson. They came, turning northwards to avoid the Jallonka wilderness, to the wild mountains of Dindikoo, now shapes of quartz serrating all the forward sky. Through and under the ledges of these they tramped as June wore on. Each night they halted and lighted fires, seeking to dry garments soaked with the rains of the day. The soldiers would shiver in cold and other dreads as around the villages and encampments with the coming of the dark they heard the cough of prowling lions or the howling of wolf-packs, hungry in the rains.

The rivers had swollen, sweeping away the native fords. The hired porters stole what they would, and vanished. At one river a crocodile almost ended the life of the guide, Isaaco; because he could not proceed with a guide lacking, Mungo doctored the black with such patience as he had paid to none of the dying soldiers. In early August they neared the Bambarran borders.

Soldiers lay down and died in the forests; Mungo left them to die, himself carrying out the work of a score, tireless, his vision ever forward on the unseen Niger. But beyond the Bambarran borders his brother-in-law, Alexander Anderson, fell ill, and him Mungo found he could not abandon. Despite the consequent delays to the expedition, he mounted Anderson on his own horse and walked beside him, holding the fainting man in the saddle. Once, so walking, they encountered three lions. Mungo fired at them with a musket, and walked towards the beasts standing astounded but unhurt. They growled their displeasure

and took to the bush as the dour Scot plodded past. He had
no time to waste on lions.

The weather cleared as they came to a village, Koomi-
koomi. They believed that the worst of the rainy season was
over. Instead, it was scarcely begun. Recommencing, the
rains recommenced the decimation of the soldier-guard
from Goree. By the 19th of August scarcely more than half
a dozen survived. But that day, as they climbed through
mountains, Mungo halted his stride and stared, and gave a
long sigh. Far off, flowing through the forests down to
Sego, he saw the Niger again.

XVII

There followed interminable discussions and arguings with
the envoys of King Mansong, now from this village, now
that, on Niger-bank. For the expedition was not allowed to
descend to Sego itself. Mansong was willing to take presents and to promise canoes, but laggard in fulfilling his
promises. Finally, early in September, he gave permission
for Mungo and his people to descend to Samee, there to
await the canoes.

Mungo had his ailing brother-in-law put in a canoe
(Scott had died back in the last forests) and ordered the
other survivors to march along the bank under the command of the mutinous Lieutenant Martyn. He himself sat
down beside Alexander, and they were rowed down
through rainy weather to the shelter of a village at least a
little nearer the end of his journey. Soon the great canoes
promised by Mansong would follow them, and then—

The river ran full and deep and strong, in flood. Still the
canoes did not come. Then Mungo obtained permission to
hold on to Sansanding (where, ten years before, he had
been offered raw eggs to eat), and there dispose of his trade
goods. He set up a shop and Sansanding flocked to purchase. Cheerful, Mungo proved an admirable shopkeeper,

every now and then running out to look for the promised canoes, to glance into the hut where Ailie's brother lay.

At length the promised canoes arrived – two rotten and heat-frayed hulks. Mungo stared at them aghast. But there would be no others forthcoming. He stared at his small store of tools and then resolved on the impossible. He and the one sane, unsick soldier who still survived, a man named Bolton, must saw the two canoes in half and make of them one trust-worthy boat.

It was impossible. But it was done. They laboured through sweating days at the river-front of Sansanding while the waters slowly sank. As steadily, Alexander Anderson did the same. On the morning of October the 28th he died while Mungo stood beside his bed. For a moment that occurrence wrung his heart. Then he turned to his canoe-building again.

At length all was ready. He had engaged a fresh guide, Amadi Fatoumi, to go with them as far as the Houssa lands. The canoe was loaded with the two surviving soldiers, Mungo, Martyn, the guide, and a slave purchased for paddle-work. They embarked on the Niger on the 19th of November, 1805, and the current rapidly swung them east and south.

XVIII

Thereafter, day on day, it is a record of battle, murder, and sudden death. Mungo had resolved to land at no point unless he was pressed for lack of provisions. Gone was his desire to walk the streets of templed Timbuctoo, the outlet of the Niger now his single concern. Again and again, deep in the country of the Moors, canoe-loads of bowmen and spearmen attempted to stay their passage. Mungo appears to have made no parley. He ordered his companions to fire into the brown of the natives, and this they did, beating a way through. At Dibbie this happened, at Kabara, the port of Timbuctoo. Then the river swung southwards. They were now on a river not only never before sailed by white men, but beyond the utmost rumours of Europe.

Day on day the canoe swept down the Niger, through low scrub land, through desert, through tracts where thin forests sentinelled the shore. Sometimes they stopped and purchased food. At the least sign of hostility the muskets were used, always effectively. Finally, they found themselves in the Houssa country. Here the guide Fatoumi must turn back.

Mungo landed him at the village of Yaour, neglecting to send presents to the king of that country. The king, enraged, resolved on an ambush. He despatched an expedition across a 'bend' in the land to lie in wait for the canoe of the white men at the rapids of Boussa.

So the saga, the strangest and most terrible in many ways in all the history of exploration, came to its end. The canoe approached the rapids, sighted the waiting natives, and presently the battle opened. But the aim of the white men was uncertain on that dancing tide above which the currents foamed. Presently the canoe grounded. At that Mungo and Martyn consulted. Then each seized a soldier – the two remaining soldiers could not swim – and jumped into the water, striking out for the distant banks.

They were never seen again.

XIX

News of Mungo Park's death at the Boussa rapids took several years to filter back to Europe. A son of his went in search of him, and died; another relief expedition came on the guide Amadi Fatoumi and learned, doubtingly, his version of the tragedy. Even now it is doubtful what part treachery and betrayal played towards the enactment of that last scene at the Boussa rapids.

Neither of the two heroic journeys settled the question of

the Niger's outlet; but they pointed definitely enough towards that solution which Richard Lander carried out in 1830, when he trekked from the Guinea coast to Boussa, embarked there and sailed down the river to the spraying outlets of the great Niger delta. Masked in that Delta it was that the Niger for long centuries had attained the Atlantic, no great and visible outrush of waters.

If his life and death contributed greatly towards the solving of that supreme mystery of West-central Africa, his chronicles carried to Europe from the gossip of Benowm tidings no less startling, if disillusioning, regarding fabled Timbuctoo. No city of magic and mystery, but a decaying, dusty mart, mud-built, odoriferous, squalid . . . And in such likeness indeed Major Laing found it in 1822 when he journeyed there from Tripoli.

Cool, impassioned, cowardly courageous, imperturbable, Mungo Park's character in analysis after a hundred and forty years disintegrates into fragments seemingly irreconcilable enough. The fire that integrated them was the Niger, Timbuctoo, search of the mystery river to the mystery city; and when knowledge of both was in his grasp the fire burned through from its dark shrine and destroyed him.

He never appears to have made any attempt to grasp the philosophy of those 'idolators' by whom he was surrounded. He never appears to have heard of Confucius or Lao-Tze. Buddha was to him the idol of a god. He was incapable of identifying even the Singhalese Buddha and the Fo of remote Shen-so – though their similarities are so obvious. His command of four languages there is little reason to doubt, and their very possession is the more damning against him: with these as his tools he might indeed have brought a rich work of delineation and interpretation out of the East, beyond that painted veil that covered it from European eyes. But the soul-quality of the Venetian was unequal to the task.

Even so, his record remains one of the great travel records, the narrative of one of the earth's earliest true conquerors – in a sense indeed that Marco would have been incapable of apprehending. His book remains still authoritative – confirmed and re-confirmed as it has been by the modern world from other native scripts – on the life and being and surface appearance of that distant East.

Very slowly the ideas in his record spread and were apprehended by other eager and questing minds. Beyond the confines of Asia Minor was not merely India and a wild and deserted land, but Empires of wealth and high civilisation, innumerable islands, lands of wonder stretching on and on, lit by strange suns, into the infinite, as it seemed to those early minds . . . Lands innumerable, and of all most fascinating those Spice Islands of the Venetian's – surely the very Fortunate Isles of old.

A century and a half after muffled feet had carried Marco to his last rest in San Lorenzo, a child of the Italian enemy-city he had hated would sit long hours above his *Travels* and pore over the story of those islands.

Don Christóbal Colon and the Earthly Paradise

I

SOMEWHERE REMOTE IN the Old Stone Age, perhaps ten thousand years before Christ, the hunting clans of the Yenisei in Siberia commenced a slow northwards and north-eastwards drift in pursuit of game or merely in happy-go-lucky migration. They were folk of mixed Mongol and Armenoid stock, tall and lank, perhaps without that gravity that later became a characteristic of their race; they were hunters and trappers, wielding chipped weapons and tools; they went naked and unashamed, men of the Golden Age, without culture or rigorous custom, without religion or superstition, kingship or classes, social problems or social convictions. As they moved north and north-eastward through hundreds of years they followed a gradual amelioration of the climate of that time: the earth was recovering from the rigours of the Fourth Ice Age. By the time they reached the vicinity of what is now the Bering Straits it is possible that they found those straits green and verdant, low swampy lands, sea-washed, stretching remotely into the hazes of sunrise. They went into that sunhaze and all unwitting their achievement crossed the landbridges from the Old World to a New Continent hitherto untrod by the feet of men.

This continent was America. Wandering south slow millennium on millennium, the hunters passed down the length and breadth of the Americas, reaching at last the remote forests of the Amazon and the chilly pampas of Tierra del Fuego. They split and differentiated into multitudinous language-groups, though not into nations, for nationhood was as unknown as culture or war. They hunted the beasts of this strange continent and made themselves shelters in caves and by breakwinds, fished in the seas of the Mexican Gulf, bathed in the waters of the Pacific, and lived and died in countless generations through that hard yet happy life that had been the life of all their species since first men climbed, by accident of arm and eye, to mankind's status.

They were in a continent geographically remote from the rest of the world, separated by long seas from the wandering incursions of other tribes of Old Stone Age folk. This till the accident of the discovery of civilisation in the basin of the Nile led to the greatest revolution in human affairs.

For those kindred groups of the Old World discovered

civilisation. They originated agriculture: they spread abroad Europe and Asia in quest of Givers of Life. They invented boats, and by 500 BC wandering drifts of them, divinely led, were adventuring out into the waters of the Pacific. Culture and cruelty and economic security and slavery had come into the world; but for long America remained untouched.

Yet, as we know now, beginning somewhere around the time of the birth of Christ in distant Syria, the first of those Archaic explorers, Proto-Polynesians or Chinese, reached the coasts of America in a stretch of a century or so, by half a dozen different routes. There they explored and settled and searched for metals and gems; and wherever their feet trod some variant of the Archaic culture rose anew – a culture in America founded on the cultivation of the maize, a culture with dim gods that speedily became Americanised whatever their Asiatic ancestry. Then the stream of Polynesian-Chinese raiding and exploring appears to have dried up for a time.

But about the seventh Christian century there was a great cultural ferment in India and beyond in Cambodia and all the East Indies. Mariners of those countries sailed and traded remotely into the Pacific. They reached America – at Panama, along the Mexican coast, at Africa in Peru by way of Easter Island – bringing fresh cultural strains to the lowly Archaic civilisation. From those fresh cultural impetuses grew up to considerable heights of achievement the notable civilisations of the Maya, the Nahua, the Inka and Pre-Inka. Then once again the changes of time and fortune cut adrift those communications across the Pacific: the Mongols of Kublai Khan had flung all Eastern Asia in a ferment and the cultural capital and the cultural leisure of Asia no longer sent forth its missionaries into that strange country of rumour and legend of which the Chinese Buddhists told, and which we now know to have been America.

Remote in the north-east Leif the Lucky, as we have seen, came exploring in quest of the Fortunate Isles, and discovered them in the continent of North America. The tale of that discovery filtered back to Europe, there to mix inextricably through four centuries with the legend of the Fortunate Isles themselves, with – more concrete, yet kin – the story of the great Spice Islands of the East. Towards the close of the fourteenth century two Venetians, Nicolo and Antonio Zeno, sailed as far north as the Faröes, and there (according to a descendant) heard of Iceland and Greenland. Visiting these lands, they heard yet again of another country distant in the south, Estotiland, where the Norse were settled, and of a country, remoter yet, 'where the inhabitants had a knowledge of gold and silver, lived in cities, erected splendid temples to idols, and sacrificed human victims to them'.

Mythical or otherwise the Zeno's adventures, conviction grew stronger, century on century, in each imaginative European mind, that somewhere out in the dark Atlantic, did a man but steer far enough, he would come to a land of wonder, of strange gods and self-sown wheat, the Fortunate Isles, the Islands of Spice. Those spices, eastward brought, were authentic enough. And for hundreds of years the Atlantic European had found drift out of the west, in the accidents of storm and tide, strange things that confirmed his curiosities. Carved sticks and the trunks of trees came, the bodies of men of un-European, un-African race, this and that item of flotsam to keep wonder kindled. It is even possible – and indeed probable – that now and again a non-Norse ship in the North Atlantic, coasting north or south, was driven from its course across the whole wide stretch of the Atlantic and glimpsed strange alien shores, and returned with the tale of them, to be half-believed and disbelieved and remembered for a little and half-forgotten.

So, long before the publication of Marco Polo's *Travels*, telling of a thousand-islanded sea beyond Asia, there was belief in an islanded Atlantic. America, untrodden perhaps by all Europeans but the Norse, was nevertheless a land of definite and continuous rumour, known through meagre fact and abounding fantasy. The geographers of the fourteenth and fifteenth centuries dotted the remoter Atlantic with islands – 'Antilia' the most popular – and it was regarded as a truism that if the sphere were the true form of the earth practice and theory might indeed be linked, and, sailing westwards from Europe, a man come in time to those islands of Brandan and Brazil, of Antilia, the Wineland of the Norseman – and beyond them to the Spice Islands and the unremote Cipangu of Marco Polo.

But it was also recognised that it would be a foolhardy and unprofitable venture because of the immense distances to be covered, the terrors and uncertainties of weeks at sea on an uncharted waste of water.

II

The man who was to solve and annotate those puzzlings and affirmations of the European geographers was born in the city of Genoa in an uncertain year that was perhaps 1448. His father was a wool-carder, a cheesemonger and a publican – and but poorly equipped for all three professions, for he suffered from frequent bankruptcies. His mother is no more than a name – Suzanna Fontanarossa – though it may be from her that the young Columbus acquired his energy, his faith, his fluency. His mendacity – he was to develop into one of the world's great liars – was probably self-sown and reared and cultivated, shade and shelter for the cloudy surmisings and vague visionings of that poet's soul which was truly his.

He was apprenticed to the more stable of his father's trades – wool-carding – at the age of eleven; he ran errands about the Genoese streets, he touted cloth samples up and down the Italian roads . . . and in intervals of the press of existence read and pondered every one of the scanty books on which he could lay his hands. He learned Latin to aid

that reading – the later Christopher of the booming mendacities was to affirm that he attended Pavia University to
do that learning – and devoured tales innumerable: particularly tales with a background of geographical speculation. They kept him alive in the dust of the sweating card-
room, the sweat of the dusty roads, those lands of mystery
and imagination. Sometime, we may imagine him affirming, he himself would achieve their like – did he ever escape
the draggled toil and poverty of Genoa.

He endured the life of a wool-carder for a long three
years and was then shipped to the Levant as tout in the
employment of the great house of di Negro and Spinola.
This was 1475. Next year he was despatched, in a convoy of
Spinola ships, on a trading adventure to England. En route,
the convoy was attacked, sacked, looted and half destroyed
by a Gascon admiral-freebooter. Christopher narrowly
escaped with his life – his ship was rescued by the Portuguese and sailed into the safety of Lisbon harbour. Refitting
next year, it proceeded to England . . .

Beyond that are three years of doubt and surmise. He
was to affirm that thereafter he visited Iceland, that he
traded down the Guinea coast, that he entered the employ
of King René of Provence as a privateer captain. Menda-
ciously, unendingly, confusingly, he poured abroad this
biography in later years that accepted it with a conviction it
now fails to carry. For one who visited Iceland his ideas of
the Atlantic remained singularly archaic: for a privateer
captain his navigation singularly inefficient. Indeed, like
Admiral Peary, there is no proof that he was ever a sailor or
understood the handling of ships. Instead, we have a
picture throughout those years of a bookish young chapman dreaming vision on vision as he raised his eyes from
the pages of this and that fantastic glomeration of fable –
visions of the Fortunate Isles, the Earthly Paradise lying
awaiting discovery a few days' journey westward there in
the Atlantic sunset . . .

Presently fortune sent him wandering to Lisbon, where his brother had taken up the trade of map-making.

Lisbon at the time was the centre for all the adventure-some and skilful pilots of Europe. From Lisbon had been directed those grandiose explorations of the African coast which were to give Portugal such remarkable commercial ascendancy over the rest of Europe through two long centuries. In Lisbon, on the fringe of all this activity, were hosts of map-makers, geographers, and the like fauna. In Lisbon it is possible that the remarkable project to realise his dreams and sail directly westwards across the Atlantic first seized hold on the imagination of the youthful Columbus.

But there is excellent reason to believe that the project was not inspired until some four years later. Columbus settled to map-making: fantastically bad maps on which he let loose the products of his imagination in great monster hordes. He knew little of seamanship, less of the world, but much of the Earthly Paradise. Had not the Northmen touched it, the Land of Wine, had not perhaps Marco il Milione glimpsed it in the islands beyond Cipangu? Cosmographically muddled, geographically out-dated, hampered by a poor education and lowly social status, Christopher clung to those convictions with the proud, pathetic tenacity of his unfortunate social compeers the self-educated men in all ages. Presently he was spreading his beliefs abroad in a social class other than his own.

Through some accident the map-maker had encountered the Perestrellos in Lisbon – Perestrello the Governor of Porto Santo, father of an attractive daughter, Filepa. They were nobles. A poet was noble as well. Christopher, in the hearing of astounded brother Bartholomew, invented himself a lineage on which even the Perestrellos looked with respect. He was descended from Colonius, the Roman commander who conquered Mithridates; his first cousins had been nobles and admirals – the admirals Casenove

Coullon of Gascony, Columbus Pyrata Palæologus of Greece – witness the kinship of their names. And the sea was in his blood as well – witness his many voyagings.

Of some such fabric was self-woven the legend of Columbus. Tall, ruddy, ardent, blue-eyed, engaging, he captured the hearts and minds of his new friends. They liked his piety, his exploits, and his gentle birth. The first of these at least was authentic – it was to be the central drive behind the great quest of his life.

So the far-straying son of the Genoese wool-carder had presently wedded the gentle Donna Felipa, the daughter of the Portuguese navigator who had been made the first governor of Porto Santo. Presently they moved from Lisbon to Porto Santo itself, Columbus stepped into his father-in-law's shoes of property, if not of power, and set to earn himself a livelihood by the making of maps and charts in the approved custom of the time. He was on the high-road to the Africas, and the maps may have sold well to uncertain or doubtful navigators hastening south slave- and gold-raiding along the kingdoms of the blacks.

And there, at Madeira, it seems that a remarkable piece of good fortune was granted him. He encountered a nameless pilot (nameless to us) who had a strange story to tell. This man had been blown across the Atlantic in his ship in a great storm, and, after the storm had died down, had come on a litter of islands in that western sea. He had made no attempt to name or claim or explore them; instead, had sailed back for Europe. Nameless and enigmatic, he sails away from Madeira, leaving to our imagination a kindled young man staring after him. No mere rumour or theoretical quibble of the geographers, no mere imagined land of faery, but *reality* whatever its reality, Cipangu, India, Antilia, the Earthly Paradise – there at the thither side of the world, awaiting discovery and conquest!

So it seems the great inspiration came on him. He made his first proposals for this deliberate adventure out into the

Atlantic to the State of Genoa. But Genoa appears to have declined with singular brevity either to finance the expedition or grant Columbus the honours he adjudged fitting for that expedition's commander. He was still to the Genoese, if recognised at all, only the wool-carder's son. Nothing daunted, his vision shod with the solid shoes of fact, he next forwarded his scheme to King John the Second of Portugal. King John was engaged in the serious business of warfare but paid the project some attention. An amusing project. But Columbus's claims outrageous. Doubting, the King referred the matter to a committee of Portuguese geographical experts.

The committee was headed by the Bishop of Ceuta. Columbus presented himself personally to plead his case. The Bishop examined it in detail, demolished it with ease. Cipangu – Antilia distant only a few hundred miles? Messer Colombo was perilously antiquated in his cosmographical notions (the Bishop was entirely in the right). Report to King John: a hare-brained scheme.

The king was unsatisfied: the project had intrigued his fancy. It was merely that he had balked from Columbus's astounding claims: the title of Grand Admiral, the title and power of viceroy of all new lands discovered, a ten per cent share in the trade with all such lands. Thereon the wily Bishop suggested that it might be a good idea not to send an expensive expedition out into the Atlantic under the command of the excitable young Italian but to despatch a single caravel to investigate the western seas. King John, somewhat faithlessly, acceded to the suggestion: a caravel was secretly despatched.

It returned in the space of a week or so. Frightened on the verge of the great cliff of ocean up which, homeward-bound, their vessel would never be able to climb again, the sailors had refused the expedition and put back into Lisbon.

III

It was 1484. Donna Felipa was dead. Columbus, disgusted at the treatment meted out to him by the Bishop of Ceuta, resolved to remove himself together with his son Diego to Spain. Meantime he appears to have made a compact with brother Bartholomew. The brother was to go to England and lay before Henry VII the same proposals as Columbus himself was to carry to the Spanish court.

That court was at Cordova, actively engaged in preparations for the last campaign against the Moors in Spain. Ferdinand and Isabella had other tasks in hand than to pay overwhelming attention even to the highly vouched-for proposals of the skilled Genoan pilot, Messer Colombo. For Messer Colombo, his piety his guerdon, had found friends very speedily in Spain – lay, noble and ecclesiastic. His poet's fiery vision passed readily to imaginative, impractical people of like calibre to himself. He persisted; his friends persisted; and the king and queen were at length led to summon a junta of cosmographers at Salamanca in 1487 – a junta deputed to test the claims and pretensions of the Genoese.

Columbus appeared before this junta, but with no more success than he had appeared before the council in Lisbon. He was later to represent it as packed with the orthodox flat-earth fanatics to a man. More probably there was hardly a member of the junta that did not believe the earth round. What they balked at was not the planet's sphericity, but Columbus's unsubstantiated statements that India was distant but a few days' sail across the Atlantic. Hard though the old legend dies, it is plain that the junta did not regard the Genoese as a 'round-earth irresponsible' but merely as a romancer and an incompetent. In both accounts they were as correct as they were mistaken in dismissing the romancing as inconsiderable.

They decided that the project was 'vain and impossible,

and that it did not belong to the majesty of such great princes to determine anything upon such weak grounds of information'.

Columbus's counter-arguments are not recorded. It is probable that indeed they were not very convincing. For of all things it is plain that the pious young poet was as poor a theoretician as a seaman – his cosmographical ideas were medieval, long years behind those of the junta. He seems to have urged nothing more original than that to the west there lay great tracts of island and unknown country (the Madeira pilot had supplied him with proof); and perhaps backed up this statement by invoking the authority of that Marco Polo who had spoken of the many-islanded Pacific.

However, his persistence won from Ferdinand and Isabella the statement that they did not definitely reject his proposition. When the war was ended . . .

From camp to camp and city to city, as the campaign progressed, Columbus pursued the court through a long five years of solicitation. He must have become a wearying figure in the sight of one at least of their majesties of Spain. Yet they were impressed: his poetic earnestness and devoutness impressed, if his cosmographical arguments seemed feeble. Various sums of money were granted him for his private expenses, he was billeted near the court as a public functionary. Ceaselessly he argued and intrigued, attempting to make influential friends, to obtain introductions here and encouragement there. Juan Perez de la Marchena, guardian of the monastery of La Rabida near the little town of Palos, became a close friend. Perez had once been the confessor of Queen Isabella. Now he agreed to take young Diego and educate him while tall, ruddy, mendacious, scoundrelly-poetic Christopher pursued his two loves – the courtship of the favour of the Queen, and the seduction, courtship and marriage – in that order – of the pious, complacent, and poverty-stricken Beatriz Enriquez de

Arana. (Beatriz, wedded and bedded, was thereafter alternately maltreated and mislaid.)

But at length he left the court in complete despair, and repaired to Palos to fetch Diego. He had determined to depart to the French court and try his fortunes there – his brother had failed with singular completeness to impress the cautious-minded King of England. Arriving at Palos, he told of this project to Perez and the chief shipowner of Palos, one Martin Alonzo Pinzon. For different reasons they were dismayed – Pinzon also had transatlantic venturings in mind. Perez wrote to the queen begging her once again to pay heed to the suit of Columbus; and once again the kindly Isabella consented, remitting sufficient money to allow him to return to the court. Negotiations (as they might now be termed) were resumed.

They were speedily broken off. The cost of the expedition was negligible and easily raised: the personal claims of Columbus were considered outrageous. The dispassionate observer of later times can hardly fail to agree. Like most visionaries and poets, Columbus was as mercenary as he was mendacious. He believed very vividly he might attain the Earthly Paradise – failing it, Cipangu by a westwards voyage of a few days' duration. And for such kingly attainment should there not be a kingly award? . . . Tall, ruddy, greying of hair, he would expound his sureties in the Palos monastery, in the Cordova Court, and believe them all very truly himself. But now and again, perhaps in the dead of night – he would wake up and stare a moment of bewildered fear at his true foundationings – the affirmations of a strayed sailor foisted upon the book-learnt visionings of a Genoan cloth-chapman . . .

He set out a second time for France; piqued, Queen Isabella had him again recalled, and again opened negotiations. Ferdinand, the sardonic Ferdinand, kept apart from the negotiations. He seems to have had little liking and less respect for Columbus: he was merely another of Isabella's hare-brained paupers . . . But now the negotiations proceeded apace. An agreement was drawn up and signed: an agreement which conceded Columbus all his demands, on the understanding that he himself was to pay an eighth of the cost of the expedition.

The total cost of that expedition, on which Columbus had spent seven years of debate and argument at the Spanish court, was less than £400. Wool-carder Colombo of Genoa rode down to Palos Admiral Cristóbal Colon.

Palos was ordered to provide two of the vessels, and a third one was chartered. The enrolling of crews proved a difficulty. Death by drowning was as little popular in that day as in this; and, whatever the imaginings of Isabella, seamen at least knew the Admiral no sailor. However, a proclamation of immunity from all civil and criminal processes was issued for all persons taking part in the expedition. As a result, the more desperate of the criminals and debtors of Spain flocked down to Palos. The Pinzon family proved active in providing men and materials: those friendly Pinzons whose friendship was to fail the test of the voyage.

None of the three vessels was of more than a hundred tons burden. Only one, the *Santa Maria*, in which the noble Don Cristóbal Colon himself took up residence, was decked throughout. For navigator and captain – he himself hardly capable of navigation – he chose one Juan de la Cosa. The other two ships, the *Pinta* and the *Niña*, were half-decked caravels under the commands of Martin Alonzo Pinzon and Vincente Yanez Pinzon. The total numbering of the expedition was a hundred and twenty souls, including an Irishman, William Herries, and an Englishman, Arthur Lake.

On the 4th of August, 1492, the expedition set sail from the Bar of Saltes, commissioned under the new admiral, not, as was afterwards told, to reach the coast of Asia, but 'to discover and acquire certain islands and mainland in the Ocean'.

IV

The Canaries were reached in the course of a few days. The weather was mild and beneficent. Yet the caravel *Pinta* had unshipped her rudder, apparently at the instigation of her commander, Martin Alonzo Pinzon, who had began to regret his share in the undertaking. Columbus, fuming, half scared perhaps already to be actually launched, must halt while the *Pinta* was repaired. News was brought him that three Portuguese ships were lying off the Canaries, Government vessels which intended to intercept the expedition, for Columbus was venturing out on *mare incognita* which was under the dominion of Portugal. The Admiral seems to have been little perturbed: with chance, tide, and the terror of navigation to face, what were a few Portuguese? The convoy again in order, he sailed from Gomera in the Canaries on the ninth of September.

Thereafter the tale of the voyage is largely an abridgment from that doubtful journal which only doubtfully can be ascribed to Columbus's own hand. Greatly helped by the north-east trade winds, he sailed on day after day, almost due west, into the unknown waters. Such was the speed of the vessels that Columbus – apparently with the complicity of his navigator, for he could not have done it alone – commenced a remarkable deception. This was the keeping of two logs – one for his own private record, one to deceive the sailors. In the sailors' log the distance was falsified and minimised as much as possible, in order that their unquenched fears of the Ocean might not overflow. (Such is the story: but what of the logs of the *Pinta* and the *Niña* under the hostile Pinzons?)

Still, unhastening but unceasing, the trade wind blew the three small ships westwards over that untenanted sea of great waves and dipping stars. September nights came down cool and quiet and unruffled over the mysterious flow and glow of the combers. On the evening of the 13th it was found that the compass needle had declined to the north-west. On the morning of the 14th the declination was abruptly to the north-east. It was the first time this variation had been noted by Europeans. On that 14th also the sailors on the *Niña* looked out and saw two great birds hovering in the sky – tropical birds such as were common to Africa, they thought, and never seen far from land. Land must be near.

In the evening of the next day a great meteor woke the twilight of the sky, flashing ensaffroned in the sea ahead. The sailors' fears received a stabbing poignancy. Was it a sign from God of His displeasure? Columbus paced his deck, apparently stolid and cool, inwardly probably the prey of acute fears. What now of his belief in the nearness of Antilia – what if there were *no* Antilia? He soothed his crews and the ships sailed on.

Next day, the 16th, they found themselves on the verge of a great plain of seaweed, stretching remotely to the horizons. In the morning light those plains rose and shook their strange forms, as though alive, and to the sailors it seemed they had come to a place neither land nor sea, but a swamp on the verge of the Abyss. All day the three small ships ploughed steadily westwards, still with the north-easter behind them, cutting through the clinging weeds of the Sargasso Sea. Night sank on the great green plains, unended. Next morning they found themselves still sailing the great weed-fringed lagoons. This morning they caught a crab, from which the admiral 'inferred that they could not be more than eighty leagues from land'! His certainty had returned: he would lie himself to the ends of the Ocean.

His remarkable inference appears to have calmed his companions. Next day many birds were seen in the sky and a great massing of clouds. Drizzling rains – land rains – came with nightfall. Land was certainly near.

But still there came no land. Columbus was made privy to a plot hatched on his own ship – 'that it would be the best

plan to throw him quietly into the sea, and say he unfortunately fell in while he stood absorbed in looking at the
stars'. He guarded himself accordingly, knowing that his
companions' fears were like to mount into madness because of that very wind which drove them still steadily
westwards. They had come to the conclusion that there
were no winds on those seas to take them back to Spain.

But a contrary wind arose, calming this fear, and with
lessened speed the three small ships beat forward into it.
Drifting grass patched the sea. Far in the south-west arose a
great shadow on the sky. Columbus altered his course to
make it. Land was near.

But it was no land, only a cloud-shape that altered and
melted as the *Santa Maria* drew nigh.

On the 3rd of October there were again signs of land, and
the crew would have had Columbus stop and beat about in
search of it. But he had been deceived too often. In later
days he was to ascribe that determination to sail still further
west to his determination to reach the 'Indies'. Rather we
may be certain it was merely a confusion of his own
uncertainties.

But now the crew of the *Santa Maria* at least was quite
definitely mutinous, and Columbus had to set himself to
pacifying them by as strange a collection of threats and
promises and lies as ever the commander of an expedition
addressed to his followers. What would happen to them in
Spain should they indeed sail back without him – or against
his orders? What would their women-folk say of them?
Think of the riches of these lands in the west that awaited
their conquest . . . Day after day, and hour after hour,
between the times of those nervous pacings of the deck, he
argued and soothed the mutineers. But at last it seems that
they refused the direct westwards course. Martin Alonzo
Pinzon came from the *Pinta* and headed the mutineers. A
compromise was arrived at. On the 7th of October the
course of the vessels was altered to the south-west.

Four days later, and still the seas were untenanted. Then, the thirty-third day of sailing from the Canaries, a 'table-board' and a carved wand, the carving apparently wrought by 'some metal instrument' were fished up over the side of the *Santa Maria*. (Or did the Admiral drop them over the side and then fish them up again?) Sailors in one of the caravels about the same time saw a drifting branch 'with berries fresh upon it'. Land was certainly near.

v

And at last, indeed, those fragments of flotsam and jetsam were justified. The afternoon passed with no sign of land ahead, but at night, near ten o'clock, while Columbus was pacing the poop he saw a light low in the west, and called Pedro Gutierrez to witness it. The two of them stood there and peered into the still night-smother, and again the light flashed and winked low down in the waters . . . They make a fine and significant picture, those first of deliberate explorers from the Mediterranean, seeing that first gleam betokening human habitation in the unknown Americas.

They called the 'overlooker' who had been deputed by the Spanish court to witness all the actions and transactions of Columbus, and Rodrigo Sanchez came slowly and unwillingly and stood between the Admiral and Gutierrez, and with them looked into the west. Once again the light flashed, and Columbus in some excitement drew Sanchez, attention to it. At first the cautious 'overlooker' professed himself unable to see anything. But in a little even he could not deny the evidence of his eyes. Light it was – 'it appeared like a candle that went up and down, and Don Christopher did not doubt that it was the true light, and that it was on land. And so it proved, for it came from people passing with lights from one hut to another.'

There was no sleep on board the three vessels standing off with furled sails that night. Of Columbus's thoughts we may guess: What was this land – Antilia, Cipangu, Wine-land, or (Mother of God! he crossed himself in the dark) the Fortunate Isle, the Earthly Paradise itself . . . And he, *he*, the non-sailor, the cloth-chapman of the Levant, had been guided by God to its shores . . .

A reward of ten thousand maravedis had been promised by the Queen to whosoever should first sight land. At two o'clock in the morning of the twelfth a sailor on the *Pinta*, one Rodrigo de Triana, called out that he saw land ahead; he was not mistaken. A low shore, tree-clad, was coming up out of the mists of dawn. The vessels stood in towards it and cast anchor.

It was the greatest moment in the life of that strange, ruddy, grey-haired, devout and scoundrelly poet who was the Admiral. He had the boats manned and himself clad in full armour and carrying in his hand the royal banner of Spain was rowed to the shore. The Pinzons, also banner-bearing, put out from the *Pinta* and the *Niña*. The armed crews blew on the lights of their match-locks and stared over the shoulders of the rowers at the nearing beach – no deserted beach at all, but one in the morning light crowded with a throng of men and women such as no Europeans had ever seen – tall and naked and staring their surprise in silence upon the newcomers.

Perhaps they gave back a little, those nude primitives, as the strangers landed. Columbus fell to his knees as soon as his foot touched the strand of the unknown country, and offered up thanks to his God for having so preserved him and justified him. All the rest of the Spaniards knelt as well, and then pressed round the Admiral, excitably, many of them in tears, to cry his pardon for their doubts of him and their threatened mutinies. It was an affecting moment, and no doubt the simple islanders, standing watching, thought it so as well. They little realised how prophetic it was – those tears shed by the first white men who came to their island.

The scene may be best seen through the eyes of the

islanders of Guanahani – that island that is now Watling
Island of the Bahamas. They had lived all their lives on that
island, as their fathers before them through long millennia,
a corner and outpost of the human drift, almost the last
men of the Golden Age that survived in the Central
Americas. They were without tools or weapons, classes
or wars, gods or kings, simple and kindly children of the
earth and sea, Natural Men as once were all our fathers.
And up out of the morning had come sailing those strange
beings, so strangely shrouded and clad, who were yet
evidently men like themselves, albeit overmen as well. They
saw the strange beings kneel and cry aloud in strange,
harmful ways, as though in fear or pain, and drew a little
nearer, helpfully. But the incantations were no more than
the spoken words with which the Admiral was taking
possession of the land in the names of their majesties the
King and Queen of Spain.

The Spaniards saw they had nothing to fear from the
natives who flocked about them in simple friendliness. By
signs Columbus gathered that the name of the island was
Guanahani. Calmly obliterating its name even as he had
annexed its territory, he re-christened it San Salvador. The
sun was shining and the air clear and sweet; and looking
over the heads of the naked islanders he saw all their land
behind them in 'the likeness of a great garden'. He looked
at the children of this second Eden, and for perhaps a while
saw them with strange clarity as the innocent and happy
souls they were, paradisal folk whose paradise his coming
was to end for ever. But that moment passed quickly
enough:

> Because they had much friendship for us, and be-
> cause I knew they were people that would deliver
> themselves better to the Christian faith, and be con-
> verted more through love than by force, I gave to
> some of them coloured caps and some strings of

beads for their necks, and many other things of little
value, with which they were delighted, and were so
entirely ours that it was a marvel to see. The same
afterwards came swimming to the ship's boats where
we lay, and brought us parrots, and cotton threads in
balls, and darts and many other things. These they
bartered with us for things which we gave them, such
as bells and small glass beads. In fine, they took and
gave all of whatever they had with good will. But it
appeared to me they were a people very poor in
everything. They went totally naked, as naked as their
mothers brought them into the world.

They were tall and red-skinned and handsome folk; they
painted themselves, for amusement, agreeably; they knew
nothing of arms or warlike practices – one took hold of a
Spanish sword by the blade, and hurt himself. Even their
darts were merely for the chase. 'And I believe they would
easily be converted to Christianity, for it appeared to me
that they had no creed.'

Even so, they had also an obvious independence and
wildness that gnawed a little at the edge of this good
opinion. It was the wildness and intractability of the free
wild animal. Satisfied that their island contained nothing of
note or worth, Columbus had the ships weigh anchor. All
the surrounding seas they saw as they coasted slowly down
Guanahani in the sun of that day, islanded unendingly.
Columbus remembered back into his early readings. Could
these, the islands of the Madeira pilot, be also the islands of
Marco Polo?

Five leagues from San Salvador, that re-christened Guanahani, they came to another island, which the Admiral
named Concepcion. Here, even at such close quarters, he
found a slightly different type of life than at Guanahani.
Here the natives were cultivators of the Archaic Culture –
that culture that was slowly seeping though the Americas

from its focal points in Central America and Peru. It had been carried to the West Indies by the Caribs, who themselves had acquired it far up in the head-waters of the Amazon, where that river's tributaries rise in Peru. Raiders and headhunters, the Caribs had settled here and there amidst the Golden Age peoples of the islands. Some islands – such as Guanahani – they had missed entirely; some – as portions of that Cuba now undistant from the *Santa Maria's* course – they dominated entirely. Concepcion was in a midway condition: the state of happy, primal innocence had been lost, but it was still a benevolent thing, this new culture, ruled benevolently by its little sun-kings.

And now the Iron Age had come upon its world.

VI

In one of the Islands of Santa Maria de Concepcion the eyes of the Admiral and his crews feasted on the sight of some trivial golden ornaments which the natives wore. These were regarded by the folk of the Archaic civilisation (we know) not as jewels or money, but as mystic Givers of Life. To Columbus's Spaniards gold also was a Giver of Life – but in no mystic sense at all. With eagerness they questioned the natives: where did the gold come from? 'From Cubanacan', was the answer, the natives pointing south.

Incredibly enough, Columbus took this word for a corruption of Kublai Khan – the great emperor of Marco Polo's journey, dead two hundred years. He hastily assembled his ships and coasted hurriedly southwards to the court of Cathay.

Island on island confirmed the tidings: southwards was the land of gold. Sometimes the name Cubanacan was varied greatly. But at length they came to the shores of the veritable El Dorado itself.

It was Cuba.

They coasted along the north-eastern part, questioning the natives who put out in canoes. Gold? – gold came from the interior, from the mines of Ciboa.

The Admiral despatched two discoverers into that interior – one a Jew who spoke Hebrew, Chaldee and Arabic, and so would be able to converse with Kublai Khan on the terms of the utmost familiarity. The 'discoverers' came on neither Mongols or gold; instead, the first recorded Europeans to view the practice, they came on tribes which indulged in tobacco-smoking, an astounding and wizard-like practice. Everywhere in those clearings of the Archaic folk of the Americas they were treated with kindness and hospitality.

Meantime, in the vessels, things had gone not so well. Martin Alonzo Pinzon and the *Pinta* disappeared. Anchored off the territory of a chief called Guacanagari, Columbus had the *Santa Maria* wrecked in a shore-wind; he and his crew decamped to the crowded *Niña*. Only one vessel was left with which he might return to Spain, and his crews, their enthusiasm considerably cooled, were becoming more and more insistent that he should set about that return. He resolved to establish a colony on Guacanagari's land. Still news of Kublai delayed.

Then the Jew returned: No Kublai, no golden city, nothing but leagues of bush had been encountered. The Admiral scolded him bitterly: the poet was fading to a ghost below the armour of the gold-seeker . . . And now he might delay his return no longer.

The timbers of the *Santa Maria* were salvaged and the fort of La Navidad built. Forty men – including the Englishman and the Irishman – were left to garrison it. Then, on the 4th of January, 1493, the Admiral launched the *Niña* on her return voyage.

VII

Meantime Pinzon in the *Pinta*, deliberately separating himself from the company of the Admiral (whom he appears to have despised very thoroughly) had set out in search of the rumoured islands of gold. Several days' sailing the Cuban coasts had brought him no fabulous mines or cities, but southwards, in an unknown bay, he had encountered natives who possessed the metal in considerable abundance. Probably they looked a sturdy breed, well able to defend themselves, not the unarmed and fenceless primitives of Guanahani. Instead of securing the gold by force Pinzon obtained a fairly large supply by barter, and turned the prow of the *Pinta* homeward.

It is a remote quarrel, that of Columbus and Pinzon, in which geographers for four hundred years have found it good to debate. Little sympathy has been given to Pinzon: he has been portrayed, unendingly, as a mean and evil personage sabotaging the schemes of the high-minded dreamer and planner who commanded the expedition. But we may see the matter with clearer eyes. Pinzon owned the *Pinta* and probably the *Niña*; it was at Pinzon's suggestion – or perhaps command – that the expedition had turned southwards on October the 7th and so come on land at all. Possibly he considered himself as well qualified as Columbus to claim the discoveries. And he had certainly more than the shadow of a case.

Unfortunately, homeward bound on the 6th of January, in the teeth of a head wind, his look-out sighted the *Niña*. Both ships, almost simultaneously, had to put about and shelter behind a headland, and Pinzon, to his chagrin, discovered the Admiral was on board the other caravel. He re-submitted himself with surly apologies to Columbus's command, though it does not seem that he shared out the gold with the second ship. Nor does it seem that Columbus pressed him hard in the matter. But discovering half a dozen natives in the *Pinta* whom Pinzon had abducted from an island, intending to carry them into slavery across the Atlantic, Columbus commanded that they be released. He refused, with a singular clear-eyedness, to disturb that harmony in which the natives had received them. The Indians who ultimately accompanied them back to Spain were volunteers.

Ten days later the head-wind abated. Coasting Hayti, the Admiral reluctantly abandoned further research along those alluring shores. The wind blew now for Spain.

But presently it died; they fought back in the teeth of adverse breezes. The *Pinta*, with her rudder uncertain as of old, retarded the passage. On the 12th of February they encountered the first of the great Atlantic storms. For three days it raged, the caravels scudding before it with bare poles. On the night of the fourteenth the signal-lights of the *Pinta* disappeared, and Columbus's own crew on the *Niña* gave up all hope of their own safety, relapsing into one of those sudden and easy despairs characteristic of their period and religion. But the ruddy, grey-haired, mendacious poet who commanded them lost neither his fortitude nor his faith. He commanded that they load the empty water-casks with sea-water, the better to ballast the caravel; and in a prayer swore that as soon as they sighted land he and his crew would walk barefoot, in penitential garments, to the first church dedicated to the Virgin. The Atlantic, soothed by this promise or restrained by the providential ballast, drove the *Niña* headlong eastwards, but declined to devour it.

Even so, the Admiral appears to have reflected that there were mischances between both of these powers which he had called to his aid. Accordingly, he wrote out a brief account of his voyage and discoveries, enclosed it in wax, sealed it in a small cask, and consigned it to the deep. Scarcely had he done so than the greater fury of the storm abated. The curling green monsters that had hurled them into the night had tamed by the morning of the 15th of February. Land was sighted – and almost instantly lost again in the smother. It was the Azores.

On the night of the seventeenth other islands were sighted, and the *Niña* lost an anchor in endeavouring to bring up under their coasts. But when the next morning came they succeeded in anchoring off the Portuguese island of St Mary.

Here, landing in accordance with their vow, half of the crew, barefoot and clad in their shirts, were making pilgrimage to the chapel of St Mary when they were ambushed by the Portuguese and taken prisoner. Breechless, they appear to have put up no resistance whatever. The Admiral, left on the *Niña* with only three sailors, had the anchor raised and beat away from St Mary's. But presently his ardour and determination revived. It was impossible that the Portuguese should flout the royal warrant of Ferdinand and Isabel. He sailed back and held a parley with the governor of St Mary's. Reluctantly that individual agreed that Spain and Portugal were at peace and that the seizure of the be-shirted crew had been unwarranted. They were restored to the *Niña*; Columbus steered for Spain.

More storms intervened to stay the voyage. The coasts of Europe were strewn with wrecks. But again, as that morning at Guanahani, it was Columbus's hour. He rode the *Niña* in triumph into the mouth of the Tagus on the 4th of March, 1493, after eight months absence from the shores of Spain.

VIII

The Portuguese king proved more than friendly: he claimed that Columbus had acted as one of his own pilots. For was not all that stretch of the Ocean under the rule of Portugal? The Admiral declined to recognise the plea, and sailed for Palos.

On the 15th of March he sailed into the port where the

expedition had been raised and staffed with the criminal off-
scourings of the Spanish prisons. Two Pinzons he brought
back, but the other, together with the rudderless *Pinta*, had
apparently vanished in the troughs of the Atlantic. Columbus hastily indited letters to the king and queen, then at
Barcelona, and prepared himself to set out for court.

But meantime Martin Alonzo Pinzon, undrowned, had
succeeded in steering the damaged *Pinta* into Bayonne.
From there, almost at the same day as Columbus reached
Palos, he despatched letters to Barcelona describing his
voyage and discoveries, and making no mention of Columbus. It seemed a neck and neck race: never did Columbus's fortunes hang so precariously in the balance. But
the Court without any hesitation recognised their duly
appointed commander: Pinzon received an order not to
appear at court except in the train of the Admiral. Coupled
with other ills suffered in steering the *Pinta* across the wild
seas the news was too much for the Palos shipmaster. He
lay dying in Bayonne on the day when Columbus marched
in triumphal procession through the streets of Barcelona,
his six Indians, parrot-laden in his train, staring their
astonishment and disquiet upon this strange world in the
maw of the sunrise.

Ferdinand and Isabella received him as a conquering
prince. He was granted a coat of arms; the title Don was
bestowed on him and his brothers and descendants for ever
after. He was made a handsome allowance and was served
at table as a grandee.

He was the most honoured man in all Spain, and the
most sought after. Sometimes, perhaps, he communed still
at night with the Levantine chapman. Sometimes, drowning away from his own eyes all glory in his achievement,
must have come memory of his mistreatment of the Pinzons, knowledge that though he had found new lands by the
chances of luck and mislore he had still no notion what
lands they were. Supposing one were the Earthly Paradise

itself cravenly abandoned by him? . . . He would turn to prayer and new resolves for the new expedition.

His title of Viceroy of the new lands was confirmed, and he was appointed to command the new venture hastily prepared. For Portugal was laying serious claim to the discoveries. Ferdinand and Isabella, having finished with and finished the Moors, were eager to acquire new lands and convert fresh batches of the heathen. (Columbus's six natives were baptised with great enthusiasm, and one of them, dying shortly afterwards, was solemnly adjudged the 'first of his race to enter Paradise'.)

Seventeen ships were chartered or commandeered for the new expedition. Mattocks, spades, seeds, and plants were loaded aboard them for the colonisation of the islands. Men flocked to volunteer for the new expedition – in the end the squadron sailed with a complement of more than fifteen hundred men. Among these were twelve priests, sent to convert the natives – the 'Indians', as they were already called, for at last it had been decided by the cosmographers that the Admiral's discoveries had been in the neighbourhood of India.

The Admiral himself seems to have been less sure – he wavered in belief between Cipangu, India, and the outskirts of the Grand Khan's dominions. But for the urgings of the crew of the *Niña*, he gave it out, he might even have sailed into the harbours of golden Opir or scriptural Havilah. He had done no more, he affirmed, than touch on the outermost and barbarous fringe of a great and wealthy continent, where there was great treasure to be found and great hosts of souls to be saved.

In that conviction – and indeed, though in another sense, it was to be justified by the subsequent adventurings of his countrymen – he sailed west in command of the new expedition from the harbour of Cadiz on the 25th of September, 1493.

IX

They sailed a prosperous passage, untroubled but by one brief storm. Holding south of the route of the first expedition, on Sunday the 3rd of November they had their first sight of the New Lands. The island they came to was one of the Lesser Antilles, and christened Dominica by the pious Admiral from the fact of it being discovered on a Sunday. It was uninhabited. Cuba, with its colony and fort of La Navidad, he knew lay to the north-west, and cruised slowly along the Lesser Antilles group in that direction. The perfection of the weather held and with it the high spirits of the thousand and a half adventurers aboard. Their eyes were dazzled with the sheen of brilliant seas and brilliant vegetation, the colourful sunrises and sunsets of those sleeping sea-lands that verily seemed 'islets of Paradise' to their ocean-weary eyes.

But landing at a new island, Guadaloupe, they discovered horror. The inhabitants were no simple primitives, but cannibal Caribs of a high scale of culture, with well-built huts and roads, and parcels of dried human flesh hung in those huts. Guadaloupe's menfolk were absent on some sea-raid, and the explorers saw only the women and children. They embarked after a hasty and horrified search and hastily sailed north.

Passing clusters of small islands on the way, they came to one lovely and large and fertile – St John, as the Admiral named it, though it was afterwards re-named Porto Rico. In its loveliness, as in Guadaloupe, only man was vile: cannibalism was the mainstay of the Carib populace. Originally, as we of a later day know, this cannibalism had been religious and ceremonial in origin among the Carib tribes in the valley of the Amazon. But it had developed beyond that ceremonial usage. Large animals which could be used for food were scarce in the Lesser Antilles: anthropophagy, inaugurated by religious ritual, had become an economic way of salvation.

But the Spaniards knew nothing of these facts. To them it was a terrifying and disgusting practice, the mark of beasts, not men. It may be that it was in Porto Rico and in Guadaloupe that there developed that first savagery towards the West Indians which led to their ultimate extermination. That the primitives of the northern islands, the Bahamas, were neither Caribs nor cannibals mattered little to the Spaniard in pursuit of gold or slaves. He could salve his conscience and every murder by thinking of his victims as eaters of men.

The squadron coasted along Cuba and reached La Navidad. The fort had disappeared: it had been razed to the ground. The forty who had been left to man it had vanished – all but a few poor skeletons and rusting fragments of armour. While the dismayed Spaniards surveyed the ruins of the fort messengers came to them from Guacanagari with the tale of La Navidad's end. The forty whom Columbus had left to seal the friendship of Europe and America had from the beginning displayed an amazing insolence and licentiousness. They had wandered the island, taking what they would, interfering with the Indians, loud, braggart and boastful. Finally a neighbouring chief could bear with them no longer. He had raised an army and marched it against the fort, destroyed it, and killed the garrison. Guacanagari himself had been wounded in defence of the white men.

Such was the story. Possibly Guacanagari himself had played a less innocent part. Even so, it seemed even to the Admiral, remembering the quality of those he had left behind, that the chief might have been justified. It was plainly impossible to think of rebuilding La Navidad. The native Cubans had soured of the white men and their ways.

But a site and the building of a town were essential, for the overloaded convoy already groaned with sick and wearied men who cried for land, sight of the treasures which had drawn them from their homes in Spain.

Columbus turned the squadron about and coasted down to Hayti. At Cape Haytien he anchored and set about disembarking stores and men on the jungly beach, there to rear the first European city of the New World, Isabella.

Isabella progressed but slowly. The men were tired and sick. But now the Admiral came out in less pleasing colours than in those days in Spain when he had been the gracious magnate receiving colleagues in a golden enterprise. He drew up regulations for labour, and enforced them ruthlessly, himself the while maintaining all the ceremonial state which he considered a viceroy's due. Isabella progressed amidst quarrels and dissensions. Provisions ran short; medical supplies gave out, and it was soon obvious to Columbus that the financial strain of the colony would be very bitterly resented in Spain. Accordingly, he despatched an envoy to Ferdinand and Isabella with the proposal that the current expenses might be paid for by capturing hordes of the cannibal Indians and shipping them to Spain as slaves. This, he thought, 'would be very good for their souls' . . .

He was a poet, with the ruthlessness and shiftiness of the poetic temperament. Like factors conditioned his greed – there was no strange and abrupt transformation of Paradise-seeker to slave-trader. He remained sincerely and righteously both – the slaves an economic necessity both for the quest of God's City on Earth and the maintenance in due state of the seeker God-appointed.

Slave hunting developed rapidly as a commercial activity among sea-parties despatched from Isabella. Specimens of the cattle were shipped to Spain. Meantime, the gold mines of Ciboa had been found and workings there had begun under the Spaniards, the natives having been violently dispossessed. Columbus concluded that the new settlement might be left to its own defences a while; and in mid-April himself put to sea in search of the golden land.

For five months he cruised to and fro the Jamaican seas,

discovering Jamaica itself and a host of islets amidst which his squadron almost foundered. On this voyage it was that he came to an island off which a strange craft was seen – a canoe with sails, manned by cotton-clad canoemen. They gestured that they came from still further to the west, and the heart of Columbus, seeing their evident degree of civilisation, rose high within him. What could they be but natives of Cathay?

However, he had no time to pursue investigations in that still unknown west. Isabella called him back. First cruising across the Lesser Antilles, he set his men slave-catching among the cannibals, then turned towards Hispaniola.

Hispaniola he found in confusion and turmoil. A gang of malcontents whom he had sent from Isabella to survey the country had roused all the Indians against them. Everywhere the enraged natives of the Archaic Civilisation were rising against this new horror that the Iron Civilisation had brought. One of their chiefs with a numerous array was marching on Isabella itself.

Columbus was down with fever when his squadron put in at Isabella. But at this news of the natives in arms he bestirred himself with a pious energy, confident that God would give the victory to His Christians. Brother Bartholomew had arrived from Spain. Leaving him in command of Isabella, the Admiral marched against the Indians.

It was a day of broiling heat and in the still air the corslets of the Spaniards were stiflingly hot. But they winked with a dreadful sheen in the eyes of the Indians with their stone-tipped spears and wicker shields. The natives charged with great bravery, and the Spaniards opened fire.

In a few minutes the fate of the battle was decided, the Indians flying in rout, hotly pursued by the Admiral's Christian bloodhounds. Four shiploads of slaves were captured, whipped back along the tracks to Isabella, and then despatched to Spain.

Caonabo, who had destroyed the fort of La Navidad, was also in arms. The Dons Bartolomeo and Cristóbal Colon marched against him with two hundred men, defeating him with great carnage. Everywhere the Indians were vanquished and those captured in arms enslaved. Caonabo himself was captured by treachery, and despatched to Spain for judgment as a 'rebel'. Maliciously he insisted on dying during the voyage, thus escaping the wheel or the stake, the first of the heroic native soldiers of the Americas who were to resist the invaders. His place is with Mochcovoh the Mayan, Quatemoc the Aztec, and the great 'Stony-Face' of Peru.

Tribute was now imposed on the Indians of Hispaniola, and a general system of vassalage, land-slavery, implemented for those unfortunate denizens of the Utmost Americas. With a pious wish to save their souls and keep in being his correct number of footmen, the Admiral who four years before had spoken of the 'free and simple folk' of Guanahani, now instituted a regular and unceasing trade in human flesh on a scale which would have made the cannibals of Guadaloupe blanch with horror.

But things in the colony itself went from bad to worse. They are hardly the concern of the record which deals with geographical quest not that pitiful tale of insult and blood and tears that has marched with colonial conquest. But their effects on the fortunes of the exploring Admiral were profound, if they left his strangely scoundrelly-idealistic nature unchanged.

In consequence of the complaints against Columbus's insufferable despotism a commissioner was despatched to Isabella by the King and Queen. He arrived in October of 1495, heard the evidence preferred against the Admiral, and drew up a report. There was no lack of evidence. Settlers and thieves, colonists and Indians, flocked to him with the terrible tale of the vivid injustices suffered under the rule of the devout Genoan, whose poetic soul was sorely vexed at the island's ingratitude. He resolved to return to Spain and justify himself before the court.

He boarded the *Niña*. At that Aquado, fearing lest his report might be forestalled, boarded another caravel. A passion for evacuation seized the Spaniards. Loaded caravels put out one after the other from Isabella, seeking the Atlantic loaded with misfortune and complaint. Bartholomew was left to misgovern Hispaniola.

Provisions grew scarce as the voyage proceeded. The ships were loaded with Indian slaves whom the crews threatened to kill and devour. It seemed that the Christians had become infected with anthropophagy as well. Columbus, heedful to the value of his cargoes, dissuaded them, and the starving convoy reached the Bay of Cadiz in safety.

Here, with that practical unimaginativeness that stamped his quality, Columbus decided on marching through the country in such triumphal procession as had witnessed his return from the first expedition. He proceeded towards the court in glittering garments, on horseback, followed by chaingangs of Indians. But everywhere he was greeted with reproaches or derision, for news of these two years' failures was well known in Spain. Men shouted insults and women reproaches. Where were the gold mines of Havilah? Where was the Earthly Paradise? Was that Indian the Grand Khan – and that other – a Grander Khan? Where were their husbands, their sons, lured across the seas by his promises, hanging roasted and dead in some cannibal hut? . . . The reception accorded him by the King and Queen was courteously polite, no more. He was not placed on trial as Aguado and Bishop Fonseca would have liked. But his pleas for money for a further expedition were put aside into a limbo of innumerable delays.

He was a broken man. Some few of that great flock of imaginative mendacities he had unloosed upon the world had come home to roost. Here, to all seeming, ended both his quests and his discoveries.

X

But behind that sanguine mask (that had acquired in his brief years of success a haughty pride) there was still indomitable if indefinite will, indomitable faith in his own fabrications and the romantic readings of the wool-carder chapman. If the Earthly Paradise sank a little from hope his cosmographical notions were still medieval. No less so were his historical notions. He was convinced that beyond those islands that had brought him little but false hope and disaster lay the golden lands of Ind or the pearly lands of Cathay. And it was his duty as a Christian to seek out those lands and win the inhabitants to the true faith – winning for himself a due pittance in wealth as reward.

For two years he badgered the court; and at length began to wear down the resistance of Ferdinand and Isabella, fundamentally kindly people, a pair who could not forget the vague glory that the Admiral's discoveries had attached to their names. It was true that except as a breeding-ground for criminals and a spawning-ground for a very ineffective kind of slave, the Indies as yet had proved of little value. But what if the Admiral were right in his further assertions – that as yet they had but touched the fringes of the great Western lands that might verily be the Eastern lands of rumour and wealth?

Indeed, it was now more than rumour that a great Western mainland existed. Sailing with English ships, Sebastian Cabot had set eyes on the North American continent and cruised along a wide section of its shore. Columbus, now that the king and queen had acceded to his fresh demand, determined to sail to the south, 'well under the equinoctial line, for I believe that no one has ever traversed this way, and that this sea is nearly unknown'.

(This sentence shows his uncertainty, his landsman's brief unfaiths in the dominant poet-prevaricator. For, as has been said, even before his first voyage all the western

Mediterranean had been filled with rumours of the Atlantic lands. And it was no impossibility that some such sailor as that Madeira pilot had indeed traversed these infra-equi-noctial waters long before.)

With three ships he put out from the Cape Verde Islands on a voyage and in a spirit singularly reminiscent of that which characterised his first sailing. The trappings of vice-roy were put by for the time. He was again the simple if inefficient commander of his ship, pacing the decks, staring at the bright Atlantic stars, shivering in the chill of a dense fog that fell on them on the 4th of July, 1498 – a fog that 'cut as with a knife'. Presently the ships were again traversing those immense fields of shining seaweed – though now on their southern fringe. The wind died and a glassy calm came on the seas.

The ships moved slowly – as though some under-water current moved them, for the air was windless. To the Spaniards the eerie motion was terrifying. The heat grew stronger as the days went west, slowly, with limping feet, across the glassy stretches of water. Presently it became so dreadful that the crew refused to descend into the stench of the caravel's interior – even in order to succour their provisions and water. Men went mad and cried to God for relief from the burning intensity of the skies – a sky like a great inverted brazen bowl. Then at last, when it seemed that the expedition could endure no longer, a faint breeze rose and strengthened. It sent the scud flying and bellied out the heat-frayed sails of the ships. It drove them steadily west.

Three days later in the evening of the 22nd of July the look-outs saw great streaming flocks of birds against the sunset, homing towards the north-east. Land was again near, Columbus adjudged, despite the like portents on his first voyage which had betokened no land. Another week went by, bird-flights every evening dotting the signature of the sunset. Once a great albatross with wide-spreading wings came to rest on the rigging of the Admiral's own ship. Still there was no sight of land.

But on Thursday, the 31st of July, Columbus's outlook, Alonzo Perez, cast his eyes westwards from the mizzen and cried out that he saw land – far off, low down in the sea, three great peaks rising warmly coloured. It was that headland that later ages were to name Cape Cashepou, verily backgrounded by the three great peaks of Trinidad.

Columbus caused the vessels to cruise close in to the shore, but finding no suitable anchorage held on his course to the west. The shores of Trinidad unreeled before the staring eyes of the crews – shores with cultivated fields backgrounded by well-built huts. The Caribs ran and stared an even greater amazement than the Spaniards. Then darkness came down over the slow spread of Trinidad and the squadron kept on its cautious course still west.

Morning found them still coasting Trinidad. So much had the ships shrunk in the heat of the mid-Atlantic that they leaked like sieves and the Admiral scanned the coast with anxiety in search of a suitable harbourage for careening. Anchoring and taking in fresh water near Point Alcatraz, he obtained his first view of the coasts of the American continent – a long, low line of land with the running surf of the Orinoco a bright limning all along it. He took the continent for an island, and gave it the name of Zeta.

Coasting the richly cultivated and peopled coast, he entered the Gulf of Paria – entering it involuntarily through the high-ridged pressures of the Serpent's Mouth, where the autumn waters are caught betwixt Trinidad and the South American coasts and pour forth with impetuosity. The light ships of the Spaniards danced like corks, to the consternation of their crews. A canoe-full of Indians had put out from Trinidad that day to stare at the ship; the Admiral, wishing to attract them, and doubtlessly abduct them, had his men play on a tambourine and dance on the poop. Recognising these as indubitably warlike demonstrations, the Indians loosed a flight of arrows in reply and returned to the shore.

Inside the Serpent's Mouth, in the Gulf of Paria, the three ships cruised slowly up the American coast for several days finding the shores littered with heavily populated villages. Coming to the Paria Point, Columbus, repaying the natives their hospitality, abducted four of their number, and held on in search of Cipangu. At last they reached the second opening out of Paria, the Dragon's Mouth, and passed that in safety, coming again in the lie of the Lesser Antilles.

Asia and Havilah still delayed, but Margarita showed up the following day a blur upon the sea and sky. Columbus, albeit with absent-mindedness, reconnoitred its shores. But all the sailors, the soldiers, the pilots – and probably the cabin-boys – on board the three vessels had been confusing his never too-lucid mind from the moment they entered the Gulf of Paria. Sight of its raging waters – fresh water – had at first convinced the Admiral that what he had at first taken for an island was in reality a continent, and that continent of course Asia. He had proclaimed to the fleet that at last they had reached the richest land in the World. The fleet had been more than dubious. Some thought they had sailed round the shallow rim of the earth and were again near Africa. Some thought they were remote in the seas that fringe – of all places – Scotland . . .

Columbus's mathematics collapsed under the strain of uncertainty. Desperately he resolved to sail at once and seek for Hispaniola – unless it also had vanished in some crinkle of the maps.

So Margarita was given but the most cursory of surveys; the Admiral fled northwards from his kingdoms of fantasy in search of recognisable geography.

XI

For three years after reaching Hispaniola Columbus remained in control there. It was three years in which all that
was best in Columbus – the visioning explorer, the attractive, if mendacious poet, the sincere, if fantastically romantic religious enthusiast – became obscured in the rôle of
haughty governor and heaven-ordained viceroy. More
darkly, they became obscured in the slave-trader. On the
least pretext the miserable Indians of Hispaniola and the
surrounding Islands were driven into rebellion, pursued
with horses and bloodhounds, captured in hundreds and
shipped to Spain for sale in the market of Seville.

At last this practice reached such limits that Ferdinand
and Isabella – for their time enlightened rulers unless
heretics were at hand – could bear with it no longer. They
forbade a great sale in Seville and paid more attention to the
constant stream of complaints that were launched against
Columbus.

So serious were these and arriving in such volume that it
was decided to despatch an investigator. He had no very
definite orders, the Comendador Francisco de Bobadilla,
but he was a fiery individual, and quite as egotistic as
Columbus himself. Arriving in St Domingo on the 23rd
of August, 1500, he took possession of the Admiral's house
and summoned Columbus and his brothers to appear
before him to answer innumerable charges.

News of this command flew abroad Hispaniola. The
miserable Spanish colonists flocked to testify against their
oppressor – the Genoan foreigner who had starved and
bullied and beaten them while he himself lived in luxury
surrounded by his brothers and favourites. These were
the colonists. But some of the Catholic priests spoke for
the Indians – Indians who had been left unbaptised in
order that they might be enslaved, Indians on whom
Columbus had raided and warred without cause or

pretext till in the course of a short eight years he had
transformed that sleepy garden of the Archaic Culture
into a hell on earth . . . Bobadilla, cold and contemptuous, heard the spluttered defence of the greying Admiral: and then ordered his arrest. His brothers were
arrested at the same time, flung in chains, and shipped
aboard a vessel bound for Spain.

With the chapman's plebeian theatricalism ousting the
unauthentic aristocrat, Columbus insisted on wearing
those chains even on board the vessel; he insisted that
he would never have them removed except by royal command. The Spanish settlers crowded to watch him pass to
the vessel and shout their execrations upon him. Flushed
and haughty and tired, he walked through their midst
without a glance.

News of the fashion in which he had arrived in Spain was
carried to the court. The King and Queen, shocked at the
arbitrary methods of Bobadilla, ordered him unchained
and sent to the court in all honour.

Ferdinand, never the friend of the plausible, poetic
Genoan, refused to grant him an audience. But Isabella
received him semi-privately, and listened to his defence,
and replied in words astounding enough in their reason-
ableness and humanity:

'Common report accuses you of acting with a degree of
severity quite unsuitable for an infant colony, and likely to
excite rebellion there. But the matter as to which I find it
hardest to give you my pardon is your conduct in reducing
to slavery a number of Indians who had done nothing to
deserve such a fate. That was contrary to my express
orders. As your ill fortune willed it, just at the time when
I heard of this breach of my instructions, everybody was
complaining against you, and no one spoke a word in your
favour . . . I cannot promise to reinstate you at once in your
government. People are too much inflamed against you,
and must have time to cool. As to your rank of admiral, I

never intended to deprive you of it. But you must bide your time and trust in me.'

Bide his time . . . when on the tip of his eager tongue was a great project to push still further west than the islands, on a fourth great expedition which would bring him, by way of a 'strait' of which he had heard, to those dominions in Asia which the Portuguese, sailing eastwards, were already exploiting . . . The Spanish rulers listened with some doubt to weary months of pleading, and at last and again surrendered. That golden tongue riddled every shield of sanity and reason opposed to it.

On the 9th of May he sailed from Cadiz with five ships.

He was strictly interdicted from putting in at Hispaniola or meddling at all in the affairs of the colonies. But was he not the Admiral? On the pretext that one of his ships required repairs he determined to make Isabella. En route, he looked at the skies and saw certain signs of the coming of one of the great Atlantic storms. Unless he found shelter for his squadron—

Ovando, the new governor who had superseded Bobadilla, refused to allow the squadron shelter in the harbour. He refused, equally, to delay the sailing of a great treasure-fleet loaded with gold from the mines of Ciboa. On board it sailed a cloud of the Spanish adventurers including Bobadilla. Two days out at sea a great tornado smote it. One ship escaped, having seen her companions whelmed in the great Atlantic mountains. Columbus had proved a true prophet.

Escaping the worst of that storm himself by sheltering under an unknown headland, he held on in the course of his fourth expedition of discovery. Jamaica was reached on the 14th of July, 1502. Still he held westwards. But presently the fleet almost foundered in the maze of cays and islets that littered those seas – islands flowering a rank green or glimmering rocky and inhospitable under the burning summer. The winds died away.

For over two months the worm-eaten, leaking ships

tacked to and fro amidst those islets, seeking a wind to help them escape. Scurvy came on the crews, and men sickened from drinking the brackish waters of the islets. The summer was one of exceptional heat. Presently mutiny grew loud-voiced. Had the Genoese clown brought them here to perish in company with his idiot self? . . . Columbus paced the deck, now white-haired, but vision-rapt and unapproachable as ever, confident in the guidance of God and the sureties of his own mendacity.

At last an easterly wind sprang up. The caravels moved out into the Western Caribbean, hitherto unexplored. In the course of a day's steady sailing they sighted a small island. It was Guanaja, off the coast of Honduras. Columbus, giving it a cursory survey, for he had already seen the dark limning of the continental mass in the west, was about to sail on, turning towards the north but for an accidental encounter. This was with a boatload of Indians from the mainland – cotton-clad Indians, traders in flint arrow-heads and copper axes.

By signs the Admiral entered into communication with them. Their leader, an ancient of imposing mien, appeared to understand perfectly, though Spaniards and Indians had no word of common vocabulary between them. Columbus by signs inquired if Cathay and the court of the Grand Khan lay near? By equally impressive signs the ancient in command of the canoe signalled Yes!

Close at hand was the land the strangers sought – a land much frequented on the further shore by ships like the Admiral's own – and he would guide the Spaniards thither.

XII

Had Columbus steered north-west, as had been his first intention, he would have made Yucatan where the great Asiatic-inspired civilisation of the Maya was slowly sinking into decay. But instead, under the guidance of the volubly sign-making Indian ancient, he steered southwards along the coast of Honduras, bright with tamarinds and the ferns of rocky headlands. This was the coast of the authentic Americas, but Columbus believed it merely another island, though one of great extent. Southwards, somewhere, lay the strait leading to the Grand Khan's dominions.

For three months, in a confusion of place-names that have now vanished, he cruised up and down the Panama neck seeking the strait or the country of gold 'frequented by great ships' of whom the Indian had told him. It is possible that the Indian had re-told a rumour of trading vessels from Asia seen on the Pacific side of the Isthmus. As we now know, Asia traded with America into remote historic times and there is nothing improbable in rumour of stranger ships in the Pacific having been noised abroad throughout Honduras. But that, at the best, had been beyond the reaches of the impassable Isthmus.

Mosquitos plagued the crews by night, heat by day. The rotting vessels made slow headway even with favourable winds. Once, anchored off a creek, Columbus was attacked by the Indians; once, seated in conclave with them, still querying the whereabouts of Kublai, he observed the natives indulging in a soothing pipe, and was somewhat alarmed believing them magicians making spells against him. In early December came a great storm, the waves bursting over the leaking vessels in phosphorescent floods and driving Columbus back to the shelter of the coast which at last he would have abandoned.

Born of this minor mischance, however, came gold at last. They had anchored off the territory of a chief named Quibia – perhaps a heritor of the degenerate Coclè culture of Panama. Gold was everywhere evident. By barter and actual excavation large quantities of the ore were procured, and the Spaniards, changeable and as easily enheartened as downcast, were enthusiastic for remaining on those shores. A village of huts, Bethlehem, was built on the bank of a stream, and there the Admiral determined to leave a garrison of eighty men while he returned to Spain for supplies and reinforcements. Bartholomew was left in charge and the Admiral put out to sea.

Unfortunately, Quibia, maltreated by the Spaniards, had gathered his forces and prepared to attack the settlement. Braves crept forward under the cover of darkness and sank the few leaky boats left for the use of the colonists. A dozen Spaniards up the reaches of Bethlehem stream were massacred. Frightened, the settlers would have communicated with Columbus still lingering in sight of the shore and awaiting a favourable wind. But there was no means whereby to communicate.

In this strait they were aided by the uneasiness of Columbus himself, fancying that all was not well in the settlement. His own boats were incapable of making the three-mile passage to the shore, but the pilot Ledesma, the solitary hero of the expedition, leapt overboard and swam through the shark-infested waters till he reached Bartholomew. Columbus's ships were signalled shorewards again, and the expedition re-embarked.

Before they could sail again, however, a caravel, leaking too desperately, had to be abandoned to the winds and tides.

The ill-fated Bethlehem settlement hull down in the north west, Columbus coasted the Darien Peninsula for a short while longer; then, abandoning still another caravel, steered for Cuba towards the end of May. The sieve-like ships staggered drunkenly through the squalls of the Caribbean. In the mist of one night the two remaining ships collided head-on, and for a while were like to sink with all hands. Indomitably the Admiral had them re-patched. Hunger assailed the crews; land was lost for days. But at last, weary and forsaken, they sighted the southern coast of Cuba, where food was obtained from natives still hospitable enough to succour the needy, even though these might be the white devils from the sea.

With that coming to Cuba there ends the tale of Columbus the explorer, the seeker of the Earthly Paradise, even as there begins a long record of him as marooned mariner, cowardly courageous commander, and – persisting to the end – mendacious egomaniac. Behind him, westwards, the Americas drowsed in sleep, the war-rent lands of the great Maya civilisations with their scrolled temples and strange gods, the sun in its full splendour before sunset on the strange aberrant splendours of the Aztec genius in floriferation, the Inka confederacy dominating Peru and the surrounding lands, immense and seemingly impregnable; that, and the league-stretching plains of North America, the forested immensities of Amazonia, the little patches by river and mountain where still, as in the Bahamas, the last of the great groupings of Natural Man lived that free and happy and animal-like existence which was soon to end for ever as the tides of a newer and crueller civilisation rolled eastwards in the track of the Genoan's chance discovery.

XIII

But the shell of the poet-explorer cannot pass beyond our horizon without a glance of interest. From that southern anchorage at Cuba, Columbus, despairing of making Hispaniola, crossed the straits of Jamaica and ran his ships on shore, embedding them in the sand. Then he sat down and wrote letters to Ferdinand and the Governor of Hispaniola, asking for aid and describing the wonders of Panama in the usual terms of overflowing optimism and exaggeration.

These letters were carried by his lieutenant, Mendez, after numerous encounters and flights and fights and travails, to San Domingo. Months went by and no news of relief came to the two ships stranded off Jamaica. The natives grew less friendly, suffering from the depredations of a scoundrelly Spaniard, Porras, who had quarrelled with the Admiral. Porras finally decided to seize the ships for himself and his fellow-mutineers. He attacked from the woods and a pitched battle on the sands was witnessed by the assembled Indians. Porras was defeated and captured, mainly through the instrumentality of brother Bartholomew, and on the 28th of June two caravels arrived from San Domingo to carry the shipwrecked sailors from Jamaica. Columbus, with a happy disregard of the actual situation from which he had been rescued, sailed in apparent confidence that in Hispaniola Ovando the Governor would give way to the superior authority of the Viceroy.

Ovando displayed no such inclination. There followed a month of wrangling, the haughty and ageing Genoese opposed to the cool and dried Ovando, a typical Spanish Grandee. Then Columbus took ship from the Indies, and never saw them again.

Even on this last voyage misfortune dogged him. The Atlantic was swept with storms and great seas beat on the deck of his ship. Ill with a fever which came with gout, Columbus lay in his cabin and listened to the thunder of the weather and turned a weary head to seek rest again, disillusionment at last upon him.

Nor was that unwarranted. The court sent no summons for him to appear. He had wasted the fortunes of the fourth expedition, he returned with no news of the imagined strait or having penetrated to the elusive dominions of that elusive Kublai who had been sleeping the last sleep in dusty Peking two hundred years. Columbus was carried to his house in Seville, to the attentions of that devoted family which held by family feeling with a strong Italian tenacity. Had he been able to sink himself in the care of his neglected Beatriz or the devotion of his sons, Diego and Ferdinand, he might even then have escaped to life and health.

But such grace and greatness was beyond the Genoese, unabandoned still by his own febrific fabrications of fantasy. For him life had become the pursuit, ever westwards, of the golden kingdoms of myth and imagination. He was incapable of resting and taking his case. Presently Diego was dispatched to the court to plead his case. He had little time for effective pleading. Isabella, the only person likely to listen again to the Admiral, was dying. With her death on the 26th of November his last hope of receiving either reinstatement or funds for a new expedition vanished.

He lingered on two years more, white-haired, pain-racked, insatiable still of reinstatement. At Vallodolid in early May it became plain that his time was short. He had a priest summoned and received the offices of his Church with the same fervent devoutness as had characterised all his life; he looked round at the faces of the family which encircled him, and forgot them, staring in spirit still westwards; then his thoughts strayed from even that worldly longing. His last whisper was 'Into Thy hands, Master, I commend my spirit.'

And when that enigmatic spirit had sailed into the dim seas to its utmost bourne, surely his Earthly Paradise at last, they buried the strayed chapman of Genoa in the monastery of Las Cuevas of Seville.

XIV

The consequences which followed the discovery of the sailing-route across the Atlantic focused on their discoverer more attention than has been paid to any other of the earth's conquerors. He has been viewed through innumerable works and innumerable eyes, from innumerable viewpoints. He has been acclaimed as the hero that son Ferdinand saw him; as the sly trickster whom Las Casas viewed. But his greatness has seldom been disputed. His feet may be feet of clay, heavy poet's feet splashed with the blood of human suffering, but they are planted certainly enough upon that 'New World beyond the wave' which he gave to Castile and Leon.

Yet he was not the first European discoverer of America: Leif Ericcson, on a similar quest, had preceded him; the mythic Irish voyagers of the seventh and eight centuries may have preceded him; and – more seriously – the strayed pilot whom he met at Madeira had preceded him. His discovery was not of a New World – which all his life long he strenuously denied and disbelieved. His discovery was of the sailing route across the Atlantic.

Even so, it was great enough. It loosed upon the sparsely inhabited American continent the hungry hordes of over-populated Europe. It loosed new motifs in art and science and perhaps religion. It ended for ever those great and strange experiments in civilisation on which the native Americans were employed. And for all Europe it meant a great lifting and widening of horizons, cultural and geographical.

It meant the vanishing from the minds of men for ever of the flat-earth hypothesis, did that hypothesis still lingeringly endure; it meant the breaking down of a great and elaborate synthesis of thought regarding the earth's origins, the origins of all men, the connection of the facts of ethnology and history with the Mosaic myths. Nothing has been so fruitful of discussion and discovery as the question of the origins of the Red Indians and their various strange cultures. America, where the last of the great masses of Natural Men – neither savage, barbarian, nor civilised – were encountered as a consequence of the establishment of the transatlantic route, influenced profoundly contemporary and subsequent political and politico-sociological thought. It may be said, indeed, with its influence upon Thomas More and Rousseau and the Encyclopedists, that Columbus fathered the French Revolution and modern humanitarianism. He was (a ruddy, horrified shade) the godfather of modern Rationalism, the Diffusionist School of History, the philosophy of Anarchism.

These were no more than undreamed consequences. His

own stature was not great: it was as fantastically puny as his cosmography was fantastically irrelevant. Europe had dispatched to the Far East in the person of Marco Polo a bright and hard young Venetian merchant-adventurer as its envoy to the Kingdom of Wonder; to the west it dispatched in quest of the haunting Fortunate Isles which Leif had looked upon a dream-ridden, inefficient Genoese woolcarder who suffered from an inferiority complex and a congenital inability to refrain from prevarication. But beyond and above the pitiful clown with the numerous footmen in Haiti, the theatrical chains at Seville, there abides very essential and real the Explorer whose horizons the undiscovered West so vexed: there is the Columbus of the First Expedition who paced his decks and saw the falling star and was undaunted as that strange beacon of God beckoned him on the Americas, the light of whose native peoples he quenched.

The End of the Maya Old Empire

THE EARLY NINETEENTH century witnessed a remarkable reversal of judgment on the American pre-Columbian cultures. Prescott's romantic histories and Lord Kingsborough's monumental *Mexican Antiquities* are inspirations of earlier and less sceptical eras. Such pleasing imaginings as that the Spaniards 'overthrew in Mexico a greater civilisation than their own' received scant support from the archeologist who had displaced the antiquary, or from the critical historian who interpreted him. Dr Robertson summed up the verdict of the new investigators: 'The inhabitants of the New World were in a state of society so extremely rude as to be unacquainted with those arts which are the first essays of human ingenuity in its advance towards improvement.' He characterised Cortes' 'emperors' as 'headmen', the gorgeous palaces of the Conquest as 'huts or mounds of rubble', the Aztec Empire as a 'league of primitive tribes'. Research, both among the ruins of the Mexican Valley and in the histories of the more prosaic conquistadores, established a singular lack of anything on the pre-Columbian continents which could be described as other than a tawdry barbarism. Lord Macaulay, no Americanist, and therefore doubtless following Robertson, when reviewing Major Sir John Malcolm's *Life of Robert Clive* (1836) and comparing the achievements of Clive with those of Cortes, wrote: 'The victories of Cortes were gained over savages who had no letters, who were ignorant of the use of metal, who had not broken a single animal to labour, who wielded no better weapons than those which could be made out of sticks, flints, and fish-bones.'

Although it is now known that the manufacture and use of all metals except iron were fairly common among the native peoples of the two continents, the last hundred years of American archeology has substantiated rather than modified such statements as Macaulay's. America at the time of the coming of the Europeans contained nothing that might be classified as a true civilisation. But that this had always been the case is by no means certain. The labours of innumerable investigators – explorers, archeologists, ethnologists – begin to reveal that something which was either civilisation, or rapidly approaching that indefinite cultural horizon, once flourished in the Central American forests.

A hundred years ago all Mexican and Central American ruins were still spoken of as 'Aztec', in spite of the hauntings of the ghostly 'Toltecs'. The Maya of Yucatan were given little space by either Robertson or Prescott. They were presumed to have been an Aztec-influenced tribe at a slightly lower level of culture than the Mexicans. They had been mentioned by Cortes and Bernal Diaz, conquered by the two Montejos, and their history – the usual thin comminglings of fantastic legend and fable – written by two clerics, Lizana and Cogolludo. Remote on the lands of the Pacific coast the Quiché were also recognised as a tribe of Mayance blood, and – even from a modern point of view – justly assessed as 'barbarous'. But the land lying between the Pacific coast and Yucatan was almost without note in the histories.

This stretch of land, watered by the Grijalva, Usamacinta and Pedro joining in confluence to flow into Campeche Bay in the north-west, and by the Rios Hondo, Belize, Grande, Motagua and Chamelicon, flowing into the Gulf of Honduras in the southeast, is a swampy and densely forested region, partly comprising the Mexican state of Chiapas, partly British Honduras, and partly Guatemalan territory. Guatemala in the eighteen-forties was still a part of the old Central American Republic. Between the issue of Sir John Malcolm's book and Macaulay's review, and while Prescott was completing his *History of the Conquest of Mexico*, it was the scene of the explorations of John Lloyd Stephens, an American traveller and diplomat, who, in the intervals of seeking a stable government with which to negotiate some nebulous proposals of the President of the United States, visited eight ruined cities. He was accompanied by the English artist, Frederick Catherwood. The account of his explorations, was principally of interest because of Catherwood's remarkable illustrations. These disclosed the fact that the strictures passed on the pre-Columbians had been altogether too severe, that something incompatible with barbarism, in point of architecture, sculpture, and the possession of an extraordinary hieroglyphic script, had once existed in the Usamacinta basin and surrounding country. Its remains – identified, of course, as 'Aztec' – had indeed been pointed out previously by Charnay and others, but Stephens and Catherwood were the first to make them generally known. In spite of innumerable differences, not so much in type as in technique, and a common script supplying the surest link, these remarkable cultural evidences were soon brought into connexion with the ruined cities of the historic Maya of Yucatan.

Among modern Americanists there is now something approaching unanimity in the belief that in the tract of land under consideration – a great inverted triangle in the heart of Central America, with a line drawn from Comalcalco to Tikal as base, and Copan in Honduras as apex – the first and greatest cultural climb of the pre-Columbians took place. What was at least the great semi-civilisation of a settled and highly organised people blossomed into the rearing of scores of building-complexes which are supposed to have been the religious centres of long-vanished cities built otherwise of wood or adobe. From the middle of the eighth Maya cycle to the end of the tenth, a period of some 450 years, sculptural and architectural art in those 'complexes' passed rapidly from an archaic phase to a naturalistic, from a naturalistic to a formal, from a formal to a flamboyantly archaistic, and then ceased altogether. Stated more cautiously, the datings in the curious calendar and script which accompanied those art manifestations ceased, a little after the close of the tenth cycle, to appear on the monuments of the region.

This, according to Professor Morley, was not a 'sudden cessation of the monuments in the individual cities when each was at its cultural and aesthetic apogee, but a gradual abandonment of the region as a whole, covering a period of about a century'. The cities were presumably deserted, the great cultivated lands left to be reclaimed by the jungle. The survivors of the catastrophe or catastrophes which led to the abandonments apparently fled northeastwards into the barren peninsula of Yucatan and there carried on an attenuated culture until the arrival of the Europeans at least a thousand years later.

'The Maya,' says Dr Spinden in his exhaustive survey of

Old and New Empire art, produced one of the few really great and coherent expressions of beauty so far given to the world, and their influence in America was historically as important as was that of the Greeks in Europe.' The consequences of the overthrow of the first American essay at civilisation in that territory variously known as the Old Empire and as Xibalba – the latter perhaps a misnomer from Quiché myth – may have been more analogous to those produced by the collapse of Rome. There probably took place the destruction or dispersal of such organised skill and documented knowledge as were never again available to the pre-Columbian nations, though on the fragments of the destroyed culture were built the magnificent barbarisms of Toltec, Aztec, and Yucatecan Maya.

The event has been explained by at least a score of contradictory theories. Of those, five at least still find champions among modern Americanists. Concerning neither the end of the Old Empire, nor its 450 years of history, is there a scrap of contemporary record extant which can be interpreted – even should the sculptural inscriptions of the ruined cities contain historical data. In the middle of last century a clue to the glyphic writing appeared to have been unearthed with the discovery, by the Abbé Brasseur de Bourbourg, of the three-centuries old manuscript *Relacion de las cosas de Yucatan*, compiled by Bishop Landa, one of the earliest and ablest clerics to come in contact with the New Empire Maya after the Spanish Conquest. The manuscript explains the Maya calendrical system in part and purports to provide a Maya 'alphabet'. But the calculiform signs set down by Landa have proved no Rosetta stone for the decipherment of either the few surviving New Empire codices or the glyphs on the monuments of the ruined cities. Neither New nor Old Empire Maya appear to have possessed an alphabet: the glyphic writing enshrines some sort of syllabary. In spite of years of research, carried out with or without the doubtful aids of

Landa, and along the lines laid down by Forstemann and Seler, only a few signs, mostly astronomical, have so far been transliterated or interpreted. The Maya scholar examining the ruins of an Old Empire site is in the position of a millennial Malayan investigating the remains of London with no better equipment than a knowledge of our calendar and systems of notation. He can read the dates on the public statues and buildings, but is quite unable from the associated legends to identify a single individual or be certain of the purpose of a single building.

The correct correlation of Old Empire dates with the modern Christian (Gregorian) calendar is still uncertain, a process attempted with the aid of New Empire datings contained in the *Books of Chilan Balam*. These are Yucatecan tribal histories reduced to writing by Christianised Maya *after* the Spanish Conquest, and set down in Latin script. Their evidence is frequently contradictory and has given rise to widely-divergent correlations. Certain German archeologists still place the beginning of the eighth Maya cycle as late as the tenth Christian century, thus bringing the end of the Old Empire close to the opening of the Spanish conquest. But no such populous region as Xibalba of the thousand cities was discovered by the conquistadores: the Usamacinta and Guatemalan cities had been abandoned long before Cortes' famous march from Mexico to Honduras Bay. He certainly encountered no Maya whatever except the transplanted Itza on Lake Peten. At the moment two other correlations are in vogue – the Spinden-Morley, which places the beginning of the ninth cycle in AD 176, and the Bowditch-Joyce, which places it 270 years earlier, in 94 BC. To the present writer, influenced by Sahagun's dating for the coming of the Toltecs to the Mexican Valley – though it is by no means certain that this event had any connexion with the Old Empire's fate – the Bowditch-Joyce correlation appears the more probable. But the matter, together with the complicated calendrical systems in general, is outside the scope of this article. A Maya cycle covered nearly 400 years, and the city-civilisation of the Old Empire triangle appears to have come into being at or about the opening of the Christian era and to have closed towards the end of either the third or fifth centuries AD. Rome and Copan, the dominant cities of the dominant empires of two continents, may have fallen on the same day.

The origin of the remarkable Xibalban culture is as mysterious as its downfall, and important in that it may offer some clue to the latter event. Professor Morley brings the old Empire Maya from the north, on the evidence of a small statuette dated towards the end of the eighth Maya cycle. This was found north of the Old Empire tract, in the state of Tuxtla. Still further north, on the Gulf of Mexico, is the tract of country inhabited at the time of the Spanish Conquest by the Huaxteca, a primitive people of Mayance speech. Professor Morley (who, like most Americanists, denies extra-American influence in the formation of the Xibalban civilisation) marches his Early Maya down from the Huaxteca region. A progressive branch of the proto-Maya stock, they came southwards into Central America, acquiring en route their distinctive script and sculpture, and arriving in the Usamacinta basin prepared for the first adventure of civilisation in the New World.

Of this migration there is, however, no trace apart from the Tuxtla statuette, which may well have been an export from the Xibalban region. The Huaxteca are beside the point; to the west and south-west of Xibalba lay the territory of the barbarous Quiché, also of Mayance tongue. Neither they nor the Huaxteca had any knowledge of the script or fully-evolved calendar. If the Quiché also originated in the Huaxteca territory, and shared in the civilising southwards migration, only racial amnesia would explain the complete absence of its influence in their primitive buildings and sculpture.

Dr Gann regards as the Old Empire Maya the descendants of the 'Archaic' peoples of the Central American highlands; a branch migrated from those highlands to the sea-coast, acquired culture, and commenced city-building. He admits, however, an immediate lack of proof; there seems to exist far less connexion between the primitive pottery of the 'Archaic horizon' and Old Empire art than between the nebulous ancient culture and that of the Nahuatlaca (Toltec and Aztec) of Mexico, who were certainly late immigrants from North America. Neither Professor Morley nor Dr Gann attempts to explain why it should be that their Xibalban Maya, originating somewhere near the Gulf of Mexico, yet reared their earliest city – so far discovered – at Uaxactun, remote on the borders of British Honduras.

Captain Joyce believes the Xibalban culture was evolved in the region where it is found, even though there are no traces of a period when the script and calendar were in a primitive state (they appear as highly developed on the first inscription as on the last). Other theories derive the Xibalbans from the Mound Builders of the Mississippi and from 'Antilia', a fragment of submerged Atlantis itself submerged early in the third century BC. But in both cases the one certain requisite – a calculiform inscription – is missing. As part – an integral part – of the diffusionist heresy, Professor Elliot Smith and Dr Perry account for the Old Empire through the civilising agency of the 'Children of the Sun', a culture drift of ruler-groups from across the Pacific, and with its original inspiration in ancient Egypt. But between any development of Egyptian picture-writing and that of Xibalba there is no similarity whatever. They are racial vehicles of thought evolved in the completest ignorance of each other.

Some two centuries before the opening of the Christian era, therefore, a people of quite untraceable antecedents on the American or any other surviving continent, in possession of an elaborate script and the most highly developed calendar yet known to us, began to build their great temple-complexes in a sporadic fashion in the triangle of Xibalba. Of their calendar Dr Spinden says: 'The Maya calculated an almost exact correction for the excess of the true year over the vague 365 day year. The excess amounts to about .24 of a day, and their correction seems to have been one day in four years for ordinary purposes and 25 days in 104 years for longer stretches of time. The latter correction is more accurate than that of the Julian calendar and nearly as accurate as that of the present Gregorian calendar put into service as late as 1582.'

They used a vigesimal system of notation, apparently with considerably more skill than such a system warrants, and had discovered, in advance of Old World mathematicians by at least a thousand years, a sign for zero. The 'Venus-count' of their calendars suggests a more highly developed technique in planetary observation than was possessed by any other culture before the invention of the telescope. They erected on the hills above Copan the gnomons of the greatest sundial in the world. These, Drs Spinden and Gann seem to suggest, were used for regulating the seasonal clocks of their civilisation. In the same city there is an altar-freize which appears to portray a city-wide congress of astronomer-priests, met for that great rectification of the Maya calendar so frequently mentioned in Yucatecan tradition – 'the putting of Pop in order'. Such a congress of scientists at that time would have been impossible in any part of the Old World except China.

The first date of the Maya era (Spinden-Morley correlation) was 3485 BC. Americanists generally regard this date as too remote to have historical significance, and as probably an invention of the Maya mathematicians for the purpose of synthesising their various calendars into the elaborate unity attained by that calendar at least 500 years before its use on the monuments of Xibalba. But this

reformed calendar is arranged for, and is capable of, dealing with periods of time as great as five million years. Such a
concept of *elapsed* time in the world's history is the greatest
achievement of the Early Maya mind of which we have any
knowledge, and suggests to the imaginative the possibility
that the Xibalbans may have had some knowledge of the
earth's geological phases.

As in ancient Egypt, architectural science was mostly
devoted to the erection of temples and temple-adjuncts; the
frequent Xibalban 'towers' may have been observatories.
Certain other structures, perhaps used as priestly colleges
or libraries, were also built in the 'central complex' of each
city. Those 'colleges' have been compared to the North
American Indian 'long-houses', the tribal council-houses.
There is good reason to believe that they were never, in our
sense, palaces, though this term is frequently applied to
them.

In spite of his achievements in abstract mathematics, the
Xibalban had not discovered the principle of the true arch.
The corbelled arch in use throughout the region made the
building of a second storey almost, though not quite,
impossible, and left all rooms exceedingly narrow and high.
Also, it is doubtful if in the whole of the Old Empire tract
there was ever an architect with a knowledge of bonding
corners.

The phases of Xibalban sculpture have already been
noted. It was undoubtedly a religious or temple art, even,
perhaps, in the case of the elaborate stelae. These were
menhirs sculptured, in greater or lesser degree, to the
likeness of statues – sometimes undoubtedly portrait-sta-
tues – and were raised at regular intervals in the plazas of
the cities, and profusely dated and inscribed. Captain Joyce
assigns Old Empire sculpture, especially as manifested on
the panels of the Palenque palaces, a higher technical level
than Babylonian or even Egyptian. That it was ever other
than formal, the portrayal of types, not individuals, has

been denied. But the extraordinarily individualised sculptures discovered in an underground chamber in Comalcalco in 1926, by Messrs Blom and Le Farge of the Tulane University expedition, effectively prove the contrary. Some of the Palenque statues probably represent women.

Whether on temple walls or on stelae the sculptured figures are apparently always those of priests or priestesses. None of the figures in the Central Xibalban or southern area is portrayed with weapons. Captain Joyce concludes that the Maya Old Empire was singularly peaceful, and probably under some central government. The building-complexes have no appearance of being fortified. Dr Spinden and Professor Morley point out, however, that not all the scenes portrayed are of peaceful character. In north-western (and presumably border) towns such as Piedras Negras representations of tortured warriors bound to trees and of disarmed and dejected captives squatting in front of triumphant conquerors have been discovered. The border position of the cities containing such sculptures must be emphasised. There is no good reason to think that civil war was common in Xibalba. Possibly the government of most of the cities, whether or not these were leagued in a political as well as a cultural 'empire', was theocratic in character. Except for the members of a priestly militia, the warrior had probably passed entirely from the Maya scene.

The general type of portrayed Xibalban has a full, heavy face, a retreating forehead – head-malformation was undoubtedly practised – blank and rather expressionless eyes – the statues were probably painted – and ears distended with great copper plugs. This was evidently the dominant type of Old Empire Mayan. Dr Gann, in the course of his yearly explorations in Central America, has come to the important conclusion that the bulk of the populace differed both in race and origin from the ruling caste. The sculptured figures of subsidiary priests, apparently not of the dominant race, are fairly frequent, and possibly represent freedmen elevated from a subservient race of helots. The Palenque stuccos are rich in portrayal of sacrificing or worshipping priests standing on the backs of crouching grotesques who are possibly slaves. Substantial proof that two distinct races did indeed occupy the Old Empire tract simultaneously might also provide an important clue to the end of that Empire – a possibility which Dr Gann does not pursue.

From excavation and the evidence of the sculptures a little is known of Xibalba's manufactures in pottery and textiles. But we still know nothing, directly, of its religion, social organisation, agriculture, or – a matter of keen dispute – its knowledge of metals – though the astronomical and mathematical achievements of the Old Empire Maya would place them high in at least semi-civilised status were their implements and weapons proved to be sub-Macaulayan. Gold was worked. A few ornaments of copper or 'accidental' bronze have been unearthed. In view of the amount of flint and obsidian tools and utensils discovered, reinforced as these discoveries are through judgment of the ruins by certain artistic criteria, it is usually maintained that the buildings were raised and the sculptures and inscriptions executed with the aid of stone implements only. Mr Hyatt Verrill, writing of his researches among the ruins of the apparently Maya-influenced Coclé culture of Panama, makes a disturbing interpellation in the unanimity of archaeologists:

On one occasion I selected several hundred stone tools and implements obtained from the site of the Coclé temple, and, outlining a coarse, simple scroll upon a fragment of soft stone which was a portion of an elaborately sculptured column, I set four of my Indians to work upon it with the prehistoric tools. Although the four were unusually intelligent and skilful men, and despite the fact that they worked

and laboured diligently for a week, and broke or wore
out all of the stone implements, their united efforts
failed to result in any noticeable carving or even in a
recognisable pattern in the stone.

The dense forests which immediately surround the Xibalban
ruins at the present time are re-encroachments of jungle upon
originally cleared spaces. In view of the amount of labour
necessary to rear the great temple-complexes, Professor
Morley calculates that the population of the Old Empire
tract was at least 500 times as great as at the present day. On
the analogy of Chichen-itza and other New Empire cities at
the time of the Spanish Conquest, Copan and Palenque may
each have numbered its citizens by the hundred thousand.

To support such populations the presumed maize-plantations must have stretched for leagues around each city.
Considering the number of those cities, and the certainty
that still more will be discovered, even the more conservative Americanist finds himself compelled to picture the
whole of the Usamacinta basin – to take only one region –
as almost one vast garden at the height of the Old Empire's
prosperity, with the forest-lands reduced to narrow strips.
Dr Gann believes that some form of intensive cultivation
was practised in the neighbourhood of the cities.

With such-like aids of scattered fact and deduction an
uncertain glimpse is obtained, through the darkness of
fifteen centuries, of the flowering of a civilisation at once
childish and precociously mature. Superficially, it had
every evidence of vigorous life and promise of spreading
abroad its cleruchies all over Central America. Its traders
had probably reached as far north as New Mexico; Sr Max
Uhle discovers Maya cultural evidences remotely south in
Ecuador. And then, in ones and twos, unrelatedly, the
Xibalban cities are abruptly abandoned, the Old Empire
tract entirely deserted, and, in the opinion of Professor
Morley, left so deserted for over 800 years.

The first defection occurred in 9.13.0.0.0 (AD 163 in the Bowditch-Joyce correlation) when Palenque, the Old Empire Florence, ceased to date its monuments and was presumably abandoned. It had had a life history of barely sixty years, and during that period gives evidence of having risen to cultural heights unsurpassed by any other Xibalban city. It is possible that Comalcalco, in the extreme northwest, was abandoned at the same time. There followed a pause. Then, between 9.18.0.0.0. and 9.19.10.0.0. (AD *c.* 262–293) the first American civilisation appears to have suffered blow after staggering blow. First, about AD 267, the great southern city of Copan, the cultural and possibly the political capital of the Empire, ceased to date its monuments. In the same year Menche (Yaxchilan), lying far in the north, midway the cities of the Usamacinta basin, was abandoned. Five years later gives the last date found at Ixkun. In 9.19.0.0.0. Piedras Negras in the north, Uaxactun in the east, and Quirigua in the south, separated by almost the entire stretch of Xibalban territory, the guardians of the surviving triangle, were extinguished. Naranjo went next, in 9.19.10.0.0. Of the whole Empire only Seibal and Tikal were left.

This list of dates, the hour-strokes for the death of the great pre-Columbian culture, is amplified by no direct historic data whatever. In AD 301 two events, faintly illuminating, apparently took place: Benque Viejo and Flores were *founded*, the former destined to last a brief twenty years, the latter forty. For by 10.2.0.0.0. (AD 340) the two elder cities of Seibal and Tikal, together with the short-lived Flores, had also been abandoned, and the entire Xibalban territory presumably depopulated.

No clear view of the magnitude of this tragedy can be gained without stressing the astronomical and mathematical achievements of the Xibalbans and the density of population which the city-centres must have possessed. The catastrophes or catastrophe which burst on the Central

American triangle depopulated the region of no sparse and barbarous tribes: it killed the promise of a high civilisation and may have affected the fortunes of millions. Whatever the remnants of Xibalban culture transported to Yucatan, whatever the number of fugitives which formed the Great and Little Descents of Yucatecan legend, it is certain that thousands of Old Empire Maya, including probably most of the members of the dominant and cultured castes, perished. In the founding of such minor sites as Flores and Benque Viejo it is possible to see temporary gatherings of refugees, but behind, in the great basin of the Usama-cinta and surrounding country, from Quirigua to Tikal, either wholesale extermination or equally wholesale relapse into barbarism overtook the Maya.

Dates later than 10.2.0.0.0. survive outside the Xibalban region at three sites, Tuluum and Chichen-itza in Yucatan, marking the founding of cities by eastwards-straying refu-gees, and Quen Santo, remote in the west, on the Chiapas border, a city which appears to have lasted a bare twenty years.

The supreme difficulty in finding a theory to explain the facts satisfactorily is the sporadic fashion in which the cities appear to have been abandoned. Captain Joyce hazards a guess at a southwards descent of barbarians – the 'Toltecs' – as part-cause. Somewhere towards the end of the third century AD according to Sahagun's dating of the Mexican traditions, new tribes (now considered to have been of Shoshone blood and of the same Nahuatl racial stock as the later and more famous Aztecs) were reaching the Mexican Valley, slaying the quinametin, or giants, and bringing records of migration from an unidentified Huehuetapallan. These tribes seem to have ranged in culture from the palaeolithic savagery of the Chichemacs to the compara-tively advanced barbarism of the Toltecs, or 'Builders'. (The name of the latter suggests the fantastic possibility that they may not have been of pure Nahuatl stock, but partly composed of descendants of the Mississippi Mound-Builders). It is therefore possible, though not very probable, that by the end of the ninth Maya cycle either these invaders or some autochthonous tribes displaced by them, were pressing on the northwestwards outposts of the Old Empire. But it is hardly likely that effects of the Nahuatl invasion were felt in Central America as early as 163, when Palenque was abandoned.

Further, as Captain Joyce himself has pointed out, the temple-complexes show no trace of forcible capture by invaders. Against this might be urged the likelihood that such invaders, burning and destroying the wood and adobe cities, would probably, through motives of religious dread, leave the stone-built centres intact. In the circumstances the possibility of a great pre-Toltec raid across the Grijalva to the destruction of Comalcalco and Palenque cannot be ruled out entirely. But it could have been little more than a raid, seeing that most of the other Xibalban cities survived it by at least a century.

Copan may have been overthrown by southern barbarians, but the fall of Menche, far in the north and at the same time, cannot be explained by any theory of invasion. Piedras Negras, still further north along the Usamacinta River, survived it a good five years. Yet Piedras Negras itself, together with Uaxactun and Quirigua, impossible for a common enemy to attack – Uaxactun could have been attacked only from Yucatan and it is fairly certain that the Peninsula was still uninhabited – were all abandoned in the same year. Nor, if Uaxactun was violently overthrown by foreigners, is it possible to explain why Tikal, twelve miles distant, should survive the older city by a good sixty years and then be itself extinguished.

Dr Spinden is explicit: 'The explanation of the eclipse of all that was finest in Maya civilisation is not far to seek. Any long-continued period of communal brilliancy undermines morals and religion and saps the nerves and muscles of the people as a whole. Extravagance runs before decadence and civil and foreign war frequently hasten the inevitable end.'

Professor Morley is equally explicit:

> While it is undoubtedly true that flamboyancy in decorative motives increases steadily during the Great Period (of Xibalba), reaching on the last monuments at the different cities to an almost bewildering ramification of detail, it does not follow that the Maya could not have carried out this extravagance of design even further if they had had more time in which to do so; and, so far as technique, treatment, and the like are concerned, the latest monument in each city is technically the best, showing no loss in skill and proficiency in technical processes up to the very end.

He himself accepts, tentatively, as do Messrs Blom and Le Farge, the theory which has perhaps the most supporters at the moment. This is that the Xibalbans' methods of agriculture, probably as primitive and wasteful as those of their descendants in Yucatan, gradually exhausted the land surrounding each city. Populations multiplied and the circles of cultivation grew tough mats of grass and weed impossible for the Maya hoeing-stick to penetrate. Agriculturists had to push further and further out into the jungle, bring more plantation stretches under cultivation, and in time find those stretches also grow barren in their hands. Ultimately, huge concentric rings of unproductive grassland surrounded each city and civilisation broke down on the problem of transporting, without the aid of domestic animals, the produce of the leagues-distant plantations to the teeming centres. The populations therefore abandoned the cities – the oldest sites earliest since these were surrounded by the widest circles of unproductive land – and drifted eastwards into Yucatan in search of virgin territory.

There are certain serious drawbacks to the acceptance of

this theory. We know nothing of Xibalban methods of agriculture. It is doubtful if the primitive methods ascribed to the Old Empire Maya were practised extensively even among their degenerate descendants of the New. The Old Empire cannot be judged by study of modern Maya – degenerate descendants of degenerates. Dr Gann's Maya, with some knowledge of intensive agriculture, seem much more probable. Further, the respective ages of the cities are far from supporting the theory of soil-exhaustion. Palenque was abandoned after a bare sixty years of occupation, Quirigua after eighty-five, Ikkun after thirty. And it is unlikely that the soil of Benque Viejo became exhausted in twenty years while that surrounding Uaxactun remained productive for over four hundred.

Dr Gann leans to the belief that the Xibalban Maya abandoned their homes and set out on the stupendous eastward exodus at the command of their priests, in the fulfilment of 'ancient prophecies'. He cites, as analogous, instances of modern Maya tribes suddenly abandoning prosperous regions for obscure religious motives and also quotes what has long been thought to be the classic New Empire example of 'abandonment-complex' – the desertion of the great metropolis of Uxmal by the Tutal Xiu, who decamped overnight to the miserable nearby townlet of Mani. But it is safe to assume that no people abandons such habitat as Xibalba, hallowed as it must have been with memories of the greatest triumphs of the race, under no other compulsion than priestly prophecy. The priests themselves, town-dwellers to a man, would have been the first to suffer in such voluntary migration. Certainly, if they instigated the abandonment of the Old Empire cities, their prophetic powers were at fault, for in the resultant confusion of centuries the presumed theocracy of Xibalba was succeeded by the congerie of warrior-ruled states in Yucatan. Whatever the aberrations of modern Maya tribes the Tutal Xiu appear to have had reasons urgent and cogent enough for their flight from Uxmal: the abandonment took place immediately after the great pestilence described in such grisly detail in Landa's *Relacion*.

The pestilence theory to account for the depopulation of the Old Empire is no longer entertained seriously. It, also, fails to explain why the cities were neither suddenly nor progressively abandoned, but given up haphazard, without regard to grouping or position. Nor would a great pestilence have taken nearly 150 years, from 9.13.0.0.0 onwards, to sweep the country.

Professor Morley devotes a considerable amount of space to a detailed examination of the belief of Dr Huntington that about AD 600 (which fits in with the Spinden-Morley correlation of 10.2.0.0.0 as AD 610) climatic changes on the Pacific coast of the United States resulted in a rapid decrease in the rainfall, reducing great stretches of country to desert land. At the same time, apparently as some sort of equipoise, the rainfall in Central America, and especially along the basin of the Usamacinta, increased and stimulated forestal growth to such an extent that the jungle advanced and devoured the plantations. Maya agriculture found itself faced with entirely incomprehensible seasonal conditions and staggering difficulties both in weeding and reaping. With the increased rainfall, transforming great regions of the cultivated Xibalban garden into swampy forest land, the breeding-grounds of the mosquito were greatly extended. As probably happened with Rome, the Old Empire was assisted to its fall by the failure of a primitive medical science to combat the spread of malaria.

Undoubtedly great areas in the vicinities of the cities show evidence of natural re-afforestation. But this may have taken place – would, in the nature of things, have taken place – without any increase in the rainfall. Climatic conditions in such regions as the Tikal-Uaxactun at the present day seem quite incompatible with the southwards extension of Dr Huntington's ingenious theory. Dr Gann and other archeologists make constant reference to the lack of water near the Old Empire sites: exploration has to be carried out in a country at once parched and clothed in luxurious vegetation. The possibility of an entire failure of the water supply appears more likely than an increase in the rainfall.

Individually inadequate, most of the theories of abandonment can yet be grouped in a plausible explanatory mosaic. Art grown flamboyant and decoratively archaistic may be no proof of decadence, but it points, at the least, to a flagging of the cultural impulse, a low spiritual vitality, and it is not too much to assume a lessened power of resistance to violent change as their concomitants. Xibalban agriculture may not have been of the excessively primitive character imagined; yet, faced with sudden and incomprehensible climatic changes – of whatever nature – in an era when the creative spirit was at its lowest ebb, it may indeed have proved unable to cope with the situation. Cities may have starved and under such desperate circumstances priestly leaders prophesied lands of plenty in the uninhabited and unexplored Yucatecan peninsula. Additional spurs to exodus may have been supplied by the sporadic raidings of barbarians or the incursions of equally sporadic pestilences.

Even so, the piecemeal evacuation seems to lack a central motive. A development of Dr Gann's contention that more than one race peopled the Old Empire tract may supply a clue. The high culture which raised its first monuments in Xibalba *circa* 200 BC, may have been of extra-American (though apparently neither Asiatic nor European) origin, and the script, calendar, and mathematical systems originally un-Maya. The mysterious culture-bringers may have enslaved the autochthonous Maya – of the same stock as Huaxteca and Quiché – and ruled as an alien theocracy in the Central American forests for nearly five hundred years. The subject race, from the sculptures seemingly a slight and undersized race having little resemblance to the tall, Cro-Magnon-like dominant caste, was probably, even at first, as numerically superior to its conquerors as the English to the Normans.

All the evidence leads to the conclusion that the dominant Xibalbans – like the Babylonians – were warriors only under pressure. Established in control of a highly-organised helot state, they may have abandoned arms entirely for those astronomical, religious, and mathematical passions to which their ruined cities bear witness. As a ruling, alien caste, their history may have paralleled very exactly that of the Aryan Brahmans in India, until freedmen, inevitable in a slave or serf state, gradually formed a third class in the Xibalban communities. An upwards infiltration of helot blood may have followed, till finally sharp distinctions of descent were lost and the ancient culture weakened. Even before the archaistic efflorescence there seems evidence of a mind, in some fashion semi-alien, influencing sculptural motif. A certain coldness and clumsy dignity has been lost. The technique is indeed maintained, but an eager, showy quality has entered both concept and execution. Absurd mistakes in the datings of inscriptions become frequent.

A state with a ruling caste and culture weakened, but still half-alien to the body of the serf populace, and subject to helot-risings: this may have been the Xibalba on which disasters descended from external sources and finally drove long drifts of refugees into Yucatan in confused hijra under the leadership of half-caste rulers.

No new theory or subtheory, however, can assume other than a questioning-explanatory attitude. Confirmation or refutation may come with the decipherment of the inscription texts. Even should these, as is probable, contain historical data, there seems little or no chance that any sculptor-scribe of the last sixty years of the Old Empire realised that he was living history and made record of the

confusion around him, the fall or abandonment of neighbouring cities, the waves of anger and hope and terror that
must have swept through the forested lands as the Maya
civilisation crashed to its fall. Nevertheless, there are remote possibilities that investigators in the country south-
west of Bakhalal may yet unearth or uncover some such
record – that, indeed, a cast of it may already repose,
unread, in some American or European museum!

For it seems that even part-solution of the most fascinating problem in American history must be prefaced by still
more intensive and organised study of the glyphic writing,
elucidation one by one of each calculiform sign, and – a
task hardly yet begun – codification and elaborate cross-
referencing of those signs in a glyphic dictionary.

Yucatan: New Empire Tribes
and Culture Waves

IN THE FIRST of these papers dealing with certain problems in the history and archeology of Ancient America an
account was given of the Maya Old Empire and the possible
causes which lead to its collapse in the fourth or sixth
centuries AD. The whole tract of Xibalba was probably
deserted, its inhabitants scattered, and the alien theocracy
which had inspired a great semi-civilisation destroyed.

But to the north and south of the Old Empire area there
presently ensued a diffusion of Mayoid culture impossible
but for the catastrophe or series of catastrophes which
depopulated such great sites as Copan, Uaxactun and
Palenque, leaving them abandoned for 1500 years to the
investigatory prowlings of snakes, pumas, and, culminat-
ingly, of such fauna as that Noah O. Platt whose name J. L.

Stephens found carved on the walls of the Palenque palace. 'From archeological evidence it would appear that Maya culture spread by way of Oaxaca up to the Valley of Mexico. Here, fostered by the Toltec, it took root and flourished with such vigour that, at a still later period, it had a profound influence on the arts and crafts of the Totonac of Vera Cruz.' Southwards, like influences appear to have inspired the Coclé culture of Panama and even spread through the Panama neck into South America, leavening the beginnings of the Andean pre-Inka barbarisms. Meanwhile, the Xibalban city-builders themselves disappeared without further record.

It is again necessary, however, to emphasise the fact that Old Empire history is entirely without record, apart from the innumerable datings on its monuments. The very name Maya was probably unknown in Xibalba. Not only has no contemporary written account of its history and downfall been found and transliterated, but, in subsequent American cultures apparently inspired by it, there is no scrap of tradition that can be definitely identified with the Old Empire. The myths of the barbarous Quiche of the Pacific coast do indeed allude to a nebulous 'Xibalba' which the present writer accepts as a reference to the Old Empire. But such an acceptance is only tentative, and one with which few Americanists agree.

Yet, in spite of lack of reference to an historic Xibalba, the Spaniards who landed in America a thousand years after its collapse discovered on the neighbouring peninsula of Yucatan a race now generally identified as the descendants of the Old Empire population. The identification cannot be regarded as more than partially proved. The thousand years of Yucatecan history is a blur of uncertain traditions, myths, legends – some of which point towards cultural and racial influences radically un-Xibalban. Yucatecan art, architecture, sculpture, script and calendar appear not so much debasements of their Old Empire counterparts (the architecture has improved in technique as it has degenerated in imaginative concept) as half-alien variations on a half-forgotten theme. In consequence of the curtailment of the ancient calendar, Yucatecan buildings lack the profuse datings of the Old Empire sites, with the result that Yucatecan tradition-history is almost entirely dateless but for the record of a single family-group – the Tutul Xiu, whose name suggests an un-Mayan origin and whose apparently meaningless wanderings across the antique Central American scene still induce almost as much confusion among Americanists as they probably did among the Xius' contemporaries.

The purpose of this paper is to suggest an outline of the Yucatecan cultural phases and the racial and migrational causes from which those phases originated. The multitude of material uncorrelated in any such framework remains productive not only of ludicrous perennial theorisings in the popular press on the subject of 'mysterious' Yucatan, but leads such authorities as Captain Joyce and M. Genet to identify the great figure of Quetzalcohuatl-Kukulcan variously as 'the ripple or catspaw, born of wind and water, the aspect of which suggests feathers, and the motion a snake', and as an actual Toltec general, with biography and pedigree!

Some synthesis is required of the data available to the modern world from the following four sources: *The Books of Chilan Balam*, laconic and frequently contradictory records of the history of the Tutul Xiu family-group already referred to, written in the Zuyua (literary Yucatecan) tongue but in Latin characters; the legends and myths collected by the early and mid-occupation Spaniards, especially the clerics Landa, Lizana, Cogolludo, and the historian Herrera; the scanty datings, according to the Old Empire 'long-count' system, found in two, or perhaps three, Yucatecan sites; the architecture and sculpture of the New Empire ruins.

The *Chilan Balam* record opens with the statement that in a 'Katun 8 Ahau' (probably AD 163) the Tutul Xiu, under the leadership of Holon Chantepeuh, set out from Nonoual, 'to the west of Zuiva and in the land of Tulapan'.

All three localities have been identified with various portions of the New World. The Abbé Brasseur de Bourbourg would have Nonoual in Oaxaca, Toltec territory, and sees Holon Chantepeuh's exodus as a drifting raid of aliens into Maya country. MM Genet and Chelbatz substantially agree with their countryman, but place Nonoual in Acallan, west of the Laguna de Terminos. Captain Joyce, on the other hand, finds it 'at present unidentified, but almost certainly somewhere in the Central Maya area'.

The French historians, believing in a Nahua origin for the Tutul Xiu, conclude that 'Tutul' probably meant 'Toltec'. It is certain that long years afterwards the enemies of the Xiu, the Cocomes and other Itzas, were in the habit of dubbing the Xiu 'strangers', in the sense of the Greek 'barbaroi'. Also, the Xiu notabilities themselves seem to have religiously eschewed the 'Tutul' from their personal names, e.g. Nachelxiu.

Now, in AD 163, if the Bowditch correlation of the Old Empire and Gregorian calendars is correct, Palenque, the Xibalban Florence, ceased to date its monuments and was presumably deserted, as were possibly other northern sites such as Comalcalco and Ococingo. The eruption of the 'Toltec' Xiu may have had connexion with a great barbarian raid upon those cities – a raid from which the Xiu did not withdraw, for forty years later they settled at 'Chacnouitan', another unknown site, but one, it is safe to conclude, somewhere on the borders of Xibalba and the still uninhabited peninsula of Yucatan. As early as AD 200, as is now known from the recent discovery of various small sites, emigrants from the still-flourishing Old Empire cities of northern Chiapas were slowly advancing towards the Rio Hondo and its confluents. 'Chacnouitan', with the Tutul

Xiu in the role of 'Mayaized' barbarians, may have been one of those emigrant settlements.

This synchronisation of events is justified if the dates in the various *Chilan Balam* records be treated selectively. For, about 100 years later, *c.* AD 300, the Tutul Xiu are stated to have abandoned Chacnouitan, and by AD 300 the Old Empire was crashing to its fall; Copan, Uaxactun, Menché, Quirigua, Ixkun deserted, possibly in a wild confusion of famine and civil war which also affected the Xiu settlement. But of those events the Xius, if implicated in them, left no account. They emerge out of the darkness of over another hundred years with the laconic statement that, *c.* AD 420, they 'discovered (and presumably settled in) Zian Caan' – another name for Bakhalal in southern Yucatan.

There, for the moment, they may be left, while consideration is given to the movements of other refugees from the fall of Xibalba. As has been stated before, the Yucatecan Maya, though obviously culturally influenced by the Old Empire, had no definite record of racial relation with it. But it is at least possible that the traditions of the Great and Little Descents were based on facts, and throw some light on the fate of the Xibalban survivors.

No such possibility of myth enshrining history was regarded as warrantable by most of the Americanists of last century, headed by Dr DG Brinton. Dr Brinton imposed on nearly every American tradition or legend a 'sun-myth' interpretation which still lingers. But the theory of the inevitable creation of gods or symbolical heroes to fit the facts of natural phenomena is, if not discredited, recognised in American archeology as only partially explanatory. The deification of culture-heroes must be regarded as at least complementary to their creation.

According to Lizana the legend of the Great Descent describes the invasion of Yucatan by Itzamna and his following. This invasion came from the west. MM Genet and Chelbatz, accepting the Great Descent as the migration of actual tribes, assign its origin to the Laguna de Terminos. Though their *Histoire* is in some respects rendered valueless by an unfortunate 'Toltec complex', and an apparent ignorance of the results of the last fifty years of excavation, it is at least possible that refugees from the middle and lower Usamacinta sites of the Old Empire pressed northwards into Yucatan in a great host or hosts through the Laguna de Terminos region. Civilising the country and settling Champoton en route, Itzamna (an idol borne in a litter at the head of the invading tribes or an actual leader bearing the name of his god) passed northwards through the barren limestone wastes of modern Campeche, and built at a suitable spot the city of Chichen Itza – the Wells of the Itza.

No dates are, of course, given for this migration. But Chichen Itza, Tuluum on the eastern coast of Yucatan, and (a doubtful case) the small site of Xcalumkin are the three New Empire localities which possess buildings inscribed with dates according to the Old Empire calendar. The Chichen Itza date is approximately AD 350, the Tuluum one approximately AD 300.

Either, therefore, the Great Descent was in the nature of a rapid march of refugees from the scene of the Old Empire collapse, reaching northern Yucatan several years before the final abandonment of Xibalba, or – the generally accepted belief – Tuluum and Chichen were cleruchies of some Old Empire city, colonised by sea before its fall. Itzamna and his tribes of Maya Itza may not have arrived on the scene until at least AD 400, and either captured these cities or re-peopled them.

It was a desolate enough country into which the Great Descent had come from the riverine cities of Xibalba. There is little or no surface-flow of water in Yucatan, but cenotes, great natural wells, appear in the limestone. Round these, or, where they did not exist, excavating the artificial chultunes, the Itza commenced to rear the single-storied temples and palaces of the Old Empire. What proportion of the invaders was composed of artists and craftsmen who had escaped the Xibalban débâcle it is impossible to tell, but the spiritual impulses behind the art manifestations of the ancient culture were certainly more than half-forgotten. Carving of the distinctive statue-stelae of the Old Empire soon ceased. Of Sayil, probably one of the early cities built – in company with Itzamal and Zama – by the Maya of the Great Descent, Dr Spinden says 'the sculpture is very flat and crude, but the free and easy postures indicate that the crudity comes from decadence rather than inexperience.' The 'katun count', a crippled version of the complicated ancient calendar, and signifying an almost complete loss of mathematical attainments, came into vogue. Nothing is certain of the personnel of the migration, but there were probably few pure-blooded survivors of the distinctive class or race which, there is good reason to believe, had ruled Xibalba as a gigantic theocracy. The warrior cacique, the halach uinic or 'real man', had appeared in Maya history, owning feudal allegiance to Chichen or some such centre, ruling his town or village in which a degraded class of masons and artisans still built and decorated, priests – heirs probably in little more than name to the artists and astronomers of the Old Empire – sacrificed and prophesied. The mass of the population, probably serf-agriculturists, cultivated the milpas or maize-plantations round each centre, forgot Xibalba, and already regarded the leader of the Great Descent, buried in the Mausoleum of the Itzamatul at Itzamal, as divine.

This is a possible picture of northern Yucatan in the sixth century AD. Both architectural and sculptural evidences are uncertain, owing to the overlaying of later centuries, but careful research, especially in the centre of the region of modern Campeche, may reveal indubitable examples of the building and art motif of this period.

But this settlement appears to have accounted for only one portion of the Old Empire refugees. From the east, according to Lizana, a new leader with a group of followers descended on northern Yucatan. Such descent (unless, which is extremely unlikely, it was a raid of Caribs across the sea) could have come only from the southeast, from the region of Bakhalal, where the Tutul Xiu had settled.

The Books of Chilan Balam appear to confirm the separate tradition. They record that, *c.* AD 500, the Xiu 'discovered' Chichen Itza and 'were accepted as lords of the land'. This, there can be little doubt, was the Little Descent, probably made by the Xiu at the head of a host descended from the inhabitants of the northern Chiapas and Honduras cities of the Old Empire. Possibly Chichen was forcibly captured and the surrounding country laid under tribute. There is no record of this but it is stated that the Tutul Xiu, no doubt in a politic endeavour to conciliate the surrounding Itza Mayas, 'called themselves Itzas'.

Whatever cultural influences the Little Descent brought are now unidentifiable, but the Tutul Xiu appear to have remained obstinately alien in Itza eyes. About 120 years after its capture Chichen, according to one version of the Tutul Xiu chronicles, was 'abandoned', according to another 'destroyed'. The Xiu were, in fact, probably driven from the capital by an uprising of the subject Itza populace and set to wander Yucatan for another eighty years until, *c.* AD 700, Champoton was 'seized' by them.

If brevity be the soul of wit, the *Books of Chilan Balam* are among the most mirthful records in existence. At this point their brevity introduces a new complication, and one that appears to have entirely mislead such modern Americanists as Dr Gann and Mr J. Eric Thompson. The Xiu who came with the Little Descent to the conquest of Chichen thereafter 'called themselves Itzas', and it is as 'Itzas' that they are thereafter referred to by their chronicles. Accordingly, the abandonment of Chichen, *c.* AD 620, has been taken as a desertion of the land by the Itza populace, another example of the mysterious 'desertion complex'. As careful study of the records show, there is no warrant for this belief. So far from deserting Chichen, the Itzas probably re-occupied it again, while the Tutul Xiu, the 'barbaroi' who had remained unamalgamated in spite of their desire for naturalisation, were evicted.

For nearly 250 years after recording the seizure of Champoton, the Xiu chronicles maintain a complete silence. It is two and a half centuries of complete darkness in the history of the Yucatecan Maya, and it is indeed improbable that even the most intensive archeological research and excavation will succeed in illuminating it. As has been said, New Empire buildings are mostly undated, and in consequence any judgement of the art of this period is rendered almost impossible. Probably it neither remained static nor (so far as architecture was concerned) declined, as has been supposed. Profiting by ages of experience, living in years otherwise a cultural coma, and without distracting considerations of elaborate mural decoration or group rhythm, the Maya mason succeeded in gradually widening, heightening, and altogether 'fining' his buildings. Pottery-making and textile-making probably remained at the general level of Xibalba. Priests conned the ancient scripts and copied them. Serfs tilled the great plantations. City batabs or governors, the 'real men' of the country, hunted and possibly indulged in occasional civil war though the settlements were grouped in a loose hegemony under the leadership of Chichen.

The ruling Chichen family of this period MM Genet and Chelbatz identify with the Cocomes, later the rulers of Mayapan and the principal enemies of the Tutul Xiu. These Cocomes the French historians not only place at the head of the Itza insurrectionists who had evicted the Xiu from Chichen, but trace their pedigree from the kings of an ancient Laguna de Terminos 'city'! It is hardly necessary to say that there is little or no basis for such pedigree-hunting, or that any account of New Empire existence from the time of the eviction of the Xiu until the middle of the tenth century is by nature almost purely speculative.

Then the Xius appear for a moment in the light again. Champoton (*c.* AD 950) is abandoned. The Xius are driven out, and, breaking into almost voluble record, the *Books of Chilan Balam* tell how the 'Itzas' (*i.e.* Xius) wandered the forests, homeless, living upon leaves and roots. Some catastrophe had smitten the western sea-board of Yucatan.

Its nature MM. Genet and Chelbatz connect with a great Toltec invasion of the peninsula under the leadership of the Mexican hero, Topiltzin Axcitl Quetzalcohuatl, whom the Maya were to remember as either the god Kukulcan or the bringer of his worship. In the acceptance of this Quetzalcohuatl as an historical personage, MM Genet and Chelbatz follow Landa, who is responsible for recording the Yucatecan tradition. Mr Thompson also believes Kukulcan may have been the leader of a culture-invasion. To Dr Brinton and the orthodox Americanists generally Quetzalcohuatl-Kukulcan, like the Toltecs themselves, remained a 'euhemerised sun-myth'. Captain Joyce believes the 'bird-snake' of the Old Empire sculptures to have been a symbol of Kukulcan, and, accepting him as a personification of natural forces, considers him an Old Empire god.

Consideration of events in the Mexican Valley at this time may provide some means of escape for this confusion of gods and heroes. By the middle of the tenth century at least it appears probable that the power of the Toltecs, the great Xibalban-inspired 'Builders' who possibly originated in the Mississippi valley, had been definitely broken by an incursion of barbaric tribes into Mexico. Tula or Tollan, the legendary Toltec capital, was overthrown and its last king, Huemac, murdered.

Side by side with this tradition of the Mexican Valley there survived a curiously complementary one telling how, at the time of the fall of Tollan, the great culture-bringer Quetzalcohuatl, in flight before the barbarians, journeyed down to the sea and took ship into the east – to return, in the Aztec imagination six hundred years later, as Cortes.

This Quetzalcohuatl MM Genet and Chelbatz, as has been said, consider an historical personage – an opinion with which the present writer is tentatively in agreement – and make him, not a gentle reformer, but the leader of the defeated Toltec army meditating a settlement in Maya country. But, considering the subsequent influence of the Kukulcan worship which it seems likely he carried into Yucatan, the matter requires some further elucidation.

In spite of there seeming to be little warrant for the contention of the 'diffusionists' that the first American semi-civilisation owed its inspiration to Asia, it is probable that, in the centuries following the fall of Xibalba, Chinese or Cambodian cultural influences played with considerable strength on the Mexican Pacific coast and the art and ethic of the Toltec tribes. This is, of course, denied by most authorities, though Mr Thompson hints at it as a possibility in his paper on 'Central America and the Children of the Sun'. The figure of Quetzalcohuatl suggests as many affinities to that of the Buddha as do the atlantean sculptures of the Toltec palaces to those of the Cambodian, and it is possible that the coming of his legend to Central America considerably antedated the adventurings of the Toltec hero who may later have borne his name. In spite of the usual sanguinary rites associated with his worship he seems to stand as a definitely alien god in the Central American pantheons.

The Kukulcan of Landa, therefore ('Kukulcan' is a literal translation into Maya of the Nahuatl word 'Quetzalcohuatl') may have been both a hero with the name of a god and, in the spirit of the early Mohammedans, a missionary of that god. MM Genet and Chelbatz, following Las Casas in this particular, land him after his sea-voyage across a neck of the Gulf of Mexico at Xicalanco – certainly the region towards which Toltec refugee tribes appear to have congregated in those years. Thereafter their acceptance of the literal truth of the legends collected by Las Casas and Nunez de la Vega, flatly refuted as those legends are by the evidence obtained from modern archaeological spade-work in the Usamacinta region, can be no longer followed. For they lead the Toltec general Quetzalcohuatl to the conquest of the cities of the Usamacinta basin and the founding of Palenque – Palenque, which, according to any modern interpretation of Old Empire chronology, had been abandoned some five hundred years, and more probably some eight hundred!

Assuming Landa's Quetzalcohuatl-Kukulcan to have had the human character credited to him, however, and associating him with the undoubted eruption of Toltec influences into Yucatan, it is possible that the Xiu eviction from Champoton in *c.* AD 950 may have been connected with the landing of the invaders. The Nahua Napoleon may have come by sea and for the first time in history Nahua and New Empire Maya faced each other.

Yucatan, as we have seen, was probably fairly unified under the Itzas at Chichen, except for such pockets of independence as the Xiu-garrisoned seaport of Champoton. But neither Xiu nor Itza would have been capable of offering effective resistance to the invader, for it seems certain that neither the bow nor the spear-thrower was known to the Maya. Minus those weapons the Itza levies were probably easily out-classed and dispersed. Toltec bow and spear-thrower may have proved as demoralising as did the Prussian needle-gun in the war of 1871. Freely interpreting Landa, it seems that the Toltec army marched through the country, captured Chichen Itza, and laid the surrounding Maya under tribute.

Quetzalcohuatl-Kukulcan commenced to prove himself a statesman as well as a soldier. Abandoning Chichen Itza he had Mayapan built as a kind of federal capital. This was in AD 989, according to the independent account of Herrera. A year later Uxmal was founded a score or so of miles south of Mayapan, and, in conjunction with Mayapan itself, Itzamal, and Chichen, formed the new Yucatecan Federation or League.

This brings us again to the record of the Xiu chronicles. According to one version of these, the Tutul Xiu, *c.* 990, 're-established Chichen Itza'. According to another Ahzui-tok Tutul Xiu, the Xiu Moses who brought to a close the many wanderings of his tribe, founded Uxmal in 990. The latter happening, coinciding with the Kukulcan legend and the fact that Uxmal had been for centuries before the Spanish Conquest regarded as an exclusively Xiu city, is the more probable. Quetzalcohuatl-Kukulcan may have deliberately invited the straying Xiu tribe to settle in the region of Uxmal in order to counterweigh the power and pretensions of the Itza.

For some years he himself appears to have ruled the League from Mayapan. Then he disappeared from the scene, probably in company with the greater part of his Toltecs, and the Itza Cocome family ruled in Mayapan as senior members of the League.

So far the materials for the filling in of this outline have been almost entirely written or traditional. But the League period is recognised by all archaeologists as marking a definite florescence of New Empire art. The great buildings of the Casa Colorada and the Caracol at Chichen are usually assigned to it, as are the principal architectural achievements of Uxmal, Labna, Kabah, Hochob, Chac-multun. Façade decoration comes into its own again, though now in the form of intricate formal mask panels. Decorative stone lattice work appears. The vertical roof structure becomes common.

It is impossible that this New Empire Renascence came into being except through outside influences. But recognition of this fact is not yet by any means general. The painstaking investigator of sites and ruins is apparently but seldom acquainted with the mass of Yucatecan tradition and legend collated by the Spanish fathers. Unless the Kukulcan legend is, for the time being, accepted as at least partially based on historic events, the causes of the Renascence might well be relegated to the benevolent urgings of the Yucatecan gods alone. Captain Joyce and Mr Thompson do not admit Toltec cultural influences in Yucatan until *after* the collapse of the League, and then in the form of diffusion from Toltec-garrisoned Chichen.

But the serpent columns and characteristically Nahuan ball courts of Uxmal and other cities are almost certainly League work. Open-work decoration on the top of temple walls is not only characteristic of Mexican architecture, but possibly Asiatic in origin. Though atlantean supports, flat roofs, and low relief sculpture showing the processional groupings of warriors may have come later, the phallic picotes of Uxmal and the phallic columns and ornaments of Labna and Chacmultun cannot well be ascribed to any other origin than the Mexican tribes, or any other period than that covered by the duration of the League of Mayapan.

Spite the frequent representations of the 'snake-bird' there are no very plausible evidences that the god Kukulcan was known to the Old Empire Maya, and, on Landa's authority, his worship in Yucatan now became general – a strange avatar indeed for Sakya Muni, if the origin of the Toltec deity was Asiatic. Probably human sacrifice as a seasonal rite of importance was also imported by the Maya from Mexico in the League years. There is a carving at Piedras Negras, in the heart of the Old Empire territory, which appears to portray a victim on the sacrificial altar, but this unrelated instance does not greatly modify the apparently general belief held in Yucatan that human sacrifice came with the 'strangers'.

Ceremonial cannibalism, the almost inevitable concomitant of human sacrifice, did not, it is possible, become common until after the wars of the League and the second incursion of a Toltec host. Mr Payne showed with considerable plausibility that in a culture which reaches to town-building and town-dwelling in a country devoid of large domestic animals the development of some such conditions as those which prevailed among the Nahua, where slaves were regularly kept in pens and fattened on maize for the table, was to be expected. But there is no record of such an appalling custom in Yucatan.

For two hundred years, until about AD 1200, the League of Mayapan endured, probably held together in the vibrant equilibrium of the cities' jealousies. Then comes in the Xiu *Books of Chilan Balam* record of a series of events in which the Xiu themselves appear to have played at first a neutral part. Hunac Ceel, the Cocome ruler of Mayapan, attacked and overthrew the rule of Chac Xib Chac, the 'king' of Chichen Itza. The League fell apart. In the first uncertain course of the conflict Hunac Ceel called in an army of mercenaries from Tabasco. These, after the defeat of Chac Xib Chac, he established in Chichen as a permanent Toltec garrison.

To this event is generally ascribed the Toltec cultural evidences throughout the peninsula, and it is indeed possible that a few new motifs in architectural decoration and in sculpture may have been brought to Yucatan by these mercenaries, practised by them in their stronghold of Chichen, and copied by the surrounding Maya cities. But such influences, except perhaps in the domain of religious rite, were probably slight enough. By another hundred years these Nahua appear to have been absorbed in the surrounding Maya populace. For, at the end of that space of time, *c.* 1300, the Xiu abandoned their neutrality, appear to have placed themselves at the head of the revolt of the Itza nobles, and 'Mayapan was destroyed'. There is no mention of the Cocomes receiving aid from their Toltec garrison in Chichen.

Probably it was at this time that the gradual splitting up of the peninsula into the states which the Spaniards found began. The Cocomes of Mayapan fled to Kimpech (Campeche), apparently a settlement also ruled by Cocomes. The Xiu, after an unsuccessful endeavour to induce the Itza nobles to accept their overlordship, retired to Uxmal again. Mani, the state which they built up around that city and their older capital, remained the dominant power in Central Yucatan.

Meantime it is probable that culture was already on the decline throughout the length and breadth of the New Empire. Mayapan, in which only the Cocome power appears to have been destroyed, was held by now this adventurer, now that. The Cocomes plotted in Kimpech. Elaboration of temple rites – the Maya temple now dominated by the hybrid Quetzalcohuatl deity – went steadily on. Cozumel Island, probably an independent 'state', had acquired through all Central America a reputation for sanctity, and, as Bernal Diaz was later to record, pilgrims from remote, un-Maya lands came to worship at the island shrines and invoke the island oracles. The great pilgrim highway between Chichen and the sea-coast opposite Cozumel was probably built at this period.

Then, *c.* 1350, an obscure version of the *Books of Chilan Balam* record that 'cannibals came'. This probably refers to a descent of Caribs on the eastern shores, in the state of Ekab and south of Ekab. They may have seized Tuluum, and been responsible for the later growth of the hybrid 'Tuluum culture' which left the sea-coast of eastern Yucatan strewn with dwarfish temples. There can be little doubt but that it was among the descendants of these cannibals, hardly yet 'Mayaised', that Valdivia and his companions, the first Europeans to come in contact with the New Empire, were wrecked nearly 150 years later.

The history of that 150 years, the closing phase in the adventure of the great lost expedition of civilisation which had appeared so mysteriously in the Chiapas forests some 1700 years before, is in portions still obscure enough. Early in the fifteenth century the Cocomes, backed by an army of barbarian Tenochcas and Xicalanques lent them by Mexico, returned to Mayapan and ruled there for a short time. This third army of mercenaries to appear in Yucatan was not even Toltec in name; the Toltecs were by then legendary figures in Mexican memory. It seems to have been composed of Nahuas at a low stage of culture, and probably, terrorism apart, they exerted little or no effect on the life of the Maya.

They constituted Yucatan's last group of invaders, and their's was the last eddy of the many culture-waves which had flowed across the history of the New Empire. The subsequent course of that history is accordingly outside the province of this sketch. How the Itza again revolted, again invoked the aid of the Xius of Mani, and again evicted the Cocomes from Mayapan; how the last vestige of political coherence vanished from the peninsula, and a host of small states arose; how the Mexican mercenaries forced their way to the northeastern coast and established themselves in the district of Kanul, there to retain their reputation for ferocity until the coming of the Spaniards; how a remnant of the Mayapan Cocomes established themselves in Tibullon and engaged in endless warfare with the surrounding Itza and their ancient enemies, the Tutul Xiu of Mani; how first a great storm laid waste all Yucatan, how on its heels followed a pestilence which wiped out half the population, how one hundred and fifty thousand Maya perished in a culminating civil war – of these happenings Landa and other historians already cited tell in detail.

One morning, the priests of Cozumel, tending their

temple altars looked up and saw far out to sea the passing of monstrous sea-houses gleaming in the sun.

It was the year 1493: those were the ships of the Portuguese.

The Buddha of America

THERE ARE FEW such instances of unwarranted shrinking from publicity as that displayed by the angel Moroni, inspirer of the Book of Mormon. On the night of September 1, 1823, Moroni appeared in a vision to Joseph Smith, a farm-labourer in the State of New York, and communicated to him news of staggering import to every student of ancient American history:

'He said there was a book deposited, written upon gold plates, giving an account of the former inhabitants of this continent, and the source from whence they sprang . . . Also there were two stones in silver bows . . . and the possession and use of these stones were what constituted *seers* in ancient or former times; and that God had prepared them for the purpose of translating the book.'

Next day, led by the vision, Joseph arrived at 'the village of Manchester, Ontario county', where stood 'a hill of considerable size and the most elevated of any in the neighbourhood. On the west side of this hill, not far from the top, under a stone of considerable size, lay the plates, deposited in a stone box.'

Joseph was next commanded to extract the plates and, with the aid of the *seers*, to set about translating them. They were inscribed with characters 'in general of the ancient Egyptian order'. Divinely equipped, Joseph speedily translated these characters into pseudo-English – a translation which now constitutes the American Bible of the Church of Latter-Day Saints.

Up to the point of revealing the whereabouts of the plates, the conduct of Moroni may be regarded as irreproachable. From thence onwards, however (viewed from the standpoint of the Americanist), he deteriorated rapidly. He gave strict injunctions to Joseph not to show the plates to any 'unbelievers' on the penalty of the translator being 'cut off'. That open-minded examination, comparison and criticism essential in testing the authenticity of archaeological finds was strictly forbidden; and Joseph seems to have taken the threat of his mystic mutilation to heart. He guarded the contents of the stone box with jealous severity. No sooner was the work of translation done than Moroni hurriedly appeared again, collected the plates, and vanished with them; leaving Joseph to publish the translation and found a new religious sect on the strength of the revelations therein contained.

No satisfactory explanation of Moroni's suspicious exclusiveness has ever been advanced by the Church of Latter-Day Saints. Even the helpful, if infidel, suggestion that the angel was so ashamed of the execrable style and grammar of the engraved account that he shrank from its examination by any other than farm-hands, is not fully satisfactory. The fact remains that but for Moroni's unaccountable sensitiveness we should now be in possession of a Rosetta Stone with which to unpry the secrets of Ancient American history. Stylistic criteria apart, it is impossible to believe but that in more competent hands the plates would have yielded up quite other things than the dreary record of a tribe of stray Hebrews magically – and altogether unwarrantably – conveyed across the Pacific to American shores in 590 BC. Undoubtedly they accounted for those most mysterious happenings in pre-Columbian history – the origin and extinction of the Maya Old Empire in Guatemala; the building of the great megalithic city of

Tiawanako in the Peruvian Andes; the whereabouts of Leif Erikson's landfall in Labrador; and undoubtedly they settled once and for all the true origin, nature and fate of that personage who haunted and bemused the mind of the Ancient American almost as much as he haunts and bepuzzles the imagination of the modern enquirer – Quetzalcoatl, the Feathered Serpent.

No mystery, indeed, to which Moroni could have supplied the key is quite so fascinating as identification of the last named. The general reader encounters him but seldom – in the pages of Prescott's suave history of the Spanish Conquest, in General Lew Wallace's novel *The Fair God*, and such-like. But, these genteel commentators apart, there has grown up round Quetzalcoatl in the last three centuries a stupendous literature of comment and suggestion – generally, it is to be feared, as turgid as erudite, and quite obscuring the unspecialist interest to which the Feathered Serpent, most alien god in the native American pantheons, may lay claim.

The background and ancestry of his avatar appears to have been briefly this:

By the end of the sixth century AD, the Maya Old Empire in Chiapas and Guatemala, the only tract in America bearing anything worthy of the name of a civilisation, had crashed to its fall. Great cities and palaces and painted temples, the work of generations of skilled artisans and artists, were abandoned overnight. In flight before some unexplained catastrophe, the Maya dispersed to north and south of their ancient habitat in urgent exodus. The majority of them forced their way eastwards into the neighbouring peninsula of Yucatan, there to salvage some part of their culture and wait for another thousand years to bring them the ships of Cortes and their conqueror, Francisco de Montejo.

The northwards-making refugees, however, appear to

have constituted no pressing hijra of tribes. Instead, they percolated through the jungle of the Tehuantepec neck in a thin trickle into the Valley of Mexico. There they seem to have encountered, advancing southwards in straggling migration, new tribes descending from the North American plateau. These tribes were Nahuas – kin to the much later and as yet unapparent Aztecs.

A fusion of refugee Maya and barbarian Nahua took place. The Nahuas were probably barely advanced beyond the ancient food-gathering stage common to all communities of the ancient world. In contacts with the shrunken remnants of the Maya civilisation they abandoned a nomad existence for tentative settlements, a sketchy agriculture and – inevitable concomitants – the breeding of priesthoods and warrior-classes. Within two centuries their masonic technique was such that to north and south, and far in the deeps of ages yet unborn, they had fame as Toltecs – 'the Supreme Builders'.

Improved in like manner was temple-technique; with it, the ritual calendar inherited from the Maya – a calendar red-spotted in no unsanguinary characters. Human sacrifice was the crown and essence of every feast and festival. Warriors continually led out fresh expeditions in search of captives to feed the altars of Tula, the great Toltec capital; slaves tilled the wide-spreading maize-plantations which supported the great priesthoods; and the fires smoked unendingly on the summits of the pyramidal temples . . .

This was the scene when, according to the legends collected by the Spanish fathers, town after town of the Toltecs, and finally Tula itself, was peacefully brought under the control of a personage who bore the name or title Quetzalcoatl – the Humming-Bird Snake. A stranger and an alien, none of the diverse accounts vary greatly in their description of him. He was tall, pale-skinned, black-bearded, and accompanied by other strangers who wore black cassocks 'spotted with red crosses'. For a time the stunned Toltecs appear to have accepted him and his mission with an incredible docility.

That mission, assuming the stranger to have been himself an American Indian, is startling enough to read of in the myths of people who, it must be remembered, did not regard their rites of human sacrifice as shameful orgies of cruelty, but as sheer necessities to ensure the life of the sun and the productivity of the soil. Across the blood-stained Toltec republics, in that continent as yet unapprehended by Europe, Quetzalcoatl marched as a blasphemer and reformer. He forbade human sacrifice – 'as an insult to God'. Instead, flowers and fruit were to deck the altars – offerings to the sun 'who himself provided them'. (Strange agnostic sentiment on such a continent and among such a race!)

But he went further, this black-robed reformer dominating for a time the cities of that astounded Amerindian semi-civilisation. War was an abomination – 'he stopped his ears when he was spoken to of war.' In place of it there was to be cultivation of the arts of peace, and of those arts Quetzalcoatl himself was a master.

He brought new methods of tillage and weaving and metal-working. He reformed the calendar. He instituted a college of priestly 'Followers'. In Tula the hideous idols gazed down on strange sacrifices from orchard and garden where once the screaming captive had been stretched across the concave blocks of black basalt. Immersed in those reforms, Quetzalcoatl took no heed of the fact that Mexico was moving and seething from two causes – Toltec discontent with his teachings and a fresh irruption of barbarian hordes from the north.

Huemac was ruler of Tula and war-chief of the Toltec tribes. For a time vassal and 'Follower' of the pale reformer and blasphemer, the position and reforms alike irked him. He encouraged an alliance of the Toltec party of reaction with the savages from the north. The combined hosts marched on Tula.

News was brought to the Humming-Bird Snake of the armies coming up against him. Thereat, refusing companionship, he left Tula and set out for the sea; which sea, the Pacific or the Gulf of Mexico, is uncertain of identification in the legends. Behind him, the barbarian hordes marched down on Tula, and Huemac, too late, turned to defend the city against his erstwhile allies. Tula was sacked and burned; perhaps the reformer looked back and saw its flames in the midnight sky.

Legend followed him, dogging his steps on that journey. At one point he halted, and there till the time of the Spanish Conquest an impress of his wearied hand might be seen on a rock. 'And in one spot he bent over a pool and looked at his face in the waters. And he saw that he was old.'

At the sea-coast a raft of serpents awaited him. Embarking, he passed into the setting sun.

Such is a brief synthesis of the legends prevalent at the time of the Spanish Conquests. For, as was soon realised, the legend was not Mexican (Aztec) only. In Tlascala was a God Camaxtli, in Chiapas a Votan, in Guatemala a Gucumatz, in Yucatan a Kukulcan – all four of them with attributes and myths definitely identifying them with the mystic Quetzalcoatl. And among all four nations, as among the Mexicans, the worship of this god had remained a thing apart from the orthodox state religion – a god and a religion by nature unassimilable in Red Indian theology, yet persisting with a strange tenacity.

Three main explanations of the phenomenon of Quetzalcoatl and his mission have been advanced and defended with an astounding wealth of erudition and acerbity. In the first place, the Spaniards had no doubt whatever about the identity of the reformer. He was a Christian missionary; according to Nuñez de la Vega, St Thomas the Doubter in person. St Thomas, after converting India, not only voyaged across the Pacific and helped to overthrow an

Amerindian Tower of Babel which the sacrilegious natives were building on the Gulf of Mexico, but later returned to Rome, interviewed the Pope on the subject of his labours, and then set out again for the scene of those labours. This fascinating hypothesis is unfortunately rendered valueless by the failure of the Vatican to keep a record of St Thomas's visit.

There is a *variorum* reading of the Christian claim: Quetzalcoatl must have been a Nestorian missionary. Nestorians early wandered far afield in the Far East; and whence the black cloaks spotted with red crosses but from some Christian descent on the Pacific Coast?

The crosses, however, appear in only one legend – Camaxtli's; whatever the colour of the cloaks, the crosses are undoubtedly politic superimpositions of the Spanish fathers. Further, no Christian missionary of any Church would have temporised with alien gods, contemptuously and indifferently, as did Quetzalcoatl.

The hunt went on. The seventeenth and eighteenth centuries indefatigably posed, questioned and read the riddle of this Occidental Sphinx. Quetzalcoatl was variously identified as a Carthaginian, a Welshman, and an Irishman. Each identification, so soon as made, lapsed into disrepute, in spite of constant assertions that Welsh-speaking, Irish-speaking tribes were to be found on the North American continent (the Carthaginians did no more than flaunt their beards from the temple-walls of Chichen-itza). The method of identification was no doubt generally pursued in the best of faith, but awoke serious doubts as to credibility. To identify a Red Indian tribe with the ancient Hibernians on the strength of the well-known Irish ejaculation 'bedad' being almost exactly similar to the tribal 'bagat' – the name, say, for a porcupine – was ingenious, but unsatisfying.

In the early nineteenth century the sun-myth hypothesis burst in splendour on the archaeological world. The record of its rise and fall is one of the most amazing things in human speculation. Nearly everything, human, divine and demoniac, could be traced in origin to a sun-myth – an anthropomorphic explanation of the sun's passage across the heavens, his positioning and power with the waxing and waning of the seasons. Applied to Ancient Egyptian and Babylonian myth, it reduced the gods to ashes, laid low Red Riding Hood and Osiris in one fell swoop, and then descended upon the New World, with Dr Daniel G. Brinton, the great Americanist, the wielder of the sun-bolt. First of victims on the American continent was Quetzalcoatl.

He was the sun. Pallid, as is the dawn, he came on the dark night of Toltec barbarism. He brought gifts, he ripened the fruits and flowers. He reigned supreme: the noonday sun. He grew old, and the hosts of darkness gathered against him: late afternoon. He returned to the sea – and saw that his face was old: the sunset. Kukulcan, Camaxtli, and all the other variants of the myth were not products of slightly varied records of the advent of a single human personality. They were myths explanatory of natural phenomena, separately built up by separate peoples, and owing points of similarity to no better reason than the similarity of the phenomena dealt with.

It is probable that future ages will speak of the sun-myth dogma as itself a myth. At its noonday splendour, however, few dared attack it. On the modern American continent, where there is a Monroe doctrine in archaeology as well as in politics, it attained enthusiastic acceptance. Earnest museum experts, North-American and Latin American, whose ancestors had massacred the native populations as brutish savages, defended with astounding vigour the ability of each of those populations to evolve unaided a complicated mystic and mysterious symbolism to explain to itself satisfactorily the ordinary phenomena of the heavens! Famines, it is said, were common in ancient Mexico and

Yucatan. And this is little to be wondered at, for, absorbed in the manufacture and study of these stupendous sun-myths, the Central American peasants could have had but little leisure in which to till their maize-fields.

Few sciences are static, however, and archaeology, that handmaid of history, still wielded her spade vigorously while listening in docile agreement to the sun-mystics. And gradually, out of her labours of ground-excavation coupled with research among the documents of the early Spanish fathers, certain facts emerged:

The fall of Tula of the Toltecs under Huemac was probably an actual historical event. For, about the same year in which the legend of the Humming-Bird Snake may be dated (*c.* AD 950), the neighbouring peninsula of Yucatan felt the effects of the Toltec debacle. A great refugee migration of Toltecs appears to have drifted southwards through the Tehuantepec neck and there heard something of the riches and splendour of Yucatan. Acquiring a leader, transforming themselves from a drift into an invading host, the Toltecs descended on the coast of Yucatan, captured the seaport of Champoton, marched inland, and took the great Maya city of Chichen-itza.

Now, the leader in question was Topiltzin Axcitl Quetzalcoatl – an astounding outrage in polysyllables at which even the Maya baulked, contenting themselves with translating the last name into Kukulcan. He was obviously a general named after a god, not the god himself, but it is not too great a stretch of probability to imagine Topil as member of some family which had known the mystic Feathered Serpent in the flesh.

Indeed, the Toltecs were more than invaders; they were missionaries spreading the creed of Quetzalcoatl. But it had suffered a sea-change. Quetzalcoatl was introduced to the conquered Maya, who had long eschewed human sacrifice themselves, as the greatest of gods, albeit alien, and one who demanded constant sacrifice of human hearts. The rites were accepted, God Kukulcan became and remained in Yucatan a high favourite long after the Toltecs had disappeared, *and, side by side with the ferocious forms of his worship was still kept alive the story of his gentleness, his agnosticism, his hatred of war and bloodshed*!

But now comes the crux of the story, as revealed by modern research. Those Toltec invaders under Topil did not introduce a new religion alone. They brought their characteristic arts and crafts. They reared new types of palaces, pillared and pilastered in styles unknown to the Maya. Squat little atlantean figures supported the roofs and doorways; above those doorways appeared stone screens of lattice-work. The Maya civilisations, both Old and New Empire, had been civilisations built with stone tools; the invading Toltecs brought copper and bronze implements to the peninsula. Sculpture had long died out among the Maya; the Toltecs revived it – something different in both concept and technique from anything of the Old Empire Maya, as the modern traveller may find by examining the walls of Chichen-itza and comparing them with earlier Palenque. The Toltecs have left in Yucatan evidences obliterated by the barbarians in their own land of Mexico – evidences of having absorbed details from a civilisation not only extremely advanced, but *extra-American*.

And that extra-American origin, if one is to accept the very plain proofs, was Eastern Asiatic – from Cochin-China or Cambodia through the medium, presumably, of the Philippines and Hawaii. Sculptural motif and decoration in the Toltec temples in Yucatan are so closely paralleled in ruined Funan of Cambodia (where Buddhist sculpture was at its zenith from the sixth to the eighth centuries AD) that it is impossible to doubt their common inspiration. Some time, as early perhaps as the days of the Maya Old Empire, stray sailors from Eastern Asia found their way across the wide surfs of the Pacific, landing astounded on the unknown coasts of Central America. They came back again throughout the centuries – though in no great numbers, one is to presume. Here and there, on the Mexican coast, they may even have had trading stations. Cortes states that on the Pacific seaboard Aralcon saw ships 'which had pelicans of gold and silver at the prow, also merchandise; and they thought they were from Cathay and from China, because the sailors of the ships gave them to understand by signs that they had had a journey of thirty days.'

This Asiatic-Amerindian intercourse was probably limited enough. Yet it seems to have continued into the time of the Aztecs who replaced the vanished Toltecs. The Aztec chess-game *patolli* is almost certainly the Indian *pachesi*. So is the Aztecan turban Indian, and so, perhaps, the Aztecan skill in gold-work. The Old World sprayed an intermittent cultural stream on the sea-board of the New. Eastern Asia witnessed invasions and upsets enough of its own for the memory of the far trading posts among the Red Men to be occasionally forgotten for centuries, perhaps, and then rediscovered. Or in Central America cataclysms of racial migration and inter-tribal war may have led to massacres of the traders; so that many years might elapse before another venturesome ship, Chinese or Javanese junk, came sailing out of the sunset to trade with some feather-cloaked American cacique of the coasts.

On the intellectual and religious life of the ancient Americans this trade apparently left no trace at all – *unless it be that Quetzalcoatl was the Buddha*.

The reasons for belief in early communication between Asia and America have been enumerated, the life of the Feathered Serpent sketched. Was he the Buddha – to whom he bears, even in Amerindian dress, such striking resemblances – or perhaps some Buddhist missionary? Is the tale of Quetzalcoatl the tale of Gautama translated from the hill-slopes and jungles of India to the hill-slopes and jungles of Mexico?

It follows close parallels. The Feathered Serpent's indifference to the gods is Gautama's agnosticism; his organisation of a special priesthood is the institution of the begging monks; his dislike of war and his half-contemptuous injunctions concerning fruit and flower sacrifices – these are of the stuff of that philosophy expounded in the Deer Park of Benares a thousand years before the burning of Tula half a world away. And the Mexican spirit-journey is, modified scarcely at all, the wanderings of the soul in the Buddhist purgatory . . .

On the other hand, the account of Quetzalcoatl's arrival from the west – a thoughtless act which definitely spokes the wheels of the sun-myth chariot – his pallid-faced, bearded followers of like kind to himself, his bringing of new arts and crafts, his absorption in these to the neglect of his growing unpopularity – all suggest the adventurings of an actual human being, some lost Cambodian philosopher-savant-missionary, rather than the transplanted adventures of the Indian Buddha.

Strange last avatar of Sakya Muni if either of these hypotheses enshrine some vestige of the truth! For perhaps, long years after the Toltec republic was a myth among the Aztecs and kindred tribes, some other Buddhist wanderer came to Mexican shores and was made prisoner, and carried to Mexico City, and in some cell of the Quetzalcoatl temple recognised words and forms that went with adoration of the Master and the Eightfold Path. Or, in the open air, witnessed the hideous ceremony at some altar when the heart of the sacrifice was torn out and held to the lips of the grinning idol – Gautama . . .

Buddha or Buddhist, it is doubtful if in all the history of religion there was ever such ironic counter-climax as that!

One may close with a suggestion and a prophecy: That the last word, all other speculations apart, is still with the angel Moroni; and that, among students of Ancient America at least, there is little likelihood of a great influx into the Church of Latter-Day Saints until the inspirer of the Book of Mormon descends again from the astral planes, summons a committee of archaeologists, and hands them definite instructions as to where lie re-buried those plates which no doubt elucidate the mystery of America's Buddha.

William James Perry:
A Revolutionary Anthropologist

DR WJ PERRY, today Reader in Cultural Anthropology at University College, London, is one of those 'modern influences' who elude the descriptive headline. If it cannot be said of him that he has taken all knowledge for his field of study, certainly his researches have drawn him into remote deeps whence originated most of the sciences, arts, and beliefs of mankind. So 'anthropologist', unless qualified, is too narrow a term, albeit 'revolutionary' is a somewhat incongruous qualification.

Yet it has justifications. For, in the company of the historian, the archaeologist, the anthropologist reared and bred and spoon-fed on the curious superstitions fathered upon the world from the tentative theories of Charles Darwin and Lord Avebury, the name of Perry is apt to raise the condescending smile that covers uneasiness. If the names of Elliot Smith and Rivers, those two other arch-infidels, be coupled with it, one is made as conscious of having perpetrated a shocking blasphemy as would a casual visitor voicing the names of the Black Trinity in a Presbyterian Chapel.

This is as it should be, for one of the main psychological axioms on which Perry and his colleagues build *their* theory is that man is by nature conservative, a hater of change, one who clings passionately to the outworn belief as sacrosanct – all unaware that that belief does no more than enshrine some stray and superseded fragment of archaic science.

NEW CLUES IN HISTORY

The part of William James Perry – he was born forty-five years ago, son of the Rev Dr Perry, late headmaster of St Anne's School, Redhill – in thus acting the iconoclast began while he was an undergraduate at Selwyn College, Cambridge, working for the Mathematical Tripos between the years 1906 and 1910. Ethnology aroused his curiosity. In 1910 he approached Dr Haddon, then head of the department, on the possibility of undertaking some original research. And Dr Haddon, all unaware of effecting a most momentous introduction, referred him to the late Dr WHR Rivers.

Now, Rivers, freshly returned from an anthropological expedition to Melanesia and kindred Pacific groups, had arrived at Cambridge convinced, among other startling convictions, that the rough stone monuments (megaliths) scattered throughout the islands of Oceania had been left there in the track of a culture-wave coming from the west. . . . This does not sound very startling. But in an archaeological world that accepted it as an axiom that almost every people automatically passed through the cultural phase of building lowly stone monuments, without outside aid or urge, it was a belief more than revolutionary. For observe its implications; it implied remote sources for the practice: it implied, more remotely, that much which we call civilisation is artificial – in the sense that man has no innate urge to it, that it is a super-imposition, acquired with reluctance, or without essential need.

But – whence the source of this artificiality which had given birth to all the ancient civilisations and was foster-mother of the modern?

Now (and these details are essential to understanding the career of that young research student who was sent to Rivers for advice) by a curious coincidence, Rivers' friend and colleague, Elliot Smith, working quite independently in Egypt, a sphere remote from Rivers's, had arrived at the conclusion that the megalithic monuments in the lands surrounding the Mediterranean – in Sardinia, in France, in North Africa – so far from being crude experimentings that ultimately led to architecture were rather crude *imitations* of a more finished product. The greater had preceded the lesser: civilisation had preceded barbarism, a fine technique a lowly one. And the home and origin of that fine technique had been Egypt of the Pyramid Age – the single spot on earth where seed of civilisation, accidentally planted, watered, and nurtured by chance and coincidence, blossomed forth into those cultural activities – agriculture, irrigation, architecture, religion – which transformed the life of mankind.

Nor did Elliot Smith limit the scope of his theory to the Mediterranean countries. If the megalithic monuments of Syria were imitations, was it not obvious, seeing the same basic principles always pursued in building them, that *all* such ancient monuments outside the Nile Valley were imitative? Syria and Sumer learned from Egypt, India and China from Sumer, Indonesia and the Pacific from India, Ancient America from the Pacific.

And, of course, not only stone-building, surely, had each of these lands learned from its sponsor, but other arts and crafts. Perhaps all arts and crafts? . . . It was a staggering vision that rose to the eyes of Elliot Smith: the sleeping primitive world of 5000 BC and then, ripple on ripple, like eddies from a stone thrown in a pool, the archaic civilisation of Egypt ebbing across it.

HIS FIRST RESEARCHES

From the adventures of the ancient travellers and voyagers of the first civilisation to Rivers advising the young Perry in Cambridge in 1910? The connection was to prove acute. Rivers and Elliot Smith, both convinced of cultural diffusion, realised one missing link in the chain of evidence. This was the East Indies, the Malay Archipelago. If the ancient civilisation of the Pacific was derived, not a home-grown product, then the great cultural wave that had carried it into those remote islands must surely have left some traces in the Malay Archipelago?

And this, Dr Rivers suggested, should be Perry's first field of research. Let him learn Dutch and study the literature of the Netherlands East Indies with particular reference to the old stone monuments of which theory demanded the existence.

The young research student took the advice offered him. He learned Dutch; he plunged into study. And by 1914 his notebooks were filling with evidence of the reality of the passage of the stone building peoples of ancient times through the Malay Archipelago. Elliot Smith and Rivers had found a valuable lieutenant. For various reasons the results of these researches were not made public until 1918, and then appeared as 'The Megalithic Culture of Indonesia', published by the Manchester University Press.

Perry is seldom an author very easy to read. The average layman, plunging into 'Megalithic Culture', has probably the feeling of a strayed traveller at the bottom of a quarry where a landslide is taking place. He is pelted with solid chunks of information. He glimpses astounding things in the rain of the strata boulders. And he crawls forth dazed, bruised, and dishevelled. . . . Piece by piece, immensely, laboriously, and impartially, the author details the evidences of cultural diffusion through the East Indies, and critically examines that evidence. It is not easy stuff to read, but it was written for neither amusement nor entertainment, and its comparative neglect by contemporary historians and archaeologists – generally so ready to acclaim erudition undecorated and undisguised – is criterion for their bias. It is criterion for that stupendous mental laziness that is the normal condition of all of us, that hatred of readjustment and fresh thinking. We have shored up and planed down the jagged edges of the quarry of history and prehistory, seated ourselves at the bottom and prepared for a picnic and a sleep in the sun. And these three tactless Titans – Elliot Smith, Rivers, and Perry – go scrambling amid the ledges with pick and shovel, digging out inexplicable fossils and exposing unseemly strata of impossible fact. And what is the good archaeologist to do but turn his back on such rude labours and go to sleep in the sun again?

THE GLAMOUR OF GOLD

In 1914 and 1915, after leaving Cambridge to become mathematical master at Pocklington School in Yorkshire, Perry entered into correspondence with Elliot Smith (Rivers had gone back to Melanesia) regarding the results of his researches, then still unpublished as 'The Megalithic Culture'. Elliot Smith he found engaged on the book which was to embrace in first draft the results of *his* researches along similar lines. This was 'The Migrations of Early Culture'. Early in 1915 he sent Perry a draft map showing the geographical distribution of megalithic monuments throughout the ancient world, together with places where the practice of mummifying the dead – so often associated with regions of the ancient stone landmarks – had once been prevalent. Perry was at once struck by an odd coincidence. For Elliot Smith's map coincided remarkably with that in the Oxford Economic Atlas, showing the ancient distribution of gold and pearl shell and jade.

Here was another and very vital link in this theory of

cultural diffusion that was being built up so gradually yet surely. Why should the Ancient Egyptian originators of civilisation ever have adventured beyond the Nile Valley and spread the seeds of civilisation and (weary for home and its glories) built with native labour crude imitations of the Nilotic monuments? And why should the Sumerians, inheritors from Egypt, have sent out their ceaseless expeditions into the uncharted wilds of India and across the waste Roof of the World? Obvious to the new school of Diffusionists that they had done so. But why?

Now here was explanation. The answer was in the ancient world what it is in the modern: the Glamour of Gold. Civilisation and its religious practices imposed a quite arbitrary and unwarranted value upon gold, upon shells and pearls and their supposed 'life-giving' qualities, and, especially by the time the treasure-seekers reached across the Pacific to Ancient America, upon jade – green, the life-colour of the corn. The Sumerian packed his primitive equipment and went into India for the same reason that the Anglo-Saxon prospected Alaska – in search of gold.

REDISCOVERY OF THE GOLDEN AGE

So, in those war-time years when civilisation reeled and tottered, Elliot Smith outlined the story of its origins and Perry filled in the outline, a laborious mosaic of unimpeachable evidence. They re-oriented history from the darkness that overcast it, traced in ever more and more convincing detail the passage across the world from that strange eruption in Ancient Egypt of every art and craft which goes by the name of civilisation, of every belief that is associated with religion and patriotism, class-divisions, kingship. All had originated fortuitously. Had there been no Nile, no river that flowed northwards from warm regions into cool, flooding at a certain season and day, impressing on the Nilotic primitives its processes, there would have been no civilisation. The world and men would still be as they were in 5000 BC.

And what indeed had been the nature and condition of those uncultured primitives the world over in 5000 BC.?

It was the next inevitable question on which the Diffusionists upraised the lamp of the new method of research. And by its light was revealed a world unexpected enough – not a world of (to quote HJ Massingham) 'these savages whose brutalities keep our circulating libraries on a sound financial footing', but genial humanity; not the howling primordial beast, but the Golden Age. In the words of Elliot Smith to the present writer: 'At an early stage in his work Perry became deeply impressed by the fact that in the heart of Borneo there still survived a people (the Punan) physically and intellectually well-endowed, who, in spite of the fact that they were surrounded by one of the most cruel and blood-thirsty groups of head-hunters, were genial, peaceful, well-behaved nomads, almost entirely devoid of culture and social organisation. This led him to undertake an extensive survey of the world to compare the various cultureless peoples. . . . Hence he was led to revive the ancient idea of the peaceful habits of primitive peoples and the essential goodness of human nature.'

War, cruelty, exploitation – all man's inhumanity to man is a thing imposed by civilisation, not sprung from innate savagery . . .

In two papers, 'The Peaceable Habits of Primitive Communities' (1916) and 'War and Civilisation' (1917), he expounded the results of his researches along these lines. But it was between the years 1919 and 1923, while Reader in Comparative Religion in the University of Manchester and in intimate association there with Elliot Smith, Wilfrid Jackson, and others of that brilliant group whose temporary localisation gave to the Diffusionists the somewhat misleading alternative name of the 'Manchester School', that he engaged on those two books which expound his leading ideas – 'The Children of the Sun' and 'The Growth of Civilisation', both published in 1923.

HIS ACHIEVEMENT AND CREDO

This sketch of their author's life has indicated the main purport of these books and must serve as tentative assessment of them. But to assess with any completeness either Dr Perry or his work is probably beyond this generation. His work demands so vast a readjustment of conventional ideas that the greatness of his achievement has never received the acknowledgment it deserves. He stands a little overshadowed by the immense reputation of his senior colleague. But, to quote again that senior colleague: 'Dr Perry has established the true conception of human nature and illuminated every aspect of early human thought and aspiration.' And these are no mean feats!

And to what conclusions that bear intimately and sharply on the modern world have his researches led him? In 'War and Civilisation', his answer is unhesitating:

This process of exploitation and domination of the many by the few will last until the common people of the earth recognise their condition and become aware of their power. The spread of education has caused the masses in every civilised country to develop a class-consciousness which is destined to produce the greatest revolution in the world's history. The day when the peoples of Europe say to their rulers and dominant classes 'We will no longer work to maintain you; we care not one jot for your quarrels and refuse to be parties to them; we will not be your instruments to enable you to plunder our neighbours' will see the end of war.'

So be it.

VI

In Brief

Controversy:
Writers' International (British Section)

A discussion was begun in the December Left Review *on the statement of aim adopted at the conference which established this section of the Writers' International, and this discussion is continued. The text of the statement was published both in the October and the December issues of* Left Review.

FROM LEWIS GRASSIC GIBBON

A GREAT PART of the thesis seems to me to propound ideas which are false, and projects which are irrelevant.

It is nonsense to say that modern literature is narrowing in 'content'; there was never in the history of English letters such a variety of books on such a variety of subjects, never such continuous display of fit and excellent technique. One need do no more than glance through an issue of *The Times Literary Supplement* to be convinced of this.

To say that the period from 1913 to 1934 is a decadent period is just, if I may say so, bolshevik blah. Neither in fiction, sociological writing, biography (to take only three departments) was there work done half so well in any Victorian or Edwardian period of equal length.

So-called revolutionary statements on decadence (such as that contained in the resolution) seem to me to be inspired by (*a*) misapprehension; (*b*) ignorance; or (*c*) spite.

It is obvious that such revolutionists imagine that modern fiction means only Aldous Huxley, modern drama Noel

Coward, modern biography the Lytton Stracheyites, and modern history the half-witted Spenglerites.

So much for misapprehension and ignorance. But the spite is also very real. Not only do hordes of those 'revolutionary' writers never read their contemporaries (they wallow instead, and exclusively, in clumsy translations from the Russian and German) but they hate and denigrate those contemporaries with a quite Biblical uncharitableness and malice. With a little bad Marxian patter and the single adjective 'bourgeois' in their vocabularies they proceed (in the literary pages of the *Daily Worker* and like organs) to such displays of spiteful exhibitionism as warrant the attentions of a psycho-analyst. From their own innate secondrateness they hate and despise good work just as they look upon any measure of success accruing to a book (not written by one of their own intimate circle) with a moronic envy.

Not all revolutionary writers (I am a revolutionary writer) are cretins. But the influence of such delayed adolescents, still in the grip of wishfulfilment dreams, seems to have predominated in the drawing up of this resolution. Capitalist literature, whether we like it or not, is not in decay; capitalist economics have reached the verge of collapse, which is quite a different matter. Towards the culmination of a civilisation the arts, so far from decaying, always reach their greatest efflorescence (the veriest tyro student of the historic processes knows this).

That efflorescence is now in being. It is not a decayed and decrepit dinosaur who is the opponent of the real revolutionary writer, but a very healthy and vigorous dragon indeed – so healthy that he can still afford to laugh at the revolutionist. If revolutionary writers believe they can meet in fraternal pow-wows and talk the monster to death by calling it 'bourgeois' and 'decadent' they are living in a clown's paradise.

Having said all this in criticism, I'll proceed to a little construction:

First, I'm in favour of a union of revolutionary writers. But this union would

(*a*) Consist only of those who have done work of definite and recognised literary value (from the revolutionary viewpoint). It would consist of professional journalists, novelists, historians, and the like, who before admittance would have to *prove* their right to admittance.

(*b*) Exclude that horde of paragraphists, minor reviewers, ghastly poetasters and all the like amateurs who clog up the machinery of the left wing literary movement.

(*c*) Set its members, as a first task, to drawing up a detailed and unimpassioned analysis of contemporary literature and the various literary movements.

(*d*) Be a shock brigade of writers, not a P.S.A. sprawl. I hate capitalism; all my books are explicit or implicit propaganda. But because I'm a revolutionist I see no reason for gainsaying my own critical judgment – hence this letter!

A Novelist Looks at the Cinema

PERHAPS, IN THE interests of truth and alliteration, this should read A Philistine looks at the Films.

As becomes a good Scots novelist, I live in a pleasant village near London; and, in the intervals of writing novels for a livelihood and writing history for pleasure, I attend of an evening the local cinema. It is popularly known as the bug house; the jest having long staled, there is no longer even a suggestion of vocal quotes around this insulting misnomer. For it is certainly a misnomer. The seats are comfortably padded, even for ninepence; a girl with trim ankles and intriguing curls comes round at intervals with a gleaming apparatus and sprays the air with sweet-smelling savours; the ashtrays are large and capacious; and it is amusing, in the intervals, to brood upon one's neighbours and consider the wild growth of hair which furs the necks of women who neglect the barber.

But at this point the Big Picture comes on. In the first hour we have witnessed two news reels; a speech by Signor Mussolini, simian and swarthy (why has Hollywood never offered him adequate inducements to understudy King Kong?); shots of a fire in a London factory, taken from the roof of a nearby building which was surely a public-house owned by a pressing philanthropist, so desperately poor is the photography and so completely moronic the camera-man in missing every good angle of vision; and No. CVII of Unusual Jobs, showing the day-to-day life of an Arizonan miner who has turned an empty gallery into a home for sick and ailing bats. Then has followed the Travelogue.

Travelogues in English bug houses (for I'll keep the homely misnomer) deal with only two portions of this wide and terrible planet of ours. We are never shown the Iguazu Falls or the heights of the Andes or the snows on Popocatepetl; or North Africa and the white blaze of sunlight across Ghizeh; or S Sophia brooding over Constantinople; or Edinburgh clustered reeking about its hill; or London in summer; or the whores' quarters in Bombay; or the bleak and terrible tracks that were followed by the Alaskan treks of '98; or Mohenjo-Daro, the cradle of Indian civilisation; or the Manger in Bethelehem at Christmas time, with the pilgrims swopping diseases on the holy stones; or the pygmies of the Wambutti; or the Punak of Borneo, a quarter of a million of them, naked, cultureless, happy, the last folk of the Golden Age; or the dead cities of Northern England, cities of more dreadful night than that dreamt by Thomson; or . . .

We are shown instead, wearyingly, unendingly, *ad infinitum* and *ad nauseam*, the fishers of Iceland and the dancing-girls of Bali. A strange, unrecorded tabu has smitten the travelogue-makers; the rest of the earth, those two islands apart, is forbidden their observation. So, with faith and fortitude, twice a week, we sit in the bug house and watch Iceland – mostly female Iceland – grin upon us over the salted cadaver of the unlucky cod; we gaze upon unending close-ups of gigantic buttocks bent in arduous toil; we blink upon geysers and giggling Scandinavian virgins . . . Or, in Bali, we watch the Devil Dance. The girls appear in masks; the novice film-fan deplores these masks till later he sees a group of the girls without them. Then he understands that even the devil has an æsthetic eye . . .

Next, Mr Laurel and Mr Hardy have entertained us with a desperate vigour. They have sawn themselves in halves, fallen down chimneys, eaten gold-fish, married their sisters, committed arson, or slept in insect-infested beds. And gradually, whatever the pursuit, the grin has faded from our faces. We are filled with awareness of a terrible secret unknown to the lords of the films: that the dictum on art being long and life short was never intended for injudicious application to a single-reel comedy . . . Mr Hardy has discovered fleas in his bed. Excellent! We laugh. The flea has infested the skirts of the Comic Muse since the days of Akhnaton. But Mr Hardy is still horrified or astounded. Yard upon yard of celluloid flicks past, and we await fresh developments. There are no fresh developments. The film, we realise, was made for the benefit of a weak-eyed cretin in whose skull a jest takes at least ten minutes to mature.

Then we have had Mickey Mouse . . . and remember Felix the Cat. Rose-flushed and warm from heaven's own heart he came, and might not bear the cloud that covers earth's wan face with shame, as Mr Swinburne wrote. But some day, surely, he will return and slay for us this tyrant. How long, O Lord, how long?

But now the Big Picture is coming. First, a lion has growled convincingly or a radio tower has emitted sparks or a cockerel has crowed in a brazen I-will-deny-thee-thrice manner. The heraldic beasts disposed of, we come to the names of the producer, the scenario-writer, the costumier, the sound-effects man; we learn that Silas K Guggenheimer made the beds, Mrs Hunt O'Mara loaned the baby, and Henryk Sienkiewicz carried round drinks. The fact that we here in the bug house care not a twopenny damn for any of these facts, that we never remember the names except as outrageous improbabilities in nomenclature, is unknown to Hollywood or Elstree . . . It is bad enough to have the printer's name upon one's novels. But what if he printed page after page in front of the title, telling how Jim Smith set the type and Rassendyll Snooks read the proofs and Isobel Jeeves typed the correspondence, and the printer's boy who had belly-ache was treated with a stomach-pump in St Thomas's?

Lists of actors and characters, confusing, and (a noted name or so apart) quite meaningless. Then, with tremolos, a distant view of New York – always the same view, film directors gallop madly round to each other's studios to borrow this shot . . . or a distant view of London; also, always the same view. Then – the picture . . .

Like most intelligent people I prefer the cinema to the theatre. Stage drama has always been a bastard art, calling for acute faith from the audience to supplement its good works. The film suffers from no such limitations; it presents (as is the function of art) the free and undefiled illusion. A minor journalist and playwright of our time, St John Ervine, denies this with some passion. His flatfooted prose style (relieved by a coruscation of angry corns) is employed week by week in a Sunday sheet to carry bulls of denunciation against the Whore of Hollywood. (Can it be that Hollywood has refused to film Mr Ervine's works as – with a far greater ineptness – it has refused to film mine?) But Mr Ervine's poor tired feet are needlessly outraged. The Whore has righteously our hearts – if only she would practise the courtesan to the full, not drape her lovely figure in the drab domestic reach-me-downs of stage drama.

Too often – in fifteen out of twenty of the Big Pictures that reach our bug house – she is clad not even in reach-me-downs. Instead, she is tarred and feathered or sprayed with saccharine in the likeness of a Christmas cake; and unendingly, instead of walking fearless and free, she sidles along with her hands disposed in a disgustingly Rubens-like gesture.

But – we had *Le Million*, and enjoyed its cackle; we had *Gabriel Over the White House*, the courtesan in dust-cap and mop, spring-cleaning her back-garden as even a Muse must do. We had *Man of Aran* which – apart from the fact that the characters never had any sleep and the sea suffered from elephantiasis, and every gesture and every action was repeated over and over again till one longed to go for the projector with a battle-axe – was a righteous film. And a month ago we had *As the Earth Turns*, which ought to be crowned in bay, in spite of some deplorable photography and an occasional sickly whiff of sugar-icing.

Between whiles our Big Picture is the Muse in tar and feathers.

Synopsis of America before Columbus

Author's Note on the Synopsis

The synopsis shows the scope of the book: the presentation of the history of pre-Columbian America as an integral whole.

The last work (in English) built on a similar, or somewhat similar plan, was Paine's *History of the New World called America* (1892–99). But Paine disputed the fact that America possessed anything in the nature of 'true history', his book is mostly a philosophical dissertation on the origins of civilisation, and forty years of research and excasation have now left it very much out of date.

McGee and Cyrus Thomas's *Prehistoric North America*, issued in 1905, was limited to 1000 copies. It dealt with North America alone, and more with culture than with history.

It is intended to make of *America Before Columbus* a book both authoritative and interesting to the non-specialist.

It is intended to have it adequately, but not profusely, illustrated.

*   *   *

J. Leslie Mitchell

is Americanist to the archaeological quarterly *Antiquity*, is author of a series of five papers entitled *Ancient America*, is author of a speculative essay 'Hanno', or the 'Future of Exploration' and of four novels: *Stained Radiance, The Thirteenth Disciple, The Calends of Cairo, Three Go Back.*

*   *   *

Synopsis of
A History of
AMERICA BEFORE COLUMBUS

Introduction   1,500 words

I   *America Before Man*   6,000 words
An outline of the geology, geography and topography of the Americas and their clues to the past non-human history of the continents. The geological ages, their

distinctively American fauna and flora. The closing-in of the land-bridges. Simian origins probably in North America (Wyoming). The question of the anthropoid ape in the Americas.

II *Man Comes to America* 7,500 words
The antiquity of Man in America. The Calaveras skull. The evidence of the Cuzco gravel-beds. Sr Ameghino and his school. The generally accepted belief that man is a late immigrant into the Americas, *c.* 20,000–10,000 BC. Theories of immigration: The origins of Man – geographical distribution of the human race in 20,000–10,000 BC.

Australasia: Uncolonised.

Europe: Cro-magnards displace non-human Neanderthalers, and are themselves forced northward. Possibility of a wave of late Palaeolithic (long-headed) immigrants from Europe to America via Greenland and vanished land-bridges.

Asia: Differentiation of races in the Tarim basin. A mixed drift of Mongoloid and Alpine peoples into North-eastern Asia about 15,000 BC at least an ethnological possibility, but no more.

III *The Races of America* 1,500 words
Do they prove a common origin? The so-called 'invariables' in the Indian race point to a Mongoloid origin. 'Invariables' – skull-formation, bone-build, hair – not invariable.

List of the great Red Indian language-groups, North, Central and South American, with consideration of the groups who used these languages.

North America: Mongoloid, but in the East with Esquimaux (European?) and possibly slight Norse modifications.

Central America: The usual basic stock, but with apparently a definite Caucasian element. Consideration of its origins left to a later chapter
South America: Mongoloid, but great proof of Polynesian

Language-affinities.

IV   *Culture Comes to America*   30,000 words
The archaic culture of the world and its rise and antiquity in America.

The archaic culture a phase, or series of disconnected evolutionary points, into which most races passed after the Palaeolithic period.

Its characteristics: Polished stone implements, ultimately metals, the beginnings of agriculture and horticulture, domestication of animals, differentiation of classes inside the human community, and either the resultant creation of priesthoods and divinities, or a crystallisation of vague superstitions into theology.

The two principal theories regarding the origin of culture and civilisation:

(a) The evolutionary school: Men, the world over, have much the same mental and physical equipment, and, providing environment is propitious, will, in their various groups (and those in groups independently one of the other) pass from Old Stone Age conditions into the beginnings of agriculture, etc. The climb from the beast and savagery.

(b) The diffusionist school. Men, the world over, have much the same mental and physical equipment, but even a lunatic in Tierra del Fuego does not make clucking sounds like an alarum-clock unless he has met the wares of a Birmingham factory. Man has no urge (innate) to take to agriculture and to polishing stone weapons: Agriculture and the beginnings of civilisation were an accident, originating in the Nile basin and from thence, slow century on slow century, welling eastwards and westwards across the world. Ultimately, this bastard archaic culture reached the shores of America, *c.* 500 BC.

These two theories in flat contradiction. Moreover, the first holds that man is by nature a ravening beasts held in the bonds of discipline and culture. The other declares that the innate sanity of Palaeolithic man the world over was twisted and debased as the result of the organisations and divisions consequent on the coming of culture.

The American evidence on the matter:

Pottery making: The utmost 'archaic horizon' in North America, ofeten [with e scored through in ink] dated 1,500 BC.

Ditto in Central America: Dated 2,000 BC. Ditto in South America: Dated as remotely as 5,000 BC.

Basket-making, textiles, etc., etc., in the same regions of the 'archaic horizon.'

Summary of the contra-diffusionist argument. Examination of its dates. Conclusion that these are mostly unwarranted guess-work.

The diffusionist case in America: Agriculture (maize-growing) first began in Central America and the coast of Peru. Tradition and excavation to substantiate this.

The likeness and obvious kinship of the American religions (detailed in later chapters).

Ditto of unwarranted customs and rites, inexplicable unless handed on from tribe to tribe: The couvade as the most irrational example. etc.

The Caucasian element in Central America – 'Polynesised' Asiatics? Polynesian affinities in South America.

Conclusion that the diffusionist's case, very greatly modified from its orthodox concept, explains the facts.

IV *Maya and Nasca-Chimu*:   57,000 words
    The First American Civlisations:
    Their appearance and characteristics.

The Maya Old Empire considered, for the moment, without chronology.

Its appearance and characteristics: The building of great temple-complexes – Uaxactun, Copan; Wuirigua; possession of a complicated glyphic script; possession of a calendrical system unsurpassed until the Gregorian; sculpture at first fairly crude, quickly attaining great artistic beauty. And so forth.
Whence did the Old Empire Maya civilisation originate?

Five Answers: (1) From the Huaxteca region of Mexico; (2) Locally; (3) From the Mound-Builders of the Mississippi; (4) From 'Atlantis' via the Antilles; (5) From Asia via the Pacific.

(1) The Huaxteca had only a later linguistic affinity with the heirs of the Old Empire civilisation.

(2) If locally would be traces of the script and calendar in archaic phases of semi-development. There are none.

(3) The Mound Builders, like the Huaxteca, had no trace of the fully-developed script and calendar which appears in the Old Empire area.

(4) No trace of even Mayoid influence in the Antilles.

(5) The Asiatic case: Stone-working as in Funan; the Mayan 'elephants' the turbans; the 'Greek' designs; the Sivaistic sculptures. Portrait-sculptures, on the other hand, generally late Chinese in appearance.

Against the Asiatic case: the fact that the script bears no resemblance to anything Asiatic. This may be bridged by certain calendrical resemblances.

The Conclusion: 112,500 words
That it is still uncertain who the Maya culture-bringers were, but most probably aliens, probably (as culture-bringers) themselves *not Maya*, though afterwards absorbed by the general populace.

The Naschu-Chimu culture appears in being on the

Peruvian coast, from Tumbiz to Arika. Probably the Chim the oldest. Our knowledge of it derived from pottery remains, mostly, owing to the fact that it built in adobe. Its characteristics: Naturalistic painting and pottery-sculpture at a high level; pyramid-building; maize-cultivation; irrigation; textile-weaving.

These arts presumably spreading south to the Nasca region, where the sculpture quickly became formalistic, and colour took the place of line.

Whence the Nasca-Chimu?

Two answers: (1) Local Development from the 'archaic horizon'; (2) Imported from Polynesia.

(1) The 'archaic' horizon probably a diffusion of higher cultures, not their sponsor.

(2) The culture-waves of Oceania. Easter Island. Conclusion that much of the Nasca-Chimu culture was imported.

The first Two American Civilisations considered together:

Sciences: Husbandry, irrigation, and the like.
Arts: Their highest attainments in sculpture.
Were the Maya glyphs used for literature? No script among the Nasca-Chimu.

Organisations and classes: A theocracy in the Maya Old Empire, as later possibly among the Nasca. But the Chimu probably under a warrior-aristocracy.

Religions: The Sun and all variants of sky-worship;

Development of the monster-gods. Phallicism and the serpent art-motif.

The more complicated South American scene:

25,000 words

The Chimu 'sun-rulers' replaced by a Nascan theocracy. Meantime, in the mountains, a warrior-aristocracy grows up at Tiawanako – a Polynesised Mayoid culture.

Apparent decline of Nasca-Chimu: Tiawanako takes control. The end of a great artistic civilisation.

VIII   *The American Dark Ages:*   25,000 words
       Aftermath of the fall of the first civilisations. The Maya Exoddus from the Old Empire tract, into Yucatan, through the Tehuantepec meck into Mexico. There they encounter tribes of Nahaus, perhaps up-rooted Mound Builders, marching down from the north. Maya influence among the Quiche of the Pacific coast.

       Peru: The spectacular rise and fall of the Tiawanako 'empire'.

       Consideration of dates: Period in this section probably closes – For Yucatan, 800; For Mexico, *c.*850; For Peru, *c.* 900 AD.

IX   INTERLUDE: *The Norsemen in America*:

10,000 words

A consideration of Lief Erikson's and other landfalls, and their influences on the American continent.

X   *The Central American Renascence*:   172,500 words
The rise of the 'Empire'. The Maya refugees from the
Old Empire tract into Mexico join with the Nahua
tribes to raise the new civilisation of the 'Toltecs' – the
'Builders'. This was probably profoundly influenced,
almost from its inception, by new culture-waves from
across the Pacific.

A detailed analysis of the Toltec civilisation: 25,000 words
The question of the human origin of the great god of
America – the Feathered Serpent. The coming of the
barbarians and the overthrow of the Toltec power.
Toltec refugees under Topiltzin invade Yucatan,
c. 950 AD.

Yucatan: Its history since it was entered by the Maya
refugees in two great waves, the Great and Little
Descents. An account of the apparent retrogression
of the descendants of the Old Empire Maya.

The invading Toltecs unify the country under the
hegemony of Mayapan and introduce their characteristic science, arts and religion. A detailed analysis of the
Toltec-Maya civilisation of Yucatan.

Final Shapings in American History: 197,500 words

North America: Displacement of tribes, resulting in
probably the overthrow of the Mound Builders. The
Nahuas, including the Aztecs, migrate into Mexico.
Settlement and war among the Nahau tribes amid the
ruins of the Toltec Empire.

Rise to power of the Tezcucans and Aztecs. The
Texucan Golden Age: Nezahualcoyotl. The Aztec
ascendancy.

Yucatan: Its fortunes and history from 950 AD to 1400 AD. The fall of the Mayapan hegemony; new 'Toltec' waves; civil war; eviction of the Cocomes; ascendancy of the Tutul Xiu; return of the Cocomes; final destruction of Mayapan

Guatemala and the rest of Central America: 20,000 words The Quiche peoples and the coming of Nahaus into Nicaragua.

South America: On the coast the rise of the Late Nasca-Chimu civilisation, apparently without external stimulus, and its culmination in the Kingdom of Chan-Chan. Simultaneously, out of the welter of confusion in the Andean region, a theocracy, the Inkas, at the head of a typical Keshwa tribe, gradually gain power.

Account of Inka conquests up to 1400 AD

The Last Hundred Years of Amer-Indian History:
5000 words
The tribal confederation known as the Aztec Empire, its rise, its character, its civilisation, its religion, its possibilities of development. Its influences to north and south, and the state of North America. The Maya in Yucatan: Degeneration again. Civil war and incessant plagues.

The Empire of the Inkas, Tawantin-Suyo. Its of the coast, Quito, Ecuador, Northern Chile. Character and civilisation. The sole American experiment in collectivism.

The state of the rest of South America.

The American Indian as Inventor and his Contributions to the World's Civilisation:

Artistic. Scientific. Agricultural and Horticultural. Literary.

Columbus' Landfall   250,000 words

History of the Continents of America before Columbus

I   *Introduction by Professor G Elliot Smith*

II   *America Before Man*

III   *Man Comes to America*

IV   *Culture Comes to America*

V   *Maya and Nasca-Chimu: The First American Civli-sations.*

VI   *Diffusion and Degeneration*

VII   *Bibliography*

VIII   *Index*

II   *America before Man*

This section will outline briefly the geology, geography and topography of the Americas and the clues to the past non-human history of the continent

i.   The geological ages, their distinctively American
     fauna and flora.   500
ii. The closing-in of the land-bridges and the
     question of 'Atlantis'.   200

iii. The possibility of Simian origins in North America (Wyoming) and the spread abroad of the plane great ape stocks.   300

iv. The anthropoid ape unknown in America. A brief sketch of his development elsewhere, the rise of the hominidae, and the evolution of homo sapiens the while America lay untenanted.   300

III *Man Comes to America*

This section will deal with the various theories of antique immigration, and the character of those antique stocks.

i.   The Calaveras skull.   100
ii. The evidence of Cuzco gravel-beds.   150
iii. Sr Ameghino and his school.   150
iv. General conclusion that these three claims for an excessively remote antiquity of Man in America are unproven, and that Man was a late immigrant, *c.* BC.   100
v.   Australasia at that date: Uncolonised.   100
vi. Europe at that date: Occupied by the Cro-Magnard-Aurignacian peoples of the Old Stone Age. Possibility of a wave of these flowing from Europe into America via Greenland and the vanished land-bridges.   200

      2,100

Asia

vii. Probability [that] a mixed drift of Mongol Alpine peoples then occupied Eastern Asia, and that eddies from that drift washed across the Behring land-bridges into America, forming the basic stock of the future populations.   300

viii. Modifications to the above conclusion (a) North America, a 'Caucasian' element that can possibly

be ascribed to the Norsemen. (b) 'Caucasian'
element in Central American, that is possibly
Later Asiatic. (c) The Melanesian and Polynesian
language-affinities of South America.   300

ix. Character of the first great drift of immigrants:

  (a) Palaeolithic in culture, a hunter, a wielder of
unpolished stone implements. Agreement as
to these elements, but the sharp cleavage
between the evolutionist and historical
schools as to the ethic and moral character
of Primitive Man.   200

  (b) The case of evolutionists: Arguing from
the 'tooth and nail; animal struggle of the
jungle, and from the character of modern
savage races, they envisage Primitive Man
as an unsocial, cruel and jealous animal,
his society in Palaeolithic times being gradually welded into tribal organisations through
the domination of the strong upon the
weak.   200

  (c) The case of the historical school: This case
received its greatest impetus with the discovery of America by the Europeans. That discovery gave rise to the philosophy of
Rousseau and the Humanists: The belief that
the primitive state of Man was a a Golden
Age of simplicity and kindliness.   200

For on the American continent those tribes
which were still in the Palaeolithic stage of
development – and therefore presumably at
the stage of the original immigrants into the
Americas – were discovered to be as lacking
in cruelty as in culture, without gods or
warfare, priesthoods or social classes.

Argument of the historical school – from evidence, not biological theorising and confusion of the savage with the primitive – that such was the original state of man generally. 100

(d) Acceptance of the latter point of view, and, from such acceptance, a brief sketch of the life and livelihood of members of the immigrant races. 500

3,900

IV   *Culture Comes to America*

This section considers the archaic culture world and its rise and antiquity in America.

i.   The archaic culture was a phase, or series of disconnected evolutionary points, into which most races passed after the Palaeolithic period. It was characterised by the use of polished stone implements, metal implements, the beginnings of agriculture and horticulture, domestication of animals, pottery-making and a crystallisation of vague superstitions into temple-religions. It came into being in different areas at different times. 500

ii.   As with regard to the original nature of man, the two principal schools of enquirers propound radically different explanations of the origin of culture and civilisation.

(a) The evolutionary school: Men, the world over, have much the same mental and physical equipment and, providing environment is propitious, will, in their various groups (and those groups independently one of the other) pass from the Old Stone Age conditions to the beginnings of agriculture, etc.

This is the 'inevitable climb from savagery'. 350

(b) The diffusionist (historical) school: Men, the world over, have much the same mental and physical equipment, but even a lunatic in Tierra del Fuego does not making clucking noises like an alarum clock unless he has met the wares of a clock-factory. Man has no innate urge to take to agriculture and to polishing his stone implements: Agriculture and the beginnings of civilisation were the result of an accident, originating in the Nile basin and from thence, slow century on slow century, welling eastward and westward across the world and ultimately reaching the shores of the Americas. 1000

iii. The American evidence in the matter: Excavations of the lowest cultural stratum in old sites give evidence of a culture characterised by the making of rude pottery, basket-work, and a somewhat rude and ineffective agricultural method in dealing with the typical American crop, maize. 400

        6,650

In North America modern investigators frequently date this early 'horizon culture' as early as 1500 BC, in Central America as early as 2000 BC, in South America as early as 5000 BC. 200

iv. From this evidence the evolutionary school concludes that in the Americas, from 5000 BC onwards, various tribes, in different regions, and without external stimulus, were slowly ascending the cultural scale towards civilisation. 200

v. The diffusionist school begins by questioning the dating of the evidence, (as will the present writer in some little detail) and showing that such dates have no geological warrant but are ascribed by the evolutionists as reasonable time periods to allow for an entirely hypothetical evolution. 500

    They go on to show that in certain important areas – the Maya Old Empire generally, the Toltec coast-sites Nasca and Chimu in South America – not only is there no evidence of the clumsy 'archaic horizon' culture, but that evidences of a high culture are quite often overlaid by evidences of a lower, arguing not evolution, but degeneration. 500

vi. Conclusion of the present writer that, while the rest of America remained at the Palaeolithic level, and no 'horizon culture' was in existence, civilisation arose spontaneouly, without American warrant or ancestry, in two distinct areas. 100

V   *May and Nasca-Chimu: The First American Civlisations.*

This section describes the uprisal of Guatemala-Honduras civilisation, and the Peruvian Littoral civilisation.

i. *The Maya*:

The appearance and characteristics of the Maya Old Empire in Central America: The building of the great temple-complexes of Uaxactum, Copan, Quirigua; possession of a complicated script and calendrical system; sculpture at first crude but speedily attaining great artistic beauty; nearness of the sites to pearl-bearing rivers, gold veins and the like. 1500

(a) Whence did the Maya civilisation originate? 9650

(b) Five answers: From the Huaxteca region of Mexico; locally; from the Mound-Builders of the Mississippi; from a remnant of 'Atlantis; or the Antilles; from Asia via the Pacific. 500

(c) Answers considered:

The Huaxteca: Their connection with the Central American Maya is, racially and linguistically, close. It is fair to assume that the whole of Central America and Mexico was once settled by Mayoid tribes. But among the Huaxteca there is no evidence whatsoever of an antique culture, though, were American culture self-developed, they are much more propitiously placed for such development. 200

The Mound Builders: Give no evidence of either the sculptural technique or mathematical attainments of the Maya. Nor are their settlements of any great antiquity. 200

Atlantis-Antilia: The traces of 'Mayoid' culture in the Antilles are obviously those left by the Caribs, the great traders of Precolumbian America. Their trading did not begin until long after the fall of the Maya Old Empire. 200

Locally: If locally there would be traces of the script, and calendar in archaic phases of development, of pottery and architecture in like phases. There are none. 150

Asia: Asiatic similarities: The Maya ku, or pyramid temple, is the 'ziggurat' that originated on the Euphrates and reached remotely into South-Western Asia; the stone-working is modified and with less imaginative feedom, that of Funan and such-like Cambodian sites; the Quiriguan 'earth-monster'; is the Indian makara; sculptured turbans, dress, and regalia Indian or Indonesian; the vigesimal notary system is that of South-Western Asia, modified. 700

(d) Conclusion: That the Maya culture-bringers were not Maya at all, but 'Polynesised' Asiatics who crossed the Pacific, settled among

the autochthonous Maya in temporary settlements while searching for 'Givers of Life',
and were absorbed and modified and changed, they and their culture, much as the
Normans were by the Anglo-Saxons.

ii. *The Nasca-Chimu* appeared in being on the
Peruvian coast, from Tumbez to Arika.

(a) The civilisations of the two cities are essentially one, though there are certain differences that suggest an earlier and later
settlement. Chimu probably the older.

300
11,900

(b) Our knowledge of this civilisation mostly
derived from pottery and textile remains,
and from burials. The Nasca-Chumu built
rarelyin stone, but in sun-dried brick. They
had large and well-planned cities; pyramidal
temples; naturalistic painting and pottery
sculpture at a high level of attainment;
maize-cultivation through irrigation; and
very brilliant powers in the weaving of textiles. 1,500

(c) When the Nasca-Chimu?

(d) Two answers: Local development from the
'archaic' horizon; imported from Polynesia. 300

(e) Answers considered:
Local development: As we have seen, there are
no 'archaic horizon' remains at all on the
Peruvian Littoral. The civilisation appears
without traceable American ancestry. 200
Polynesian: The pyramid-temples of Nuka-
Hiva match those of the American Littoral;
the practice of mummific-[line end] ation
among the Chimu-Nasca is the Polynesian
practice; The meré weapons are Polynesian. 500

    (f) Conclusion that the Nasca-Chumu culture
         was imported from Polynesia at a date before
         the Polynesian cultures had dwindled and
         while they were still fresh-drenched with
         the influence of South-Western Asia.   100

iii. The first two American civilisations, Maya and
     Nasca-Chimu, compared, their points of resem-
     blance and difference. Doubtful legendary matter
     apart, we have no knowledge of their gods, social
     classes, priesthoods – *no knowledge committed to*
     writing before the time of Columbus.   600

     But the Maya Old Empire, judged by sites, was
     essentially peaceful. The figures on its sculptures
     go unarmed. And, though we have no direct
     knowledge of its gods, the sculptures hint at
     sun and element deities intermingled with frag-
     ments from theology. It is fair to assume that the
     Maya Old Empire was ruled by an alien theocracy
     or its descendants.   600

     These matters in connection with the Nasca-
     Chimu are even more obscure. The paintings
     suggest that the monster-deities of the Pacific
     faintly guised as American super-fauna; they
     suggest a cultured and alien class dominating
     the subservient masses; and they give no evidence
     of the warrior, at least in the earlier periods.   500

     16,000

VI *Diffusion and Degeneration*

This section concludes the book and shows how civilisation
spread abroad the Americans from the Maya and Nasca-
Chimu foci, and of the progressive degeneration that every-

where succeeded its first florescence.

i.   Accepting the precedence of the Maya Old Empire upon the so-called 'archaic horizon', it now seems certain that it was from the Old Empire sites that agricultural civilisation flowed northwards into Mexico, transforming the lives of the Golden Age hunters. Adventurers and explorers from the Maya settlements bore it in the train of their searchings and excavatings for precious metals. By land and sea it passed up country, crossed the Rio Grande and penetrated amidst the tribal areas of North America. But, the further it went from the focus, the fewer the elements that took root in each new settlement. North America, beyond the Pueblo region, never learned to build in stone; the script and calendar became barbarously mutilated on the Mississippi; and in whole tracts of country, hearing only faint rumours of this new thing in life, the ancient hunters wandered unfettered as before.   1,500

Honduras and Panama show evidences of the southwards flow of Mayoid influences. In Panama the Cocle culture uprose, aided perhaps by fresh trans-Pacific influences. The tide of archaic civilisation flowed into South America and in Ecuador appears to have come into contact with discussion of elements from the Nasca-Chimu cities of the Peruvian Littoral.   1,000

ii.   By 800 AD the Americas were studded with these sites where men had learned to tame the maize and their fellowmen. Fresh incursions of adventurers appear to have crossed the Pacific – as indeed they did for long ages up to the coming of Columbus. In Alaska, in British Columbia, they left traces of their influence. They inspired the art and metal-craft of the Mexican Toltecs who overthrew the Maya Old Empire and perhaps the religions and certainly the social philosophy of the Tiawanakon highlanders who became the Inca and ended the domination of Nasca-Chimu. 700

19,700

iii. For those ancient civilisations, the Maya Old Empire and the Nasca-Chimu, degenerated rapidly through lack of stimulus and exchange with other civilisations, and through the fact that implicit in their own peaceful organisations was yet that element which made inevitable the rise of the warrior class. They fell, and despite fresh stimuli from the Old World that reared the magnificent barbarisms of Toltec, Aztec and Inca [*sic*], civilisation in the erated into the strange, aberrant darkness-cultures that Europeans discovered with the coming of Columbus.   1,000

iv. But the history of that thousand years of change and degeration belongs to another volume than one that sketches merely the beginnings in America.

20,700 words

VII *Bibliography*

VIII *Index*

*Preliminary Precis of a Still Untitled
History of the Conquest of the Maya*

PART I: THE CIVILISATION OF THE MAYA

I. *The End of the Maya Old Empire*

i. The Maya appear, with civilisation fully developed, in
Central America, *c.* 200 BC
ii. The unsolved question of their origin: Native Americans, strayed Asiatics, or survivors from Atlantis?
iii. The nature of their cultural achievements, mathematical, architectural, literary, etc.
iv The glories of the Maya Old Empire.
v. The mysterious catastrophe which suddenly depopulates
it.
vi. Flight of the survivors into Yucatan.

II. *The Maya in Yucatan*
i. The fate of the refugees.
ii. The building of new states and cities, and part-salvage of
the ancient civilisation.
iii. The mysterious un-Mayan tribe, the Tutul Xiu, rises to
dominance.
iv. Maya civilisation spreads north and south of Central
America after the Old Empire debacle.
v. The Toltec semi-civilisation in Mexico.
vi. Its overthrow by barbarians.
vii. Toltec refugees invade Yucatan.
viii. The adoption of human sacrifice, ceremonial cannibalism, [and tot-]al brutalisation of the Maya.

ix. The three-city league of Mayapan.

x. It [ends]

xi. Two hundred years of civil war. xii. The great plague.

xiii. The aberrant Maya civilisation in 1493.

(Part I will probably amount to about 20,000 words.)

PART II: THE FEET OF THE STRANGERS

1. *The First Europeans*

i. Columbus's discovery.

ii. Colonisation of the West Indies and Panama.

iii. Rumours of the American mainland.

iv. The wreck of Valdivia's ship on the coast of the state of Ekab, in Yucatan.

v. The Thirteen survivors captured by the Maya of Tuloom city.

vi. Fattened on maize for sacrifice.

vii. Half of them escape and cross the mountains into the interior.

viii. Seized and enslaved by another Maya cacique.

ix. The sailor Guerrero and the priest Aguillar alone survive the hardships: Guerrero becomes a Maya prince, Aguillar a harim-attendant.

11. *The Explorers*

i. Cordoba in search of slaves.

ii. He arrives at Cape Catoche in Yucatan, and is repulsed by the inhabitants.

iii. Sails along the coast, 'studded with temples and cities'.

iv. Lands in view of one of these cities – Champoton.

v. The first piched battle between Europeans and Maya.

vi. Mochoovoh, the Maya leader, defeats Cordoba.

vii. Cordoba, wounded, takes to his ships and returns to Cuba.

viii. Grijalva, with the historian Bernal Diaz on board, sails on Cordoba's track.

ix. They land at the island sanctuary of Cozunel.

x. Sail round coast.

xi. Encounter Mochoovoh: second battle.

xii. Grijalva withdraws, worsted.

xiii. Grijalva sails up the Mexican coast and hears of the riches of the Aztec Empire, founded by the barbarians who overthrew the Toltecs.

xiv. Cortes equips an expedition against the Mexicans.

xv. Lands at Cozumel Island en route and forcibly converts the Maya islanders to Christianity.

xvi. Hears of Guerrero and Aguillar, prisoners on the mainland, and sends ransoms for them.

xvii. Guerrero refuses to be ransomed.

xviii. Cortes sails for Mexico.

(Part 11 about 15,000 words.)

PART III: THE CONQUEST OF THE MAYA

1. *Expedition of Montejo the Elder*

i. 1516: state of Yucatan; four paramount princes.

ii. The Maya aware of Cortes' conquest of Mexico, but incapable of sinking their differences to meet the attack against themselves.

iii. The attack materialises: Francesco de Montejo, with small force of cavalry, artillery and bloodhounds disembarks at Cozumel Island.

iv. Character of Montejo and his companions; their expectations of treasure.

v. They cross to the mainland and capture a town.

vi. Resolve to march into the interior.

vii. The Maya raise the country.

viii. Guerilla warfare. ix. Battle of Tami inconclusive.

x. Spaniards seize the town of Ti-hoo and are besieged.

xi. The chief of the Tutul Xiu state of Mani at enmity with the rest of the Maya.

xii. Marches to Montejo's aid. xiii. Raises siege of Ti-hoo.

xiv. Subjugation of all Yucatan, except the Can country, by Spaniards and Tutul Xiu.

11. *Eviction of the Spaniards*

i. The Spaniards partition the states. ii. Little treasure.

iii. Quest of the Golden City.

iv. Montejo despatches Davila towards the Can country in search of treasure.

v. Guerrero chief warrior of the Cans.

vi. Organises them against the Spaniards.

vii. Eighteen months of guerilla warfare.

viii. Death of Guerrero, the Hispano-Maya.

ix. Montejo recalls Davila.

x. Yucatan in revolt against Spanish oppression.

xi. Spaniards besieged in Chichen-itza, the chief city they have seized.

xii. Driven into citadel. xiii. They starve.

xiv. They chain a dog to the clapper of a bell, and escape at night.

xv. Maya discover how ringing is caused, and pursue.

xvi. Montejo attempts to lead his shattered forces to the refuge of Mani.

xvii. Fails, and is driven to the sea-coast by Maya armies.

xviii. Embarks, and sails to Mexico.

111. *Expedition of Montejo the Younger*

i. A great plague follows the Spaniards' departure.

ii. Civil war between the Tutul Xiu, 'the friends of the scum from the sea,' and the other Maya.

iii. Spanish priests arrive on the coast from Mexico.

iv. Montejo's son equips an expedition.

v. Lands at Campeche. vi. Is joined by the Tutul Xiu.

vii. Great battle near Mayapan. viii. Rout of the Maya.

ix. Spaniards' orgy of massacre.

x. Thousands of Maya trek southwards into the bush.

xi. Yucatan brought under civil jurisdiction.

xii. Death of Ahpula Tutulxiu, the last high priest.

(Part III about 30,000 words.)

PART IV: THE LAST FREE MAYA CITY

i. Flores on Lake Peten, deep in the Honduras bush.

ii. Founded by the Itza Maya tribe – refugees from north Yucatan in pre-Spaniard times.

iii. Accessions during the Spanish conquest of Yucatan.

iv. Its population and culture. v. Its inaccessibility.

vi. First, second, and third Spanish expedition against it.

vii. Finally captured by the troops of Martin Ursua, 1697, 150 years after the conquest of the rest of Yucatan.

(Part IV about 10,000 words.)

Epilogue

Notes

Bibliography

The present writer is in possession of a large supply of suitable maps and illustrations.

Brief Synopsis of
A HISTORY OF MANKIND

I. THE BACKGROUND OF HUMAN LIFE

i. Men have been considering the size, the shape and the appearance of their background for some 300,000 years.

ii. For 297,000 out of that 300,000 it was probably no more and no less than the average mammal bestows on his habitat.

iii. Civilisation the origin of 'cesnic curiosity'.

iv. The earth some 2000 million years old.

v. Its place in space and time. vi. A finite universe.

vii. Theories regarding its origin and extinction.

viii. The origin of the earth. ix. The planet cools down.

x. The apparently mechanical origin of life – an accident in a little by-pass of the chemical processes.

xi. Methods of reconstruction. xii. The geological ages.

xiii. Life seeks the land.

xiv. Consideration of the urges to change: the power of environment, the power of desire. Modern reflexology and its light on habit-formation.

xv. The Proterozoic. xvi. The Palaeozoies. The amphibians develop 'land-habit.'

xvii. The Mezozoic. The world of the dinosaurs, herbivorous and carnivorous.

xviii. Its duration throughout 2000 million years.

xix. Evolution within this period.

xx. The first birds representing small and harried beings take to feathers and the air.

xxi. The ancestral mammal-type, also harried to the colder fringes of the world, takes to scale-modification and the production of hair.

xxii. The coming of the Great Ice Age.

xxiii. The Cainozoic, the world of the mamals.

xxiv. Its floriferation.

xxv. Its assailment and modification by the coming of four ice ages.

xxvi. The lemurs of 'Lemuria'.

xxvii. The evolution of the monkey.

II. THE ASCENT OF MAN

i. The original home of the Primates – Wyoming, Borneo, or the Malay Peninsula.

ii. The first anthropoid apes in Africa. Early strayings of the primitive apes.

iii. Specialisation of the early anthropoid in the Siwalik Hills, in the Early Miocene.

iv. The great westward ape-drift from Inds, in the early Pliocece.

v. First European apes, Dryopithecus and Pliopathecus.

vi. Ancestral ape-forms of Gorilla and Chimpanzee drift into Africa.

vii. Simultaneous life of the first representatives of Homo – Taungs Man in Bechuana, Pitheoanthropus in Java, Sinanthropus in China, Piltdown Man in England, Heidelberg Man in Germany.

viii. The earth roamed by stray hordes of half-men for many millenia before 500,000 BC.

ix. Causes of the rise of the Human Species.

x. Climatic and food changes.

xi. The specialisation of the hand.

xii. Hand and brain interacting.

xiii. Life in the days of Heidelberg Man.

xiv. The appearance of Europe, the food hunted, the degree of intelligence attained, the probable character of the early half-men.

xv. The appearance of a specialised Man, Home Neanderthalensis on the European and West Asian scene a hundred thousand years ago.

xvi. His specialisation to a fruit-eating diet.

xvii. His re-specialisation to changing conditions with the Fourth Glacial Age.

xviii. His probable appearance and character and degree of intelligence.

xix. A fire-using, tool-making animals.

xx. The Neanderthaler's tools.

xxi. Appearance of the first specimens of Homo Sapiens, our ancestors, in France, Spain, North Africa, Palestine, Hungary.

xxii. Contemporaries of the Neanderthaler and using Neanderthaler tools.

xxiii. Possibility of interbreeding discussed: Neanderthaloid types in Homo Sapiens.

xxiv. Appearance of Europe at the time of the appearance of Homo Sapiens on the scene.

xxv. Palestine or Mesopotamis his probable place of origin.

xxvi. His supplanring of the Neanderthaler.

xxvii. Origin of the races of Mankind – The Golden men migrate into Europe, blonds and brunets: the ancestral negroes into Africa, ancestral Chinese into the Tarim basin, etc.

III. THE STONE AGE

i. Definition of the term: The Stone Age the period through which Man and Near-Man manufactured and used implements and weapons chipped, knapped and smoothed from stone.

ii. Its two divisions: Lower Palaeolithic, tools used by Near-Men and Ancestral-Man; and Neanthropic, tools used by True Man.

iii. The Lower Palaeolithic endured from perhaps 500,000 BC to 20,000 BC.

iv. A period characterised by the slow improvement and alteration in technique.

v. The early shapeless eoliths give place to the Chellean implements, these to the Acheulian, to the Mousterian. Identification (tentative) of stone cultures with various races of Near-Men.

vi. The Neanthropic endured from 20,000 BC until (in Western Asia and Egypt) about 6,000 BC.

vii. Its division into Aurignacian, Solutrean, Magdalenian, Asilian, Capsian, in Europe.

viii. Contemporary cultures in Egypt and Palestine; the Tasians and Natugians.

ix. The people of the Neanthropic cultures: Their remains apart from implements.

x. The paintings and sculptures of Cro–Magnard and Magdalenian.

xi. Similar art-manifestation in North and Central Sahara.

xii. Their burials and care for the dead. xiii. Their material well-being.

xiv. The inter-connection of all their various cultural phases – one invention slowly spread abroad and subdued all others.

xv. Early trade in flints, shells, and the like.

xvi. Neanthropic Man a Primitive Man.

xvii. Difficulties in assessing him, his thoughts, his beliefs, his dreads, his hopes.

xviii. Commonly described as a 'savage.'

xix. Character of surviving savages in 20th century.

xx. Doubts as to comparisons with modern savages – iron-using peoples eith a long tradition.

xxi. The search for the lowliest type of human being alive today: stone-using, cultureless.

xxii. List of such peoples.

xxiii. Probability that they are the direct cultural and temperamental legateess of Neanthropic Man.

IV. THE ARCHAIC CIVILISATION

xiv. The Tasians. xv. The Badarians. xvi. The Amratians.

xvii. What drove men in great numbers into the Nile valley?

xviii. Desication in North Africa: the Nile a primitive Eden.

xix. Peculiarities of the Nile: flowing from equator northwards.

xx. Conclusion that wild cereals were markedly ripened and irrigated in front of the eyes of primitive man in the Nile basin.

xxi. Conclusion that agriculture may first have been practised here.

xxii. Conclusion that Badarians, Amratians, represent outlying attempts learned from Nile-bank.

xxiii. Mesopotamian and Egyptian datings compared.

xxiv. When did civilisation begin?

xxv. The Sothic calendar.

xxvi. The first villages and overlords.

xxvi. Development of the kingship.

xxvii. The Gods arrive. xxviii. The search for Life for crops and men.

xxix. Building. xxx. Metal-working. xxxi. Social classes.

xxxii. The great adventure of Mankind begins.

xxxiii. Footnotes of caution on position of Egypt as focal point.

xxxiv. State of present day archeological research.

xxxv. Conclusion that no future research can uncover alien beginnings for the Egyptians, at least, as all beginnings are present on Nile Bank.

V. SPREAD OF THE ARCHAIC CIVILISATION

i. The world in 3000 BC.

ii. Food-producing communities in Mesopotamia, Asia Minor, Crete, the Indus Valley, Egypt.

iii. Rest of the world still at the hunter and fisger stage.

iv. The diffusion of civilisation: mechanism.

v. Nomads, traders, explorers, miners.

VI. THE EMPIRES OF WAR AND GOD

iii. The home of war owing to the crowded nature of the delta.

iv. Continual war of the city-states from the First Ur Dynasty onwards.

v. Arrival in the First Ur Dynasty of a new cultural motif – the over-riding kingship.

vi. The king as Sun god.

vii. Slaughter of dependents at his death.

viii. This motif diffused from Egypt.

ix. In Egypt the rise of the Sun God King.

x. Expansion and conquest motifs associated therewith.

xi. The first invading armies of an Empire.

xii. The Egyptians in Libya and Syria.

xiii. Semitic invasion of Lower Mesopotamia.

xiv. The Empire of Hammabi, the first military Empire.

xv. Peaceable nature of the earlier Sargonic Empire.

xvi. The Semites invade Egypt. xvii. The Hyksos.

xviii. The New Empire. World-wide diffusion of cultural motifs in the New Empire.

xix. Diffusion of Egyptian motifs in Crete and Greece.

xx. The Minoan age in Crete.

xxi. Characteristics of a singular island civilisation.

xxii. Final overthrow of the Cretan Empire by raiders from its own colonies in southern Greece.

xxiii. The great conflict between Egypt and Asia.

xxiv. Fortunes in the fifteenth century conflict.

xxv. The rise of Assyria. xxiv. The first Empire of Aberrant Motive. xxv. Her conquests and overthrow.

xxvi. Migrations of nomads and highlanders during this period: the Early Greeks descend on Greece, the Celts on Western Europe, the Huns on China.

xxvii. Character and influence of these nomads.

xxviii. Their disintegrating influence on the Empires of War and God.

xxix. Development of the fundamentals of modern civilisation in the great Empires.

xxx. Origins of the script.

xxxi. Origins of the Sun and War Gods.

xxxii. Origin of organised cruelty.

xxxiii. Development and diffusion of the material bases of culture.

xxiv. The world in 600 BC.

VII. THE DAWN OF INDEPENDENT REASON

i. The world-wide enslavement of the human mind to the archaic concepts of science which were the great State Religions.

ii. The mind of man in the Archaic Civilisation: its narrowness within a circle of fearful fears and equally fearful hopes.

iii. Examination of the essentials of the great State creeds of Egypt, Babylonia, Early Aryan India, China.

iv. The origin and development of the idea of immortality.

v. The break down of the great state system in various localities.

vi. The Ionians of the small city communities.

vii. Consequent humanisation of 'divine' earthly rulers.

viii. Consequent humanisation of the gods.

ix. Consequent evolution of partial democracies.

x. The rise in Lonia of the leisured man, in slavery neither to a court, a temple, a trade.

xi. An assured and independent freeman.

xii. His speculations.

xiii. The first independent thinkers in Ionia – Thales, Anaximenes, Anaximander.

xiv. Their atheism and belief of in a mechanistic world.

xv. Their cosmic concepts.

xvi. Their views on human relationships.

xvii. Simultaneous speculation in Babylonia, as preserved in the Jewish scriptures.

xviii. Speculation almost entirely on the relationship of God and man.

xix. Evolution of Jewish ethical codes.

xx. Little doubt of an inter-connection of influences between Ionia and Babylon at this period.

xxi. The new thought leavening the ancient world.

xxii. Rise of Gautama in India at same period.

xxiii. His amplification of Thales and the Jews: the Eight Fold Path.

xxiv. Close inter-connection of the Ionian and Buddhist atheism with the monotheism of the Jews.

xxv. The trade routes to China.

xxvi. The life and sayings of the great Lao Tse.

xxvii. Undoubtedly influenced from Mesopotamia.

xxviii. Lao Tse's rediscovery of the Golden Age.

xxix. His apprehension of the fundamental kindliness and justice of uncivilised human nature.

xxx. Contemporary life of Confucius.

xxxi. Stimulation from orthodox State religion, modified by Lao Tse concepts.

xxxii. Confucius the 'bourgeois reformer,' Lao Tse the revolutionist.

xxxiii. The Code of Confusius.

xxxiv. Fundamental similarities in the teachings of all thesereformers.

xxxv. Undoubted cultural connections between all regions.

xxxvi. These philosophical-religious speculations the return of freedom and anarchy to human thought.

xxxvii. Spread and distortion of the doctrines: The Ionians pass on into scientific speculation, fathering Plato and Aristotle; the Buddhism of Gautama becomes a dogma: Confucianism becomes a State Religion.

xxxviii. Survivals and repercussions.

VIII. THE SECOND EMPIRES

i. Greece and the Greeks.

ii. Constitution of the Greek State.

iii. Life in a city of the Ancient Greeks.

iv. Greek colonisings in the Black Sea, in Hagna Graeca, in North Africa.

v. Greek culture originally Cretan-Egyptian of inspiration.

vi. The long history of Greek political warfare.

vii. The menace of the Ancient Empires.

viii. Rise of Macedon.

ix. The Adventure of Alexander the Great. vi. His Empire.

x. Its diffusion of fresh cultural elemants from Libya to the Indus and Central Asia. Its short endurance and collapse.

xi. The Empire of Asoka, built on Greek political model and Buddhist teachings.

xii. Its short endurance. x. Its fathering of the Gupta era.

xiii. Its influences in Indo China and Indonesia.

xiv. The rise of the Man Dynasty in China.

xv. The unification of China under Shi-Hwang-ti.

xvi. Quality of the Second Chinese Empire.

xvii. Its cultural influences on Japan, and beyond.

xviii. Its collapse. xvii. Its Seleucid political inspiration.

xix. The world of Western Europe.

xx. The Bronze (Archaic) Civilisation stretching from the Shetlands to Central Germany.

xxi. The Etruscans and Phoenicians come to Italy and North Africa.

xxii. Character of their cults.

xxiii. Rise of Rome. xxiii. Subjugation of Italy.

xxiv. Subjugation of Phoenician Carthage.

xxv. Quality of the Roman mind under the Republic.

xxvi. The Caesarian adventure and the beginning of the Empire.

xxvii. The world at the time of the birth of Christ; North Africa at the stage of Archaic civilisation, Europe under Graeco-Roman empires, Asia Hellenised, Australasia in the Archaic civilisation, America in the Archaic civilisation.

xxviii. The Archaic civilisation in America.

xxix. The rise of Nasca Chimu on the Peruvian littoral.

xxx. The rise of Tiawanako I in the highlands.

xxxi. The Cocle culture in Panama.

xxxii. Development of the non-State religions under the second Empires.

xxxiii. Buddhism. xxxiv. Hellenistic philosophy.

xxxv. Lao-tse teachings westernised.

xxxvi. The expectations of Judaism.

xxxvii. The problem of Christianity's origin.

xxxviii. All its elements present in the ancient world before the reputed coming of Christ.

xxxix. A synthesisation of State Religion and Independent Thought.

xxxx. Personality and Life of Christ.

Synopsis of Memoirs of a Materialist
(about 80,000 words)

GENERAL EXPLANATION

This, (of course) is intended as something new in auto-biographies. The terms borrows from the films are almost self-explanatory. Briefly, however:

REEL I: 1906–16

The Camera Eye (i)	The author, born in a farmhouse in the North of Scotland in 1901, centres his principal childhood memories around a heroic incident in which he figured at the age of five – the attempt to harness his pet cat to a small waggon which he had constructed for her. The Camera Eye makes direct shots of the incident and its accessories: farm, parents, district, etc.
Scenario Script (i)	An essay on the country and country folk of Scotland, their origins, qualities, decay.
The Camera Eye (ii)	Direct shot of the author as schoolboy.
Scenario Script (ii)	Essay on education of that time and of the present – Education scholastic, sexual, community.
The Camera Eye (iii)	A day in the life of a Presbyterian boy twenty years ago.
Scenario Script (iii)	An essay on Scotland as a nation and the the Scots as a people.

Still (i) Portrait of CM Grieve ('Hugh MacDiarmid') as the typically untypical Scot.

REEL II: 1916–18

The Camera Eye (iv)	Direct shots of the author's first job – a War-time cub-reporter in Aberdeen, doing the round of the harbours.
Scenario Script (iv)	An Essay on the relation of letters to life, as viewed by the author in these (Phase I)
The Camera Eye (v)	Again direct shots of the author's life in his second job – reporter in Glasgow.
Scenario Script (v)	Essay on the class war from the viewpoint of one who in origins (peasant) was outside the war.
Still (ii)	Portrait of HG Wells – principally as the inspirer and bamboozler of youth. Direct shots of HG in action – on God, on the author, on Communism at three o'clock in the morning.

REEL III: 1918–21

The Camera Eye (vi)	Direct shots of the author, at the age of seventeen, on a troopship bound for Mesopotamia.
Scenario Script (vi)	Essay on the most cowardly, helpless, and brainless of beings – the English soldier.
The Camera Eye (vii)	The author in charge of a provisions barge which every fortnight journeyed up and down the Tigris, between Baghdad and Basra, during the Arab Revolt.

Scenario Script (vii)	A consideration of how and where civilisation first arose – in Mohenjo-Daro, in Mesopotamia, in Egypt.
The Camera Eye (viii)	Shots of a visit to Bethlehem on Christmas Eve in 1921.
Scenario Script (viii)	Essay on religions; on the Christs, their origins, their messages; on atheism as a religion.
Still (iii)	Portrait of an acquaintance, a Russian White officer, as the typical representative of a vanquished class.

REEL IV: 1921–8

The Camera Eye (ix)	The author in Egypt: A morning after a night genteelly engaged in touring the Pyramids and the brothels.
Scenario Script (ix)	An essay on the bounds of the physical world; on exploration as the escape from self; on the new physics; on (the author contends) the essentially mechanistic properties of the relativitist universe.
The Camera Eye (x)	Shots of the author's wife dying in hospital.
Scenario Script (x)	A consideration of the relations between men and women, men and men, men and semi-men.
The Camera Eye (xi)	The author mapping in Yucatan. Shots of Palenque and the ruined Maya lands.
Scenario Script (xi)	An essay on the last great groupings of primitives – the

Americans – as they lived before the coming of Columbus.

Still (iv)   Portrait of Elliot Smith as the great historian and humanist.

REEL V: 1928–34

The Camera Eye (xii)	The author in England again. As a short story writer; as a novelist.
Scenario Script (xii)	An essay on the relations of letters to life, as viewed by the author at the present day (Phase II)
The Camera Eye (xiii)	Shots of the author and his wife as Communist agents in a general election.
Scenario Script (xiii)	An essay on the Future.
The Camera Eye (xiv)	Shots of a journey to Scotland by automobile, in company with a French M.P. (1934); A distinguished author's receptions.
Scenario Script (xiv)	A consideration of the instruments with which we view and measure and assess the world without. Bekhterev popularised in opposition to Pavlov.
Still (v)	Portraits of two representative 'literary lights'.

No synopsis can give any idea of how a writer will deal with a subject. But in the present case reference to other books of the author will indicate, here and there, the general line of treatment. For example:

Early days	*The Thirteenth Disciple* (novel)	1931.
The Essay form	*Scottish Scene* (Gibbon)	1934.
Biographical method generally	*Niger* (Gibbon)	1934.

The Scottish sections   *Grey Granite* and other
                         Gibbon novels.   1932–1934.
Historical reconstructions.   *The Conquest of the*
                              Maya Earth Conquerors. 1933.
Autobiographical excerpts   *Gay Hunter* (novel)   1934.

Synopsis of
The Story of Religion

NOTE: All synopses are unsatisfactory. The following pages attempt little more than outlines of the origins of the various religions.

They omit, for lack of space, those details that will make the portraits in the book itself 'come alive'.

They omit (though these are integral to the stories as they appear in the book) most of the drama of personal hates and hopes, triumphs and crises, in the careers of the prophets.

And perhaps they omit to show that the author's method will be as severely objective as possible, so that the cultured Confucian will be as little likely to take offence as the cultured Christian or Communist.

I. THE COMING OF THE GODS

This will open with a short prelude in pre-history and an enquiry into the thoughts of men before they became men. Did they fear the thunder and the volcano and dimly dream of gods when the Old Man of the tribe, being dead, yet haunted them in sleep? Did Sleep bring them the first intimations of immortality, trailing clouds of glory from afar?

Elucidation will be attempted by comparison with the

mind-states of surviving primitives, or primitives who until recently survived. From this the conclusion will be drawn that Natural Man was fundamentally irreligious: he had no gods, he did not bury his dead, he neither feared hell nor hoped in heaven. He was an animal unvexed by the mystery of existence. For him the mystery had no existence, and existence had no mystery.

But gradually certain geographical happenings concentrated Early Men in great numbers in the Valley of the Nile, and Agriculture was invented. With its coming came the greatest of revolutions in the minds of men. They saw interconnection between their food-supply and the flooding of the River and the prophesying of the First Irrigator. Dimly, they apprehended the Divine.

Slowly (yet all accomplished in the space of a few centuries) the first Fertility Cults – the first of all religions – arose. Sacrifice and propitiation were the gifts demanded by the divine for the continuation of favours: fruitful crops and wombs and the ever-renewed potency of the God Irrigators.

Then came the spread of the first civilisation abroad all the Old World and ultimately to the New. Everywhere it carried, changed and altered in outward form, in essence the same, the rites and beliefs and rituals of the Egyptian agricultural cult. Central in this was the ever re-enacted drama of the Divine Trinity – Osiris, Isis, and Horus.

Development of the Old State Cults. Accretion of Gods, for monotheism was the original state, polytheism marked advancement. The same God shed attributes that new gods might arise possessing them. Everywhere the King and the Theocracy reigned supreme. The Gods were remote, terrible, cruel and implacable, only to be propitiated by human pain. They had no heed for the individual, for the sorrows of death and decay, no consolation for the all-pervading sense of frustration that haunts human life.

II. AKHNATON FINDS ADONIS

We are still in Ancient Egypt. Its civilisation is at its zenith. It produces beautiful jewel-work and architecture. Its artists are skilled and competent – if uninspired. Its soldiers have conquered more than half of Asia Minor. Its temples cover the land.

But, to the young, the imaginative, the rebellious, it is a civilisation of terror and weary frustration. The Gods are Immutable Laws, heedless and cold. Their priests are tyrannous and rapacious. Art is bound hand and foot by theological conventions – bound to a sterile symbolism. Conduct is weighed down under a mass of ritual. Conquest is merely rapacity.

It is the year 1375 BC. Thothmes IV, the great architect and soldier, is newly dead. He is succeeded by his almost unknown son, Amenhotep – small and deformed, an epileptic married at the age of thirteen to a barbarian princess of Aryan blood.

On the throne, he proceeds to launch one of the greatest and most colourful attempts at revolution that have ever been recorded. He loves his wife – and insists in riding through the streets of Thees in the state chariot, holding his wife's hand. He fondles his children: he insists on sculptors depicting the fact. He believes in tempering justice with mercy: he insists on the courts carrying his belief into effect.

But more: he insists that Heaven shall conform as well. His boyhood broodings in company with his young wife have convinced him that the horrific Gods are false. There can only be the God that is Joyous Life. His symbol: the sun. Therefore, Amon-ra shall be suppressed, he and all his satellites, and the name and image of the Atar, the Effulgence of the Sun, exalted in their stead.

So it is done. Astounded, resentful Egypt bows before the dreamer. The old Gods are banished. A reign of naturalism in all relationships, human and divine, is proclaimed. The Pharoah alters his name to Akhnaton. And he and his wife set out for the western deserts to build the City of Atar, the City of God on Earth.

It is built. But Akhnaton's spirit grows weary as his epilepsy increases. And outside the Golden City the storm of reaction rises. Syr is in revolt. The Priests are in revolt . . .

Death of Akhnaton and destruction of the New Faith.

III. GAUTAMA BREAKS THE CHAIN

A brief resumè of the history of the next seven hundred years. The waning fortunes of Egypt, where no new Akhnaton arose. The rise and fall of the Assyrians. The coming of the Greeks to Greece, of the 'Aryans' to India.

In that period Cnossus is burned, Troy is overthrown, and the first eclipse noted. But there is no record in all the West of any great change in the attitude of men towards the Unknown which they have called the Divine.

With one exception. In a tiny enclave on the coasts of Asia Minor, in an obscure Greek city, the philosopher Thales broods on Life and the Cosmos, the first of the Rationalists. He preaches and writes and his words are borne on the winds of trade and scandal and priestly gossip remote into Asia . . .

Gautama Siddhartha is born in Kapila-vastu of Benares in 560 BC. The heir to the principality, he is brought up to avoid the unpleasant entirely – from lice to lions. Condition of the society into which he is born: the caste system at its most rigorous, the great and pitiless Hindu pantheon.

Gautama, happily married, rides abroad and sees the horror of life – poverty and disease and death, the unending Cycle of Pain. What part have the Gods to play in it? How can they ever alter these immutable monstrosities? How if (as the travellers from the West suggest) the Gods themselves are prisoners in the Chain?

He takes leave at night of his wife and son, rides out of Kapila-vastu, changes clothes with a beggar, and sets out an outcast to seek the truth.

In pursuit of it he tortures his flesh in dreadful austerities, abandons these as useless, loses his followers, and still seeks on. Then, under the bo-tree, the vision comes to him of the Eight-Fold Path whereby the pain of life may be foregone, the causal Chain broken forever by the serene abandonment of individuality.

He preaches the doctrine in the Deer-Park of Benares, acquires a great following – including his wife – and before he dies sees his creed of Life-Defiance spreading over India like a great conflagration.

Beyond the borders of India, northwards, that conflagration kindled at the fires of pity and despair encounters in its path the bulwark of another new Godless religion.

IV. THE ROAD OF K´UNG-FU-TZE

This new religion which spreading Buddhism encounters in the kingdoms of the Chinese rivers is Confucianism. Its founder, Confucius, dies six years before Gautama Buddha . . .

He is born nine years before the Buddha into a Chinese society in much the same condition as Gautama's – except that the State Cult lacks the horrific pantheon of the Hindu. The Fertility Gods were early in China decentralised: fertility was left in the hands of the individual's Ancestors, whom he worshipped and propitiated.

But the political oppression and corruption in China is far worse than in India. Here individualism, with the break down of the necessity for the Great Gods, has run riot. Chinese society of that day is a mixture of a bear-garden and a bandit's den.

The young scholar of the family of K'ung surveys the tumult. Intensely conservative quality of his mind. He marries at eighteen, is a public official at 20. Then, in his fashion, he (like Gautama) sets out to seek the Truth.

Visits Ho-nanfu and encounters the great mystic Lao-tze. Considers his creed of Tao insufficient for the times. Beginnings in his mind, as he wanders from state to state, city to city, of his own 'school' of thought. What creed is it well for a man to hold as a guiding light through the troubles of life?

First, that the Gods are beside the question. They may exist: that is their concern. The Unknown is the concern of the Unknown. In the Barbarian Universe the Cultured Man will run on no dangerous imaginings: He will honour his Ancestors, act prudently and wisely, be diligent, be courteous, hold as close to the truth as his own safety reasonably admits, avoid extremes and distrust extremes in both thought and action.

It is a creed, unlike Akhnaton's or the Buddha's, that is a retreat from the investigation of the Dark Background. But to the Chinese its appeal is overwhelming.

Confucius's mixed political and family life. Final sanctuary in Lu. Dies with the opinion on his lips that his creed will fall for lack of philosopher-kings to carry it through.

V. CHRIST AND THE FATHERHOOD OF GOD

For five hundred years these two great products of the Far Eastern mind, Buddhism and Confucianism, are the only virile intellectualist religions in the world. But even in the Far East itself they struggle with doubtful success (except at the price of compromise or mutilation) against the decaying Fertility Cults. Neither of them ever penetrates beyond the borders of Persia to the Near East or Europe.

Yet in Europe, Egypt, and the Near East the old Cults are also decrepit. Their place has been taken, for the dull and the conventional and commonplace, by new religions centring around some semi-divine Redeemer, who takes away the sins of the world. Such a Redeemer is Mithras and his religion is the great slave and proletarian one. For the educated, the imaginative, religion has almost vanished from the scene. In its place the cultured man turns to some code of ethic such as Stoicism or Epicureanism.

This is Europe and the Near East. But in Judaea is the Hebrew enclave. The quality of the Hebrews unique. Their narrow monotheism, originally a military necessity, is nevertheless forced towards mysticism on the one hand, and Redeemer-faith on the other. Judaea is a Roman province. Many Redeemers, some warlike, some pacific, rise to free the populace from the aliens.

Jesus Christ, one of these Redeemers, considered as a Man (the only aspect in which History may view him), not – which may be true – as an emanation of the Divine. His birth and childhood and probable contacts with non-Hebrew thought. The beginnings of his mission to preach a Reformed Judaism.

He encounters John the Baptist and is hailed by him. His Reformed Judaism broadens and alters in scope. He brings something new into religious teaching – he teaches and proclaims that that Dark Unknown is God, non-malignant God, God who is towards Man a loving Father. He teaches love as the terrestrial motive, and by means of it the attainment of the Kingdom of God on earth – for the kingdom of God within each breast can lead to no other result.

He goes to Jerusalem, performing wonders by the way. The Sermon on the Mount. The Last supper. He is seized and tried, refuses to defend himself, and is crucified as a malefactor.

VI. MANI SEEKS THE LIGHT

For two hundred years Christianity, with varying success, besieges the outposts of the Roman world. Bred betwixt the two great empires of the time – The Roman and the Parthian – its success eastward is slight.

Condition of affairs in the body politic, Roman and Parthian. Huge slave populations bitterly oppressed, an unending warfare between a crude capitalism and a brutish aristocracy, an equally unending war between the New Religions which have succeeded the Old Cults – Christianity, Neo-Platonism, Mithraism.

Birth of Mani (Kubricus) in Babylon, amidst the decayed splendours of the old Two Rivers civilisations. Born a Zoroastrian, he has intense religious curiosities. He encounters Christianity and studies it. He resolves to travel and study many religions. Like Gautama and Confucius, he sets out in search of Truth.

His far wanderings lead him to India and across into China. He returns to Persia with a creed slowly shaping to being in his mind, a breathless belief that is stamped by a vision.

Life is an unending fight – between evil and good, darkness and light, death and life. In this unending conflict Light (representative of God, who in the birth of time was overthrown by Satan and still struggles to reclaim the world) manifests itself age after age through great Prophets – Noah, Abraham, The Buddha, The Christ, and – Mani. The Dark Unknown is an evil thing – but it lessens and shrinks. By a combination of the Light creeds – a synthesis of Buddhism, Christianity, Zoroastrianism – men may have the perfect creed.

He preaches this throughout the Parthian Empire. Shapur, the Emperor, takes the new religion under his protection, and it flourishes exceedingly. Offshoots from it leaven Christianity. Mani is launched as the Prophet Triumphant.

But the dynasty of Shapur and Hormizd perish: to Bahram I Manichaeism is an evil heresy. He had Mani arrested and tortured.

He is crucified and flayed alive.

VII. PROPHET OF THE PITIFUL

For four hundred years after the death of Mani the history of religion in the West is the history of the growth of Christianity. It is not a steady and uninterrupted growth; and the young Churches are rent by schisms, many of them traceable to the doctrines of the prophet who was crucified by Bahram. But gradually Christianity succeeds in extirpating all rival creeds in Europe and the Near East. It achieves this result at the expence of its own original purity and simplicity, and by absorbing many details of rite and ritual from the old Fertility Cults.

In the Peninsula of Arabia Jewish and Christian colonies are powerful and influential. But the Arab of Mecca and Medina and the great coastal and hinterland regions is still a pagan, with that variety of the fertility religion adopted the world over by the nomad. His Gods are Rain and Robber Gods, his ethic confused and barbarous. Consciousness of this fact is deep in the minds of the more intelligent. These turn more and more towards Judaism or Christianity.

But a Meccan camel-herd and trader, Mohammed, is following an ancient path of inquiry. Trading in Syria, in Nejd, in Aden, he seeks for religious Truth. His employer, the widow Khadija, sympathises with her grave and epileptic herdsman. They marry and retire together to the caves of Mount Hira, seeking revelation.

Revelation arrives in a vision from Gabriel. He reveals to Mohammed, in this world over-run with colourful and foolish cults and gods, the true ONENESS of God. There is no God but God, pitiful and compassionate, and between him and Man there can arise no intermediaries, priestly or profane.

Excepting Mohammed. Evicting Mani from the list, he proclaims himself the last of the Prophets (of whom Christ is acknowledged hitherto the greatest).

He carries out five years of propaganda in Mecca. The result is fifty converts. Then he and the converts are violently evicted from Mecca and fly to Medina. There Mohammed organises the arm of the flesh. He raises an army and returns to Mecca, slays his enemies, establishes himself as theocratic ruler – and receives fresh visions from God. Ceremonial and ritual have entered his creed. The Pitiful God he finds also a Merciless and Revengeful God, and reveals him accordingly.

His creeds spreads abroad Asia and Mohammed dies in the midst of triumphant success.

VIII. THE LIFE AND DEATH OF CALVIN

For a thousand years thereafter Christianity versus Mohammedanism is the principal religious alignment of the West. Islam obtains an uncertain footing in Europe, but elsewhere, in Africa, the Near East and Central Asia, is all-conquering. But it also has its full share of schisms and religious wars, acquiring heretical tenets from Zoroastrianism and Christianity, even as Christianity itself is constantly threatened with reform by sects drawing inspiration from Mani and the like alien theologian.

Principally, the struggle within Chrustianity is the struggle of the individual man to assert himself, to claim direct communication with God, unhelped and unhindered by rite and priest. This is the motif backgrounding the rise of the Lollards of England, the Hussites of Prague, the Anabaptists of the Low Countries, the Lutherans of Germany. The main weakness of those movements (except, to some extent, Luther's) is that they are obviously sectarian movements from the main body of Christianity: They possess no rigorous code to differentiate them from the orthodox Catholic.

But in 1509 John Calvin is born in Noyon of Picardy, and grows up to become the second great prophet within the

Christian faith. He becomes a priest of the Catholic Church, attains advancement, and is singularly devout until, at Bourges, he falls to reading a Greek Testament. Thereon he becomes a protestant.

There follows ten years of preaching and persecution throughout which Calvin retreats more and more from Catholic doctrine. Gradually he builds up a great body of Law or dogma on which the True Christian must base his faith. Flying to Switzerland, he succeds in converting the town of Geneva, and becomes its dictator. Then he issues the principal tenets of his faith.

These are (1) Particular Election (2) Particular Redemption (3) Irresistible Grace (4) Final Perseverance.

Geneva becomes the first of modern theocracies. It introduces into life a concept of stern individualism, contract between the Unknown and the favoured individual, a business relationship of honesty and fair dealing. It eschews the God of love; it becomes the battle cry of the rising commercialist classes of Europe.

Calvin dies at the height of his power.

IX. JOSEPH SMITH AND THE ANGEL MORONI

For two hundred years more the history of Christianity is largely the history of the Protestant movement and its qualified success. At its core is Calvinism, sternly rationalist outside the orbit of its own peculiar dogmas. For the Anglo-Saxon populations at least the Unknown called God is no longer Mysterious: it is assessed, named, and signatory being to a contract.

In that two hundred years the continent of North America is colonised by the Anglo-Saxons – largely Protestant Anglo-Saxons. The habit of Protesting is in their nature. In the peculiar cultural and geographical circumstances of their new habitat their schisms from orthodox Christianity are apt to assume strange forms. They are the heirs and successors to an alien race, the Red Indian. The culture and origin of that race intrigues even the most thoughtless. And even the unimaginative, gazing on the great earth-tenples of the Mississippi Mound-Builders, is apt to speculate on the relation of the Amerindian to the Unknown . . .

Joseph Smith Junior, is born in 1805 at Sharon, Vermont. The son of a small farmer, he is profoundly pious, his only literature the Bible and some confusedly romantic histories of the early English and Spanish conquerors. Until the night of September the 31st 1833 there is nothing remarkable in his life.

But on that night the Angle Moroni visits him in a dream, and reveals to him the whereabouts of certain gold plates containing the religious history of the Ancient Americans. These, the Angel makes known, had been descended from one of the lost Tribes of Israel, but had lapsed from worship of the True God. Joseph is bidden to dig up the plates, translate them, and make known their contents to the Gentile.

This he does, translating the plates into pseudo-Biblical language. These translations become the Book of Mormon and the Bible of the Church of Latter-Day Saints.

Their main tenets are: Continuance of Miracles; the coming of the Millenium in an American Zion; the speedy Second Coming of Christ.

Joseph and a small band of adherents set about propaganda for the Neo-Christian faith he has originated. Presently he has a considerable body of followers, and builds the first temple. He is persecuted, tarred and feathered, and flies. A second temple built at Nauvoo in 1841. Here, the editor of a paper, the Expositor, criticises the Mormons. Joseph has the paper's buildings razed. Arrested himself, he is murdered in a cellar of Carthage gaol.

X. KARL MARX AND THE KINGDOM OF GOD ON EARTH

The subsequent heroic history of Mormonism – heroic in its great faith and endeavours – nevertheless reveals a curious fact. New faiths are apt, in the nineteenth century world, to become localised. World religions appear things of the past. This is proved once again on the American scene with the rise of still another Neo-Christian Church – the Church of Christ Scientist.

All over the world, as industrialism intensifies, there comes a loosening of the bonds of belief in any of the Gods – any of the names and personifications applied to the Unknown. In the welter of the Industrial Revolution, personification especially is doubted.

In place of worship of the Unknown arises Humanism, the worship of Man, belief in his goodness and perfectibility. Liberalism, fathered by Rousseau, and Socialism, fathered by d'Holbach and Owen, enshrine this new belief. But both, as with early Protestantism, are handicapped for lack of the discipline and faith-inspiration of a rigid dogma.

This is to be supplied by Heinrich Karl Marx, the son of a Christianised Jewish family. Born at Treves in 1818 he receives an excellent education, and early embraces Radical and Humanist ideals. The quality of his mind astonishes contemporaries to admiration.

Presently, editor of a Rhineland Liberal paper, he is forced to fly from Germany through a case of political persecution. He goes to Paris and discusses Socialism with the French Utopians. He goes on to London and meets Fredrich Engels. This meeting determines his life-work.

He settles down in the British Museum to study the origin and nature of the great forces which condition Human History. In *The Communist Manifesto* of 1841 he and Engels expound the result of his researches, the tenets for an atheistic Living Church of History:

Economic change is the supreme motivation. Human history is the history of class war. The last class but one is now in the saddle. Below it, the last class, the Proletariat, rises to overthrow its oppressor. Then, in a classless world, Equality will come, the Millenium be established.

He creates the First International, rules the Socialist forces of Europe, dies in obscurity: but thirty years after is the deified inspiration of a great Church embracing millions of followers – the Communist International.

Notes for a
Stained Radiance Sequel

CHARACTERS:

Deeps, the novelist: HG Wells
A Lesbian female writer: Norah James
A fat florid publisher: Hale
Kyrle, The American: Newman
Kyrle's wife: Lover for Garland

COURSE OF STORY:
Kouza reads about the landing of Russian Cruser & near break-up of Lab. Gov. What he reads. Descript on of said Government & members. Reads about the arrival of the Prince Koupa: 'Saved!'

John Garland awakens in his bed by the side of his wife. Thoughts on love. Their morning greetings.

He arrives at the Communist Party office. The C.P. How its prestige went down as hunger rose. Garland reads about the Prince. Resolves to have him mobbed when he appears in public.

A hotel servant goes into the Princes room & is surprised at the mud there & the changed appearance of the prince. What the Prince says when he wakes up. He looks out at London.

★

The newspapers hear of the Prince. Description of newspaper & its proprietor – a South African with a face like a dissolute Neanderthaler. Publicity for the Prince.

★

The Prince is mobbed & Garland does not know him. It is next Sunday. Description of Garland is contingents. Individuals among them. The march.

The Prince has given an interview to a paper: 'How I shot down the bolsheviks with my own hands!' He sits gnawing his thiumbs when the communists come for him. Storm the hotel and throw out most of the staff. Kouza rapes a maid en route.

Next morning the Press thunder [?] for protection of the Prince. But the end of the Government is at hand. In two days time a strange, sick [unintelligible] upon [unintelligible]. It is the Prime Minister.

Some details of the PM.

Known as The 'Bhoy of Bahooley' – a Bhaooley Bhoy was I born & a Bahooley Bhoy shall I die.'

★

The Dean of Thames-side & his sexual obsessions. Genitalia swung between him & the crocs. He prowled the parks at night & had couples arrested. He comes upon Garland and his wife and gives them in danger[?]

★

Visit to Whipsnade. Small, white man in charge of beasts.

★

The Jews as reviewers – ultra-Englismen. Sussex beared brawn.

The General Election draws on. Storman in it; Koupa in it; Garland in it with the American.

How the people voted in the slums. Their enthusiasm for the Tory.

★

Garland's last vision of the survey[?] away & the end of civilisation. Smash it with [unintelligible?] and return to the earth's sparse hunting groups – the remedy.

★

Koupa's progress as the Prince At a country house. Steals the spoons. Speaks a weird dialect. Meets Jew reviewer. – (Ralph Straus) a homosexualist, who loved little boy authors. Recommended to obtain naturalisation through his Mansen [Hansen?] passport.

★

Garland & his American in love with one another. Thea told of it – in no doubt: They thrash it out. All agreeable. Garland cannot believe there is so much sense in the world!

*

Shocked communists hear of it. Expel Garland. Newspaper howl.

*

Storman in the Phoenician & the meaning of the Script. What a [unintelligible].
Storman holds a publishers party & meets The prince. Norah sleeps with him.

*

The Bhoy of Bahooley bestows a peerage on the Prince. Delight of BB to associate with royal blood. Koupa proudly conscious of blood.

*

Robert Gozford hoins the Franciscans. Life in the monastery. Sleep. The falling away of the Roman Catholic Church.

*

The archaeologists conference & the half-wits who meet there.

*

Deeps left preach Free Love providing it is monogamous.

*

The Epimeshean[?] Soc meeting on Sexoloag better go to Mouncey Hill.

Notes for
Domina

Though some aspects of the story of Domina Riddoch are complementary to those of Malcom Maudslay, as related in *The Thirteenth Disciple*, Domina's history is nevertheless her own, as Malcom's was his.

J.L.M.

TENTATIVE OUTLINE
Born 1900.

I. SUR LE PONT D'AVIGNON
The history of Domina from the day of her birth to the time when she left France at the age of 11.

II. LEEKAN
In Scotland. At Leekan. At Dundon. Schooling up to 1917, when she leaves for London University.

III. THE HOSTEL
Domina in London. At the University. At the hostel. Friends. Stuart Isham. Dorota Maxwell. The Gordon sub. The final episode.

IV. B.Sc.
Dom. in flat with Stuart and Dorota. Graduation. Job. work. Two lovers, both married. Domina discovers diffusionism. Dom. in own flat.

V. MALCOM
Dom. meets Malcom. Holidays away from him. That metal. Pain and its discovery. Opinions on her work. Gradually abandons the loveliness of lust. Arguments with Stuery and Dorota. We grow up, I suppose.

VI. SECULAR CONTROL.

Domina in Germany. Dom. back in England. S.C.G.
Descriptions of people. Malcom. Work. Disputes. Renewed faith. Marriage with Malcom. His departure.

VII. TWO VOICES

Domina about to have a baby. Work still. No news from
Malcom. Satisfactory metal. Doesn't expect to hear of
Malcom again. Night of birth of son. Stuart with her.
The morning.

FURTHER NOTES FOR DOMINA

1. In Avignon – Her mother a rationalist, her aunt a
Catholic. Domina remembers later its unimportance.
2. Domina talks with Stuart and Dorota: Domina about
men as the god-makers. Women had always more sense.
Stuart on the unimportance of men, anyhow. A biological
freak – the male. Be possible to do away with him in time.
Dorota: A Genitalian parasite? Stuart: Exactlt. Domina:
Well, it will be a pleasant world in many ways, Stuart,
where one can get on with chemistry and not bother with
males. Child – pleasant and amusing injection of synthetic
serum. But I believe he is more than a biological freak. He
is a pleasant person with slightly varied biological function, but a mind like mine. Stuart: Maudslay? Yes, but
there are few Maudslys. Something has happened to him
to shock him into a kind of flaming justice towards all the
world.
3. People at the hostel: Hobbs and Robey (Mobbs and
Crowley) who are Lesbians; Dorothy (Evelyn) much as she
is; Stuart, Dorota; The lunatic 'chaste' girl; Billy; Elsie.
4. Dom's first honeymoon – Robey's bungalow. Rain. The
green water.

Notes for Three Stories

THE LOST WHALER

The young, dour captain marries the fresh, simple girl who has never left the land. They set out for the Arctic.

No whales. The captain refuses to turn about. The girl grows very silent.

Whales.

They turn south. The captain here's his wife below singing 'There is a green hill far away'. He goes down to her. She is mad.

GYPSY

The fisher-girl wishes to marry the gypsy. Her parents refuse to have any thing to do with the matter.

Parents discover couple together in embarassing circumstances. Girl hints that they'd be compelled to marry.

Father and lover go out of room. Mother and daughter talk. Mother hints that her daughter is daughter to a gypsy also. Advises daughter to marry *her* lover.

Daughter and lover discuss matter afterwards. Daughter laughs over strategem – there is no necessity for them to marry.

SCOTS SHORT STORY

Scene: Mountains

Jean Mintie lying ill. Thinks of John, silent, devoted. Thinks of her reputation and the times she had. Clucking of neglected chickens. Stern niece goes out. Ushers in old friend: Small, hesitant. Witheread.

The anniversary of Jean's husband's death. They discuss it. Maggie's confession: 'There was something between me and John.'

Eh? John – Jean's scorn.

Maggie tells how, while Jean gallivated around she would come across the moor and tend to his cattle and so forth. How, when Jean's first baby came into the world she comforted John that the baby after all might be his.

How she loved him, but repressed even shewing because he adored his wife and wait up for her and her return from drunken bouts.

Maggie: Can you forgive me?

Jean: There's nothing to forgive. He never loved me – though I him a the days he was on earth. It was pity for me.

Maggie – pity only because I'd found out his secret. He told me on our marriage night you were the only lassie could ever love.

Notes for
The Rooftree

The falling Walls of Maiden

1. In 1643 the second wall fell. The great storm of winter and the wreck of the ship below Maiden, after a fight with an English vessel.

2. The news brought by the rescued Puritans Hugh Sibbald. The war is out. John Walcar and Geillis resolve to ride south to suucour the succession.

3. They leave Hugh Sibbald recovering. He and Geillis fall in love.

4. Magnus on the road to the south – Christ and the Covenant.

5. Edinburgh and the news. Montrose one with the king. Magnus resolves to enlist.

6. Geillis and Hugh on what they will do to recl the Maiden lands.

7. Magnus at Marston Moor.

8. Geillis and Hugh at Dunnottar – Guests.

9. The march for Inverlochty.

10. The wasting of the Howe. Geillis and Hugh's consummation. Hugh's horror and departure.

Notes for
Men of the Mearns

Field of Flowers
Achadg-nam-blaith
Maghcircin – Mearns

OUTLINE AND NOTES
Place: Principally the Mearns; elsewhere Scotland.
Period: 1636–1688.
Essential places: Auchinblae; The Field of Flowers.

WARS:
1. National Covenant.
2. 1639; Scots Covenanting Army march to Duns Law. Treaty of Berwick with king. 15/2/39. Marischal Covenanter.
3. 1643 Solemn League and Covenant with England. Montrose goes south to help King.
4. 1644 Marston Moor.
5. 1st Sept 1644. Montrose's victory at Tippermuir.
6. 2nd Feb 1645. Montrose wins Inverlochy.
7. 1646–7. 19th March Montrose wins Dunnottar. Wastes countryside. Jan. 1649. Execution of Charles I.
8. 1650. Montrose executed. Charles II at Dunnottar
9. 1651. Second visit.
10. 3rd Sept Regalia in Dunnottar.
11. May 1652. Siege by Cromwellians. Capture.
12. 1660. Restoration.
13. 1685. Covenanters in residence. – 24th May–10th July.

THE SAND BANK FORT

1. First hundred – ends with the carrying of Statouns message to Huntly.
2. Second – ends with wasting of Dunnottar ten years after.
3. Three – ends with capture of Dunnottar by the Cromwellians.
4. Four – ends with the death of Richard Cameron.
5. Five – ends with the Covenanters in Dunnottar.

1. GM– 14
2. 1645 – 19
3. 1652 – 26
4. 1680 – 54
5. 1685 – 59

VII

Speak of the Mearns

Book I

WHEN THE ROMANS came marching up into Scotland away far back in the early times they found it full up of red-headed Kerns with long solemn faces and long sharp swords, who rode into battle in little carts, chariots they called them, of wicker and wire, things pulled by small ponies that galloped like polecats and smelt the same, scythes on the hubs; and the deeper they marched up through the coarse land and less they liked it, the Italian men. And by night they'd sit down inside their camps and stare at the moving dark outside, whins and broom, hear the trill of some burn far off going down through Scotch peats to the sea, and wish to their heathen Gods that they'd bidden at home, not wandered up here. And next morning they'd dig some more at the camp and pile up great walls and set up a mound and mislay a handful or so of pennies and a couple of bracelets and a chamber pot to please the learned of later times, and syne scratch their black Italian heads and make up their minds to push further north.

Well, the further they got up beyond the low lands the wilder and coarser the wet lands turned, the Caledonians had wasted the country and burned their crops and hidden their goats far up in the eyries, even sometimes their women, though women weren't nearly so valuable as goats, all that you needed to breed a fresh woman was a bed and a loan of your neighbour's wife, long faced and solemn as yourself. So the Romans jabbered at the women they got, and built more camps and felt home-sick for home, Rome, and its lines of wine shops, till they came in the lour of a wet autumn day up through the Forest of Forfar, dark, pines lining the dripping hills in a sweat, and saw below them the Howe of the Mearns, along dreich marsh that went on and on and was sometimes a loch and sometimes a bog, the mountains towered north, snow on their heights eastwards, beyond the ledge of more hills, came the grumble and southwards girn of the sea . . .

*

. . . their creash into the red Mearns clay as it well became the lowly-born, pointed by God to serve the gentry.

By then the long Howe was drying up, here and there some little tenant of the lords would push out a finger of corn in the swamps, and dry and drain and sweat through a life-time clearing the whins and the twined bog roots, working his wife and bairns to the bone, they'd not complain, there wasn't time, from morn to night the fight would go on, at the end of a life time or thereabouts another three acres would be hove from the marsh and a man would be easing his galluses, crinkled and bent and half-blind, and just be ready to go a slow stroll and take a look at the work of his life: and the canny Mearns lairds would come riding up 'Oh, ay? You've been reclaiming land here?' And the tenant would give them a glower, 'Ay.' 'Then you know that all lands reclaimed in this area belongs to the manor?' And the tenant if he had any wisdom left from the grind and chave of his sweating day would 'gree to that peaceful and pay more rent; if he didn't he was chased from the land he held and hounded south and out of the county, maybe strayed to Fife and was seized on there and held a slave in the Fifeshire mines, toiling naked him and his wife and bairns, unpaid, unholidayed in the long half-dark. For that was the Age of God and King when Scotland had still her Nationhood.

And here and there a village rose, with a winding street and a line of huts, each fronted by a bonny midden-pile,

along the coast rose St Cyrus, Johnshaven, Bervie, Stonehaven, Stonehaven's middens the highest and feuchest, in
the days of the Spanish Armada a lone and battered ship of
that fleet crept up the North Coast on a foggy night, the
Santa Catarina, battered and torn; and maybe she'd have
escaped to her home and her crew got back to their
ordinary work of selling onions up and down the streets
but that she came within smell of Stonehaven and sank like
a stone with all hands complete.

But about the times of the Killing Time the castle of
Dunnottar was laid seige by the English, men of that
creature Cromwell came up, him that had warts on his
nose and his conscience, and planted great bombards
against Dunnottar where the crown and the sceptre of
Scotland were hidden. And George Ogilvie was the childe
in command, he said he wouldn't surrender, not him,
though the heavens fell and the seas should yawn, he
was ready to sacrifice his men, the castle, the land, Kinneff
itself, rather than yield an inch to Cromwell. And the
English, aye soft-headed by nature, prigged at him to yield,
they didn't want blood, only the crown and the sceptre, that
was all. But while they were prigging he'd those fairlies
lifted and carted off to another place, the minister's wife,
Mrs Grainger hid them, carting them off in the hush of one
night to the Headland of the Howe, soft laplap went the sea
in the dusk as she rowed the boat in under a crumbling wall
and ruined dyke lone and pale in the light of the moon, here
Maiden Castle once had arisen. And as she climbed up the
eyrie track and over the long deserted walls, something
moved queer in her heart at the sight, she turned and
looked from the walls to the sea and the moon sinking low
and wan; and made up her mind she would mind that place
till the time she died.

She did the minding before that came. The English grew
tired of besieging Dunnottar and brought up their bombards and trained them and fired them; and George Ogilvie

gave a skirl of fear and surrendered at once and the English came in and ransacked Dunnottar from top to bottom, not a trace of the regalia stuff; and not a trace had any for years, till the Restoration came and the King and the Graingers howked the regalia stuff from the place where it had lain under the floor of the kirk; and when they came to ask for reward Mrs Grainger asked that she have the land where Maiden Castle stood by the sea.

Now the Grainger woman had been a Stratoun, she was big and boney with black thick hair, a bit like a horse, only not so bonny, and she planned to settle her goodson Grant in Maiden Castle, could they get it re-built, and plough up the tough land on the landward side and get him to do a bit fishing or smuggling or stealing or a bit of pirating and keep himself in an honest way. So with the little she'd saved in her life, her man the minister a fusionless old gype mooning and dreaming and thinking of God and rubbish like that instead of getting on, she set up Grant in Maiden Castle, they built a fine Scotch farm-house, half that and half a laird's hall it was; and Grant she had alter his name to Stratoun; and there was laid the beginning of folk who sweated a three hundred years in that parish douce and well-spoken, if maybe a bit daft. The littlest of lairds in changing Kinneff, they would lift their heads as the years and the generations went by and see changes in plenty come on the land, it broadened out from the old narrow strips into the long parks for the iron plough, horse-plough-ing came and at last a road, driving betwixt Bervie and Stonehaven, filled with the carriages of the gentry folk; and here and there a new farm would rise, to spoil the lands of the little crofters. And by then Kinneff had two kirks of its own, and a schoolhouse and a reputation as a home for liars so black it would have made a white mark on charcoal.

Stonehaven had grown the county town, a long dreich place built up a hill, below the sea in a frothing bay, creaming; and it had a fair birn of folk in it by then, bigger

it had grown than any other Mearns place, even Laurencekirk with its trade and its boasting; and a Stonehaven man
would say to a Laurencekirk man: 'Have you got a Provost
in Laurencekirk man?' and the Laurencekirk childe would
say 'Aye, that we have; and he's chains.' And the Stonehaven gype would give a bit sniff, 'Faith, has he so? Ours
runs around loose.'

Bervie had mills and spinners by then when the eighteen
eighties opened up; and it was fell radical and full up of
souters ready to brain you with a mallet or devil if you spoke
a word against that old tyke Gladstone. It lay back from the
sea in a little curve that wasn't a bay and wasn't straight
coast and in winter storms the sea would come up, frothing
and gurling through a souter's front door and nearly swamp
the man setting by his fire, with the speeches of Gladstone
grabbed in one hand and Ingersoll under his other oxter.

Now these were nearly the only towns that the folk of the
Howe held traffic with, they'd drive to them with the carts
for the market, cattle for sale, and bonny fat pigs, grain in
the winter, horses ploughing through drifts, and loads of
this and that farm produce. And outside it all was an antrin
world, full of coarse folk from the north and south.

The Howe

I

Now here was the line of the curling coast, a yammer of
seagulls night and day, the tide came frothing and swishing
green into the caves that curled below; and at night some
young-like ploughman childe, out from his bothy for seagull's eggs, swinging and showding from a rope far down

would hear the dreich moan of the ingoing waters and cry out to whoever was holding the rope: 'Pull me up, Tam. The devil's in there.'

But folk said the devil maybe wasn't so daft as crawl about in the caves of The Howe when he could spend a couthy night in the rooms and byres of Maiden Castle, deserted this good ten years or more, green growing on the slates and a scurf from the sea grey on the windows and over the sills. The last Stratoun there had been the laird John who drank like a fish, nothing queer in that, a man with a bit of silver would drink, what else was there for the creature to do if he was a harmless kind of man? But as well as that his downcome had been that he swam like some kind of damned fish as well, he was always in and out of the sea and the combination had been overmuch, one night his son, John was going to bed when he heard far low down under the wall a cry like a lost soul smored in hell. He waited and listened and thought it some bird, and was just about to crawl under the sheets, douce-like, when the cry rose shrill again. It was summer and clear, wan all the forward lift over the sea; and as young John Stratoun ran down the stairs he cried to his mother 'There's a queer sound outside. Rouse the old man.'

His mother cried back the old devil wasn't in his bed to rouse but out on some ploy, John should leave him a-be, he'd come on all right, never fear the devil aye heeded to his own. And with that the coarse creature, a great fat wretch, she could hardly move for her fat, folk said, a Murray quean, they aye run to creash, turned over and went off in a canny snooze. The next thing she know was John shaking her awake. 'Mother, it's faither and I'm feared he's dead.'

So she got from her bed with a bit of a grunt and went down and inspected the corpse of her man, ay, dead enough, blue at the lips, he'd filled himself up with a gill of Glenlivet and gone for a swim, and been taken with cramp. And folk told that the Stratoun woman said 'Feuch!

You were never much, Sam lad, when you were alive and damn't, you're not even a passable corpse.'

But folk in the Howe would tell any lies, they'd a rare time taking the news through hand, Paton at the Mains of Balhaggarty said the thing was a surely a judgment, faith on both the coarse man and his coarse-like wife, the only soul he was sorry for was the boy. And at that the minister to whom he was speaking, nodded his head and said 'Ay. You're right. Then no doubt you'll have no objections, Mr Paton, to contributing a wee thing for the creature's support? They've been left near without a penny-piece.' So Paton pulled a long sad face and had to dig out, and it served him well.

They didn't bide long in the place after that, the stock and the crops and the gear in the castle were rouped at the end of the Martinmas, the Stratoun woman would have rouped Maiden Castle as well but she couldn't, it descended to John the son. So instead she left the place stand as it was, no tenant would take it, and went off to the south, Montrose, or foreign parts like that, to keep the house for her brother there him that was a well-doing chandler childe. And sleep and rain and the scutter of rats came down on Maiden and there had bidden for a good ten years, till this Spring now came, a racket of silence hardly broken at all but that now and then on a Sunday night when the minister was off to his study for prayer and the elders prowling the other side of the parish and the dogs all locked up and even the rats having a snooze, after their Sunday devotions some ploughman lad and his bit of a lass would sneak into the barn and hold their play and give each other a bit cuddle, frightened and glad and daft about it: and if maybe they thought they saw now and then some bogey or fairley peep out at them there was none to say that the thing wasn't likely Pict ghosts or the ghosts of the men long before peeping from the chill of that other land where flesh isn't warm nor kisses strong nor hands so sweet that they make you weep, nor terror now wonder their portion again, only a faint dim mist of remembering.

II

Now the nearest farm to Maiden Castle was the Mains of Balhaggarty along the coast, you went by a twisty winding path, leftwards the rocks and the sea and death if you weren't chancy and minding your feet, right the slope of the long flat fields that went careering west to the hills to the cup of the Howe, and, bright in Spring, the shape of Auchindreich's meikle hill. The Patons had been in Bahaggarty a bare twelve years and had done right well though they were half-gentry, old Paton an elder, precentor, he stood up of Sabbath in the old Free Kirk and intoned the hymns with a bit of a cough, like a turkey with a chunk of grain in its throat, and syne would burst into the Hundreth Psalm, all the choir following, low and genteel, and his wife, Mistress Paton, looking at him admiring, she thought there was no one like Sam in the world.

Folk said that was may be as well for the world, Paton was as mean as he well could be, he'd four men fee'd, a cattler and three ploughmen, and paid them their silver each six month with a groan as though he were having a tooth dug out. But he farmed the land well in a skimpy way, with little manure and less of new seed, just holding the balance and skimming the land, ready for the time when he might leave and set himself up in a bigger place. He'd had two sons, or rather his wife, you'd have thought by Paton's holy-like look his mistress had maybe had them on her own, the elder would never have been so indecent as take a part in such blushful work. The one of them, William, was a fine big lad, a seven years old and sturdy and strong, with a fine clear eye that you liked, he'd laugh, ' 'Lo, man, Losh you've got a funny face.' And maybe then you wouldn't like him so much, queer how fond we all are of our faces. But he was cheery young soul for all that, aye into mischief out in the court, or creeping into the ploughmen's bothies and hearkening to the coarse songs they'd sing, about young ploughmen who slept with their masters' daughters and such like fairlies, all dirt and lies, a farmer's daughter never dreamed of sleeping with a ploughman unless she'd first had a look at his bank-book.

The second son Peter, a six years old, you didn't much like the look of, faith dark and young and calm with an impudent leer, not fine and excited when you patted his head but looking at you calm and cool, and you'd feel a bit of a fool in the act. But you never could abide those black-like folk, maybe they'd the blood of the Romans in them or some such coarse brood from ayont the sea. The wife, Mistress Paton, was an Aberdeen creature, she couldn't help that nor her funny speak, she called *buits beets* and *speens* for *spoons*, they were awfully ignorant folk in Aberdeen.

Well, that was the Mains of Balhaggarty, and outbye from it on the landward side lay the little two-horse farm of Moss Bank, farmed by a creature, Cruickshank the name, that was fairly a good farmer and an honest-like neighbour except when his temper got the better of him. He was small and compact and ground out in steel, blue, it showed in his half-shaved face, with a narrow jaw like a lantern, bashed, bits of eyes like chunks of ice, he'd stroke his cheeks when you asked his help, at harvest, maybe or off to the moors for a load of peats, and come striding along by your side to help, and swink at the work till the sun went down and the moon came up and your own hands were nearly dropping from their dripping wrist-bones. And if your horse might tread on his toes with a weight enough to send a ordinary man crack and make him kick the beast in the belly, he'd just give a cough and push it away, and get on with his chave, right canty and douce. And at last, when the lot of the work was done he'd nod goodbye, not wait for a dram, and as he moved off call back to know if you'd want his help the morn's morning?

You'd think 'Well, of all the fine childes ever littered give me the Cruickshank billy, then' and maybe plan to take a bit rise out of him and get him neighbour-like, for more work. But sure as God in a day or so some ill-like thing would have happened between you, a couple of your hens would have ta'en a bit stroll through the dykes to his parks and picked a couple of fugitive grains and laid an egg as return, genteel, and turned about to come away home. And Cruickshank would have seen them, sure as death, given chase and caught them, and a bird in each hand stood cursing you and the universe blue, might you rot in hell on a hill of dead lice, you foul coarse nasty man-robber, you. And just as the air was turning a purple and the sun going down in a thunderstorm and all the folk within two miles coming tearing out of their houses to listen, he'd a voice like a foghorn, only not so sweet, had Cruickshank, he'd turn and go striding back to his steading, a hen in each hand, with a soulful squawk, and clump through the oozing sharn of the court, heavy-standing, deep-breathing his bull would be there with a shimmer and glimmer of eyes in the dark. So into the house and brush past his wife and cry 'Hey, bring me a pen and some paper.' His wife, a meikle great-jawed besom, nearly as big and ugly as Cruickshank, and of much the same temper, would snap back 'Why?' And he'd say 'My land's being ruined and lost with the dirt that let loose their beasts on me. Me! By the living God I'll learn the dirt – hey, where's that paper?' And that paper in hand he'd sit and write you a letter that would frizzle you up, telling you he held your hens, and you'd get them back when you came for them yourself and paid the damage that the brutes had made. And for near a six months or so after that when he met you at kirk or mart, on the turnpike, he'd pass with a face like an ill-ta'en coulter. There was no manners or flim-flams about Cruickshank at all, and sometimes you'd think there was damn little sense.

They'd had two sons, both grown up, the one Sandy bade at home with his father and ran a kind of Smithy at Moss Bank, coulters and pointers and the like he could manage, not much more, the creature half-daft, with a long loose mouth aye dribbling wet, and a dull and wavering eye in his head like a steer that's got water on the brain. He'd work for old Cruickshank with a good enough will a ten or eleven months of the year and then it would come on him all of a sudden, maybe shoeing a horse or eating his porridge or going out to the whins to ease himself, that something was queer and put out in his world, and you'd hear him give a roar like the bull and off he'd stride, clad or half-clad, and Moss Bank mightn't see him for a month or six weeks, the coarse brute would booze his way away south and join up with drivers off to the marts, and vanish away on the road to Edinburgh, and fight and steal and boast like a tink. And then one night he'd come sneaking back and chap at the door and come drooling in, and the father and mother would look at him grim and syne at each other, and not say a word, real religious the two of them except when cursing the Lord Himself for afflicting decent honest folk that had never done Him any harm with a fool of a son like this daftie, Sandy and a wild and godless brute like Joe.

Now Joe had been settled in Aberdeen in a right fine job with a jeweller there and was getting on fine till the women got him, next thing there came a note to Mossbank that Joe would be put in the hands of the police unless his thefts were paid to the hilt. Old Cruickshank near brought a cloud-burst on the Mearns when he read that news, then yelled to his mistress to bring him his lum-hat and his good black suit. And into the two of them he got like mad, and went striding away down the road to Stonehaven, and boarded a train, into Aberdeen, the jeweller said he was very sorry, what else could he do, Joe was upstairs, and the sum was twenty five pounds if you please. And old Cruickshank paid it down like a lamb, if you can imagine a lamb

like a leopard, and went up the stairs and howked out Joe
and hauled him down and kicked his dowp out of the
jeweller's shop. 'Let me never look on your face again, you
that's disgraced an honest man.'

Joe was blubbering and sniftering like a seal by then, 'But
where am I going to go now, Father' and old Cruickshank
said to him shortly, 'To hell,' and turned and made for the
Aberdeen station.

Well, he went there, or nearly, it was just as bad, he
joined the army, the Gordon Highlanders, full up of thieves
and ill-doing men, grocers that had stolen cheese from their
masters and childes that had got a lass with a bairn and run
off to get-out of the paying for't, drunken ministers, schoolmasters that had done the kind of thing to this or that
scholar that you didn't mention – and faith, he must fairly
have felt at home. So off he went to the foreign parts, India
and Africa and God knew where, sometimes he'd write a
bit note to his mother, telling her how well he was getting
on; and Cruickshank would give the note a glare 'Don't
show the foul tink's coarse scrawls to me. Him that can
hardly spell his own name, and well brought up in a house
like this.'

For Cruickshank was an awful Liberal man, keen to
support this creature Gladstone, he'd once travelled down
to Edinburgh to hear him and come back more glinting and
blue than ever, hating Tories worse than dirt, and the
Reverend James Dallas worse than manure. Now, the
Reverend James Dallas was the Auld Kirk minister, the
kirk stood close in by the furthest of the Mossbank fields,
huddling there in its bouroch of trees, dark firs, underneath
were shady walks with the crunch of pine cones pringling
and cool in the long heats of summer and in winter time a
shady walk where the sparrows pecked. Within the trees lay
kirk and manse, the kirk an old ramshackle place, high in
the roof and narrow in the body, the Reverend James when
he spoke from the pulpit looked so high in that narrow place

you'd half think sometimes when the spirit was upon him he'd dive head first down on your lap. And all the plough-men away at the back would grunt and shuffle their feet, not decent, and the Reverend James would look at them, bitter, and halt in the seventeenth point in his sermon till the kirk grew still and quiet as the grave, you'd hear the drone of a bumble bee and the splash of a bead of sweat from your nose as it tumbled into a body's beard. Then he'd start again on Hell and Heaven, more the former than the latter for sure, and speak of those who came to the Lord's House without reverence, ah, what would the last reward be in the hands of GED? For the Lord our Ged was a jealous Ged an the Kirk of Scotland a jealous kirk.

You thought that was maybe true enough, but it wasn't half so jealous as the Reverend himself, he'd a bonny young wife new come to the Manse, red-haired and young with a caller laugh, a schoolteacher lass that he'd met in Edin-burgh when he was attending the Annual Assembly; and he'd met her at the house of her father, a minister, and fairly taken a fancy to her. So they'd wedded and the Reverend had brought her home, the congregation raised a subscrip-tion and had a bit concert for the presentation and the first elder, Paton, unveiled the thing, and there it was, a brave-like clock, in shape like a kirk with hands over the doors and scrolls all about and turrets and walls and the Lord knew what, a bargain piece. And the Reverend James look a look at it, bitter, and said that he thanked his people, he knew the value of time himself as the constant reminder of the purpose of Ged; and he hoped that those that presented it had thought of time in eternity. And some folk that had paid their shillings for the subscription went off from the concert saying to themselves that they'd thought of that, he needn't have feared, and they hoped that he would burn in it.

If he did folk said he would manage that all right if only he'd his wife well under his eye. For he followed her about like a calf a cow, he could hardly bear to let her out of his sight though while she was in it he paid little attention, cold and glum as a barn-door. She'd laugh and go whistling down through the pines, him pacing beside her, hands at his back, with a jealous look at the cones, at the hens, at the ploughmen turning their teams outbye, at Ged himself in the sky, you half-thought, that any should look at his mistress but him.

Well, that was the Reverend James Dallas, then, and his jealousy swished across the Howe and fixed on the other kirk of the parish, the wee Free Kirk that stood by the turnpike, a new-like place of a daft red stone, without a steeple and it hadn't a choir, more like a byre with its dickie on, than a kirk at all, said Camlin of Badymicks. The most of the folk that squatted in it, were the shopkeeper creatures that came from the Howe villages and the smithies around and joineries. The kind of dirt that doubted the gentry and think they know better than the Lord Himself. The only farmer in its congregation was Cruickshank of Mossbank sitting close up under the lithe of the pulpit, his arms crossed and his eye fixed stern on the face of the Reverend Adam Smith, shining above him in the Free Kirk pulpit like a sun seen through a maiden fog.

The Reverend Adam was surely the queerest billy that ever had graced a pulpit, in faith. He wasn't much of a preacher, dreich, with a long slow voice that sent you to sleep, hardly a mention of heaven or hell or the burning that waited on all your neighbours, and he wasn't strong on infant damnation and hardly ever mentioned Elijah. Free Kirk folk being what they are, a set of ramshackle radical loons that would believe nearly anything they heard if only it hadn't been heard before, could stick such preaching and not be aggrieved, especially if the minister was a fine-like creature outside the kirk and its holy mumble, newsy and genial and stopping for a gossip, coming striding in to sit by the fire and drink a bowl of sour milk with the mistress. But the Reverend Adam neither preached nor peregrinated, your old mother would be lying at the edge of death and say 'Will you get the minister for me? There's wee bit thing that I'd like explained in the doctrine of everlasting damnation; forbye, he might put up a bit of a prayer.' And off you'd go in search of the creature, and knock at his door and the housekeeper come, and she'd shake her head, he was awful busy. You'd say 'Oh? Is he? Well, my mother's dying,' and at last be led to the Reverend's study, a hotter and hotch of the queerest dirt, birds in cages and birds on rails, and old eggs and bits of flints and swords and charts and measurements, a telescope, and an awful skeleton inside a glass press that made your fairly grue to look on. And the Reverend would turn round his big fat face and peer at you from his wee twink eyes, you'd tell what you needed and he'd grunt 'Very well' and his eyes grow dreamy and far away and start on his scribbling as before. And you'd wait till you couldn't abide it longer: 'Minister, will you come with a prayer for my mother? She's sinking fast' and he'd start around 'Sinking? What? A ship off the Howe' – the fool had forgotten that you were there.

And when at last he'd come with the prayer and you'd take him along to your mother's room and she'd ask him the point about burning forever, instead of soothing her off, just quiet, with some bit lie to soothe the old body and let her go to hell with an easy mind, he'd boom out that there were Three Points at least to look at in this subject, and start on the Early Fathers, what they'd said about it and argued about it, a rare lot of tinks those Fathers had been, what Kant had said, and a creature Spinoza, the views of the Brahmins and the Buddhists and Bulgarians, and what that foul creature Mohammed had thought, him that had a dozen women at his call and expected to have a million in heaven. And while he was arguing and getting interested your mother would slip from under his hands, and you'd pull at his sleeve. 'Well, sir, that'll do. No doubt the old woman's now arguing the point with Kant and Mohammed in another place.'

Faith, it was maybe more that and a chance, folk said, that the big-bellied brute was keen on Mohammed. What about him and that housekeeper of his, a decent-like woman with a face like a scone, but fair a bunk of a figure for all that. Did he and her aye keep a separate room, and if that was so why was there aye a light late in hers at night, never in his? And how was it the creature could wear those brave-like clothes that she did? And how was it, if it wasn't his conscience, faith, that the Reverend Adam was hardly ever at home? Instead, away over Auchindreich Hill, measuring the Devil's Footstep there, or turning up boulders and old-time graves where the Picts and the like ill folk were buried in a way just as coarse as Burke and Hare.

East, landwards of the Free Kirk rose Auchindreich, spreading and winding back in the daylight, north along the road was the toun of the Howe, and south-east before you came to it two small crofts and a fair sized farm. Now the childe in the croft of Lamahip was a meikle great brute of a man called Gunn, long and lank with a great bald head and a long bald coulter of a red-edged nose, he farmed well and kept the place trig and his wife and three daughters in a decent-like way. And, faith, you'd have given him credit for that if it wasn't he was the greatest liar that ever was seen in the Howe or the Gowe. If he drove a steer to the mart in Stonehyve and sold it maybe for a nine or ten pounds, would that be a nine or ten pounds when he met you down in the pub at the end of the day? Not it, it would be a nineteen by then, and before the evening was out and the pub had closed it was maybe nearer twenty-nine; and he'd boast and blow all the way to the Howe, staggering from side to side of the road and sitting down every now and then to weep over the lasses he had long syne, the lasses had aye liked him well, you heard, and he'd once slept with a Lady in Tamintoul, she'd wanted him to marry her and work their estate, but he'd given it all up, the daft fool that he'd been, to take over the managership of a forest in Breadalbane – had you heard about that? And you'd say 'God, aye, often,' and haul him to his feet and off along the road again, up over the hill that climbs from Stonehyve in the quietude of a long June night, you looking back on the whisper and gleam of Stonehaven, forward to the ruins of Dunnottar Castle, black and immense against the sky, the air filled with the clamour of seagulls wings as they pelted inland from a coming storm.

His wife was a thin little red-headed woman, canty and kind and maybe the best cook that ever yer had been seen in the district, she could bake oatcakes that would melt between your jaws as a thin rime of frost on the edge of a plough, baps that would make a man dream of heaven, not the one of the Reverend Dallas, and could cook that foul South dish the haggis in a way that made the damn thing nearly eatable, not as usual with a smell like a neglected midden and a taste to match, or so you imagined, not that you'd ever eaten middens. And she'd say as she put a fresh scone on the girdle 'But they're not like the fine cakes you had from your Lady, are they now, Hugh,' with a smile in her eye, and he'd answer up solemn, No, God, they weren't, but still and on, she did not so bad. And she'd smile at the fire, kneeling with the turning fork, small and compact, and keeping to herself, you couldn't but like the little creature.

Faith, that was more than the case with the daughters, the oldest, Jean, had a face like a sow, a holy-like sow that had taken to religion instead of to litters as would have been more seemly. But God knows there was no one fool enough in the Howe to offer to bed her and help in that though she'd seen only a twenty-three summers and would maybe have been all right to cuddle if you could have met her alone in the dark, when you couldn't see her face, you don't cuddle faces. But she never went out of a night, not her, instead sat at home and mended and sewed and read Good Works and was fair genteel, and if ever she heard a bit curse now and then from old Hugh Gunn or some lad dropped in to hear the latest or peek at her sister she'd raised up her eyes as though she suffered from wind and depress her jaws as though it was colic, fair entertaining a man as he watched.

But her sister Queen was a kittler bitch, dark and narrow with a fine long leg, black curly hair in ringlets about her and a pale quiet face but a blazing eye. She was a dressmaker and worked the most of the day above the shop down there in the Howe, sewing up the bit wives that wanted a dress on the cheap without the expense of going to Stonehyve, or needed their lasses trigged out for the kirk, or wanted the bands of their frocks let out when another bairn was found on the way. And Queen Gunn would sit and sew there all day and at night would sit and just read and read, books and books, birns of the dirt, not godly-like books or learned ones, but stories of viscounts and earls and the like and how the young heir was lost in the snow, and how bonny Prince Charlie had been so bonny – as from the name you had half-supposed. And in spite of her glower and that blaze in her eye she'd little or no time at all for the lads; and the Lord alone knew what she wanted, the creature.

Now the second of the crofts in that little bouroch was Badymicks that stood outbye the land of Cruickshank, a little low dirty skleiter of place, the biggings were old and tumbling down, propped up here and there with a tree or so, or a rickle of bricks or an old Devil Stone brought there by Arch Camlin from one of his walks. He was the only Camlin that had come in the Howe and faith, folk said that that was as well, one of the breed was more than enough, the Camlins were thicker in the Howe than fleas, farmers and croppers and crofters and horse-traders, horse-stealers, poachers and dairymen, and the Lord knew what, if a Camlin stole your watch at a fair and you cried on a bobby to stop the thief it was ten to one, in Fordoun or Laurence-kirk, the bobby would be of one of the Camlins too, and run you in for slandering a relative. Well, Arch was maybe the best of the lot, a forty years or so old, swack and lithe, with a clean-shaven face and meikle dark eyes. He'd married a second time late in life, a creature from the way of Aberdeen, she'd come to Badymicks a gey canty dame, with fine fat buttocks and a fine fat smile, she'd been a maid to a couple of old women that had worn away through a slow slope of years as worms wear off from sight to a grave. They'd left her a couple of hundred pounds and just as she was wondering what to do with it along came Arch Camlin on some ploy or other and picked up the two hundred in his stride, so to speak, and the poor lass with them and carted the lot away to tumbledown Badymicks. And there for a while it had been well enough, Arch was land-mad, at it all day criss-crossing his ploughing with a sholt and a cow and planning the draining of the sodden fields, he could work the average man near to death. And coming from the fields to his supper at night he'd dally with the woman and give her a squeeze and she put on a fine dress and smile at him soft, and all had been well for a little time.

But Arch had been married long afore that, his first wife had died and left a wee lass, Rachel, that Arch had put out to suck with an old widow woman in a village of the Howe. So now Arch brought this quean Rachel home, short and dark with a sallow skin, black-haired, black-browed, with a bit of a limp, and her eyes wide with a kind of wonder, you couldn't make up your mind on the lass, but Mistress Camlin made up hers at once, she couldn't abide her and would hardly heed her, the little lass would follow Arch all day long out in the fields, in the flare of sun, in dripping rains on autumn's edge, keen and green on a morning in Spring you'd hear her cry him into meat. She was only five when she came to Badymicks and the next year the new family started to come, first a loon and then a lass, and there was every sign in this year as well that another bairn was hot on the way. And no sooner had the first put in its appearance that the gentility went from poor Jess. She grew whiny and complainy and bunched in the middle and seemed hardly to ken her head from her feet, and even if she did what to do with either, and she'd stare at Eda, Bogmuck's housekeeper, and shake her head and wonder aloud how any women could get pleasure out of *that*.

Bogmuck was the second biggest place in the parish, and the man that had ta' on it on the new thirteen years' lease was a well-set up and well-doing childe, Dalsack the name, from a bothy in Bogjorgan. He was maybe a forty, forty-five years old, with whiskers down the side of his face, decent, and aye wore a top-hat on Sundays, an elder at the kirk, and a fine, cheery soul. He made silver as some folk made dirt or bairns, Dalsack had had over much sense for the latter, he'd never married and never would, over shy to be taken in by any woman. He was a knowledgeable and skilly man, cheery-like and the best of neighbours if maybe a wee bit close with his silver. And why shouldn't he be? It was only dirt that brought themselves to paupers' graves that would fling good money about for nothing. Well, God, if that was the case, as they said, there was little chance of Dalsack a pauper, he'd smile, big and cheery but careful to the last bit farthing there was, as he paid out the two fee'd men of Bogmuck or the money the housekeeper wanted to pay for groceries and the like brought up from Bervie. For a good six years he'd had a housekeeper, a decent young woman though awful quiet, that did right well and never raised scandal, no fear of that with Dalsack about, he must nearly have fainted with shyness, you thought, when first he found himself in his mother's bed: in the bed of another woman, faith, he'd dissolve into nothing but one raddle of a blush.

So things were canty and quiet enough till the January of 1880 came in, and then the housekeeper left of a sudden, nobody got to the bottom of it, she packed her bag and went trudging away, folk saw her come past the houses of the village with her face white and set, could it be that she had the belly-ache? And one or two cried to her to come in and sit her down for a cup of tea – was she off to Stonehyve then, would it be? But she just shook her head and went trudging on and that was the last of her seen in the Howe.

And faith, Dalsack didn't meet her marrow. Instead, he fee'd to Bogmuck a quean whose capers were known all over the Howe, Eda Lyell, a shameless limmer, she came from Drumlithie, a bonny like quean, but already with three bairns on her hands and each of them by a different father. Folk shook their heads when they heard of her coming and the Reverend Dallas went to Dalsack and told him bitter that the parish would be tainted and riven with sin if he brought this woman to Bogmuck, a foul insult in the face of Ged. But Dalsack just gave his nose a stroke and smiled and said canny that he didn't think so. And come she did in a week or less, trailing over the head of Auchin-dreich hill with her three weans clinging on to her skirts, half-dead with the voyage through the whins and broom; and the whole of the village made a leap for its windows and stared at her as she panted by, the foul trollop that she was, said all the women, and the men gave a bit of a lick at their lips, well, well, fine buttocks and a fine like back.

But she'd more than that, some thought it clean shame-ful, for before she had been a three months in the Howe Eda was a favourite with every soul, big and strapping with a flushed, bonny face and hair like corn, ripe corn smoothed out in flat waves in sun under the ripple of a harvest guff, and a laugh that was deep and clear and snell, snell and sweet as a wind at night. There wasn't a more helpful body in the Howe, or more obliging, she worked like a nigger indoors and out – ay, Dalsack had fairly a bargain in her. Near the only creature that still looked down on her was the Reverend James Dallas, as you may well have guessed, he met her out in the parks one day, her spreading dung under the coming of April, a white-like morning, dew about, and the peewits wailing and crying like mad. And he said to her 'Are you the woman of Badymicks,' and she nodded to him blithe, 'Ay, sir, I am that.' 'Then see there are no more fatherless bairns brought into the world by you to your shame. Give you good-day' and he went striding off, leaving Eda staring after him, big and tall and sonsy and flushed, frozen a minute, a ploughman was by and heard every word and told the tale. And when folk had heard they said it was shameful, who was he to slander the poor quean like that? Maybe he was mad that for all his trying and the guarding of that Edinburgh wife of his he couldn't bring a single bairn in the world, let alone a healthy bit three like Eda's.

Now the village was hardly a village at all, long lines of houses fronting the road and across that the tumbling parks of the farms and the crofts, the rigs of Badymicks, the curving whin lands seeping to Bogmuck, beyond that far and a two miles off the sea and the high roofs of Maiden Castle. One end of the village was the school and schoolhouse where old Dominie Moncrief lived with his daughter, him an old creature near to retiring, her a braw lass awful keen on the lads. Betwixt was the line of the cottar's houses for roadmen and folk of like ilk and bang at the other end of the line the village shop and post-office in one, a fine big place where you'd buy anything, tow and tea and marmalade, and gingham strips and crinolines and baps and bags of peasmeal and rice and hooks and eyes and needles and stays, boots for the bairns for going to the kirk, and anything from a flea to a granite gravestone. The Munros were the folk that ran the place, father and son, and old Munro, that was Alick, was fair dottled by then and mixing up time and space and all, he'd come peering

behind a bale to serve you, his runkled old face in the light
of the crusie looking like one of the salted fish the shop sold
in such stores for the winter's dinner. He aye wore a
nightcap upon his head and fingerless mittens on his hands,
poor stock, and he it was the postmaster, Johnnie his son
carried round the letters. Folk had made a bit rhyme about
old Munro—

> He wears a nightcap on his head
>   And muggins on his han'
> And every soul that sees him pass
>   Cries Mighty, what a man!

But he'd never heard that, the thrawn old tyke, and thought
himself right well respected, and would read any letter that
came to you all over from back to front of the envelope with
a sharp like look as much as to say 'And who are you to be
having letters and disturbing a man at his real work, then?'
So he knew all the things that were going on, some said that
he and his son, young Johnnie, steamed open every letter
there was, God knows they got little for their pains if they
did.

Young Johnnie was a bit of a cripple, like, thin and
souple, but his right leg twisted on back to front as though
he'd made up his mind to go back and never come into the
world at all. But faith, Mistress Munro had beaten him at
that, out into the world he'd come at last, a thirty years
before that time, and his mother had taken a look at him
and then turned her face and just passed away. And Munro
was once telling that tale in the shop and a ploughman
childe said he didn't wonder, it was the kind of face to turn
even a mother. And Johnnie the cripple foamed with rage
and went about swearing for days what he'd have done if
that ploughman had stayed – he was awful for thinking
himself a terror, poor Johnnie.

Well, whether or no it was true that they steamed the

letters it was from the post office that the news spread round, a two months before the Lammas came in, that the Stratouns were coming back to the Howe, to Maiden Castle down by the sea that had lain lost and empty ten years. John Stratoun the son was coming back, he'd a wife and three bairns and was coming from Montrose to farm the land and put it to right and establish the Stratouns on the land again.

The Stratouns

I

Alick was eight and Peter five and Keith just turned a three years old the spring when John Stratoun left Montrose and carted the family and gear he had to Maiden Castle. He'd been foreman for the contractor in the new drains they were laying in Montrose, had father, he'd been doing that kind of work for years, but never much satisfied, he thought little of towns; and never he could take a walk on a Sabbath outside the town through the greening parks but that he would stop and dawdle and peer down at the earth and test the corn-heads and nod his own head at the nodding corn, 'Aye, God, but it's canty stuff to look at.'

Mother would say in her sharp-like way 'Don't swear like that in front of the little 'uns' and father would say 'Od, lass, did I swear? Well, well, they would hardly know what I meant' and give Alick's hair a bit of a tug, or make out he was thrappling Peter's long throat; but you were only a baby then, Keith, and he'd pitch you up in the air, high, suddenly the fields rose high, you saw Montrose and the gleam of the sea, flat and pale, and gave a scream, not frightened, you liked it, just couldn't help the scream. Mother would give another snort, such awful conduct on a Sabbath, this, what ever would the neighbours say if they saw?

Well, the stay in Montrose came suddenly to an end, Granny that bade at the other end of the town, in a little house like a lop-eared hare, died at last at her kitchen table one day, with a meikle bowl of brose before her and a coarse-like book spread out on her lap. She'd fair been a right fine granny, Keith thought, she never come into the house but she brought a man sticks of candy to suck right to the end and make himself sick, but Mother you thought didn't like her much, you'd heard her say to father once that of all the coarse creatures she'd ever set eyes on his mother, she thought, was nearly the worst.

Father had just said in his quiet-like way, "Od, lass, and maybe you're right, 'od, aye' and mother had looked mad enough to burst, if there was a thing that she couldn't abide worse than somebody to argue with her it was somebody who gave in all the time. And she'd skelped Alick's ear for leaning over the fire, and swooshed Peter out of her way from the table, and no doubt would have given you a shake as well if it hadn't been you were sitting good as gold, in a corner, cuddling the big cat, Tibbie. 'Right? Ay, I'm right. And a bonny look out to think that such blood runs in the little 'uns.' You wondered what kind of blood it was, Granny's, you thought it blue, not black, her hands were white and skinny and thin and you could see the veins when they lay at rest; maybe Mother thought blue blood awful coarse.

Well, Granny died and all the house in Montrose was fair in a stew for a day or so, mother coming and going and weeping now and then, loud out she wept, just like yourself, 'Oh, it's awful, awful, poor creature, poor creature,' she meant Granny, and father patted her shoulder 'Wheesht, lass, wheesht, she's safe and at rest.' But Mother just wept a

bit more at that, and Alick that was making a face behind
her, making on he was weeping as well, real daft, was so
funny that you and Peter burst out in a laugh. And at that
Mother stopped from her greeting at once and wheeled
round and smacked Alick one on the ear, and you and Peter
got a bit of a shake. 'Think shame of yourselves, you coarse
little brutes. Laughing and your granny new in her grave.
Whatever would the neighbours say if they heard?' And
father said quiet and bit wearied-like 'Och, they'd just say it
was Granny's coarse blood.'

But syne Father found he'd been left nearly three hundred pounds, he'd never suspected, neither had Mother,
that Granny had nearly as much as that, and they sat up half
the night whispering about it, Mother loud out saying 'Yea'
and 'Nay', father in a canny whisper, low, so that you and
Peter and Alick wouldn't waken in the meikle box bed
ayont the fire – you were all three awake and hearing each
word and tickling each other under the sheets. And whenever father might raise his voice a wee, Mother would
whisper fierce 'Wheesht! You'll waken the bairns, man'
herself loud enough to waken the dead.

And what they were arguing and bargying about was
whether or not to leave Montrose and trail away up through
the Howe to some place that father called Maiden Castle.
Mother was just as keen as father, but she wouldn't let on to
that, not her, she'd to be prigged and pleaded with half that
night and most of the next day, and again next night till at
last father said with a bit of a sigh 'All right, lass. Then we'll
stay where we are.'

At that Mother flared up 'Stay here in a toun when
you've a fine farm away in the Howe? Have you no spunk at
all to try and make you improve yourself?' and father said
nothing, just smoked his pipe, and mother started singing a
hymn-tune, loud, she aye did that when blazing with rage;
so you knew that father had won the battle.

II

Father was a meikle big man with a beard, or so you aye
thought, but Alick didn't, he said the old man wasn't bad,
but only a wee chap, and couldn't fight a bobby. But father
had fought worse than bobbies in his time, when Granny
came down to live in Montrose he'd gone to school and
grown tired of that and then worked in a flax-mill and tired
of that, till Granny had asked him in the name of God what
did he think there was to turn his useless hands to, then?
And father had said 'The land' and Granny had said that
was daft, he couldn't be a ploughman, the Stratouns had a
name to keep up in the Howe. So father had borrowed
some money from her and emigrated to a place called
America, awful wild and full up of buffaloes and bears and
wolves that at night came snuffling under the doors of the
sheds where father and others slept, snuffle, snuffle in the
moonlight. If they peered through the cracks they'd see the
glare of the eyes below. But father said he hadn't been
feared when he'd tell you the stories, and you knew he
hadn't, he'd just thought 'Ay, losh, but the poor beasts are
famished' and turned over to sleep in the other side. There
was an awful queer lot of men there, Germans and Poles
and such-like folk, father hardly knew a word they said, that
wouldn't have scunnered him, the farming did. For it
wasn't real farming at all, he told, just miles and miles
of sweet damn all, prairie and long grass and holes in the
horizon, and a bleak, dull sky night and day, hardly a tree
and at night a moon so big and red it seemed to a man the
damn thing would come banging down on the earth. And
the ploughs were the queerest and daftest things, the cattle
were scrawny and ill-kept beasts; and after six years John
Stratoun looked about and decided he'd just have a look at
Scotland. And off he set and home he had come, in a cattle-
boat, with ninety pounds of his savings tied up in a little
pock under his arm-pit, awful safe, but when he got into

Glasgow he'd forgot to keep out any change and nearly had to take all his clothes off in the railway station to pay for his ticket.

Well, he got back to Montrose, still the same, the feuch of it he smelt from the railway carriage, he'd never much liked the place, you knew, though father had a good word for near everything, every place, every soul, he ever had known, he'd have said that the devil wasn't maybe so bad, it was just the climate of hell that tried him. But as the train came coasting the sea and Montrose was below father looked out, it was harvest time, they were cutting the fields, a long line of scythemen and gatherers behind, and one of the gatherers straightened up and looked at the train and father at her, and it was mother, though she didn't know it, father did, he made up his mind at that minute, he would say, that she was to be mother (and Alick in bed would snigger about that, and say funny things and you couldn't but laugh).

She wasn't much taller than father was, but well-made, a fine-covered woman with flaming red hair and sharp blue eyes and full red lips and white strong teeth; and father thought her the bonniest thing he'd seen in all the days of his life. And he'd hardly got into Montrose with his things and knocked up Granny, she'd said 'Oh, it's you? Shut the door John, I can't abide draughts' than he was out of the place again, and bapping away back by the railway track through the long haycocks that posed to the sun and over soft stubble and so to that park.

And he made himself acquaint at the place, and got a fee there and wedded mother. And they finished the feeing and came into Montrose, to work at contracting, and that father stuck till Granny was carried at last to her grave, she's a stone above it; and years after that Keith once had a spare hour on his hands, autumn, dripping with rain and a sough of the soft and slimy sea wind from the sea of Montrose was a scum on the roofs, and he wandered into the graveyard,

dark, and looked for that stone and found it and read, queer
and moved:

Ann Stratoun.

Aged 89.

'And still he giveth his beloved sleep.'

III

It was late in the jog of an April day when our flitting of
Montrose came through the Howe, over the hill of Auchindreich and into the crinkly cup of the village, shining
weather, far up all day as we came rode little clouds like
lost feathers, high, as though some bird were lost in the lift,
moulting maybe, and beyond it the sun, and clear and
sharp all about the roads the tang and whiff of the sun-
touched earth, warm and stirring, little mists riding them
by the Luther bridge, and the teeth of a rainbow came out
and rode the seaward hills by Johnston Tower. I couldn't
see it though Alick held me up and pointed it out from the
back box-cart. And then I was sleeping to the chug and
sway of the horses' hooves and the moving cart and on the
three carts rumbled along together, father sitting in the
lead, behind him the gear he'd gotten for his farming and a
dozen hens locked up in a coup, and two ploughs dis-
mantled and loaded up and high towering about it all the
bit of the furniture that wouldn't go into the second cart, a
great oak wardrobe from Maiden Castle carted away from
there thirty five years before when Granny moved from the
place to Montrose.

And there was Laurencekirk all asleep, with its lint-mills
and its meikle bobbies about, with their big straw hats and
their long-falling beards. Now and then we met in with
some creature traipsing along the turnpike, a tink with bare
feet and hardly a stitch, his rotten sark sticking out from his
breeks, behind him his wife with a birn of bairns, they'd cry
out for silver and father would nod ''Od, aye we can surely

spare you a something.' Mother was mad and said it was wastery, what would tinks like that do with your bawbees that you'd earned yourself by the sweat of your brow? Spend it on drink, the foul stinking creatures. And Father said agreeably 'Oh ay, no doubt' giving his long brown beard a bit wipe, his brown eyes, mild, lifted up to the hills, his hands soft on the reins of the new mare, Bess.

Alick came behind with the second cart, awful proud and sitting up there like a monkey, chirking away at the gelding, Sam, Sam paying no heed but flinging his legs fine and sonsy and switching his tail and stopping now and then to ease himself, the tail switched up in Alick's face. The furniture and gear was piled in that cart and the meat we'd need when we'd gotten to Maiden, and all our clothes and the like of things, Mother as well, sitting up genteel, dressed in best black and her eyes all about, sharp and clear on everything, only her hair was just like a flame that didn't seem somehow to go with the eyes, said Geordie Allison, our new fee'd man. And he said Ay, God, she no doubt led old Stratoun a dance and fairly believed that she wore the breeks.

Geordie Allison himself drove the last of the carts, a well set-up and stocky man with a long moustache and a long red neck, he'd worked for father once in Montrose though he was a ploughman and like father couldn't stick a job that wasn't out on the land. He was awful old, we all of us thought, maybe thirty or forty or nearly a hundred, Mother didn't like him much, we were sure, she'd been awful shocked by the way he spoke to the minister man outbye from Mondynes.

We'd newly come through the wee toun of Fordoun when we met the minister, out for a walk, with his black flat hat and his long black clothes, he stood to the side of the road, and father lifted his hat to him and mother bobbed, as folk had to do when they met in with a minister childe. The minister held up his hand and father hauled at the head of

Bess and the whole three carts came showding to a halt while the minister ran his eyes over us all, wee pig eyes and not very bonny, and asked where we were going, where we'd come from, what were our ages, were we godly folk. And father just sat and looked at him douce, but mother bridled and answered him short, and at last Geordie Allison cried out from the back 'Are we standing all day with this havering skate? If he's no place to sleep let him take to the ditch, we've to get to Maiden afore the sun sets.'

Mother had been awful ashamed and red, she said after that she was black affronted, whatever would the minister say about them? them that had aye been decent folk. But father just chirked to make Bess get up 'Ay, no doubt he'll have a bit tale to tell, the lad had a nasty look in his eye. But ministers aye are creatures like that, they've nothing to do but stand and claik.' And Mother said wheesht, not to talk that way and her trying to bring up the bairns God-fearing. And Geordie Allison muttered at the back there was surely a difference between fearing God and fearing the claik of a flat-faced goat with a flat bottom bulging out his black breeks.

Then we came to a ridge between the hills, early after-noon, Peter only asleep, snoozing dead to the world, so tired, on the shelvin lashed to the back of the cart. And father said 'Well, we'll stop a while here and have a bit feed,' and Mother said no, she wouldn't have folk think they were tinks, they could eat a piece as they went along. But father just gave his brown beard a stroke and led the carts in by the side of the road, a burn flowed and spun and loitered below, minnows were flicking gold in the shadows, far up over Geyriesmuir hill there were peewits crying and crying, crying, the sound woke Peter and he cried as well, lost and amazed a minute, in the midst of the bright, clean, shining land where only far off in other parks were the moving specks of men at the harrows. And Mother came running and lifted him down and nursed him and said that he was her dawtie, he didn't much like it, Alick was sneering 'Aye, mammy's pet' and I was grinning, he could sleep his head into train oil, Peter.

But Geordie Allison was out and about, gathering broom roots and hackles of whins, and coming striding back for the kettle and tearing off down to the burn with it and setting it loaded over the fire, tea hot steaming in a mighty short while, all sitting around to drink from the cups, and eat the fine oatcakes. Mother could make better oatcakes and scones than any other soul in the Howe, or so she was to think till she got to the village and heard of the reputation of Mrs Gunn. We'd brought a great kebbuck of cheese as well, old and dried, full of caraway seeds and with long blue streaks out and in, all crumbly, and we all ate hearty, father sitting by mother and as he finished he gave her a smack on the bottom as she stood to pour him another cup 'Faith, creature, you can fair make a tasty meal, even though it's only by the side of a road.'

Mother said 'Keep your hands to yourself and don't haver. What would folk say if they saw you, eh?'

''Od, they'd go blue at the gills with envy. Let them see, let them see. Well, Keith my man, what do you think of the Upper Howe?'

But you just yawned and were sleepy again and a little bit frightened of the horses, the place, the clear cold crying of the long grey birds, all this business of going to a farm where Alick said there would be great big bulls to gore you to death, and swine that ate men, a swine had once eaten a man in Montrose, and maybe lions and wolves and bears, in an awful old Castle full of ghosts and golochs and awful things. But you chirped up 'Fine, faither' and he said you were a gey bit lad, a man before your mother all right, and then as your face grew all red and flushed he rose and carried you away from the rest, round the corner behind the whins. Other men didn't do that kind of thing, but father did, he hadn't any shame. Mother said it sometimes left her just black affronted the womanish things he could turn to. But you liked it, you gripped his hand coming back, and he patted your head, his eyes far way, forward and upward to the cup of the Howe.

And the horses were bitted and the cart-stands let down and father and Geordie lighted their pipes, blue puff-puffs, and mother smoothed down her dress, looking this way and that, with sharp, quick eyes, in case a neighbour might be looking on, though there wasn't one within twenty miles. And you all piled into the carts again and went on through the long spring afternoon, hardly it seemed it would ever end, down past Drimlithie, white and cold and sleeping under the Trusta hills, here the Grampians came marching down, green-brown, towering in snow far in the peaks, beyond as you turned by the farm of Kandy, far up and across through rising slopes, rose Auchindreich all dark and wild with the winding white track that climbed by Barras to the end of our road.

Bunches of firs in long flat plantations, the road all sossed where they grew each side, and then you were through the Fiddes woods and turned up right to tackle the hill, the sun going down and greyness coming over the hard, clear afternoon. Mother got down from the second cart and came and wrapped up the bairns, tight, in plaids, they could hardly move, Peter didn't care, just snored on, he snored with his mouth wide open and you would sometimes watch the waggle of a thing inside like a little red frog, to and fro, and think what an awful thing was a mouth, you'd queer-like fancies even then.

And looking out from the plodding carts as the last of the little farms passed you saw the dark was following you along the road and between the whins, like a creeping panther or a long black wolf, pad-pad in long loping shadow play, what if the thing were to catch you here? And as you thought that it rushed and caught, the carts were in darkness, slow thump, thump, hares were running and scuttling across the deeps of the road and far away, miles off in some lithe sheltered peak a cow was mooing in the evening quiet. Then lights began to prink here and there as they rose and rose, to the roof of the world as it seemed, though only the lip of the Howe, up and up to the long flat ridge where in ancient times the long-dead heathen had built their circles and worshipped their gods, died, passed, been children, been bairns and dreamed and watched long wolf-shapes slipper and slide about their habitations in dark, un-friended, unguarded by such a one as Geordie Allison with a fine long whip and a fine long tongue; he wasn't frigh-tened at anything, Geordie, the dark or a horse or even Mother.

You went rumbling through the Howe in the dark, father striding ahead with a lantern, mother following leading Bess. Bess hungry and dribbling soft at her hand, Mother saying 'Feuch, you nasty brute' as the mare wetted her fine Sabbath gloves; and then was sorry in the way she would be, 'Poor lass, are you wearied for your stable, then?' At that Bess nibbled some more and snickered, then shoved down her head and went bapping on, no meat till the end of the road, she knew.

Father hadn't been down that road since nearly a thirty five years, last time running and sobbing up this brae, past Badymicks to the village to send for a doctor to come look at his father dead and spread out by the barn of Maiden. But he hadn't forgotten it, striding ahead, the lantern gripped sure and canny in his hand, no fairlies vexed him minding that last time, there was nothing from the other world ever vexed a decent man if he minded his own business and hurt no one, he would face up to God at the Judgment Day, Father, and knock the shag from his pipe; 'Ay, Lord, this is fairly a braw place you have,' kind and undisturbed and sure as ever, sometimes there was some-thing in that surety of his that half-frightened Mother, was there ever such a man? And she'd cease to scold him and fuss around, seeing to his boots or his breeks or his meat, and creep against him, alone at night, and his arm go round her corded and strong 'Well, lass, tired lass?' Oh – a fine lad, John, but she mustn't be a daft, soft fool and think that.

And Mother gave Bess's reins a tug, Bess heeded nothing, swinging along, past Badymicks and the smells of Bogmuck. Father sniffed at the smells of the midden, ay, they'd fairly a fine collection of guffs, fine for the crops, fine for the crops. And already he was half-impatient to be home and settled in and get on with the work – God, man, what a smell was dung at night thick and spread on the waiting land!

But now a new smell was meeting the carts, sharp and tart and salt in the throat, the smell of the sea, and then its sound, a cry and whisper down in the dark as you wound by an over-grown rutted lane, a weasel came out and spat at Father and once the long shape of some sheep-killing dog snarled at him from the lithe of a hedge, but he paid no heed, going cannily on. He'd fallen to a wheeber, soft and quiet, a song he'd often sing to the lads:

> Oh, it's hame, dearie, hame, fain
>   wad I be,
> Hame, dearie, hame, in my ain
>   countree,
> There's a gleam upon the bird
>   and there's blossom on the tree,
> And I'm wearin' hame
>   to my ain countree.

And suddenly, great and gaunt, owl-haunted, Maiden Castle.

The boys were never to forget that spring, it wove into the fabric of their beings and spread scent and smell and taste and sound, till it obscured into a faint far mist all their days and nights in the town of Montrose. And it seemed they had bidden at Maiden forever, and would surely bide there forever. Alick would say By God he hoped not, he would rather bide in a midden, he would.

The three loons slept in the meikle box bed set up in the kitchen of the windy Castle, so long and wide with its clay floor and its low wood beams, all black and caked, that at night when you looked out from the blankets it seemed you slept in the middle of a park, far off across its stretching rigs the fire gleamed low by the meikle lum, the grandfather clock by the little low window was another door and the moonlight crept and veered and flowed on the ground, nearer and nearer, you could hear it come. And above that sound, unending, unbegun, the pelt of the tide down under Maiden, soft and whispering, where dead men were, fishes, and great big ugsome beasts, without feet or faces, like giant snails, they crept out at night from the caves in the rocks and came sniffling, sniffling up the rocks, sniffling and rolling, they'd get in at the window, you could hear the slime-scrape of a beast on the walls. And you'd bury your head below the bed-clothes and cuddle close to the sleeping Peter, he in the middle, Alick far at the side. You were only little and had to lie in the front, no defence. And Peter would stop in his snoring a minute and consider, and give a grunt and a torn groan, and start in hard at his snoring again till you'd think in a minute his head would fall off, clean sawn through – Losh, how he could sleep!

And at last so would you, curled up and small, and the next thing you know that the morning was come, five o'clock and father and mother up, a windy dawn on the edge of the dark, the dark rolling back from the sleeping Howe parks like a tide of ink, a keen Spring wind breenging and spitting in from the sea, gulls on its tail – ay, rain today. And Father would button up his jacket and grab a great horn lantern in each hand, and cry up the stairs, 'Are you ready, Geo man?' and Geordie Allison come clattering down and out they go to tend to the cattle, the horses, the pigs, tackitty boots striking fire from the stones in the close as they waded through the midden over to the dim sleeping cattle court, frosty in steam from the breath of the kine.

Behind in the kitchen Mother, a scarf wrapped round her flaming hair, would be shooting to and fro and back and about and up again, collecting pails and sieves and pans, and oilcake for the calves and a little dish to give the cats that bade in the byre, five of the brutes, a taste of milk. And at last, with a guano sack about her, as an apron, and her frock kilted up high, she'd go banging out of the kitchen door; and Alick would groan from the far side of the bed: 'The old bitch would waken Kinneff Kirkyard,' he was funny, Alick, aye fighting with Mother.

Father and Geordie would be meating the horses, four of them now, fat and neighing, waiting their corn and straw steamed with treacle, as Mother opened the door of the byre and went in to the hanging lantern there, and banged down her pails on the calsay floors. The cats would come tearing out to meet her, mewing and purring, and mother would say 'Get out of my way, you orra dirt!' and kick them aside, but not very hard, and get the leglin down from the wall and stride over the sharn to the big cow Molly. 'Get over, lass,' and Molly would get over, and down Mother would sit and start to milk, slow at first, then faster and faster, the milk hissing, creaming, into the pails, the five cats sitting in a half-circle below, watching, or washing their faces, decent, and now and then giving a little mew, and the kittens dabbing at the big one's tails.

Father would bring in bundles of straw and throw them in the stalls in front of the kine, 'A fine caller morning with wind in the loft. We'll need to take advantage o't. Can you hurry up the breakfast, lass?'

Mother would turn her head from the cow, 'Hurry? And

what do you think I'm doing now? Having a bit of a sleep in the greip?'

''Od no, you're fine. But just have the breakfast right on time. We're beginning the meikle Stane Field today.'

So mother would be tearing down to the house in less than ten minutes, skirts flying, pails flying, nearly flying herself, crying to the boys 'Aren't you up yet? Think shame of yourselves lying there and stinking. Out you get, Alick and Peter.' Peter would grumble 'Well, you told us to lie and not mess about in your road in the morning' and Mother would snap as she shot to the fire and stirred in handfuls of meal in the pot: 'None of your lip, you ill-gotten wretch,' and Alick would mutter 'And none of yours,' but awful low, Mother was a terror to skelp.

So out the two of them would get from the bed, gey slow, Oh God, it was awful, just a minute longer and they wouldn't have felt as though their faces would yawn from their heads. They'd have mixed up their clothes the night before as they went to bed, Alick would have lost his breeks or his scarf, Peter had kicked his boots under the bed, and they'd have a bit of a fight while they dressed, and Peter would say from his solemn fat face 'Punch me again and I'll tell mother.'

'Oh, aye, you would, you mammy's pet. You're worse than Keith.'

'I'm not.'

'You are. Who's feared at the kine? Who's feared at a punch? Even Keith could make you greet if he tried.'

Mother would cry 'None of your fighting. Alick, get out and open the hen-rees, and mind that you don't chase the chickens. Peter, come and give the porridge a steer. Are you wakened, my dawtie little man?'

You would whisper from the bed 'Ay mother, whiles' it was true enough, sometimes you'd hear and see for a minute, then there came a long blank, you were swimming about, down into darkness, up into light of the cruse-lamp above the fire. But now Mother had dowsed that, it was nearly daylight, through the kitchen window you could see far off the parks all grey in that early glim, waiting and watching like tethered beasts, with a flick of their tails the line of seagulls rising and cawing in by Kinneff. And Mother would pull out the meikle table, well-scrubbed and shining, and get down the caps, big wooden bowls with horn spoons, and lift the porridge pot off the fire, black and bubbling, pour out the porridge, set the great jug of milk in the middle and breakfast was ready and out on the close was the sound of the feet of father and Geordie coming for it, and behind them Alick, he'd let out the hens, nobody looking and shooed them and tried a new swear-word on them, and slipped into the stable, given Bess a pat, taken a draw at Geordie's pipe left alight in the top of a girnel, been nearly sick, walloped a calf that looked at him nasty-like in the byre, and eaten a handful of locust beans he'd nicked from the sack in the turnip-shed. And now he came looking as good as gold and quiet, and Mother said 'That's my man. You're fair a help. Sit into the breakfast.'

Then father would bow his head above the table, big brown beard spread out on his chest in tufty ends, and say the grace, decent and quiet:

> Our Father which art in heaven
> Hallowed be thy name
> And bless these mercies for our use
> For Christ's sake, Amen.

But the boys didn't know that these were the words and for years after that you would sit and wonder what God was doing with a chart in heaven and why father should swear at the end of the grace, folk only used the name of Christ when a horse kicked them head first into a midden or they dropped a weight on their toes and danced, or a flail wheeled round and walloped them one as they flung up an arm at thrashing-time. Only you knew Father couldn't be swearing, not really, else Mother would have been in a rage, instead of sitting there perky and quick, flaming hair, Geordie Allison said if ever fire failed them here in the Maiden they could warm their nieves at the mistress's hair.

'So you're tackling Stane Park this morning then?'

Father said 'Ay we'll be at it all day. Can you send out the dinner at twelve, would you say?' and Mother said couldn't he come home for it, like a decent man, he'd be tired enough, her eyes upon him in that way that she sometimes had, it made you ashamed that anybody should look at father, like that. But father shook his head, no time, they were far behind with the season as it was, must hash on ahead and try and catch up. 'Ready, Geo?' and Geordie would nod 'Faith, nearly, when I've sucked down the last of the brose. Right, Maiden, then, I'll be following you,' he called father Maiden and it sounded queer till you learned that all the farmer folk were called by the names of the farms they had, you were glad that you bade in Maiden Castle and not at a place like Bogmuck, you thought awful to have folk call father muck.

So off the two of them would stamp together, up across the close to the stable door, the four horses standing harnessed within, champing and clinking, father would chirk 'Come away, then, Bess' and Bess, at the furthest end of the stable would back down slow in her stall and turn and come showding down to the stable door. Behind her Sam and Dod and Lad, and as Bess came opposite Father would twist his hand in her mane and shove his boot in her swinging britches, and vault on her back with only a swing, Geordie couldn't, he'd to stop his horse and climb on with a stone to help, he said father was the swackest man he knew and folk wouldn't have guessed it, him stocky as that.

Through the close they'd ring and out into the road that led winding up to the heights of Stane Park, broom-sur-

rounded, a woesome place, whins and broom and a schlorich of weeds had crept from the coarse land year on year as
Maiden lay fallow as any maid; and this park Father set to
break in with a double plough and fresh-sharpened socks,
every day it was Alick's job to take socks and coulters to the
smithy at Moss Bank for Sandy, the daft-like creature, to
sharpen. So wild was the park with knife-grass and weeds,
and great boulders that tried to lie down in the grass and
scape the drive of the plough as it came. But midway the
park were the stones from old time that gave the place its
unco name, a circle of things flat and big, where the
heathen had worshipped and had a fair time dancing,
and singing and worshipping the sun, the foul creatures,
instead of going decent to kirk with fine long faces and
wearing lum hats.

And all about, the morning rising, other teams would be
out in the parks, near at hand the straining teams of
Balhaggarty shoring the slopes, team on team, with the
gulls behind, their cries coming down the wind and the
sound as the childe wheeled round the harrows and turned:
'Gee up, there, wissh.' 'Come on, you brute.' Beyond these
slopes was a wink of the land of Badymick, Arch out in his
fields, whistling, his whistle clear in the air, in the sky, him
and the larks both daft together, whistling away for dear life
up there, and a little dot trotting at the heels of him as he
drove the sholt and the cow in the harrows, that would be
Rachel, the daughter creature, small and sallow and a
queer-like bairn to come of the red-faced stock of the
Howe. Cruickshank's men one would hardly see except
as Father turned at the foot of the park to go back up the
drill and then he could see on the edge of the cliffs, poised
between earth and sky in that light, the team that Cruickshank drove to work, a mule and a sholt and in front of
them, tracing, the old wife herself, by God.

Father would take off his jacket and fold it and yoke the
horses to the swingle trees and spit on his hands, high and

clear the sky, the horses straining, waiting the words, 'Come away then lass, come away then, Lad,' off they'd go curling the furrow behind, and behind that Geo Allison sweating and swinging, one foot in the drill and another out, and crying to the Bees of horses to steady, God damn't, did they think they were hares, not horses? And the sun would be rising, the sea-mists going, wheeling, they would look down on Maiden Castle with its old walls skellaching over the sea and Father would think a minute, maybe: 'That thing'll be dangerous, I shouldn't but say,' but not severe or meikle disturbed, his was the nature to trust even a tower.

No sooner were the men folk out of the way then Mother was in a stew to get things redded up, hens meated, calves out, the kye new-bedded, the milk churned, Alick and Peter got ready for school, all at one and all at the same whip. And she'd do it too, like whirlwind, just, and Alick and Peter would be held and scrubbed till the skin gey nearly peeled from their noses and their breeks pulled up and their galluses fastened and asked if they'd been to the you-know-where, and they'd say, ashamed 'Och, aye,' even it if wasn't true; and Mother would say 'Have you got your books? Here are your pieces and off you go. See you behave yourself with the Dominie.'

They'd cry back 'Och aye. Ta-ta, mother. Ta-ta, Keith' and you would run to the head of the courtyard where bare and white stone circles lay to take the stacks at the harvest's end: 'Ta-ta!' and they'd wave and Alick, if Mother wasn't looking, would put his fingers to the end of his nose and spread them out and add the fingers of the other hand and stand on one leg and wheel round about, making fun of the Howe and Maiden Castle, the teams in the parks and the sun in the sky, he was fairly a nickum was Alick, said Geo Allison.

Father once caught him doing that and said ''Od, laddie, is your nose so ticklish?' Alick said that it wasn't, but father said it must be and caught Alick under his oxter, gentle, and upended him and rubbed his nose in the earth, to and fro and Alick howled and father dropped him and stroked his beard: 'I'll ay be pleased to help you, Alick.'

Alick stood up and went away grumbling, but he said he didn't mind the old man, if it had been Mother caught him at that she'd have deaved the backside from a sow about it, him-disgracing-the-house-and-taking-the-Lord's-name-in-vain, just-awful-and-what-would-the-neighbours-say-about-it.

When they'd gone it was your chance to ransack the place and play the devil, and climb down the rock with hands holding the grass, down and down to the water's edge, the tide going out, far on the rocks shells and fine things littering the beach, fill all your pouches, there was a seagull, 'Shoo away, creature' slow flap-flap it rose, yourself up the rock and round the mill-course and spread out your shells in the sun. By then the cats would have crept from the byre and come round in a circle to watch you a while, but whenever you'd your house with the shells built up they'd mew through the middle and knock it down, they were awfully ignorant creatures, cats.

You'd weary a while of the playing then, and lie flat on your back and look up at the sky, pale-grey, and wan in the slight spring sun, rooks cawing about the firs, high and far, caw-caw, unending; and there, a blink on the edge of the day, a thing like curtains sweeping on Maiden. You'd seen it before and knew what it meant and would race for the shelter of the cart-shed and watch, the curtain would wheel and the sun shine through, there rainbows glimmer and then the wash of the rain was pelting the roofs and sweeping up inland across the Howe, drooking the parks a minute, passing. Father and Allison wrapped a minute in the flay and sweep of the water, shining out next minute not hurted at all. It must be fine fun to be a man.

At eleven o'clock Mother would have made the dinner,

porridge again, or stew of a rabbit, and loaded that into a pail and that into a great big basket with plates, four spoons, a bit of the kebbuck of cheese, a flask of the ale that she made herself; and slung the basket over her arm and cried 'Come on, Keithie, we'll away with the dinner.'

You hated her to call you Keithie, but trotting beside her her hand was kind, helping you up the chave of the road and on to the track that led to Stane Park. Father would see the two of you coming and draw in the horses at the tail of a drill, and Geordie Allison follow him in that, they'd loosen the harness and wipe down the horses and then come and sit under the lithe of the broom while mother dished the dinner out, sharp and quick with her scornful eye and her big red face and her thick-lipped mouth. 'Ay, well, it doesn't look as though the two of you've done much in spite of all your haste to be out.'

' 'Od, woman, I'm sure we haven't been idle. What think you, Geordie?'

'Well, damn't, man Maiden, you must speak for yourself. Maybe you lay down and had a bit snooze, I didn't or else my memory's going.'

'That'll do, Geordie Allison. Here, here's your plate. Fill up your gyte and give's less of your din.'

And they'd all sit and eat, the horses nibbling grass, the sun flaring, the team in the other parks would have loosed and going swinging up to their biggings far off in the bothy of Bahaggarty some childe would be singing as he made his brose:

> And Jean, the daft bitch, she would kilt
>   up her coat
> From her toes to her knees, from her
>   knees to her throat
> And say to her lad, as blithe as you
>   please—

And Mother would say it was just disgusting, those tinks of ploughmen and the things they sang, bairns hearing them too. You wished that you could have heard what the lass said, but father just nodded and said 'Od, aye, he'd never seen much fun in singing that kind of stuff about your lass, even though she's been as kind and obliging as the singer said, there was a time and place for these kind of pleasures, and the time to sing about them was when you were having them.

Mother would turn redder than ever at that and said 'For shame, Maiden, you brute,' and father give his beard a slow stroke and say 'Well, lass, I've sang with you, and you with even less on your back than the lass in the song of that bothy billy.'

Father was sore behind with his fields, but he was winning as the Spring drew on, the Stane Field at last had been ploughed and harrowed, and a day came when bags of the new manure were carted from Stonehaven down to Maiden and from there out along the top of Stane Park and edgeways on to the long moor fields, two of them and the narrow one that fronted the sea and was needed for turnips. Father planned to manure the lot, the land had lain fallow in fine condition, but a touch of manure would kittle it up. And you would come out and watch them at it, still Spring, and still the fine weather holding, father swinging the hamper in front and broadcasting the manure with swinging hands, Geordie Allison toiling behind him and the sacks with a pail in each hand to replenish the hamper, the manure flying out in white clouds as they worked, shrill and queer down by the sea the clamour of the tide returning again, to you it seemed sometimes those afternoons would never end, on and on, till the sun at last, wearied with manure, sunk half-way down and looking out on the winding track that led to the Howe you would see two specks that moved and loitered and halted once a little way and stopped and considered, a long half-hour, Peter, Alick –

coming home from school and digging out their boots from the ditch where they'd hidden them as they set out for school, Mother had intended them to be decent but at school the scholars had laughed at them, they went barefoot day in and day out and Mother would sometimes see their feet, at night and say 'Well, God be here, however did you get your soles scratched like that?' And Alick would say 'Och, we just had a game. Mother, can I have some supper now.' And Mother would say 'Supper at your age? Away to your bed, let's have no more of you.'

But before that came had come loosening time, the four horses, unyoked from the harrow or ploughs and brought champing in through the cobbled close, caked with sweat, father in the lead as they stopped and drank at the meikle stone trough. 'Steady on, Bess. Don't drink so fast,' he was as careful of a horse at the tail of the day as he was of one at the early morning. But Geordie Allison would be crabbed and tired: 'Come on, you old brute' he would say to Lad, 'God Almighty what are you standing there doing. Praying?' and gave him a clap in the haunch that would send old Lad through the close at a trot and breenging like a one-year old into the stable. Father never said a word, for he knew Geo tired, as some folk could be, he himself never. So the two would meat the beasts in the half twilight and rub them down and water them, and straighten up and look at each other, and take down their jackets from the stable door.

'Ay, man, well, I think we'll away in for supper.'

'Faith, Maiden, I think we've half earned it.'

Summer and the cutting of the short wild hay, there'd be no time to lay down clover, Father got out a couple of heuchs and he and George Allison were at it all day on the long salt bents that rose from the sea beyond the peaked curl of the castled Headland. Then came broiling weather and the water failed inside the yard of Maiden Castle, the well went lower and lower each day till at last father had the roof taken off and he and Mother and Geordie looked down, the thing was old and green-coated, far down the water shone in half-mirk. Father took off his coat and went down, Mother watching, white faced, crying to him not be a silly-like gawpus now, as he usually was, and not spoil the water.

She and George Allison lowered pails while Father stood to the knees in mud and loaded the pails and had them pulled up, pail after pail through a long summer day, when he came up at last he was caked with dirt but canny and kind and calm as ever. 'Aye, well, we'll tackle the rest the morn.'

And tackle it they did, father again went down with a spade and pails and moiled in the half-dark and cleared out the mud and stones and dirt that clanjamfried the bent of the well. Geordie Allison pulled them up to the top and flung out each pailful over the dyke, spleitering out in the long wide arc to the boil and froth of the sea below, you thought it fun and at every throw let out a scream till Mother came running, flame-hair and red face gone white, and thrashed you because you had feared her so. And Geordie said when she'd gone to the house never to fear, you'd grow up yet and be able to thrash a woman himself, that would be some consolation like for the aching doup that you had at the moment.

So they cleared out the well and the water started slow to come in, Geordie Allison was made to load barrels in a cart and go up to the village and borrow there while father stayed and watched the well. And at first the water was a dribble, slow and then it came in jets and bursts, and father went down the rope to taste it and came back with his face a bit sober like. And he cried out 'Lass,' and mother came. 'The water in the well – just have a look in.'

So mother looked in and you did as well and nearly fell head first over the coping, seeing the pour and spray of it. And Father told Mother the water was salt, the sea had got in and the well was finished.

They sent off that night for a ploughman childe that sometimes worked on Balhaggarty, an old, slow stepping, quiet-like man, and he came down that evening as the light grew dim and chapped at the door and spoke to Father. And he said 'Well, well, it's my wee bit stick you need, I doubt,' and drew out a moleskin case from his pouch, the three boys crowding round to look. And inside the case was a bit of wood, no more, Alick said aloud what was the daft old gype thinking he was doing with that.

But he and Father went out from Maiden and walked slow up and down in the park out from the Castle where the headland rose. And after a while the ploughman childe pointed at the stick he held in his hand, it was wriggling about like a snake alive. 'You'll find water here, and not over-deep. And my fee'll be five shillings, man.'

Father said there was nothing else for it; and they dug the well through the month that followed, whenever they managed to get back from the work, digging and hafting in the evening light, Geordie Allison swearing under his breath by God when he fee'd he'd fee'd as a ploughman not as some kind of bloody earth-mole. But Father was the queerest man to work with, he never answered, just looked at him kind, with far away look that was somehow fey, and made a body fell silent to wondered, and felt ashamed to have vexed the man – aye, God, a queer character, Stratoun of Maiden.

And when at last the well was finished and sweet water flowing in Father said that they'd have a day off, what would Geo Allison do with the money if he had a ten shillings given him? Geordie said that apart from fainting with surprise he'd take the lot into Aberdeen and have such a real good blinding drunk he wouldn't know a known man's face. Father brought out his wallet and counted ten shillings into Geo's hand, Geo standing with his lower jaw hung down like a barn door that was badly used. Then he habbered 'Well, Maiden, well man, this is fine,' and turned and went off to the bothy room. Mother had seen and heard it all and she was in an awful rage at Father: 'You heard what the creature said he would do?' And father gave his beard a bit stroke and mother a bit of a clap on the bottom ''Od, aye, lass, I heard, as I'm not very deaf. And what for no? Let every man follow the gait of his guts.'

Mother said she never heard such coarse talk and father should be ashamed of himself, how would his bairns grow up to behave if they heard him say the like of that? Father said they'd no doubt trauchle long; and he didn't expect that Geo, sonsy man, would be as daft as behave as he'd said.

But faith, that was just what Geo did, next morning he wasn't to be found in Maiden, and the long red farmer childe of Bogmuck was out in the seep of the autumn morning, taking his ease, he'd had an awful night with eating over meikle salt fish to his supper, when he saw a man going over the hills, bapping it away Stonehaven way. And that man was Geo Allison and no other, he walked the whole way to Aberdeen, canny-like, to save his silver, through the Dunnottar woods of Stonehaven that scent in green all the countryside, Stonehyve itself was asleep as he passed but for a stray cat or so on the prowl and a couple of lasses that lay in the gutter, mill-lasses caught and ill-used by the fishers the night before, with their petticoats torn and their breasts sticking out, a dirty disgusting sight, Geordie thought, why couldn't the foul slummocks have stayed at home? They were just beginning to waken up but he paid them no heed and went shooting through, up the long road by Cowie and Muchalls, through Newtonhill with never a rest, the sun had risen and the teams were out, blue rose the smoke from the morning pipes as the scythe-men bent in rows to the hay, here and there Geo Allison would meet with a tink or a gentry creature in a fine bit gig, and he paid heed to neither rich nor poor and near two o'clock in the afternoon looked down and there under his feet was the grey granite shine of Aberdeen, smoke-clouded, with the smoke of the sea beyond, a gey fine place though awful mean, and as full of pubs and cuddlesome whores as the head of a Highlander full of fleas.

And Geordie started on the first pub he came to and worked on canny into Aberdeen, outside the fifth pub was a cart and horse and Geo jumped in and drove off in the thing, careering over the calsays a while till he tired of that and the folk all shouting, so he halted the thing in a quiet-like street and went into another pub, near and convenient, and said to the man 'A nip of your best.' And when the man drew the nip and set it down Geo of a sudden took a scunner at his face and gave the barman one in the eye to waken him up and teach him better than carry a face like that in public. It took the barmen and three other folk to throw Geo out on his head on the calsays, it did Geo no ill, he staunched the blood and crept round the back of a shed for a sleep, he woke up just as the dark was coming and counted his change, he still had four shillings. So he started in through the lighted street, and had here a drink and there a cuddle, pubs and whores as thick as he'd thought, then it all faded to a grey kind of haze, he'd a fight with a sailor, and he and a lass had gone and lain on a heap of straw, a gey fine lass though she thought him drunk and tried to rape his pouches for him, he'd given her a cure that cured her of that, and syne the mist had come down again, he'd argued with a policeman, and held a horse and stood in front of a stall for a while, singing, till they told him he'd better move on; and at last, in one of the last of the pubs, or thereabouts, he'd suddenly thought how full up this Aberdeen was of Tories, the scum of the earth, the dirty Bees. So he started telling the pub about it, and next time he woke up the stars were fading, a windy dawn grey over Aberdeen, he was lying in a puddle of urine in the street, and he'd been so thrashed and kicked about he thought for a while he could hardly walk. But faith, he could, and turned him about, and

picked out the north star, and turned his back, and started
on the road for home again.

And that was Geo Allison's day in Aberdeen, Father
laughed when he told him the tale, "Od man, you got little
for your silver, I think.' Geo Allison said that Maiden was
mistaken, he'd got a change, and changes were lightsome as
the monkey said when he swallowed the soda.

By September the Maiden Parks on the uplands were
rustling in long green-edged gear that every evening lost
some of the green and turned a deeper and deeper yellow,
though Stane Hill loitered behind the rest and scratched at
its rump and slept at its work and wouldn't waken, a real
coarse Park. Father went the round of them and looked at
the earth in the evening light, the crumbly sods and the
crackling corn and the rustle far down through the forest of
stalks as some hare lolloped off, filled up, to its bed. Above
the sky a shining bowl of porcelain, flecked and tinged in
blue, Father stroking his beard and nodding eyes far off on
the shining slopes where Auchindreich climbed up purple
into the coming of the darkness' hand. 'We'll start the
cutting the morn's morn.'

They hired a band of tink creatures from Bervie, ragged
and lousy and not over honest, they'd nip in the hen-
houses and steal mother's eggs if she weren't looking, the
clothes from the line, the meal from the barn, and the dirt
from under your fingernails. And Alick going in, in the
quiet of an evening to steal a handful of locust beans came
tearing out with his face all red 'Father, the spinners have
been stealing the beans,' in a fury about it, but Father not.
He took Alick's ear in his right hand, soft, "Od, have they
so? And not left some for you?' – Mornings, right on the
chap of six, the bouroch of tinks were in Maiden close,
waiting for the master the Geo Allison and the man they
had hired from the village, warm, a cool wind up from the
sea drifting through the clouds of the warmth as the lot set

off for the Tulloch Park, or Joiner's End or at last Stane Muir.

And Father would halt inside the gate, the lot behind him, and take off his jacket, roll up his sleeves, and whet his scythe, the ring of it echoing up through the half-light, all the ground grey and dry and waiting, scuttle of little birds deep in the corn, Geo Allison whetting his scythe behind him and the man from the village with a spit and growl using his whetstone and telling the tinks to stand well back if they had the fancy to keep their legs. Then Father would bend and swing out slow, and cut and the sheaf of corn would swish aside, quicker and quicker, till at last he got the pace for the bout, behind him the other two following, uneven at first till they got the rhythm, the gatherers following, gathering and binding, quick and sure, their thin white faces straining and white, gasping as they flung the sheaves aside. Behind, if they looked up a dizzied moment they'd see on all the parks of the Howe the glitter of far scythe-blades, shining, gleaming, ay, man a fine sight, a real good harvest and the weather holding.

You would come out with Mother whiles when she brought the pieces for the harvesters, oatcake and ale and a bite of cheese for the gatherers, they called her Mem to her face, what they called her behind her back she never guessed, you did, you heard one and your heart nearly stopped, frightened and angry and wanting to cry. But for Geo and Father there were white sheaves and scones, milk and great yellow dollops of butter, Alick and Peter were on school holiday and would come tearing in about as well and sit and stare and look fearfully starved, Mother didn't heed, if they couldn't stay and help in the parks they could wait for their dinners at the ordinary times.

Then one noon a great black cloud like the hand of a man fast-clenched in rage rose up above the shining humps of the Grampians far way in the east, across the haste of the harvesting Howe, folk stopped and stared at the thing and

swore, it wheeled and opened and gleamed in the sun,
bonny you thought it, only a kid, you didn't know better,
Geo Allison swore 'God damn't, that's the end of harvest
today.' The hand was unfolding and whirling west, a little
wind went moaning in front like a legion of kelpies, the
devil behind, over the hill of Auchindreich, the sun went,
bright and shining a minute, dark the next, then the swish
of the rain. Father cried to you 'Run for the house, my
man,' you ran, legs twinkling in and out, fun to see your
own legs twinkling, fell twice, didn't cry, too brave, you'd
show the damned rain, couldn't catch you, there was the
barn door and Peter and Alick standing inside crying
'Come on, Doolie,' they called you Doolie, and you them
Bulgars under your breath, an awful word you mustn't let
mother hear.

It rained for nearly two days and nights, the sea well
frothed over and out of the streaming windows of the tower
the sea looked like the froth of a soup tureen, far away as the
evening closed the fisher boats of Stonehyve and Gourdon
reeled into safety with drooked sails, the fog horn moaned
down by Kinneff and the gatherers all went back to Bervie.
Father sat in the barn, twisting ropes out of straw, Geo
Allison or Alick fed the straw, father twisting, fun to watch,
when you grew up you'd do that as well and be a big farmer
and have a brown beard and marry mother and sleep with
her and give her a smack in the bottom, like that, when she
was in a rage about something or other.

You thought that the harvest was finished then, you'd
stay in the barn day on day and twist up ropes, lonely
playing, and listen for rats, Towser and you, he wagged his
tail and cocked his ears and looked at you, sly, you the
same, squeak the rat, the dirl of the rain swooping over the
byres, go on for ever and when next Spring came you'd be a
big man and go to school. But then the rain cleared off in a
blink, late in the evening, father went out the round of the
parks, you hung on his hand, still all the fields except that

up in Balhaggarty a bothy childe was singing clear, to the soft drip-drip of the bending corn-heads.

The whins were a dark green lour in the light and father stopped and looked up at them, and smelt the wind, and looked down the fields at the glisten of the sea as it drew into dark and pulled its blankets over its head. And just as the two of you stood and listened there came a thing like a quiet sigh, like a meikle calf that sighed in sleep, grew louder, the wet head of the corn moved round and shook, father nodded. 'Ay, fine, it'll be dry ere the morning, Keith.'

And next day they started in on the harvest again, and got through it afore October was out, all cut and bound and set in stooks, great moons came that hung low on the plain above the devils stones in the old Stane Park while Geo Allison and father led by moonlight driving out Bess with an empty cart through the scutter and flirt of the thieving rabbits, the brutes came down in droves from the hills and ate up stooks and riddled the turnips, through the plaint and wheesh of the peesies flying, dim and unending through the moon-hush, to the waiting lines of the sound-won sheaves. Then they'd pack the carts full and plod back to the close and set to the bigging of the grain-stacks there, the harvest moon lasted nearly a week and one Sunday night Father looked at the sky and said they'd better take advantage of the grieve weather that lasted. Mother was in all her Sabbath clothes, she said to Father 'Think shame of yourself. Lead on the Sabbath, there would come a judgment on us.' Father said 'Well, lass, maybe there will. But it's work of necessity and mercy, you ken,' and mother said it was no such thing she was sure, but just clean greed, and whatever would the neighbours say?

But 'od, the creatures had no time to say a thing, the scandal of that night was soon all over the Howe, no sooner did dusk come down that Sabbath over all the touns than canny folk who had been to the kirk and stood up there right decent by the sides of their women, snuffling the Hundredth Psalm right godly, took a taik indoors and off with their lum hats and their good black breeks and their long coats with the fine swallow tails and howked on their corduroys and their mufflers and went quet from their houses out to the stables, and yoked up the horses, whistling under-breath, and took out on the road to the waiting stooks. And all that night the Howe was leading, ere morning came there wasn't a standing stook in the Howe, all the harvest in and well-happed and bigged; and a man had time to sit down with his paper and read of the Irish Catholics, the dirt, them that wanted Home Rule and the like silly fairlies, the foul ungodly brutes that they were.

The Potato harvest was next on the go, Geo Allison said to Father, 'Maiden, if we want to be clear of the rot this year we'll need to howk up and store fell early, I can feel in my bones a wet winter's coming.' Father said Faith then, he was sorry about the bones, but it was real kind of them to give the warning, he and Geo would tackle the potatoes the morn. And so they did, Alick and Peter and Mother to help, you yourself ran up and down the drills and looked at the worms, big ones, pushing their heads out of holes and watching the gatherers, you liked worms, but Mother said 'Feuch, you dirty wee brute' when you showed her your pockets full up of them. So you took them away to the end of the park and laid them all out on a big flat stone, they wriggled and ran races, fun to tickle them, but they wouldn't speak to you, they were awful sulky beasts, worms, when they were offended, like.

Geo Allison said that of all the foul coarse back-breaking jobs ever invented since Time was clecked potato-gathering was surely the worst, he'd a hole in his back above his dowp where his spine and his bottom had once joined on. Mother turned right red when she heard him say that and told him 'None of your vulgar claik', but father just said Geo must

bear with the thing and fill up on fried tatties throughout
the winter, funny man, father, Alick said he was daft,
messing about with the drills at the end and going all over
the land again and making as sure as a sparrow with dirt
that there wasn't even a little wee tattie left, when Alick was
big he wasn't to stay at home here, he was going to grow up
and get a fee as a farm-servant on a place down the Howe,
and drive big Clydesdales and every night go and sleep with
a lass at the back of a stack, same as the Reverend Adam
Smith did with his housekeeper.

That was at the end of the potato harvest he said that, the
three of you sitting round the tattie pits, sorting out rotten
tatties from the fresh, clean ones, a snell wind blew. And
Alick boasted some more about what he would do, Peter
listening half asleep as usual, you yourself began to speak as
well, you said you wouldn't sleep with anybody, ever, when
you were big, but alone by yourself, and you'd be a cattler
and look after bulls. And Alick said 'Go away and not
blether, Doolie,' Alick was a cruel beast and you thought
sometime when you were grown up, maybe ten or eleven,
you'd get him alone you with father's gun, and blow off his
head, right, with a bang, and that would teach him, that
would.

But you caught a cold out by the pits that afternoon on
November's edge, it closed and choked about your wind-
pipe, Mother cried that God, the bairn was smoring when
you sat at supper and caught you up, something red with a
long forked tail seemed running and scuttling up and down
your throat and then you saw father rise from the table, face
all solemn, and cry to Geo Allison. Then you were taken off
to bed, Mother's room, mother carrying you, sometimes
you didn't like her at all, now – only with her safe and alone,
if only she would hold you all the time, in darkness you
woke and screamed for her and she held you close, funny
texture her breast, smell of it, long hair about you, but the
devil was back, fork-tailed, racing up and down your throat,

low in the hush of one night you woke with the blatter of sleet on the window-panes, sudden in that hush the cry of an owl.

So you saw little or nothing of that year's end, Hogmanay for you was blankets, hot drinks, father's grave face, did he think you'd die? You closed your eyes a little and waited and then the funniest thing started to happen, the room and chairs began to expand and explode all about you, growing bigger and bigger, you looked at your arm, like the leg of a horse, you could see it swell and swell as you looked till it filled the whole room and blotted out everything, then Mother reached down shook you, 'Keithie, here's your broth.'

So Hogmanay went by, you heard skirling in the kitchen, somebody singing, somebody laughing, whistle of strange sleet one morning as you woke and looked out and there it was snowing white, ding dong out and across the happed lands, through the wavering pelt you could see from the window the smoke rise far from Balhaggarty, from the bouroch of trees that hid the kirk, black things, the crows, flying above it, oh, winter had come and you couldn't go out, you'd wanted to play in the snow.

Father said to the Doctor will the little'un die? and the Doctor was big and broad and buirdly, he'd ridden from Bervie on his big fat sholty, he shook his head 'Faith no, not him. He's spunk in him, this bit son of yours, But he'll gang a queer gait by the look of him.' Father asked how and the Doctor said 'Faith, have you never used your eyes on him? He's as full up of fancies and whigmaleeries as an egg of meat, he's been telling me his dream and his fancies, – faith, that's a loon that'll do queer things in the world.' Father said 'Well, well, if he' does no ill, he may do what he fancies, I'll not bar his way.'

But after that Father and Mother were queerer, they'd look at you queer now and then and syne nod, and you hear the story about the doctor and couldn't make out what they meant at all you'd just had a dream, every body had dreams. But you were growing up, oh, that was fine, a bairn no longer, to school next year, this first year at Maiden Castle put by.

Book II
Schooling

AS THE NEW YEAR came blustering into the Howe, folk
took the news of the parish through hand, standing up
douce and snug in the bar and watching the whirl and break
of the flakes that the wind drove down from the hills to the
sea like an old wife shake the chaff from a bed. Ay, God
there hadn't been a winter like this, said Gunn of Lamahip,
since 'yt, he minded it well, he was fee'd at that time up in a
place in Aberdeen, called Monymusk, one morning he
woke and looked out of the bothy window, b'god, the farm
place had vanished entire, nothing about but the shroud of
the snow. So he'd louped from his bed and gotten a spade
and hacked his way from the bothy door and set to
excavating the lady, gey rich and stuck up, that owned
the place. Well, he chaved from morning nearly till noon
and at last got a tunnel driven through, and reached the
front door and broke down that. And the lady said she'd
seen many a feat, but never that kind of feat before, and
raised his wages right on the spot and hardly left him a-be
after that, maybe running in to see him in the bothy, he got
scunnered of her after a while, though a gey soft keek and
canty to handle—

Arch Camlin of Badymicks had come in, he said 'God,
Gunn, are you at it again? Cuddling the jades'll yet be your
ruin.' Gunn gave his great big beard a bit stroke, 'Faith,
man, it might once, but I've gotten by that. Did I ever tell
you of that sawmill place that was owned by a countess
creature in Angus. Well, one day she said to me, "John,
man"'

Young Munro, the nasty wee crippled thing said 'Faith, she was making a doubtful statement,' and Gunn turned round and said 'Faith, and what's that?' and Munro said 'That you were a man. Ay, God, Lamahip, you can fairly blow.'

That was a nasty one for Lamahip, folk sipped their drams slow and squinted at them, and wondered if Gunn would take the crippled creature a bit of a bash on his sneering face to teach him better manners, like. But he couldn't well do that with a cripple, and God, it was doubtful if he'd understood the nasty bit insult of the nasty creature, he went stitering on with the tale of his women, folk yawning and moving away from him and watching from the window a childe or so coming swinging up from the storm-pelted road into the shelter and lights of the bar. There was Dalsack of Bogmuck that fine-like childe, his boots well clorted up with sharn, he'd been spending the day mucking out the cattle-court and came in now eident and friend-like and shy, and said to Craigan back of the bar 'A wee half, Jim. Faith, man, but it's cold. Have you heard the newsy-like tale from Moss Banks?'

Folk cried out 'No, what's happened down there?' and Dalsack took a bit sip at his dram and told them the tale, folk crowding about, God damn't, now wasn't that fairly a yarn? The poverty laird of Maiden Castle had got a right nasty clout in the jaw.

His horses had near gone off their legs with standing about the winter in the stable, snuffling at the scuffle of rats in the eaves and tearing into great troughs of corn, gey sonsy beasts, and he fed them well, him and that tink-like man of his, Geo Allison, ay, that was his name. Well, yesterday, when the snow cleared up, the Stratoun man had made up his mind to let out the horse for a bit of a dander, frost on the ground and a high, clear wind, and Geo Allison had set about the bit job, with the midden loons clustering at the stable door. The big mare had been led out by Allison, and the man was standing chirking at the door to cry out the others, all patient and fine when one of the loons, that big one Alick, had stuck a bit thistle alow the mare's tail. No sooner she felt that than, filled up with corn, her heels rose off the ground in a flash and planted themselves on Geo Allison's chest. He sat down saying un-Sabbath-like words, and b'god the world was full of horses' legs, the rest of the brutes, unloosed in the stable, no sooner heard the clatter of the mare's flight than they themselves tore like hell from the stable, scattering the two Stratoun loons like chaff, and careering round the court like mad, nearly running down Mistress Stratoun in the clamour. She cried to the brutes weren't they black ashamed, but damn the shame had one of the horses, they found the close gate and went galloping out, nearly tumbling head first down the old well, syne wheeling like a streek of gulls for the sea, gulls above it, cawing and pelting, Geo Allison scrambled up to his feet and tore after the beasts, crying to them to stop, the coarse Bulgars that they were and get their bit guts kicked in. Well, the mare was in the lead and she stopped and took a bit look out over the sea and syne another back to Geo Allison and kicked up her heels and took a bit laugh and turned and went racing across the ley field, making for the moor, the others behind her, and so vanished like the beasts with the chariot of fire, Geo Allison pelting like hell at their heels, folk living up here in the clorty north had only themselves to blame, the fools, instead of biding in the fine warm south.

Well, the horses fairly enjoyed themselves, they went over the moor of Balhaggarty and took a bit keek in at the kitchen window where Mistress Paton was making the sowans, she thought it was one of her churchyard ghaists and gave a yowl, and at that the mare gave back a bit nicker and showed her teeth and turned round, fair contemptuous-like and rubbed her backside against the window and ate a couple of flowers from a pot, and seemed to ponder

the next bit move. Well, b'god, she'd soon a flash of
inspiration, and raised up her head and looked over the
hill to where the lums of Moss Bank were smoking, far
away, a smudge by the tracks. And she gave another neigh
and set off, the douce black plodding at her heels, gey quiet,
the old gelding and the young mare skirting behind, stopping now and then to kick up their heels and look back at
the figure of Geordie Allison, no more than a blue and
blurring dot, far across the snow and turning the air blue as
he cursed all the horses from here to Dundee, the daft-like
dams that had given them birth and the idiot stallions that
fathered them.

Well, you all know the kind of a creature Cruickshank is
when he'll sight just one of your hens taking a bit of a stroll
before breakfast and maybe casting one eye on his land. He
was out at the tattie pits when he heard the coming of the
Maiden horses like the charge of the cavalry at Balaclava, he
looked up and cursed and turned white with rage. His wife
heard the grind and clatter as well and came running out to
stand beside him, the two of them just statues of fury,
watching the mare nose round the close and nibble the hay
from one of the stacks, and kick down a gate and look over
at Cruickshank, one ear back and the other forward, a devil
of a horse if ever there was one, just putting her fingers to
her nose at him. But Cruickshank was fairly a skilly childe,
he came out of his stance of sheer amaze and ran for the
house and a pail of hot water and dosed it well with treacle
and brought out slow across the close and put it in the
middle of the cattle court. The smell was enough for all
four of the horses, a bit thirsty and cold-like from their
winter caper, they trotted nickering into the court and
Cruickshank banged up the gates behind them and
nodded, 'Ay, well, when you next get out, it'll be with
your owner's written apology.'

Mistress Cruickshank cried 'Ay, and his pay for the
damage,' and Cruickshank said 'Get into the house. When

I need your advice, I'll maybe ask for it' and they stood and glowered one at the other, frosty and big, fair matches for each other, till they both sighted Geo Allison coming dandering in about on the look-out for the Maiden horses. He cried out to ask if Cruickshank had seen them and Cruickshank glunched at him, Ay, oh, ay, he'd seen the coarse foul stinking beasts, where had the dirt come from, would it be?

Geo Allison was a bit ta'en aback ay that and said that they'd come from Maiden's, of course, where the hell else, out of the sea? At that Cruickshank told him he wanted none of his lip, but he could take home this message to his master: If he wanted his foul, mischeivous beasts he could come and get them, he'd not get them else.

Faith, Geo Allison didn't like the look of him and tailed away home with his tail 'tween his legs, and was hardly at Maiden than back came Maiden himself from his tear away over to Bervie. No sooner was he back than he heard the story, a funny devil Stratoun, and worth the watching. And all that he said was 'Well, well, we'll see,' and set out himself for the toun of Moss Banks.

The two of them met in the cattle court, Cruickshank had a straw skull full of neeps and was carrying them up to the door of the byre, big and squash, the sharn rising brown under his boots, when Maiden cried to him canny to stop. So he stopped and set down the skull, face black as thunder, and started in with hardly a pause for breath to ask what the hell he meant by it? Was this the way to treat an honest man, the stinking, half-gentry dirt that he was? Mistress Cruickshank came tearing out to watch, and all three looked at Stratoun and they thought him gey feared, he stood stocky and quiet, giving his beard a bit stroke, and syne nodded 'Well, well, I'm sorry for that. But I doubt I'll need my horses back again.'

Cruickshank said 'You'll get them back when you pay for them,' and Maiden just stood and shook his head, 'Faith, no man, I'll take them back just now,' and sure as death there'd have been murder then, Cruickshank was just taking off his coat and Maiden was fairly a sturdy billy, but that Alick, the biggest of the Maiden sons, came tearing through the yard at that minute, crying 'Father, father, you've got to come home. Keithie's ill again, and spewing up blood,' his mother had sent him, he'd run all the way. Stratoun turned round and went striding out of the close and across the hills, the loon at his heels, forgetting everything about the horses.

Geo Allison would have tailed out after him but that Cruickshank cried 'Hey, what's your hurry? You can surely lead a pair of them back yourself. I'll take the other pair back for you.' And while Geordie Allison stood and gaped b'god Jim Cruickshank lead out the horses that he'd sworn he wouldn't part with at all, and got ropes to lead and followed Geo, and they sludged back douce across to the Castle, and stabled the horses up slow and quiet, not to raise a din with a bairn sick. And when he had finished with doing that Cruickshank went down to the kitchen door and lifted the sneck and went cannily in and asked Mistress Stratoun was there anything he could do, they hadn't a sholt here at Maiden, should he drive down to Bervie and bring up the doctor?

And what thought you of that of the Cruickshank childe? For off to Bervie b'god he had driven, as anxious to help with the saving of the loon as he'd been to knock John Stratoun's teeth down his throat a bare half hour afore. Faith then, when he'd broke down the ice there would maybe other folk go down to Maiden, an ill-like thing with the bairn dying, 'twas said he wouldn't last out the week.

Book III

DRIFT AND COLOURED clouds and a long queer time that
you tripped and stumbled, shamble and slip, down a long
cave that was littered with bones, dead men here, dead men
there, thick air so you couldn't breathe, choking and
stumbling for lack of breath down and down to the dark
of the cave. And then you were out, for a minute up, and
opened your eyes, and there was mother, funny man beside, with a basin all blood, awful stuff blood, it must be the
doctor, they did coarse things to little loons, you screamed
and screamed while they held you and soothed you, and
you fought some more and went back to the cave.

Alick and Peter, as they told you later, could hardly sleep
for the din you raised, like a calf with the scour, and them
both so sleepy. And they couldn't get to their beds that
night, anyhow, for the gallons of hot water that had to be
boiled on the open fire, Mother flying about the place with
her skirts kilted up and her face all red, flinging the
furniture out of her way, not safe to be anywhere near
the daftie, Alick had whispered low to Peter. Father had
just sat down in the chimney-corner, Geo Allison over at
the other side, there was nothing they could do and they
took it calm, but mother was all in a fash that when the
doctor came down he could wash his hands and the blood
from the knives he'd been cutting you with, and not find the
place looking like a bit of a barn. Father gave her a pat on
the bottom 'Don't fash, it'll come to all the same in the end.
We've all of us got to pass some time, and he's the only one
that we've lost.'

Mother rounded on him in an awful rage: 'Who've we

lost? He'll outlive you all, and do things in the world you'll never do.' Father said 'Well, well, if that's the case, why are you getting ready to rub down the corpse?' and Mother told him not to be a daft fool, this wasn't for a corpse, but the doctor man.

And when he came down he was washed and fed and said he thought you'd maybe survive, and Geordie Allison trying to be newsy, struck in 'Och, ay. There's a lot of killing in a kyard,' and mother gave him a look that nearly blasted him, you were always Mother's pet, yes you were.

Well, it was that night while you were sleeping and the snow was on again, that the village began the first of its visits, Dalsack and his Edith, the housekeeper lass, came down from Bogmuck, stitering through the drifts, Dalsack with a load of a kebbuck of cheese, for the invalid, like, and Edith with a pot of jam, Mother had heard all about her, a Real Coarse Quean, and was maybe a bit short when they were shown in. But losh, Peter thought her awful bonny, he'd sleep with her when she'd grown up, she'd red hair and fine round legs and arms, and she sat down and hoisted up her skirts and warmed herself at the fire and spoke and Mother thawed out, and sat down for a rest. And no sooner had she done that than Edith herself jumped up to her feet and started getting a meal ready for them all, Mother that wouldn't let another help gave her a nod, 'Oh ay, if you like.' Dalsack and father were at it on the land, about the best time to muck it and the short-eared corn, would it be a decent crop in the Howe? And just as they were getting on fine there came another scuffle at the sneck and in came stamping the Cruickshanks of Moss Bank, Father and Mother and another one. Mother would hardly speak to them at first and she and Mrs Cruickshank eyed one the other like a couple of hens about to fight, Mrs Cruickshank big as Bess, gey near, and with an awful face to match; but Father cried her into a seat and they all sat down, and the third one from Moss Bank, a young-like childe, was in-

troduced, awful exciting, you couldn't guess who he was
. . . You said yes you could, and Alick said you couldn't
you were lying upstairs all cut up with knives and dripping
blood like a new killed pig. So you couldn't guess, see? . . .
And the man was the son of the Cruickshanks, William,
that had been a jeweller up in Aberdeen and had run away
and joined the soldiers and fought all over the world,
Blacks, and Chinese, awful brave, when Alick was grown
up he'd do the same, steal things from jewellers, only he
wouldn't be such a fool as get caught. So *he* sat down as
well, and the old Cruickshank cuddy and Mrs Cruickshank, hell, what a face, and they claiked and claiked till
they wearied the lads, Mother wouldn't let them go to their
beds in the corner, it wouldn't have been decent, though
they were nearly yawning their heads off with sleep and
pulling up the corners of the blind and squinting out at the
ding of the snow, the squeege of the sea worse than ever
that night, like the kind of daft beast you'd said it was like.

Father had cried out to Peter to ask ' 'Od man, you're gey
white about the gills. What is't that's got you?' and Peter,
the fool, had told the story you'd whispered in bed, before
you were ill, of the ill beasts without eyes, great slimy
worms, who rose from out the sea in the night, wet squelch
and scuffle over the Maiden walls, snuffling blind hungry, a
grue in the dark. And all the folk in the kitchen listened, and
looked a bit as though they'd grue themselves, Mistress
Edith gave a shiver and covered her eyes and old Dalsack
even took a keek over his shoulder at the rattle and
smoulder of the black night wind snarling outside the
kitchen door, for a minute they all listened, even father,
to the whoom of the storm in the lum, beneath it, below it
the surge of the water rising up from the caves of the sea,
even Mother had her red face queer a bit, with its flitting
eyes and that nasty smile frozen on her jaws, and the
Cruickshank fright neighed out it wasn't canny, a laddie
like that, not much wonder he was lying up ill. But Father

just smiled placid at his pipe and so did Jim Cruickshank, they didn't fear anything, Alick thought it was a pity they hadn't had that fight he'd stopped when he brought the news of your illness, they'd plenty of guts for a fight the both of them.

Then William Cruickshank, that was sitting by Dalsack's housekeeper, Edith, started to tell of the queer fairlies he'd seen and heard in India, an awful antrin place, the creepers came down and moved at night with things like hands of flesh, if a man was caught in a jungle alone those coarse-like plants would strangle him. And he told of the heat and the thirst of the days, the pallor at night like spilt buttermilk, buttermilk sprayed on a summer midden, full of ill smells, about the trees watching and waiting, the thump of your heart nearly sickening your stomach, and far off down the bit track you had took the thump and thud of following feet, following quick and sharp on your track through the glow and flow of the moonlight, daren't look back, could only go on, maybe a tiger, maybe worse, he himself had once been tracked that way, he could hear the pad of the beast close behind and at last he swung round and faced and God—

And Soldier William stopped when he got to there, cheery and buirdly, but his voice now solemn, you'd have heard a pin drop, and Mistress Edith behind him was gripping his arm, he looked down at her hand and then at her face and gave the hand a pat, she mustn't fash, guess what the bloody thing was after all? Only a wild pig, a sow at that, maybe tame once and grunting at his heels in the hope he'd have a bit offal to give it? But Jesus, it nearly had turned his wame!

That was a fine enough story, eh? but his father that silly old sumph, Cruickshank, God who would have him for a father, said sharp 'Ay, maybe you've had your adventures, that's no reason to take the Redeemer in vain. If you've come home to bide at Moss Bank with us you'll bide as a well-favoured, God-fearing lad.' And even Peter and Alick felt shamed, Moss Bank speaking that way to a grown-up man like his son, but he didn't seem shamed, just laughed and said in his English-like way 'Don't worry, father, I feared God enough that night when I thought the tiger was with me.' And then he told another story that mother and Cruickshank both thought right fine, about a soldier in his regiment, a decent-like chap, who'd said he was an atheist, didn't believe in God. Well, he caught a fever and was taken to a hospital and his last words were 'Give me the Book.' And when he asked 'What book' he said 'There's only one Book – my bank-book, of course,' and then laughed at them, the coarse devil had known they expected he'd say the Bible. And he'd died right like that, an awful warning.

Mother said 'Yes, the foul stinking swine', Alick said she would like to cut folks throats for Jesus, so would Moss Bank, they both looked as solemn as hens choked on dirt, but Alick took a look at the soldier, William, and he was looking at Mistress Edith and just at that minute he gave her a wink, and Alick looked at the others then, Father was staring up at the couples, Geo Allison was blowing his nose gey loud, Alick said to Peter in bed later on he thought that that soldier Bulgar was just making fun of Mother and Moss Bank. And whether that was true or not he'd no right to look at Edith like that, Alick himself was to have her for his lass when he'd grown up and robbed some jeweller and pushed mother off the Maiden cliff, so he would sometime, he was sick of her nagging, and owned Maiden himself when Father was dead, so he would, Peter and you would be just his ploughmen, he was the eldest.

Well, they'd all had a late bit supper then and Mother gone up to have a look at you, and Mistress Edith with her, tall, and ruddy, you'd opened eyes to the dazzle of light, stopped your blowing of little red bubbles, to stare at the woman beside Mother, bigger, with her fine face and laugh, she whispered 'Poor man, oh, poor wee man' and you stared and stared and tried to speak and then tumbled in to

the cave again. But Mother had thought you were getting
on fine, and taken Mistress Edith down again, a meikle
supper spread in the kitchen, ham and oatcakes and some
of the Dalsack cheese, and father sat in to say his grace and
they all ate up and had a claik, Dalsack said with his shy,
fine smile 'That must be an extraordinary laddie, your
youngest, Mistress Stratoun,' and Mother said 'Och, just
ordinary, ordinary' she didn't want folk to think you queer.
But Geo Allison said b'god you weren't that, with the
queerest havers and stances and answers, a funny bairn,
no doubt you'd get on, into a daftie-house, maybe in the
end. Father said 'No fear of that. Though, faith, I will say
he's a queer-like nickum. He'd speir the head from a Devil
Stane or a creel of fresh herring back into the sea. 'Od, he'll
be a handful to the teachers, I warrant, when we send him
up to the village school this Spring.'

You'd always remember till the day you died that queer,
quiet evening in middle March that father took you out to
the fishing, the first evening you'd been letten out, pale for a
breath of air, Father wrapped you up in a blanket and
carried you, rod and tackle over one arm, you over the
other, the sun had gone down saffron behind except for
some tint on the verge of the sea, it was sleeping in a little
foam of colour and far away on the dying edge of the white
wings of the Gourdon fleet went home, you stared and
stared at it all, at the quietness that was rising a dim wall in
the east, creeping up the sky and overtaking and drowning
in blood the lights behind the fisher boats. Father set you
down and stepped in the boat, tucked you up, and sat down
and picked up the oars. 'Fine, Keith lad?'

You said 'Ay, father,' and looked over the thwarts to the
little hiss of the water, out, down to the shag and sway and
green gleam of the bottom of the sea where the fairlies bade.
But there were none to be seen at this, it was clear and open
and you looked up and saw far along the fringing cliffs the

place where the seagulls wheeled and cried out over the brinks from Dunnottar Castle it came on you this was maybe the sea, the beasts only silly dreams after all, light and the gulls and white hiss of the sea. Your stomach still felt awful funny inside you, as though Bess the mare had stepped on it, the smell of the sea made it turn a wee, but you didn't let on, Father would have turned and taken you back.

Instead he took the boat out to the point, beyond it, suddenly, the evening wind came, it blew a little spume in your faces, your nose and cheeks stung to its touch, a little smother of blood on the sea, soaking and pitching under the keel, Way way way! the gulls crying. You said 'Father, why do they aye cry that?' and he stopped and listened from unlimbering the tackle, 'Cry what, my mannie' and you told him 'That – Way, way, way!'

Father said well, 'od, he didn't right know, the beasts and birds had funny-like cries, it was maybe some kind of speaking of theirs. You said 'Oh. But have they all lost their way?' and father gave you the funniest look, he said that you were a gey queer lad, and bent to his tackle and then straightened again, listening to the gulls and stroking his beard, the sunset behind him on the sea.

You drowsed a bit then and opened your eyes, father was pulling a fish aboard, a great gaping brute that blinked at you and worked its jaws and floundered and gasped, you drew up your legs away from it, Father didn't notice, the beasts were coming in bourochs, fast as he let down the lines for them, blue and grey rising out of the sea, fluttering and flicking, paling and dying, now the great wall behind the horizon's edge had blackened and blackened as though some Geordie Allison out there with a pail and tarbrush in the other hand had mistaken the sky for the barn wall, through the tar there came a glimmer of a star funny things stars, lights far away, God lighted them at night with a spunk from the box in a pocket of his breeks, striding backwards and forwards the roof of heaven, he'd a long brown beard like Father's just, but he wasn't so fine, sometimes you were dead feared of him. Father turned round 'Not cold are you then,' and you said you weren't, neither you were, just frozen in a wonder looking at the sky, arching and rising in the coming night. What if God made a bit slip some time and cracked the sky and came tumbling through, box of spunks still gripped in his hand and splashing the water so high from the sea it went pelting high up across the Howe—

And then you were feared, you held your breath, tight, there was the crack, growing wider and wider, a splurge on the lift, the dark behind, light in front, the splurge blue and yellow, the gulls had stopped that daft crying and crying and the wind had stilled, why didn't father see, He was coming, He was coming.

Boom!

Something flickered from the crack, and father raised his head.

"Od, we'll need to be holding back. There's the thunder, Keith, it'll frighten your Mother.'

That thunder-pelt was the beginning of the wettest Spring that had come on the Howe for many a day, all that night it thundered and rained, in turn, when one had finished with splitting the sky and scarting its claws along the earth and over and through the dripping parks, the other came down in blinding pelts, the swash of it warping through roofs and walls, the cattle court of Balhaggarty was flooded out and half the stock drowned, at Moss Bank Sandy the dafty had come home gey late from a boozing ploy and gone into the smiddy where the coals still glowed and sat him down for a bit of a warm before sneaking up the stairs to his bed. And faith if he didn't fall fast asleep and was woke with a smack of cold water in his face, the smiddy swirling with a thing like a wave, he thought between the coals and the water he was surely in hell at last, not fair and went yammering out of the place to the kitchen door of Moss Bank to beat and clamour till letten in by his brother William who'd been the soldier. William asked what the hell was he up to, the fool, screeching around like a sheep half-libbed, and Sandy yabbered and dribbled and shook and said that coming by Dalsack's, he minded, he'd heard an awful commotion and cry and decided the devil was in there at last, getting at Dalsack for sleeping with his housekeepers, but he'd never thought Auld Nick would follow him here.

William said 'Here, what's that that you say. Dirty lout,' and near bashed him one, Mistress Edith a fine and upstanding girl that wouldn't look at a rat like Dalsack. But Sandy only moaned and yabbered some more, and at last Will put on his breeks and leggings and his reefer coat and set out for Moss Bank, near blind with the flare of the lightning sizzling and pelted with a slow dry wind that blew steady and strong, 'twixt the gusts of rain. In the Bogmuck kitchen a light was shining, he chapped at the door and went in and found out then what the commotion was about, Dalsack had had water taken in his kitchen, with a fine pipe and the Lord knew all the arrangements, and been a bit proud at being civilised: but early that night as they went to their beds the whole damn arrangement had burst in the rain, that was the commotion that Sandy had heard, the bed of the bairns in the kitchen drenched, Dalsack had come tearing down in his sark, naught else, and tried to light a candle, and the bairns had thought that he was the devil, coarse tinks creatures to think that of the man because he had whiskers like a yard of broom, syne Edith had come and tried to comfort them, and stop the flow of the water from the pipe, from them, an awful soss. Well, William was a skilly man with his hands, he'd learned in the Army to do all kinds of things from mending a pipe to cutting a throat, he shot about and stopped the flow, and took a sly look at Edith in her nighty wet, it stuck to her bonny chest with the points of the nipples sweet and showing, wet hair down her back like a Viking maid, by God, he made up his mind at that moment he'd get her and have breasts, hair and all, though the whole of the Howe was to be one long howl. Dalsack smiled shy through his whiskers and sark and said he was awful obliged to him, a fine childe, Dalsack, he dug out the whisky they sat drinking that till the morning came and William would stride back again to Moss Bank, through a Howe that was just a soss and a puddle and under the lour of a sky like lead.

And going back he followed the ridging track and went round and through by the Auld Kirk lands, and there a gey antrin sight met his eyes as he looked over into the old kirkyard where the folk of the Village had been laid in earth since ever the memory of man began, there ere old stones there that leaned this way and that, with daft-like inscriptions and curlicues, stones from the days of Christ's Covenant, one with a picture graved in the stone of an old-time brig in full sail, fair daft, that had been the ship of a Captain Stratoun; and the grass grew high and rank and dreich, choked round with the flat, bland blades of docken, a fine kirkyard and seldom disturbed except for the hares that had their holes there, maybe lairing there young in some coffin place in the bones of a woman once young and bonny, as Geddes Munro, the cripple, had once said, the foul young beast, so William remembered, he'd said it no doubt for a spite of the fact he'd never lair *his* body in any woman's. But now as William Cruickshank looked over the wall under the drip of the dreich dark yews, it looked like a hotter in a cattle shed, stones had been flung down here and there and a tide of water swashed through the place, flinging up the end of a new-buried coffin, that would be the coffin of a joskin man from the Home Town back of the village. In the thin wet glimmer of the March morning it looked an evil and fervid place, and Will Cruickshank shivered and turned in a half-run till he saw something that near made him sick, the figure of a woman over by the church wall, pressed up against it, a woman in white, in a nighty, hair down about her shoulders, bonny-gleaming, and weeping and weeping as though her heart would break. God damn't, what was she doing there? For it was the Reverend James Dallas's wife.

Well, he nearly stept over to question her on't, and was just giving his soldier's mouser a twist afore he did that, a fine figure of a man, when she turned and went out of the place by herself, bare-footed, he saw the gleam of her bare feet, she passed down into the shelter of the avenue trees, the morning was hardly breaking, white, he stood with a prickle of skin and stared after, had he really seen her or was it a fancy?

So he went back to Moss Bank and told the tale of the riven kirkyard, but not of the weeping minister's wife, he kept that till later, and Moss Bank said it was the just the kind of a thing that would happen in a proud and sinful place like an Auld Kirk, you'd not find the like of that in the field where the Reverend Adam Smith buried the Free Kirk men. And just as he said that the postie came in about, young Munro with his white, sneering face, and asked if they'd heard the news from the Howe? They hadn't, and so he began to tell them, – they knew of that daughter of Gunn of Lamahip, Queen, the dressmaker, so dark and stuck-up, a Gypsy-like bitch with her quiet airs? Well, where do you think she had spent the night? – at her shop in the village, not going home, she said that coming on of the storm had stopped her. Faith, maybe so it had, but did that account for the fact that as the morning broke and the Dominie's servant lassie, Kate, was getting up with a wearied yawn and taking a keek down the street she saw the door of Queen's shop slide open and who should come out, rubbing his eyes, unshaven, with a gey dreich look on his face, but the Reverend Adam Smith himself, that fat coarse ill-living Free Kirk loon. – Cruickshank of Moss Bank said

'G'way with your lies,' but young Munro just sneered at him coarse. 'Lies? Fegs, there was lying enough there last night – your Free Kirk man in the bed of Queen Gunn.'

And afore that Saturday was done the news of the ploy was all over the parish, men meeting one another on the top of boxcarts cried it out, they cried from hedges and stacks, and the tops of barns they had set to repair, at Balhaggarty Mrs Paton greeting in her dairy where all her cheese had been spoiled by the water and the eggs piled up like a ready made omelette, dried up to listen to her servant lass, and then ran to carry the news to the elder, Sam Paton, solemn, rubbing his stomach, he's awful pains below his waistcoat this morning, he said it was just the kind of thing he expected to have happened to a Free Kirk minister, and rubbed his stomach some more and looked round, and went down to Maiden to see how they were, so he said, but really just to pass them the news, awful kind of him, Mrs Stratoun said, ay, God, a right handsome bitch of a woman and had brought three fine sons intil the world, though they said that the youngest one was a daftie.

The storm had nearly missed Maiden Castle, except the loft where Geo Allison bade, Geo said that it smote in on him at midnight like the angel of God, by the look of his face he and the angel weren't on good terms, he sat and shivered the day by the fire. When he heard the story of the two bit kirks, the auld one with its dead in resurrection and the Free one with its minister acting spry and quick, he said he expected that from ministers, did they ever work like other folk and use up their juices and go tired to bed? – Not them, they'd had to be randy to live. John Stratoun said 'Od, that might be so, but he hardly saw that the fact would account for the Reverend James Dallas at the least getting out of his bed in the middle of the night and tearing up a coffin or so, just to prove that he was a vital man. And Sam Paton gave his stomach a bit rub, and a glower at Geo Allison, sour as his wame, and said he'd no liking for blasphemy. And Geo Allison mumbled 'Your stomach won't stand it,' but not over loud, he was only a joskin and not a gey big farming man.

The only place in the Howe that day that hadn't heard the two scandals till late was Archie Camlin's at Badymicks, the couples of the byres had tumbled in and nearly killed a couple of his kye, and Arch was up in the roof giving them a mend with wee dark Rachel standing below, carrying the nails and her eyes on Arch as though on Elijah coming from the clouds when Sandy Cruickshank took a wamble in there and cried up the news, teething and dribbling and mouthing. Arch said b'god he saw nothing in that, couldn't the Reverend Adam have a sleep where he liked or the dead in the kirk of the Reverend Kames go out a bit stroll if it took their fancy? 'Get away home, Sandy, man, to your bed, and not blether that kind of dirt to me with the lassie there standing by and listening.' Sandy looked at Rachel and mouthed and yammered 'She over-young to understand' and Arch called down 'Away home with you. Bairns ken well enough from the womb, I think, all the ways that got them there. And I've little fancy for her growing up to snigger and sniffle around every tale of every auld childe that sleeps with a woman.' So off poor Sandy had to waddle through the glaur, all the thanks that he got for his story, and what did Arch Camlin mean by his say, would he have the quean Rachel grow up a fair heathen and not know the difference between right and wrong?

Next day there was such a power of folk in Free Kirk at ten as hadn't been there since the news of Balaclava, near, the Reverend Adam climbed into the pulpit and peered down at them over his stomach and the two-three chins he wore over his collar, and puffed, and then drew out his great hankie, and blew a blast on it like the Last Trump's blast, and then preached them a sermon from Numbers, fegs, all about figures and descents and ascents and a creature called Jeanie Ology, would she be one of his lasses,

would you say? It was more than likely, but heard you ever
the like, him introducing into the pulpit the name of
another lass after that night he's spent in the cuddles of
Queenie Gunn.

The Auld Kirk itself was nearly toom, the Reverend James
Dallas preaching bitter on the traipse that creature Lot had
had when he went out of the City of Sodom, there was
hardly a soul in the pews that day, pine shadowed, the sun
shone through flying blinks of rain, forward under the pulpit
head the choir sitting upright, genteel, behind them the pew
of the Badymicks folk, Arch Camlin there with his little lass,
and God she had a right unco stare, her with her boots and
her funny limps and her dark-like skin, like a nigger's near,
you couldn't wonder if the mother in law wasn't so keen
about the bit creature. Midway was the pew of the elder,
Sam Paton, with his wife prinked out in all her braws and
jingling when she moved like a horse at a show, and behind
that the seat of the Lamahip folk, would you believe there
was Queen Gunn sitting there distant and quiet and dark,
her eyes staring out of her face like live lumps of coal, only
quiet coal, up at James Dallas as he preached from the
pulpit, down from him to the seats in the corner where sat
the folk from the manse themselves, the mistress and her bit
maiden Ella, and further back still in their gentry's pew, the
folk from Maiden, John Stratoun himself and his red-faced
wife her head bent genteel but her eyes sharp and flitting on
everything about her, their three weans beside them, all
dressed up and starched. And over and above them all there
thundered the tale of that creature Lot, his life, his death,
and the coarse thing she'd done with that daughter of his in a
bit of a cave. Folk put up their hankies to hide their yawns
and poked their bairns to keep them awake, all except Arch
Camlin with his dark quean Rachel, her head had fallen
forward on the desk in front, sleeping the creature and over
the way the youngest of the Stratouns sleeping, as well, that
laddie that had nearly died a month back.

Ah well, they were gey young for the kirk. They were going to school inside the next week, and fegs that would waken them up for good.

You thought it an awful funny place, the school, the Dominie was big and bald and thin, with glasses perched on a long thin nose, he stood in the playground between the two walls that separated the lasses' playground from the lads', and rang a bell and afore you could blink there were scholars tearing in from all directions, out of the hedges and over the walls, and tearing out of the lavatories where they'd been drawing funny pictures and up from the post-office tattie-pit where they had been throwing things at the post office, big loons and little ones and medium ones, and lassies with long plaits and legs, didn't like it, thought you'd maybe cry for a bit, and felt awful lost till you sighted Peter. You ran to him and took his hand but he was ashamed and pushed you away and said 'Your place's with the bairns, see?'

So you'd to line up last of all the lines and were awful ashamed, they put a lassie beside you, little and dark, and she looked at you queer and you stared down at your boots, fine boots, Mother had brought them in Bervie for you. And minding mother you nearly cried again, till you thought of the piece that you carried in your bag, for dinner, bread and butter and jam and a big soda scone with treacle inside it. So maybe you'd like the school after all.

Inside Miss Clouston took the little ones, she was awful thin and stern and fierce and the scholars said she wore red drawers and kept her strap in brine to pickle, she wasn't young, and looked about a hundred, and if one of the little ones messed up the floor she'd flush up red and say 'Dirty, go out' and near frighten a little 'un out of its life. But she didn't with you, she liked you from the first and was awful kind and took you to the fire and you warmed up and newsed with her and told her of the fish father catched in the sea, and had she ever seen the Maiden Mare Bess, losh, you was a horse, last month you were ill, it was awful queer, the doctor cut you, you liked better sleeping on your own for all that, had the Missie ever slept by herself, did she ever hear the queer beasts at night that came creeping up out of the sea, snuffle and slide, Father said they weren't real, hadn't that loon a funny face, 'My brother Peter says you wear red flannel drawers.'

Miss Clouston said sharp 'Well, that'll do, Keith. Now sit down here beside this wee girl, her name's Rachel, and see you don't fight.' So down you'd to sit beside a lass, fight, you wouldn't fight with a quean, and you said right out that Alick said a quean couldn't fight a kipper off a plate, they were over weak in the guts. And there was a snicker of laughing all about and next minute you thought your head would fall off, Miss Clouston had smacked you so hard in the ear, she was a bitch and you cried a bit.

And while you were doing that and Miss Clouston, red faced, was taking the first of the lessons, singing, they'd all to stand up and she banged the piano and said 'Do Ray' and they all said 'Do Ray' the little quean Rachel tugged at your sleeve and said not to mind and not to be feared, she herself wasn't feared at any one. So you dried your nose on your sleeves and said you weren't feared, you weren't feared at anything, one night you were out, it was awful dark and a great big dog had come leaping to bite you, and you'd taken an axe and killed it dead, you were gey strong. Rachel said 'Oh losh, that was awful brave' and you told her some more of the things you'd done till Miss Clouston barked 'No talking there among the little ones,' that meant you two and you just sat wearied.

But syne she started lessons for you two and drew three funny pictures on the blackboard and told you to draw them as well, awful hard, they looked all wrong, one was a funny man called A, standing the way father sometimes stood, and another B, would that be the daft Bee that

Geordie Allison would call the horses, the third was C, and was just daft, sea wasn't like that, oh, it was awful school, you minded sudden the sea and its greensy splurge out over the rocks and the gulls crying. But then you saw Rachel was drawing the daft-like stuff on her slate, so you had, and some more after that, and it wasn't so bad, though you fell asleep afore dinner-time.

At dinner you sat at the foot of the playground on the edge of the hedge and listened to Alick saying what he'd do to a lad, Jockie Elrick, that had said that he could fight Alick easy. And Alick finished his dinner quick and said to Peter 'Look after Ma's Pet' he meant you, and took out a great gully knife from his pouch and started to sharpen it on the sole of his boot, loons standing around and gaping at him, he was going to libb Jockie Elrick with it and then cut his throat from ear to ear, so he said, you cried out 'Ay, hurry up,' for you'd never seen that done afore to anyone. And over at the other side of the playground Jockie Elrick was sharpening his knife as well, the lads all said there'd be an awful lot of blood.

But the bell rung afore they could get to grips, and you'd the long afternoon to get through. Miss Clouston brought you a book of pictures, one was a train, you'd like to drive a train, and one was a beast that you didn't know, like a great big dog. Rachel knew more than you, she spelled it out and said it was a lion, her father had told her a lot about lions, they bade in a place called Africa and ate up black men, you asked why, it would surely be nicer to eat white, Rachel didn't know, that was just the way with lions. And then Miss Clouston called 'Children, you mustn't talk,' so you had a little bit sleep instead, and woke up with Alick shaking you awake, he'd come to take you home your first night.

The bairns were pouring out of the school and down in the playground going mad with delight at being freed from the Dominie and Missies, one had a kite, he'd let it high up, and two loons crept through the lower hedge and stole a handful of the Dominie's tomatoes, and Peter took out his knife again, sharp, and waited for Jockie Elrick, they circled round each other, knives all ready, Peter said that Jockie Elrick was a Bulgar, and Jockie said that Peter was another, see, and then they both nodded 'Wait till the morn' and separated, and you all held home, lasses trailing along in groups with their arms wound round one the other's shoulders, awful big, they petted you, you were over wearied to tell them you didn't like lasses, except maybe Rachel, she was fine.

She came down the Badymicks road behind you and Peter and Alick and you twice looked back, and saw her limp, and felt awful sorry, she looked dark herself in the fading light, would the folk in Africa that the lions are be like her, would you say? And you looked back again and felt feared for her, and ran back to her side and took her hand, 'I'll take care of you if the lions come.' She said that was awful fine of you, but there weren't any in Scotland, she thought, you said 'Maybe no, but this is the Howe' and held her hand down to Badymicks, she put her arms round you and kissed you then, liked it, but Peter and Alick had stopped and looked back and started mocking you. 'Och, look at the lassies slobbering and kissing,' and the Bulgars tormented you all the way home.

Mother asked how you'd gotten on, and you said 'Och, fine' though you were so wearied, you fell asleep at the supper table and dreamt you were chasing Miss Clouston up the Howe with a gully knife in your hand, only it wasn't Miss Clouston but a great big beast, a lion from Africa, and it in its turn was chasing Rachel Camlin, pant and pant, you heard its great slobber, but you were gaining, gaining on it quick.

And then you woke up in the kitchen bed, dark in the early gliff of Spring morning, beside you Peter and Alick asleep, and far underfoot with shoggling surge the tide in the darkness taking its turn.

And still the rains of that Spring came down, at School every morning the bairns of the Howe sat and steamed like ill plates of porridge, and far and near through the tumbling runnels the water poured from the drooked lands to leave room for a fresh pelt coming at noon, piles of water tumbling and falling with a wheeling of rainbows and a cawing of gulls. To plough was to wade in mud to the knees, Arch Camlin digging up a bit of his moor fell into a bog and was nearly laired, he'd have died there but that Rachel was here, a Saturday, and ran for help to the figure of Dalsack across in his fields, ploughing and steaming with a blowing pair. Dalsack cried 'What? Well, well, thet's gey coarse' and came stepping canny across the fields and looked down at Arch Camlin pinned in the hole under a weight of lever and broom. 'Fegs, man, we'll need to howk you up out of that.' Arch Camlin said he was awful kind, but wouldn't he first like a draw at his pipe? So Dalsack was a wee bit nipper then, and howked out Arch, clorted up and down from head to feet and over his head, shivering with cold.

Dalsack would have let him stagger off home, but Edith had seen the whole play from the kitchen and came running out and invited him in, 'Dalsack, you old Bulgar, help the man to tir.' And she ran and made him a hot berry drink while Arch stripped off every clout he wore and got into a baggy old suit of Dalsack's, Rachel sitting by with her staring eyes, Edith big and bonny bustling around, caring nothing for naked men, seeing that Dalsack gave all his help. And Arch Camlin, coming away a bit later, thought back on the way that Edith behaved, 'od, yon was a funny-like way for a housekeeper to act with her lawful master, now.

He met in with Cruickshank from Moss Bank up the road and stopped to pass the news of the day, and said what he'd thought about Edith and Dalsack. Jim Cruickshank said 'Damn't, and what's funny? She's a fine lass, Edith, but a whore for all. I'se warrant she warms the old sinner's bed.'

Arch wouldn't have that, No, no, a fine lass, and Cruickshank said she was fine enough, but a whore by nature, she'd burn yet. So he drove off and Arch Camlin went home, Fannie trailing about like a wee dish cloth. He told her the tale of his time in the moor and all she said was 'Faith, did you then? Eh me, and now I'll have to wash up your breeks and sark,' b'god that was all that worried her.

So Arch took a bit of a stroll out that evening, walking canty along the dripping paths, and came to the high still ridge in the dripping silence of the cease of the rain, below the lights of Maiden were twinkling, he'd take a bit taik in about there, he thought. In the yard Geo Allison was watering the horses, the poor brutes skirted up over their dowps, and they stood and had a bit news a while till Maiden himself came out of the byre and cried 'That you, Arch? Come away in.' And into the kitchen Arch Camlin stepped, and who should be there, either nook of the fire than that Edith of Bogmuck and the soldier-childe, William, the ill-doing soldier-son of Moss Bank, looking chief as a cock and hen at each other, Mrs Stratoun tearing around at her work, the lads all snuggled in their beds already. Faith, it seemed the young Cruickshank hadn't the objections to Edith that his ill-tuned father had.

But Arch thought that little business of his and started with Maiden to take through hand the threshing mill that was coming to the village in a week or so, to Badymicks first, Bogmuck, and syne Maiden, then across the moor to Balhaggarty, from there along to Lamahip, Moss Bank said he would thresh his own. Edith and young Cruickshank sat and listened, young Cruickshank ignorant about things like this, he asked if they'd ever thought a time would come when a place like Maiden could drive its own thresher with electricity up from the sea? John Stratoun said "Od, maybe we will, but we'll leave that over a year or two yet,' giving his beard a bit of a stroke, ay, a dry soul, Maiden, Arch Camlin thought.

So out at last he went taiking home, and young Cruick-shank and Edith rose to go with him, outside the rain had passed, stiffly blustering a great wind was darting up the Howe, they'd to bend their heads to the tingle and blow and fight their way to the long hedge-dripping track. At the break of the roads that led east and south, Arch Camlin cried out he'd take Edith home, but young Cruickshank said 'Ho no, I'll come with you. Fine evening for a bit of a stroll, you know.'

Faith, if that was the thing that he wanted he ended up with a sappier touch, looking back when he parted with them outside Bogmuck Arch Camlin saw him with Edith close up, tight in his arms as though he would mince her and kissing her lips in a fashion not decent, was that the way to behave to a lass that was good enough, but just a plain whore?

Notes to Speak of the Mearns

1.

Balhaggarty – Sam Paton & wife (Strachan) – two young sons, William & Peter
Moss Bank – Jim Cruickshank & huge wife. Two sons: Sandy the daftie & Joe the soldier
Auld Kirk – Rev James Dallas. Young, pretty wife
Free Kirk – Rev. Adam Smith. Housekeeper
Lamahip – Gunn; Bright wife; daughters Jean (religious) & Queen (mysterious)
Badymicks – Arch Camlin, his wife, & daughter Rachel.
Bogmuck – Dalsack & Edith
Howl [a name he sometimes applied in the draft to the village near Maiden Castle] – Munros, The Postmaster & son.

2. *Development of Story:*

Sam Paton and his wife of Balhaggarty: Paton develops cancer. He was always full of wind and water. Mrs Paton sees more and more ghosts.

Jim Cruickshank and his wife of Moss Bank: They are drawn into the drama of Joseph's love of Edith, and finally flee the district. Towards the end, Cruickshank is out with a gun to kill Dalsack of Badymicks.

Reverend James Dallas of the Auld Kirk and his wife: The Rev grows more bitter and narrow, a sadist who ill-treats his wife and refuses her sexual intercourse. An afflicted imagination with the horrors of the Old Testament. Mrs

Dallas ultimately consoles herself with young Munro of the Howe and his tormented sneers change to love.

Reverend Adam Smith of the Free Kirk summoned to console the mystic Queenie Gunn is confirmed in his dislike of all hatred not thoroughly dead. He goes digging in Stane Park and uncovers an ancient grave: the man done in with a blow at the back of the skull.

Stephen Gunn of Lamahip continues his lies. But in the end the old liar proves to have told the truth – some laird woman remembers him. At the Big House. Religious Jean with a baby. Queen goes to London and becomes a preacher.

Arch Camlin of Badymicks continues whistling and working. His complaining wife has another baby at which Mrs Stratoun attends.

Dalsack of Bogmuck and his housekeeper. Edith and Joe continue their flirtation. Edith reveals the father of her child as Dalsack. Marriage with Joe.

The Paralysed Pinto of Adam's Castle: His forester, Johnson, his keeper, McGrath. Hatred between the Stratouns and Pintos.

3. *Incidents*:

(1) Steam-mill. All the people of the Howe there. Water carrying. Chaff. Hum of the engine. Sights out beyond.
(2) Wedding of Joe and Edith.
(3) The horse that tumbled over the cliff: Geo Allison and Bess.
(4) Annual Games and Dance.
(5) Sunday School Picnic.
(6) Prize-giving.
(7) Tree-sawing in the woods – steading trees.

(8) James Dallas's discovery of his wife in Munro's arms.
(9) The hanging of Stephen Gunn.
(10) Burns' Nicht supper.

New Characters
The Laird
Forester Johnson
Keeper McGrath
Gunn of Lamahip as old Scorgie plus old Hodge.

Notes

TEXTUAL NOTE: The items in this section are from *Scottish Scene or The Intelligent Man's Guide to Albyn* (London: Jarrolds, 1934). Some had been published earlier: 'Greenden' in *The Scots Magazine* Dec 1932, pp. 168–76; 'Clay' in *The Scots Magazine* Feb 1933, pp. 329–39; 'Sim' in *The Free Man* 2 (10 June 1933), pp. 5–7.

CURTAIN RAISER

p. 3 Gibbon moved to the 'pleasant village' of Welwyn Garden City in 1929. MacDiarmid lived in Whalsay, Shetland from 1933 until 1942. On MacDiarmid and *Scottish Scene* see Alan Bold, *MacDiarmid* (1988), pp. 314–16.

THE ANTIQUE SCENE

p. 3 Gibbon's Diffusionist beliefs are explored in this essay; see Douglas F. Young, *Beyond the Sunset* (1973). Diffusionists argued that there was a Golden Age until the coming of civilisation, when agriculture diffused its corrupting influence from the Nile delta throughout the world. Grafton Elliot Smith (1871–1937), a professor of Anatomy, explained Diffusionism in *The Ancient Egyptians* (1911) and *The Migration of Early Cultures* (1915). His ideas were developed in HJ Massington, *The Golden Age* (1927).

p. 4 The publications of Karl Kaltwasser (b. 1894) include *Das Schicksalsbuch* (1937) and *Vomtätigen Wort, eine Rede* (1938), on German intellectual life.

p. 4 Guild-towns refer to Scottish burghs.

p. 5 Maglemosian culture, named after finds at Maglemose in Denmark, marked a shift between Palaeolithic and Neolithic cultures.

p. 5 Cro-Magnard refers to Cro-Magnon man, whose remains were found at Cro-Magnon in the Dordogne. His long-skulled, short-faced physical type has survived up to the present day.

p. 5 Magdalenian, named after La Madelaine, a cave on the Vézère, refers to the upper Palaeolithic culture.

p. 6 Celt, as a term, was first applied to people from Gaul, then extended to mean people from Celtic-speaking groups, including Breton, Cornish, Welsh, Gaelic, Irish and Manx. See Nora Chadwick, *The Celts* (1997). Gibbon harbours a strong prejudice against them.

p. 7 Pytheas of Massilia (*fl.* 4th century BC) was a Greek seafarer, who sailed to Thule (possibly Iceland), travelling past Spain, Gaul, and eastern Britain.

p. 7 Calgacus (*fl. c.* 84) was the leader of the Caledonii at the battle of Mons Graupius.

p. 7 Kenneth MacAlpin (*fl.* 9th century) succeeded his father, Alpin, as king of the Dalriada Scots in 834.

p. 7 The Picts are central to Gibbon's writing. This ancient people of Scotland, associated with the North East, were noted for their distinctive decorated stones. See Anna Ritchie, *Picts* (1989). The area where Gibbon was raised is rich in archaeological sites, including the cairns on Mont Goldrum (Camp Hill) and beside Cluseburn farm and the Standing Stone on Murrystone Hill. See IAG Shepherd, *Aberdeen and North East Scotland* (1996).

p. 8 The 'Scoti', who came from North East Ireland to Kintyre and Mid-Argyll *c.* 500, used the name 'Dalriada' (their homeland) for their new territories. The kingdom lasted until Kenneth MacAlpin united Scotland, by conquering the Picts. See John Bannerman, *Studies in the History of Dalriada* (1974).

p. 9 Christianity came to Scotland with Columba (521–97) and the North East was one of the earliest Christianised areas. St Drostan, a disciple of Columba, founded the Abbey at New Deer. See James Porter, ed., *After Columba – After Calvin* (1999).

p. 9 The Scottish reformer John Knox (*c.* 1513–72) was hugely influential in the establishment of Protestantism in Scotland in 1560. He is equally known, as Gibbon says, for opposing Mary Queen of Scots. See Edwin Muir, *John Knox, Portrait of a Calvinist* (1929) and *John Knox* (1975), ed., D. Shaw.

p. 10 The Pictish stone at Aberlemno Churchyard, Angus, shows a spectacular battle scene involving two Pictish armies. See W.A. Cummins, *The Age of the Picts* (1995), pp. 133–5.

p. 11 Good introductions to the development of languages within Scotland include David Murison, *The Guid Scots Tongue* (1977), J. Derrick McClure, *Why Scots Matters* (1988) and Derick Thomson, *Why Gaelic Matters* (1984).

p. 11 Malcolm III, Canmore (*c.* 1031–93) was the son of King Duncan. Raised in Northumbria, he succeeded to the throne of Scotland in 1057, when Macbeth was killed. See Gordon Donaldson, *Scottish Kings* (1961) on Malcolm, and the other monarchs here.

p. 11 St Margaret (*c.* 1046–93) was Canmore's second wife. She was born in Hungary, the daughter of Edward 'the Exile' of England. She engaged in extensive reforms of the Scottish church, built Dumfermline Abbey and refounded Iona.

p. 11 Four of Malcolm's nine sons succeeded him

p. 12 Andrew of Wyntoun (*c.* 1355–1422) wrote the rhyming *Orygynale Cronykil of Scotland* at the end of the fourteenth century, describing the history of Scotland from the Creation to his own time.

p. 12 John Barbour (*c.* 1320–95). His long poem *The Bruce* is a major source on this king's life.

p. 12 Blind Harry (*c.* 1440–*c.* 1492) wrote *Wallace* (*c.* 1477), a poem which celebrates the Scottish patriot and his nation. It was inspirational for later poets like Burns and Hogg.

p. 12 The War of Independence usually refers to campaigns between Scotland and England from 1296 to 1328. See Raymond Campbell Paterson, *For the Lion* (1996).

p. 12 William Wallace (d. 1305) defeated the English invaders at the Battle of Stirling (not Cambuskenneth) Brig (11th September 1297). As Guardian of Scotland, Wallace was defeated by the forces of Edward I at Falkirk (22nd July 1298). See Andrew Fisher, *William Wallace* (1986).

p. 13 The English cleric John Richard Green (1837–1883) wrote a popular *Short History of the English People* (1874), revised and reissued in four volumes (1877–80).

p. 13 The Army of the Scots Commons refers to Wallace's forces.

p. 14 Villeinage is the tenure or status of a villein, or (from the 13th century onwards) a serf, free in relation to all but his lord.

p. 14 The notion of clan in Scotland involves loyalty to the chief, from the tenant-retainer, based on common ancestry. See I. Grimble, *Clans and Chiefs* (1980).

p. 14 The Auld Alliance between Scotland and France against England began in 1295, and was renewed again on several occasions, including that which led to Flodden. See Gordon Donaldson, *The Auld Alliance* (1985).

p. 15 James IV (1473–1513) was known for his stable and culturally rich reign, including his patronage of William Dunbar and Gavin Douglas. Having renewed the Auld Alliance with France, James died facing the forces of Henry VIII of England at Flodden (9th September 1513), along with many of Scotland's prominent nobles and an estimated 12,000 troops. This is remembered in the lyric, 'The Flowers of the Forest' (the best known version is by Jean Elliot).

p. 15 Henry VIII (1491–1547) of England engaged in

'monk murdering' when he suppressed the English monasteries between 1535 and 1536.

p. 15 In August 1542 Henry VIII attempted to invade Scotland, but was repelled by George Gordon, the fourth Earl of Huntly (*c.* 1510–62) at Haddenrig.

p. 15 At the Battle of Solway Moss (24th November 1542), Scottish troops, led by Maxwell (d. 1546), Warden of the West March, surrendered to the English. Many of the captured men joined the 'Assured Scots' (allies of Henry VIII). See GM Fraser, *The Steel Bonnets* (1974).

p. 15 The disheartened James V is said to have predicted the end of the Stuart dynasty in Scotland, on the birth of his daughter, Mary, with Mary of Guise-Lorraine (8th December 1542).

p. 16 Mary Queen of Scots (1542–87) claimed her kingdom of Scotland in 1561, recently widowed from Francis, the Dauphin of France. See Jenny Wormwald, *Mary, Queen of Scots* (1988).

p. 18 The National Covenant of 1638 rejected Charles I's conditions of worship for Scotland, and was followed by the Solemn League and Covenant of 1643. There was an upsurge of Covenanting activity after the Restoration. The brutal 'Killing Times' have been treated by many Scottish writers. See Walter Scott, *Old Mortality* (1816), James Hogg, *The Brownie of Bodsbeck* (1818), John Galt, *Ringan Gilhaize* (1823), SR Crockett, *The Men of the Moss Hags* (1895) and, most recently, James Robertson, *The Fanatic* (2000). Gibbon planned a novel on this period, *The Men of the Moss Haggs* (see below, 'In Brief'). See Ian B. Cowan, *The Scottish Covenanters* (1967).

p. 19 Charles II (1630–85) was crowned King of Scotland in 1651, and came to the throne of England and Scotland in 1660. The Restoration Settlement led to an upsurge of Covenanting activity in Scotland. See KDH Haley, *Charles II* (1988).

p. 19 Battle of Rullion Green, 28th November 1666, at

which Sir Thomas Dalyell (*c.* 1599–1685) defeated the Covenanters.

p. 19   John Graham of Claverhouse, 1st Viscount of Dundee (*c.* 1649–89), 'Bonny Dundee' or 'Bloody Clavers' depending on perspective, was a professional soldier. He joined the Prince of Orange's horse-guards in 1672, returning to Scotland in 1677 to join the forces of the Marquess of Montrose, his cousin. Beaten by the Covenanters at the Battle of Drumclog (1st June 1679), he saw them defeated at the Battle of Bothwell Brig (22nd June 1679) and ruthlessly routed those who survived. He received a fatal wound at the Battle of Killiecrankie (27th July 1689). See Alistair Norwich Tayler and Henrietta Tayler, *John Graham of Claverhouse* (1939).

p. 20   Andrew Fletcher of Saltoun (1655–1716) opposed the Union of the Parliaments, proposing a federal union between England and Scotland. See WC Mackenzie, *Andrew Fletcher of Saltoun* (1935).

p. 20   See John Prebble, *The Darien Disaster* (1968).

p. 21   John Erskine, the 11th Earl of Mar (1675–1732), was known as 'Bobbing John'. He was Secretary of State in 1705, Commissioner for Union in 1706 and supported George I in 1714. However, Mar raised the standard for James VIII on the Braes of Mar in 1715. After Sherriffmuir he left for France and he later changed sides again.

p. 21   At the Battle of Sherriffmuir (13th November 1715) the Jacobites, under Mar, were forced into a retreat by the Duke of Argyll's government forces.

p. 21   Charles Edward Stuart (1720–88), Charles III or the Young Pretender, landed in Scotland on 12th July 1745. See SM Kybett, *Bonnie Prince Charlie* (1988).

p. 22   Jacobite clans included the Macgregors, Macdonalds, Macphersons, Stewarts and Robertsons. See C. Petrie, *The Jacobite Movement* (1959).

p. 22   The Jacobites reached Derby in December 1745. Due to the lack of French support, and the strength of the opposition, they retreated to Scotland.

p. 22 At the Battle of Culloden (16th April 1746), the Jacobites forces were swiftly and decisively defeated and then routed, by 'Butcher' Cumberland. See John Prebble, *Culloden* (1961).

GREENDEN

p. 23 This story and those which follow (particularly 'Clay') bear witness to Gibbon's wonderful recall of farming methods, and terminology, in the North East Scotland of his childhood. The North East places mentioned, in the stories and essays below, are in the area around Lawrencekirk, where Gibbon grew up. See Ordnance Survey *Pathfinder Maps 273, Stonehaven and Inverbervie* and *285, Laurencekirk and Fettercairn*. On traditional farming techniques and land management, see Alexander Fenton, *The Rural Architecture of Scotland* (1981); *The Shape of the Past* (1985–86); *Scottish Country Life* (1999). See too *Farm Servants and Labour in Lowland Scotland 1770–1914*, ed., TM Devine (Edinburgh: Donald, 1984).

p. 23 The Free Church of Scotland was founded at the time of the Disruption (1843). In 1900 most of its members joined the United Free Church but a minority remained as the 'Wee Frees'. See GNM Collins, *The Heritage of our Fathers* (1974).

p. 24 The rig and furrow system, also known as runrig, was prevalent throughout Scotland until the eighteenth century, and lasted in isolated places beyond this time. Each tenant was allocated a number of rigs which were intermixed and sometimes reallocated between tenants.

FORSAKEN

p. 46 'Eli, Eli, lama sabachthani' (Matthew 27: 46) is Christ's cry of despair: 'My God, my God, why hast thou forsaken me?'. Eloi is also the name of the idle race in Wells's *Time Machine* (1895).

p. 46 The Samaritans were traditionally the enemies of the Jews; Jesus was insulted by being called a Samaritan

(John 8: 48). Jesus spoke with, and preached to, Samaritans several times (see John 4).

p. 47　Proverbially, all Scots are Jock Tamson's bairns.

p. 49　Pa is compared to Peter. Originally called Simon, Peter was a fisherman from Bethsaida in Galilee. He occupied a special place among Jesus' disciples.

p. 50　Mary Magdalene was the sister of Lazarus and Martha. Jesus expelled seven demons from Mary (Mark 16: 9; Luke 8: 2) and she is the quintessential reformed sinner of the Christian tradition.

p. 52　The mother is appropriately compared to Martha, the sister of Mary and Lazarus, from Bethany. She was the worker of the household (see Luke 10: 38–42).

p. 52　Jesus, of course, is supposed to have been a carpenter before he began his preaching (Mark 6: 3).

p. 52　On Lascar dock-workers from India, see Bashir Maan, *The New Scots* (1992).

p. 52　The son of the family is Paul (Saul of Tarsus), a Roman patrician. Saul underwent a conversion experience on the road to Damascus when Jesus appeared to him (Acts of the Apostles 9).

p. 53　Sanhedrin: a Jewish council or court, especially the supreme council and court at Jerusalem.

p. 53　Agitprop is pro-Communist Agitation and Propaganda.

p. 54　This Biblical concept is expressed in the Acts of the Apostles (2: 44): 'And all that believed were together, and had all things in common.'

SIM

p. 57　The spinners of Segget feature in *Sunset Song* (1931).

p. 59　Brose is proverbially the food of the poor farm worker.

p. 62　The term days were, traditionally, the four days of the year when leases and contracts of employment began and ended in Scotland. They are Candlemas (2nd February), Whitsunday (15th May), Lammas (1st August) and Martinmas (11th November).

p. 66 Dundon features, too, in *The Thirteenth Disciple* (1931). It is a thinly disguised Aberdeen.

CLAY

p. 69 This story contains much detail about the farming culture of Gibbon's lifetime, from methods of manuring, to harvesting practices, involving women and men, to cross-ploughing (see Glossary).

p. 75 Rachel's bursary is a reference to the kailyard convention of the lad o'pairts being offered a place at the university.

p. 77 Stonehive is the North East name for Stonehaven.

p. 79 On early burial customs, see CR Wickham-Jones, *Scotland's First Settlers* (1994), especially pp. 117–18.

p. 80 Clay, in the Bible, is associated with human life. See Isaiah (45: 9): 'Woe unto him that striveth with his maker! . . . Shall the clay say to him that fashioneth it, What makest thou?'

THE LAND

p. 82 Kailyard is the cloyingly sentimental school of writing associated with SR Crockett (1859–1914), Ian MacLaren [John Watson] (1850–1907) and JM Barrie (1860–1937).

p. 83 Ptolemy listed sixteen groups of people living in Scotland, including the Venricones.

p. 84 The quote is from *The Thirteenth Disciple* Book I, IV. The reference is to Gilbert Keith Chesterton (1874–1936), Catholic man of letters and novelist, satirised in MacDiarmid's *A Drunk Man Looks at the Thistle* for his girth and complacency. 'Chela' is a Hindi word for slave or servant. Azilian: belonging to a transition between Palaeolithic and Neolithic, named after Ariège, where objects of this culture were found in a cave.

p. 84   Phthisis is an infectious disease, producing lesions of the lungs.

p. 85   The turtle dove is the quintessential Biblical symbol of innocence; in the Song of Solomon (2: 10) the lover is asked to rise up as 'the time of the singing of birds is come, and the voice of the turtle is heard in our land.'

p. 87   Spartacus (d. 71 BC), one of Gibbon's greatest heroes, was a Thracian shepherd, captured by the Romans and sold at Capua to become a gladiator. He escaped from captivity in 73 BC and led a revolt of the slaves. See Gibbon's novel *Spartacus* (1933) and his poem of that title in Songs of Limbo.

p. 89   Gibbon's description of the Glen of Drumtochty recalls John Ruskin (1819–1900) on the distinctive qualities of Scottish streams. See *Fors Clavigera* vol 3 (1903) ed., E. T. Cook and Alexander Wedderburn, pp. 593–95.

p. 90   Tyre was a Phoenician settlement, South of Beirut. An important centre for trade, it was famous for the 'Tyrian purple' dye.

p. 90   Quoted from 'Crowdieknowe', *The Complete Poems of Hugh MacDiarmid*, pp. 26–27.

p. 91   Alexander the Great (356–323 BC), king of Macedonia and the Greek mainland campaigned across the Jaxartes, a great river of Central Asia.

p. 91   Chichen-Itza was the power centre of northern Yucatan, with its main period of occupation being between *c.* 1000 and 1250.

p. 92   Fray Bentos: canned corned beef.

p. 93   Oswald Spengler (1880–1936), the German writer, wrote *Untergang des Abendlandes* (1918–22), translated as *The Decline of the West* by C F Atkinson (1926–29). His idea of cycles is that all cultures, and civilisations, are subject to growth and decay.

p. 94   Gilbert White (1720–93), the English naturalist and cleric, wrote a popular *Natural History and Antiquities of Selborne* (1789).

p. 94   Harold John Massingham (1888–1952) was a writer and essayist, author of *The English Countryside* (1939).

p. 95   In 1685, one hundred and sixty seven Covenanter men and women, followers of the deceased preacher Richard Cameron, were imprisoned for nine weeks in the small vaulted cellar now known as the Whigs' Vault, at Dunnottar Castle, near Stonehaven. See Alastair Cunningham, *A Guide to Dunnottar Castle* (1998), pp. 14; 32–33.

p. 95   The Appian Way was the main thoroughfare between ancient Rome and Greece, built by Appius Claudius Caecus in 312 BC.

GLASGOW

p. 97   Siva is the destroyer and life-giver, third God in the Hindu triad.

p. 97   Xipe Totec is the god of spring and renewal according to the Aztec. In Aztec rituals connected with Xipe people were sacrificed by flaying.

p. 97   In *The Thirteenth Disciple* (1931) Mitchell describes Glasgow as 'that strange, deplorable city which has neither sweetness nor pride, the vomit of a cataleptic commercialism' (Chapter 3).

p. 98   Camlachie, Govan and the Gorbals were all notorious slum districts in Glasgow.

p. 99   The Morlocks are a group of spidery underground men, in HG Wells' *The Time Machine* (1895). They do all the work while the Eloi are idle but, during the night, sometimes climb up the ventilating shafts to feed on the Eloi.

p. 99   The line 'where he and his true love will never meet again' is from the well known tragic lyric, 'The Bonnie Banks of Loch Lomond'.

p. 100   *The Modern Scot* was published from 1930 to 1936. Adam Kennedy was involved in this periodical. His work includes *Orra Boughs* (1930).

p. 100　　Kelvingrove is one of the most desirable districts of Glasgow.

p. 101　　Douglasism, based on CH Douglas' ideas – advocating an 'economic democracy' and 'socialising credit' to decentralise finance and make the individual economically independent – is discussed in detail in MacDiarmid's *Scottish Scene* essay 'Representative Scots (2) The Builder – Major CH Douglas'. MacDiarmid had much more faith in Douglas than did Gibbon.

p. 101　　Wendy Wood (1892–1981), leading campaigner for Home Rule in Scotland.

p. 101　　Sir (Edward Montague) Compton Mackenzie (1883–1972), the novelist and broadcaster, settled in Barra in 1928 and, latterly, lived in Edinburgh. A supporter of the Scottish Nationalist Party, his comic works include *The Monarch of the Glen* (1941) and *Whisky Galore* (1947); novels about society, economics and politics *include The Four Winds of Love* (1937–45). See A. Linklater, *Compton Mackenzie* (1987).

p. 101　　George Blake (1893–1961). Novelist, magazine editor and publisher, born in Greenock and worked in Glasgow and London. His novels about west coast Scottish working class culture include *The Shipbuilders* (1935).

p. 101　　James Maxton (1885–1946). Politician, born in Glasgow. Chairman of the ILP in 1926 and MP for Bridgeton from 1922 up to his death in 1946. Pacifist and conscientous objector; imprisoned for trying to organise a strike of shipyard workers during the First World War. Maxton's works include a book on Lenin (1932). See William Knox, *James Maxton* (1982).

p. 102　　Robin McKelvie Black edited *The Free Man*, a Social Credit Weekly. See Bold, *MacDiarmid* on Black.

p. 102　　Hunterian Museum of the University of Glasgow, based on the museum and art collection of William Hunter (1718–83) is the oldest public museum in Scotland; it opened in 1807.

p. 103 Jozef Isräels (1824–1911), the painter, was born in Gröningen. He was well known for genre paintings, especially of fisherfolk, like his *Children of the Sea* (1857).

p. 104 Sir John Everett Millais (1829–96) was an English painter associated with the pre-Raphaelites.

p. 104 Kelvinside, Woodsidehill, Hillhead and Dowanhill are all districts in the fashionable West End of Glasgow.

p. 104 Springburn, Bridgeton and Mile End, as Gibbon explains, were parts of shipbuilding and industrial Glasgow.

p. 105 Guy Alfred Aldred (1886–1963), Non-Parliamentary Anarcho communist; argued from the doctrines of Mikhail Bakunin (1814–76), the Russian anarchist, who opposed Marx in the Communist International of 1872 and was expelled.

p. 105 The National Party of Scotland was formed in 1928 and merged with the Scottish Party in 1934 as the Scottish National Party.

p. 106 Sir Harry Lauder (1870–1950), the Scottish comedian, made his name composing and singing songs like 'Roamin' in the Gloamin' and 'I Love a Lassie'. He is compared here to Baal, a god of the Phoenicians, often used to imply a false god.

p. 108 The Molendinar Burn, and the Isle of Bute.

p. 108 Heptarchy is government by seven persons. This was supposedly the system of the English kingdoms of Wessex, Sussex, Kent, Essex, East Anglia, Mercia and Northumbria.

ABERDEEN

p. 109 Mitchell enlisted in the Royal Army Service Corps on 26th August 1919, and served in Mesopotamia, Palestine and Egypt between 1919–1923.

p. 111 Aberdeen's geography is described with precision here, from the Duthie Park to Marischal College to the statues described.

p. 115 Mitchell worked as a junior reporter on the *Aberdeen Journal* between 1917 and 1919, when he took up a post with the *Scottish Farmer* in Glasgow.

p. 115 The Aberdeen journalist George Fraser recalled the founding of the Aberdeen Soviet, in a letter to John Manson in 1933, confirming Gibbon's anecdote: 'Alexander Catto, the Chief Reporter, had sent Leslie to report on a meeting of the cell and when the young reporter was somewhat long in returning, his chief decided to go along himself to see if all was well with the lad. To his amusement he found him actually addressing the meeting', quoted in John Manson, 'Hugh MacDiarmid and Lewis Grassic Gibbon's Politics', *Cencrastus* 50 (Winter 1994), pp. 39–42.

p. 115 '*O tempora, O mores*' is from Cicero's *Catilinam* Speech 1: Chapter 1: 'O the times, O the manners'.

p. 118 Footdee is one of the oldest fishing ports in the North East, by Aberdeen.

p. 119 Brachycephalic means broad headed, associated with Pictish stock.

p. 119 *The Press and Journal*, Aberdeen's leading paper, founded in 1747.

p. 120 St Machar's Cathedral, in Old Aberdeen, is close to the Kittybrewster market (now demolished, along with the slum areas Gibbon mentions below).

p. 120 Olaf was the name of five kings of Norway, starting with Olaf I Tryggvessön (*c.* 965–1000), who participated in the Viking expeditions against Britain and succeeded to the throne of Norway when he overthrew King Haakon in 995. King Arthur, of course, is the legendary king of the Britons, supposedly buried (among other places) in the Eildon Hills, in the Scottish Borders.

p. 120 Donald, the Lord of the Isles and claimant to the Earldom of Ross, was defeated by the Lowlanders of the North East at the Battle of Harlaw in 1411.

p. 121 Mannofield and Cults are still desirable districts in Aberdeen, particularly for the modern oil executive.

p. 122 Red Biddie is a mixture of red wine and methylated spirits.

LITERARY LIGHTS

p. 123 Alan Porter (1899–1942) was a poet and critic; his work includes *The signature of pain and other poems* (1930) and, as editor, *John Clare: poems, chiefly from manuscript* (1820).

p. 123 Vladimir Michail Bekheterev (1857–1927) was a psychologist. His work includes *General principles of human reflexology: an introduction to the objective study of personality.* Ivan Petrovich Pavlov (1849–1936), best known for studying conditioned, or acquired, reflexes associated with the brain.

p. 123 George Bernard Shaw (1856–1950), Irish Socialist playwright, critic, journalist, essayist and a leading member of the Fabian Society.

p. 125 Sir Rabindranath Tagore (1861–1914), the Indian poet, philosopher and Nobel Prize winner (1913).

p. 126 Eric Linklater (1899–1974), the Orcadian novelist, journalist and broadcaster, set most of his work in Northern Scotland, including *White Maa's Saga* (1929) and *The Men of Ness* (1932).

p. 126 *Hatter's Castle* (1931) by Dr AJ Cronin (1896–1981) originally from Dumbartonshire. *The House with the Green Shutters* (1901) by George Douglas [Brown] (1869–1902) is a virulent attack on the Kailyard school of sentimental Scottish rural fiction.

p. 127 The editor of *The Modern Scot* was JH Whyte. In 1936 the periodical merged with the *Scottish Standard* to form *Outlook*.

p. 127 Paul Einzig (b. 1897) was a political economist, whose work includes *The Economic Foundation of Fascism* (1933) and *Economic Problems of the Next War* (1939).

p. 127   (Ignatius) Roy (Dunnachie) Campbell (1901–57), South African poet and journalist. He fought with Franco during the Spanish Civil War.

p. 127   Johnsonese refers to the sometimes laborious style of Samuel Johnson (1709–84).

p. 128   (George) Norman Douglas (1868–1952). Novelist and travel writer, born at Tilquihillie near Banchory, who spent much of his life in Italy. His works include *South Wind* (1917) and *Old Calabria* (1919).

p. 128   Robert Bontine Cunninghame Grahame (1852–1936): essayist, politician and travel writer. Born in London to a Scottish and Spanish family, he married the Chilean poet, Gabriela de la Belmondiere, and travelled widely, particularly in South America. Cunninghame Grahame was the Liberal MP for North West Lanarkshire (1886–1892) and was jailed for six weeks in 1887, after participating in the Trafalgar Square riots. A close friend of Keir Hardie, Grahame was the first president of the Scottish Labour Party in 1888. After the First World War, he joined the Scottish Home Rule Association, was president of the National Party of Scotland in 1928 and first president of the Scottish National Party when the NPS merged with the Scottish Party in 1934.

p. 128   Dr James Bridie [Osborne Henry Mavor] (1888–1951), the Glasgow playwright, was chair of the Glasgow Citizens Theatre.

p. 128   Edwin Muir (1887–1959), Orcadian poet, novelist and critic. Moved with his family, at 14, to Glasgow. Member of the ILP, contributor to AR Orage's *The New Age* and married to the novelist Willa Anderson.

p. 128   Dr Charles Murray (1864–1941) was an Aberdeenshire poet who worked in South Africa, known for his evocative poems in North East Scots.

p. 129   WH Hamilton was an early critic of MacDiarmid. He edited an anthology of mostly minor poets called *Holyrood: a Garland of Modern Scots Poems* (1929).

p. 129   Naomi Mitchison (1897–1999). Edinburgh born, hugely prolific novelist and poet throughout her long life. Her interest in folklore, particularly in the classical period, is reflected in *The Corn King and the Spring Queen* (1937); *The Conquered* (1923) was her first novel, set in the distant past. *Black Sparta* (1928) is also broadly historical in tone.

p. 129   Neil Miller Gunn (1891–1973) from Caithness. Gunn's semi-allegorical work investigates Scottish culture, often among the Northern fishing communities, drawing connexions between the past and the present (Gunn posits, like Gibbon, that a Golden Age existed in Scotland in the past). *Sun Circle* was published in 1933, and other works include *The Silver Darlings* (1941) and *The Well at the World's End* (1952). See Douglas Gifford, *Neil M. Gunn and Lewis Grassic Gibbon* (1983).

p. 130   Willa Muir (1890–1970), née Anderson, was a novelist and social critic. She married Edwin Muir in 1919. Her works include, with Muir, translations of Franz Kafka (1883–1924) and other European writers. Her novels include *Imagined Corners* (1931) – a detailed exploration of the situation of unconventional Scottish women – and *Mrs Ritchie* (1933). *Mrs Grundy in Scotland* (1936) is a caustic look at Scottish culture and *Belonging* (1968) is Muir's memoir. See Margaret Elphinstone, 'Willa Muir: crossing the genres', *A History of Scottish Women's Writing* (1997), ed., Douglas Gifford and Dorothy McMillan.

p. 130   John Buchan (1875–1940), Lord Tweedsmuir of Elsfield, was a novelist, journalist, editor and critic. Buchan's work ranges from historical novels like *John Burnet of Barns* (1898) to adventure novels like *The Thirty-Nine Steps* (1915) and the disturbing *Sick Heart River* (1941). See A. Smith, *John Buchan and his World* (1979).

p. 130   Sir Henry Rider Haggard (1856–1925). Novelist, born in Norfolk. Worked in Africa between 1875 and 1881, and known for his sensational, adventure novels including *King Solomon's Mines* (1885).

p. 131 Catherine Roxburgh Carswell, née Macfarlane (1879–1946), the novelist, biographer and critic, was born in Glasgow and married the journalist and critic Donald Carswell (1882–1939) in 1917. Her works include a controversial *The Life of Burns* (1930) and *The Savage Pilgrim: A Narrative of D. H. Lawrence* (1932) as well as the psychological novels of Scottish women's identity *Open the Door!* (1920) and *The Camomile* (1922). See Glenda Norquay, 'Catherine Carswell: 'Open the door!', *A History of Scottish Women's Writing*.

p. 131 John Middleton Murry (1889–1975) was a poet, essayist and critic.

p. 132 Ethel Mannin (b. 1900) was a writer and educationalist whose work includes *Common-sense and the Child* (1931) and *Falconers Voice and Other Stories* (1935).

p. 132 Gilbert Frankau (1884–1952) was a poet and novelist. His works include *City of Fear* and other poems (1917) and *Farewell Romance* (1936).

p. 132 The *History of Aneurism* was AJ Cronin's thesis for his MD at Glasgow University (1925).

p. 132 Sir James George Frazer (1854–1941), the social anthropologist, was born in Glasgow, and educated at Cambridge. His works on allegedly primitive cultures includes *Totemism and Exogamy* (1910) and, most influentially, *The Golden Bough* (1890), revised (1911–15) and abridged (1922)

p. 132 Sir Edward Burnet Tylor (1832–1917), the anthropologist, was born at Camberwell and travelled in Mexico. His best known works are *Primitive Culture* (1871) and *Anthropology* (1881). See RR Marett, *Tylor* (1936).

p. 133 Muriel Stuart's works include *Christ at carnival, and Other Poems* (1916), *The Cockpit of Idols* (1918) and *Fool's Garden* (1936).

p. 133 Francis Thompson (1859–1907). His work includes *Poems* (1893), *New Poems* (1897), an *Essay on Shelley* (1909) and *Life of St Ignatius* (1909).

p. 133   Hugh MacDiarmid [Christopher Murray Grieve] (1892–1978), the poet and polemicist; Gibbon's friend and key figure of the Scottish literary renaissance.

p. 133   (James) Lewis (Thomas Chalmers) Spence (1874–1955) was an anthropologist, poet, and magazine editor. Writing on the customs and mythology, in Britain and beyond, his works include *Mythologies of Mexico and Peru* (1907), *Dictionary of Mythology* (1913), *The History of Atlantis* (1927), a pamphlet *Freedom for Scotland* (19–) and *Collected Poems* (1953).

p. 135   William Soutar (1888–1943), the Scottish poet, served in the Navy during the First World War; where he exhibited the symptoms of the spondylitis which would keep him bedbound from 1930. His later poetry is largely in Scots, often geared towards children.

p. 135   The *via terrena* is, literally, the way of earth; the earliest form of Roman road: a track worn by the feet of people and animals.

p. 135   Synthetic Scots is the term used to describe the literary blending (from everyday life as well as dictionaries of the language) in Scots during the literary renaissance.

p. 135   James Barke (1905–58), Scottish novelist and author of *Major Operation* (1936) and *The Land of the Leal* (1939). *The World his Pillow* (1933) was his first novel, but he was most successful with a five volume sequence on Robert Burns.

p. 136   Donald Sinclair (b. 1855) published Gaelic works, including the comedy *Domhnull nan trioblaid* (1936) and *Suiridhe Raoghail mhaoil* (1929).

p. 136   The work of Duncan Johnston (1881–1947) includes *Cronan nan tonn* (1997) with foreword by AN Currie.

p. 136   John MacFadyen was a Gaelic poet and songwriter, whose work includes *Sgeulaiche nan caol* (1902) and *An t-eileanach* (1890).

p. 136   Alexander MacDonald [Alasdair Mac Mhaighstir

Alasdair] (c. 1695–1770) was a poet and a teacher from Moidart. His best known work includes 'Birlinn Chlann Raghanill', a detailed description of a sea voyage from South Uist to Carrickfergus.

p. 136 Duncan Ban MacIntyre [Donnchadh Bàn Mac an t-Saoir] (1724–1812) was largely unappreciated in his lifetime, but now recognised as one of Scotland's finest poets, writing in Gaelic. Best known for his nature poetry 'Moladh Beinn Dònhrainn' celebrating his favourite mountain.

p. 137 Fionn MacColla [Thomas Douglas Macdonald] (1906–75), the Scottish novelist and headmaster, wrote novels of Highland life. The Albannach (1932), deals with the struggles of a Free Church elder's son, while And the Cock Crew (1945) is set during the Highland clearances.

p. 137 The full quotation, from Virgil's Aeneid 9, 1.941 is 'Macte nova virtute, puer, sic itur ad astra': 'Blessings on your courage, boy, that's the way to the stars'.

THE WRECKER – JAMES RAMSAY MACDONALD
For fuller details on Ramsay MacDonald, see Austen Morgan, J. Ramsay MacDonald (1987) chapter 7, 'The 1931 financial crisis' and David Marquand, Ramsay MacDonald (1977).

p. 137 The French writer Anatole France (1844–1924) [Jacques Anatole Thibault] won the Nobel prize for literature in 1921 and was literary critic for Le Temps.

p. 137 The 'Nominalist and Realist' controversy was between those who argued that reality is composed of individual parts and that abstract entities (universals) lack reality (Nominalists) and those who believed that universals exist without specific objects. Leading Nominalists included William of Ockham (c. 1285–1349) and one of the best known Realists was Duns Scotus (c. 1266–1308).

p. 138 This passage, describing a North East landscape, from MacDonald's Margaret Ethel MacDonald (1911) p. 220, is quoted from Mary Agnes Hamilton, J. Ramsay MacDonald (1929), revised from The Man of Tommorrow

(1923), pp. 9–10. Gibbon draws extensively on this 'Lady Biographer' in this essay. Subsequent passages are from Hamilton p. 9 (MacDonald's Morayshire roots); p. 12 (MacDonald's grandmother) and p. 37.

p. 139 August Weismann (1834–1914), the German biologist, developed the theory that organic hereditary substances are transmitted between generations.

p. 139 According to Tantric Buddhism, the human passions (desire, aversion) can be purified, to lead to the practitioner's spiritual development.

p. 139 Mesozoic: of the Secondary geological period, including the Triassic, Jurassic and Cretaceous systems.

p. 139 Cassell produced a 'National Library' series in the late 19th century. There was also a 'Pocket Library' and a 'Cassell Biographies' series of the 1920s and 1930s.

p. 140 The Independent Labour Party was founded in 1893; the Scottish Parliamentary Labour Party was founded in 1888 by J. Keir Hardie.

p. 140 Sir James Arthur Thomson is Sir John Arthur Thomson (1861–1933), the biologist and naturalist. Thomson was Regius Professor of natural history at the University of Aberdeen (1899–1930). He wrote, broadly, on evolutionary issues, including *The Science of Life* (1904), *The Bible of Nature* (1909) and *What is Man* (1923). Between the Wars, Thomson was criticised as an old-fashioned biologist by some but was, by others, used as an exemplary scientist with a sense of religion; I am grateful to Sean Johnston for this information.

p. 140 The anthropologist and anatomist, Sir Arthur Keith (1866–1955), who was educated at the University of Aberdeen, specialised in fossilised humanoids. His work includes *Human Embryology and Morphology* (1902) and *Ancient Types of Man* (1911). *New Discoveries* (1931) stated that modern humans began in the early Pleistocene period.

p. 141 Dr Samuel Smiles (1812–1904), from East Lothian,

was editor of the *Leeds Times*. Influenced by Richard Cobden (1804–65), he was interested in social reform. His best known work is *Self Help* (1859).

p. 141 Hugh Miller (1802–56), from Cromarty, was a geologist, journalist, and editor of the Free Church publication *The Witness* from 1840. He recalled his autodidactic background, as a stonemason, in *My Schools and Schoolmasters* (1854).

p. 142 The reminiscences of Ramsay MacDonald (1866–1937) include *Wanderings and Excursions* (1925), a collection of essays about Scotland and the world.

p. 142 Dr GB Clark, the Radical MP for Caithness, was Chairman of the London branch of the Scottish Home Rule Association; MacDonald was honorary secretary to the Association. Clark later joined the Scottish Labour Party.

p. 142 MacDonald was involved with the Social Democratic Federation from 1885. His involvement with the Fabian Movement began in the late 1880s.

p. 000 (James) Keir Hardie (1856–1915), from Lanarkshire, began work as a miner in 1866. A journalist, and agitator for a miner's union, he was a founder-member of the Scottish Labour Party (later merged with the Independent Labour Party). He gained a parliamentary seat in 1892, lost this in 1895, but re-entered parliament as MP for Merthyr in 1900. As a trade unionist and believer in Home Rule for Scotland and Ireland, Hardie was a highly controversial figure. See Kenneth O. Morgan, *Keir Hardie* (1975) and on the history of the Labour Party, AJ Davies, *To Build a New Jerusalem* (1996).

p. 143 Oliver Cromwell (1599–1658), the English Parliamentarian, invaded Scotland as part of his political consolidation, after the execution of Charles I in 1649. His regime became increasingly unpopular.

p. 143 John Hampden (1594–1643) was a moderate English parliamentarian. Hampden was one of the members

Charles I tried to seize in 1642 (a crucial event in the outbreak of Civil War in England).

p. 143 William Penn (1644–1718), was the English founder of Pennsylvania, and an ardent Quaker.

p. 143 Edmund Burke (1729–97), the Irish statesman and philosopher, wrote the hugely influential *Reflections on the French Revolution* (1790).

p. 143 The two Labour MPs elected at the 1900 General Election were Keir Hardie for Merthyr and Richard Bell, secretary of the Amalgamated Society of Railway Servants, for Derby.

p. 143 MacDonald's Socialist tracts and books include *Socialism and Government* (1909) and *Socialism: Critical and Constructive* (1921). Gibbon evidently was familiar with a wide variety of his work.

p. 144 Gregor Johann Mendel (1822–84), the Austrian biologist, developed the law of dominant and recessive characters: the basis of modern genetics.

p. 145 Arthur Henderson (1863–1935), the Glasgow born politician, was chairman of the Labour Party and served in the Coalition Cabinets of 1915–17. He was Home Secretary in 1924 and Foreign Secretary from 1929–31, but refused to join MacDonald's National Government in 1931.

p. 145 Marie Correlli (1855–1924) [Mary Mackay] was a popular English novelist.

p. 147 Vladimir Illyich Lenin [Ulyanov] (1870–1924), the Russian Revolutionary, led the Bolsheviks from 1903. Although the rising of 1905 failed, the October revolution of 1917 meant the collapse of the Provisional Government and the Bolsheviks coming to power. In 1922 Lenin began the 'new economic policy', allowing Russia limited free enterprise; he died two years later.

p. 147 At the Third International, or Comintern, established in Moscow in 1919, principles were established regarding co-operation with the peasants, and a need for centralised control.

p. 147 Frederick John Napier Thesiger, 1st Viscount Chelmsford (1863–1933), occupied various establishment posts, including Governor of Queensland (1905–09), Governor of New South Wales (1909–13), Viceroy of India (1916–21) and was appointed First Lord of the Admirality in 1924.

p. 148 Lord Salisbury: the political dynasty of the Cecils began with the first Baron Burghley, William Cecil (1520–98). The family was represented in Gibbon's lifetime by Robert Arthur James Gascoyne Cecil, 5th Marquess of Salisbury (b. 1893), who was Foreign Under-Secretary in 1935.

p. 148 John Campbell edited the *Workers' Weekly*; the official paper of the Communist party. He was arrested in early August 1924 for printing an article arguing that British soldiers should not 'turn your guns on your fellow workers' in a class or military war. On 13th August the prosecution was withdrawn; MacDonald's actions, however, came under scrutiny. See Marquand, pp. 364–77.

p. 149 The General Strike of 1926 began on Monday 3rd May at 11.59 pm. On MacDonald's actions, see Marquand, pp. 434–40.

p. 149 Stanley Baldwin, 1st Earl Baldwin of Bewley (1867–1947), the English Conservative politician, became Prime Minister in 1923. In the MacDonald Coalition (1931–35) he was Lord President of the Council. See Keith Middlemas, *Baldwin* (1969).

p. 149 Labour Representation Committee, formed in 1900.

p. 149 Joseph Stalin (1879–1953) [Iosif Vissarionovich Dzhugashvili] gradually built up his political position after the 1917 Revolution. On Lenin's death in 1924, he took control, and ruthlessly eliminated his many perceived opponents.

p. 150 In 1929 MacDonald was the first British Prime

Minister to visit the United States of America. The Republican Herbert Clark Hoover (1874–1964) was 31st President of the USA, from 1928. He was beaten by Franklin D. Roosevelt (1884–1945) in 1932.

p. 150 MacDonald argued for a National, or Three Party coalition, Government in the General Election of 27th October 1929. Labour lost 1,500,000 votes, and their representation dropped to 46 members. Over 80 per cent of backbenchers elected were Conservative. MacDonald was still Prime Minister, and the Cabinet was split between 11 Conservatives, 4 in the National Labour Group, 3 Samuelite Liberals and 2 Simonites.

RELIGION

p. 154 The four Veda are the holy books of the Hindus.

p. 154 Henry Grey Graham, *The Social Life of Scotland in the Eighteenth Century* (1937).

p. 156 The Mayan people (*c.* 592–900), based in Southern Mexico and Guatemala, were particularly noted for their ceremonial architecture.

ENVOI

p. 168 Sauria is an order of reptiles.

p. 168 The Auld Lichts were opposed to the New Lichts, with the religious split of 1799. Auld Lichts were in favour of establishmentarianism (the state upholding the church); New Lichts believed in disestablishmentarianism (church and state should be independent).

p. 168 For MacDiarmid's opinions on London Scots see *A Drunk Man Looks at the Thistle* (1926) in *The Complete Poems*, pp. 81–167.

p. 170 Walter Elliot (1888–1958). Conservative politician, writer and broadcaster. Secretary of State for Scotland (1936–38) and Minister of Health (1938–40). His publications include *Toryism and the Twentieth Century* (1927).

PART II: SONGS OF LIMBO

TEXTUAL NOTE: The following poems are all printed, by kind permission, from the typescript in the National Library of Scotland, MS 26058, with the exception of the last one, which is by permission from Aberdeen University Library 2377/1/31. All the poems in this section originally appear in two versions: a draft and a fair copy. I have followed the fair copies. Most of the changes between verses are small, affecting punctuation (commas into inverted commas; dashes omitted or added). Only significant changes – altered words, additional or removed verses – are noted below.

IN EXILE

p. 173 This poem was written to commemorate Gibbon's twenty-first birthday.

p. 174 After verse 7 of the draft there is an additional verse, scored through:

> And in your eyes a thousand fairy lights,
> Clear-burning, sweet;
> Fit lamps upon the Alabaster Shrine
> And greeting meet.

LINES WRITTEN IN A HAPPY THOUGHTS ALBUM

p. 174 Ré is Gibbon's wife, Rebecca Middleton, who grew up at Hareden, near to the Mitchell's farm at Bloomfield. They married in 1925.

p. 174 In the draft version, Mitchell has counted the syllables in these lines, marking his scansion pattern of '10 4 10 4' beside the lines. The pattern seems to be a flexible form of iambic pentameter, with a lyrical flavour, and I am grateful to Alan MacColl for pointing this out to me.

p. 174 Line 14 is originally 'empulsed in pangless pain'; the 'empulsed' is deleted.

p. 175 Line 16 is originally 'When memories dream'; the 'When' is deleted.

p. 175   Line 40 is originally 'Gilden Age', followed by 'I near' (presumably typographic errors).

SIX SONNETS FOR SIX MONTHS
  II IN MEMORIAM, RAY MITCHELL.
p. 177   In *Leslie Mitchell: Lewis Grassic Gibbon* (1966), Ian S. Munro quotes a moving letter from Mitchell to his wife, dated 11th February, while she was in Purley Cottage Hospital, pp. 43–44.

  III MICHAEL
p. 177   The archangel Michael is prominent in the apocrypha as the protector of the Jews. In the book of the Apocalypse (12: 7) Michael leads the angelic hosts.

VIMY RIDGE
p. 183   Vimy Ridge was recaptured by the British Army in April 1917, as had been agreed with Joffre in 1916, in preparation for the offensive in Flanders.
p. 184   The name Calvary is derived from the Rheims *New Testament* translation of 'calvariae locus', the Latin for Greek 'kraniou topos', the place of the skull (Golgotha) where Jesus was executed (Mark 15: 22).

SPARTACUS
p. 186   On Gibbon's hero Spartacus, see above (*Scottish Scene*, 'The Land').

LOST
p. 187   See the treatment of this theme in 'Forsaken'.

A SONG OF LIMBO
p. 190   In line 7 of the draft, this reads 'Come back! . . . And it seems that we hear,'; in the fair copy this also appears but 'And it seems that' is scored out and, in ink above, Mitchell adds, 'And dreaming,'.
p. 190   Line 11 of the draft is 'Their voices call as they called of old,'.

RUPERT BROOKE

p. 190   Rupert Brooke (1887–1915), the English poet, published his first book, *Poems*, in 1911 and died, tragically young, while serving with the Royal Naval Division.

p. 190   Lycomedes was the king of the Dolopians; he lived on the island of Scyros when the Trojan War was being fought.

p. 190   Pyrrhus the Redhead was the name of Neoptolemus, son of Achilles.

p. 191   In Greek mythology Adonis's coveted beauty led Aphrodite into conflict with Persephone. He was fatally wounded by a wild boar while in his youth.

THE COMMUNARDS OF PARIS

p. 199   The Communards were communists, adhering to the Paris Commune of 1871, rising against the National Government, maintaining that each city or district should be ruled independently by its own commune. See *The Communards of Paris 1871* (1973), ed., Stewart Edwards.

THE ROMANTICIST

p. 199   Line 1 of the draft is 'the thing I loved'.

ON THE MURDER OF KARL LIEBKNECHT AND
ROSA LUXEMBOURG

p. 200   In the draft, the title is 'On the Death of . . .', 'Death' is scored out and replaced with 'Murder'. Karl Liebknecht (1871–1919) was a German barrister and politician. A member of the Reichstag (1912–1916), he was imprisoned during the First World War for his pacifist beliefs. He participated in the Revolution of 1918 and was murdered in Berlin, along with his co-leader of the Spartakusbund, Rosa Luxembourg (1871–1919). Luxembourg was a German revolutionary, born in Poland, and wrote *Akkumulation des Kapitals* (1913). See Gilbert Badia, *La Spartakisme* (1967).

WHEN GOD DIED

p. 201　In the draft, the paper is torn and the last four lines are missing.

NOX NOCTES

p. 202　The title is, perhaps, an ironic reference to the 'Noctes Ambrosianae' series in *Blackwood's Magazine*.

DEAD LOVE

p. 203　The draft has a piece of sellotape over the first verse, making it difficult to read, but there seem to be some minor changes. Line 1, for instance, seems to read 'you nor I' rather than 'my dear and I'.

p. 204　Line 8 of the draft originally read 'Fire the dark valleys far beneath': this is scored through and the substitute line handwritten beneath.

p. 204　In verse 8 of the draft 'the breaker' is scored out and 'On last tides met' is given as a final line, also scored out.

p. 204　Line 33 in the draft is 'for we' rather than 'for me'.

p. 205　Line 46 in the draft is 'be Love's leaf' rather than 'by Love's leaf'.

VERSES TOWARDS 'KNOWLES LAST WATCH'

p. 206　Norla, as a character, appears in the *Polychromata* series (see below, 'Vernal').

DUST

p. 210　Cnossos, in Crete, is thought to have been the site of the court of Nausicaa, featured in *The Odyssey*, see below (Polychromata, 'He Who Seeks').

MORVEN

p. 212　Morven features in the Ossianic poetry of James Macpherson (1736–1796), as part of the Scots ancestral homeland. See *The Poems of Ossian and Related Works* (1996), ed., Howard Gaskill.

THE PHOTOGRAPH

p. 213　Eros, the god of Love.

p. 000   Ares, the Greek God of War, also identified as Mars.

TEARLESS
p. 215   The draft version has these additional verses, omitted in the fair copy:

> Being dead: song ceased forever,
> Past like a wind-blown feather,
> A crumpled, downy feather.
> Only her body lay
>
> On that fringe of Cairo's night.
> (Soul, gone from sound and sight,
> Was it darkness drowned you or light,
> Night or an undreamt day?)
>
> And the moonlight shuddered and passed,
> And the brooding shadows massed,
> And gathered and flooded at last
> The blackness where she lay.

RONDEL
p. 217   The sunstone men are the Picts.
p. 217   Jason's *Argo* had to pass through the Symplegades, or the Clashing Rocks, to enter the Hellespont. The rocks moved, crushing ships; the Argo was the first ship to pass through them and, after this, the rocks never moved again.
p. 217   The Argo was sailed by the Argonauts, who were Jason's companions as he searched for the Golden Fleece.

ON A VERNACULAR SOCIETY
p. 218   An auroch is the extinct wild ox or urus, sometimes used in error to refer to the European bison.
p. 218   Odin was the Norse god of battle.

PART III: POLYCHROMATA

TEXTUAL NOTE: Gibbon worked with the Royal Army Service Corps in Mesopotamia, Palestine and Egypt from 1919 to 1923. The stories in this section are all set in Cairo, most around the Khalig el Masri, the city's main thoroughfare, showing Gibbon's knowledge of this area and its landmarks, including the Pyramids. Gibbon enjoys using local phrases and spellings, such as *jinni* (genies). The Polychromata series was published in *The Cornhill Magazine* between 1929 and 1930.

HE WHO SEEKS

p. 223 Mount Olympus, in Thessaly, is traditionally the home of the greater Greek gods and so, by extension, heaven.

p. 223 Rameses II, the Great, was of the 19th Egyptian dynasty. He ruled between 1292 and 1255 BC, having come to terms with the Hittites at Kadesh. His reign is remembered for its monuments and temples, including the mortuary temple of Seti I at Luxor, the hall of the Karnak temple, and the rock temple of Abu Simnel.

p. 224 Tovarishii are comrades.

p. 229 Hagia Sofia was built in Istanbul (532–537) as a Christian cathedral. It became a Mosque at the time of the conquest of the Byzantine Empire in 1453.

p. 233 The *Odyssey*, composed probably at the end of the 8th century BC, is believed to be the composition of Homer. It describes the ten year journey of Odysseus, home to Ithaca after the Trojan Wars.

p. 233 The Evening Star is Venus.

THE EPIC

p. 236 Incidentally, there was a St Conan of Iona (d. *c.* 648) who was, traditionally, venerated in the Hebrides.

p. 238 The Sphinx was a monster in Greek mythology with the body of a lioness and the head of a woman; she asked travellers to solve riddles and, when they failed, strangled them.

p. 240 Friedrich Wilhelm Nietzsche (1844–1900), the German philosopher, philologist and poet, was opposed to the 'slave' values of traditional morality. He developed the idea of the 'superman': rational, liberated and the creator of a 'master' morality.

p. 241 The Pharaoh Akhnaton [Amenophis the Fourth] was King of Egypt in 1350 BC. Akhnaton aimed to introduce a peaceful and philosophical society to Egypt, but his innovative culture was opposed by Thebean politicians, including the ousted Amon priests. The kingdom fell and Akhnaton disappeared.

p. 241 Cleopatra (69–30 BC) was Queen of Egypt (51–30 BC).

p. 241 Ferdinand Marie, Vicomte de Lesseps (1805–1894), the French diplomat and celebrated engineer, was in charge of the construction of the Suez canal (1859–1869).

p. 241 The Mameluks were a powerful group in Egypt; there were two main ruling dynasties, divided on ethnic lines: the Bahri (1250–1382) and the Burji (1382–1517). In 1517, when Selim I, the Sultan of Ottoman Turkey, defeated Egypt, it came under Turkish power but the Mameluk *beys* (governors) still retained power. Napoleon defeated the Mameluks in the Battle of the Pyramids (July 21st 1798) and Mameluk power was finally broken by the massacres in 1805 and 1811 at Cairo.

p. 241 The Tartars merged with the Mongols, after their joint invasion of parts of Europe and Asia in the 13th century to form the Kipchak Empire (the Golden Horde) which ruled most of Russia till the 15th century.

p. 242 Aubrey Vincent Beardsley (1872–1898), the English artist, is known for his unique and imaginative visual style.

p. 243 Boyars were members of the old Russian aristocracy; before the reforms of Peter the Great.

p. 244   A mujik is a Russian peasant.

THE ROAD

p. 251   Prominent members of the Pre-Raphaelite Brotherhood (est 1848), who sought to restore modern art to a purer state, included Dante Gabriel Rossetti (1828–1882), William Holman Hunt (1827–1910) and John Everett Millais.

p. 253   The Haj is the Mohammedan pilgrimage to Mecca.

p. 253   The Jihad is the holy war for the Mohammedan faith.

p. 253   A bey is a Turkish governor.

p. 257   A thaumaturgist is a miracle worker.

p. 258   Aryan means Indo-Germanic or Indo-European; in the Nazi context, non Jewish Copts are the Christian descendants of the ancient Egyptians.

A VOLCANO IN THE MOON

p. 267   A selenographer studies the moon's physical features.

p. 267   A caliph is a spiritual leader of Islam; a successor of Mohammed.

p. 268   Marie Curie, née Maria Sklodowska (1867–1934) was the Polish-born pioneer in research on radioactivity, and won the Nobel prize in 1903 along with her French husband Pierre.

p. 272   Ramadan is the Mohammedan month of fasting by day.

p. 278   The Spartacists was the name of an extreme German communist group in the revolution of 1918, as well as that of the followers of Spartacus in the Third Slave War against Rome (73–71 BC).

THE LIFE AND DEATH OF ELIA CONSTANTINIDOS

p. 283   Tommaso Campanella (1568–1639), the controversial Dominican writer and philosopher, born in Calabria, Italy. His works include *Prodromus Philosophiae instaurandae* (1617) and *Atheismus triumphatus* (1631). See, too, *The Sonnets of Michael Angelo Buonarroti and Tommaso Campanella*, translated into rhymed English by John Addington Symonds (1878).

p. 283 Samos, Ionia, was the birthplace of the mathematician and philosopher Pythagoras (*c.* 569–475 BC).

p. 299 A loggia is a covered, open arcade.

COCKCROW

p. 301 Proto-Semites: the first Semitic peoples.

p. 301 Marco Polo (1254–1324), the Venetian traveller, spent twenty four years in Asia, including a period serving in the administration of Kublai Khan (1214–94).

p. 301 Phidias was one of the three architects of the Parthenon (*c.* 477–438 BC) the other two being Ictinus and Callicrates. He was supervisor of all the building work at the Acropolis.

p. 301 Aristotle (384–322 BC), the Macedonian philosopher, studied under Plato.

p. 302 Aldous Huxley (1894–1963), the English novelist and essayist, is best known for his futuristic and distopian novel *Brave New World* (1931).

p. 302 Ernst Heinrich Haeckel (1834–1919), the German biologist and philosopher, heavily influenced by Darwin, used evolution as the basis for his theories of biology and in a wider context.

p. 302 The Titans were descended from Uranus and Gaea, and were the older gods and goddesses overthrown by Zeus.

p. 303 The Greek philosopher Plato (*c.* 428–347 BC), the founder of the Academy in Athens (387 BC) was one of the most influential Western thinkers.

p. 303 Samurai are members of the Japanese military caste.

p. 303 A sarcomata is a tumour from connective tissue, or any excrescence of flesh.

p. 308 Carcinomata are cancers.

p. 310 Prometheus was one of the Titans, who created humanity along with his brother Epimetheus. He gave fire to humanity, angered Zeus and was chained to a rock in the Caucasus where an eagle continually ate him alive, until he was freed by Hercules.

GIFT OF THE RIVER

p. 317 Pierre Abélard (1079–1142), the Breton philosopher and theologian, had a tragic love affair with Heloise, the niece of Canon Fulbert.

p. 317 Leander of Abydos was in love with Hero, a priestess of Venus who lived on the opposite side of the strait separating Asia and Europe. She lighted a torch nightly, so he could swim to her, but one night he drowned in a tempest. His body was carried to her European shore, and she drowned herself in despair.

p. 319 The idea of a 'flexible, synthetic World-speech' was the subject of much debate in the 1930s. The international language Esperanto had been invented in 1887 by the Polish oculist, Dr Ludwik L. Zamenhof.

p. 322 The English poet Algernon Charles Swinburne (1837–1909) is known for his highly charged, and metrically skilled poetry, from the sexually resonant *Poems and Ballads* (1866) to the political *Songs before Sunrise* (1871).

p. 327 The Roman poet Virgil (70–19 BC) wrote the epic *Aeneid*, the pastoral *Eclogues* (37 BC) and the *Georgics, or Art of Husbandry* (37–30 BC).

p. 327 Gabriel D'Annunzio (1863–1938), the Italian playwright, novelist and poet. His works include the joyous poetry of *Canto nuovo* (1882), and the play *Gioconda* (1898). He supported the Italian Fascist movement.

p. 327 Romaic means of, or relating to, modern Greece (particularly its language).

EAST IS WEST

p. 334 Daedalus was the mythical artist who created the Cretan labyrinth.

p. 334   La Manche is also known as the English Channel.

p. 334   Nicolaus Copernicus (1473–1543), the Polish astronomer, discovered that the earth revolves around the sun (the heliocentric system).

p. 335   The mummy of King Oomas, found at the Pyramid of Oonas at Sakkarah, is probably the oldest mummy in Egypt, and is now in Cairo.

p. 336   An ornithopter is a flying machine with flapping wings.

p. 342   All pioneers of flight. Icarus, the son of Daedalus, flew from Crete on wings partly made of wax, which melted as he flew too near the sun, causing him to fall into the sea and drown. Otto Lilienthal (1848–1896) was a German pioneer of gliders.

p. 344   The Brahmin is one of the highest, or priestly, castes among the Hindus.

p. 344   Saheb is a term of respect: gentleman.

p. 347   *Per ardua ad astra*: through hardship to the stars.

VERNAL

p. 353   Anthony Trollope (1815–1882), the English novelist, explored the world of the upper class in the Victorian period.

p. 357   The Coptic Church refers to the main Christian sect in Egypt.

p. 361   Anatoli Vasilievich Lunacharsky (1875–1933) was the USSR's first Commissar of Education. Known for his powers of oratory, he played a key role in the 1917 Revolution.

DAYBREAK

p. 370   The quote is from the song by Allan Cunningham (1784–1842), 'My ain countrie' which has passed into oral circulation.

p. 375   The khamsin time refers to the season in Egypt when a hot south or south easterly wind blows, for about fifty days from the middle of March onwards.

p. 376 A dragoman, in Eastern countries, is an interpreter or a guide.

IT IS WRITTEN

p. 384 See Gibbon's novel *The Thirteenth Disciple* (1931).

p. 387 A gillyflower is a flower that smells like cloves

p. 387 Gethsemane is the garden on a hill where Christ spent the night after the Last Supper, before being betrayed.

p. 388 Members of various churches: the Chaldean, Armenians and Nestorians (often regarded, by the established churches, as heretical). The Nestorians, for instance, followed the teachings of Nestorius, patriarch of Constantinople (438–31) who taught that the divinity and humanity of Christ were not united in one personality.

p. 389 The Manicheans followed the teachings of Manichaeus, from Ecbatana (*c.* 216–276) who taught that everything was derived from two principles: light and darkness or good and evil.

p. 399 Ormudzd was the chief god of the ancient Persians: the Creator and Lord of the Universe.

THE PASSAGE OF THE DAWN

p. 403 A Tuareg is a nomadic Berber from the Sahara.

PART IV: ONE MAN WITH A DREAM

TEXTUAL NOTE: 'A Stele from Atlantis', 'The Woman of Leadenhall Street' and 'The First and Last Woman' all appeared in the *Masterpiece of Thrills* ed., John Gawsworth (1936). 'Roads to Freedom' was first published in *The Millgate* 26 (1931). The other items all first appeared in *The Cornhill Magazine* between 1929 and 1930. 'The Lost Constituent', 'The Floods of Spring' and 'Revolt' all reappeared in J. Leslie Mitchell, *Persian Dawns, Egyptian Nights* (1932) reprinted, ed., Ian Campbell (1997).

A STELE FROM ATLANTIS

p. 423   Atlantis is a legendary island in the Western Ocean, near to the Pillars of Hercules. Plato mentions the island in two dialogues, the *Timaeus* and *Critias*. Atlantis was supposedly an ideal commonwealth state.

THE WOMAN OF LEADENHALL STREET

p. 429   *Homo sapiens*: the one species of people still in existence.

FOR TEN'S SAKE

p. 461   A hakim is a physician, or an official.

THE LOST CONSTITUENT

p. 490   Janissaries were the soldiers of the Turkish footguards (*c.* 1330–1826).

p. 490   The Gregorian calendar was reformed by Gregory XIII (1582) from the Julian calendar introduced by Julius Caesar and modified by Augustus.

p. 494   Chryselephantine means made of gold and ivory

p. 000   Mandragora is a genus of plants: the mandrake.

THERMOPYLAE

p. 522   King Leonidas of Sparta marched to Thermopylae to face the troops of Xerxes, the son of the King of Persia, in 480 BC, in a mountain pass. The three hundred-strong Spartan force (including Leonidas) were all killed, but their self-sacrifice allowed the Greek forces to consolidate and, finally, repel Xerxes.

p. 523   A khan, in this context, is an Eastern inn, or caravanserai.

PART V: THE GLAMOUR OF GOLD

TEXTUAL NOTE: The first three essays here are from *Nine Against the Unknown. A Record of Geographical Exploration by J. Leslie Mitchell and Lewis Grassic Gibbon* (London: Jarrolds, 1934). 'The End of the Maya Old Empire' and

'Yucatan' appeared in *Antiquity* (1930), 'The Buddha of America' in *The Cornhill Magazine* (1932) and 'William James Perry' in *The Millgate* (1932).

THE BUDDHA OF AMERICA
p. 714   See Henry Mayhew, *The Mormons* (1851).

WILLIAM JAMES PERRY, M.A., D.SC., A REVOLUTION-
ARY ANTHROPOLOGIST
p. 726   See too William James Perry (1864–1922), *Social Organization* (1924).

PART VI: IN BRIEF

TEXTUAL NOTE: 'A Novelist looks at the Cinema' first appeared in *Cinema Quarterly* (1935) and 'Controversy: Writers' International (British Section)' in *The Left Review* (1935). The synopses which follow are all from NLS MS 26066.

CONTROVERSY: WRITER'S INTERNATIONAL (BRITISH SECTION)
p. 738   The works of Sir Noel Pierce Coward (1899–1973), the English comic playwright of upper class life, include *Private Lives* (1930) and *Design for Living* (1931).
p. 738   Giles Lytton Strachey (1882–1932), the English biographer, essayist and critic, author of *Queen Victoria* (1921) and *Eminent Victorians* (1928).

A NOVELIST LOOKS AT THE CINEMA
p. 740   Benito Mussolini (1883–1945), the Italian Fascist, was the Prime Minister of Italy from 1922 and head of the Italian Socialist Republic (1943–45).
p. 742   The Irish playwright, novelist and critic St John Greer Ervine (1883–1971). His works include *Boyd's Shop* (1936), and a biography of *Charles Stewart Parnell* (1925).
p. 744   The films referred to here are *Le Million* (1931), dir. René Clair; *Gabriel Over the White House* (1933), dir.

Gregory La Cava; *Man of Aran* (1934), dir. Robert J. Flaherty; and *As the Earth Turns* (1934), dir. Alfred E. Green.

DOMINA
p. 804 A continuation of the story of Malcolm Maudsley, *The Thirteenth Disciple* (1931).

THE ROOFTREE AND MEN OF THE MEARNS
pp. 808 & 809 Both set during the Covenanting period.
p. 810 Richard Cameron (1655–80), the prominent Covenanter and leader of the Cameronians.

PART VII: SPEAK OF THE MEARNS

TEXTUAL NOTE: Ian Campbell published this, in its full version, in 1982. Set in the world around Stonehaven, it deals with the same landscape as the *Scottish Scene* stories.

BOOK I
p. 815 On the hiding of the crown and sceptre of Scotland, as described here, see Alastair Cameron *A Guide to Dunnottar Castle* (1988), pp. 28–31.
p. 817 William Ewart Gladstone (1809–1908), born in Liverpool into a Scottish family, was the leader of the Liberal party after 1867, and four times Prime Minister
p. 817 Robert Green Ingersoll (1833–1899), the American lawyer and orator, was known as the Great Agnostic due to his distinctive religious beliefs.

II THE HOWE
p. 820 The precentor led the choir's singing in traditional Scottish services.
p. 826 Elijah (*fl.* 9th century BC), the Hebrew prophet.
p. 827 The philosopher and rationalist Benedictus de Spinoza (1632–1677).
p. 828 Burke and Hare, the famous Irish resurrectionists of Edinburgh, tried in 1828, who supplied corpses to the

anatomist Dr Knox. James Bridie (mentioned in 'Literary Lights') wrote a play on the subject, *The Anatomist* (1931).

p. 829 Stonehyve is the North East name for Stonehaven, sometimes spelt Stonehive by Gibbon. (Today it is also known as Steenie.)

p. 831 Ploughing with a pony and an ox was fairly common in Scotland in the past. See the photo of ploughing with horse and stirk, c. 1910, reproduced in the CD ROM *Northern Folk*.

III THE STRATOUNS

p. 847 The ponderous way Bess moves suggests she is a heavy horse, usually a Clydesdale, which were so popular with the North East farmers. See the CD ROM *Northern Folk*.

p. 882 Gourdon is a fishing community south of Stonehaven, on the North East coast.

p. 889 At the Battle of Balaclava (25th October 1824) in the Crimean War, the British lost control of their major supply road but their opponents, the Russians, did not achieve their goal of capturing Balaclava, which supplied the British, French and Turkish forces.

NOTES

p. 900 Burns' Nicht Suppers: celebrating the birthday of Robert Burns (1759–92), Scotland's national poet, on 25th January.

Glossary

Note: Lewis Grassic Gibbon had a huge knowledge of North East Scots, and he used the language in a distinctive way. Some Scots words are anglicised in spelling, if not in their sound: *ower* becomes over; *braw* is brave. His spelling is inconsistent: e.g. *tackèd-boots* or *tackitty boots; swivel tree* or *swingle-tree*. Still, the range and depth of Gibbon's Scots is evident, particularly regarding farming life.

a-be	alone
abide	stand
aboot	about
abune	above
abysm	abyss
a-cower	cowering
ae	one
afore	before
agley	off the straight and narrow, wrong
ahint	behind
aiblins	perhaps, possibly
aik	oak
ain	own
alow	below
alowe	alight, glowing
ane	one
antrin	eerie, strange
aught	anything
auld	old
awa	away
awful	very much
aye	always, ever
ayont	beyond
backerty-gets	backwards
bade	lived
bairn	child
balk	shy away from
band	waistband
bap	roll (bread)
bap	to plod
bapping away/on	not wasting time over

bargy	bandy words about; argue
bawbee	halfpenny
ben	inside, in
bent	open field; slope/hollow of a hill
Bervie	Inverbervie
besom	broom; contemptuous term for a woman
betwixt	between
bidden	remained, stayed
bide	wait, stay
big	construct, build
biggings	buildings
billie, billy	lad
bind	tie up bundles of grain at harvesting
binder	machine for bundling up grain
birl	whirl
birn	load, burden
bit	small (with affection, or contempt) or necessary
bitted	fed
black affronted	very ashamed, mortified
black-like	dark
blash	splash, heavy shower, torrent
blatter	rattle
blawn	blown
bleezin	boastful, blazing
blether	chatter, foolish nonsense
blithe	cheerful, happy
blow	brag, boast; swell
blushful	embarrassing
bobby	policeman
body	person
bogie	scary ghost, phantom
bonny	pretty, beautiful
booze	drink (alcohol)
boss	bunch/tuft of grass; frame of wood on a saddle
bothy	separate farm building for unmarried workers
bothy billie	unmarried male farm worker
bothy childe	unmarried male farm worker
bouroch	bonds; rope tied round a kicking cow's legs whilst milking; cluster
bout	the range of land covered as a plough moves across the field
box bed	built-in bed, enclosed with panels, with a curtain or hinged panel at the front
box-cart	cart made to tilt (long-carts were unyoked to tilt)
brae	hill
braid	broad
brave-like	handsome
braw	grand, handsome
bree	stock, soup
breeks	trousers, breeches

breeng	drive on, rush forward
brig	bridge
britchen, britches	straps passing round the hinder-part of a shaft-horse, so it can push backwards
broadcast	cast out, throw out (e.g. seed or manure)
Broo	Unemployment bureau, dole
broom	shrub, *Cytisus scoparius*
brose	dish of oat or pease-meal with hot milk or water, butter and salt
buirdly	burly
buit	boot
bulgar	an expletive; bugger
bunk	a chest used as a seat
by his/her lone	alone, with no companion
bye-thought	passing thought
byre	cowshed
ca	call
caller	healthy, vigorous; fresh
calsay	cobbled area (of street/in front of byre/ stable)
canny	cautious, careful
canty	cheerful, pleasant
capers	goings on
carrying	pregnant
cattler	cattleman
caw	call of a bird
chancy	(in negative) unlucky, unfortunate
chap	knock, tap
chave	toil, work hard
cheery	cheerful
childe	lad
chirk	to make a harsh noise, gnash teeth
chitter	shiver, flicker
chug	pull, jerk
claik	gossip
clang	clung
clanjamfrie	rabble; junk
clean	completely, absolutely
cleck	bring forth, invent
clort	dirt
close	farmyard or entry passage to a tenement; or mean, tight-fisted
closet-bed	box bed
clour	thump, blow
clout	blow, punch; or cloth, rag
clutter	confusion, mess
coarse	rough, boorish, disagreeable
coddle	cuddle, embrace
coldrife	chilly
cole	cut, clip, shear; put hay into cocks
con	squirrel
cope	incline
corded	to accord; a thin rope

corn	oats
cottar	tenant in a cottage without land tied to it; married farmworker whose house is part of his fee
cottar house	tied cottage
coulter	iron blade in front of a ploughshare
coup	fall over
coup	coop
court	courtyard; covered enclosure for cattle
couthy	pleasant, agreeable
crack	talk, conversation, gossip
cratur	creature
creash	fat, grease
creel	deep basket for carrying, e.g. fish or peats
cricks	cracks
croft	small farmstead
cross-plough	to harrow a field across the ploughing
cruse lamp, cruisie	boat-shaped lamp
cry	call
cuddlesome	cuddly
cuddy	donkey or horse
curlicue	curl
curling	curving motion given to a curling stone
cushant	wood-pigeon
cutting	reaping
daft	stupid
daftie	simpleton, fool
daftie-house	asylum
daft-like	foolish
dander	stroll
dawdle	linger
dawtie	pet, darling
deave	deafen/stun with noise
dee	die
den	a narrow valley, especially with trees
devil stone	standing stone
dickie	dickie suit, tuxedo
dight	rub, wipe; ready, put in order
ding	beat, strike
dirl	rattle, vibrate
dirt	contemptuous term for a person
dishcloot	dishcloth
docken	a wild plant; the dock
dollop	portion, large piece
dominie	schoolmaster
doolie	ditherer; a hobgoblin
doon	down
dottlet/dottled	mentally feeble, senile
doubt	fear, be afraid; uncertainty
doubtful	dubious
douce	pleasant
doun	down
doup	backside, buttocks
dour	stern, relentless

downcome	downfall
dowse	extinguish
dram	small drink, usually whisky
dreich	dreary, bleak
drill	ridge with seeds or growing plants
drook	soak
drummle	to make/be muddy or disturbed
dux	best pupil in the class, or school
dyke	ditch, or boundary wall
eident	diligent, busy
eirde	earth-house
ere	before
eyen	eyes
fa'	fall
factor	property manager, land steward
fair	completely, certainly, quite
fairely	marvel, stange sight
fairlies	marvels
fairly	quite
faither	father
fash	trouble, fret
feared	frightened
fee	to hire as a (farm) servant; a servant's wages
fegs	in faith, indeed
feint the	devil the
fell	extremely, very or strong, fierce
fettle	good order
feuch	yuk, ugh; foulness
fey	doomed, other-worldly
fine	very well; well mannered
flare	glare
flaunting	quivering with excitement, agitation
flay	strip, flay
fleer	ogle
flim flam	insubstantial substance, air
flit	shift, remove
flitting	removal
flyte	scold, disapprove
forbye	besides
forenicht	evening, early nighttime
fouk	folk
frae	from
frere	brother, friend
friend-like	friendly
frock	dress; fisherman's jersey
fu	full
fumblements	fumblings
fusionless	weak, dried up, lacking substance
gait	way
galluses	braces (for trousers)
galumph	to march along, exultingly (Lewis Carroll's coinage)
gang	go

gang a hard/queer gait	follow a hard/unusual path
gant	stutter, stammer; yawn
garred	made
gather	bring together corn to make a sheaf
gawpus	simpleton
gear	belongings, possessions, stuff
gentry	people of rank, gentlefolk
get-up	outfit, clothes
gey	great, rather, very (often ironically)
ghaist	ghost
gied	gave
gimcrack	tawdry, fantastic
girdle	griddle
girn	grimace, grumble
girnel	chest for storing meal/grain
glaur	mud, dirt
glen	narrow valley between hills, usually with a stream and often trees
gley	squint, glance
gliff	a gust; moment
glim	glimmer
gloamin(g)	twilight, dusk
glower	glare, scowl
goloch	ground beetle, or earwig
goodson	son in law
gorlin	unfledged
gowk	stare (to), cuckoo, fool
graip, greip	fork, with iron prongs, used in agriculture
grand	fine, first-rate
grat	cried
gree	settle
greet	cry
grieve	farm baillif, overseer
grieve-weather	good weather for working
grue	shudder, shy away from in horror
grumph	grunt
grun	ground
guff	reek, smell; puff of air
gully knife	a large knife
gurl	growl, roar, howl
gutter	mud, mire
gype	a fool, idiot
gyte	mad with joy or rage
habber	stammer, stutter
hack	troublesome cough, crack
hackle	straw
hae	have
haft	heave, lift up
hald	hold
half	half pint
halfin	stripling
ham	back of thigh (especially animal's), hock
hame	home
hantle	a considerable number (of folk)

hap	wrap up, cover, tuck up in bed
hash	mess, muddle, confusion
hash on	press on
haugh	level ground on a river bank
haver	chatter, speak nonsense, gossip
haycock	haystack
heed	pay attention to, bother about
hen-ree	hen-run
heuch	reaping hook
hid	had
hind	farmservant (married)
hing	hang
hirple	limp, hobble
hoast	cough
Hogmanay	New Year's Eve
hoose	house
hoots	exclamation of doubt, irritation
horn spoon	spoon made of horn
hotch	infestation; slovenly woman
hotter	jostle; swarm
hove	heaved, flung
howe	hollow, low-lying land, plain surrounded by hills
howk	unearth, dig out
howlet	owl
hurl	wheel
i	in
ilk	kind; same as the person/thing just mentioned
ill	cruel, miserable; harm
ill-gotten	illegitimate, badly begotten
ill-like	evil, suspicious
ill-ta'en	resented
ill-tuned	bad tempered
ill-used	badly treated
in a way	in a state
ingathering	collecting, gathering in
ingleneuk	corner by the fireside
ingoing	going in, entering
intil	into, inside
ither	other
jade	woman
jaloose	suspect
jangle	to chatter, prattle; dissonant clanging (bells)
jog	jag
joiner	carpenter, woodworker
joinery	joiner's workshop
joskin	farmworker, yokel
kale	curly-leaved cabbage
kebbuck	a whole cheese
keek	glance, peek
keen	cruel (weather); brave (people)
keen and green	brave and eager
kelpie	water spirit (often in the form of a horse)

ken	know
kilt up	tuck up
kine	cows
kin'ly	kindly
kirk	church
kirkyard	churchyard
kittle (up)	to tickle, to strike up (a tune)
kittler	more provoking, teasing
kyard	vagrant, rough person
kye	cows
lair	mud, mire; grave; to lie or rest
laird	lord, landowner
laist	last
Lammas	quarter day, 1st August
lang	long
lang dune	long ago
lank	lean
lanky	gangly
Lascar	Eastern (usually Indian) sailor
lave	rest, remainder; wash
laverock	skylark
lea	fallow, unploughed land
lead	carry in harvest
leal	true, loyal, faithful
leather	thrash with the tawse (leather belt)
led	carted crops to the farm land
lee	shelter
leglin	lade-gallon (used as a milk pail)
letten	left
letten a-be	left alone
ley	lea
lib, libb	castrate
licht	light
lichtsome/lightsome	cheerful, lively; trifling
lift	sky
limmer, limner	rascal (of child), disreputable woman
lithe	shelter
littered	born
littered bed	portable bed which can be carried by horses
loch	lake
lollop	lope
long	tall
lood	loud
loon	lad
loose	untie, loosen, let go
loosening time	quitting time; the end of the working day
lope	spring, leap
losh	Lord
loup	leap, jump
lour	overcast weather, threatening rain; frown
lowe	flame, burning
lug	ear
lum	chimney
lum-hat	top hat, tall hat

maiden	virgin, spinster
malagarouse	disorder, rumple up
man	husband, man
manse	minister's house
marrow	match, equal
mart	agricultural market
Martinmas	Day on the Feast of St Martin (11th November)
maun	must
meal	oatmeal
meat	food, meal
meating	feeding
meck	penny, cent
meenistair	minister
meikle	great big
Mercat Cross	Market Cross
mettle	spirit, calibre
midden	refuse heap, dunghill
Mighty	the Almighty
mill-course	circular path trodden by horses driving a threshing-mill
mind	remember, pay heed to
minnow	a small fish
mirk	twilight
moil	toil
mony	many
moon-hush	in the still of the moonlight
moonlight flit	removal by night, without paying debts
moose	mouse
the morn	tomorrow
the morn's morn	tomorrow morning
most-like	probably
mouser	moustache
muck	manure, dung
muckle	much
muddle	to work fussily, doing little
muggins	woollen stocking leg, used to protect the arms
mune	moon
nae	no
nane	none
naught	nothing
near	almost
neb	nose, beak
neighbour-like	neighbourly
new-bedded	given new bedding
newsed	chatted
newsy	gossipy
nicht	night
nick	steal
nicker	cracking/clicking sound
nickum	scamp, rascal
nieve	grasp, grip; fist
nighty	nightgown

the night	tonight
nip	dram
nipper	sharper
nook	corner
nought	nothing
nout	ox, steer (singular); cattle (plural)
o	off
och	expression of weariness, regret
od	God
oe	grandchild, descendant
on-ding	downpour of rain or snow
on-goings	goings on
oor	our
orra	spare, superfluous
outby(e)	away from the farmsteading; a little way off
outgoing	going out
over	too, excessively
overdear	expensive
overmuch	too much
ower	over
oxter	arm pit
paich	gasp, pant
palaver	fuss, trifle
park	enclosed land, field
peasmeal	flour made from ground pease
peat	fuel, cut from boggy moorland
peesie	lapwing
peewit	lapwing; the cry of the lapwing
pelt	sped/work energetically; downpour
pictures	movies
plait	pleated hair
plash	splash, sudden downpour of rain
play	amusement, sport
pleiter	mess
ploughchilde	ploughman
ploy	scheme, undertaking
pluffer	pea-shooter
pock	bag, parcel
pointer	leading man of a team of reapers or the strip of corn he cuts
pose	place in a specified position
postie	postman
pouch	pocket, purse
precentor	leader of church congregation's singing
press	large cupboard
prig	plead, beg
pringle, prinkle	thrill, tingle
prink	twinkle
puddock	frog
put out to suck	put to be nursed
quean	young woman (usually unmarried), girl
queer	strange
quet	stealthily
quick	alert, alive

quietude	still
raddle	to fuddle, stupefy
ramshackle	unkempt, untidy
rank	overgrown
rape	cheat
rax	reach, stretch out
reaper	reap
reckon	count on, enumerate
ree	pen, enclosure
reef	itch, scab
reek	smoke
redd up	settle, tidy; scold
rickle	loose heap, pile
riddle	coarse, agricultural sieve
ridging track	track along a high ridge
rig	strip of ploughed land
rig-end	the lower end of a rig
right	very
rime	hoar frost
rise	a piece of fun, joke
rive	tear, plough up; fallow
roan	of a variegated colour
roller	machine for flattening turfs
roup	sale/public auction of (a farm's) goods, often due to bankruptcy
roust	stir into action
runkle	wrinkle, crease
Sabbath	Sunday
sae	so
sair	sore
sappy	fleshy, soft
sark	shift, undershirt
scafe	pare off
scart	scrape
schiltroun	squadron of armed men
schlorich	unsavoury mess (of food)
scoriate	reduce to dross or slag from metal smelting
scour	diarrhoea, especially in farm animals
scunner	disgust, repel
scutter	muddle, pointless dawdle
seemly	fitting; pleasing in appearance
seep	drip, ooze
set	sit
shackle	wrist
shag	tobacco
shamed	embarrassed
shammle	shamble, walk clumsily
sharn	dung (semi-liquid)
sheeny	shiny; discarded lover
shelvin	extra boards fixed onto the sides of a cart to increase its capacity
shielin	high summer pasture, usually with a shepherd's hut
shift	move, hesitate

shoggle	sway unsteadily
sholt, sholtie, sholty	pony; young horse
shoon	shoes
short	short-tempered
showd	sway, rock
sic	such
sicna	such
silver	money
sin	since
sin' syne	since then
skellach	small bell, handbell used by a crier
skelloch	shriek, scream
skelp	slap
skeugh	askew
skilly	experienced, skilled
skimpy	mean, corner cutting
skirl	shriek, shrill sound (associated with piping)
skleiter	heap, messy pile
slaver	saliva
sleeked	cunning, sly
slummock	slattern
sma	small
smeddum	strength of character, spirit
smiddy	smithy
smokie, smoky	smoked haddock, associated with Arbroath
smore	smother, suffocate, choke
snae	snow
sneck	latch
snell	smart, sharp, sarcastic
snib	fasten, bolt
snicker	snigger, snort
snifter	sniff, snivel
sock	ploughshare
soft	feeble-minded
sonsy	fine, cheerful
sore	difficult, hard, painful
soss	mess, dirt, confusion
sough	sigh (of the wind)
sound	narrow channel; swoon
souple	nimble, supple
souter	cobbler, shoemaker
southron	southern
sowans	dish from oat husks and meal steeped in water for a week, strained to leave a solid mass
speak	the talk/gossip (of a place)
speir	ask
spew	vomit
spleiter	splash
splurge	splash
spume	spray
spunk	spark, spirit; match
squatter	squat, sprawl
squeege	twist, out of shape

stack	peat stack; hay stack
stammy-gaster	shock, great disappointment
stance	position
stane	stone
stany	stony
start	sudden move
stave	a short song
steek	shut, close
steer	disturbance, bustle; stir
stert	to start
stirk	a steer
stite	rubbish, nonsense
stiter	stagger
stock	fellow
Stonehive, Stonehyve	Stonehaven
stook	a shock of sheaves
stooking	making a shock of sheaves
store the kin	(in negative) not survive, not keep the human race alive
stot	young bull or ox; castrated bull
stour	dirt, swirling dust; struggle
streek	stretch
stricken	suffering
suck	suckle, nurse
sudden-like	suddenly
sumph	oaf, sulky person
swack	supple, active
swash	splash
sweir	lazy, loathe to work
swing	walk with a heavy gait
swink	work hard, toil
swish	splash; dash
swivel-tree:	swingle-tree of a plough
swoosh	sweep aside
syne	next, then, presently; since, before now
ta'en	taken
taik	stroll, saunter
tail	end
tailer	hand turnip-cutter
tackèd-boots, tackitty boots	hobnailed boots
take [that] through hand	discuss/deal with thoroughly
tares	tear/cut by a plough (referring to the angle of adjustment between the coulter and point of the ploughshare which regulates the cut in the furrow)
tarn	a small mountain lake
tash	damage, spoil
ta-ta	bye bye
tattie	potato
tattie-shaws	leaves/stalks of potatoes
team	team of animals at ploughing
tear	speed; work energetically
term	start of lease/employment contract
thocht	thought

thole	bear
thrappling	throttling
thrash	thresh
thrawn	contrary, obstinate
thunder-pelt	thunderstorm
tink	travelling person, pedlar (derogatory)
tint	lost
tir	to strip off clothes
tosh	(make) neat, tidy
toun	farmsteading; town
tow	rope, cord
traipse	trudge, shuffle, tramp
trashy	worthless, disreputable
trauchle	toil, labour
trig	trim, neat
trigged out	kitted out
tulloch	mound, hillock
turn	become giddy, dizzy
turnpike	turnpike road
twa	two
twink	to twitch, jerk
tyke	cur, dog
ugsome	loathsome, disgusting
unchancy	unlucky
unco	strange, awful
undocht	weak, ineffective
unlimber	to spread out
unloose	untie
vennel	a close, narrow alley between houses
vex	distress, worry
wabble	wobble, go weak
wallop	thump
wamble	stagger
wame	stomach
watch	guard
weet	wet, drizzly
well	right
well-happed	well built
well set-up	well built, determined
wha	who
wheeber	whistle
wheep	whistle (often of bird/wind)
wheesh	a rushing noise
wheesht	be quiet
whigmaleeries	fancies, whims
whiles	sometimes, now and then
whin	furze, gorse
whirlimagig	whim
whist	be quiet, still
whit owl	barn owl
whoom	roaring sound
wink	window
wife	woman, usually middle-aged (disparaging), married woman

wissh	quiet, steady
wonder	marvel, object of wonder
wynd	narrow street, alley
yabber	chatter, gossip
yammer	rumble, chatter
yavil	flat, prone part
yer	you
yon	that
yow-trummle	cold spell during sheep shearing time in early summer, literally 'ewe trembling' time

CANONGATE CLASSICS

Books listed in alphabetical order by author:

Grampian Quartet (The Quarry Wood, The Weatherhouse,
   A Pass in the Grampians, The Living Mountain) Nan
   Shepherd
   ISBN   0 86241 589 6   £8.99 $14.95
Consider the Lilies Iain Crichton Smith
   ISBN   0 86241 415 6   £4.99 $11.95
Listen to the Voice: Selected Stories Iain Crichton Smith
   ISBN   0 86241 434 2   £5.99 $11.95
Diaries of a Dying Man William Soutar
   ISBN   0 86241 347 8   £5.99 $11.95
Shorter Scottish Fiction Robert Louis Stevenson
   ISBN   0 86241 555 1   £4.99 $11.95
Tales of Adventure (Black Arrow, Treasure Island, 'The
   Sire de Malétroit's Door' and other stories)
   Robert Louis Stevenson
   ISBN   0 86241 687 6   £7.99 $14.95
Tales of the South Seas (Island Landfalls, The Ebb-tide,
   The Wrecker) Robert Louis Stevenson
   ISBN   0 86241 643 4   £7.99 $14.95
The Scottish Novels (Kidnapped, Catriona, The Master
   of Ballantrae, Weir of Hermiston) Robert Louis Stevenson
   ISBN   0 86241 533 0   £6.99 $11.95
The Makars: The Poems of Henryson, Dunbar and Douglas
   JA Tasioulas (ed.)
   ISBN   0 86241 820 8   £9.99 $16.00
The Bad Sister: An Emma Tennant Omnibus (The Bad
   Sister, Two Women of London, Wild Nights)
   Emma Tennant
   ISBN   1 84195 053 X   £7.99 $15.00
The People of the Sea David Thomson
   ISBN   0 86241 550 0   £4.99 $11.95
City of Dreadful Night James Thomson
   ISBN   0 86241 449 0   £5.99 $11.95
Black Lamb and Grey Falcon Rebecca West
   ISBN   0 86241 428 8   £12.99 $19.95
The King and the Lamp: Scottish Traveller Tales
   Duncan and Linda Williamson
   ISBN   1 84195 063 7   £7.99 $15.00

ORDERING INFORMATION

Most Canongate Classics are available at good bookshops.
You can also order direct from Canongate Books Ltd –
by post: 14 High Street, Edinburgh EH1 1TE, or by telephone:
0131 557 5111, or fax: 0131 557 5211, or email:
                   salesandmark@canongate.co.uk
   There is no charge for postage and packing to customers in
the United Kingdom.